Tough as Nails:
The Complete Cases of Donahue

Frederick Nebel

TOUGH as NAILS

THE COMPLETE CASES OF DONAHUE FROM THE PAGES OF BLACK MASK

FREDERICK NEBEL

Illustrations by
ARTHUR RODMAN BOWKER

Edited & Compiled by
ROB PRESTON

Introduction by
WILL MURRAY

Series Editor
KEITH ALAN DEUTSCH

Boston • Philadelphia • New York
2012

© 2012 Altus Press • First Edition—2012

DESIGNED AND PUBLISHED BY
Matthew Moring

BLACK MASK SERIES EDITOR
Keith Alan Deutsch

PUBLISHING HISTORY
"Introduction" appears here for the first time. Copyright © 2012 Will Murray. All Rights Reserved.
"Bibliography of the Works of Frederick Louis Nebel" appears here for the first time. Copyright © 2012 Rob Preston. All Rights Reserved.
Owing to limitations of space, permissions to reprint previously published material appear on pages 573-575.

Published by arrangement with Black Mask Press/Keith Alan Deutsch (keithdeutsch@mac.com).

THANKS TO
John Benson, William G. Contento, John Desbin, Keith Alan Deutsch, Stefan Dziemianowicz, Doug Ellis, Larry Estep, Ron Goulart, Perry Grayson, Doug Greene, Paul Herman, Rich Kahl, Timothy Lantz, Dave Lewis, Steve Lewis, Denny Lien, John Locke, Joel Lyzeck, Ken McDaniel, Walker Martin, Will Murray, Lynn Myers, Rick Ollerman, Bill Pronzini, Dan Roy, Kevin Burton Smith, Bob Wardzinski, Robert Weinberg, Robert Wheadon, and John Wooley.
The Publishers wish to express many thanks and much appreciation to Rob Preston.

ROB PRESTON WOULD ALSO LIKE TO ACKNOWLEDGE THE FOLLOWING
RESOURCES IN COMPILING THE FREDERICK NEBEL BIBLIOGRAPHY:
E.R. Hagemann's *A Comprehensive Index to Black Mask,* Michael Cook & Steve Miller's *Mystery, Detective and Espionage Fiction,* Leonard Robbins' *The Pulp Magazine Index,* The Fictionmags online index, and Rara-Avis mailing list.

Visit altuspress.com for more books like this.
Printed in the United States of America.

Table of

CONTENTS

Introduction

WILL MURRAY

IT was a tough time. It was a very tough time.

The Great Depression of the 1930s fostered some very hard-boiled writers. Dashiell Hammett. Raymond Chandler. Paul Cain. Horace McCoy. Others too numerous to mention.

One of the greatest of these, and most overlooked, was Frederick Lewis Nebel (1903-1967). Like Hammett, Nebel came out of the Roaring 20s, specifically the period when the sleepy pulp fiction field exploded. New publishers, new magazines abounded. Prosperity drove those twenty and twenty-five cent magazines into circulation heights never to be seen again.

Nebel was one of the coming writers for Fiction House, an upstart new pulp publisher that rode prosperity like a cowboy rides a bucking bronco. Their editorial motto was "Action stripped to the bone."

Young and ambitious, Nebel had skipped college and knocked around the world some—which was the preferred background for the aspiring pulpster. A teenage stint as a farmhand in his great uncle's homestead in the Canadian north woods gave him all the background he needed to break into Fiction House's *North-West Stories,* so-called because it featured tales of the Wild West and the Northwest both. It was rugged he-man adventure, and the reading public ate up these tales of strapping two-fisted outdoorsmen.

Nebel stuck to the Northwestern side of *North-West Stories* early on. Before long, he was spinning yarns for Fiction House's stable of thick magazines, creating characters like the Driftin' Kid for *Lariat* and hosts of others for *Action Stories* and *Air Stories.* He was still in his early 20s.

Writing about one of his early Yukon heroes, Nebel once observed: "This may sound ancient in these days of ultra-modernism. But rough men, elemental men, men who could hold a grudge until doomsday—they are the men that built empires and tramped a broad road 'round the world." [1]

That was the kind of pulp-paper hero Fred Nebel espoused. And on which he made his early reputation.

In the summer of 1926, a new editor took control of *Black Mask*, a Fiction House rival that mixed detective, western and adventure stories. Joseph Thompson Shaw sought to refine his new charge, already featuring the popular works of Carroll John Daly, Erle Stanley Gardner and Dashiell Hammett. The ball was rolling. Shaw had only to guide it forward.

Fred Nebel climbed aboard that year. He had contributed only one story prior to Shaw, "The Breaks of the Game." Soon, he would become one of the magazine's most reliable and prolific contributors. Maybe it was the excitement that was growing in the magazine's pages. Or perhaps in Shaw, Nebel discovered a kindred spirit.

For Shaw wished to offer the American public a new kind of hero. One, he wrote, "…who knows the song of a bullet, the soft slithering of a swift-drawn knife, the feel of hard fists, the call of courage." [2] That description was standard pulp, if somewhat poetic. Shaw aimed to take pulp heroism to a new level.

In the post World War I era, readers were shucking off the old conventions. Nowhere was this more true than in the moribund detective field. Where the public had been satisfied with eccentric deductive geniuses, the amateur criminologist who ran rings around police and professional crooks alike, now male readers wanted raw meat. Some had known the horrors of war. Others had only read about it. But they demanded more raw realism in their escape fiction.

Carroll John Daly had been giving it to them since 1922 through his super-violent private detective, Race Williams. Dashiell Hammett tempered that approached to a realistic level that defined this new school of "hard-boiled" writing. Joe Shaw believed that the cool, tough but dispassionate Hammett approach was the future of the detective field. So he set out to transform *Black Mask*.

Out went the last of the old formula detective heroes. From then

1 North-West Stories, *October 22, 1927. pg. 117.*

2 *Frank McShane,* The Life of Raymond Chandler *(New York: Penguin Books, 1976) pp 46-47.*

on, only real detectives—whether official or private—would be admitted to *Black Mask's* austere pages. Newspapermen, lawyers, professional adventurers and other tough types were also permitted. The only other qualification: they had to be two-fisted.

As Shaw described the *Black Mask* ideal, "He is vigorous-minded; hard, in a square man's hardness; hating unfairness, trickery, injustice, cowardly underhandedness; standing for a square deal and a fair show in little or big things, and willing to fight for them; not squeamish or prudish, but clean, admiring the good in man and woman; not sentimental in a gushing sort of way, but valuing true emotion; not hysterical, but responsive to the thrill of danger, the stirring exhilaration of clean, swift, hard action—and always pulling for the right guy to come out on top." [3]

In this groundbreaking new writing environment, Fred Nebel fit right in. He had lived, and he could write. How much of the lean Fiction House approach to action writing infiltrated *Black Mask* is unclear. But Nebel was a natural.

Fred Nebel might have become only one of *Black Mask's* regulars, like the half-forgotten Roger Torrey or the utterly neglected Ed Lybeck, but for the fact that Dashiell Hammett was not long for *Black Mask*. Hardcover fame and Hollywood glory would soon beckon him to better money and markets.

Nebel first emerged as a significant voice with the first installment of an extended story, "The Crimes of Richmond City," which introduced Police Capt. Steve MacBride. "Raw Law" kicked off the semi-serial in the September, 1928 issue.

A regular series followed, which only grew in popularity when Nebel expanded the role of the inebriated comic-relief reporter, Jack Kennedy of the *Free Press*. Soon, Fred Nebel was one of Joe Shaw's stable of regulars.

As contributor Tom Curry once observed, "Shaw was one of those editors who believed in using staff writers rather than buying whatever the mails brought in. He picked eight or ten men, and bought from them steadily.... Shaw gave his writers the reign, let them do the writing while he did the editing. He had to cut out crudities, and such; that was only right. Hammett wrote one brand of stuff, Gardner another, Daly a third, Nebel his own; and Curry had his line. There

---

3   *ibid.*

was real variety in the magazine. It was refreshing." [4]

Then Shaw lost Dashiell Hammett completely in 1930. Hammett's departure left an unfillable void that nevertheless had to be filled.

To replace the departed Continental Op, Fred Nebel introduced "Tough Dick" Donahue in "Rough Justice." The new series kicked off with the November, 1930 issue. It was the final story in that issue. Hammett's last Op yarn, "Death and Company," led off that same issue. It was as if Joe Shaw was deliberately orchestrating the passing of the hard-boiled torch.

Cut of very different fabric than the Op, yet comfortably in the same sub-genre of shady-side-of-the-law lawman, Donahue is a disgraced ex-New York City police detective working for the Interstate Detective Agency as private investigator. Familiarly, he was called "Donny." It was Shaw who called him "Tough Dick" Donahue in the story blurbs. Nebel never did.

"Rough Justice" introduces the streetwise Irishman out of his element, in a sweltering St. Louis. The tale is not merely a prime example of Fred Nebel's brittle approach to hard-boiled storytelling, but showcases one of his favorite fictional devices—the use of weather as a dramatic accompaniment—if not counterpoint—to the action. This may have been a reaction to Fiction House's editorial strictures. Its editors told their writers: "No weather reports." Freed of that restriction, Nebel raised meteorological atmospherics—whether it be heat, hail or thunderstorms—to high art. "Rough Justice" is a prime example.

A three-part storyline followed. Nebel wrote new Donahue yarns in bursts of three or four, which Shaw invariably scheduled in consecutive issues. Typically, many of them followed the Hammett formula of novelettes presented as connected stories. Not exactly serials, they allowed for better plot development without violating the Depression-era editorial taboo against serials.

Ironically, the series almost ended prematurely with the seventh tale, "Death's Not Enough", when a new rival to *Black Mask,* Popular Publication's *Dime Detective,* offered Nebel four cents a word to inaugurate a new P.I. series, featuring Jack Cardigan of the Cosmos Detective Agency. He was virtually a simulacrum of Donahue, except that Cardigan operated out of St. Louis.

---

4   *"It's Your Own Show "by Tom Curry.* Writers Year Book, *Vol. 1, No. 16 1945 pg 88.*

After a year, Nebel relented and new Donahue stories began appearing in *Black Mask,* starting with "Shake-Up." They continued until 1933, when Nebel again retired "Donny" Donahue with "Champions Also Die."

With the Depression making life hard and ordinary people even harder, the hard-boiled characterization that was so refreshing in the 20s seemed triply appropriate in the 1930s. It was as if Joe Shaw and his writers had been ahead of their time and hard times had caught up with them.

In his laconic style, hard-boiled characters who could be tough yet breezy, honest but also semi-scrupulous, Fred Nebel was Hammett's natural heir. Some readers preferred him to Hammett. And unlike some failed *Black Mask* writers, like James H.S. Moynahan (of whom Shaw once said, "Jim is so far wrong that his machinery creaks and groans."),[5] Nebel was no Hammett imitator, but an authentic voice in his own right.

That he never achieved Hammett's stature was a matter of professional choice. In 1933, with Fiction House temporarily out of business and other pulp magazines folding under the great groaning weight of the deepening Depression, Nebel broke into hardcover with *Sleeper's East.* New novels emerged from his typewriter in 1934 and 1935.

Then Nebel succumbed to the lure of the slicks. The money was better than what the hardcover houses paid. The chances of a sale to Hollywood were about equal, or better. The slick circulations were also suffering. Older, more expensive contributors were being cast aside in an austerity move. Seasoned pulp scribes were sought to bring in new readers. *Collier's* and *Redbook* opened their doors to Nebel's work. It would be only a matter of time before he cracked the top slick market, *The Saturday Evening Post.*

Still, loyalty kept Nebel contributing to *Black Mask.* Kennedy and MacBride continued their cockeyed adventures. And pulping for *Dime Detective* was nearly as lucrative as slicking for *Redbook.*

Yet the indefatigable Donahue again refused to perish. A final case straggled out in 1935. A close reading of "Ghost of a Chance" however, proves conclusively that this is a rejected Cardigan story. Donahue is said to be working for the Cosmos Detective Agency, not Interstate.

---

5   *"Lester Dent: the Last of Joe Shaw's Black Mask Boys"* Clues, *Vol. 2, No. 2. Fall-Winter 1981, pg. 130.*

Fred Nebel continued the Kennedy and MacBride stories until Joe Shaw's abrupt departure from *Black Mask* in August 1936. Ironically, Nebel's final submission was rejected by *Black Mask's* publisher over Shaw's objections in these final months. Its title is unknown, but it could have been a last Donahue, one supposes.

Again demonstrating deep loyalty to Shaw, Nebel severed all relations with *Black Mask.* He was all but out of the pulps in 1937.

After that, Frederick Lewis Nebel was a slick man. He never looked back. Even when Joe Shaw assembled his historic *Hard-Boiled Omnibus* in 1946, Nebel steadfastly refused to allow one of his best Kennedy and MacBride stories to be reprinted in its pages, essentially stifling his own literary posterity. Essentially, he turned his back on the genre that made his name, and it likewise returned the favor.

In a letter dated December 8, 1945, Nebel gave his reasons:

"The reason why I don't want to see my old *Black Mask* stuff between boards is because I think it served its purpose well when it was first published but I honestly cannot see what purpose it would serve now. These times have moved fast. The stories, published between ten and fifteen years ago, seem now to be dated. The very sense of timeliness that made them good does not, I think, make them so good now. I can work up no enthusiasm."

Shaw pleaded with Nebel to reconsider:

"I'm in one tough spot," he wrote. "Simon & Schuster have asked me to write an introduction as to what made *Black Mask* and its recognized distinctive style click. Well, that's the story of you and Dash, particularly, and Ray Chandler when he came along later. It isn't my story—I never 'discovered' an author; he discovered himself. I never 'made' an author. He made himself. And you and Dash made that first distinctive style… How the hell am I going to tell about it if you are not there?" [6]

But Fred Nebel stood as firm as one of his pulp protagonists.

While Nebel later relented, permitting a half-dozen Donahue tales to be reprinted in the 1950 collection, *Six Deadly Dames,* he had already been left behind, a fading memory in the minds of his readers, while Hammett, Chandler and others went on to become celebrated, then legendary.

Fred Nebel belongs equally in that august pantheon. Joe Shaw put

---

6 *Shaw to Nebel, December 11, 1945.*

it this way in 1945: "Every worth while editor in the country knows you were one of the highlights in creating that distinctive type and style, along with Dash and Ray; a pretty good triumvirate in any man's language." [7]

With this complete collection of "Tough Dick" Donahue's cases, perhaps at last he will.

---

7 *ibid.*

Rough Justice

A hard-boiled, fighting dick trails his man through the dangerous by-ways of St. Louis' underworld.

Chapter I

DONAHUE came in through the door from the outer office and stood with his hat in one hand, using the other hand to mop his face with a wrinkled handkerchief. He was a big lanky man with black hair, deep-set dark eyes, a long jaw and a long straight nose. He wore a lightweight dark gray suit, no vest, a white oxford shirt with soft collar attached, and a blue crepe tie. He looked hot and uncomfortable and there were two lines attesting to that between his rather wiry eyebrows.

"You Stein?" he asked with half a grumble.

The small dapper bald man behind the shiny oak desk nodded and the motion of his head made the daylight flash on his horn-rimmed spectacles in a way that for a moment hid his eyes.

"I'm Donahue."

Stein said, "Oh, yes. I had a wire from Hinkle."

"Here's a letter," said Donahue as he crossed to the desk.

He sat down in an arm-chair facing Stein while Stein tore open the letter and read a few lines.

Stein nodded and said, "Oh, yes." He folded the letter, laid it on the desk and crossing his hands on the desk said, in a gentler tone, "Yes—yes, indeed."

Donahue was fanning himself with his straw hat. He saw a water-cooler in a corner beyond Stein's right shoulder. He said, "It's hot," and got up and went to the water-cooler. He drew out a glass of water, tasted it, carried the glass back to the chair and sat down again. He looked squarely at Stein, took a long draught, said, "Ah," and put the glass down on the desk. He smacked his lips and said, "Ah, that's good. St. Louis is not a burg for a cold-weather guy." His tawny face, which had been lowering, gradually brightened, and suddenly he

1

smiled, showing long hard teeth.

Stein smiled back at him. Stein's smile was not spontaneous. It did not reveal his teeth because his lips did not part. It was a gentle, fixed, surface smile not particularly friendly.

Donahue said, leaning forward, "I suppose Hinkle just introduced me. He said you'd be a lot of help. We've got something hot, and of course you'll be on hand if I get in trouble. But aside from that, he said you'd see I met the right guys."

"Of course," said Stein. "But just what sort of right guys do you want to meet?"

"A cop that can be smeared. A cop that knows this burg up, down and across—and"—he lowered his hard blunt voice—"a cop that'll keep his jaw shut after he's smeared and stay out of the way. No harness bull. A bigger guy."

Stein said, "Anybody with you?"

"No. This is a lone tail and no small fry."

"Did Hinkle say how much you're to spend?"

Donahue shook his head. "No. He said you'd reason that out. If you spend too much, you'll argue with him. All I want is a cop in the know, and he's not going to know too much about what I'm after."

Stein picked up a paper cutter and probed beneath a thumb nail. "What are you after?"

"Let that slide," said Donahue. "If I get in Dutch I'll tell you."

Stein shrugged. He scaled the paper cutter back on the desk, picked up the telephone and called a number. When he had the connection he said, "You, Luke?... Say, listen, I've got a friend here from New York. I want you to treat him right.... Sure, he's okey. Where can you meet him?... Huh? Oh, yeah. That's okey. When?... In an hour.... What?... Of course. If he wasn't I wouldn't tell you.... Okey, then. In an hour."

He hung up and said, "Luke Cross. Plain-clothes. He'll meet you in Constantine's. That's a Greek joint in Sixth Street."

"Where's that?"

"Well, when you go out of this building, turn to the right and walk three blocks. Then you're at Sixth. Turn left and walk four blocks and you'll see the sign. Go in and tell the Greek you're waiting for Luke Cross."

"That's jake. I'm staying at the Braddock. I'll be seeing you."

Donahue got up, put on his straw hat and went out through an office where a stenographer punished a typewriter. He descended in an elevator, passed through a lobby into the broiling street, and turned to the right He crossed the street and turned south into Sixth. He stopped at Market against traffic, took off his hat, wiped the sweaty band, wiped his forehead, glowered at nothing and crossed the street putting on his hat when the traffic cleared. Opposite a parking lot he saw a green board sign with the word *Constantine's* on it. He crossed the cobbled street, pushed open a glass door with green curtains, and entered a long, narrow room with a lot of porcelain-topped tables. At the right was a counter with a cash register and a cigar case. A fat swart man stood behind the counter smoking a cigar.

Donahue said, "I'm waiting for Luke Cross," and went on to a table in a corner farthest from the counter.

The Greek followed him and grinned and said, "You wait for Luke Cross?"

"Yeah."

"He's friend of me."

"Yeah."

The Greek wiped the table with a soiled napkin and said, "Warm, ain't it?"

"Hot as hell."

"You like a bottle beer?"

Donahue looked up at him, half grinned. "Got one?"

"Sure."

"Let's see it." Donahue put his hat crown down on the table, blew out a breath, squirmed in his coat, ran a finger around his muscled neck beneath his collar band. He stood up and took off his coat and hung it on the back of the chair. His shirt was dark with dampness. He sat down, pulled at his trousers until the cuffs were up to the tops of his socks. The Greek brought a bottle of beer, poured a glassful, grinned, and Donahue raised the glass, said, "How," and emptied half of it.

"Not bad," he said.

" 'S very good," smiled the Greek. "You want paper?"

"Yeah, got one?"

The Greek went over to the counter, brought back a copy of the *Globe-Democrat*. Donahue thanked him. It was all out of order; fell open at the editorial page, and Donahue scanned the editorials, the daily column, then came to H.L. Phillips and chuckled between draughts of beer. He was finishing up the funnies when the door opened and a man came in. The man was short and fat, dressed in a shiny alpaca suit that was open revealing a round paunch and a blue-striped shirt. A narrow-brimmed hat of soft brown straw was tilted over his forehead. His face was chubby with red cheeks, a bulbous nose and little blue eyes that looked across the room at Donahue. Donahue said:

"Hello, Cross."

The man said nothing but thumped slowly across the room, pulled up a chair and sat down opposite Donahue. He took a toothpick from a glass on the table, put it between his fat lips and said:

"Donahue?"

"Yeah."

"Well, how do you like St. Louis?"

Donahue said, "How about a bottle?"

"Sure."

"Flag the Greek."

But the Greek was on the way over and Donahue ordered two bottles. He lit a cigarette, exhaled sharply, eyed Cross with blunt eyes hard like round brown marbles.

"Stein says you're okey, Cross, so let's talk business."

Cross picked his teeth. "I'm listening." He did not look at Donahue. His small blue eyes wandered back and forth across the table absently. When the Greek brought the two bottles and poured out two glasses, Cross picked up his with a fat reddish hand, grunted and drank noisily. He set the glass down but kept his hand around it, looking at the glass with his small blue vacant eyes.

"Like this," said Donahue, placing both elbows on the table. His voice was low, throaty, earnest. "I'm looking for a guy named Mickey Shane. I tailed him from New York to Cleveland and Indianapolis. Shane's an alias he's been using and he may be laying up in this burg under the name of Shannon. Shannon's his real name, but he cuts it up into Shane, or Hannon, or O'Shane. It's been Shane on the way West."

"What's your racket?"

"Racket? Don't make me laugh! Say, Cross, I'm just a working guy like yourself. I used to be on the cops—yeah, for two years. New York, sure. But I got canned. I raided the wrong gambling joint one night and wounded a guy that tried to kick me in the belly. He was a Mick too—like myself. Well, Cross, I'm a private dick now—these last four unholy years. Interstate Agency."

"Oh, them guys."

"Yeah."

"Well." Cross continued to stare at his glass.

"Well, what do you say, Cross? I've got a hunch that this guy Shane is laying up here because he bought a ticket to St. Louis with stop-over privileges, and he's been stopping over. You know the joints and you ought to have an idea where a gun would lay up if he came here. This guy is a gun and no fooling."

"What you want him for?"

Donahue grinned broadly and his dark eyes sparkled. "Come on, Cross, why be a guy like that? I just want to get this guy where I can talk to him." He reached back into the inside pocket of his coat, took out a soiled large envelope, and laid a photograph on the table. "That's the guy."

Cross's face, for all its red chubbiness, was about as animated as dough. His small blank eyes passed over the picture.

Donahue hammered home his argument—"Stein will fix you up, Cross. Our outfit retains him, and if I get in Dutch he'll fix that too. But I won't get in Dutch. And you and I don't have to be seen together. Just get me a line on this guy, you've got stoolies of your own, and give me a ring at the Braddock Hotel. You'll be clean, Cross."

"Well." Cross picked up the photograph, stared at it, then threw it back on the table. Then he drained his glass of beer, wiped his fat lips with a fat hand. He said, "Well," again and shoved back from the table. He laid his palms on the table, looked at them dully, as if in phlegmatic indecision. Then he cleared his throat and rose, saying, "Well, I got to get back on the job."

He shifted his straw hat to the back of his head, took a handful of toothpicks, said, "Braddock Hotel."

"Yeah," said Donahue

Cross turned and moved towards the door, his big fat body rolling from side to side on short fat legs. The Greek called, "S'long, Luke." Cross muttered, "Um," and went out through the door.

Donahue was chuckling to himself.

Chapter II

THE room had two windows over-looking Locust Street. The windows were open and there were screens of fine mesh, more a bulwark against coal dust than insects. An electric fan on the wall swung slowly in something less than a half circle and droned monotonously. The room was green; bed, desk, carpet, chairs were green. The drapes in which the windows were framed hung motionless. A bar of hot sunlight slanted obliquely through both windows. The corridor door was open, but there was another door with horizontal blinds, fastened by a hook, intended to stimulate circulation. It was August in St Louis. It was eighty-eight Fahrenheit in the room—worse in the street.

Donahue lay on the bed, stripped but for a pair of blue trunks. Around him were spread the *Post-Dispatch, Judge, The New Yorker, Time* and the *New York Sun.* On the desk which he had drawn up beside the bed were two bottles of Perrier, three-fourths of a bottle of bourbon, a couple of glasses and a bowl of cracked ice. Donahue lay motionless on propped up pillows, hands behind head. It was his third day in St Louis, the third day of an insufferable heat wave in a city whose summers are never clement His black hair was rumpled, and beads of sweat glistened on his forehead. He stared meditatively at the blank green field of the ceiling. Even the motor horns in the street below sounded hot and muffled.

When the phone rang Donahue merely blinked, did not budge a

muscle. The bell stopped. Donahue watched the shimmering disc of the electric fan. When the phone rang again Donahue made a face. He turned his face towards the phone, regarded it with a scowl. It rang boisterously, insistently.

"Hell," muttered Donahue, and reached for it. Into the mouthpiece he said, "Hello."

"Donahue?"

"Yup."

"Stein. I'm coming up."

Donahue frowned, then said, "Come on." He hung up, his face a little puzzled. He rose and walked over to unhook the door with the horizontal blinds. He went back to the bed, sat down on the edge of it, picked up a rumpled packet of cigarettes from the desk, took one out and put it between his lips. He tore a paper match from a book of matches, struck it, lit the cigarette and lay sidewise on one elbow.

When Stein knocked he said, "Come in."

Stein came in, small and thin and neat in a suit of Palm Beach cloth and a broad-brimmed Panama hat. He let the door close behind him and stood looking at Donahue. His thin face with the shiny horn-rimmed glasses looked grave and portentous.

"Well," he said, "what do you think happened?"

"Sit down," said Donahue.

"Cross got bumped off." Donahue finished taking a drag on his cigarette and let the smoke lazily from his nostrils.

"Did he?"

"Yes."

"Nothing in the papers."

"He was found about two hours ago in an alley down by the river. He must have been bumped off last night."

"That's tough."

Stein took off his hat, walked to a chair and sat down. He stared levelly at Donahue. "Now what the hell are you after?"

"What's that got to do with Cross?"

Stein's glasses flashed. "Listen to me, Donahue. That cheap outfit you work for has retained me in this city to help out any of its operatives who might need help here. I've a right to know what you're after. You're primed to get in Dutch, so I might just as well know. Play ball."

"I told Cross to get a line on a guy named Micky Shane, alias Shannon, alias Hannon, alias O'Shane."

"All right. Why?"

"I'm looking for Micky Shane."

"That's no answer."

Donahue got up, poured some bourbon into a glass, threw in some cracked ice, made the glass half-full with Perrier. He half-turned.

"Want a drink?"

"No!"

Donahue sat down on the bed with the drink, looked at Stein, began to smile and then grinned.

He said, "How the hell will I get in Dutch?"

"That Greek Constantine was a friend of Cross's. You met Cross there, didn't you? The gumshoes will poke around to all the joints and the Greek might remember that you and Cross had a talk the other day. If I'm going to be your lawyer, I want facts or you and the whole damned Interstate can go to hell."

"Calm yourself, Stein—calm yourself! On a hot day like this! I get hot watching you. Don't worry about me, old-timer. I can find my way after dark. Calm yourself! Think of your temperature!"

"I don't feel like joking, Donahue, so cut it out!"

Donahue took a drink. "When I get in Dutch, Stein, I'll tell you about it. But just now I'm all right. If you think Hinkle will tell you more, there's the telephone. Ask for long distance. The number is Beekman double-o-six-o."

Stein stood up, slapped on his Panama. He pulled a silk handkerchief from his breast pocket and mopped his face. He regarded Donahue with sharp eyes behind large glasses.

"Just a bull-headed Mick, eh?"

"Don't get sore, Stein. Have a drink."

Stein said, "Go to hell," and strode out.

Chapter III

AT Police Headquarters in Clark Avenue Detective Hocheimer sat at a battered desk and gnawed at the stem of a corncob pipe. He sat in shirtsleeves, bald head splotched with red heat-spots and high blood-pressure, white hair above the ears damp, thick jowls hanging over a soiled stiff collar, big round eyes bleary.

A head poked in the door, "Guy wants to see the guy on the Cross job."

Hocheimer erupted to say, "Well, ain't I the guy?"

"What I said."

"Who is he?"

"Dunno. Want to see him?"

"Well… well, send him in."

The head disappeared. A little later Donahue came in, fanning himself with his straw hat

"Hot, ain't it?" he remarked.

"You're about the tenth guy's asked me that. What you want? Who are you?"

Donahue pulled a swivel-chair around and sat down. He laid his hat on the table, took time off to wipe his face and neck with a damp handkerchief.

Hocheimer looked like some modernized fat Buddha, sitting there hunched in his chair, with fat hairy arms dangling towards the floor, and big round eyes drooping biliously from their sockets.

His voice was rough, asthmatic. "Well, well—who are you? What do you want?"

Donahue took out his wallet, took from it a card, passed the card to Hocheimer. Hocheimer glared at the card, glared at Donahue, pulled in his lower lip and let it go with a wet smacking sound.

"Yeah. Well?"

"I knew Cross."

"Yeah, yuh did?"

"Yeah. I had a few drinks with him the other day in a Greek speak in Sixth Street."

"I know the place. The Greek says Luke met a guy there. So you're the guy."

"I'm the guy. I'd met Cross a couple times before when I was in this burg, and I called him up and made a date. I thought he could help me out."

"And what are you here for?"

"I'm looking for a guy. I thought Cross could give me a steer. He was a good egg."

"What guy? What do you want him for?"

Donahue pulled his chair six inches closer to Hocheimer. He tapped Hocheimer's knee. "Not so fast. Listen. I may be able to give you a break if you give me one. I'm not going to go into detail, so get that straight."

"You might be in a tough spot, buddy."

"Not at all. I haven't done anything except ask Cross to give me a steer on a guy I was tailing. There's nothing to show that he got bumped off because of that, and even if he did, it's no fault of mine. Have you had a line-up yet?"

"No. We're picking up a lot of guys and we'll go over them in the morning."

"Good," said Donahue. "Now if the guy I'm after is in that line-up, I'll tip you off, provided—*provided*—you give me an hour alone with him before you get your hooks in him."

Hocheimer sat farther back in his chair. He raised his fat hairy arms and laid them across his bulging thighs. He lowered his head and his jowls lay almost against his shoulders. His thick, shapeless mouth twisted.

"You trying to bargain with me, Donahue?"

"What's it sound like?"

Hocheimer sat up straight, put his elbows on the arms of the chair, thrust his huge face forward.

"You got a hell of a nerve, Donahue!"

"My eye! I'm giving you a break!"

"Suppose," said Hocheimer with a gentleness that did not fit his voice or bulk, "I lock you up on general principles."

Donahue's eyes darkened, but he shrugged. "You wouldn't be such a fool."

"Wouldn't I?"

"Well, maybe you would be a fool. Try it."

There was a long moment of silence during which Hocheimer bulged motionless in his chair, his fat wet eyes sliding back and forth across Donahue's brown muscled face, his breath wheezing in his throat behind a lower lip that hung loose and shiny and revealed his lower teeth. Donahue's brown clear eyes never wavered. They did not squint. They regarded the fat mass of Hocheimer's face with blunt, bold frankness. About his neat wide mouth was the vaguest spectre of a droll smile.

"Wouldn't I?" croaked Hocheimer thickly.

"Try it. The Interstate has lots of money behind it. You haven't got a leg to stand on except suspicion, and I'd be out inside of eight hours, and just for spite I'd let you try finding this guy yourself.".

"Yeah?"

Donahue suddenly made an impatient gesture. "You hick cops are the berries, believe me! Well, what are you going to do, pinch me? If you are, go to it. Or if you want to get a break, play ball."

"Who is the guy?"

"If he's in the line-up you'll find out."

"And if he ain't?"

"Hell, we'll both be out of luck."

Hocheimer creaked in his chair, put fat palms together and massaged them. "If he ain't, Donahue, you and me will have a long talk. I got no use for private dicks that come out here from New York and cause a lot of trouble. If he ain't, remember, you're going to spring your whole story."

Donahue laughed. "But a hell of a lot of good that will do you!"

"Remember," said Hocheimer hoarsely, "if he ain't."

Donahue said, "Be your age, Hocheimer!" and grinned with all his straight hard teeth.

Chapter IV

SUMMER rain....

Donahue stood by the window watching the sheets of rain thrash against the glass. Clark Avenue was barely visible through the smeared panes. Thunder rumbled afar, drawing nearer, and rapiers of lightning impaled the wet gloomy murk, and automobile horns complained in a half-dozen different tones.

When the door opened Donahue did not hear it. Hocheimer, grinning loosely, barged in and rocked across the floor and slapped Donahue on the back. Donahue turned his head without turning his body.

Hockeimer jerked a thick thumb over his shoulder. "Take a go at him, Donahue."

Donahue turned then and put his hands on his hips and grinned at Hocheimer.

Hocheimer said, "You ain't such a bad guy, Donahue."

Donahue still grinned. Then he took hold of Hocheimer's arm.

"Lead me, brother."

Hocheimer chuckled and they went out of the room, through a corridor, into another room that was small, gloomy. There was a dusty desk, two straight-backed chairs. A young man sat on one of the chairs. He had yellow hair and a thin white face, and his mouth was thick and red-lipped, loose, rather weak. His eyes were insolent. His hands were manacled together. A policeman leaned against the desk.

Hocheimer said, "All right, Schwartz."

Schwartz twirled his stick and strolled out of the room. Hocheimer looked at the pale-faced youth on the chair, looked at Donahue, winked one of his fat watery eyes, said, "Okey," and went out.

Donahue turned slowly to stare at the door. He stared at the door for fully a minute. Then he crossed to it, put his hand around the knob, turned the knob and opened the door. Hocheimer was standing there. He coughed behind his hand, waved the hand, said, "Okey, Donahue." Donahue grinned at him. Hocheimer chuckled hollowly, coughed again, then walked away whistling.

Donahue closed the door, turned and leaned against it, slipping one hand into his jacket pocket and letting it lounge there. His dark deep-set eyes settled on the pale-faced youth and studied him keenly. The youth's eyes were mutinous and he was trying to make his mouth hard. Thunder rumbled roughshod over the roof. Lightning blazed in the room. The pale-faced youth blinked his eyes and appeared to cringe momentarily. The thunder tumbled away, diminishing, growling afar.

Donahue left the door, picked up a chair and dragged it across the room. He put it down in front of the youth, straddled it, put his arms on the back of it. His back was to the window, his face dimly in shadow.

"Hard guy, eh?" he said offhand.

The youth spat one word.

Donahue said, "How long have you been out of diapers?"

The youth repeated the word.

Lightning blazed whitely in the room. For one split-second the youth's face was a white frozen mask. Thunder exploded overhead, shook the room. Another flash showed the youth's thick, soft red lips agape, his eyes wide.

Donahue's chuckle was low. "Little boy afraid of lightning?"

"—for you!"

"Ah, don't be tough, Micky," chided Donahue. "I'm a good guy, no kidding. Let's be friends."

"—for you!"

"Honest, a guy like you, just out of stir, should be careful. What did you want to get caught in this line-up for? I'm ashamed of you."

"Don't be a wisenheimer!"

"I'm no wisenheimer, Micky. I'm just a poor guy trying to make a living. Now be nice. Why did you leave New York?"

"You're so wise you ought to know."

"Well, I know a few things. I know about that shooting in Ninth Street, when they almost got you. And I know about that other shooting in Harlem when they tried to get you again. You sure bear a charmed life, kid. Yeah, I know you blew the town to come out here and lay up, but there's something else I want to know, Micky, that seventy-thousand-dollar diamond engagement ring."

"Jeeze!" It was an expression of disgust

"You know about it, Micky. You've got it. That's why your boy friends tried to get you. You were holding out on them."

"I was like hell!"

"Kid, the insurance company hired us to watch you as soon as you came out of stir and we've been watching you. When you pulled that job in Westchester two years ago, I'll admit you got a tough break. You did the inside job, blew the safe, and your buddies on the outside breezed when the cops came. You got away by the skin of your teeth but the cops got you a week later. They got all the jewelry except the seventy-thousand-dollar hunk of ice. I'll say you had guts to plant that and take the beatings they gave you. I don't blame you for holding out on the guys that left you in a tough spot. You needed the jack when you came out, and that hunk of ice was big enough to bring you fifty thousand from a fence. All of that is okey. But, kiddo, I'm on a salary to get that ring or find out where it is. And I'm going to get it."

Micky snarled, "You're all wet. I haven't got it. I never had it. I'm flat broke."

"Let's tune out the bed-time story, kid. The guys who stuck up the house with you were after you when you came out. I tailed you here and got Cross to help me get a line on you. Hocheimer's got you for that job, with a good motive. You found out that Cross was looking for you and you let him have it."

"That's a lousy lie. I never saw Cross, and I didn't know he was looking for me. I left New York because those guys were after me. Them yaps thought just like you—that I'd planted the ring before I went up and got it when I came out. But I didn't. For crying out loud, d'you think I'd come out here if I had a hunk of ice worth fifty thousand at a fence's price? Snap out of it!"

"You'd go anywhere to save your hide, and I don't blame you. Listen here, kid. You're in bad now. You come across to me and I'll do everything I can to get you a break. My job is to get the ring, and not the killer of a cop that didn't watch his tricks."

Thunder banged against the roof. Lightning crackled, spat, flashed in the dim room. Micky jerked on his chair. His voice rushed out as the thunder stumbled reluctantly away.

"Jeeze, I tell you I'm broke—flat, on my uppers! I never saw the damn' ring! So help me, God, I never saw it!" He suddenly began to blubber, to choke, to cry. His head fell down to his chest.

Donahue reached out, put the heel of his hand against Micky's forehead, and shoved the head up, saying, "Cut it out!"

The head fell down again. Donahue shoved it up again.

"You goof, cut out bawling! What a hell of a chance you'll stand against Hocheimer!" He stood up, stepped in front of Micky, grabbed a handful of hair, jerked the head up and held it back, peering down into the pale, tear-and-sweat smeared face. His voice came low, husky: "Get this, lad. You're in a pinch. Come across about that ice and I'll do anything I can for you. I'll get you a lawyer. Listen, Micky. You could never stand the gaff here. Hocheimer'll whale hell out of you and they'll hang you sure as hell! Use your head. Listen to me, do you hear! *Listen to me!* I'll—"

Thunder exploded. The window rattled. Sheet-lightning blazed luridly through the window. Micky cringed, sobbed. The rain thrashed violently.

"For God's sake, let me go!"

"You listen to me!"

"Let—me—go! I tell you, I didn't—I don't know anything about—"

Thunder seemed to bang through the room. Micky jerked. The chair fell over and Micky fell with it. Donahue hung on to his chair and followed him to the floor, stopping on one knee. Micky lay panting. His lips blubbered and sweat poured down his face.

"Micky, think hard. I'm a guy can make things easy for you."

" I — d o n ' t know! I didn't get that ring! If I had it, I'd tell you. But I haven't got it. I never had it. I don't know anything about it. I don't. I—I— Lemme go! I tell you, lemme go! Lemme...."

Donahue said, "Hell," without emotion, and let the head drop to the floor. He knelt, looking down at Micky, forearm resting on knee, hand hanging motionless. There was a dark scowl

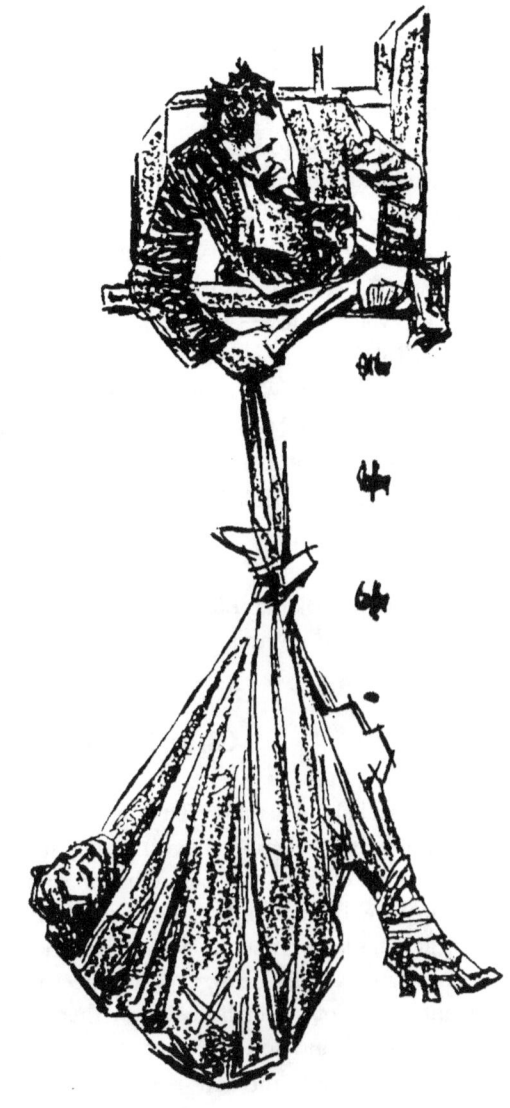

between his eyes. His mouth was unpleasantly bent. His dark eyes scintillated. He said, "Hell," again, this time deeper in his throat. He motioned his lips. He pulled out a wrinkled handkerchief and ran it over his face. He combed his fingers back through his hair.

Suddenly he snarled, "You're a damn' liar, Micky!"

"No—no! God's honest truth—"

"Stow it, you hop-head!" His teeth shone between curled lips. He stood up. He leveled an arm down at Micky. "Just before they hang you, baby, I'll come around and maybe you'll tell me for the good of your soul."

Micky scrambled to his feet, stood shaking on them, moving his manacled hands up and down. "And—they won't hang me! Because I didn't kill Cross!"

"Didn't? Well, they'll hang some guy for the killing, and you'll do as well as any. I'll do my little bit towards seeing you do hang."

Micky's voice grated—"Frame me, eh? Frame me, eh?"

"Sure. Think that over." He bowed and smiled with mock obsequiousness. "Shall I tell Hocheimer you'd like an audience with him?"

Thunder boomed. Lightning blazed in the room. Micky cringed, gasped, stood shivering.

Donahue laughed shortly, without humor. "Little boy afraid of lightning?"

"You—you—"

"Ah, for cripes' sake, lay off! That gutter language is out of date. Sit down"—he started towards the door—"before I knock you down."

Chapter V

STEIN sat behind his shiny flat-topped desk and probed abstractedly beneath a thumb nail with a long, slender paper knife. The thunder storm of three days before had in some measure broken up the heat wave. It was still hot, but not unbearably so. Stein looked very neat in his light tan summer suit, with a henna-colored tie trimly meeting a tan silk collar. Below in Olive Street a trolley car bell clanged petulantly, a lot of motor horns blew. Then a police traffic whistle shrilled, and bell and horns stopped.

A girl appeared in the door that connected Stein's private office with the outer office.

She said, "Mr. Donahue."

Stein looked up at her, looked down at his finger nails. He threw the paper knife on the desk and sat erect, picked up some papers and bent his brows over them. He looked annoyed.

But he said, "All right."

The girl disappeared.

Donahue appeared. He came in strolling, hands in jacket pockets, stiff straw hat clamped between left side and left arm. He was smoking a long, thin panatela of a very light brown color. He was strolling, but the expression on his face was not a strolling expression.

He stopped midway between the door he had entered and the desk at which Stein sat looking very absorbed in the papers before him. But Stein looked up, nodded curtly, said, "Hello, Donahue," and went on reading.

Donahue said nothing. He rolled the light brown panatela from one corner of his mouth to the other and stared with dark, hard brown eyes at the bald pate of Stein. Stein went on reading with an amazing show of intense concentration. He turned sheet after sheet in a brusque, businesslike manner. He made quick notations with a pencil.

Donahue stood motionless, feet planted a little apart, hands idle in pockets, smoke rising in a thin gray column between his eyes. His long, lean face looked very brown, very mask-like. The muted noise of traffic in the street below rose and fell in waves of varying sound. The electric fan in the office droned with the hot monotony of a bee. The typewriter in the outer office began clicking spasmodically.

Stein shifted his horn-rimmed spectacles, twitched his eyebrows. The spectacles seemed to annoy him. He took them off, took the silk handkerchief from his breast pocket, polished the glasses, held them up and looked at them and beyond them, at Donahue.

"Little cooler, Donahue?"

"I didn't come here to talk about the weather."

"One talks about the weather from force of habit."

"One two-times from force of habit, too."

Stein put on his glasses, was very fussy about the way they fitted. He took pains to fold the silk handkerchief before returning it to his breast pocket. He coughed behind a small white well-kept hand. He motioned to the chair at the opposite side of his desk.

"Won't you sit down?"

"You don't have to be polite."

"I'm not. I want to talk to you."

"Talk."

Stein picked up the paper knife, leaned back in his chair, poked idly at the desk blotter with the point of the paper knife. He pricked six holes in a row, then pricked six more at right angles, and then threw down the paper knife.

"Well, Donahue, business is business, you know," he said airily.

Donahue nodded very slowly. "Yeah, two-timing is two-timing. You call it what you like. It's still two-timing."

"Don't be an ass."

Donahue ripped his hand from his pocket and slashed it shortly away from his stomach. "I'm no ass! But you're a —— damned double-crossing kike!"

Stein remained calm, casual. "Now, Donahue, please—"

Donahue took three hard steps that brought him to the desk. The hand that he had ripped from his pocket became a fist and the fist landed dully on the desk and remained there at the end of a rigid arm. His wiry brows almost met above his nose, and dark fury burned in his eyes, his lips thinned against his teeth.

His voice rapped out swiftly, deep-toned, rough-shod—"I know I'm in a rotten game, Stein. I'm not defending it. I don't know why I'm in—but I'm in it. It keeps me in butts and I see the country and I don't have to slave over a desk. I get places. It's not a pretty game, and no guy ever wrote a poem about it. But it's the only hole I fit in."

He stopped. He turned, strode to the connecting door and closed it. He came back to the desk, put his palms flat down on it, and leaned on his arms.

"Stein, I may be a bum, but I'm not the bum that you are."

"Now, now, Donahue—"

"Shut up! I'm talking! My boss sent me out here with your address. I came here. I told you what I wanted. It was none of your damned business what I was after and you knew it. If I got in Dutch, I got right out of it—and without your help. You wanted to make a case right off the bat, so you could get some easy dough from the Agency. But there was no case. You got sore at me because you couldn't buffalo me."

"Donahue, I tell you—"

"I told you to shut up! For two cents I'd break a chair over your head! I've been up against crooks, guns, and I've double-crossed them to get what I wanted. That's what my game is. It's not a polite business of question-and-answer bunk. You work against crooks and you've got to beat them at their own game. But now—now, Stein—I'm up against a different proposition. I'm up against a smooth-tongued kike who's double-crossed me!"

Stein's spectacles flashed. "You take it easy, Donahue! I'm not standing for any loose talk from a cheap Mick gumshoe, and you and your agency can go plumb to hell. Get out of my office!"

"You get this, Stein! You went to Shane because you knew I wouldn't tell what I was after. You're his lawyer now, and I know damned well you wouldn't work for charity. There's money in this job. You know what I'm after. You know what Shane has, or you know that he's got money that represents what he did have. And you're figuring to get that money by taking his case and saving him from the gallows!"

Stein smiled his thin, artificial smile. "Yes, I am Shane's attorney. Beyond that you're just a big bag of wind."

"Am I? Well, don't let that idea run away with you. You're not going to get that money, Stein. I haven't been spending all of my time in bed, and you're going to land so hard that it ain't even going to be funny. Stuff that down your belly and see if it doesn't give you indigestion."

Stein put his fingertips together. "Now will you get out of my office?"

Donahue gave him a short, harsh laugh, walked to the watercooler, poured out a drink and turned and looked at Stein while he held the glass in his hand. He was breathing heavily and perspiration gleamed in silvery streaks on his brown face. He took a drink, licked his lips, flexed his body in his sweaty clothes. He made a motion with the glass and some of the water slopped out and slopped to the floor.

"So don't spend too much time on Shane," he said. "You'll lose money on him."

"On your way out, Donahue, please leave the door open."

Donahue laughed, finished the drink, set down the glass. He strode to the door, stopped with his hand on the knob, looked at Stein. Stein sat with fingertips lightly together, face expressionless, daylight shining on his spectacles and hiding his eyes.

Donahue said, "Shane claims he's innocent, doesn't he?"

"Read the papers, didn't you?"

"Yeah. Wouldn't it be funny if he is?"

Donahue pulled open the door and went out chuckling.

Chapter VI

DONAHUE had been getting on well with the Greek Constantine. Hocheimer had okeyed Donahue, and the Greek knew on which side his bread was buttered. He supplied Donahue with beer and cigars—gratis, but Donahue was looking for information, too....

"I'm still working on this case, you know," he said, two days after the seance with Stein.

"'S too bad about Luke. 'S too very bad."

"Yeah. Luke was a nice guy."

"Very nice guy."

Donahue started a glass of beer. "You know, I don't think the case is settled yet."

"Yeah."

"No."

"Oh, yeah.... No."

"That's right. I don't think it's all settled. Say, did Luke used to meet any guys here?"

"Some, yeah."

"Who?"

"Well, Luke use to meet... let's see. Um. Oh, was Charley Hart from de newspaper. Um. Was Luke's brodder-in-law, Meester Coombs. Um. Was Tony Nesella. Um. Was Johnny Murphy from over de station-house. Um. Guess dat's all."

"What's Nesella do?"

"He was waiter down de place by de river dey call de *Show Boat Club*. I ain't seen Tony."

"Where's this *Show Boat Club?*"

"By de river. Let's see. She's on Second Street. She's crazy club. I tell you, de likker she ain't no good dere. But maybe you see Tony you tell him my name, he give you some good."

"Night-club, eh?"

"Yeah. De nigger band. Yeah. Like dat. Make whatcha call whoopee."

Donahue laughed. "Well, I feel like making whoopee."

"She's open only de night. De women"—he grimaced and shook his head—"no good. Tony tell me." He grinned, patted Donahue's arm. "Good-lookin' guy like you no play around women like those."

"Never can tell." Donahue took another drink.

A waiter yelled, "Cash!" and the Greek made a bee-line for the cash register.

Donahue went down to the *Show Boat Club* that night

It crouched in a slanting cobbled alley a couple of blocks from the river. A damp warm mist had come up from the Mississippi. It hung motionless in the cobbled alley. Street lights were few and far between, and brick houses, dark-windowed, stood irregularly along the alley, and a blue glow hung over the doorway before which a taxi deposited Donahue. The blue glow revealed a square board sign with the words *Show Boat Club* painted in large letters. There were a half-dozen cars parked in the alley, and a man in a wrinkled white duck suit stood leaning outside the doorway.

Donahue had no trouble getting in. The place was wide open. A man inside took his hat and gave him a check. Another led him down a musty hallway where blue lights glowed. This man opened a big door and led him into a large room on the walls of which were painted a hazy idea of a show boat and some plantation scenes. The tables were rough board, without covers, and lined three walls. Against the fourth wall was a raised platform that was supposed to look like the stern of a show boat. Negro musicians sat there and mopped shiny black faces. Four wooden propellers thrashed beneath the ceiling and stirred the second-hand atmosphere.

As Donahue sat down at a table he muttered to himself, "Joint."

The waiter said, "What?"

Donahue looked at him. "Tony Nesella around?"

"No."

"Off?"

"He don't work here."

"He did."

The waiter looked at the table. "What you want?"

"Pleasant guy, ain't you?"

"What you want?"

"Well, give me what you've got. It's probably new bourbon or bath-tub gin, but I'll take a Brody. And some Canada Dry."

The waiter walked away.

The jazz band cut loose. Couples got up. Some looked like clerks and their girl friends out to paint the town. Others looked as night-club patrons look. All perspired and danced. The floor was not waxed. It was just a floor and feet scraped harshly against it. At a table near the jazz band sat two girls. One had had things done to her hair and it was now blonde. The other had hair black as jet that fitted her head like a helmet, showing the lower half of each ear and running around her forehead in severe bangs. Her cheeks were a bad paint job.

Donahue got up and went over and asked her to dance. She had nice teeth and used them. They stepped around. She danced formally, or what might have been her idea of dancing formally—breast high, stomach in, chin up, eyelids lowered.

Donahue said, "Call that dancing, kid?"

She laughed with her teeth together. When the round was over Donahue steered her to his table. She sat down and waved a handkerchief in her face. Sweat stood out on Donahue's face. He grinned through it.

"You're pretty good, kid," he said.

"Oh, you think so?"

"Yeah. Take some nourishment. Hey, waiter!"

When the waiter had come and gone she said, "You can step yourself, big boy."

"I admit it."

"That sounds Irish."

"I admit that too."

She laughed. "Now I can expect a line."

"Not unless you want it."

The waiter brought her drink and she looked at Donahue and said, "Here's how."

He drank with her and set down the glass, scowled at it. "Mouth wash! When Tony Nesella was here a guy could get a drink."

She took another drink and said nothing.

Donahue said, "Where is Tony?" and threw a packet of cigarettes on the table.

She took one and Donahue struck a match for her. She said with a puff of smoke, "Tony? I guess he left."

"That's too bad. He was a nice guy. I'd like to see him."

Out of the side of his eye Donahue saw a big rangy man standing in the doorway with the waiter who had brought the drinks. The big rangy man had fuzzy red hair. Donahue thought he saw him raise a hand and move a finger.

Donahue looked down at his drink. After a minute the girl said, "Excuse me, big boy," and went out through the door.

Donahue did not send his eyes after her, did not rise. He leaned on his elbows and moved his glass back and forth over a wet smear on the table. The jazz band exploded again. Couples grew on the floor. One couple reeled against Donahue's table. He caught a whiff of perfume saturated with perspiration. He watched the contents of his glass creep sinuously across the table. A youth's loose face leered down at him over a girl's red hair.

"Sore, bud—sore?"

Donahue looked up. "Sore?... No."

"Was gonna bust you if you were."

The girl said, "Billy... Billy!..."

Donahue laughed. "I'm licked, bud."

The couple reeled off among other reeling couples. The trombone booed. Feet threshed the floor.

The girl with the black tight hair and the bad paint job came back to Donahue's table and sat down showing her teeth in an intimate grin. Donahue ordered more drinks. He put his hand on the girl's hand and squeezed it. He smiled at her.

"I'm going to like you," he said.

"Oh, yeah?"

"Sure. You're the berries, kid, no fooling."

The waiter brought their drinks.

Donahue said, "I think I'll get tight. Want to get tight?"

"Do you want to get tight?"

"Yeah. I'm on a spree. I feel like making hey-hey, and I've got the jack to make it on."

She rubbed her palm over the knuckles of his hand. "You're nice, big shot—you're sure nice."

They danced again. The big man with the fuzzy hair came to look in through the door. He had pale glassy eyes beneath beetling brows. He wore a white silk shirt with purple arm garters, white flannels, black-and-white shoes.

Donahue and the girl went back to the table after the dance and ordered more drinks. She said her name was Eva. Donahue drank in big gulps. He drank two and sometimes three glasses to the girl's one. He ran his hand through his hair until it became disheveled. His dark face became shiny with sweat. When, at the end of an hour, they danced again he staggered, and they returned to the table before the end of the number.

He lounged back in his chair. His eyelids drooped and he gazed around the room blearily. The big man with the fuzzy hair appeared in the doorway again and looked at him. The girl Eva looked at the man in the doorway and raised her eyebrows. The man in the doorway nodded.

Donahue groaned and put his head down on the table. The girl put a hand on his wet hair and said:

"Maybe the heat's getting you in here, honey. There's a cooler room upstairs, on top. Want to rest up?"

Donahue mumbled, "Yeah…. You're a good kid, Eva."

"Well, come on, hon."

Donahue got up, looking very drunk, very wilted. The girl took his arm and steered him through the door into the blue-lit hallway. Donahue walked with his head hanging, his feet lagging.

"Here's the stairs, hon."

"Yeah."

He climbed the stairs in fits and starts, hanging to the banister. He reached the top and stood swaying in the hall there.

"This way," said the girl.

He stumbled after her to the rear of the hall. He stopped and waited while she opened a door. As she entered a dark room he lunged in after her, caught the door, fell back with it, shut it with a bang, remained leaning with his back against it, his hands behind him.

The girl found the switch and turned on the light. The bedroom contained a single bed, a wash-stand, a small table, and two chairs. Donahue lurched across the room and stopped with arms braced against the sill of the one window. He put his head out and looked down. They were on the second story.

The girl was tugging at his arm. "Come on, hon, lay down on the bed and rest. Take your coat off."

He turned around slowly and blinked sleepily at her. He grinned. He put his arms around her and hugged her. She smiled up into his sweaty brown face.

"You're some dame, Eva."

"Glad you think so big boy.... Come on, lay down."

She urged him towards the bed. He dragged his feet towards it and when his knees touched the edge of it he half-twisted and sank down. But he dragged the girl with him. She protested.

"Please, honey—"

He swung her down on the bed with sudden violence and a low curse. One big hand smacked across her mouth and stifled a cry and he heaved up to bend his leg and plant the lower part of it across her legs. Her eyes sprang open with sudden terror.

He laughed bluntly. "Well, you little ——, I didn't think they were so dumb as this even in the sticks."

With his free hand he drew a handkerchief from his breast pocket, bent over her, forced it beneath the hand that stifled her mouth and then gradually forced the handkerchief into her mouth. She heaved and writhed and gagged, but he got all of the handkerchief into her mouth. Then he rolled her over, yanked her hands behind her back, took a pair of manacles from a hip pocket and snapped them on her wrists. Then he rolled her on her back and stood up.

He drew a key from his pocket and held it up and said, "Didn't you hear me lock the door as we came in?... So you think that a quart of bath-tub gin can get a good man tight? Well, sister!"

He laughed heartily, lifted her from the bed and laid her on the floor. Her face worked as she tried to yell, but not a sound came from her gagged mouth. He pulled a counterpane and two sheets from the bed and tied them together. The end of one sheet he tied to the bed. The end of the counterpane he lashed around the girl's waist. He moved quickly, surely.

He carried the girl to the window, shoved her out, and gradually lowered her to a dark yard below. When the tension on the improvised line lessened, he stood up. He went back to the door and inserted the key but did not turn it. As he was moving towards the window a fist rapped loudly on the door. He looked back once but kept on towards the window. He swung a leg out, then another, then grabbed the line and lowered himself to the yard, where the girl lay.

Bending down, he untied her and hauled her to her feet. He unlocked the manacles and put them in his pocket. He dragged her over two fences and five minutes later came into a dark, mist-ridden street. Here he paused to draw the handkerchief from her mouth. She whirled on him.

He shoved the muzzle of his automatic against her stomach. "Sister, this rod will be in my pocket. You're going places with me, and if you let out a chirp I'll let you have it. Come on."

"You ——!"

"Such language!"

He yanked her through the dark street.

Chapter VII

THE electric fan in the room in the Hotel Braddock had a subdued drone.

The girl lay on the bed sobbing, an arm across her face. Donahue stood at the foot of the bed, holding a tall glass of ice water, and looking darkly at the girl. He had taken off his coat and tie and rolled up his shirt sleeves.

He growled, "Cut out that bawling!"

She took her arm from across her face and sniffled. Her face was red as a beet and the rouge had run. Strands of black hair were pasted wetly on her forehead.

"What—what do you want me for?"

"I want Tony Nesella."

"I don't know where he is."

"You're a damned liar! Why did you want to get me in that room?"

She broke out crying again and put her hands to her face. Donahue cursed, slammed his glass down on the desk, sat on the edge of the bed, grabbed her hands and pulled them from her face. He leaned over her, spreading her arms until the hands were at either side of the bed. He glared down into her wide terrified eyes with hard round brown ones.

"You listen to me, sister! I saw all that by-play of yours with that big mutt in the doorway. When I mentioned Nesella's name to that flat-mugged waiter he shut up like a clam. When you first came over to my table, I saw the big mutt give you the high-sign and you went out. Nesella's name spelled trouble there and getting me in that room was a frame. Now get this: You come across to me and you'll walk out of this room as you are. You tighten up and I'll call in the police."

"You—you're hurting my wrists!"

"I'll hurt more than your wrists. Who was Tony Nesella?"

"A waiter at the—"

"I mean, outside of that."

"God, I tell you I don't know!" Her breath was hoarse in her throat, pumping out of an open mouth. "You—you can't do this to me!"

"Who's going to stop me?"

"Please... let me go!"

"You'll go, baby, as soon as you give me a line on what's behind all this damned monkey business. I mean it. Now cut out this sob stuff and use your head, because you're in a tough spot."

"Please—"

"Stop saying please! Get it into your nut that I mean business! Why did my mentioning Nesella's name start things?" He shook her. "Why did it? You hear me—why did it?"

"Oh ... it's so hot! Stop. I—I'll pass out—"

"And I'll give you a bath to bring you back. Come on, sister. Play ball."

She looked haggard, miserable. She shook her head slowly. "No... I don't know a thing... a thing."

He kept at her for an hour, mercilessly. And at the end of the hour he was perspiring as much as she.

And she said, "Not a thing.... I don't know...."

He got up from the bed, walked over and stood beneath the fan. His face was almost sullen. He pulled off his shirt and threw it across the room. He rubbed his hands down his arms. He went into the bath-room, got a towel and rubbed that down his arms, around his neck, down his chest beneath his undershirt. He went back into the bath-room with the towel, drew a glass of ice-water, carried it to the bed.

"Here's a drink," he said.

She said, "I don't want it."

He sat on the edge of the bed, put an arm around the back of her neck, made her sit up and held the glass against her lips. Then she drank, draining it. He got up and let her fall back.

"I'm damned if you'll pass out," he growled.

She closed her eyes and groaned. Donahue walked around the room aimlessly, flung black looks at her, stopped at the foot of the bed and said:

"Will you come across?"

"I don't know—anything—anything."

He put his hands to his head and said, "My God!" and then went to the telephone. He called a number. The girl on the bed turned her face and looked at him. She bit her lip.

"You've still got time," he said.

She went on biting her lip.

"Hello," he said into the mouthpiece. "Hocheimer there?… Yeah, put him on."

He leaned towards the girl. "How about it, sister?"

She was still biting her lip.

Donahue came back to the mouthpiece. "Hello, Hocheimer. This is Donahue.… I'm all right, sure. But get a load of this. You know that *Show Boat* joint down near the river.… No, I didn't say a show boat was on the river. That joint, I mean—that so-called night-club.… Yeah, that's it. Well, listen. I've just been down there and I've got something hot. I was poking around on that Cross killing, and on a tip—went down there looking for a guy named Tony Nesella.… What right have I to poke around? Be your age, Hochie. I got the hunch that maybe Shane didn't kill Cross.… Well, I know you have, but if Shane's innocent, why hang him?… Oh, shut up and listen.

"When I got down to this club I asked a waiter for Tony, thinking that Tony was a waiter there too. Well, he used to be, but no more. But after I'd mentioned his name the waiter acted dumb. Then a broad shared nourishment with me, and I mentioned Tony's name again. A big frowzy-haired guy high-signed her into the hall. She came back to my table and I began to act tight. After a while she got me to go upstairs to a room. I tell you, they were scared stiff about me. But I got out of the room. Yeah, and I took the broad with me, but she won't spring.… Where am I? Down in my hotel room with the broad.… No, don't come over here. Go down to the *Show Boat Club* and pinch that frowzy-headed bum that framed me.… Yeah, I'm listening." He leaned back in the chair, nodded, said, "Um," or, "Yes," and finally, "All right, Hocheimer. I'll bring her over."

He slipped the receiver quietly into the hook, put his hands on his knees, and grinned broadly at the girl.

He said, "Little Eva, you might have gotten out of this by telling me that Tony was a stoolie of Luke Cross's. Hocheimer of Headquarters is going down to see Brennan, that big bum of a friend of yours.

Primp up, chicken, while I put on a shirt."

She had not moved since Donahue finished talking with Hocheimer. Her eyes were round as saucers, her lower lips drawn in between her teeth. A pallor was creeping through the flush on her face, and her hands were fists, white-knuckled. Her eyes followed Donahue as he crossed the room whistling and pulled open a dresser drawer.

Then she spat, "You—!"

Donahue, still whistling, looked around at her as he lifted a shirt from the drawer. He shoved long brown arms into crisp clean sleeves, began singing in a low voice the chorus of the song he had just whistled.

She sat up and cried, "I hope they kill you, cut your dirty heart out!"

Donahue buttoned his shirt, bowed gently, and switched back to whistling as he put on a tie.

She rasped, "You dirty Irish—"

Donahue wagged a finger at her. "Naughty—naughty! Papa spank!"

In blind fury she swept the heavy glass water pitcher from the table beside the bed and hurled it at Donahue. He caught it neatly with both hands, set it down on the dresser, crossed swiftly to the bed, grabbed her by both arms and swung her to her feet on the floor. Then he rushed her towards the bathroom.

"Wash your neck for a change," he growled, "and behind your ears, and don't use my comb."

Chapter VIII

EVA sat disconsolately in an arm-chair in a room at Police Head-quarters. Donahue sat on a desk, dangling his legs. From time to time he looked at his strap-watch, and he smoked many cigarettes. The hot dark night hung outside the open window, and a greasy, corroded electric fan hummed on the desk.

Eva had gone on a diet of absolute silence. Donahue had nothing more to say to her, wherefore he said nothing. There was a bad squeak somewhere in the electric fan. He turned the fan off. Then because the motionless air became too hot, he turned the fan on again.

When a sudden scuffle of feet and a rumble of voices sounded outside the door, he slipped from the desk and stood behind Eva, looking at the door over her head. The door banged open, and a knot of men came lunging in. Blood and bruises were visible.

Hocheimer's straw hat had a broken crown. He slammed Brennan, the frowzy-haired man, into a chair and slapped his fat palms together. A couple of policemen rough-housed two other men into chairs. Hocheimer took off his broken hat, looked at it, looked daggers at Brennan, threw the hat on the desk, and looked at Donahue.

"Well, there y' are, Donahue—there y' are."

Donahue smiled, bowed and spread his hands. "You seem to have had a hot time."

Brennan was glaring at Eva and cursing silently with his lips.

Hocheimer said, "When we got down there the joint was closed, so we knocked and knocked and got no tumble. Then we went around in the back and crashed through a window. Before we knew it there was a free-for-all in the dark. You should have seen it! One of my men found the lights, and when the lights went on some bum pulled a gun. I let him have it. It was all so sudden. I wasn't looking for fight, I just wanted to ask some questions. But them bums had other ideas. We had to kill two of them, and one of my men had to be took to the hospital, and here's the rest. Hell, Donahue!" He mopped his fat face.

Brennan snarled at Eva, "What a fine broad you turned out to be!"

"I didn't—"

"You didn't! Hell! You double-crossing tramp!" He looked up at Hocheimer. "Take it from me, fat boy, that frail is going to get hers! This squeal cooks her. Get this: She came from Peoria a year ago. She was married to a guy she didn't like. His name was Joe Corson. He worked on the railroads. One night he was found dead in a crashed flivver outside of Peoria. He was drunk. This frail was driving the car. She gave the car the gas and jumped. Her husband was sound asleep beside her, and the flivver was doing fifty when it socked a stone wall. When the wreck was found she was beside it, with scratched knees and a couple of cuts. There was no case at all."

Hocheimer opened his eyes wide. The girl had gone dead white. Her hands crept to her cheeks and the fingernails clawed at her cheeks. Suddenly she screamed.

Brennan laughed. "That for you. You would double-cross me, eh? You would pull a fade-out with this dick and send Headquarters down on me? Ah, I should have broken your neck long ago!"

She stared at him with terror-stricken eyes, shaking her head, mumbling. Then she cried:

"I didn't tell him anything!" She flung at Donahue, "Did I?"

Donahue grinned. It was a strange, insinuative grin, and he kept shifting it from Eva to Brennan. But he said nothing.

Brennan snapped, "You think I'm a goof? With the whole police force busting into my place! All right, all right! But by tomorrow, kiddo, the Peoria cops will come down here, and I hope to hell they burn you!"

The girl jumped up, making fists of her hands. Color flooded her face. Her voice grated harshly:

"You dope, you! I didn't say a word, but now I will. And you'll hang. Officer, this man killed Cross. Brennan killed Cross. The gun he used is buried in his cellar beneath an old ice-box. Him killing Cross was a mistake. He meant to kill Tony Nesella because he thought Tony was stooling to Cross about the liquor they were running on the river. It was a dark night and pretty misty. Brennan followed Tony to that corner in Commercial Alley, and he saw Tony alongside a pole. He fired and missed and Tony jumped. He thought it was Tony jumped into the open again, but it was Cross, who was leaning behind the pole waiting for Tony. And Cross got his and Tony ran. Brennan ran after Tony and got him down by the river. He crushed his skull, tied a rock around his neck and pitched him in the river. He came back to the joint shaking like a leaf and he said to me, 'My God, I killed Luke Cross!' That's what he said. Mike, you made me do this! Till now I didn't say a word."

Brennan fell back in his chair, horror widening his eyes. Eva put her hand to her eyes, staggered, collapsed on the floor. Brennan looked down at her, dazed, speechless.

Donahue chuckled and said, "Hell, Hocheimer, this has been some merry-go-round!"

Hocheimer swallowed hard. "I never expected this."

"Neither did I."

"Yeah, but you sure stirred up a pot of trouble."

"It's your name gets in the papers, Hocheimer. You've got no kick. Hell, you should thank me!"

"Yeah. Yeah, I s'pose I should."

Donahue said, "Look," and counted on his fingers. "You get credit for nabbing the killer of Cross. For nabbing the killer of Tony Nesella. For nabbing a hubby-killer from dear old Peoria. Hocheimer, old boy,

I shouldn't be surprised if they made you a sergeant or whatever they make good detectives in this burg."

Hocheimer actually grinned—a sort of shy, embarrassed grin that made his fat face ludicrous. But he promptly banished that and assumed an air of heavy dignity. He said to the policemen:

"Lock these birds up for a while." He looked down at Eva, who was stirring on the floor. "Give her a drink."

When he and Donahue were alone, Hocheimer sighed into a chair and opened his shirt.

"You're a good egg, Donahue," he said. "You must be one of those amateur detectives a guy reads about in books. You go after things for the love of the game."

Donahue, sitting on the desk and dangling his legs, broke into uproarious laughter. "Don't be that way, Hocheimer! And where the hell do you get the amateur stuff? Say, if you think I'm a Good Samaritan you're off your trolley. So far you've got everything out of this show. I haven't got a thing except a lot of trouble."

"Well, you were wrong on Shane. He didn't even know this gang."

"Sure I was wrong. How was Shane picked up?"

"Kelly picked him up on a hunch, that's all. And he was packing a gun."

"He can get a bondsman easily enough for that."

"Sure. He'll be out tomorrow."

Donahue stood up. "I'll be around here. I want to know just when he goes out."

"Listen, Donahue," complained Hocheimer. "For God's sake, don't start any more trouble!"

"Cross my heart," grinned Donahue.

But Hocheimer looked worried.

Chapter IX

AT noon Micky Shane walked out of Headquarters into bright hot sunlight. He needed a shave. He stood on the curb for less than a minute, then started east on Clark. A moment later Donahue came out, spotted him, crossed the street but followed in the same direction. Micky turned south into Tenth Street, then east into Spruce, passed Ninth and Eighth and turned south into Seventh. He continued south and was held up by a string of truck traffic that had come over the Free Bridge and was rumbling west on Chouteau. After a minute he crossed Chouteau, walked west on the other side of the street and then swung south.

Donahue, stopping on the corner behind a pole, saw Micky enter a three-story dirty red brick house. Two minutes later Donahue moved towards that house, drifted past, got the number, crossed the street and entered a rundown cigar store. He bought a couple of cigars and a newspaper and hung around inside the store reading the paper, though he was able to see the red brick house through the window. The proprietor sympathized with him about the weather, and Donahue bought a bottle of soda pop.

He killed an hour in the store and began to weary of it, having drunk in the meantime four bottles of soda pop that did not set well on his stomach because the aftermath of his bout with a quart of bath-tub gin still remained with him.

He was on the point of going out and trying to walk off the gin when he saw a yellow taxi draw up before the red brick house. He saw Stein get out, very dapper in a tan suit and Panama hat.

As the taxi moved off Stein entered the red brick house.

Donahue remained motionless chewing thoughtfully on the stub of his cigar. He remained that way for fully three minutes, then pushed open the screen door, flung away his butt and crossed the street. He loafed up to the hall door, looked up the front of the building, then walked into a dark hall that was cool and damp in comparison with the street. He stopped and blinked, trying to accustom his eyes to the darkness.

At the back of the hall a door was open and a baby was crying. Donahue moved towards the open door, stopped outside and knocked. Presently a fat negress appeared wiping her hands on a greasy blue-checked apron.

"There's a man named Shane living here, isn't there?"

"Shane? Nossuh, Ah don' know dat name."

"Maybe it's O'Shane, or Shannon, or Hannon—something like that."

"Well, dere's a Mistuh Hannon, but I reckon he ain't home. He done gone away, Ah reckon, but he'll be back, 'cause his bag is still dere."

"I think he came back today. I'm a friend of his."

"Well, suh, then he's on de top flo', de back o' de hall, way back."

Donahue said, "Thanks," and left her and climbed to the top floor.

He walked softly towards the rear of the musty hall and stopped before a door that barred his way. He put his ear to the door. There were voices beyond the door, and he recognized the tone of Stein's voice, but not the words. When Stein's voice stopped he heard Micky Shane's. Then Stein's again. Stein talked most. There was an insistent strain in the tone of it.

This kept up for ten minutes while Donahue crouched outside the door. Then there was silence, then moving feet. Presently a key turned in the lock. Donahue stepped to one side, in the deeper shadows, and his hand went around his hip, came around front again holding his gun.

The door opened and light rushed into the hall. Stein stepped out putting on his hat. Micky Shane came behind him and turned to insert the key in the outside of the door.

Donahue said, "Let's go back in a minute."

Stein stiffened. Micky whirled and bumped into Stein. Donahue stepped out of the shadows and looked at both of them. They looked at him. Stein's face was shadowed down to his mouth by the broad brim of his Panama. Micky Shane had not yet put on his hat. His eyes popped.

"In," said Donahue.

Stein said, "I am leaving, Donahue. I came here to confer with my client."

"You are not leaving, Stein," smiled Donahue.

"I tell you—"

"Get in!"

He straight-armed Stein into the room so fast that Stein almost lost his balance. He jammed his gun into Micky Shane's stomach and backed him step by step into the room. He reached back with his left hand and quietly closed the door. He leaned indolently against the door, a crooked little droll smile on his lips.

Stein was a cool bird. Having regained his balance, he drew out a silk handkerchief, patted his lips, coughed gently into the handkerchief, then tucked it carefully back into his pocket.

Micky Shane was rattled. He kept licking his red soft lips and rubbing his hands against hips. His eyes burned feverishly on Donahue.

"Donahue," said Stein in a platform voice, "you know you are more than overstepping your province."

"Who the hell ever said I cared whether I did or not?"

"Donahue, I demand that you get away from that door and permit me to go about my business."

"Honest, Stein, I get a great kick out of you."

"And I don't care for your cheap repartee!"

"Oh, that's what you call it?" Donahue chuckled with genuine good humor. "Ah, Stein, you're a trick—you sure are a trick. I'd like to let you go. In fact, I don't care a damn whether you go or stay… after I get what I came for."

"I don't know what you're talking about."

"That's a worn-out answer, Stein."

"Donahue, step aside so that I may—"

"Lay off!" Donahue darkened suddenly. He took a step from the door and stopped. "You punk kike, you can't hand me a line like that! I got this kid in jail and I got him out. And I didn't get him out because I like him or to pass the time away. I got him out to get what he's got. I want it, Stein! By God, I want it! I've pulled some bones in this burg since I came here, but now I've got him and you in a jam and I don't want to hear a lot of hot air!"

Micky Shane snapped, "You big bum, there ain't nothing here! Stein bailed me out and come down here to talk to me! Of all the wet-blankets I seen in my time—"

"Enough out of you, hop-head!" cut in Donahue.

Stein began, "Donahue, in the name of reason—"

"To hell with reason!" roared Donahue, getting darker. "Shut up, both of you! You, Stein, take your clothes off! Strip!"

"Why, I—"

"Strip!"

Micky Shane said, "Don't you do it, Stein. This guy's just a bad smell."

"Donahue," rasped Stein, "I won't submit to this humiliation!"

Micky Shane yelped, "Don't you, Stein!"

Donahue took one quick step. His gun rose, came down hard against Micky's head, and Micky hit the floor with glazed eyes. Stein made a leap for the door. Donahue jumped after him, caught him by the collar, yanked him back and sent him spinning across the room.

Stein hit a chair, tumbled over it, banged his head against the window sill. He lay panting and gibbering, holding his head.

"Get up," said Donahue. "Get up and take your clothes off. If you don't want to take them off, give me what I came here for. Get up!"

Stein drew his knees up to his chest, crouched on the floor. Donahue went over, grabbed a handful of Stein's shirt and heaved him to his feet. He shook him violently.

"All right, keep your pants on, but raise your hands!"

"Donahue, stop this. You can't—"

Donahue jammed a hand into one of Stein's coat pockets. It came out empty.

"Keep 'em up, Stein!"

Micky Shane was crawling on hands and knees. Donahue heard him and twisted about. Stein drove a fist to Donahue's ear. Donahue shook his head, swung back on Stein. Micky flung himself at Donahue's legs. Donahue went down like a felled tree. But in falling he grabbed one of Stein's legs and Stein went down too.

Micky planted his teeth in Donahue's leg, and Donahue yelled, "Damn you!" and twisted violently. Stein had a foot to use and he walloped it against Donahue's head. Donahue clenched his teeth and wrenched Stein's leg so hard that Stein cried out in pain. Micky let go of the leg and threw himself farther up on Donahue, striking the back of his head with hard little fists. Stein was kicking Donahue in the face, and Donahue reached back, caught one of Micky's arms and forced him off his back. He muscled around dragging Stein with him, his gun beneath his stomach. He recovered his gun, suddenly heaved towards Stein and rapped the barrel against Stein's head as Micky was scrambling to his feet. Stein grunted and lay flat on his back, and Donahue was on one knee when Micky kicked him in the jaw. The blow drove him tumbling back over Stein, but he rose in the midst of Micky's next attack, blood dripping from his face, and with his left hand caught Micky by the throat. With his right he clubbed the gun twice on Micky's head, held him for a moment with his left hand, then let him drop limply to the floor.

He stood for a brief moment breathing heavily, while drops of blood from his face stained the front of his sweat-soaked shirt. He was a little numb, blinking his eyes and moving his jaw from left to right. He coughed, then sneezed, and rubbed his nose.

He put his gun in his pocket and got down slowly to his knees beside Stein. He went through Stein's coat pockets, drew out a leather wallet, dropped it on the floor. He went through Stein's trousers pockets. He found nothing he wanted. He picked up the thick wallet and opened it, pulled out a lot of cards. Then he pulled out a lot of bills. A ring fell out with the bills and rang lightly on the floor. Donahue snatched it up, rose, stood looking at it. He smiled at it, tossed it into the air, caught it and shoved it into his pocket.

He went over to a wash basin, poured water from a pitcher, leaned over the basin and with his hands splashed water into his face. He put his face down into the water, holding his breath. He backed away from the basin, shook his head, groped for and found a towel and dried his face. He looked at himself in a cracked mirror. A couple of cuts were bleeding.

There were black and blue welts on his forehead and jaw. He took out his handkerchief and patted the cuts gingerly, making a face.

Stein and Micky Shane were still prostrate on the floor. Donahue looked at them without interest. He shrugged. He picked up the basin of water and drenched Micky Shane's head. He threw what remained in the pitcher into Stein's face. He lit a cigarette and sat down on a chair.

Ten minutes later Micky Shane sat up looking like a man in the throes of a hangover. He held his head between his hands and grimaced and said, "Oh, hell."

"Hell's right," said Donahue.

"Oh-o," groaned Micky.

Donahue stood up. "I'm blowing, little bad boy. Stein's not so used to getting socked on the dome." He drew the ring from his pocket and held it up between thumb and forefinger. "See, Micky? See?"

Micky Shane stared bleakly at the ring. "Okey, Donahue."

"You should have got rid of it in New York."

"I couldn't. The only fence I knew was a friend of them palookas that was my buddies. I was looking for a fence here I knew about, but he's been in stir for three months."

"And Stein said he'd find one for you, eh?"

Micky groaned, "Oh-o," again and held his head.

Donahue walked to the door, opened it, said, "Good-bye, little boy. And stay out of big time. And tell Stein for me when he comes around that I enjoyed my visit in St. Louis. Thank him for the way he went out of his way to make my visit interesting."

"Oh-o," groaned Micky, and lay down on the floor holding his head.

Donahue took a cab to his hotel and sent a wire that said: *"Got it. Leaving tonight."*

Then he spent half an hour in a cold tub reading all about how Detective Rudolph Hocheimer of Police Headquarters had tracked down and apprehended the murderer of Detective Lucas Cross and Antonio Nesella. There was also the story about Eva. Hocheimer got a big hand all around, with his picture on the front page.

Donahue got a big laugh.

The Red-Hots

*An unsuspecting artist, a girl
on the make, two rodmen
and—tough dick Donahue.*

Chapter I

THE taxi slopped and skidded through brittle slush and its right front wheel grated against the curb as squealing four-wheel brakes dragged it to a stop. Grimy water splashed the sidewalk.

Donahue, lurching in the darkened back, said, "Never mind the trimmings, brother," and then pushed open the door.

The driver said, "These lousy streets," with a grievance, while reaching out a hand to take a dollar bill Donahue thrust through the connecting window. When the driver returned fifty cents Donahue gave him a dime, stepped out into the freezing slush and banged the door.

Donahue climbed the narrow stone steps of the gray-faced house in Waverly Place. The glass vestibule door was open, but the door behind it was locked. Beside this door was a white button which Donahue pressed.

Presently a figure materialized behind the white-curtained glass door, and then the door opened and a small, plain-looking man of middle years said, "Yes, sir?" inquiringly.

Donahue said, "I'd like to see Mr. Crosby."

The man opened the door wide and said, "He's on the top floor in the studio apartment—number fifty-two."

"Thanks," said Donahue.

He went halfway down the hall and climbed three staircases. Number fifty-two was at the back of the hall, and there was a streak of light between door and threshold.

He knocked and heard some movement inside. But it was fully a minute before the key turned in the lock. Then the door opened and a small youngish thin man, neatly dressed in blue serge, looked at him.

Donahue asked, "Mr. Crosby?"

The man smiled with white agreeable teeth and said, "No, he's not in."

Donahue looked at his strap-watch. "He was to be. It's eight-thirty. We had a date for eight-thirty. I'll park."

He walked in without waiting to be asked, took off his brown Borsalino. His black hair was thick and had many shining undulations. His face was long, lean, tawny-brown and his eyes were nut-brown beneath wiry black brows. He threw his hat on a wide divan and opened his raglan coat.

The small neat young man closed the door, and still wearing his agreeable smile, said cheerfully, "Have a seat. Crosby ought to be back if you say you have a date with him…. I didn't get the name?"

"I'm Donahue. My boss sent me down here. Crosby called up late this afternoon and asked to send a man down…. You a friend of Crosby's?"

"We room together."

Donahue dropped into a huge leather easy chair beside a fireplace in which red embers glowed. He snapped a match on his thumb-nail and lit a cigarette. Throwing the match into the fireplace, he said offhand, "What's worrying Crosby?"

The neat young man was standing with his back to the door eying Donahue quizzically. "Was something worrying him?"

Donahue looked up sharply. "Enough to want a private dick."

"Oh… I see." The neat young man put his hands on his hips. "He just came back from Paris, you know. We haven't seen much of each other. But he looked worried. I didn't know. Didn't he say anything over the telephone?"

"No. He just said send a dick down."

"Then he *must* be worried!" The neat young man left the door, crossed to the bathroom, came out a minute later and said, "He should be back any minute. He went out to get a bite to eat. I've a date. Hope you don't mind waiting alone."

"Not at all."

The neat young man put on a blue ulster and a derby and pulled on yellow gloves. "Make yourself at home. Cigs in the box there, and some cigars, I think. Tell Crosby I'll be back late."

"Okey."

The man said, "Well, good-night, Mr. Donahue," smiled agreeably, opened the door and went out.

Donahue swung the chair around to face the fire and stuck his feet on a split log. When he finished the cigarette he opened the humidor on the low brass Moorish coffee table and helped himself to a cigar. He lighted it complacently.

The bronze clock on the mantel said nine-thirty when he tossed the cigar butt into the grate and stood up with an impatient grunt.

A soft knock on the door made him turn abruptly and look at it. Then he crossed to the door, opened it and stood looking down at the face of an incredibly beautiful girl. She was smiling, but a glimmer of surprise showed through her smile.

When she said nothing, Donahue said, "Yes? Do you want to see Mr. Crosby?"

She nodded. "Ye-es."

"He's not in, but I'm waiting, too, so you may as well join me… though"—as she walked in—"I was just on the point of leaving."

His eyes slanted down at her, appraised her with satisfaction, and he was closing the door when she turned around and stood with her back to the fireplace. She wore a mole coat and a dark snug cloche hat. She was very small, with small white teeth, brown big eyes and olive satin skin, and there was a distinct odor of liquid-heavy Shalimar perfume.

Donahue smiled, showing long narrow teeth. His dark eyes glittered, and he bowed, saying, "You might as well sit down."

"I'll get warm first," she said, and shivered, adding, "Miserable weather!"

He said brightly, "Yes, rotten out. It's been comfortable by the fire. Crosby should have been in long ago. We had a date. Guy lives with him asked me to wait and then breezed… he had a date."

She said, "Oh, yes?" in a far-away voice, and threw a series of veiled looks around the room.

"You know Crosby well?" Donahue asked bluntly.

"Rather well. He telephoned me he was back from Europe. I just dropped in… wasn't certain of finding him. Since you have a date with him perhaps I'd better go."

"Nonsense! Hang around."

She sighed. "Mine is not important… merely a hello call. Did his friend say when Mr. Crosby'd come back?"

"No. No, he didn't. He just said he figured he'd be back if we had a date. He was a nice agreeable little guy."

Her eyes clouded and her lips tightened for the briefest of moments. Then she said, "Well… I'll be going. I have an appointment uptown at ten."

He said in a disappointed voice, "Well, if you must…" and moved with her to the door. "I'll tell him you called?"

"If you will. He'll know me… Leone Tenquist's the name."

Donahue said he would tell Crosby, and the woman went out leaving a faint smile and a breath of Shalimar perfume.

When the room was quiet again, the ticking of the bronze clock audible, Donahue muttered, "Don't know what's keeping that guy," and started pacing up and down irritably. Ten minutes of this and he began looking around for a telephone. There was none in the living-room. He lit a match and prowled into the adjoining room. It was large and bare, with a skylight, and a dais and the paraphernalia of an artist. He found a button, switched on lights. He saw no telephone, but there was a room beyond. He entered this, couldn't find the switch, struck another match and fumbled towards a small table beside a bed. He dialed a number in the Beekman exchange, waited, then said:

"Hello, Burt…. This is Donahue. Say, what time was I to call on this Crosby job?… I see. Well, it's damned near ten now and nobody's here…. Sure I'm in the place. His pal let me in…. Well, I'll hang around till ten and then I'm breezing. Okey. 'By, Burt."

The match had gone out. Donahue grumbled, swore, struck another and carried it towards the door. Before he reached the door he saw part of a man's trousered leg lying on the floor. He swung towards it, and the match's dim light began to include thighs, waist, chest, head.

Bending down he saw that neck and shirt-collar were soaked with blood.

Glazed eyes stared at the match.

The match went out.

Donahue said, "Hell!" furiously in the darkness.

Chapter II

HE rose and lit another match, found the light-switch, turned on the lights. He took another look at the dead man, had to step over him to get to the farther side of the room. There was a hooked rug lying twisted on the floor as though it had been mixed up in a scuffle.

A closet door was open, and clothes lay on the floor. A yellow suitcase was open, its lining slashed apart in several places. A Gladstone had undergone similar treatment. Drawers of a highboy were open; shirts, collars, undershirts, pajamas, handkerchiefs were jumbled on the floor. A steamer trunk, open, had its insides hacked up after the manner of the suitcase and the Gladstone. Four hats lay on the floor, their sweatbands turned inside out. Red leather bedroom slippers had been slashed.

Donahue prowled around with a keen predatory look in his eyes. He touched nothing. He came back to the dead man and rolled him over with a foot. The man's pockets had been pulled out. Bills and loose change and a rifled wallet lay on the floor near him.

Donahue sloped into the studio, snapped dark eyes around, stood spreadlegged in baffled chagrin, swinging a clenched fist at his side. Canvases on plain wooden frames were strewn about. Everything was in disorder—but in this studio it might have been put down to the artist Crosby's recent homecoming.

Cruising the living-room and the bathroom, Donahue finally came to the corridor door, glared at it, then yanked it open and went running down four staircases. He did not know where the houseman lived, so he opened the front door, pressed the button.

A minute later the man who had first opened the door appeared, and Donahue said, "Come upstairs with me."

The little man followed, complaining that he was getting old, that it was a hard climb to the top floor. Donahue did not argue, but led the way up and then on into Crosby's apartment. When he piloted the little old man to the bedroom he did not have to point out the dead man lying on the floor.

The little man gasped, "Mr. Crosby!" in a horrified voice.

"Just wanted to make sure," Donahue said, then asked, "What's your name?"

"It's—Adler."

"Okey. Now come into the living-room with me." He took the little old man by the arm and marched him out of the bedroom, across the studio, and into the living-room. "Sit down," he said briskly, and pointed to a straight-backed chair. When the man seemed not to have heard, Donahue put a hand on either shoulder and pressed the man down into the chair with firm, gentle persistence.

"Mr. Crosby!" the little man moaned. His face twisted up and a tear fell from each eye.

Donahue was crouched over him, shaking his shoulder. "Come on, Mr. Adler—snap out of that."

"Uh—Mr. Crosby...."

"I know, I know all about that, but snap out of it. He was probably a good guy, lived here a long time, and you liked him a lot. Okey. But don't slop all over the place now. You can do that later. But brace up.... Listen. My name's Donahue. You hear? It's Donahue. I'm a private cop. You hear me? I said I'm a private cop. Mr. Crosby called up the Interstate this afternoon and asked them to send a cop down. They sent me down. You get all that?"

Adler sat straight in the chair now blinking through his small spectacles. He sniffled. He gulped. "You're—a private detective?"

Donahue slapped the man's shoulder. "There! You've got it now! All right. Now pay attention. You remember when you let me in?"

"It was eight-thirty."

"Okey. There was a man in this room when I came up. He said he roomed with Crosby."

"No—nobody roomed with Mr. Crosby."

"I know that—now—but I didn't then. Now what time did you let that man in?"

"About seven-thirty."

"He didn't give a name, did he?"

"No. He just snapped, 'Mr. Crosby.' Like that. He was a big hard-looking man—"

"What? I mean, you say he was a big man?"

"Well, big as you... six feet... heavier than you, though."

Donahue's dark eyes glittered. "All right. He came in at seven-thirty. Now the man in here was a small man, no taller than you. What time did he come in?"

"I didn't let anybody in but the big man."

Donahue stood up and jammed fists against hips. He looked at the door and said, "This ain't even funny," and his upper teeth chewed on his lower lip. Then he looked down at Adler.

"Mr. Crosby came home from Europe—when?"

"Monday—three days ago."

"Did you ever see or let in a small young man—say about twenty-eight—with hair black as mine only smoother. He has very white even teeth and a pleasant agreeable face. His voice is high but nice on the ear, and it's a lively voice."

"No, I don't remember. I'm sure I didn't."

"All right. Now how about a woman a little smaller than you, say about twenty-six, with a small face, neat pointed chin, small teeth, and large brown eyes?"

"Well, I didn't let a woman like that in. But I came in with mail for Mr. Crosby yesterday and a woman like that was sitting in that leather chair by the fireplace. I think she came over on the boat with Mr. Crosby or met him in Europe or something. He was over there four months, you know."

"How old was Crosby?"

"Maybe thirty he was, and very successful, he was. He made covers for magazines. And he was so cheerful and seemed much younger than he was... like a boy, Mr. Donahue. And he was good to me. He's lived here for six years, and I've been here ten. He used to give me clothes o' his—lots of them that was almost new. And hats. And I could wear his socks. Sure, it was just yesterday morning he gave me a suit and a couple of hats with London labels and some socks. Ah, poor young feller!" Adler wiped an eye. "Somebody'll be having to notify his uncle up in Westchester—Mr. Amos Crosby, a fine upstanding old man that loved young Mr. Crosby."

Donahue's voice was low and husky saying, "It was rank murder,

Mr. Adler—and somebody was looking for something Crosby had—something he probably brought from Europe." He shrugged, slammed fist into palm. "Well, now the police."

He strode through the studio, into the bedroom, paused to stare moodily at the bloodied body, then went on to the little table and picked up the telephone. He called the district station-house, and when the connection had been made he said:

"Hello, is this you, Riley?... This is Donahue. Say, a guy's been rubbed off down in Waverly Place. Real butcher's job.... Number 14. Guy name of Crosby—artist.... No, I don't think it's a crime of passion.... How did I? Well, Crosby called up Hinkle this afternoon and told him to send a man tonight. I came down.... No, we didn't know why he wanted us. He's just come back from Europe. So I came down, and when I got here Crosby was cold.... Yeah, I'll hang around till you send the plain-clothes over."

He hung up, rose, went over and stood beside the dead man on the floor. Among the articles that had been emptied from the wallet, was a small pin seal book with gold edges. Donahue knelt down, picked it up, flipped the pages. It was an address book with alphabetical indentations. He turned to C. He found Amos Crosby, Westchester 0040. He turned to T. He found L. T. scrawled in pencil, beneath it, Avalon-Plaza, and a Schuyler telephone number. He returned to the telephone and called that number.

When a voice said, "Hotel Avalon-Plaza," Donahue said, "Will you connect me with Miss Tenquist?" There was a long pause, then the voice saying, "Sorry, sir. Miss Tenquist does not answer." Donahue said, "Thanks," and hung up.

He dialed the Agency next and said, "Burt. Hello, Burt. This is Donahue. Crosby's been croaked.... Yeah. It's a long story and the plain-clothes'll be in any minute. All the time I was waiting for him he was dead in another room.... Absolute. A guy I've seen, a broad, and another guy I haven't seen, are mixed up in it. Crosby has an uncle in Westchester. Money, I guess. We may get a job if you call him up and notify him of his nephew's death. Spread it thick. Tell him the boy had engaged us. Number's West-Chester 0040.... Okey, Burt. Be seeing you later."

When he got back to the living-room, Adler was still sitting on the chair, head in hands. A bell rang loudly somewhere distant, and Adler started, got up.

"The front door," he said, and hurried out sniffling.

Donahue was standing before the fireplace lighting a cigarette when the door opened. A man in plain-clothes came in followed by two uniformed policemen. The man in plain-clothes was tall, lank, lantern-jawed. He wore a faded gray overcoat and a soft hat that had been made shapeless by many rains.

"Hello, Donahue," he said glumly.

"Hello, Roper."

"Where's he?"

"Across the studio."

Roper had his hands in his pockets and his shoulders huddled up to his ears, as though he were chilly. The two cops were young, in bright uniforms. They followed Roper.

Adler came in rubbing his hands slowly together against his meager chest. He looked helplessly at Donahue. Donahue smiled reassuringly but said nothing.

Roper's heavy slow footfalls came back across the bare studio floor, and then he came into the living-room.

"That's nice," he said. He looked at Adler. "Who's this?"

"Houseman," Donahue said.

Roper said, "Yeah?" and then moved towards the fireplace, pulled a chair up close to it and sat down with his back to the fire huddling his big bony shoulders. He looked mournful and detached.

"Now," he said, "let's go over it."

Donahue, holding the little black address book in a clenched hand in his pocket, smiled with long narrow teeth and said, "Sure, Roper," amicably.

Chapter III

WHEN Donahue left the house in Waverly Place, it was ten-twenty, and the morgue bus was drawing up to the curb. There was no crowd, since no commotion had attended the quiet murder of Crosby, and crowds in Waverly Place are rare anyhow.

Donahue crunched stout shoes on freezing slush as he headed west, turned into Sheridan Square. He crossed the Square and went down into dark windy Grove Street. Where a dim yellow light glowed from a door submerged five feet beneath the level of the sidewalk. Donahue turned down the flight of stone steps, passed through the open doorway, turned right against a closed door, opened it, walked ten feet down a narrow corridor, opened another door, and entered a long bar at which stood eight scattered men.

The slack-faced barman, who was idly picking his teeth, said, " 'Lo, Donny."

"Bunt," Donahue said. "Scotch and soda."

"How's the racket?"

"On the up and up."

While the barman was uncorking the Scotch, Donahue walked the length of the bar, entered a telephone booth. The sound of the nickel dropping in the slot was audible outside the booth. Donahue talked for a minute, hung up. Then another nickel made a noise. He talked again, hung up, came out and picked up a pickle from the lunch counter on his way to the bar. He downed the Scotch straight, chased it with soda, rang a half dollar on the bar.

He said, "Be seeing you, Bunt," and walked out.

Returning to Sheridan Square, he went down a West Side subway kiosk, took a northbound local to Fourteenth Street, left the local and caught a northbound express. Ten minutes later he left the express at Seventy-second Street, took a local to Seventy-ninth, got off and climbed the stairway to Broadway. He walked one block west and turned south into West End Avenue.

The Avalon-Plaza was a small apartment-hotel better than middle class, just short of swank. Donahue passed a braided doorman, pushed a revolving door around, climbed three marble steps, turned right and climbed three more, and then walked down a narrow quiet foyer. To the corpulent complacent man at the desk he said, "Will you tell Miss Tenquist that Mr. Donahue is calling?"

The man said, "Certainly," and repeated the names to the switchboard operator. When he turned back to Donahue saying, "Yes," Donahue asked, "What number?" And the man said, "A-455."

A small silent elevator whisked Donahue to the fourth floor, and the elevator boy leaned out to point and say, "Down that way, sir, around the bend."

There was a brass knocker shaped like a harp on the door marked A-455. Donahue raised it and let it fall back to its brass base.

The latch clicked and Miss Tenquist looked quizzically at Donahue.

She had loose brown hair and wore a blue peignoir casually and becomingly.

He eyed her steadily with round hard brown eyes and showed his long narrow teeth in a fixed smile.

Without saying anything, the woman stepped aside and looked around the room vaguely, and while she was doing that Donahue walked into a small but not inexpensive living-room. To the left were two doors. One led to a bathroom; the other to a bedroom.

When she had closed the door, Donahue, hat in hand, said, "I called you from downtown."

"Yes?" She was eying him strangely, uncertainly, and color was creeping into her cheeks.

He was smiling at her fixedly. "I didn't tell you over the phone that Crosby'd been murdered."

Her small white fingers flew to her mouth but did not succeed in stopping an explosive, "Oh!" that burst from spread lips. Her brown eyes dilated wide with sudden horror. Then the lids wavered, the eyes rolled a bit. Donahue took a step toward her, arms outthrust. She backed away, putting the back of her hand against her forehead. She sank to a divan and said breathlessly, "Oh... murdered!" tragically.

"Yes," Donahue clipped. He went on rapidly in a blunt incisive voice, "He'd been murdered when you got there. He'd been murdered before I got there. He was lying in his bedroom all the time and I didn't know it."

She said, "Oh, oh," behind teeth that tried to close hard, and a harried look battled in her eyes.

"Listen," Donahue said, sitting down beside her. "You were worried when you came there tonight. Who are you? How long have you known Crosby?"

"I've known him—quite a while."

"Not so long. I happen to know you came over on the boat with him."

She caught her breath, trained her eyes on the carpet. "Yes, I did. I knew him in Europe. We met in Europe."

"Listen. When you came in tonight, how did you get in?"

She had her handkerchief pressed against her mouth now. She looked squarely at Donahue with her wide-open eyes. "Why, what do you mean?"

"I mean, ordinarily you ring the front door bell to get in that house.

You didn't. You came right in. You must have had a key."

She swallowed. "Who are you?"

"I told you my name. That's not answering my question. Did you have a key?"

She got up and started walking around the room. Donahue got up and trailed her around the room, asking, "Now did you, did you?" She whirled and cried, half in tears. "What if I did have a key?"

He stopped and spread his hands palmwise, saying, "That's what I wanted to know. Then you had a key. You must have been a very good friend of Crosby's." He smiled crookedly. "Very intimate, eh?"

She looked confused. "If you want to put it that way."

"That's all right by me," he grinned. "We'll forget all about that. But here's something else. That guy I said was Crosby's room-mate wasn't. Why didn't you tell me nobody lived with Crosby when I made that crack?"

"I still don't know what right you have to ask all these questions?"

"When I mentioned that guy, I remember you kind of tightened up—as if you knew who I meant." He lowered his voice, hardened it. "Listen to me, little girl, it's all right if you were playing house with Crosby—that was his privilege and yours. But when a guy gets his throat carved and you act dumb when I shoot questions at you—" He shook his head. "That doesn't go at all—not with this baby."

She was trembling, but she put fire in her voice when she cried, "Who—who are you?"

"Just a private cop earning his salary.... You knew Crosby well. All right. He sent for a private cop. Now you ought to know why. We don't know. He called up and said he'd explain when we sent a man down. So I went down. This smooth-faced guy let me in, saying he was Crosby's room-mate. Then you drift in. Say, who was after Crosby—and why?"

She blew her nose and shook her head and said beneath her handkerchief in a panicky voice, "I don't know! He didn't tell me anything!"

Fury leaped in Donahue's dark eyes. His hand shot out, caught the girl's wrist and he heaved her close up against him.

He snarled, "I hope to tell you you're a damned little liar!"

"Ow... you're hurting!"

He released her abruptly and she fled backwards across the room. He chopped off an oath that did not quite get to his lips and scowled darkly at the girl.

"Don't pull a song and dance on me!" he rapped out. "We can get along fine as long as you don't play me for a jackass. Come on now, break clean. What kind of a racket are you in on?"

"I—I don't know what you're talking about."

"I said don't song-and-dance!"

"I tell you—"

A knock on the corridor door stopped her. She flung a look at the door. She flung a look at Donahue. Donahue made a motion for her to open the door while his right hand went around to his hip-pocket and drew out a Colt's .38 revolver with an abbreviated two-inch barrel. He took six backward steps into the bath-room, left the door open.

The girl had her hand on the knob of the corridor door, and all color had drained from her face.

Chapter IV

SHE opened the door. Her body stiffened and her hands started towards her breast. She backed up as the small neat young man came in slowly and smiled with his agreeable white teeth. His right hand was significantly in the pocket of his ulster. He reached around back with his left hand, closed the door, stood with his back against it and turned the key in the lock.

He said in his pleasant lively voice, "Hello, Irene."

The girl had backed up against one arm of the divan, and she sat tensely against it, hunched forward, in an awkward position that had about it something of breathlessness. Her brown eyes were fixed wide on the small neat young man. His rather dark luminous eyes twinkled.

He said, casually, "Babe didn't get it."

She scraped the side of the divan with clawing fingers. Fear began to distort her face, and she kept twisting her head from side to side. Her lips opened, her teeth opened, and she began to breathe hoarsely.

The small neat young man came forward, taking his time, smiling pleasantly. He said, "And I didn't get it."

She cringed, held her arms out, palms towards the man. She crouched behind the palms.

She choked, "Babe… you didn't—"

"No, Irene. I didn't. Not that. I just slugged him…. Aren't you the two-timing little—?"

"For God's sake, Alfred… go out!"

"Don't try to kid me. Babe's not here. Babe's still in the land of nod, as the poets say…. And will it be poetic justice if I break your nice sweet jaw?"

"Alfred!…"

"I'm talking, Irene. What a jack I've been. I always knew you used to be sweet on Babe, nuts on him, but I thought that was all over—"

"I swear it is, Alfred!"

"Bah! You two-timed on me, but Babe didn't get it. Maybe he did get it. But he didn't have it. He passed it on to someone… to you."

"No—no!"

Alfred drew out a very small but business-like automatic and leveled it at the girl's breast.

He said quietly, "One of us has it. Babe hasn't. I haven't. You have!"

"Please… I swear!…"

He raised his left hand slowly and placed the fingers around the girl's throat. He pressed the muzzle of the gun against her breast. He smiled at her.

"For two-timing, Irene, you ought to get a belly full of this. I may yet. But first I want to know who has it."

"I—don't know, Alfred! That's God's truth! Go out… come back later!"

He laughed leisurely, tightened his fingers on her throat until she gagged and raised her hands to grip the arm that held her. She teetered on the arm of the divan, lost her balance, fell backward on the divan kicking up white smooth legs.

Alfred took two steps and looked down at her where she lay panting and rubbing her throat. He leaned over a bit and slapped her face. She cried, "Ow!" and she meant it. Alfred slammed the pistol against her ribs and she screeched. He stood up, took two more steps, turned on a radio. A jazz band boomed into the room. He returned to the divan and struck the girl again—with the gun. He planted a knee on her stomach and went on striking her. He did not look mad, merely interested in his work.

Donahue stepped from the bathroom, walked across the carpet, stopped behind Alfred, and when Alfred's gun hand rose, Donahue gripped it, twisted sharply and spun Alfred around to face him. Alfred's gun was in Donahue's left hand, and Donahue's gun was in his own right hand. Donahue struck Alfred playfully on the head with Alfred's gun, and when Alfred fell back grunting, Donahue grinned and said:

"Does hurt, doesn't it?"

Alfred regained his poise, smiled and said, "Yes, a bit."

The girl sat up, sobbing. She rose and burst out crying and stumbled to the bathroom.

Donahue eyed Alfred and said, "Turn off the radio."

Alfred turned off the radio. He smoothed his collar, pushed back his black smooth hair and kept looking at Donahue with mild and polite interest.

"You're a smooth——," Donahue said drily.

Alfred smiled, said, "Association," brightly.

Donahue said, "Well, I'm not smooth. And I don't like smooth guys."

"Do you mind if I light a cigarette?"

"Yes I mind."

Alfred shrugged. "You're uncommonly hard to get on with."

"I'm damned hard to get on with."

Alfred sighed. Then his face brightened. "Irene is a very temperamental soul."

"We'll discuss you right now. Never mind about Irene.... Listen, you—what the hell was the idea of handing me a line in Crosby's apartment?"

"Must we go into *that?*"

"Oh, I think we ought to—since it's very likely you carved the poor slob's throat."

Alfred laughed lightly. "Now, now, Mr. Holmes!"

Donahue took three hard steps and jammed his own gun so hard against Alfred's chest that Alfred exploded, "Ugh!" and almost fell down.

Donahue clipped, "You're not funny at all, bozo!"

Alfred got his breath back, laughed in confusion, shoved back his hair and said, "My, you're like a regular New York cop."

Donahue struck Alfred on the head and Alfred fell down on the floor, sat with his head in his hands and rocked back and forth groaning.

Donahue said, "I don't like wisenheimers."

He got down on one knee. He put Alfred's gun in his pocket and used the hand that had held the gun to pull Alfred's hands from his face. Alfred's eyes were wet and he looked peeved.

"You don't have to be so rough," he said.

"You don't have to make those musical comedy wisecracks…. Listen to me, brother. You're in a tough spot. Crosby was carved, and you were in his apartment when I got there. Crosby was murdered because he had something that you guys wanted. You're a red-hot—so is the jane… but you're hotter than she is because she came there after the murder. She came in while I was there. We notified Crosby's uncle that his nephew had got a dose, and the old boy's coming into town like a bat out of hell—and he told us to carry on with the investigation. I'm carrying on—and you're going to talk before I walk you into a pinch."

Alfred became thoughtful. He said sadly, "Say, I am in a tough spot, ain't I?"

"I wouldn't fool you!"

The girl came back into the room sniffling and saying, "You dirty little rat, trying to link me with your dirty little schemes! I told you to stay away from me—to leave me alone. I want nothing to do with you. I'm sick and tired of being drawn into your schemes, and I'm sick and tired of seeing you."

She picked up a heavy bronze book-end and hefted it. Hot scarlet overran her cheeks and her brown eyes blazed.

Alfred raised his hand. "Now don't throw that, Irene."

Donahue put in, "I thought it was Leone."

She came over and stood quivering, the book-end in an upraised arm. "You're a very small rat!" she cried.

Alfred said, "Now don't, Irene—"

Donahue looked at Alfred and said, "Just for fun I ought to encourage her."

The girl's hand came down swiftly.

Donahue felt the book-end strike his head. He knew he was reeling. He knew blackness cascaded down upon him. There was another blow, a laugh—Alfred's quiet laugh—and then there wasn't anything.

Chapter V

COMING to at midnight, Donahue lay in the darkness for a few minutes feeling his head. When he touched a bump near the crown he said, "Ugh!" and then cursed. Then he sat up. He could see two windows, the night sky beyond them, some tattered star fragments. He fumbled in his pockets for a match, found one, struck a light and then moved towards the electric switch. He snapped on the lights.

He was still in the same apartment.

He said, "Hell and damn," earnestly, and prowled around, wearing a brown predatory look. The bedroom was empty. Bureau drawers were open—empty; clothes closet was open—empty. He went around into the bath-room. It had been cleaned out except for a bottle with a little Listerine in it. Donahue poured it into a glass, added water, slushed his mouth out, spat noisily.

Alfred and the girl Irene had pulled a fade-away.

Donahue wet his hair, brushed it back with his fingers, washed face and hands and dried them. Returning to the living-room, he saw his gun lying on the divan. He picked it up, saw it was still loaded and replaced it in his overcoat pocket. His brown face was hard, sullen; he muttered diatribes in his throat behind his narrow clenched teeth. He went into the bedroom again, looked beneath twin beds, dumped out the contents of a waste basket.

He threw aside crumpled empty cigarette packets, a tooth-paste box, a copy of the *Evening Sun,* a theatre program of the Lyric showing *Fifty Million Frenchmen,* a Bascom ticket envelope, a passenger list of the *S. S. Driatic,* a dry cleaner's bill, a colored cardboard box that had contained hairpins, an empty vanishing-cream jar, an empty rose-colored bottle that had contained fingernail polish.

Donahue reclaimed the passenger list of the *S. S. Driatic.* Under the C's he found *Robert C. Crosby.* Under the T's he found *Alfred P. Tenquist;* beneath this, *Miss Leone Tenquist.* He folded the booklet and thrust it into his pocket. His dark eyes glittered as he bent to throw the other articles back into the waste-basket.

He returned to the living-room, picked up his Borsalino, slapped it carelessly on his head and cringed, exploding, "Damn!" It was the bump on his head. He drew in a breath and went towards the door, making a sour face. He passed into the corridor, buzzed for an elevator. When one stopped he got in. When the doors slid open on the main floor, a man squeezed in as Donahue was going out, and as Donahue walked away he heard a bass voice say:

"I want A-455."

Donahue stopped in his tracks, stood rooted but did not look around. Then he went on walking through the lobby, passed out into the street and turned south. Half a block away three taxis stood in a row at the curb. Donahue passed the first and walked up to the second. He handed the driver a dollar.

"This guy ahead of you may get a call any minute," he said. "Maybe I'll want you to follow him."

The driver reached back an arm and opened the door. "Okey, chief."

Donahue climbed in the back, lit a butt and watched the entrance of the Avalon-Plaza. About five minutes later a man came out. The doorman blew a whistle and the first taxi got into gear and drove up to the hotel entrance.

"Follow that guy," Donahue said.

The driver started his motor, meshed gears but held the clutch out. When the first taxi pulled away from the curb the second did likewise.

The first taxi turned east on Seventy-ninth Street, south into Riverside Drive. Donahue's man stayed half a block behind, but sped up when a Packard sport and a checkered cab got in between him and the green cab he was trailing. He passed the Packard and the checkered job and followed the green taxi around the blinker into Seventy-second Street, then south on West End Avenue. At Fifty-ninth Street, West End Avenue becomes Eleventh and shoots south past railroad yards and switching engines; becomes a rough, shoddy and dark street without traffic stops, where trucks and taxis slam recklessly on their way.

The tail turned east into Fortieth Street, crossed Tenth Avenue, roared beneath the Ninth Avenue Elevated and started to slow down just west of Eighth Avenue. The green taxi was pulling into the curb; Donahue's was a hundred yards behind, drifting leisurely. The green cab was stopped when Donahue's rolled past, and the big man was getting out in front of a lighted doorway that was flush with the street.

Donahue leaned forward and said, "I'll get out at Eighth."

When he alighted he gave the driver another dollar, then walked west on Fortieth until he came to the lighted doorway. He walked into the open lobby, looked around for a button, saw none. He got on his toes and ran his fingers along the top of the door frame. He found a button there, pressed it. A minute later the door opened and Donahue walked in saying, "Hello, buddy."

He walked on down a narrow low-ceiled corridor, passed a kitchen, entered a small bar beyond which was a dining-room where a slot gramophone was raising a lot of noise and dancing feet were shuffling.

The man who had come out of the Avalon-Plaza was standing at the far end of the short bar watching the spectacled bartender mix a whiskey-sour. Donahue put a foot on the rail a dozen feet from the man and watched him in the mirror. When the bartender came down the line mopping the bar Donahue said:

"Scotch and soda."

"Punk night out, eh?"

"Pretty lousy."

Donahue was trying his drink when the big man ordered another whiskey-sour. The big man wore a voluminous tan polo coat, a brown silk muffler, and a rakish large-brimmed brown hat. His face was big, bronzed and bulged at the eyebrows. His gimlet eyes were hidden in tight folds of flesh, and his mouth was wide and drooped at the corners. When he had drunk half of the second whiskey-sour he turned and rolled to a telephone-booth, closed himself in, talked on the telephone briefly, came out again and finished the drink. He threw a bill on the bar, said "Night," gruffly and stamped down the narrow corridor, wearing a scowl. Donahue had finished the Scotch and soda. The bartender took sixty cents out of a dollar and Donahue left the bar, pocketing the change.

When he came out into Fortieth Street he saw the big man half a block away heading east. Donahue tailed him to Broadway, where the man climbed into a yellow cab. Donahue boarded a black-and-white, said, "Follow that yellow," and sat on the edge of the back seat watching. The yellow cab turned east into Thirty-fourth Street, crossed Fifth, Madison and Park; turned north on Lexington and west into Thirty-seventh Street and crawled into the curb on the upgrade. Donahue told his driver to keep going, spotted the three story gray-stone in front of which the yellow had stopped and told the driver to pull up at the taxi stand at Thirty-seventh and Lexington.

He walked down Thirty-seventh on the left side of the street, watched the right. He was opposite the graystone walk-up when he saw lights appear on the third floor behind windows that had shades drawn all the way down. All other windows were dark—had been dark when the taxi drew up. Donahue walked a little farther down, crossed the street, came back up and climbed six stone steps to an open vestibule door. Stepping into the vestibule, he saw a brass plate with four buttons running vertically beside four niches for name. The top niche was the only one that had no name.

He pressed the top button. A minute later the door clicked and Donahue opened it, looked into a dimly lighted corridor. He stood there, reached out and pressed the button again. He listened, looking at the latch. It began clicking again. When it stopped Donahue waited another minute, pressed it again, still holding the door open. The lock began clicking. Donahue smiled to himself, his eyes narrowed shrewdly. While the lock was clicking Donahue pressed his finger against the button, held it there for half a minute. The lock stopped clicking. Donahue gave the button another short push, then shoved his head into the hall and listened. He heard footfalls somewhere above.

He stepped into the hall, closed the door, went quickly and silently to the rear of the lower hall. He turned and waited in the shadows. The footfalls came down, walked the length of the corridor above, then came down the staircase to the lower hall.

Donahue saw the big man striding towards the hall door. The big man reached the door, drew the curtains aside, peered through the glass. He listened. His actions indicated that he was becoming suspicious.

Meanwhile Donahue was sliding through the shadows, hugging the shadowy base of the staircase. His right hand came out of his pocket holding the Colt's revolver. He held the gun in front of him and was ten feet behind the big man when he said:

"Suppose you raise 'em, Babe."

The big man whirled hugely, sucking in a breath, and his right hand tightened on something in the pocket of his coat.

Chapter VI

DONAHUE'S voice was low, clipped—"You heard me, Babe! Get that hand out of your pocket! And get your hands up."

"What the hell is this?—"

"Those hands, Babe!"

The big man snarled and thrust his big hands upward.

Donahue said, "Get over here... kneel on this lower step."

"Say you—"

"Get over here!"

The big man lunged, fell to his knees on the lower step.

"Now lie down on the steps."

"I'll be—"

"Get down and keep your hands out straight beyond your head. That's the way." Donahue went through the man's pockets, took out an automatic pistol. "Now bring the hands down behind your back— and be nice."

"You're sure a careful guy, ain't you?"

"Pretty careful, Babe." Donahue clipped manacles deftly on the man's wrists, then stepped back and said, "Now get up and we'll go up to your flat."

"I don't get this at all, guy."

"I don't myself. Maybe we can figure things out. Up you go, Babe." Donahue prodded him in the small of the back with his revolver, and the man started upward, and Donahue kept the gun against his back as they climbed more stairs and then walked into a room whose door had been left open. It was the front room, the living-room that looked out on Thirty-seventh Street. It was a big room, well furnished, and behind it was an equally large bedroom.

Donahue locked the corridor door, left the key in the lock. The big man had turned and was backing sullenly across the room, big head hunched between massive shoulders. His eyes could not be seen for the puffy rolls of flesh that drew together over them, yet at times there was a faint glint.

Open French doors connected living-room and bedroom, and Donahue went into the bedroom sidewise, keeping an eye on the big man. He pulled open a clothes closet, closed it. He looked into the bath-room. Coming back towards the living-room, he paused in front of a bureau, sniffed. He looked at the things on the bureau. He picked up a crumpled lace handkerchief, put it down, proceeded into the living-room wearing a droll smile.

"Irene wears a nice perfume, Babe."

The big man growled, "Say, who the hell are you?"

"Who do you think?"

"I don't think. I don't know. The bracelets say a dick, but dicks don't bust into houses alone."

Donahue said, "I had a talk with Irene and I had a talk with Alfred. They haven't got it. You must have it."

"Got what?"

"The bulls are kind of worked up over the Crosby kill, Babe. The guy who killed Crosby got it. I got there late. You were there before me, and Alfred was there after you. I didn't get it. Alfred didn't get it. Irene was there, too, but she didn't get it. You—must have got it."

The big man knit his brows, chewed on a thick nether lip. His big nose wrinkled. He looked baffled. Donahue was a dark lean man eying him narrowly.

The big man growled, "Come on, guy, lay your cards on the table. Cut out the sparring."

Donahue smiled bleakly. "I don't have to lay any cards on any table, Babe. I'm top-dog. You do the laying."

"Suppose I don't lay?"

"Suppose you do."

"I said—suppose I don't?"

Donahue dropped his voice ominously. "A dick named Roper's on the job. He's a hard guy, Babe. I can always reach him by telephone."

The big man snarled, "You're a—stoolie trying to step into big time!"

"Okey… then I'm a stoolie. But that's got nothing to do with what you are, or what I want from you. Every stoolie has his price. You know mine."

"What do you want?"

"You know what I want. I want the same thing Irene wants, the same thing Alfred wants. They know you carved Crosby trying to get it. I know it too."

The big man's face was getting red. His breath rushed hoarsely through wide nostrils and his hands strained at the manacles.

"Did Irene?…" he choked.

"She did after I beat her a while. She said you must have got it when you carved Crosby."

The big man lunged towards Donahue, brought up against Donahue's gun. His eyes were shining dagger points in the slits of flesh.

"How the hell did you muscle in on this?"

Donahue smiled. "Open season, Babe.... Don't shove your belly too hard against this rod."

The big man sucked in a huge breath, held it, then let it gush out boisterously. "Damn it, I didn't carve Crosby! Irene's a liar!"

"Punk, Babe. You called on Crosby, turned the joint inside out and carved him. That's open and shut. You were seen going in.... Now where is it?"

"I don't know! I haven't got it! Irene or Alfred's got it. And she's a liar if she said I carved Crosby. I was down there. All right, I was down there. What the hell of it? I was Crosby's bootlegger. I was before he went to Paris. He called me up when he came back. I brought him around three bottles of Scotch because my runner was out. I never run around with the stuff ordinary. But Crosby was a good buyer."

Donahue wrinkled his brown forehead. "You might have been his bootlegger, Babe, but you got in on something bigger. You had something to do with this racket the woman and Alfred're in on. You're Irene's boy friend. You and Irene double-crossed Alfred."

"Say, fella, you know a hell of a lot about this."

"I get around, Babe."

The big man tied his face up in puzzled wrinkles. "I'm damned if you're a stoolie! You're getting more like plain-clothes every minute!"

"Do you come across, big boy, or do I put through a telephone call? If you didn't slice Crosby you know who did."

"So you're a dick, eh? So you're a dick?" The big man scowled darkly, snarled, "You can go to hell! If you think I'm a red-hot, you're all wet."

The telephone bell jangled. Donahue started towards it, then motioned the big man over.

He said, "Sit down and answer it."

"Me with manacles?"

"I'll hold the receiver for you."

The big man sat down at the library table. Donahue took off the receiver, placed it near the big man's ear, put his own ear near it.

Irene's voice said, "Babe!"

Babe said, "Yeah."

"I'm coming over! I've got to see you! I'll be over in twenty minutes!"

Donahue whispered, "Tell her sure, Babe."

Babe grumbled, "Sure, come on."

"Oh, Babe, I've had one hell of a time! I'm all in! But I'll be over—in twenty minutes."

"Sure, Irene."

Donahue hung up saying, "This is sure a break, Babe. Now be a strong silent man.... So you and the broad have been two-timing on Alfred all along, eh?"

"——for you."

"And you think I'm a dick, eh?"

"I don't know what you are. I'm beginning to think again you're a stoolie doublecrossing the cops."

Donahue chuckled drily. "We'll wait and see what Irene thinks about it." He took out a key-ring. "I'm going to plant you in that easy chair facing the door. Your hands are going to be manacled in front, and there'll be a newspaper over them. You stay in the chair, taking it easy: the prosperous bootlegger at home. I'll be in the bedroom watching you. One step out of turn and you get the works."

"I'd give a thousand bucks to know just what you are, guy."

Donahue laughed good-naturedly. "Hell, what a piker you turned out to be!"

The big man growled petulantly, "Jeeze, you're an aggravating kinda guy!"

Chapter VII

WHEN the door-bell rang the man called Babe was sitting in an easy-chair with a newspaper lying across his lap.

Donahue said, "When she knocks, just say come in to her. Don't get up."

"You're boss just now, fella."

"Okey." Donahue walked to the corridor door, pressed a brass button on a brass plate beside it. Then he unlocked the door. The entrance to the bedroom was to the left of the corridor door as one came in, and one entering would be unable to look into the bedroom until he had reached about the center of the living-room. The big man sat across the room from the corridor door but faced it squarely. One of the two front windows was directly behind him.

When Donahue entered the bedroom he turned its lights out and took up a position behind a highboy, around whose front corner he could peer into the living-room and see the big man but not the corridor door.

He called quietly, "For the time being, Babe, you're on the spot. Play ball."

The big man droned sullenly, "Okey, fella."

A moment later a light knock sounded on the door.

The big man said, "Come in."

There was a pause. Then the door banged open.

Donahue saw the big man heave in the chair, throw off the newspaper, open his mouth, start to get up.

A silenced gun popped.

The big man slammed back into the chair snapping out his legs. He toppled with the chair.

Donahue leaped across the bedroom.

Footfalls were hammering down the stairs.

Donahue streaked out into the hallway, looked over the balustrade. The feet were hurrying down the staircase below. Donahue forked the balustrade, shot down backwards, landed on his feet, raced down the next staircase. He heard someone stirring in one of the apartments. He rapped the door as he sped past and yelled, "Man shot on top floor!" He boomed down into the lower hall, burst out into Thirty-seventh Street.

There was a man racing towards Lexington Avenue, hugging the buildings. Donahue started long legs flying, swung south on Lexington. The man was half a block ahead of him. He was a small man, swift as the wind. He was Alfred.

He shot down Thirty-sixth Street, turned south on Third Avenue. The avenue was deserted. Store fronts were dark. An Elevated train threshed by overhead, southbound. Alfred reached the Thirty-fourth Street station, bolted up the stairway. Donahue hammered up behind him. When he reached the platform the train had pulled out. Alfred had crossed the tracks, was rushing through the turnstile on the northbound platform.

Donahue turned and went down the steps he had climbed, crossed Third Avenue and saw Alfred running north, now a block distant. At Thirty-eighth Street Alfred leaped aboard a cruising taxi, disappeared in the back. Donahue yelled, ran out into the street, flagged a south-bound taxi.

"Tail that blue cab, bud!" he clipped as he jumped in the back and slammed the door.

The taxi wheeled about in the middle of the block, shifted into high, roared north beneath the Elevated structure. The blue cab made a left turn into Thirty-ninth Street, turned north on Lexington. It went through a red traffic light. Donahue's cab went through a red traffic light. The blue cab swung left at Forty-second Street, skidded on streetcar rails. Alfred jumped off at Grand Central. Donahue handed the driver fifty cents, dropped off before the cab stopped, galloped on the sidewalk and shoved in through heavy swing-doors.

When he reached the rotunda of the upper level Alfred was at the other end heading into a passageway at a fast walk. When he saw Donahue he broke into a run, took the underground entrance to the Commodore, came out into Forty-second Street and headed east at a fast walk. Donahue made him break into a run again, and they raced east past the News Building.

Alfred winged a taxi at Second Avenue. Donahue stopped on the corner and watched the taxi speed south. A minute passed before he hailed one swinging out of Forty-second Street, and when they were under way the other cab was three blocks beyond. An Elevated train was crashing southbound overhead. The taxi that Alfred had taken slewed into the curb at the Thirty-fourth Street Elevated station, and Alfred leaped out, darted up the stairway as the train was pulling in alongside the platform.

Donahue leaned forward and said, "Shoot down to Twenty-third Street."

"Listen, boss—"

"No fireworks—honest, buddy," Donahue said.

Taxi sped southward between steel Elevated pillars. Train sped southward overhead. At Twenty-third Street the Elevated swings east for a block, then south again on First Avenue. Between Second and First Avenues is the Twenty-third Street station. Donahue's taxi reached it four blocks ahead of the train. Donahue got out, paid up, climbed the staircase and stood behind a partition at the platform exit.

The train pulled in slowly after having made the turn. It was pretty empty. Train gates opened—closed. Quick footsteps sounded on the platform. Alfred appeared, strode past the partition behind which Donahue crouched. Donahue took a fast step after him and said:

"All right, Alfred—quiet, now!"

Alfred stopped short when Donahue poked a gun muzzle against Alfred's back.

"Hands out of pockets," Donahue said.

Alfred took his hands from his pockets. Donahue frisked with his left hand, said, "Turn around." Alfred turned around, his small face white and breathless. Donahue reached inside Alfred's ulster, drew a pistol from the ulster's inside pocket. There was a silencer attached. Donahue shoved gun and silencer into his own inside pocket. His mouth was tight, a windy look was in his eyes.

"Now, you—we'll go places," he said.

"Listen, Donahue—"

"Down those steps, sweet man—and a wisecrack out of you and I'll break your jaw. Get!"

He grabbed Alfred's arm, walked him rapidly down the staircase. Alfred was like a man in a daze. He kept on trying to say things but somehow he seemed unable to utter a word.

But finally he said, "Where—are we going?"

"Ever hear of a dick named Roper?"

Alfred winced. "You mean—Bat Roper?"

"They tell me he bats hell out of guys."

Alfred dragged to a stop. "Cripes, Donahue—"

"You're such a red-hot, though, that maybe he won't have to bat you. Quit stalling! Come on!"

Alfred hung back, setting his small mouth firmly. Three men were coming up Second Avenue.

Donahue rough-housed Alfred. "Damn you—"

Alfred leaped at Donahue yelling, "Help! Help!"

"You—!" Donahue snapped.

Alfred clawed at him, yelling for help, struggling frantically. The three men broke into a run, shouting. They were big men—East Siders. Donahue clouted Alfred on the head with his gun. Alfred screamed. The three men came up yelling.

Donahue shouted, "Stay off, you guys!"

Alfred buried his teeth in Donahue's arm. Donahue kicked Alfred's shins. The three men landed on Donahue and whaled him with hard fists. Alfred broke away, raced down Second Avenue.

Donahue shouted, "You fools, that's a killer! I'm a cop!"

"Yeah, you're a cop!"

"Damn your souls, clear out!" Donahue roared. He whipped his gun back and forth, laying open a cheek; plunged through the men, streaked off after Alfred. Alfred swung west into Twenty-first Street. Donahue took the corner wide, saw Alfred speeding towards Gramercy Park.

He yelled, "Stop, you! I tell you, stop!"

Alfred did not stop. He was swift for a small man. But Donahue stopped, clicking his teeth together. He raised his gun, looked down it, pulled the trigger. Flame and smoke burst from the muzzle. The street boomed. Alfred reeled sidewise, fell, slid on his side into the gutter.

When Donahue came running up Alfred was crawling on his side, moaning hysterically. He was dragging his left leg. When Donahue reached down Alfred screamed like a maniac. Windows were grating open. Lights were springing to life. Alfred screamed till his voice broke—and then he coughed, choked—but kept on crawling, leaving a thin trail of blood. Donahue reached down again, grabbed Alfred's shoulder.

"A guy would think you had places to go," he said. "Snap out of it, dumb bell."

Alfred stopped crawling but screamed again until his voice broke, banged his head on the pavement and swept the air with his hands.

Donahue knelt down and grabbed him by the throat. "And you're not going to bang your brains out!"

Running footsteps came down the street. Metal buttons and a shield gleamed, and a gun shone dully as a policeman passed beneath a street light.

A bull voice yelled, "Hey, you!"

Donahue looked up saying, "Come on, copper. There's a red-hot here."

The policeman slowed to a heavy-soled walk. He was broad, stocky, young, with his cap raked over one ear.

"What the hell's this?" he growled.

"This guy smoked out a bird up in Thirty-seventh Street. I've been tailing him. I nailed him on the Twenty-third Street L station, but he got wise and tried a break."

"Yeah? And who the hell are you?"

"Don't get tough, coppy. I'm an Interstate boy. This gun's mixed up in the Crosby kill."

"That job down in Waverly Place tonight?"

"Yeah…. Better phone an ambulance. I potted him in the left leg."

"Where's his rod?"

"I've got it here—in my pocket."

"How'd you happen to get it?"

Donahue stood up. "For crying out loud, don't be a rookie, copper. I asked him if he'd mind giving it to me. He said he'd be tickled."

"You're a wise guy, ain't you?"

"Nah, I'm not a wise guy. I hate wise guys…. Do you telephone or do you want me to?"

"I'll telephone. Just don't get wise—don't get wise."

Half a dozen persons had come out of doorways and were edging nearer. The policeman strode towards them saying, "I want a phone." Somebody said, "Right here, officer. What happened?" The policeman didn't say what happened, and hurried through an open doorway.

Alfred was gibbering now. He began to bang his head against the pavement again screaming, "Mother o' God!" in a frenzied voice.

A woman's voice quavered, "Oh… the poor man."

Donahue dropped to his knees and held Alfred's head locked in his arm.

He said, "No, you don't, Alfred. No, you don't."

Alfred groaned, "Why didn't you finish me—why the hell didn't you finish me?"

"I should do favors for you!" Donahue said; chuckled, added, "Yes, I should!" He was running his right hand through Alfred's pockets. Something clinked in his fingers.

Chapter VIII

WHEN Donahue was striding past the hospital desk Roper came in huddled in his threadbare coat and stepped side-wise so that he blocked Donahue. Donahue stopped, smiled amiably and said:

"Hello, Roper."

The dour-faced precinct bull said, "Hello," dully. He spoke very slowly, way down in his throat. His big lazy eyes were expressionless. His lantern-jawed, muddy brown face was inanimate—and because of that, somehow threatening.

Donahue said, "They're upstairs swabbing out the little guy's wound. They tell me Babe Delaney got it in the belly. It's funny… he's in a room next to Alfred Poore."

Roper never changed the expression on his face, but after a pendant interval he said monotonously, "You been going places and doing things tonight, ain't you?"

"I've been getting around."

"And seeing people."

Donahue thinned his eyes. "Well, what's eating you, master mind?"

"There's a jane in the show. You know so much. Where's the jane?"

"I wouldn't know. Alfred's a secretive little guy. He got tougher too when he heard Babe wasn't dead."

Roper's lips opened slowly. "Secretive like you, eh? You knew a hell of a lot more than you told me."

"I gave you a straight story, Roper. Adler, the houseman, was there to check up…. Hell, do you suppose I'm going to let you in on a brainstorm I get?"

"Remember, Irish, it don't pay to crack bright with the precinct boys."

Donahue placed a forefinger against Roper's chest. "Remember, Roper, it doesn't pay to get tough on a guy was in on the ground floor. Alfred and this Babe guy are tight-mouthed."

"There's always the rubber-hose short-cut."

Donahue grinned. "Be seeing you, Roper."

Roper gripped Donahue's arm. "Suppose we sit down and you tell me the story from beginning to end."

Donahue reached around his right hand and closed it on Roper's wrist. "Suppose," he said, "you go over to the Twenty-first Precinct and read the blotter." He threw down Roper's hand.

Roper's face remained inanimate, but he said, "Someday you'll be sorry, Irish."

Donahue walked past him saying, "That sounds like the words to a song I once heard." He kept on walking, went out through the hospital door.

He walked a block west on Twenty-sixth Street and hailed a taxi that was drifting north on Second Avenue. He said, "Run me over to Broadway and Thirty-second Street." When he settled in the seat he yawned, stretched arms and legs, looked at the illuminated dial of his strap watch. It was three a.m.

Broadway was a deserted canyon when he alighted. Herald Square, by day a seething whirlpool of traffic, was empty and silent now. Donahue walked south, his footfalls clear-cut on the pavement. Dirty snow lay in the gutters.

He turned into the lobby of the Hotel Breton Arms. His heels rang on the tiled floor. A small bald man leaned on the ornate desk reading a paper. Donahue walked to the elevators. A sleepy Negro in a red uniform got up and walked into the elevator behind Donahue. When the elevator started Donahue said, "Ten." The Negro snapped gum with tongue and teeth. Donahue got out at the tenth floor, turned left, looked at numbers on doors. He drew a key with a brass tag from his pocket. It clinked in his hand. The oval-shaped tag said:

T

O   E

H   L

BRETON

ARMS

1046

He walked on smooth green carpets, turned left, walked a matter of ten yards and stopped before a door on which the number 1046 was printed in dull gold. He stepped back and looked up at a wooden transom that was open about six inches. No light issued.

Donahue inserted the key quietly, turned it quietly, then gripped the knob and turned it slowly to the right. Presently the door gave inward. He opened it wide, so that the light from the corridor spread into the room, revealed the corner of a green carpet and the legs of a chair. He found a button on the wall inside the door frame. He pressed it and the room lit up.

Irene lay on the bed in canary yellow pajamas. Her legs were spread, each foot tied to a corner of the bed by means of narrow but strong luggage straps. Her arms were tied similarly to the posts at the head of the bed, and a towel was fastened around her mouth.

Donahue said, "Well!" jocularly, closed the door, unbuttoned his raglan and came over to sit on the side of the bed. Irene's eyes were wide, frightened. She moved her head from side to side. Wrinkles appeared and disappeared on her forehead.

Donahue chuckled, reached around to the back of her neck and unfastened the towel. When he took that off there was a rag stuffed in Irene's mouth. He drew that out and threw it on the floor.

Irene exhaled, "Whew!"

Donahue said, "Nice pajamas you wear, Irene."

"Oh, God!" she moaned, straining at the luggage straps. "Get these things off! They hurt."

"They won't hurt if you lie still. Besides, I remember that clout on the head…. Irene, you and I are going to have a very short conversation. First, let me tell you that Babe Delaney is in the hospital with a bullet in his guts. Alfred, that nice-faced little doggie, is in the same hospital with a bullet in his leg. Alfred got Babe. I got Alfred."

She grimaced, showing her white small teeth.

Donahue went on, "The bulls have Alfred for the Delaney shoot and it won't be long before they pin the Crosby kill on one of them…. It wasn't very nice, Irene, the way you helped put Babe on the spot."

"I didn't—"

"Ah—ah!" Donahue held up his forefinger, shook it. "I happened to be listening in when you telephoned him."

She cried, "I was made to do it! Alfred stood right there with a razor held under my throat. I had to, Donahue—I swear to God I had to!"

"You little double-crosser, you were playing both ends against the middle! You were jockeying both Alfred and Babe!"

She closed her eyes, bit her lip, whimpered, "Oh… God!"

Donahue leaned across the bed, braced on two rigid arms, one on either side of Irene's waist. His brown eyes smoldered.

"You don't have to act around me, Irene," he said. "You'll get on better by coming across. The bulls have Babe and Alfred, and they're both red-hots. The houseman down in Waverly Place saw Babe come in. I saw Alfred there and I saw you there. I'm the only one knows where you are. I want the whole story from you."

"What good would that do?"

He said quietly, "It will help you a lot. You've got looks. I've got a pull in the city, and the tabloids can run you up on the sob stuff. If you don't play ball with me, I'll land on you like a ton of brick."

"Oh, I've been a fool!"

"If you only wouldn't pull those stock lines, Irene!"

Her voice throbbed when she cried, "I mean it!"

"Bah! You laid the trap for Crosby—"

"That's a lie!" she shouted.

Donahue rose, crossed to the door and closed the transom. He came back to the bed eying her whimsically. "Then are you going to tell me why it's a lie?"

Her eyes narrowed. "How do I know you can give me a break?"

"You can find out by not telling me things."

"Why—why do you want to know?"

"I'm a private cop. I work for a salary. I get a bonus on big jobs I turn. Crosby's uncle offered to pay the Agency ten thousand dollars. I get the bonus by getting to the core of things before the cops do. That's the whole shebang in a nut-shell."

She considered him for a moment. Then she said, "The trouble is, you don't believe I loved Crosby."

"All right.... I'll believe you loved him."

"You say that easily."

"Maybe I'll be able to say it easier after you've told me things."

She sighed brokenly, moistened her lips. She looked at the ceiling and said, "I did love him. He loved me. I met him on the boat train from Paris to Cherbourg. Alfred and I were traveling as brother and sister. We were only two days out when Robert told me he loved me. Alfred never loved me. We weren't like that to each other. We just— traveled together, for reasons.

"Alfred was bringing home a diamond he'd lifted from a woman at Cannes. It was worth about seventy thousand dollars. It was set in a platinum medallion, a pendant sort of thing. We got to Paris with it. We got the stone out of the platinum medallion, threw everything away but the stone.

"When we were three days out of Cherbourg, Alfred began to get one of his hunches. He was sure the Customs would pick it up. He browbeat me into planting it on Robert. I did. I didn't want to, though. I told Alfred how I felt about Robert, and he scoffed—just as you've been scoffing. He threatened to expose me if I didn't do as he said. I was afraid of the inevitable. I planted it on Robert. I worked it into one of his paint tubes, one that had been half used, with the bottom rolled up like you roll up a tube of toothpaste. I unrolled it, slit it, worked the diamond up into the paint and then re-rolled it."

"Where does Babe Delaney come in?"

"Oh… Babe." She sighed. "He was Robert's bootlegger. The first day Robert was home he called Babe up, and Babe went down to see him. He saw a photograph of me lying on the table there—one Robert had taken on board ship. Robert remarked it was a picture of Leone Tenquist. Babe said nothing to him. He came to me and asked what my racket was. I told him it wasn't anything. He said maybe I'd tell him or he'd tell Robert how things stood. Alfred and I had to let Babe in. We promised him ten thousand on sale of the diamond.

"Robert gave me a key to his flat. He said he'd be busy for a few days but that I could drop in any old time. I went down and looked for the tube of paint. I couldn't find it. I told Alfred I couldn't find it. He accused me of a double-cross. I swore I was telling the truth. Then Babe came, and when he heard the story he accused both of us. I told both of them the exact description of the tube of paint.

"Babe went down last night to look himself. He was tearing the place apart when Robert came in. Babe must have picked the lock. He did a two year stretch ten years ago for picking locks. He turned out the lights, but Robert went after him in the dark. Robert was pretty strong. Babe had to use a claspknife.

"Alfred stole the key I had to Robert's flat. He went down. He was there when you arrived. I went down when I'd discovered my key was gone. It's the truth, the God's honest truth! I couldn't get out of the racket. I tried to. I meant to after I'd gotten the diamond. I was going to let Alfred and Babe split. I was crazy about Robert."

"And what happened to the diamond?"

"Gone. Robert had cleaned up, thrown out a lot of rubbish. The diamond went that way. Nobody got it."

Donahue began untying the straps that held Irene's feet. "You have nice little feet," he said.

"Please—don't ridicule me!"

He said, "Irene, that's a swell story and it rings true. I'll repeat it word for word to the bulls. You were a girl trying to go straight, but they had you in the toils of sin. Great?… Sure! I'll boost your story fifty per cent by saying that it was you put me on the trail of Babe Delaney."

She gasped, "Oh… not that!"

"Irene," he said, untying her hands, "you want to save your skin. Babe Delaney muscled in. He was a punk. You want a fresh start in life—"

"You're ridiculing me!"

"I promise you the sweetest sob story ever told, Irene. You may even get a run in vaudeville... but you've got to tell the cops that Babe Delaney carved Crosby. That's your big and only way—out into God's country.... But why did Alfred smoke the Babe?"

"He was sure that if he didn't Babe would get him."

Donahue stood up, smiled down at Irene. "Crosby knew a looker when he saw one, honey."

Irene started to cry into her hands.

Donahue went towards the telephone saying, "Well, it's the least I can do for Roper."

Chapter IX

WHEN the door opened Roper stood there with his dour face and his lazy big eyes.

Donahue said, grinning, "You must come in."

Roper walked in hunching his shoulders in his threadbare coat. He looked at Irene. She was standing with her back to the bureau. She looked very small and very lovely in a black dress that clung snugly to neat hips. Donahue closed the door and Roper stared at Irene with his big dispassionate eyes.

He said dully, "So you're the moll in the case."

"I wouldn't call her a moll," Donahue said.

Roper did not look around at Donahue but he said, "Keep your oar out of it, Donahue."

Then he walked heavily to the bureau, gripped Irene's arm.

"You look like the kind," he said. "You look like the kind I like to get nasty with."

Donahue put in, "Why, Roper, because a good-looking jane would never give you a tumble?"

Roper turned somberly. "You looking for a punch in the jaw?"

Donahue snarled, "Ah, grow up, copper. Keep that stuff for the coked wops you're used to slapping. I gave you a break. This little pinch is yours but you've got to handle it right. This girl steered me onto Babe Delaney for the Crosby kill. You've got the guy killed him.

Why pick on the ladies?"

Roper looked at Irene. "You say Babe killed Crosby?"

She faltered, "Ye-es."

He shook her arm brutally. "Why the hell didn't you come to the police?"

Donahue said, "She thought I was a real copper, Roper. When I told her dick—I didn't say private. She and Crosby were in love. She's sidestepped a bit, but she was trying for a straight and these bums got in her way. You can see she's a good woman."

"Don't kid me, Donahue."

"I wouldn't kid you, Roper."

Roper dropped Irene's arm. His eyes hung somberly on Donahue. He said, after a minute. "Okey, Irish. You're a fast worker. If I was a younger cop, and ambitious, I might get God-awful sore. But I'm retiring soon. I'm used to routine." He turned to Irene. "Get your things on, sister."

Irene put on her mole coat and the dark cloche hat. Roper opened the door and waited in the hall. Irene went out. Donahue went out, snapped off the lights, closed and locked the door. He gave the key to Irene.

They were silent going down in the elevator. When they passed out into Broadway Roper said:

"We'll take a cab down if you'll pay the fare, Donahue."

Gun Thunder

Tough dick Donahue takes up the trail of a gang's sweet racket.

Chapter I

DONAHUE put down the whiskey-sour when he heard the muffled shot and looked at himself blank-faced in the mirror for the space of ten seconds. The bartender stopped his bar-rag half way through a leisurely stroke and put his round bald head attentively on one shoulder.

A drunk at the end of the bar stirred and hiccoughed and then made his face more comfortable in the crook of his elbow.

Roper, the precinct dick, stopped picking his teeth and scowled sourly over his shoulder at the door.

A girl sitting at a wall-table asked, "Was—was that a shot?"

"Was it?" the man with her said.

Far away, a police whistle....

Roper turned, hunched his wide bony shoulders in his threadbare dark gray coat and rapped his heels hard on his way out. Donahue followed.

Grove Street below Sheridan Square was a gloomy street walled in by low dark-faced houses and punctuated at infrequent intervals by small yellow lights indicating speakeasies.

Roper was a gaunt, lunging figure seen for a split-moment beneath one of these lights. Donahue was a slower figure six paces behind.

Northeast on Grove was a small group of people—shapes, shadows in the glow of an ineffectual street light. A shiny visored cap and metal buttons flashed beneath the light. A woman was chattering in a high, strident voice, and there was the sound of windows grating open. Heavy heels rapped the cold winter pavement and more metal buttons passed beneath the street light.

Donahue came up behind Roper. Roper had his hands thrust in his overcoat pockets, a misshapen weathered hat yanked over his eyebrows. A fresh cigar jutted from a corner of his mouth.

"You, Klein?"

"Yeah. You, Roper?"

"Yeah…. 'Lo, Mahoney."

" 'Lo."

"Guy got it, Roper," Klein said, bending over a crumpled figure in the gutter.

"Cold?"

"No foolin'. Smack through the chest… right here."

Mahoney was waving his hand. "You guys get back. Come on, everybody get back. *You*—I mean you too—"

"Ah, no you don't," Donahue said, laconic.

"Listen, baby—"

"Forget it, rookie."

"That's Donahue," Roper threw in. "Private dick. A pest… but what the hell."

"Well," Mahoney grumbled; then turned on the others. "Come on, get back! Give the guy air!"

"Ah, hell, he's dead," Klein said.

"Come on, get back…." Mahoney's shield flashed as he rocked back and forth with great importance.

The high, strident voice proclaimed, "It's murder! Oh, a man's been murdered!"

Roper half-turned with his dull long dour face. "Who's making all the noise?"

Mahoney strode towards the cluster of people and repeated the question with added emphasis. An old woman was clawing at a black shawl she wore around her shoulders.

"I saw it!" she cried breathlessly. "I saw it!"

Roper slouched over and asked, "What'd you see?"

"Him—murdered!"

"Yeah?… Where were you?"

"I was comin' down from the Square. I saw two men kind of close like. I thought first they were drunk. Then there was a shot. I heard the shot. And there was a burst of flame. I saw it. I heard the shot. This here man fell down."

"Get a look at the other guy?"

"It was dark. How could I see him? I just saw him. I mean I didn't see his face. He ran off, quick. He ran off down Bedford Street."

"Big or little?"

"He looked bigger than this one. It was hard to tell but he looked bigger. I'm sure he was bigger. He ran down Bedford Street."

Roper turned. "Anyhow, Mahoney, hike down Bedford Street and around kind of and see if any guy saw any guy running. Klein, pop up the Square and report. Tell 'em I'm here too. Tell 'em to shoot over the morgue bus."

The two patrolmen started off on the double-quick.

Roper slouched back to the inert form, knelt down and fumbled in his own pockets.

Donahue knelt down beside Roper, drew a match from his pocket and scraped it against the curb. He cupped the flame over the dead man's face. Legs of the man were on the sidewalk, the rest of him twisted down into the gutter, thin hair rumpled and moving in the winter wind.

Roper squinted and leaned closer, his long bony jaw stretching. "Hell," he muttered.

"Familiar face?"

"Kinda."

"What I thought."

Roper said, "Yeah, I've seen the man before."

Roper looked up slantwise with his dour eyes. His gaunt face was dully inquisitive.

As the match went out Donahue said, "Adler's his name." He struck another match and held it cupped over the dead man's face. "Yeah, Roper.... Adler."

"Adler, eh?... Why, yeah. Why, sure. Adler... sure. That house over in Waverly Place where this guy, this what's-his-name... Crosby—yeah, Crosby. Where Crosby was rubbed out a couple of months ago by Babe Delaney. That's right. Funny."

He went through the dead man's pockets. He took out pipe, tobacco pouch, keys, pen-knife, forty-two cents, a worn wallet containing eighteen dollars, a theatre ticket stub for a Fourteenth Street burlesque house, business cards of a coal dealer, a milk company, a radio store.

"No robbery," Roper sighed. "Nope. No robbery. No smell of booze around, either. No lush job.... Adler, eh?"

The crowd had grown in numbers and had edged nearer, restless, curious.

Roper stood up, raising his gaunt nose beneath the yellow street light. "Anybody else see this?"

"I was comin' down from the Square—"

"I mean anybody else?" Roper broke in.

Here and there—"No." "No, Officer." "No, not me," in various degrees of hushed breathlessness.

Roper's wide bony shoulders sagged. He took a limp cigarette from his pocket and stuck it between his loose wide lips. He fumbled in his pockets.

Donahue said, "Here," lighting a match, and Roper shoved out his long jaw and put the end of the cigarette into the blowing flame. He looked over the flame with his dour eyes.

"Got a smell?"

"You?" Donahue smiled.

"I asked."

Donahue snapped away the match and his chuckle was low and amused in the gloom.

"Hell," he said, "I only find smells when my boss sends me."

"Yeah. Yeah, I know that hooey, too. There was always something queer about that Crosby case. Something queer about the murder and that jane and the way the diamond disappeared and never showed up again."

"The State wanted the killer of Crosby. It got him."

"Yeah. It got him. And the ice that all the noise was about…just disappeared." He looked hard at Donahue. "Sure you ain't got a smell?"

"Nothing you haven't got. You're the big master-mind around this neighborhood. And you ask—me?"

"Ah, can it."

"Okey." Donahue shrugged.

The morgue bus came and went away bearing old Adler's shattered body. One by one the crowd broke up, vanished. Mahoney came back and shook his head.

"Nobody saw nobody, Roper. The mutt pulled a neat fade-away, that's a cinch."

Donahue stood on the curb looking intently around on the street, up and down the gutter.

Roper came over and assumed a rough intimate tone. "Have a drink before I shoot over the house."

"Can't, Roper. Thanks. Got a date."

Roper gripped his arm. "How about that smell?"

"Ah, grow up, copper!" Donahue pried loose and went away walking towards Sheridan Square.

Chapter II

ADLER… poor slob. Old Adler, janitor and resident manager of the three-story graystone in Waverly Place, where Crosby, that artist, had been carved by Babe Delaney because Crosby was supposed to have brought in a diamond which Irene Saffarrans had planted on him en route from Europe.

And that boy friend of Irene's…. Alfred Poore, that nice-faced rat who had come over with her. Irene had planted the diamond in a half-used tube of Crosby's paint, and Crosby, all unknowing, had smuggled it in.

He'd gone kind of nuts on Irene.

Babe Delaney had got wise to the stunt Irene and Alfred were up to. Saw her picture in Crosby's flat when he came down to deliver some liquor. He'd been Crosby's bootlegger before the artist went abroad. Said nothing to Crosby but hiked around to Irene and Alfred, got the story, and wanted a split.

Then things had happened… one suspecting the other of a double-cross in the series of confounding incidents that followed. And Crosby… killed in the rush.

The big rub lay in the fact that when Crosby got home from the European trip he threw out a lot of rubbish, among which was the half-used tube of paint. Adler himself had remembered throwing it out.

Now the Babe was marking time in the death house and Alfred was doing a ten-year hitch. Irene got clear. She had looks and pathos in her make-up. And Donahue, by this and that, had helped manipulate her freedom, with the tabloids back of her. Well, Irene had given him the story about Babe and Alfred and the whole scheme. And the Interstate Agency had harvested a fat sum from Crosby's moneyed uncle….

ASA Hinkle, the Interstate in person, said, "Murder, then—raw and unadorned."

"Cheap murder," Donahue nodded.

Hinkle was a large benign Jew, with white hair, diplomatic *pince-nez,* and a large, firm jaw. He held an excellent perfecto between white, strong fingers.

"After I got rid of Roper last night," Donahue said, "I chased around the alleys as far as McDougal Street, looked in ash-cans, gutters, everywhere. I asked some questions, but nobody saw a guy running. It's funny how guys run and nobody sees them."

"And you didn't find it?"

"No."

Hinkle took a slow, meditative drag. "And you think Roper never paid any attention to the fact that it was gone?"

"I don't think he did. He might have. But I don't think so."

"Odd."

Donahue scowled. "Some fine day I'm going to paste Roper. I'm going to get him off in a corner and push his dirty —— dam' face in. He's a punk, that guy—a leech. He's the lousiest cop on the Force. When I think of a good guy like Ames, who used to cruise that precinct; and then this guy Roper—cripes, I see red. No fooling. He's a louse—a stink. He never crashed any job on his own. I gave him the Delaney job—gave him the broad. And does he appreciate it?

Hell, that guy would rubber-hose a ten-year-old kid if he thought he could beat something out of him!"

"Grudge against him, haven't you?"

"Yeah, you said it. I hate having a bad smell around me all the time."

Hinkle leaned forward on his flat-topped desk, "Well, Donny, make a stab at this. Play around a while and see what turns up. If that diamond is still in circulation we may get it. If guys do murder for it, it must be worth something... and very likely its rightful owner may crop up one day. Uh—and don't be too rough on Roper. He has—you know—his uses."

"Yeah. I'll be la-de-da with him. Sure I will!"

Hinkle sighed. "You get notions, Donny...." He bent over some letters, puffed serenely on his cigar.

Donahue went out like a gust of wind. He took the elevator down to the lobby, walked out into Park Row, into a brisk winter wind and bright winter sunlight. He walked west on Chambers Street, past City Hall, crossed Broadway, and continued west until he reached Sixth Avenue, when he entered a subway kiosk. He boarded a north-bound local, watched three stations go by, and got off when the fourth station said Christopher Street and Sheridan Square. The wide square was windy. A big cop stood in the middle directing traffic.

Donahue struck Grove Street, turned into Waverly Place and walked past Gay Street. He remembered the gray-faced house, the wet, snowy night he had walked in and found Crosby dead on the floor. Now he climbed the stone steps, entered the open vestibule, rang a bell button beside the inner door.

After a while a short, stocky man opened the door and looked out with vacant, big eyes.

"You the new manager?" Donahue asked.

"Yes, sir."

"I'm Donahue, of the Interstate Detective Agency. I knew Mr. Adler pretty well. We worked together, kind of, on the Crosby murder here, two months ago.... Mind if I look at Adler's things?"

"Well, I don't think I can say... me being new here. Mr. Roper, another detective, was here this morning."

"Yes, I know Roper. I don't want anything. Just like to poke around, and you can poke around with me." He was fingering a five-dollar bill. The man looked at it, then looked away as though he had not seen it.

"Maybe... I guess...."

Donahue entered, and the short, stocky man led him downstairs to a room next to the furnace room. Here old Adler had lived his bachelor's life—with his books, his magazines, his pipe.

"Ten years, wasn't he—here?" Donahue said.

"Yes, sir—ten years. The owners are giving him burial, and his sister is on the way from Rochester to get what things he left. These.... I been packing his clothes." He nodded to a battered old trunk. "I had them all packed, but Mr. Roper dumped them all out, so I just been packing them again."

Donahue pulled over a chair beside the trunk, sat down, and drew out the garments one by one. There were some shirts with Regent Street, London, labels. There were two soft hats; one had a Jermyn Street label. There was a sweater from the Burlington Arcade.

The new manager said, "I used to know Adler. He said Mr. Crosby used to give him a lot of second-hand clothes."

"Yes, he told me that too."

When Donahue had finished searching the trunk he sat back.

The manager nodded to the table. "These here are bills and things he had in his tin box."

Donahue went to the table and ran through a sheaf of receipted bills—grocer's, butcher's, tailor's. He looked at one that was headed: "Hats Cleaned, Blocked." There was one item on it. A hat that had been cleaned and blocked. It was dated March third—four days ago. Donahue looked at other bills, shuffled the lot together and replaced the clip which he had taken off.

"Did Detective Roper find anything?"

"He didn't seem to. He asked me a lot of questions about Adler. Of course, I didn't know much."

"H'm. Adler never said he'd been bothered after the Crosby kill?"

"No."

"What's your name?"

"Homer's my name."

"All right, Mr. Homer." He withdrew the five-dollar bill from his pocket, laid it on the table. "I'll be going. May see you again sometime."

"Thanks, Mr. Donahue."

Outside, Donahue walked east on Waverly Place, turned north

into Sixth Avenue, walked one block and swung east into Eighth Street. He entered a small shop where a swart young Italian steamed a hat in the window and where another was polishing the shoes of a man who sat in one of six chairs. Farther back, behind a glass showcase displaying shoe polishes, creams, laces, and hat bands, stood another man who did nothing. Towards him went Donahue.

"You own this place, brother?"

"Shu."

"Knew that guy Adler was bumped off last night?"

"Yeah, shu. Useta come in here lots."

"Nice old guy, wasn't he?"

"Fine—a guy, shu. Kinda funny... y' know what?"

"Yeah." Donahue leaned on the glass showcase. "You remember if he brought in a hat to be cleaned a few days ago?"

The man chuckled. "Yeah, shu. Was ver' funny 'bout de hat. Say we should be moocha careful... y' know what? Shu. Was good hat. Say, you 'member dat man was slice up two mont's ago... Mr. Crosby?"

"Crosby? Sure do."

"Was his hat. Was a hat Mr. Crosby geeve dis guy Adler. So Adler say we gotta be moocha careful… y' know what?"

"I get you." Donahue nodded towards the front of the shop. "That boy clean the hat?"

"No. Was feller I chuck t'ree days ago. Joosta fire him—like dat. Gotta fresh. Was a wise guy. Yeah, shu. Nick Bonalino… no good. Moocha wise guy. Play de pool all-a time. Friends drop in and keep up de talk and Nick no do mooch work. So I fire him. Was always tell me he getta good job singing in night-club."

"What night-club?"

"Watcha call de *Hey-hey Club*—McDougal Street. Jeep joint…."

"I know the joint."

"Say, you dick?"

"Yeah, I'm a dick. Any other dick in here today?"

"No."

Donahue brightened, gave the man a cigar, and breezed out.

Chapter III

MCDOUGAL Street south of West Houston is no beauty spot. Dark as a pit at night. Narrow and dirty, honeycombed by pseudo-Bohemian night-clubs that specialize in the fleecing of late-wandering drunks and sober suckers. One or two men standing in front of an innocent-looking dark-faced house are all the signs you will find. No glitter of lights. No telephone listing. The taxicab drivers know them all. And the police. Thus the notorious *Hey-hey Club*….

Donahue passed three men leaning against the iron hand-rail of a six-step stoop, climbed the steps, pushed open a dark door, entered a dimly lighted room. Two men looked at him. They wore tuxedos and had white, watchful faces. Behind them was a booth where a blonde took Donahue's ulster and hat and gave him a check.

One of the two men guided him through gloom towards another door, and Donahue entered a low, long room that had a small orchestra platform at the farther end, tables along the side walls and sprinkled across the floor halfway to the orchestra platform. Beyond these latter tables was a space of floor about twenty feet by twenty. This was the dance-floor. Walls and ceiling were draped in purple. The tables were crowded, and at a large table near the platform sat a half dozen girls in showy evening dress. Hostesses.

Donahue was led to a table. He sat down and ordered Scotch straight with soda on the side. The waiter brought the drink and marked down on his pad: $1.50. The manager came over, leaned on the table and said:

"Want a girl friend?"

"No."

"Okey."

A group of slack-faced youths appeared on the platform, picked up instruments and started to play. Thirty couples crowded on the twenty-by-twenty floor and began to dance. Most of them were drunk. The orchestra played short numbers, and dawdled around until some drunk careened up to the platform and deposited a bill in the upturned high-hat there. Then the players grinned, picked up their instruments again, and played.

Donahue wagged his head and muttered, "Cripes!"

A waiter came over, scooped up his glass, said, "Same?" and Donahue nodded.

The band stopped. The dancers staggered back to their tables. The wall lights dimmed. A spotlight was thrown on the dance-floor.

A red-haired girl sauntered out, clapped her hands and yelled, "Now a little show, folks! A great little show! Greatest little show in old New York! Singin', dancin'—all kinds of hey-hey! Open your eyes and get an eyeful! Open your ears and get an earful! Trixie Meloy, singin' and dancin', folks—and how!"

Trixie Meloy swept onto the floor. She hadn't much on. She was a high-kicker. She danced badly and sang worse. The crowd applauded. She toured the tables and the drunks gave her tribute in crisp bills. Donahue gave her a chuckle.

Came the red-head yelling, "Now a bit of Spanish—right here in the little old *Hey-hey Club*. Castanets, folks—and other things. Watch her shake the Spanish.... Señorita Martinez, folks—hot from old Madrid!"

Castanets and Señorita Martinez whirled out on the floor. She had black, shiny hair and a fixed smile. The drunks gaped. The orchestra boys smirked. The señorita did her stuff, did an encore, made the round of the tables and collected.

Then the red-head waved her hands. "Now—now, folks. A great big surprise. Nick Bonalino, the singing waiter. He's going to sing

How Come You Do Me Like You Do?"

It was the waiter who had served Donahue. He was tall, young, handsome in a smooth, dark Italian way. Donahue settled on his elbows and watched him. The boy could sing. He didn't bother with the gestures. But his voice was rich and soft.

> *"How come y' do me like y' do-do-do?*
> *How come y' do me like y' do?"*

Donahue finished his drink, watching Nick Bonalino.

> *"Gonna lay yo' head on a railroad line,*
> *Letta train come along an' pacify yo' mind...."*

Nick was good. He had to give two encores. He made the round of the tables. Donahue put a dollar in the hat.

The side-lights went on again when the spotlight went off. The drunks got up and danced.

Nick came over to scoop up Donahue's drink.

Donahue said, "You're good, boy."

"Thanks."

"Maybe I can do things for you in a bigger way."

"Yeah?"

"Yeah. Drop around to my hotel at ten tomorrow morning. The Brooke. West Ninth Street. Donahue's the name."

"Jeeze! Wait! How do you spell it?" Nick wrote the name down on the back of a card. "Ten?"

"Ten."

"Jeeze! Thanks. I'll be around."

Donahue paid four-fifty for three drinks, got up and left the *Hey-hey Club*.

AT ten o'clock next morning Donahue was sitting in his hotel room when the telephone rang and the man at the desk said Mr. Bonalino was calling.

"Send him up," Donahue said.

Nick Bonalino looked like a sporting man when he entered the room. He wore a large-brimmed tan hat, a yellow overcoat of military cut, brown trousers that broke over buff-colored spats. He carried a Malacca stick and smoked a cigar.

"Hope I'm on time, Mr. Donahue."

"Sure. Sit down." Donahue had closed the door. He slushed red-leather mules across the carpet, picked up a pipe and crammed tobacco into the bowl. He dropped to a wide easy-chair, lit up and looked at Bonalino with mild amusement.

"You look like ready money, Nick."

"I ain't, though. A man's gotta keep up appearances."

"Yeah." Donahue leaned back comfortably. "I'm sorry I got you up here, Nick, on the pretense of getting you a job."

Nick dropped his bright-glowing face and looked confused. "I don't get you."

Donahue waved his pipe indolently. "I'm a dick."

Nick Bonalino started. "A dick!"

"Take it easy, kid. I'm a nice dick. You look like a nice guy to me. Everything will be nice."

"But, jeeze, me— I don't— Me?"

"It's this way, Nick. You look like money. And you got fired from that hat cleaning place in Eighth Street—"

"I didn't get fired. I left."

"That's better. Fits in better. Then you left. Okey... you left. Why?"

Nick Bonalino got up and glowered, darkly handsome. "Because I was through with 'at guy. Because I was through with 'im." He slashed his yellow-gloved hand dramatically back and forth.

Donahue looked amused. "From hat cleaner to singing waiter. Is that—up or down?"

"I was getting a try-out, 'at's what I was. So I had to wait on tables too. And I had to pay the boss fifty bucks to let me sing. And I went over big. And I only started there last night."

"That coat you've got on rates at least a hundred bucks. The hat's no less than twelve. The spats five. The suit looks like about eighty. How come a guy cleans hats, suddenly busts out in a rash of good clothes? How come, Nick? Huh? On the up and up now, kid."

Nick Bonalino towered in his lean dark way. His black eyes glittered. "Dicks don't act this way. I don't know much about them, but I know when they want to ask a guy questions they don't make nice dates like this."

Donahue stood up, dropping his amused look. "I'm a private dick—"

"Then you got no right to ask me all these damn questions!" He slapped on his hat, pivoted and started for the door.

Donahue slid sidewise with amazing rapidity and blocked the door. "No you don't, Nick."

Nick tightened his full lips, showed clenched teeth, and uncorked a short right jab. It landed on Donahue's jaw. His head jerked. A blaze leaped into his brown hard eyes. A twisted look of contempt jumped to his lips. Lightning-like, a one-two punch... and Nick hurtled backwards, fell over a chair, crashed into a telephone table, brought down telephone, books, and another chair.

Nick lay there, rather tangled up in the telephone wire, looking shocked and dazed, the top of his hat crushed in, the brim pressing down against his ears.

Donahue walked to the secretary, took out a Colt's .38 revolver, handled it with a negligence born of old familiarity.

"Get up, Nick. Get up, you poor dumb dago."

Nick got up, his overcoat askew, his hat still crushed on his head. Donahue picked up the telephone, set it on a chair.

"You're not a bad guy, Nick," Donahue said. "Don't try to get wise around me. I don't like it. I don't like wiseacres.... Now keep your ears open. You must know about the Adler murder... over in Grove Street, night before last. Anyhow, you cleaned a hat of Adler's a few days before he was murdered. Then you left your job. Then Adler was murdered."

"What—me—murder a guy!"

"Nah, did I say that...? But listen. You cleaned a hat, an English hat. You found something in it. You found a diamond in it."

Nick Bonalino's face turned very red. He laughed. "Ha! Me find a diamond? Ha-ha!"

Donahue moved his gun around and laid his brown gaze hard on Bonalino. "You found a diamond, Nick. I can see it in your face. You found it. If you don't come across you'll be mixed up in this murder. You found the diamond. You found that diamond. You—you have that diamond!"

"Honest to God, mister—"

Donahue took two fast steps, held the muzzle of his gun an inch from Nick Bonalino's stomach. "I said, Nick, you're not a bad Wop. Just a little wise. Just inclined to be something of a sheik. But that's all right. Twenty, aren't you...? Well, anyhow, this is murder. Want the police to slam you around? Come on, Nick, I'm a good guy, a great guy when you know me. But if you try to stall on me, I'm a louse. That diamond, Nick...."

"God, I ain't got it—"

"You had it. You stole it—"

"I didn't steal it! Adler didn't know it was there! I just spoiled the lining and I had to put a new one in, and the diamond fell out. I just—kept it."

"Where is it?"

"I hocked it. I got two hundred fifty on it. I needed these duds to make a nice appearance at one of them clubs. In tips and what I got for singin' last night I made twenty-five. I figured to get the diamond out when I had the jack and have a ring made. Kind of be nice to have a ring when I'm singin' in the spotlight."

"Too bad, Nick... but I want the diamond."

"I ain't got the jack. I only got thirty-eight bucks to my name."

"I'll get the money. I want the diamond. I'll go with you and we'll get the diamond."

"Jeeze, I didn't know! Jeeze, murder...!"

"Okey, Nick. You're a good guy. I like you." He rubbed his jaw. "You hit like a mule, kid."

"Hell, I didn't mean it. I got all steamed up."

"Yeah. So did I.... Have a drink while I put shoes on."

THE hock-shop was in Fourteenth Street. It was about the width of a railway coach, and half the length. The window was littered with cheap novelties. The interior was dark and gloomy, and behind the showcase a man sat at a high desk and regarded the insides of a watch beneath a brilliant green-shaded light. He looked around when Bonalino and Donahue entered, got down off the high stool, picked up the stub of a cigar and put it between his teeth. He was a small, slim young-old man, with a sallow gray face and big horn-rimmed glasses, black curly hair.

"I'll take this," Nick Bonalino said, laying the hock ticket on the counter.

I. Friedman picked up the stub, looked at it, looked at Nick, and went into the rear. He reappeared a couple of minutes later, opened a small envelope and poured out an oblong stone.

"It's a honey," he remarked as he laid it in Nick's palm. "I didn't expect you back so soon."

"I just needed ready cash," Nick said as he counted out two hundred and fifty dollars.

"Give you eight hundred any time you want to sell it."

"Okey. I'll think it over."

"Sure."

"So long."

" 'Bye."

Donahue and Nick started west on Fourteenth Street.

Roper stepped from a doorway and fell in beside Donahue.

"Got a smell all right, eh?"

Donahue chuckled. "Hello, master-mind. See you've stopped bothering the kids who pitch pennies in back alleys."

"Lay off!" Roper rumbled. "Who's your friend?"

"Friend of mine."

"I don't like your company."

"Go to hell."

"Who's your friend?"

"Mr. Bonalino…. Mr. Bonalino, this is Mr. Roper, a kind of detective."

"Pleased to meet you, Mr. Roper."

As they walked, Roper said, "I been over to the house in Waverly Place. I left instructions not to let any cheap private fly-cop in."

"Okey," Donahue said. "That's fine."

"Listen, you. What you been doing in that hock-shop?"

"Looking around. Mr. Bonalino is interested in the case. He's going to write a play about a good detective. So he goes around with me and sees how I work."

"Huh!" Roper grunted.

They were approaching Union Square.

"There's another hock-shop. I think we'll drop in there."

Roper slowed down. "Pretty wise, you, Donahue."

"Be seeing you, Roper, when I can't help it."

Donahue and Nick entered another hock-shop. They looked in the showcase, killed five minutes, came out and walked on.

"He's tailing us," Donahue said.

They visited three more hock-shops, asked nothing, spent about five minutes in each. They wound up at Astor Place, entered the subway, got off at Bleecker Street and walked west.

"I think we've dropped him," Donahue said. "All right. I have your address. You have mine. I'll be getting in touch with you. If this guy Roper finds you and gets funny, call me up. He's got nothing on you. Act dumb. Act indignant. If he tries to frame you I'll get a lawyer who'll make an ass out of him. So long, Nick."

When Donahue walked in on Hinkle he said, "Well, I've got the ice."

"So soon? My, my!"

Donahue rolled the diamond on the desk. "I got Bonalino in the room and talked him into coughing up. He's a good Wop, after you talk to him. He'd hocked it. Cleaned the hat and had to take the lining out. The diamond was behind the lining."

"Meaning?"

"That Irene's song-and-dance about hiding it in the tube of paint was a stall. She double-crossed Alfred. She never hid it in the paint tube at all. She hid it in the hat, the two-timing little —— "

Hinkle said, "Greenberg will be in tomorrow. He knows stones. He'll tell us the exact value. Meantime we'd better keep it in the safe."

"Yeah. Now the thing is… we've got to locate Irene. Hell knows where she is. But if she isn't behind this murder I'm a slob. I'll bet she's got another boy friend…. Roper tailed us to the hock-shop. But I got rid of him. I went into a few more hock-shops to give him the idea I was cruising the town like a regular story-book cop. That guy's going to walk into a crack in the jaw any day…. Y' know, I think I'll take a trip up to Sing Sing and see if Alfred knows where Irene's hanging out."

"Go to it, Donny. But I don't think he'll know."

"Anyhow, the ride'll do me good."

Chapter IV

AT seven that night Donahue walked into his room at the Hotel Brooke. He stood in the center of the floor for a long minute, staring at the carpet, then flung his hat on the bed, took off his ulster and hung it up in the closet. He sat down by the telephone and called a number.

"Hello, boss. Thought I'd catch you home…. Yeah, I just got in…."

No. Not a thing. I talked myself blue in the face but Alfred must have thought I was a liar. He wouldn't open his mouth. He didn't know anything about Irene. I told him she was playing around with a guy and everything. But not a rise out of him…. Yeah, I know it is…. Sure. That's all we can do…. Okey, boss. Good-bye."

He hung up, rose, took off coat and vest and unsholdered his suspenders. He put on slippers, stuffed and lit a pipe, turned on the floor lamp beside the easy-chair, and sat down with some magazines.

At eight o'clock the telephone rang. Donahue threw aside the magazines, got up, yawning, and picked up the instrument. The voice at the desk said that Mr. Bonalino was calling.

"Just send him up," Donahue said.

When a knock sounded on the door Donahue crossed the room and opened the door wide. But he did not look at Nick Bonalino. He looked at a tall, well-groomed young man who held a heavy automatic pistol in his hand.

The man took a step in, said, "Back, you—and watch your hands."

Donahue stepped back. The man entered all the way, kicked the door shut with his heel. He had a white, well-packed face, yellow eyebrows, small hard, round eyes, and firm, thin mouth.

"So you're Donahue, eh?"

"And you're Bonalino?"

"You ought to know."

"I know Bonalino."

The stranger eyed him shrewdly. "Know what I came here for?"

"I wouldn't know."

"Says you, baby. Get started. I want that hunk of ice."

Donahue smiled. "Aren't you the presumptuous —— ?"

"Get it!" the man snapped. "I didn't come up here to have you make a lot of cracks."

"You came up for a hunk of ice."

"You said it."

"Okey," Donahue said, nodding around the room. "Find it."

"That's your job."

"Guess again, brother."

The man came closer, his hand tight on the butt of his gun. "You ever get lead in your belly, guy?"

"Sure. Common occurrence."

He jammed the muzzle against Donahue's stomach. "You get that hunk of ice, you wisenheimer, and get it fast!"

"You want it, bozo. You get it."

The man gnawed his lip. Then—"Turn around."

Donahue turned around. The man felt his hip pocket. "Now stand right where you are."

"Sure."

The man went to the secretary. He was quick, and he kept an eye on Donahue while he pulled out all the drawers. He dumped their contents on the floor. Then he crossed to the bureau, pulled out all the bureau drawers, dumped their contents on the floor, knelt down and sifted with his fingers. He rose, cursing, and hauled all the clothes out of the closet. He searched every pocket. He searched two hand bags and a trunk. He turned finally and came towards Donahue.

"It's here. Where the hell is it?"

"Did I say it was here?"

"— — you, cut out stalling!"

"That's just an idea you have."

The man whipped up his gun and laid it hard against Donahue's head. Donahue wilted, tried to close with the man. The man stepped back after the manner of one used to such tactics.

"Easy, Donahue!"

Donahue stopped, looking at him beneath a corrugated forehead. A trickle of blood made its way from Donahue's hair and down across his left temple.

"Where is it?" the man asked coolly.

"I haven't got it!"

"Where is it?"

"It's not here. I don't know where it is. I haven't got it."

"Bonalino said you got it."

"He's a damned liar!"

The man came forward again, his white, hard face menacing. "I want that ice," he said quietly, evenly. "I mean to get it. You've got it and you're going to give it to me."

Donahue wore a twisted, humorless smile. "You can't bump me off here, brother. You just can't. It's nine flights down to the lobby. The house dick is down there. Everybody'd hear the shot. You'd never get away."

"I'd shoot my way out."

"You don't look like a common gun. A common gun would do that. No guy with brains would. I haven't got the ice. I don't know anything about it. It was just a bum steer that Bonalino gave you. He'd like to shove a knife in my ribs himself—if he had the guts. Lay off, brother. You're wasting time here. Besides, you don't buffalo me a bit. I know you wouldn't be crazy enough to cut loose with that rod on the ninth floor of a hotel."

"You know a lot, don't you?"

"Yeah. I've been going to night school."

The man took one step, one sure swing. His gun banged against Donahue's jaw. Donahue pitched backwards over a chair.

"That's for bright boys," the man said, walking over.

Donahue lay where he had fallen, his legs draped over the upturned chair, his back flat on the floor. Red color flooded his face, and his lips were flattened against his teeth, and blood was on his jaw. His eyes looked misty. Muscles alongside his mouth bulged. He braced an elbow against the floor, started to rise doggedly, desperately. The man leaned over and struck with the gun again.

Donahue crumpled backward, crying out hoarsely. He folded his arms across his face. The man made another thorough search of the room while Donahue lay like one dead. After a while the man stopped in the center of the room, scowling. He crossed to Donahue, kicked him in the ribs. Donahue did not stir.

The man put away his gun, adjusted his hat and coat, went to the door and walked out.

DONAHUE came to an hour and a half later. He sat up and looked at the soggy blot of blood on the carpet. He ran his fingers across his jaw. His fingers came away stained. He looked white, his lips were hueless.

He got up slowly and went into the bathroom. He looked at himself. Blood had caked from his hair down his cheek to the right jaw. Blood was still soft on the left jaw. He blinked. His hands shook.

He ran warm water into the basin. He shoved his face and head into the water, left it there for the duration of a long breath. He lifted his head, blew his lips. He looked at himself. He ran the ensanguined water out of the bowl and refilled it. He washed his face again. He took a wad of cotton, soaked it with an antiseptic fluid and swabbed his jaw and head. He dried his face where it wasn't cut. Then he took out a bottle of iodine, painted the cut on his jaw. He sucked in a breath, saying, "Cripes!" and closed his eyes hard. After a minute he parted his hair over the cut on his head, iodined it, wincing again, sucking in breath and blowing it out boisterously.

He returned to the other room, poured two inches of Scotch into a water glass and downed it straight. He took off his bloodied shirt. His undershirt was stained too. He took it off. He had a lean-muscled torso, with lots of chest.

There was a knock on the door.

Donahue half-turned and stared dully at the door. Then he walked to the bureau, took his Colt's .38 from the top. He went to the door with it, turned the knob.

Nick Bonalino towered there, out of breath. He had a blackened eye and blue welts on his right cheek-bone.

"God, Donahue!"

"Get in. Quick!"

Bonalino lunged in, and Donahue closed the door, locked it. Bonalino stood in the center of the floor, heaving up and down in an effort to get his breath. Donahue eyed him frigidly.

"Well," he said, "you got me into a nice jam."

Bonalino was looking around at the empty drawers on the floor, on the tangle of clothes, books, odds and ends.

"Me! God… me! I—I been through hell myself. I didn't tell him, Donahue! Holy Mother, I didn't! He knocked me out, but I didn't tell him. He got the card of yours you gave me. I came over soon as I could. I came in a taxi. I got off at the corner and I was coming towards the hotel here when I saw him come out and walk towards University Place. So instead of coming in I followed him. I figured if you was dead, what the hell could I do but follow him. And if you wasn't dead—well, I could follow him too. So I did."

He paused for breath.

Donahue's eyes began to glitter darkly. "Good, Nick! By God, you're good!"

"So—so he took a taxi at University Place, and then I took one. And I followed him to Thirty-eighth Street. He went in a hotel—the Redfern—on Lexington. I didn't go in. I just followed him there and came back. Jeeze… whew! Did I get a beating up? Whew!"

"He wanted the diamond, eh?"

"Yeah. I acted dumb, but he started to haul off on me. I don't know how he found me—"

"Used his head. Went to the hat-cleaning place where you worked. Got your address. *That's* the guy killed Adler. I'll bet my shirt on it. He got Adler's hat. No diamond in it. He saw it had been cleaned. He cruised the hat-cleaning places in the neighborhood. He—yes, he used his head, that guy. He's no small tomatoes."

Nick went into the bathroom, came out again holding palms up and looking woebegone. "Look at me! Just when I'm starting to sing too! I can't sing this way. Holy Mother, what a break!"

"I'll help you out till you lose the beauty spots, Nick. But I sure thought you two-timed on me. I sure did…. Take a tip. Stay away from the place where you're living. Take a room somewhere in another neighborhood for a while. That guy may look you up again. I think I'll take a room somewhere."

"Where?"

"The Redfern…. How's to have a drink, Nick?"

Chapter V

DONAHUE took a bag and went over to the Redfern that night. He got a room on the fifth floor overlooking Lexington Avenue. At eight next morning he rose, shaved, went down to breakfast. At nine he called Hinkle and gave him the dope.

Then he bought two newspapers, went into the lounge near the front entrance, and sat down, hat and overcoat on a nearby chair. He watched about two hundred persons go out and come in. At eleven o'clock he saw Irene Saffarrans pass through the lobby on her way out, and turn north on Lexington.

He rose, put on hat and overcoat and went out. When he reached the street he saw Irene a block ahead. The morning was bright with sunlight. A wind blew down the avenue. Irene looked stunning in a mole coat, well-turned legs flashing gun-metal sheer stockings in the sunlight.

She reached Forty-second Street, turned west and entered a drugstore. When she came out she carried several small packages. She walked east on Forty-second, crossed the street, and headed south on Lexington.

When Irene swung into the entrance of the Redfern, Donahue was six paces behind her. When she reached the elevator he stepped in behind her. Turning, she saw him, and surprise sprang to her face.

Donahue affected similar astonishment. "Well! Well, how do you do!"

"Hel-lo," she stammered.

The elevator rose, stopped at the fourth floor. Donahue got out, smiling amiably. Irene got out, still at a loss for words. The elevator closed.

"So you're living here, too?" Donahue said.

"Yes. Yes, of course."

She looked frightened. She had not yet recovered completely from the shock. She walked hesitantly down the corridor and stopped before a door. Donahue stepped back and slipped his hand into his overcoat pocket. The hand closed around a gun there.

Irene opened the door, and Donahue's eyes leaped into a small foyer, beyond into a large living-room. Irene shrugged and went in, and Donahue followed. There was a bedroom off the left of the living-room, a bathroom beyond the bedroom, door open. Donahue's eyes darted about. He wandered into the bedroom, saying, "Swell, Irene! Swell place!" He looked in the bathroom, in the open clothes closet, round and round the bedroom.

Irene came in, taking off her mole coat. She laid it on the bed and took off her hat. She was small, chic, good-looking.

Donahue said, "Hell, you don't seem happy to see me."

"Happy?" She laughed half-heartedly. "It all brings up old times—ugly times. I've tried to forget all that."

He followed her back into the living-room. She dropped to a divan, took a cigarette from an ivory humidor, lit up. Her face was pensive.

Donahue stood in the center of the room eying her. "I'm not rubbing it in, sister—but you're certainly high-hatting the guy who got you out of a bad jam."

She frowned, annoyed. "Oh, don't be silly! I'm not high-hatting you. I'm just thinking. In a flash—seeing you—old times are back. I've been so happy lately."

He sat down and stuffed his pipe. "I know, I know. But try to forget, Irene. It's all a rotten business. Why, only the other night that guy Adler was bumped off. Remember him?"

She thinned her eyes against the smoke rising from her cigarette.

"Yes, I remember him."

"Gunned out. In Grove Street. Some gangster's job, I guess. But I don't know. I don't know much about it."

Her eyes became thinner. She puffed rapidly on her cigarette. Said nothing.

Then she looked up at Donahue's face. "You've been fighting?"

"No. Taxi smash-up."

She looked down again. Two wrinkles appeared on her forehead. She looked worried.

Donahue lit his pipe and puffed up contentedly. Then—"I can't get over running into you! Just plain luck!"

"Luck?" She laughed wearily.

"Yeah. Sure." Smoke dribbled from his nostrils. "Say, Irene, how about giving me a little inside dope?"

Her eyes started. "On what?"

"The guy who killed Adler."

Her hand trembled. She crushed the cigarette in a tray. Her eyes became suddenly furious. "There you go—dragging me back again into the past!"

"How about it, Irene?"

"Don't be stupid! How should I know anything about who killed Adler? I'm living a quiet life here."

"Alone?"

"Of course! Of course!" She sprang to her feet, her small white hands clenched. "Can't you let me alone? Must you hound me? Can't I ever live down the past? God knows, I'm trying to!" Her small, neat body trembled, her white throat throbbed. Anguish threshed across her face.

Donahue wore an amused smile. "Irene. Irene, don't act that way. Let's be out and out."

"I tell you, I know nothing! How could I know anything? How could I?... Oh, you, you—the way you hound me! You're a devil, Donahue—a smirking devil! Let me alone! I tell you I'm living a quiet life. I know no one. I'm actually a recluse. I have no friends—nobody. And you—you come here with your insinuations and questions!"

She put her hands to her face and began to cry.

Donahue looked ceilingwards and groaned, "Oh, Lord, get a load of this!"

Irene dropped to the divan, buried her face in the pillow, sobbed. "How can—I—forget—when you—you— Go out! Don't persecute me! Go out!"

Donahue stood up, regarding her where she lay twisted on the divan.

"You have nice ankles, Irene."

"Go! Please—*please*—go!"

"You know, Irene—you're nice. Neat to look at. Swell! I could get quite interested in you—if you didn't have the bad habit of getting mixed up in murders."

She raised a tear-stained face. "Murder! What have I to do with murder?"

"You are also," he said, "the world's best amateur actress."

"I—I—"

"Shut up, Irene." His voice hardened, his brown eyes narrowed.

She cringed. "Now—now you're trying to frame—"

"Shut up! I want the man who murdered Adler! I want the man who caved in my mug!"

"Please, Donahue, I tell you I know nothing. How could I when I'm living—"

"The life of a recluse," he mocked; then snapped. "Hooey, Irene! Bologney! No matter how you slice it, it's all bologney to me.... Your playmate was tailed here last night. You can tell me where he is, or I can sit here and wait till he comes in. Makes no difference to me. Only you might be spared a little scene. Take it any way you want it, sister—but I'm going to get your sweet man."

"Oh!" she choked, and again, "Oh!"

"You're in this thing deep again, Irene. You—you couldn't keep your fingers clean—"

"I'm not! God's truth, I'm not!"

"You are. You are. I gave you a clean break after the Crosby kill. I believed all you told me about going straight. Yeah, a hard-boiled baby like me—believing you! What a cripes-awful frost!... But now I'm going to park here. I'm going to watch that door. I'm going to wait for that guy to come in, and if he so much as goes for his rod I'll blow his guts all over the room. So help me!... Unless you tell me where he is now."

She drew her legs up on the divan, curled up, tying herself in a huddled knot. All color had fled from her face. She was white—deathly white—and her eyes stood out like wet shiny coals. No woman ever looked more tragic.

Donahue curled his lip. "You put it over nice… this heavy melo-drama, Irene."

"Oh-o-o, please—please!…"

"I couldn't blame any guy for tumbling for you. I did. But now—it's all over. You're just a lousy little liar, Irene. A clever liar. Act all you want. But I'm going to get your daddy."

"You're wrong! You can see nobody else lives here. Look around. I'm alone. Do you see anybody else's clothes?"

"No. Your daddy was wise enough to keep his own headquarters. But he came here last night. He was tailed here."

She got control of herself. She tilted her small square chin. "That's a lie! I don't know what you're talking about. I'm innocent, and if you don't get out I'll call the desk and have you thrown out!"

"You wouldn't do that, Irene."

She set her lips, rose and went to the telephone. She picked up the instrument. "Are you going out, or else?"

"You wouldn't, Irene."

She took off the receiver, said to the desk operator. "There is a man in my room annoying me. Please send up the house officer." She hung up, turned and looked at Donahue with frigid eyes. "I tell you I'm innocent!"

Donahue put his hands on his hips. He chuckled. "You're rich, kid! By God, you're rich!"

When a knock sounded on the door, Irene crossed the room, turned the lock. A big man with polished pale hair looked in, bowed.

"Where is the man, Miss Saffarrans?"

She pointed haughtily. "There."

The house officer entered heavily, wearing a quizzical frown. He stopped before Donahue.

"Will you go out quietly?"

Donahue laughed in his face. "Sure."

"Do you want him arrested, Miss Saffarans?"

"No. Just throw him out."

Donahue started towards the door, looked down at Irene in passing with good-humored contempt. "Okey, sister."

She was rigid, cold-eyed. She said nothing.

Donahue went out.

Chapter VI

THEY put Donahue out, bags and all. He offered no explanation, no resistance. He moved to a hotel half a block north, on the opposite side of the street. He got a front room on the third floor, lit his pipe and sat down by the window. He had a clear, unobstructed view of the façade of the Hotel Redfern.

At one o'clock he saw Irene appear. A bell-hop carried four bags. The doorman blew a whistle and a taxi drew up before the façade.

Donahue was already on his way out of the door. He ignored the elevator, took the stairway; reached the lobby, sped through it and attained the entrance. He was still behind the glass doors when he saw the taxi bearing Irene go by. He pushed open the door, climbed into a waiting taxi outside and said:

"Follow that checker!"

"Oke."

The taxi swung around in the middle of the block, and was directly behind the checker at the Forty-second Street traffic stop. When the traffic cleared, the taxi headed north on Lexington, made a left turn into Forty-seventh and then swung north on Park Avenue. At Seventy-ninth Street it turned left again, crossed Madison and took the transverse through Central Park, came out of the park at Manhattan Square, and went on west through Eighty-first Street to West End Avenue. It turned north on West End Avenue and drew up before the West End Hermitage Hotel.

Donahue said, "Go right by and stop at Eighty-fifth."

He got off at the corner, paid up, shoved his hands into his overcoat pockets and walked south. Entering the small, cosy lobby of the West End Hermitage, he went directly to the desk. There was no one behind it. His eyes dropped to the register, and read the last inscription upside down: *Ann Logan, City*. Alongside the name was: 810. Just then the clerk appeared and said: "Yes, sir?"

Donahue asked for rates on a suite. The clerk told him. Donahue thought he couldn't pay the price, thanked the clerk, and strode out.

Opposite the West End Hermitage was a larger hotel which

Donahue entered. Off the left of the foyer was a large lounge with curtained windows looking out on the avenue. Donahue found a chair near the window, sat down and was able to peer between the folds of the curtains at the façade of the West End Hermitage. He started a cigar, leaned back. Other guests smoked and drowsed or read around him.

At half-past two he saw a man get out of a taxi. The man carried no luggage. He was the man who had caved in Donahue's face. He entered the West End Hermitage.

Donahue did not move. He sat back comfortably, showing no surprise, and continued to watch the façade of the hotel opposite. The butt of his cigar was dead in his mouth. He took the butt out, dropped it into a tray. He moved in the chair, a bit restless. But he never took his eyes from the hotel across the street.

At a quarter to four the man came out—alone. He spoke to the doorman, and the doorman hailed a cab.

Donahue got up and swept out of the lounge. He passed through the revolving doors as the man went north in a blue taxi. He crossed the sidewalk and got into a black-and-white cab. The blue one was swinging west into Eighty-third Street. Donahue gave instructions, and the black-and-white got started.

They picked up the blue cab swinging south into Riverside Drive. It turned east at Seventy-second Street, crossed town to Central Park West, south to Columbus Circle, and east on Fifty-ninth Street to Sixth Avenue, when it swung south. At Forty-fifth Street the cab stopped, and the man got out and walked west. Donahue's cab swung into Forty-fifth and rolled along slowly past numerous cheap theatrical hotels. The man entered the Hotel Brick. It had a faded frescoed entrance, four stone steps from the sidewalk.

Donahue left the cab, drifted past the Brick, turned and came back and entered. It had a small drab lobby strewn with threadbare plush divans and easy chairs. It had a couple of synthetic blondes, and a half dozen young men dressed in the mode, a little beyond the mode.

Donahue bought a paper and took a seat. He spread the paper, watched the elevator. He settled back comfortably, stretched and crossed long, lean legs.

Five minutes later the elevator opened and the man came out. He came out watchfully, his right hand in his overcoat pocket significantly.

Donahue, visibly surprised, since no doubt he had expected to wait much longer, dropped his paper and stared. The man looked straight at him, then started past him towards the door. Donahue put a hand on the arm of the chair and started to get up.

The man half-turned. Flame blew his pocket out. He broke into a run.

The two blondes screamed.

Donahue had his teeth together—hard. He held his left arm away from his side in an awkward position as he shoved up to his feet. He winced and threw startled eyes at his left arm. There was a hole in the sleeve. There was also a tear on the lapel of his coat, where the bullet had touched before striking his arm. The tear on the lapel was about where Donahue's heart should have been.

The half-dozen young men of leisure were still petrified where they lounged. The clerk behind the small desk was petrified.

Donahue lunged through the door, holding his wounded left arm between chest and stomach. In his right hand was the Colt's .38.

The man was hurrying towards Sixth Avenue. He had both hands in overcoat pockets. He looked around and saw Donahue running. He broke into a run himself. He looked wild-eyed, desperate. He swung north on Sixth Avenue, taking one hand from his pocket.

Donahue swung north after him, and people stopped and turned and conjectured loudly. Donahue had his left arm pressed hard against him. His face was a little gray, very grim. In his eyes brown fury stormed. His mouth was tight, lips thinned in a taut line against teeth that were vised behind them. He did not yell. He kept running.

The man reached Forty-ninth, turned west. Donahue was half a block behind him. The man turned north into Broadway, and at Fiftieth Street he plunged into a subway kiosk. Donahue plunged down after him.

No train was at the northbound platform. The man jumped to the tracks, crossed to the southbound platform. Donahue jumped down, but a southbound train roared into the station before he could reach the platform. He crouched between two metal pillars. The train was not crowded. He could see the people getting in. He saw the man get in.

As the train started Donahue hauled himself up between the cars, opened a vestibule door, and heaved into a half-empty car. He saw the man at the rear end. The man saw him. The man rose and plunged into the car behind. Donahue raced the length of the car. The passengers gaped. One or two rose and made for the cars ahead. The train thundered through the tunneled darkness, clicked and banged over switches and pounded into Times Square.

The doors opened. Donahue rushed out. He saw the man half-way up a staircase. He climbed after him, chased him through a wide corridor packed with humanity; chased him through turnstiles, past a bootblack, an elaborate newsstand, up a staircase, through the lunchroom in the Times Building, out into Forty-second Street.

For a moment Donahue lost him. The crowd milled around. Donahue could not run. He saw the man crossing Seventh Avenue, heading west. He burst through the crowd, defied a traffic whistle, bounded across the avenue and on down into Forty-second Street.

The man, well ahead, kept looking back. He crossed Eighth Avenue at a fast walk, with Donahue a block behind him. Both were winded. Near Ninth Avenue, the man ahead suddenly disappeared. Donahue broke into a run, trying to keep his eye glued on the spot where he had last seen the man. When he came to the spot he saw a hardware store, a cut-rate sporting goods store, and between the two a wooden door that had a single light, shaped like a lantern, above it.

A speakeasy....

Chapter VII

DONAHUE spent two minutes trying to get his breath. He was chewing savagely on his lower lip, and the storm had not left his brown eyes. His jaw was still set hard, and there was an air of recklessness about him— wild and not altogether reasonable.

He rapped on the door. He waited, his right hand gripping the gun in his pocket, his left arm pressed against his stomach. Blood had come down his sleeve and was congealing on the back of his hand. He took his hand off his gun and knocked again, then returned the hand to his pocket and gripped the gun again.

No answer....

Donahue stepped back six paces. He looked up and down the street. No one was nearby. He bunched himself, took three fast steps, then two running ones, and crashed against the door with his right shoulder. The door splintered, snarled, banged violently inward, and

Donahue hurtled into one end of a long, narrow hallway.

At the farther end was a doorway, beyond which was light and three men standing motionless, looking towards him. Then another form appeared in the doorway—quickly. Flame exploded. Donahue flopped. The bullets went over his head, out through the door, across the street and into the plate-glass window of a radio store. Glass crashed.

Donahue, twisted on the floor, fired and knocked out one of the three lights in the room beyond. The doorway was vacant. The three men—the fourth man who had fired—were not in sight. Gun smoke drifted down the corridor towards the street. Across the way, the radio dealer was yelling:

"Police! Police!"

The man heaved in the doorway again, firing. The hallway shook. Bullets splintered the wall. Donahue, crouched way down, pulled his trigger and sent two bullets into the man as the latter came thundering towards him. No doubt he had heard the call for help. He was cornered. He was trying to crash his way out to the street.

Donahue rose as the man banged into him. The man's gun went off. The powder blast singed Donahue's cheek, and the bullet walloped the ceiling. The man was a tower of strength, of mad purpose. He carried Donahue six feet towards the door by main strength, and then Donahue laid the barrel of his .38 across the man's head.

It didn't stop the man. He was caged and he was fighting for the freedom of the street and the chance of a running fight. Somewhere a police whistle blew. The man groaned and hurled himself and Donahue towards the door, which was still a matter of four feet distant. Donahue had only one hand, one arm, to use. He gave ground, but he gave it slowly.

Faces appeared and disappeared in the room beyond the hall. That was the bar. The gunsmoke filmed the doorway. There were oaths back there, startled cries, groans.

The two fighting men were nearing the front door. The killer had the strength which comes with insensate rage. Donahue had the spring-steel strength of fierce purpose. Now he was using his wounded left arm to keep the killer's gun high. No easy task. The killer was keeping Donahue's gun clear with his left hand. While they heaved, swayed, tore up the carpet with grinding, relentless heels.

Minutes... that had the semblance of hours. Seconds of chaotic agony. Both wounded....

They whirled out through the door, on to the sidewalk. People had come close. Now they retreated—rapidly, with frightened little sounds. Some took to their heels and did not stop. Others chose convenient recessed doorways.

"Police! Police!"

There was a cop coming, a block away. He had a nightstick in one hand, gun in the other. There was a man tearing along behind him. Plain-clothes.

Donahue's teeth were grinding together. The killer was forcing down his wounded arm, bringing the gun nearer Donahue's head. Donahue could see the black muzzle.

He knew he had no more strength in that wounded arm. He knew the killer would bring that muzzle in line with his brain.

He bent his head sidewise as far as he could. He put all his strength in his right arm, bent at the knees to drop lower. His left arm gave way—so abruptly that the killer's gun-hand smacked against his shoulder, the pistol scraping Donahue's ear. The gun boomed at the same instant. The shot crashed the window of the store on the right of the speakeasy. The killer heaved, roared—broke loose as the cop skidded on the sidewalk. The killer swung towards the cop. His gun blazed, and the cop was turned halfway around.

Donahue fired. The bullet tore through the killer's side. The killer whirled on Donahue. The plain-clothes man, sliding along the storefronts, raised his gun. Four explosions banged in the dark street. Four bullets hammered the killer. The killer fell backward against the impact, crashed to the gutter.

The cop sat on the sidewalk saying, "Cripes! Cripes!" over and over.

Donahue stood in the center of the sidewalk, hatless, his hair plastered over his forehead, his gun hanging at his side, smoke dribbling from its warm mouth.

The plain-clothes man came towards him with gun leveled.

"Oh… hello, Ames," Donahue said.

The plain-clothes man squinted. "So it's you, Donahue."

"Yeah. Little old Donahue."

Ames was a small, oldish man, with a small, round face. He turned the face towards the man lying in the gutter.

"Who's he?"

"I figure he's the guy killed Adler."

"That Village job?"

"Yeah."

"How come you're in on it?"

Donahue shrugged. "Dunno. I guess I just got in on it."

More cops were coming from the direction of Times Square. Ames walked to the gutter, rolled the killer over, picked up his gun. He pocketed the gun and laid his hand on the man's chest.

"Alive," he said, "but not for long, I imagine."

He rose and came back to Donahue quickly. "How many shots you put in him?"

"Three. Two in the hall. One when he went for the cop."

"And I put in one. Okey, Donahue. Is it my pinch complete?"

"Yeah. Sure, Ames."

Ames nodded. "Then I put in all the shots."

Donahue grinned. "Good old Ames."

"How are you?"

"Lousy." Donahue moved his left arm. "I can't feel this any more." His hand was caked with blood. He was unsteady on his feet.

Ames walked over to the cop. "How are you, Meyer?"

"I think I rate a hospital bed."

"I'll phone. Get this. You and me get this pinch. The guy there is Donahue, a private dick—a good egg. This gun figgers as the guy rubbed out Adler in the Village the other night. Got that straight?"

"Okey, Billy."

Ames stood up. "Riot squad."

The cops came trooping up with drawn guns.

Ames talked fast to the sergeant. Then he grabbed Donahue and steered him into the speakeasy. They went on into the bar. Half a dozen men were there, and Louie the owner. Louie was white.

"God, Ames! That guy come in, yanked his gun and said no one was to open the door! What could I do?"

Ames went behind the bar and made a telephone call.

He came around out front and said, "All you men stay here till I tell you to go.... I'll use your private room, Louie. Come on, Donahue."

He steered Donahue into a small room off the bar. "Now, quick on the details, Donny, so I can get this thing straight. How'd it all start?"

Donahue started right from the murder of Adler, gave a complete resume up until the time he broke down the door of the speakeasy.

Ames listened intently. He had a keen face, neat, sharp eyes. "And Irene—she was in on the Crosby kill?"

"Yeah. You remember, don't you?"

"Yeah. I remember. Roper'll get sore you didn't let him in on the kill."

"How could I? Besides, that guy's a frost anyhow. I'm through with Roper. Through…! I'll go up with you to get Irene."

There were feet tramping in the corridor. Ames went over and opened the door. The sergeant was there. An ambulance doctor was there. Ames beckoned the latter in.

"Look at this boy's arm, Doc, will you?"

The doctor smiled. "Banged up, too, Donahue?"

The bullet had gone through the forearm. Louie brought in warm water.

The doctor said, "The ambulance hopped off with the cop and the guy who got all the lead in his belly."

"How's the guy?" Ames asked.

"Bad. He'll hang on for the night maybe, but I doubt if he'll ever get over it…. You'd better come to the hospital too, Donahue."

"Okey. But bind it up now, will you?"

"Sure."

"Hurt?"

"Cripes… yes!"

"It's a nice wound. A neat one. No worry— Sorry!"

The sergeant looked in. "How's things?"

"Oh, fine," Donahue groaned. "Yeah. Fine. Great!"

Chapter VIII

WHEN the taxi stopped in front of the West End Hermitage the street lights began to glow. Ames got out and Donahue followed him. Ames paid the fare, and they walked casually into the lobby. Then entered an elevator.

Donahue said, "Eight."

The elevator rose smoothly, whispered to a stop. The men got out, and Donahue looked at the numbers on the doors opposite.

"Down this way, I guess," he said.

They turned left and walked on smooth carpets. They stopped before a door marked 810. Ames rapped with his knuckles. There was some movement inside. It was a long minute before the door opened.

Irene looked out. She said nothing. Only her hand went to her throat and she swallowed hard.

"Hello, Irene," Donahue said.

She said nothing.

Donahue said, "This is Detective Ames."

"How do you," said Ames. He pushed the door all the way open and strode in past Irene.

Donahue entered, looking down slantwise at Irene. He closed the door with an arm thrust behind him.

She wore a canary yellow negligee.

Ames said, "Will you get dressed, Miss Saffarrans? We'll wait."

She looked at them with wide, motionless eyes. She was still swallowing hard.

"What—what—?"

Ames said, "We just about shot apart a friend of yours. We'll want you too. Make it nice, Miss Saffarrans."

"Oh-o!" she whimpered forlornly.

Ames picked up the telephone, said into the mouthpiece, "Let me speak to the manager." And a half minute later, "Hello. This is Detective Ames. I'm in eight-ten. Don't get disturbed. Everything will be all right. I just want to know if eight-ten made a call to the Hotel Brick within the last—say—three hours…. Yes, I'll hang on." He looked up.

Irene was cringing against the wall. Donahue was smiling at her.

Ames looked at the telephone. "Yes?… I see. All right, thank you…. Yes, everything will be quiet." He put down the receiver. He nodded towards Donahue.

Donahue said to Irene, "So you saw me tail your friend away from here. You called the Brick and warned him. Well, he came out of the Brick well heeled."

"Oh-o!"

"Get ready," Ames said. "Don't bother taking your bags."

She fled into the bedroom, closed the door.

Ames and Donahue sat down, helped themselves to Irene's cigarettes, and waited. Twenty minutes later Irene appeared. Her face was tear-stained, but she looked stunning. She held her chin high.

Donahue remarked to Ames, "Dramatic little soul, Billy."

"Ready?" Ames asked.

"Yes," she murmured tragically.

The elevator boy watched them askance on the way down. The manager, the clerks, the bell-hops, stood transfixed in the lobby. Nothing was said. Nobody moved.

Irene and the men went out to the sidewalk, got into a taxicab, drove off in the growing darkness.

INSPECTOR Kaltenheimer was a pontifical-looking fat man with small steel-rimmed glasses. He sat in a swivel-chair, fat fingers of fat hands primly together.

Ames leaned against a radiator, arms folded, small face bland and attentive.

Irene sat in a chair facing the inspector across a flat-topped desk.

Donahue stood six feet behind the inspector, hands in overcoat pockets, hair still rumpled, face gray and haggard.

"Your man died," Kaltenheimer said slowly. "The gun expert, miss, has just proved that the gun found on him was the one used to murder Mr. Adler in Grove Street, the night of March fifth. Your man—discovered to be Peter Bruhard—died without saying anything. He left the telling to you."

"What is there I can say?" Irene asked.

The inspector raised a hand, all knotted except the forefinger, which jutted imperiously upward. "You were seriously linked with the Crosby murder. Two of your friends are paying—one will pay the supreme penalty in a month—Babe Delaney. The other is serving a term at Sing Sing. Now—your latest acquisition—Peter Bruhard—who has served time in California—your latest acquisition has died by the gun. What sort of conscience must you have, Miss Saffarrans?"

Her face looked drawn. "Please, please!" She held up a tragic white hand. "Don't be cruel. I tried to get out of it all—please believe me, I did."

Donahue came forward, bitter-lipped, and laid a closed fist lightly on the desk.

"That's your old line, Irene. You got Bruhard to do your dirty work. You got him to kill Adler—"

"I didn't! I didn't! I told him the diamond was in the hat. I described the hat. I didn't tell him to kill Adler. I pleaded with him to use common sense."

"Then that was all a lie about your planting the diamond in the tube of paint."

She colored. "I had to tell that lie. I was trying to get away from Alfred, and I thought that if the tube had disappeared that would be the end of it. And Peter—I just happened to mention the diamond one night. I was sick of it all. I didn't want it. He made me tell about it."

"He's dead now," Donahue said, "so he can't tell his side of the story. You lied to me. You lied to everybody. You lied to save your skin and you didn't care who paid the penalty. You're nothing but a dirty, cheap—"

The telephone on the desk rang. Kaltenheimer picked it up, said his name into the mouthpiece. Then he looked up at Donahue. "Mr. Hinkle is downstairs. Should he come up?"

Donahue shrugged. "Sure. He's my boss."

When the door opened Hinkle rolled in, puffing placidly on a cigar. He stopped short, took in the scene with one slow but sure glance, and then relaxed.

"Hello, Inspector... Ames... Miss Saffarrans.... Well, Donny, where've you been? Trying to locate you since noon."

The inspector said, "I guess he's been around. He got tangled up in a fracas. Hence Miss Saffarrans. And a chap in the hospital. Peter Bruhard. Ames there shot it out with Bruhard in Forty-second Street. Seems Bruhard murdered Adler."

Hinkle's eyes twinkled. "Good work! Splendid! You know Donny got the stone the whole rumpus was about."

Irene started.

Kaltenheimer blinked his eyes but went on looking pontifical.

Hinkle opened his overcoat, took out a large wallet, opened the wallet, took out the stone and laid it gently on the desk blotter. The light from the green-shaded electric glinted on it.

Kaltenheimer picked the stone up, turned it round and round, sat back and looked up at Hinkle.

"So this is it—the stone was hidden in the hat?"

"That's it," Hinkle said. There was a droll look around his mouth.

Irene was leaning forward, her fingers twitching, her throat throbbing, her dark eyes wide with yearning.

"But the rub," Hinkle said, "is that it's not a good diamond."

"It is!" Irene cried. "That—stone is worth ninety thousand dollars!"

"H'm," the inspector mused.

Hinkle bowed. "If you will pardon it, madam, an expert on my staff came in today and examined it closely. It is not glass. It is an inferior diamond—worth—at the maximum—four hundred dollars…. Keep it, Inspector, among the other H.Q. souvenirs."

Kaltenheimer said, "You're sure, positive?"

"Say, boss," Donahue broke in, "it can't be. That stone—"

"I'm positive, Donny. Greenberg knows stones, if nothing else."

Irene fell back in her chair, staring into space, strange dark lights knotted in her eyes.

"Well," the inspector said, turning the stone round and round, "it's often the case. Even crooks get fooled. But—anyhow—we got the murderer of Adler and"—he looked at Irene—"we have the murderer's inspiration. And this time, Miss Saffarrans—you will go behind the bars. I promise you that."

Donahue picked up his hat. "I'll be going then." He looked down at Irene. A bleak smile appeared on his gray, haggard face. "This comes of two-timing, sister. And no tabloids to help you this time."

"If I had my way—if I had my way—" His fist thumped slowly, his lip curled.

"Come on, Donny," Hinkle said.

"Sure." Donahue relaxed, turned away from the desk.

They said good-bye all around, left the room, left Police Headquarters. Walking down Centre Street, Hinkle said cheerfully:

"I know a nice quiet speak where we can get some good food and a bottle of Chablis."

"Yeah. Let's," Donahue grunted.

Then he slowed down, swayed, fell against a pole.

"What—!" Hinkle started.

"Get a cab, boss. I'm caving—"

"What's the matter?"

"Arm… here…."

"Good God, I didn't know! Why didn't you say something?"

Donahue grinned. "I was getting around to it, boss."

Hinkle held him up, shouted, "Taxi! Taxi!"

Brakes squealed.

Donahue went to the hospital.

Get a Load of This

Tough dick Donahue, of the Interstate, goes after big game in the underworld jungle.

Chapter I

THE hock-shop was on Fourteenth Street, east of Union Square. It was about the width of a railway coach, and half the length. The window was littered with cheap novelties. The interior was dark and gloomy. Behind the showcase a man sat at a high desk and regarded the insides of a wrist-watch beneath a bright green-visored light whose concentrated radiance did not extend beyond the desk.

Donahue kicked the screen door open, walked in casually, and the screen door banged behind him. He drifted down the length of a beam of spring sunlight that came in through the door. He wore a neat pepper-colored suit, a gray soft hat, and he smoked a straight-stemmed shell briar.

He leaned indolently on the counter and said, "Hello, Mr. Friedman."

The man got down from the high stool and approached the back of the counter. He was small, slim, with a young-old sallow face, horn-rimmed glasses, black curly hair.

"What can I do for you?"

Irony was in Donahue's crooked slow smile. "Remember me?"

Friedman did not look Donahue in the eye, but he said, "No, I'm afraid I don't."

"Well, don't be afraid." Donahue drew his hand from his pocket and laid a large diamond on the showcase. "Then maybe you remember this."

Friedman's eyes riveted on the stone. Lines appeared on his forehead. "I can't say I do."

"Ah, cut out the horseplay, Friedman. Sure you remember it. And you remember me. A guy named Bonalino hocked it here a month ago. I came in with him when he took it out. You said at the time that you would give him eight hundred for it any time he wanted to sell it."

"I said that?"

"You said that."

Friedman shrugged. "Maybe I did. I can't remember everybody comes in here. A lot of people hock things here."

"That diamond," Donahue said incisively, "isn't worth eight hundred. Not seven. Not six. At best it's worth four hundred, which means that your top price would be two. Now when Bonalino hocked it you gave him two hundred and fifty bucks—"

"Say, who are you?"

"I'm a private dick. You remember me now?"

"Sure I remember you now."

"Okey. How's to come across?"

Friedman frowned. "But I don't get what you're driving at."

"Your brain's not as lame as that. I'll tell you what I'm driving at. The diamond that Bonalino hocked here was worth ninety thousand bucks. You duplicated it with this hunk of cheap ice. Bonalino doesn't know a diamond from a good hunk of crystal. You knew that much. When he came back here with me to get his ice, you gave him this."

Friedman laughed. "Ah, be yourself, guy!"

"I'm being myself, sweetheart. We've got a letter from the Anglo-Continental Indemnity Company, of London and Geneva. They're looking for that hunk of ice, and this is not it."

"I don't get you at all."

Donahue wagged his finger. "Listen. A guy name Alfred Poore and a jane named Irene Saffarrans brought the diamond over here from France. Poore lifted it from a dowager duchess in Cannes this winter past. Coming over, the jane planted it on an artist named Crosby. They were afraid of the Customs. Crosby got knifed to death by a guy named Babe Delaney, who made Poore and the Saffarrans jane let him in on the racket. He'd found things out. Poore gunned for Delaney and I got Poore and they sent him to the Big House. Nobody concerned got the ice.

"It turned out that the ice had been planted in one of Crosby's hats, and when he got home Crosby gave his janitor, a guy named Adler, some old clothes—among them the hat. The Saffarrans jane got clear after Poore went up, and she hooked up with a guy named Bruhard. Bruhard bumped off Adler in Grove Street, got the hat but

not the diamond. Adler had got the hat cleaned. Bonalino worked in the hat-cleaning store, and when he took the lining out he found the ice. He hocked it here. Bruhard got gunned out in Forty-second Street, the jane got ten years. Nobody concerned got the real ice. Do you get me now?"

"No, I don't. I loaned Bonalino two-fifty on this diamond. He paid me two-fifty and got the diamond back. That's all I know, and you can believe it or lump it."

Donahue's voice rose—"I don't believe it and I'm not going to lump it!"

"Listen, master-mind." Friedman leaned on the counter and laid narrowed eyes on Donahue. "I don't know what your game is, but it's not on the up and up. I don't know what the hell you're talking about, and I don't have to carry on a conversation with you. Why don't you get a brainwave and take the air?"

Donahue got interested. "So you've decided to get tough, eh? Trying to brazen it out, eh? Well, pipe this, sweetheart: It won't work. That diamond was worth ninety thousand bucks till it reached here. Do you want to play house with me or do you want me to go to Head-quarters and tell what I know? They don't know that Bonalino hocked it. They think he had it in his possession from the beginning. I kept back the news to clear Bonalino."

"Go to Headquarters."

"Yeah? You keep books, you know. You're supposed to enter every article pawned here. You know that, don't you?"

"Sure." Friedman swung a ledger on to the counter, flipped the pages, stopped, turned the ledger around so that Donahue could read it, and laid a finger on an entry. "There it is. I valued it wholesale at eight hundred. I loaned two-fifty on it. My books are okey. Go to Headquarters."

Donahue looked up at him, smiled without humor. "Your brain's not lame, Friedman—not at all."

"There it is—in black and white."

"Okey. But I don't believe everything I read. Be seeing you some more, baby."

Donahue went out wearing a sultry look that was not without chagrin.

ASA Hinkle, the Interstate in person, looked up from his flat-topped desk when Donahue entered and said:

"You look down-hearted, Donny, my boy."

Donahue paced the floor a turn or two, scowling. He was baffled, and now that he was away from unfriendly eyes, his manner showed it. "That guy Friedman wasn't born yesterday."

"Oh, that's it!"

"I felt like caving in his mug."

"Only a city dick can do that—and get away with it. What did he say?"

"Nothing worth a damn. He made the entry in his book okey. The guy's solid and he knows it. He valued it at eight hundred. If anybody argues he can say *that* was what he valued it at. There's no proof he had the real diamond. No proof at all. It's changed hands so much that anyone might have fluked it." He dropped the bogus stone on the desk. "I guess you can let the Police Commissioner have it back. It didn't work."

Hinkle took off his diplomatic pince-nez. "That diamond must be in America, Donny. Poore and the Saffarrans woman know stones. They wouldn't have tried to bring in a fluke."

Donahue squinted. "What do you want me to do—go down and see Friedman again, get him in the back room and punch him around until the yellow runs? I'll do it! By God, I'll do it!" His dark eyes glittered, his fists were rocks at his sides.

Hinkle smiled, shook his head. "Donny, don't be so thoroughly Irish."

Donahue turned away, growled, "That's an old one of yours!"

Chapter II

DONAHUE was eating ravioli in an Italian speak in West Tenth
Street at noon the next day when Libbey, a city press association
reporter fell in through the door, picked himself up and headed for
the bar in the rear.

"Some day you'll knock your brains out," Donahue called.

"Oh, hello, Donny."

Libbey changed his course, came over and flopped down in a chair
facing Donahue. Drink had sapped the color in his cheeks. Drink
had given him that young-old face. The crown of his hat was dented
in, and his tie was crooked against his collar. He reached for the bottle
of red wine beside Donahue, poured a water-glass full, swallowed it
without a pause. He smacked his lips.

"How's the ravioli?"

"How's the wine?"

"I don't like wine…. Hey, Skinny, bring me a Bacardi cocktail, and
I don't mean rosewater…. Well, wine is all right, Donny, if there is
nothing else but water around. I feel depressed. That louse Sweeney
is God's most ungrateful man. I telephone him immediately after the
murder happens and what does he do but wisecrack and accuse me
of being drunk. I'm going to throw the job and get down to writing
a novel."

"Who got gunned out?"

"A fellow gave pennies and baubles to little kiddies. It's a shame,
Donny."

"Around here?"

"Fourteenth Street."

"Oh, yeah?"

"Yeah. A hock-shop man, Friedman."

Donahue looked up. "How'd it happen?"

"Nobody knows. Some guy just came in, apparently, and blew him
apart and went away, taking with him some loot—possibly. At any
rate, there was a chamois gem bag on the floor near the pool of blood."

"What time?"

"About eleven, I guess…. If you could see the pool of blood—"

"What's the cop on the job think?"

"Who... Roper?"

"Roper on it?"

"Yeah. Great mind, that Roper... for a moron. Well, what the hell could he think? What do I think? What does anybody think? Look now: Murder and robbery, of course. But of an odd nature. There is the chamois bag lying beside the pool of blood. But it appears that the safe was not rifled and nothing stolen from it. Then what? Well, either the chamois bag was flung down in disgust by the murderer-thief, or it was discarded after he had taken something out of it. In the latter case, it's plausible to assume—*hic*—to assume that Friedman had something shady in his possession. What was it? Who knows? Ah, my son, that is the mystery.... Well, it's about time, Skinny!"

Libbey tipped the Bacardi cocktail against his lips and drained it at two swallows. "*Encore*, Skinny.... How's to, Donny?"

"No, thanks. And what does Roper think exactly? Did he figure things out that way?"

"No. God, no! Roper? Pardon me if I seem to chortle.... How's the ravioli?"

"Fine."

"Think I'll have some spaghetti. By the way, I kidded our friend Roper a bit. I said to him, quite offhand, 'If you find it hard, Roper, look up Donahue.' You should have seen him! And do you know what he said? He said, 'Whenever I look that palooka up, it'll be to put bracelets on him.' I said bracelets were kind of effeminate; you might object. He spit on the floor, showing how he was brought—or dragged—up.... Cripes, Skinny, you take long! A guy would think this belly-wash was custom made."

Donahue paid his check and got up.

"So soon?" Libbey asked.

"I've got places to go."

Before he left the speak, however, he made a telephone call. "Hello, Ames?... Listen, Billy. This is Donahue.... I'm jake. Say, can you meet me in Fritz's in fifteen minutes?... Oh, something. I'll tell you then.... Great, Billy!"

When Donahue stepped from the booth there was a hard smile on his face. He walked briskly to a subway station and walked impatiently for a northbound train. His manner was eager and alert. He was smiling when he went down into a basement speak on Thirty-sixth street.

Ames was standing at the bar. He was a medium-sized man, blonde, casual, smiling. "Hello, Donny." He was lazy-voiced.

"Listen, Billy. D'you hear about that kill in Fourteenth Street?"

"Yeah. We got it over the precinct. Mob job, eh?"

"I wouldn't know. There's a possibility it wasn't. Want to do something for me?"

"Any time."

"Find out who was released from Sing Sing recently, and if any of the guys was a cell-mate of Alfred Poore."

"That all, Donny?"

"That's all."

"Have a drink?"

Chapter III

DONAHUE had bathed and was on his way out for dinner that night when the telephone rang. He went back to answer it.

"Yeah, this is Donahue.... Oh, hello, Roper. What's on your mind?... Oh, you do? Well, I'm going out to eat.... It can wait, can't it? Okey. I'll drop in."

He hung up, stood for a long moment with the telephone in his hand. Then he put it down, looked a little puzzled, and went out.

Roper was sitting in the back room of the station-house. Madden, his partner, and another dick named Crowley, were with him, and none of them smiled. Crowley closed the door, and Roper creaked his swivel chair. He drew a letter from his pocket, held it out.

"Read it, Donahue."

Donahue took the letter, spread it and found it to be a note written on I. Friedman's business stationery. It said:

> *Dear Benny:*
> *Business is not so good, but that seems to be the case all around. I can lend you a hundred till the first, but I've got to have it back then.*
> *My back is a little better, and I guess I'll be all right soon. Nothing has happened, except a visit yesterday by a fly cop named Donahue. He threatened me, but I laughed that off.*
> *Don't forget I've got to have that century back by the first. Ike.*

Donahue said, "H'm," handed the letter back and added, "What do you make of it, Roper?"

Roper wore a dull, inimical look. "I'll turn that question right around at you."

"And we still don't get an answer," Donahue said.

"Don't we?"

Donahue looked at him with wide-open brown eyes. "What's this—another indication of your sense of humor?"

Roper's gaunt jaw shifted. "Why did you threaten Friedman?"

"Did I threaten Friedman?"

Roper stood up, a bony man with wide, stooped shoulders, hard wrists and big-knuckled hands. "You read this letter, didn't you? This guy Friedman wrote to his brother, and he wrote you threatened him."

"It doesn't say I threatened his life, does it?"

"It says you threatened him."

"All right. I threatened to bust him in the face. What about it, copper?"

"Why did you threaten to bust him in the face?"

"It was personal. I lost my temper."

Madden came up behind Donahue and gripped his arms.

Roper said, "Come on, Donahue. Why did you threaten him?"

Red color began to creep into Donahue's face. "You guys going to get rough?"

"I'm waiting for an answer," Roper said.

"Then tell this mutt to take his hands off me!"

"Let him go, Madden."

Madden stepped back.

Roper said, "Okey, Donahue. Now tell me."

"I've told you. It's my business, and if you're dumb enough to think I'm mixed up in this job, arrest me!"

Madden grabbed him again, twisting his arms behind his back. Donahue's brown eyes got humid, and his lip curled, a dark shadow swept down across his forehead, across his face, making the red there dull and malignant.

Roper said, "I want to know what you were doing in that guy's store yesterday. This letter wasn't mailed. We found it in his store. He must have written it this morning. You've got to come across, Donahue."

"Not on your natural, Roper," Donahue snapped. "Arrest me. Go ahead. Nothing would tickle me more, because I'd be out in a couple of hours and you'd be the laughing stock of the whole neighborhood. You can't buffalo me, sweetheart. Try it on the kids you slap for pitching pennies in the back alleys."

Roper took one forward step and laid the flat of his hard hand across Donahue's face. Donahue kicked Roper in the shins and Roper fell down. Madden butted Donahue with his knee. Crowley punched Donahue in the short ribs, and Donahue, cursing, kicked sidewise at Crowley while Madden still held his arms locked behind.

Roper was getting up, his upper lip lifted wolf-like.

Donahue said hotly, "You know damned well you can't arrest me! What you want, you cheap punk, is to find out what I know about Friedman! You're using this letter as a buffer. But it only gives me a laugh. Go ahead—arrest me! Why don't you?"

"Let him go, Madden." Roper's face was somber, his voice a low growl.

Madden stepped back. Donahue smoothed down his sleeves, turned and headed for the door. Madden stepped in his way.

Donahue said, "You're another dick needs a bust in the mouth."

"Why don't you bust it?"

Roper raised his voice—"Get out, Donahue."

Donahue yanked the door open, threw a contemptuous look at Madden, at Roper, and Crowley; laughed sarcastically and went out with a toss of his chin.

FOUR nights out of each week Donahue ate dinner at Dominick's, a quiet joint where you got good chili con carne and Spanish sherry that wasn't cut but once. This was one of the four nights. Dominique was the real name, but the neighborhood was more or less Italian, and Dom himself had lived much in Genoa; and besides, the guy who'd painted the sign that hung over the narrow door was a Baxter Street Italian with a one-track mind.

It was near Columbus Park, on the Baxter Street side. It had a few booths in the rear room—the restaurant comprised two large rooms—and some lattice-work beneath the ceiling entangled with imitation vines.

Donahue found his favorite booth empty and after he'd told the waiter to bring him a Martini, Dom came over all smiling with a lot of big white teeth.

"Lady lookin' for you, Donny."

"Yeah?" Donahue laughed, broke a bread-stick. "It's happened before."

Dominick indicated a brunette who sat alone at a table in the opposite corner.

"She doesn't know me," Donahue said.

"Mebbe not. She justa ask you come here and I say sure, lots."

Donahue said, "Okey. Let her sit there. I don't want to know her."

Dominick looked puzzled. The waiter brought the Martini, and Donahue tried it, gave his order. The brunette didn't eat. She was drinking gin rickies, from time to time. Donahue spent an hour over his meal, winding up with black coffee and a tot of brandy. He paid his bill, got up and on the way out stopped to touch Dominick's shoulder.

"Remember, Dom, I haven't been in."

"I getcha. Sure."

Donahue walked out and crossed the street, stopped at the corner and waited. He waited half an hour. Finally the girl came out and walked towards him on the opposite side of the street. She was tall, had a loose-limbed walk that was not ungraceful.

He tailed her until she reached a corner where three cabs stood at the curb. She got in the first and drove off. Donahue got in the second and said:

"Tail that jane, bud."

The tail led to Julie's in West Tenth Street, and when Donahue entered the bar he could see the girl sitting at a table in the back room. A waiter was taking her order, and when the waiter came into the bar he saw Donahue and started to open his mouth.

Donahue cut in with, "Is that jane looking for me?"

"Yeah, Donny. She just—"

"Tell her you haven't seen me here in weeks."

Donahue had a beer and was finishing it when the girl got up and left. He went out a minute later and saw her walking east. She turned into Gay Street and struck Waverly Place. Familiar neighborhood for Donahue. Here Crosby had met his death at the hands of Babe Delaney. Here he had first seen Irene Saffarrans and Alfred Poore, the nice-faced rat. Here he had seen Adler, who later got smoked out in Grove Street.

The girl entered a four-story graystone near Sixth Avenue. Donahue crossed the street and watched the building. Lights on first and third floors were glowing. Two minutes, later Donahue saw two windows on the left light up. He saw the form of the girl in one of the windows for a brief moment, before she pulled the shade down. She lived on the third floor. While she was reaching up to draw down the shade on the other window Donahue saw a man in a bathrobe stretching and yawning. Then the drawn shade hid both.

After a minute Donahue crossed the street, got the number of the house, and walked to Sixth Avenue, turned north and then east into Eighth Street.

When he entered his hotel there was a letter in the box. It was on the hotel stationery.

The clerk said, "A man came in at about eight, asked for you and I said you'd gone out. He wrote a note and said I should be sure to give it to you."

"Thanks."

Donahue walked away, stopped, tore open the letter. It was from Ames.

> *Dear Donny:*
> *Tubba Klem finished a five-year stretch last Tuesday. He was Poore's cell mate. Luck. And don't forget yours truly.*
> > *Billy.*

Donahue walked to a large earthen ash receptacle, tore the note into fragments, dropped them on the butt-littered sand, and entered the elevator wearing a puzzled frown.

The man he had seen yawning and stretching was not Tubba Klem.

Chapter IV

WHO was the woman?...

"Never saw her before," Donahue said.

"That's queer," Hinkle said. "Funny, too, that when Dom said a girl was asking for you, you didn't get right up and fall right down for her."

"What am I supposed to do, laugh?" Donahue leaned back in the chair.

"If the man I'd seen was Tubba Klem I'd bite. But he wasn't, and I haven't the slightest use for that sort of a woman. They mean trouble every time and all the time and no foolin'."

Hinkle sighed. "Well, we won't go into that…. And Roper started a third degree on you, eh?"

"Yeah. And he's got a flatfoot tailing me now." Donahue stood up, strolled to the window. "He's holding a pole up now. Some rookie." He came back and stood by the desk, staring abstractedly at its hard, shiny surface. "And the guy wasn't Tubba Klem. He was a big guy, plenty of muscle, and light hair. At a glance, I'd say I'd never seen him before. The jane and the guy must be strangers in town."

The telephone rang. Hinkle answered it, then shoved it across the desk. "For you, Donny."

Donahue picked it up, said, "Hello…. Yeah, this is Donny…. Huh?… I get you…. Sure. Okey, kid." He hung up and put the telephone back on the desk. "One of my little stoolies. I know where Tubba Klem is. Tubba has come out of stir with a he-man complex. He's packing two big guns." He put on his hat.

Hinkle's face became grave. "I wouldn't get a two-gun man's goat, Donny."

Donahue laughed. He slipped his right hand beneath his left arm, drew out a long-barreled blue automatic. "Take a look at that, Asa." He laid it on the desk and smiled at Hinkle.

"Hell, man, it's only a twenty-two!"

"Ten shots, hollow-point. The best balanced gun a man can buy, and one little slug will do the trick. When a guy packs two big guns, it means to me that he's a punk shot and figures on dynamiting his way out."

He picked up the slim automatic, slipped it into the sheath beneath his arm. He took a look through the window. "First," he said, "I'll have to shake the rookie."

He went out and walked down Park Row to Broadway. He hopped a northbound Broadway street car, and saw the rookie climb into a taxi behind. The taxi followed the street car, though it had plenty of opportunity to pass it. Donahue rode as far as Worth Street, alighted and dodged traffic to the west side of Broadway, then strode west on Worth Street. The taxi passed him, and the rookie got off at the corner of Worth and Church. Donahue turned north on Church. The rookie was drifting along behind.

Donahue turned west into Franklin Street, walked one block and went down into the West Side subway kiosk. A train was standing in the station. Donahue ducked into the toilet. He waited until the train had drawn out, then pushed the door open and stood behind the turnstiles. He saw no one. He dropped a nickel in the slot and a minute later caught a northbound local. He changed to a Bronx Park express at Fourteenth Street, saw no sign of the rookie.

HARLEM was sunning itself. The spring afternoon held promise of an early summer. Little kids—three of them—sat half naked in a doorway from which issued the sound of something frying and the smell of that which was being fried. Two doors farther on a couple of tough-looking bucks leaned against a dirty store-window that had the word Pool painted on it.

Donahue passed the smelly doorway, and slowed down as he approached the pool parlor. A hall-door was ajar just beyond the big window. It indicated regions above the pool layout. Donahue pushed the door open, left it open, so that bright sunlight followed him in. He stood inside, body twisted, eyes slanted at the door. After a minute he looked up the wooden staircase.

He climbed it. The soles of his shoes made loose boards creak, and the banister wobbled when he leaned against it. On the first landing a door opened and a girl came out humming. She was high-yellow, had pretty teeth and flashing black eyes. It was the perfume Donahue didn't like.

"How yuh, mistuh big boy?"

"Yeah," said Donahue, and went on up the next staircase.

He paused at the top. The girl's heels were rapping down the stairs below. Donahue climbed a third staircase, stood at the top counting doors. Then he walked past three doors, stopped before the fourth. He knocked. He waited a minute and knocked again.

Then he took a bunch of keys from his pocket. He chose one of three master keys. It worked. He entered swiftly, closed the door and locked it.

The room was small, with one window looking out on a backyard and a panorama of roofs, clothes-lines and garbage cans, rusty fire-escapes and skeins of radio aerials.

The room itself had a cot salvaged from some army and navy store.

Two chairs, one with a broken cane bottom. A washstand with speck-led stone top, a bowl and a pitcher. An imitation-leather suitcase, new, lay on the floor. A dirty shirt lay on the bed, along with a pair of socks. The drawer of a cheap bureau was open, revealing one clean shirt.

Donahue pulled the two other drawers out. They were empty. He looked under the clean shirt. Nothing. He tackled the suitcase. There were two bottles of High-and-Dry in it, buried among more dirty clothes. He searched the clothes, making a face. Finally he closed the suitcase, stood up and let his eyes roam around. He crossed to the washstand, opened the door beneath the mottled top. Closed it. He drew his lower lip sidewise beneath his upper teeth, scowled reflec-tively, while his keen eyes stabbed the room in a dozen places. As a matter of form he turned the mattress over and searched the pillows. Nothing, of course. There was a pair of old brown shoes beneath the cot. He pulled them out, ran his hand inside each. He threw them down, disgruntled. One turned over on its side.

The sun, driving one slim rapier of brilliance into the room, made something shine on the sole of the shoe. Donahue knelt down. Gum soles. He held the shoe in his left hand, took a penknife with his right, pried out the shiny little object. He carried it to the window. He smiled—grimly, intimately.

He went to the door, unlocked it. He took one of the two chairs and placed it against the wall beside the window. He opened the window and looked down. A fire-escape led to the cluttered yard below. He looked at his watch. It was four o'clock. He dragged out his pipe, stuffed it and sat down on the chair facing the door. He lit up, and when the inside of the bowl was a red glow, he leaned back and crossed his arms on his chest, his right hand concealed by the upper part of his left arm. He hooked one heel on the edge of the bed.

AT five a key grated in the lock. The door swung open and Tubba Klem rocked in. Stopped short. Drew up one side of his broad, fat nose and wrinkled his fat eyelids over rodent eyes.

"Should lock your door, Tubba, when you go out."

"How'n hell'd you get in?"

"Door was open."

"The hell it was!"

Donahue grinned. "Honest, Tubba. How the hell do you think I'd get in?"

Tubba Klem scowled with his huge apish face, kicked the door shut and scaled his hat on the bed. He had got a haircut in stir just before leaving. His head was shaped like one end of a watermelon, hairless, corrugated in the back. He had no eyebrows, but the bone above his eyes was craggy.

"What you want, Donahue? I know you!"

"So you've gone native, Tubba?"

"What you want? I said what you want?" His mouth was huge. His teeth were huge, and primordial fire burned in his crag-shaded eyes. A broad man, wide around the middle, wearing a misshapen coat. "You got a helluva nerve, comin' in here! What you want?" He stood on trunks of legs that were spread wide, mammoth feet rooted to the floor, outthrust jaw belligerent. The room seemed to have grown smaller since his entrance.

Donahue lounged on the chair, heel of his left foot still hooked on the edge of the bed. The surface of his brown eyes was whimsical. Deeper, there was a hawk-like watchfulness.

"Don't get steamed up, Tubba."

Tubba Klem's scowl wavered. He looked almost sheepish. He laughed, shrugged, and drew a crumpled cigarette from his pocket. He lit up and dropped to the cot.

His tone was more amiable when he said, "What can I do for you, Donny?"

"I heard you were Poore's cell-mate."

"Yeah."

"I fixed him for that ride. I was wondering how he's getting on. He wasn't a bad guy."

Tubba Klem shuttered his eyes, dropped his thick lower lip so that his lower teeth appeared. For a brief moment he looked oafish. Then he said, "Oh, yeah, Al's okey."

"Hear he's trying to get another trial."

"Well, maybe. Guess he is maybe. I dunno."

"He needs jack; that's what he needs."

Tubba Klem steadied his eyes. He was thinking hard. The effort made wrinkles on his forehead. Donahue was eying him slyly. Tubba Klem looked up at him a little baffled, a little suspicious. Donahue smiled. Tubba Klem dropped his eyes, jerking them back and forth across the floor. Then he scowled and looked up.

"What you drivin' at? What you want?" He heaved up, making great fists of his hands. "I don't savvy you at all, Donahue! You go get to hell outta here!"

"Ah, calm down, Tubba. I don't want you. I just thought you might spring something about Poore's plans. Well," he got up, "I guess Poore held his trap. I just got a bum steer, Tubba."

"Well, see you stay outta here!"

"Sure. Don't get sore, Tubba. I'm wrong. I admit it." He grinned. "I always figured you got framed up the river last time. I'm sorry, Tubba."

Tubba Klem looked grieved. "Course I got framed. Ain't I tryin' like hell to get a job now? And here you gotta come snoopin' around."

Donahue held out his hand. "I'm sorry, kid. Shake."

Tubba Klem looked suspicious again. He put out his hand warily. Donahue shook it, dropped it, went to the door. He opened it, said, "The straight and narrow pays, Tubba. So long."

"So long, Donny."

DONAHUE entered the hock-shop on Fourteenth Street at a quarter to six.

A youngish man, with pomaded black hair, looked up from a ledger.

"Hello," Donahue said.

"Hello," the man said.

"Are you running this place now?"

"Yeah."

"Ike's brother?"

"Yeah."

"Benny?"

"Sure."

Donahue smiled. "I'm Donahue."

"Yeah? You're the guy came in here the other day—"

"I'm the little boy. Now hold on, kid. Don't get hot and bothered. You'd like to find out who murdered your brother, wouldn't you?"

"What's that to you?"

"Maybe I can turn the trick. Now forget I was going to punch him in the jaw. I lost my temper, that's all. I'm sorry, too. You forget it and maybe we'll get somewhere."

The man shrugged. "Go ahead. Spill it."

"Okey. When you came in here to open up, I suppose things were not in order. Was anything lying on the floor? I mean, was anything spilled?"

"As far as I can make out, nothing was swiped."

"I know. But was anything lying on the floor? Watch parts. Anything."

"Well, there was some parts scattered on the work desk in the back room."

"Let's look at 'em."

Benny grumbled, but led Donahue into the back room. He pointed to a tray. "These things were scattered on the desk. I put 'em back."

"What's this?"

"Lady's wrist-watch. I guess Ike was fixing it."

"Yeah. All the parts here?"

Benny looked at a tag. "It needed a main spring."

"Is that all?"

"That's all it says."

Donahue got down on his knees, lit a match and searched under the desk. Two fingers of his right hand slipped into his vest. Then he lit another match, searched some more, and finally stood up, asking:

"What's this?"

"Looks like a watch stem. Guess it belongs to that watch."

Donahue picked up the small watch, inserted the stem. It fitted flush with the frame of the watch. He stood back, stroking his jaw.

"Well," he said, "another blind alley, but worth a chance. Thanks, Benny."

Outside, he hopped a taxicab. Fifteen minutes later he walked in on Asa Hinkle. Hinkle was putting on his hat.

"I see no blood, Donny."

"Don't lose hope. I'm going to get a good meal under my belt and then I'm going after Tubba Klem."

Hinkle dropped his smile. "That certain."

"I dropped in Tubba's place this afternoon. He was out. I looked around and I found the smallest watch stem you ever saw. It was jammed in the gum sole of Tubba's spare shoes. Tubba came in and we talked about the weather. Then I went down to the hock-shop. The stem fitted a watch there."

"Listen, Donny, you'd better get a flock of cops—"

"No! They'll blow him apart. I just want to put him out temporarily."

"For God's sake, Donny, that guy's a killer!"

"That's tabloid talk, boss. But if he gets me, here's his address." He bent over the desk, writing.

"Donny, it's suicide—"

"Said he hysterically."

Chapter V

DONAHUE went to the dago joint in West Tenth Street for a spaghetti feed and a bottle of ink. He took on a whiskey-sour at the bar, then went into the side room, saw Libbey, the journalistic drunk, in one corner and chose another. It was one of those times when Donahue wanted to be alone.

"Why the tall millinery?" yelled Libbey.

"Hello, Libbey." Donahue spread a napkin, said to the waiter, "Spaghetti and the works."

"Oke."

"I always thought you were a conceited, high-hat—" yelled Libbey, good-naturedly. "Oh-ho!" softly.

Donahue froze on his chair.

The woman again.

She sauntered through the door, passed Libbey's table and sat down at one six feet on his right. He eyed her with the dazed look of a sot. She was stunning in a dark cloche hat, a dark tailored suit and a white blouse with black vertical stripes.

Donahue was moving one leg from beneath the table, reaching with his right hand for his hat. The waiter came with a menu.

Donahue clipped, "Gus!"

The waiter came over, and Donahue muttered, "That jane's looking for me. She'll ask for me. Tell her I don't come in here."

"Oke."

She ordered a gin rickey.

Skinny came in with Libbey's Bacardi cocktail.

Gus stopped at Donahue's table. "She did. Oke."

Donahue nodded.

At that auspicious moment the drunken Libbey again yelled across: "I say, brother Donahue, do you know class when you see it?"

Donahue dropped his eyes to the table, broke a bread stick.

The woman had started, was looking at him. Donahue kept his head down, frowning sourly.

The woman smiled, said, "Hello, Mr. Donahue."

Donahue looked up. "Speak to me?"

She rose, moved her long legs slowly on the way over, sat down at his table and took one of his cigarettes.

"Got a light?"

"You see the matches, don't you?"

She chuckled. "Just a strong, silent man, eh?"

"I'm not in the habit of having stray broads sit at my table. Give your legs a walk, sister."

"Is that a way to treat a lady?"

His nostrils twitched. "I know how to treat a lady."

She blew smoke in his face, showed even white teeth in a droll smile. "I'll bet you bite when you're really mad."

Donahue folded arms on the table, settled head between broad shoulders, bored the woman with unfriendly eyes. "Get it off your chest and then take the air," he clipped in a low, incisive voice.

"Why rush things, big boy?"

In the same incisive voice, "Do your song and dance or I'll call the boss in and tell him to throw you out. This speak is no port of call for your kind."

"So you think I'm that kind?"

"I'll take the benefit of the doubt." Looking at her, he suddenly became aware of the fact that her eyes were green.

She said, offhand, "Oh, I want that diamond, Donahue. That's all."

"You also have a sense of humor," he said, laughed shortly and took his arms off the table as Gus swooped down with steaming dishes. Gus drew the cork on the bottle of ink, flicked the woman with a sidelong glance, sighed, and shuffled off.

She said, "You switched stones, Donahue. You showed a fake to the police commissioner. Nobody switched stones but you."

"And you want it, eh?"

"I want it."

"Well, I haven't got it. And if I did have it—" He chuckled and began eating. "On your way, girl scout."

Her green eyes narrowed. "Okey, wisenheimer. This means you're on the spot."

"Okey," Donahue said cheerfully.

She leaned back, still eying him shrewdly. "A split would be all right by me."

Donahue laid down his knife and fork. "I told you to take the air! By God, if you don't, I'll have you kicked out!"

She stood up, her nostrils quivering. Her green eyes blazed. She went out swiftly, her high heels rapping on the floor.

WHEN Donahue came out of the speak into Tenth Street, his eyes swept up and down. He started off, turned into West Fourth Street and headed for Sheridan Square. He walked a bit gingerly, his dark eyes alert, darting from sidewalk to sidewalk and frequently back over his shoulder. He kept close to the shadows of the houses.

At Sheridan Square he entered the uptown subway kiosk, caught a local and changed to an express at the next station. He watched the people who entered behind him.

Harlem at night was no beauty spot. Donahue was a lean man striding purposefully through the seedier part of the Black Belt. Only this night's grim mission prevented him from having played along with the strange woman.

There was the familiar pool parlor, half a block ahead, on the other side of the street. The click of balls could be heard, and a man's harsh laughter. A few lighted windows straggled above the poolroom to the roof. A couple of Negro sheiks sauntered past swinging sticks, and whistling.

Donahue crossed the street and was about to enter the hall-door when he heard heavy footsteps above. He stepped aside, walked rapidly away and melted into the recess between two dark-faced store windows. He saw Tubba Klem come out of the doorway and walk south. A minute later Donahue followed.

Tubba Klem turned three corners and then went down a dark street. Half way down the street was the *Black and Tan Club*. Tubba Klem entered beneath the blinking electric light sign. Donahue passed the club, walked a block, turned and came back. He entered the *Black and Tan*.

There was a smoke-filled lobby, black drapes covered with silver scrolls, and black men with white teeth, white stiff shirt fronts and natty tuxedos. There were dim lights with red globes, and a hat-check girl with dusky skin and marcelled hair. And the buzz of voices.

Donahue checked his hat and hung around in the lobby smoking until the jazz band cut loose. When he heard the shuffle of dancing feet, he drew aside the folds of the black-and-silver curtains and bumped into a huge black head-waiter. The head-waiter took him to a small table far removed from the dance-floor. Donahue ordered gin and ginger ale.

Through the shifting panorama of dancers he caught intermittent glimpses of Tubba Klem sitting with a small beady-looking man with a big nose and a shiny bald pate. The little man was doing most of the talking and all of the gesturing. Tubba Klem was grinning at a brown girl who sat at a long table with five other brown girls. When the dance was over, the crowd sat down, and Donahue had to bend sidewise to see Tubba Klem. He saw the small man get up petulantly and go to a table where a girl waited.

Tubba Klem was drinking. He drank out the space of four dances. Then got up and headed for the lobby. Donahue saw him pass through the curtains.

Donahue called the waiter and paid his check. He waited two minutes, then got up and went into the lobby. He saw the front door closing, caught a fleeting glimpse of Tubba Klem in profile. Donahue got his hat, went out and saw half a dozen persons getting out of a limousine. They wore evening wraps. He saw Tubba Klem walking away.

When he had taken six steps, Donahue drew the long-barreled .22 from the sheath under his arm. He pushed the barrel into his pocket, keeping his hand on the butt. He walked rapidly, and was ten feet behind Tubba Klem when he turned in towards a doorway.

"Just a minute, Tubba," Donahue said quietly.

When Tubba Klem turned, Donahue was only five feet away from him—stopped. His hat was yanked down far over his eyes.

"Look here, Don—" Tubba Klem began.

"Shut up!"

"Damn you, Don—"

"Walk a bit, Tubba."

"Say, what the hell—"

"Get!"

Tubba Klem's hands went in towards his sides.

Donahue drew his automatic. "I said, Tubba—walk a bit."

"—Dam' you—you—" But Tubba Klem began walking.

Donahue walked at his side, a foot clear of him, half a foot behind.

"Don't hurry, Tubba…. Now, listen: Have you an alibi as to where you were at ten-thirty Tuesday morning?"

"What the hell's it gotta do with you?"

"Slower. There's no hurry… I know you haven't got an alibi. You killed Ike Friedman, the pawnbroker."

"Me? Ah, you're—"

"When I poked into your room this afternoon I found a little watch-stem jammed in the sole of one of your brown shoes. I went down to the hock-shop and the stem fitted a lady's wrist-watch that was being repaired. You picked it up with your shoe when you killed Friedman Tuesday morning. Poore was your cell-mate. He told you about the ninety-thousand dollar hunk of ice. You got to be pals in stir. You went after the ice, and Poore's split was to go toward financing a shyster for a new trial. I saw you talking with Hermie Shantz, the fence, in the *Black and Tan.*"

Tubba Klem whirled, rooting himself to the pavement on huge legs. "You're a dirty liar, Donahue! You're a doublecrossin'——!"

"Keep your hands away, you punk, or you'll get a belly-full! I'll give you a break. But I want that ice. I —"

"Ice me eye! I ain't got no ice!"

"I want that ice, brother, or I call on the cops. You're not the kind chucks a gat away after smoking out a guy. You've got the gat on you. Headquarters has the bullet killed Friedman. I get the ice or I call on the cops. You've got just one minute to make up your mind. And when I get the ice, Tubba, I wait three hours before I tip off the cops. If I don't get it, I tip them off now."

Tubba Klem's great chest heaved. His jaw worked, and little sounds strangled in his throat. His huge hands opened and closed.

"It's murder, Tubba, and you'll burn. If I get the ice you get three hours to jump any train you want to. Minute's almost up. There's a drug-store—and a telephone—around the corner."

"Jeeze, I hate your guts!"

"I think they're okey. Minute's up."

Tubba Klem's breath exploded. "You dirty —— "

"Come across—or start walking!"

Tubba Klem coughed. His big hands shook. One hand stopped against his pants belt. Two fingers slipped into the small watch-pocket, came out shaking. The hand clenched.

"I'll get you for this, Donahue! If it's the last thing I do I'll get you. I'm gonna get you! Blow your lousy heart out!"

Donahue held out his left hand. Tubba Klem smacked a ball of cloth into it. Donahue fingered the cloth open and felt a small, hard object. He flashed a quick glance at it.

"Now walk, Tubba. Walk to the next block and turn. I'll be standing right here. And if you don't want to conk out before the cops get you… then look for me, sweetheart—look for me. Get."

Tubba Klem turned and lunged off, his huge trunk swinging on his short thick legs. Donahue stood in the middle of the sidewalk, his gun in a line with Tubba Klem's back.

A man stepped from the shadows on the opposite side of the street and started across to head off Tubba Klem. Tubba Klem stopped and for a split-instant froze.

"Put 'em up, you!" barked the man.

Donahue tensed. Roper! Roper had been tailing him!

Tubba Klem let out a roar and pitched against a house wall. Both guns leaped out of his pockets. Roper raised his gun and the muzzle blast blazed in the gloom. Tubba Klem screamed, but his guns belched. Roper turned half around in the middle of the street and started falling.

Tubba Klem roared, "Now you, Donahue!" And his guns blazed again.

Zing! That was the sound of a high-speed bullet passing over Donahue's head.

Donahue jumped sidewise, danced from foot to foot. *Bang. Bang!* One of Tubba Klem's bullets chipped pavement alongside Donahue's foot. Tubba Klem was not aiming. Like most gunmen he was trying to dynamite his man down.

Donahue had his gun raised, his right arm out straight, right side in a line with Tubba Klem. He pulled the trigger. The report sounded like a small firecracker. He saw Tubba Klem sit down on the pavement, and heard his guns clatter down. He ran forward and found Tubba Klem sticking his tongue out, his eyes bulging.

A police whistle shrilled, and a cop came tearing around the corner.

Tubba Klem was like a man paralyzed. He could see. He could hear. But he couldn't move a muscle. This is what a small calibre bullet does when it strikes a man's solar plexus.

The cop came pounding up with a drawn gun.

"What the hell's the matter?"

Donahue stood up. "This gun and Detective Roper had it out. I had to shoot this guy. He's Tubba Klem."

"Who are you?"

"Donahue. Interstate Agency. Take this guy's guns. He's not hurt bad. Only his wind's knocked out."

Donahue rose and ran out into the street. He dropped down beside Roper. The dick was dead. His throat was torn out and there was blood on his stomach.

"How's Roper?" the cop yelled.

Donahue stood up and went towards the cop, saying, "He's dead."

There was another cop coming down the street.

Chapter VI

THE precinct captain was a tough nut with a reputation and a clean record. He sat on his desk with arms folded and one foot planted on the seat of the swivel-chair. Roper had gone to the morgue. Tubba Klem had been taken to the hospital.

"Roper," said the precinct skipper, "dropped in here just this afternoon. He was lookin' for Tubba Klem."

"He must have figured the same way I did."

"I don't know you, Donahue. Roper knew you well. He said you were the world's worst pest. A guy that hated city cops—"

"Ah, bologney!" Donahue laughed. "That was Roper's version of it. Listen, skipper—ask some other guys: Billy Ames, down at Times Square; Captain Hafferkamp at Old Slip; Inspector Kaltenheimer."

"Anyhow," the captain said, "I'll have to take that hunk of ice you took from Tubba Klem."

Anger leaped into Donahue's round brown eyes. "After I got it!" He stood up and glared at the captain. "Not on your natural, skipper. This diamond goes in the Agency's safe. We return it to the European Indemnity company that hired us to get it." He chuckled brittlely. "You must take me for a two-year-old!"

The captain thinned his gray eyes. "You heard me, Donahue. Stolen property when regained goes into the hands of the police for safe keeping."

"Now don't read me the law. I know the law. There are exceptions to every law, and this is one. The Agency has a rock-bound reputation, and you just don't get the ice."

"Donahue," said the captain grimly, "I want that diamond. Hand it over."

Donahue said, "Mind if I use the phone?" He picked up the instrument and called Headquarters. He got Inspector Kaltenheimer on the wire, then handed the phone to the captain.

The skipper tightened his lips, spoke into the mouthpiece. A minute later he hung up, twisted his lips and put down the phone.

"Okey, Donahue. Thanks for going over my head." He got off the desk, turned his back on Donahue and walked to a window, staring bitterly out into the street.

"The trouble with a lot of you guys," said Donahue, "is that you're not grateful. I give your precinct Tubba Klem, and still you yap."

The skipper said nothing. Donahue put on his hat, started a cigarette, and went out.

At a corner drug-store he made a telephone call.

"Billy Ames?... Hello, Billy. Donahue. Listen, I got Tubba Klem.... I'm sorry, kid, but a couple of bulls took him over, up here in Harlem.... Yeah, I'm up here now. I thought I might be able to give you the pinch, but there was no go. But listen, Billy. I'll do right by you.... Well, it's this way. Some jane was after the ice, too. She's got a boy friend. The jane handed me a tough line in Julie's tonight and said I was on the spot. Now you can take this tip or leave it.... Yeah, it sounds good to me. She and the guy are living at number —— Waverly Place. Third floor, front, left—as I saw it from the street. I'd go heeled, Billy—and maybe I'd take some boys along.... Roper? Oh, Roper got his throat shot out by Tubba Klem.... Yeah. I'll tell you about it when I see you.... Sure. Good-bye, Billy."

He hung up, went out and entered a downtown subway kiosk.

It was eleven o'clock when he entered the lobby of his hotel. He went to a writing desk, sat down and drew out the diamond. Cold fire in the palm of his hand! He took a half a dozen sheets of note paper, folded one four times around the stone, then doubled the other five around that. He slipped the lot into an envelope and sealed it. He went over to the desk and said:

"Hello, John. Put this in the safe till morning, will you?"

"Will you write your name on it, Mr. Donahue?"

"I forgot." He picked up a pen and dashed off his name.

John took a key and a letter from one of the cubbyholes behind. He said, "A lady left this note for you, Mr. Donahue."

"Thanks." Donahue tore it open while John went to the safe and put away the letter Donahue had given him. Donahue read:

> *Dear Donahue,*
> *Forget about that row tonight, will you? I was off my head. I came around to apologize but you weren't in. If you will meet me at that place in Tenth Street tomorrow night, I'll explain.*

No signature. Donahue crammed the letter in his pocket and went to a telephone booth. He called a number and when the connection was made, he said:

"Billy Ames there?… When did he leave?… I see…. No; no message."

He slammed the receiver into the hook and rolled out of the booth scowling. Ames had left the precinct half an hour ago. That meant he was already at the address in Waverly Place.

Donahue sighed, got in the elevator and was whisked upward. He stepped out into a quiet corridor, walked on thick green carpet. He took out his keys inserted one in the lock of his door. He entered and pressed the light switch just inside the door.

"Put 'em up, brother."

Donahue froze.

A man was standing in the center of the room holding a big automatic pistol. The woman was sitting on the divan, smiling.

"Why, you dirty—"

"Cut it!" bit off the man. "Close that door! Lock it!"

Donahue kicked the door shut but did not lock it. He turned and looked at the man.

"Lock it, I said!"

"Lock it yourself."

The man jerked his head. "Lock it, Clio."

The woman got up, sauntered across the room and turned the key. Donahue eyed her narrowly.

He said, "How the hell did you punks get up here?"

"Simple," she said. "I went back to the speak after you left and got talking with that drunken reporter. He told me where you lived. I came over and asked for you. You weren't in. I wrote the note and watched where the clerk put it. I could see the room number on the cubbyhole. Then I got"—she nodded to the man—"my husband, and we sprung the lock. My husband—"

"Without benefit of clergy," sneered Donahue.

"That's enough juice outta you!" barked the man. "Take his gun, Clio."

She tapped Donahue's hip pockets, then his coat pockets. She wore a puzzled look.

"Look under his arm," coached the man, and moved around to Donahue's left side.

She got the gun and stepped away.

The man with the gun came closer. "Now that ice, brother."

Donahue bit him with a contemptuous eye. "Ah, lay off that. I haven't got any ice."

"Frisk him, Clio."

The man moved around behind Donahue, pressed the muzzle of his gun against Donahue's back. The woman went through Donahue's vest pockets. She went through his coat pockets. She went through his pants pockets. Then she emptied his wallet on the table.

"Nothing, Jess," she said.

The man came around to face Donahue. He was a big-shouldered man, the same one Donahue had seen yawning in the room in Waverly Place. His eyes were glacier blue, his nose battered, his lips wide and thick. He bared a row of teeth, two of which were gold.

"I want that ice, Donahue. You got it. You switched it when you got it from Bonalino, when that Poore rat was sent up. I know you private dicks. You're a lot of crooks, and a hunk of ice like that was worth more to you than any job could pay you for a lifetime. I tell you, I want it!"

"Well, if I had it, guy, I'd give it to you. But I haven't got it. That's on the up and up."

"You know where it is, then! Where is it?"

Donahue grinned. "Sure I know where it is."

"Then where is it?"

"At a precinct in Harlem."

The man's eyes narrowed. "Yeah?"

"Yeah. You sap, you've been on a blind trail. I had the ice. I had it tonight. I took it from Tubba Klem. He was Poore's cell-mate in the Big House. He got it from Friedman, the pawnbroker. I put a bullet in Tubba's guts, and I had to leave the ice with the precinct captain. Tubba smoked out Roper, a precinct dick, before I got him. You'll see it in the first editions."

"That's just a line, Jess," the woman said. "He's stalling for time. Don't swallow that."

Jess jabbed the gun hard against Donahue's stomach. "Listen, baby. You're in a hell of a tough spot—"

"I know I am, Jess. And I'm trying to get out of it. So help me God, I'm telling the truth."

The woman laid Donahue's gun on the divan and said, "Jess, if you swallow that you're a jackass. This guy is as two-faced as they come. Let's take him for a ride."

Jess said, "How would you like to go for a ride, Donahue?"

"Come on, be your age," Donahue said. "Don't you suppose I'd cough up if I had the ice? I told you where it is. Call the hospital and see if Tubba Klem isn't there. There's the phone."

"What hospital?"

"The Harlem Hospital on Lenox Avenue."

"Look up the number, Clio."

The woman found a telephone book, nipped the pages, found the number.

"Call it," said Jess.

"What, I should call from this room? Don't be that way. Make this bright boy do it."

"Go ahead, Donahue."

Donahue put the call through, and while he was waiting for the connection Jess told Clio to take it over. Donahue handed her the phone.

In a few seconds she said, "Harlem Hospital?... I want to know how Mr. Klem is?... All right. Thanks." She hung up, scowled. "He's resting."

Donahue smiled. "As I told you."

The woman spun on him, her green eyes murderous. "So you think you're out of it, eh?" Her nostrils quivered, her whole body began to vibrate.

Jess snarled, "Snap out of it, Clio!" but his tone smacked of indecision.

She snapped at Jess, "Are you turning la-de-da?"

The man's jaw hardened, but he said nothing.

The woman clenched her hands and jerked her green stare back to Donahue. "No, you're not out of it! You're going for a ride, brother! You're going to get your guts blown out!"

Now Donahue was baffled.

Her voice rose, quavering hysterically. "You hear me! You're going for a ride!"

"What the hell good will that do you?"

"Good? A lot of good, you —— damn' dick! A lot of good! All right… the ice is safe in the precinct. But you get yours anyhow. You know what you did to get this ride? Do you?"

"No," dully.

Blue veins stood out on her forehead. "You sent my sister up for ten years."

"You're—"

"My sister! Irene Saffarrans!"

"Good God, Clio!" growled Jess. "Calm yourself!"

Donahue's brown eyes opened wide.

"Shut up, Jess!" she cried. "You've got to go through this with me. You promised. That's what we came here for. If we didn't get the ice, then we were to get this louse. You promised, Jess! You can't let me down!"

"Wait a minute," broke in Donahue. "For God's sake, sister, you're crazy—"

"And you shut up, big boy!" she snarled. "You've said all you're going to say! You hounded her. You sent her up for ten years. Ten years! You're a sneak, a dirty double-crossing yellow dog—"

"And you're a liar!" Donahue broke in hotly. "I sent her up. Yes, I did. But I managed to get her ten years instead of fifteen, which she deserved. She double-crossed every man she ever traveled with. She caused the deaths of Crosby, Babe Delaney, Bruhard, and the little old Adler. And because of her Poore went to the Big House. Don't tell me! That sister of yours was a crook—and a dirty one—from the word go! I know you janes—the whole lot of you! I wouldn't wipe my feet on you! And I know how to treat a lady, sister, when I meet one. But this lousy business I'm in—"

"That's enough," she snapped. "Jess, we'll take this guy. Down the stairs and out the side entrance. We'll walk him to the car and ride him up First Avenue and pitch him from the Willis Avenue Bridge."

Jess's eyes flickered, and muscles bulged alongside his jaw. His voice was muffled when he said, "Okey, Clio…. Put your hat on, Donahue."

"Listen, Jess—"

"Put it on!" choked Jess.

Donahue picked up his hat. His face turned gray, a humid look came into his brown eyes.

Clio went over and listened at the door. Then she unlocked it. Opened it. Jess jerked his chin, and Donahue walked past him slowly into the corridor, his lips hueless.

Clio whispered, "Past the elevator to the stairway!"

"Go ahead, Donahue," said Jess.

Donahue had taken two steps when the elevator door opened.

Chapter VII

THE three stopped. Jess slipped his gun into his pocket. The elevator door was open, but no one came out. The girl looked at Jess and Jess looked at the girl. Donahue looked towards the elevator. None of them could see its door, but all knew that it had opened.

Then it closed. It was a silent elevator. You could not hear its movement in the shaft.

Jess drew out his gun. "Mosey along, Donahue."

The girl led the way to the end of the hall, opened a door that led to a cement stairway. Their feet echoed on the way down. It was really a fire exit. Jess walked behind Donahue, his big hand white-knuckled on the gun.

Presently the girl stopped. "The next landing is the last, Jess. Shove the rod in your coat pocket. If he makes a break let him have it."

"Okey, Clio."

They went out into a marble corridor where a few lights burned. They started down an arcade lined by exclusive little shops—all dark at this hour. Glass swing-doors were at the end leading into Ninth Street. Donahue marched between the man and the woman.

Clio moved ahead when they neared the swing-doors. She pushed one open and held it open while Jess prodded Donahue into the street. Then she let the door swing shut on its silent spring, and they started east on Ninth Street towards University Place.

"Hey, you!"

The woman flung a look over her shoulder. Jess hugged his gun tight and twisted.

There was a man standing on the sidewalk in front of the hotel entrance. Even in the gloom Donahue recognized Billy Ames.

Said Billy Ames, "Put 'em up!"

"It's a frame!" the woman muttered. "That guy was waiting for us! Donahue knew it!"

Her hand jumped from the pocket of her blue coat and a small automatic spat sharply. Ames had jumped sidewise. The woman bared her teeth and sent three shots in rapid succession. One of them got Ames. He flinched, and then the gun in his hand banged.

"Oh-o," the woman grunted. One of her legs buckled, and she slumped to the sidewalk.

Jess roared and blazed away, and Ames staggered backwards, as his own gun thundered. Donahue fell on the gun in the woman's hand, tore it from her feeble grasp. He whirled on Jess, charged him and jammed the muzzle against his side, press the trigger. The explosion was muffled by Jess's clothes.

Jess heaved away, groaning. He started running. Donahue streaked after him. Swinging into University Place, Jess twisted and sent two shots at Donahue. One nailed Donahue in the left leg, and he skidded against the building. He clawed his way to the corner and saw Jess running north on University Place. He toiled after him, hopping on one foot, dragging the other. If only he had the long-barreled twenty-two!

Crossing the street, Jess turned for another shot. Donahue heard the bullet snick past his ear, heard it crash the plate glass window of a shop. Donahue fell down, lay panting at the curb. Jess ran on towards a parked car.

Donahue got up and tried to run on both legs. The experiment drew a rasp of pain from his throat that was clipped short by tightened lips. He hopped across the street, his breath clotting in his throat. He heard the cough of a starting motor, saw smoke belch from the parked car's exhaust. He clamped his teeth and tried to run again on both legs. The pain seemed to stab to his brain. It made him dizzy. But he stuck it out. Stuck it out till he reached the back of the car. But the car was starting.

Donahue grabbed the spare tire, got his arms around it. He was dragged a matter of ten yards before he got his foot clamped in the inside of the rim. He hung on grimly as the car wheeled around a corner. It was a big sedan.

East on Sixteenth Street, past Stuyvesant Square, and then north on First Avenue with the throttle wide open. Donahue hung on, his wounded left leg lying across the tail light, shooting pain through his body with each bump. After a while the car slowed down to a normal rate of speed. It made a left turn into Thirty-seventh Street and rolled past garages and dark-faced houses. Halfway up the block it swung in to the curb and came to a stop.

Donahue was already off the tire. He staggered up the side of the car as Jess pushed the door open and shoved a foot out.

"Come right on out," said Donahue, "but watch your step."

"Why, damn my soul—"

"Out Jess, or I'll finish you right here."

Jess stumbled out, one hand pressed to his side, pain on his face.

"I gotta get a doc, Donahue."

"So have I, you big bum."

Jess was breathing hoarsely, doubling up.

"But you walk now," Donahue said. He reached out with his left hand and tore the gun from Jess's hand. "Walk to Lexington Avenue. There's a hotel up there where I can telephone."

"I can't! So help me, I can't go another step!"

Donahue leaned against the car, his face drawn. He hefted the two guns. "Get, Jess—or I'll empty both these rods in your belly!"

Jess staggered away from the car. Donahue toiled after him, dragging his left leg, hopping on the right. Jess dragged his heels, bent far forward, both hands held to his side. They crossed Second Avenue, crossed Third and started up the hill towards Lexington. Half way up Jess fell to the pavement, groaning.

"Get up, Jess!"

"I can't. Honest to God, I can't! Oh-o.... God.... God!"

Donahue started towards where Jess lay, but he never made it. He dropped three feet short, and lay braced on one elbow. Jess was sitting facing him, hands gripping his side, torso rocking from side to side. The street was dark, deserted; not even a house light shone. At the next corner was the hotel.

For fully two minutes they said nothing. They could hear each other's labored breathing, see each other's sweat-smeared and pain-twisted face. Then Jess fell quietly side-wise.

Donahue looked at him through glassy eyes. The street began to fade. Jess became a dark blur lying on the sidewalk. Donahue's braced arm collapsed, and his head struck the sidewalk. He could not move it. Blackness was sweeping down on him.

His hand tightened on the gun he had taken from Jess. He pulled the trigger, kept pulling it until the hammer clicked. The echoes of the shots hammered violently in the narrow street.

Donahue's fingers relaxed. He sighed, and then there was nothing but blackness. But somewhere a police whistle shrilled.

Chapter VIII

DONAHUE came to some time later in a white hospital room. He saw two nurses, a doctor, another doctor and he saw sunlight slicing through two windows. Sunlight after darkness. The uppermost thought in his mind, tenacious after hours of riding wild nightmares, had to do with Jess crumpled on the dark pavement in Thirty-seventh Street.

"How are you, lad?"

Donahue saw the fat doctor's lips moving.

"They get Jess?" Donahue asked.

"Who?"

The other doctor leaned. "He means the gangster."

"Oh, Jess. Yes. He's in the ward now."

"Alive, eh?"

"Quite.... How do you feel?"

"I haven't felt so rotten in a long time."

The doctor said, "You were in bad shape, lad. You'll be on your back for a month… but you'll get over it."

"Butt?"

"I wouldn't—yet, lad."

"Okey." He licked dry lips, and the nurse gave him a drink of water. "How's Ames?"

"Ames?"

"The dick got shot in University Place by the guy I nailed."

"Oh, yes. Ames is quite all right. Sitting up in fact. He got two wounds, but neither of them was frightfully serious. He said he'd like to see you when you came to."

"That's fine."

The two nurses and the two doctors went out. Five minutes later one of the nurses opened the door, and a white-coated man wheeled in Ames.

Ames was smiling tranquilly. "So you got him, eh, Donny? That was guts, boy. And I got the jane. It was tough. I ducked two of her shots, but when the third got me I couldn't help cutting loose. I've never killed a jane—before. It's kind of—getting me… you know?"

"Yeah, Billy. Broads. They trick us, cheat us, and try to murder us… and when they get it in the neck, we—get a touch of heart…. How the hell did you ever happen to come over to the hotel? I never thought you'd show up."

"Well, I breezed down to the place in Waverly, but nobody was in. I hung around a while, and then I thought I'd walk over and get the details from you. I went up in the elevator. When it opened at your floor, I happened to look in the mirror that the operator uses to see if anybody's coming for the elevator. You know, it's fixed up on the side near the door."

"Yeah."

"Well, I saw you and the jane and the guy with the gun. I figured that if I stepped out then I'd have no show… and you'd get rubbed out in the rush. So I told the guy to go down again. Then I saw you hoofing out the side entrance. The papers are having a hell of a gay time about it. One thing that's got me—"

The door opened and the nurse said, "Mr. Hinkle calling."

"Sure," said Donahue.

Asa Hinkle entered with his ambassadorial air, closed the door, turned and stood looking at Donahue. He said nothing. He regarded his aide with mild, curious intensity.

Donahue reached out, lifted Ames' cigarette from the latter's fingers and took a long drag. He gushed smoke through his nostrils, said, "Pardon me if I don't seem to get up, Asa."

Hinkle chuckled, came forward smiling and laid his soft, fat hand on Donahue's lean brown one.

"You're a wonder, Donny!"

Donahue chuckled. "Now come the bouquets."

"Not," said Hinkle, sitting down, "exactly." He leaned forward. "We thought Jess had the ice, but he said you said you'd left it with the precinct skipper in Harlem. Skipper says you're a liar."

"I am. Jess told the truth."

Hinkle wagged his head, drew in his upper lip. "The skipper says—"

"Now don't worry about that," Donahue broke in whimsically. "The ice is safe. Go over to my hotel and tell the clerk to give you the letter I had him put away just before I went up to my room—and met the broad and her playmate."

Hinkle's eyes widened. "So that's it!" He placed his hand on Donahue's again. "Donny, you are a wonder! Take a long rest, boy. The reward is big. I'll cable our client immediately, deposit your share in the bank for you. It's been a long road, Donny. And a brutal one. Frankly, I'm surprised to see you alive.

"This last play was a bad one. We've got it straight now that Poore sent Tubba Klem after the ice. Poore figured that Friedman had switched it. And we've got it straight that Irene Saffarrans had a long talk with her sister and Irene figured that you'd switched the ice."

Donahue sighed. "Okey, boss… okey. Get the ice and get rid of it. It's the unluckiest hunk of ice I ever tailed. I'm on my back for a month, and I don't want to hear about it, don't want to talk about it. I'm sick of guns and gun-toting frails. When I can walk I'm going to go to the country. I know a guy up in the mountains. He's got a cabin there. And it's quiet as hell. God, Asa, it'll be good to smell the woods and forget all about business!"

Asa sat back with a reflective smile. "You know, Donny, I'd like to go with you."

Donahue glared. "Nix. You couldn't get enough newspapers, and you couldn't go an hour without talking about your life's work. Nix, boss. Just nix."

Hinkle chuckled. "I guess you're right, son."

Spare the Rod

*Tough dick Donahue is taken
for a buggy ride.*

Chapter I

WHEN Donahue came into the office Asa Hinkle, the pontifical-looking head of the Interstate Agency, looked up from the
stock quotations he was frowning over.

"I thought you'd be at Tony's," he said.

"I was learning some card tricks."

"Well, I don't suppose that could be any worse than playing the
market."

"I told the boys I'd be right back."

Asa Hinkle sat back and pulled a memorandum from the drawer.
"You have a reservation," he said, "on the Pennsy tonight—for St.
Louis. You'd better take plenty of clean shirts."

Donahue stopped a lighted match half-way to the cigarette that
hung from his lips. Then he grunted, put flame to tobacco, and snapped
the match into a cuspidor.

"Who the hell wants to go to St. Louis?" he said.

"Boy, the way my finances stand now, St. Louis is as good as any
place. You'd better take along some Scotch, too. I hear they're having
a cold snap out there and you can only buy gin and thrice-cut bourbon."

"Listen, Asa, the last time I went to that burg I almost got fogged
out. Not only that, but there was a shyster there named Stein who
double-crossed us."

"This is simple," said Hinkle. "It looks to me like nothing more
serious than being a bodyguard. The client's name is William Herron.
He's at the Apollo Hotel, in Locust Street—room 804. I think your
train gets in at five tomorrow evening."

"What's the matter, haven't they got any private dicks in St. Louis?"

"That is neither here nor there. Herron called us on long distance
just before noon today. I told him that it seemed a little irregular and

that I didn't think we could send a man out there unless we had a retainer. He said that would be given as soon as you arrived. I said that it was possible to send money over the Western Union. Half an hour ago I collected three hundred dollars that he sent by telegraph. I just wired him that Mr. Donahue would arrive about five tomorrow evening."

Donahue tipped back his Homburg. "Providing you supply the Scotch."

"I have two bottles here in the desk."

"Suppose I get in Dutch out there?"

"Go to Moss Garrity, in Olive Street. And remember, tip no more than ten per cent. And don't include any money lost in those East St. Louis gambling joints."

"I'll be good."

"I seem to have heard that before. But anyhow, start packing."

The sound of wheels rattling over switches, the slow lurching of the Pullman, the muted jangling of bells, woke Donahue up. He looked out of the window and saw railroad yards: red lights, green lights, many steel rails shining in the gloom.

He picked up a book that had fallen to the floor, stowed it in the Gladstone, took a flat black automatic from beneath a suit of pajamas and shoved it into his pocket.

The train crawled into the shed. Donahue put on raglan and Homburg, submitted to the porter's ministrations, tipped him, grabbed up the Gladstone and got off. He defied porters on the way up the platform, went through the barn-like station and came out in Market Street. He took a taxi and it rushed him to Twelfth, north on Twelfth, east on Locust. He got off at the Apollo Hotel.

He had wired ahead for a room on the eighth floor. They gave him number 812, and a black boy took the key and the bag and piloted Donahue aloft; opened a window in the room, opened the closet door, grinned with white horse teeth in a sooty black face.

"Anything else, suh?"

"I brought my own."

"Thank you, suh."

The boy left and Donahue stood for a moment staring down into Locust street, where a pall of smoke and fog dimmed the lights. Then he took off hat and topcoat and sat down at the small metal desk. He took up the telephone receiver.

"Give me room 804," he said. Presently he heard a man's voice, and said: "Mr. Herron?... This is Donahue, the Interstate man from New York. Should I come right over?... I'm down the hall from you in 812.... All right, I'll be right over."

He hung up and sat staring blankly at the instrument for a full minute. Then he rose, wagged his head dubiously, frowned with his lean-cheeked brown face. He looked like a man reacting visibly to a vague inner instinct; to an intangible warning against which his better judgment was as nothing compared with the force of circumstance. With a hoarse sigh, begrudgingly philosophical, he went to the door, opened it and locked it from the outside; went down the corridor with a shadowy forehead and slow deliberate footsteps.

Herron let him in after a moment's scrutiny through big horn-rimmed glasses.

"Well—well, so you got here; so you did get here!"

There was no handshaking. Donahue, hands thrust into jacket pockets, strolled in as though the room and Herron were a familiar ensemble. Herron locked the door behind him, quickly. Donahue walked the length of the room and turned finally when he reached the windows. The shades were drawn. The room, larger and more pretentious than Donahue's, was close, stuffy, as though no air had permeated it in a long while.

Herron, beaming with a fat florid face, chafed fat white hands and stood watching Donahue with eyes that laughed without losing their scrutiny. Donahue returned the look with candid brown eyes and immobile brown features.

"Well—well, now that you are, Mr. Donahue—now that you are here—well, sit down. Of course, sit down—anywhere."

"I've been sitting all the way from New York."

Donahue continued to stand, feet a little apart, broad shoulders slouching, hands in pockets. Herron lumbered across the room and turned on another light. He was well-dressed, a vigorous fat man whose fat was not particularly doughy. Solid white fat. Crinkly gray hair. Big eyes with a bright blue baffling look. His age might have been forty or fifty. He sat down in a mohair armchair, lit a dark cigar, began to smile reflectively.

"I suppose you think it odd, don't you?"

Donahue shrugged. "I haven't got the details yet."

"Oh, I mean—I mean my sending to New York for a private detective. Eh? Don't you?"

"I'm never surprised, Mr. Herron."

"Well, I am glad to hear that, Mr. Donahue. I am certainly glad to hear that. Yes, sir—indeed. I think you will find that it was worth your while to leave New York and come here. I have to have a man I can depend on implicitly. Eh? Implicitly! You understand that, of course."

"Yes."

"Splendid! And I am a man you can depend on too, Mr. Donahue. Depend on me to compensate your Agency for anything you do. And I might add—I will add, in fact, that a little premium for yourself will not be entirely out of order. Eh?"

"Go on, Mr. Herron."

"Of course, to be sure. These little preliminaries I think are necessary. I am a man who believes in certain preliminaries, Mr. Donahue; one might even call them courtesies, or delicacies. You appear to me to be a man of intelligence and tact and also a man of courage and tenacity. Said as much to myself the moment I laid eyes on you. And I believe in giving credit where credit is due.

"Now, Mr. Donahue—now." Herron took three quick puffs on his cigar. "My real name is not Herron. You may as well know that now, though I implore you to keep it a secret. You must at all times call me Herron. My real name is Stanley Edgecomb. As Stanley Edgecomb I was supposed to have left for Hot Springs three days ago. I didn't. I am here, in this hotel, incognito. I have not been out of this room since the night I walked in as William Herron. I want to be frank with you, Mr. Donahue."

For the first time since he had entered the room a glimmer of interest appeared in Donahue's eyes.

"Surprised—eh?"

"No," said Donahue.

"By Godfrey, you are an uncommon fellow! A man of parts you are, Mr. Donahue! 'Pon my word!" He swayed in the chair in what seemed like a paroxysm of sheer delight.

Donahue began to speak frankly, bluntly—"Mr. Herron, suppose we get down to cases. It's kind of you to spread a lot of bouquets around, to tell me I'm pretty damn' good. I know I'm pretty good, Mr. Herron. What are you driving at? In short, what is your particular kind of racket?"

"Racket, Mr. Donahue, is an ugly word. I wish you would not use it again. Stanley Edgecomb is well known in this city. He is a lawyer. I, Stanley Edgecomb, am a lawyer. A price is on my head, that price set by the head of a notorious gang. I was warned to leave this city within twenty-four hours. To all appearances, I left, deciding that discretion was the better part of valor—outwardly, at least.

"Understand, I dare not show my face on the streets. Not even my friends know that I am here. My house is closed, but I believe it is being watched. And this is where you come in. In my haste to get away from the house, I left behind some valuable papers, in my safe. I want you to get those papers."

"Anybody in the house?"

"One servant, old Jansen, who sleeps on the top floor. But you will not disturb Jansen. I will give you my keys and the combination to my safe. In the safe is a black metal box. In that box are these papers. You will bring me the box. Eh?"

Donahue frowned. "How long do you expect to stay here in hiding?"

"Until the police have rounded up the gang. It was on the advice of a policeman that I left town. He doesn't know I did not leave. He thought I would be safer while the process of rounding up was going on. I have been worried, thinking that someone might break into my house and get these papers. I think they would be safer with me. Now—here are my keys. This one opens the rear door. I will give you this one. And here is a diagram of the interior of the house, showing the room where the safe is located. Midnight or after would be the best time."

"And you got me all the way from New York—for this?"

"Of course, Mr. Donahue. The papers are valuable to me. They contain much evidence against the gang I started out to crush."

"Why didn't you hire a private cop right in town?"

"Because I am too well known here. Come, come, Mr. Donahue. If you are incredulous, inquire anywhere as to the reputation of mine. Ask anyone who Stanley Edgecomb is."

Donahue shrugged. "Well, I take the key. And let us go over the plans."

"To be sure, Mr. Donahue!"

Chapter II

AT eleven-thirty that night Donahue walked out of the Apollo Hotel and climbed into a taxi. He gave an address and the taxi turned left into Seventh Street, west on Olive. It was cold, and Donahue slouched in one corner of the tonneau, his collar up around his ears, his hat yanked down over his eyes.

Fifteen minutes later the taxi drew up at the corner of Lindell Boulevard and Kingshighway. Donahue got out, paid up, took a look at the Hotel Chase and then dodged traffic on the way across the monumental plaza. He walked west on Lindell, with pretentious homes on his right, Forest Park on his left, a cold wind at his back. His well-shod feet smacked the pavement with dogged deliberation, his dark eyes, hawkish beneath his hat brim, cruised the street and kept watching the houses. Finally his eyes settled on an imposing rough stone house with a tower on its left. Broad lawns lay before it. The windows were darkened.

But Donahue walked past, his eyes keening, jabbing the shadows on all sides. The street seemed deserted of people, though cars hummed past occasionally. The wind rattled in the leafless trees and the Park was black and silent beyond. After a while Donahue about-faced and retraced his steps. He did not slow down. He turned abruptly into the cement walk leading to the towered house and quite as abruptly went around to the rear.

Basement windows were almost flush with the cement. The door was down at the end of three steps. It was a heavy wooden door, and

Donahue inserted the key, turned it quietly, opened the door and entered. He did not lock it.

He drew out a small flashlight, the size of a large fountain pen, and played its beam on the cement floor. He went past coal bins and a warm furnace and found a stairway which he followed upward to a door that opened at his touch. He entered a large pantry, went from it into a large kitchen and then into a small serving pantry.

Next was a swing-door—and he found himself in a dining-room. He moved quickly, surely, because he had memorized the plan of the house by heart. Next a drawing-room, large and sumptuous. To the left a foyer—and across the foyer a library. He closed the French doors of the library behind him, turned out the flash, drew down four shades, and then turned the flash on again.

He crossed the room to a row of bookcases, counted off, then swung out one of the compartments. The face of a circular wall-safe glinted in the flash's beam. He took out a slip of paper and went to work. In a short moment he had the safe open. He removed a black metal box, closed the safe, swung the book-section back into place. He turned out the flashlight, raised the four shades and returned to the French doors.

In a minute he was outside, locking the basement door. He was starting around the side of the house when he saw a man leaning against a tree on the Boulevard. The man moved slightly, but remained against the tree.

Donahue pressed against the wall of the house and retreated. He held the box tightly under his left arm. His right hand tightened on the flat black automatic in his pocket. He stood for a moment in perplexed indecision. Then he peered cautiously around the corner of the house.

The man was still standing by the tree. Another man walked past slowly, and the two seemed to look at each other. There was no purpose in the walking man's footsteps; he seemed to be strolling idly.

Donahue retreated again, went farther back in the yard. He came to an arbor connecting two octagon shaped summer-houses. Beyond was a high stone wall. He would make considerable noise getting over that, would make of himself a handy target for any wayward gun. Had those men tailed him from downtown? If they had, they would know what he looked like.

Snap-judgment decided his next move. He hid the black box behind a row of shrubbery that grew close to the stone wall. Then he stood up and followed the wall. It was easy work scaling the hedge that separated the grounds of the towered house from the grounds of the next. He went back of three houses, then turned and walked boldly to the street.

Reaching the sidewalk, he looked negligently down the Boulevard and saw the man still leaning against the tree; saw the other walking idly. Donahue set out briskly away from them. Presently he heard footsteps walking rapidly behind him. Two pairs of footsteps. He did not look around. The automobiles went humming by. The men were walking faster.

Then suddenly a car drew into the curb, passed Donahue and stopped a dozen yards ahead in front of an imposing red-brick house. A tall man got out and headed for the approach leading to the house. But he stopped short and turned towards Donahue. A gun appeared in his hand.

Donahue, thinking only of the two behind, was taken by surprise.

The tall man said: "Get in that car."

"Listen—"

"Get in!"

The two men came up and crowded Donahue with drawn guns, and the tall man helped them rush Donahue into the big sedan. He landed in the seat and the tall man slid down beside him, pressing his gun against Donahue's ribs. One of the others climbed in front beside the chauffeur, and the last to come in took one of the folding seats facing Donahue and the tall man.

"All right, Charlie," the tall man said.

The chauffeur shifted into gear and the big sedan started off.

Donahue chuckled. "That was sweet work, boys."

"Put your hands up," said the tall man. He took away Donahue's gun and then said: "Where is it?"

"Where is what?"

"The stuff you came after."

Donahue shook his head. "You've got me wrong."

"Cut that!" The gun jabbed Donahue's ribs viciously.

"Honest," Donahue said. "I haven't got a thing."

"Frisk him, Pete," the tall man said.

Pete leaned forward and ransacked Donahue's pockets. After a minute he played a small pocket flash on the spoils, said: "Well, here's his wallet and a key ring and here's a loose key and here's a hunk of paper was in his overcoat pocket, and an Apollo key."

The tall man examined the articles with exasperated scrutiny. "Private shamus, eh?" he snarled. "This is certainly a new one on me!... What's these numbers mean on here?"

"Probably telephone numbers."

"My eye!"

Pete suggested, "Maybe a combination—"

"That's it!" the tall man rasped. "And this is the key."

"Hey," called Charlie from behind the wheel, "should I head out towards the river?"

"Just keep moving," the tall man said.

"I was thinkin'," Charlie said, "about them woods this side o' the bridge, just in case you want to—"

"Shut up and keep moving," the tall man growled.

Donahue said: "I hope you guys aren't fools enough to try taking me for a ride."

The tall man jabbed him again. "Listen, shamus! You were in that house! You got something—"

"Yeah, he was in that house all right," Pete said.

"Of course I was in that house," Donahue said.

"Well!" the tall man rasped.

"Well," Donahue said, "what the hell of it? Have I got anything? Pipe this, you wiseacres. I saw the guys hanging around outside. I knew it was a plant. And when I see you birds, d' you think I'd be jackass enough to walk out waving the bacon? Not in these old trousers, you dumb hoods."

"Ah, sock 'at loud-mouthed punk," Charlie flung over his shoulder.

"This key," the tall man said to Donahue. "You used it to get in, didn't you?"

"Maybe I did."

"And these numbers on this hunk of paper—"

"I can't imagine how they got in my pocket," Donahue said.

Pete said, jabbing his finger at the paper: "That's it, I'll bet. I'll bet that's it. And that there's the key. It's a big key, see. It ain't a hotel key. And his other keys are on a ring. That's the key, I'll bet. I'll bet it is."

"I think you're right, Pete," the tall man said. "Turn off that flashlight."

Pete sat back and the flash's beam swept upward before it vanished. Donahue caught a fleeting glimpse of the tall man's face. A long, narrow face, white and bony, with blue hollows on the cheeks, hueless lips, a thin nose, intense black eyes, small, feverish.

The car hummed on in silence.

Finally the tall man said: "Charlie, drive home."

He leaned back, raised his gun and struck Donahue on the head. Donahue pitched to the floor of the car and lay motionless.

Chapter III

DONAHUE came to in a large bare room. He lay on a cot, a slim dirty mattress the only thing between him and the spring. A single globe burned in the center of the room. Two green shades were drawn. He got up painfully and slouched to one of the windows, pulled up the shade. It was dark out, windy. He could see gaunt limbs of trees moving, and rolling open land beyond. The window was protected on the outside by three vertical bars. He pulled down the shade again and turned.

"That's it: keep that shade down," a man said from the doorway.

"Now look here," Donahue began, "what the hell's the use of keeping me cooped here?"

The man was small, chunky, blonde. He held a revolver in his hand and his pale blue eyes were glacial.

"I said, keep that shade down."

"The hell with the shade. What I want to know—"

"What you want to know, buddy, don't mean a thing to me."

The man's voice, like his eyes, was frigid. He backed out and closed the door.

Donahue shrugged and dropped back to the cot. He fished a crumpled cigarette from his pocket, lit up and reclined on one elbow. His brown eyes thinned down speculatively. He held inhalations of smoke long in his lungs, then let the smoke dribble out slowly through his nostrils. He looked at his strap-watch. It was half-past one in the morning.

At two he heard the sound of an automobile engine. He rose and cat-footed to one of the windows, drew the shade aside just far enough to peer out. He saw two big headlights among the trees, several shadows of men moving; heard low voices, a door open.

He went back and sat down on the cot. Two minutes later the door swung in and the tall man stood there in a baggy ulster belted tightly at the middle and a derby tilted on his head. Back of him were some more men: Pete and Charlie and the blonde and the other man who had ridden in the car.

The tall man was drawing off his gloves. The cold had put spots on his thin white face. His small black eyes glittered.

"Shamus," he said in a thin brittle voice, "you've just got to come clean."

Donahue stretched and yawned. "About what?"

"Jeeze, I'm gettin' to hate 'at guy!" snarled Charlie.

Pete said: "Keep your mouth shut, Charlie."

The tall man swaggered into the room, his face sinister in a quiet unostentatious manner, his black eyes almost luminous with a suppressed ferocity.

He said: "It was the key. It was the combination. But"—he showed thin small teeth gradually—"the stuff was gone!"

"No!"

"Just—yes."

Back of the tall thin man the others waited, rooted to the floor like images, like robots that would move at the magic touch of a single word.

Donahue stood up slowly. He swallowed once. He looked from one to another of the men slowly, dispassionately, with a strange brown-eyed candor. Then he spread his hands palmwise.

"What am I supposed to say?"

"You," came the thin brittle voice of the tall man, "know what to say."

"So help me, brother, I don't."

The tall man took a long springy step and caught Donahue by the collar in a long-fingered strong hand. His black eyes stared fiercely, his thin nostrils twitched.

"You'll tell me," he droned somberly. "By ——, you're not as fancy as you think you are! You hear me!"

The brown-eyed candor of Donahue's eyes seemed to enrage the tall man. His taut arm throbbed. He cursed and flung Donahue sprawling to the cot. Charlie whipped out an automatic and started dancing up and down like a boxer, a mirthless grin spreading his lips.

The tall man looked at Charlie and said: "Calm down, you." Then he looked at Donahue. "We've been watching that house for days. Nobody could have taken it out. Nobody left or went in the house but you. What I want to know is, how do you figure in this spread? Where do you come in? Who sent you?"

"The man who owns the house sent me. Where the hell do you think I got the key—made it?"

The tall man stepped back, bending his brows. "Stanley Edgecomb sent—"

"I guess he had a right to, since he owns the house and the property I went after."

"Where is he now?"

"Hell knows. I picked up the job in—well—Kansas City. He was on his way West—South. I was to take the stuff and put it in a safe deposit vault, send him the key and receipt. I was paid three hundred bucks in advance—"

"Ah, he's lyin'; that guy's lyin'," Charlie snarled.

"Shut up," the tall man said.

"That wiper of yours sure has a nasty disposition," Donahue said, with a nod towards Charlie.

The tall man said: "Never mind him. Why the hell did Edgecomb send you into his own house? Couldn't you've gone to his caretaker?"

"He didn't even want the caretaker to know. Listen. I'm a private cop and when I pick up a three-hundred-dollar job as easy as this looked, cripes, I don't ask too many questions. He said the house might be watched. He warned me. Now what a swell spot I'm in when I report that the stuff wasn't there. You guys have got me all wrong. I've got no grudge against you—none of you, except maybe Charlie, and he smells, or maybe he's just kind of meshuga—"

"Ixnay on them wisecracks," Charlie snarled, massaging his gun.

The tall man had calmed down considerably. He plucked thoughtfully at his lip, looking around at his men.

Pete said: "It's somethin' phony somewhere, I'll bet. I'll bet my shirt there's somethin' phony. I'll bet you anything there is."

Donahue chimed in: "You said it, Pete. There certainly is. When Edgecomb sends me to his own house to get something, and it isn't there—" He threw up his hands. "Well, every little thing isn't strictly on the up and up. Look at the hole I'm in. Listen, if I thought"—he jabbed a forefinger rigidly into space—"if I thought I was going to get mixed up in a scatter like this I'd never have taken the job. Not me." He waved his hands alongside his ears. "No, sir—not this baby!"

Charlie snarled: "Ah, this guy's just tryin' to talk himself out o' the hot grease! Let me take him for a walk in the woods."

"You," Donahue said sagely, "had better spare the rod."

"And spoil the kid, eh?"

"No. And save yourself from the hot seat, torpedo."

"Sh!" the tall man said.

There were running footsteps racing down a stairway. A man burst into the room.

"Jeeze, there's a car parked down the street—just parked. It looks like cops—"

"All the shades down?" cut in the tall man.

"Sure."

Charlie growled: "I'll get the Tommy guns—"

"You wait a minute!" snapped the tall man. "Those plates were changed, weren't they?"

"Sure," Pete said quickly. "Changed them as soon as we got back."

"What d' you do with the others?"

"Chucked them down the well."

"Okey." The tall man listened intently for a split-moment. "Now get this. No shooting. If it's the cops, let 'em in. Spread some cards on the table, and a bottle. Look contented, everybody."

He spun on Donahue. "You—you'll sit at the table with the boys. Take your overcoat off. And hold your tongue."

"Now you wait a minute," Donahue clipped crisply. "None of that stuff. You're in a tough spot. So am I. I'll play my part providing I walk out with the cops when they leave. I'll walk to their car, wait till they go, and then go with them."

"Nix on that!" Charlie barked. "This guy—"

"I'm not talking to you, you heel. I'm talking to your boss."

"You'll wait till they're gone," the tall man said.

"Nothing doing," Donahue flung back hotly. "You can't shoot me now. You can't start a fight. They'd hear it. I walk out with the cops. I tell them nothing. Take that—or leave it."

"My——!" groaned Charlie.

The tall man muttered: "Okey."

"Jeeze, you gonna let this guy—"

"Shut up, Charlie! It's the only out."

Pete said: "Somebody knocking."

"Answer it," the tall man said. "You other guys—inside. Quick! I'll do the talking."

His black feverish eyes glittered on Donahue. Donahue smiled.

"Two-time," the tall man muttered, "and I'll fog your guts."

"How about a little stud," Donahue recommended.

Chapter IV

THEY sat at a round table in a big room, holding cards, looking contented or bored. Donahue was considering a pair of aces showing, with a third in the hole, and the chunky blonde was dealing. A bottle and glasses were on the table, and cigarette smoke writhed and slithered beneath the chandelier.

Pete yelled down the hallway from the front door: "It's just Sergeant Uhl and a couple o' boys."

"Pair of aces bets," said the blonde.

"Pair of aces bets two blues," said Donahue.

A small man in a gray velour hat appeared unostentatiously in the doorway and regarded the gathering with mild blue eyes. He had a white mustache, gently inquisitive eyebrows. Two big men, younger, bulked behind him, hands in pockets significantly. The small man had his fingers loosely locked behind his back.

"Oh, hello there, Sergeant!" greeted the tall thin man, leaning back, saluting.

"Hello, Shadd," Uhl said softly. "I just thought I'd drop around and see who was living here. It's a nice night out."

"So they tell me."

Uhl looked slowly around the table. "Just a friendly little gathering."

"Won't you have a drink?"

"I never touch it, Shadd. My liver can't stand it any more. This is a nice quiet place you have. Sort of off the beaten paths. It used to be a farm here, didn't it?"

"Believe it was—at one time."

"Yes, yes," Uhl drawled, "it is a very nice place."

"You don't get out this way much, do you, Sergeant?"

"No, I don't, Shadd. And I like the country, too. So does my wife, Ella…. Now, Charlie, take your hand out of your pocket. I'm not going to hurt you."

"I was fishin' for a match," Charlie blurted.

Shadd, the tall man, slid a black look towards Charlie.

Uhl went on drawling monotonously: "We're only on a tail. A man named Jansen was killed a little while ago down on Lindell Boulevard and we thought—no offense, Shadd—we just thought you might know something about it."

"Gosh, Sarge, I'm sorry—we don't," Shadd said.

"A man in the house next door heard the shots and ran out in time to see a black sedan draw up. Two men jumped in the sedan and it headed west. It had Oklahoma pads. I noticed outside that you've got Missouri pads, but it was a sedan like yours. I noticed your engine's warm."

"I just came in a little while ago," Shadd said. "Did the car come out this way?"

"The man next door called Headquarters and the dispatcher flashed a description of the car to all outlying districts. The car was supposed to have come in this direction."

Donahue said: "Say, before Shadd and the boys came back, I heard a car go by. I looked out the window and I swear it was doing better than sixty. It was a big sedan. I couldn't tell whether it was black or dark blue."

"I guess they're heading west," Uhl said sadly. Then: "Well, we'll get along, Shadd. I'm glad to find you liking it out here. It's healthier than in the city… you know, Shadd?" Uhl almost winked; he smiled gently, said: "Well, we'll be going then. Come on, boys."

Donahue stood up. "You heading back for the city, Sergeant?"

"Yes."

"Mind giving me a lift?"

"Only too glad to."

Donahue shrugged into his raglan, smiling around the table. He could almost feel the current of suspicion, of brooding fear, that pulsed in the men.

"I'll be seeing you, boys," he said lightly.

He rolled out with the plain-clothes men into the windy darkness. They crossed a grubby lawn, passing between two huge oaks, and reached the gravel highway. A man was waiting by a big touring car, the red end of a cigarette incarnadining his nose.

"You can ride in the back," Uhl told Donahue kindly.

One of the detectives climbed in front beside the chauffeur, and Uhl joined Donahue and the other detective in the rear. Uhl stowed away two Thompson sub-machine guns in a compartment back of the front seat; they had been lying on the floor. The driver turned the car about and the big machine roared back towards the city. Donahue took in landmarks carefully.

"He was killed in the basement," Uhl said wearily. "Shot once in the chest, once in the head. He was an old man. The Edgecomb place. Edgecomb went West—or South—for a couple of months. You know him, of course: he's a brilliant lawyer." He turned towards Donahue in the dark windy tonneau. "You're a stranger here, aren't you?"

"Yes, kind of."

"H'm, I thought so.... Not too fast, Eddie. Some bad curves along here."

Donahue got off at Olive Street and Twelfth Boulevard. He walked rapidly to the Apollo and entered a deserted lobby. He stopped at the desk to ask if any telegrams had arrived; there had not; he ascended beside a sleepy elevator boy and went directly to his room. He took off hat and raglan, felt gingerly of the bump on his head, winced, swore softly, and took a long shot of Scotch straight. For a moment he paced up and down with long heavy strides, slamming fist into palm slowly, time and time again.

Then he went down the hall and knocked at Herron's door. It opened almost immediately, and he walked in. Herron closed the door, locked it. He was still dressed; anxiety and eagerness showed in his face.

"You didn't get it—"

"I got it," clipped Donahue, "but I had to plant it out back of the house. And what a sweet mess I piled into! Bodyguard? Hell!" He dropped to a chair and related briefly what had happened.

"And Jansen was killed!" exclaimed Herron.

"So Uhl says. And let me tell you that Uhl is a pretty foxy dick. One of those quiet guys. But he's got a head on his shoulders."

Herron blinked. "And Shadd! Shadd is the one! Shadd and his

rats! They were waiting, eh? They didn't believe that I had left town. And poor Jansen— It's outrageous, Mr. Donahue! Why didn't you tell Uhl?"

Donahue scowled. "I made a bargain with Shadd. Uhl's no dumb bunny. He'll get them."

"But a bargain with Shadd—"

"Was a bargain," broke in Donahue. "Those guys might have socked and planted me away before Uhl and his men came in. Don't you worry about my end of it. I'll get that black box. One bad thing—Shadd knows where I'm staying. They frisked me and I had the hotel key in my pocket."

"That is bad, Mr. Donahue, that is bad."

"I'll admit it's not rosy, but what the hell. Those guys would have a swell job on their hands trying to crash this hotel."

Herron made a sweeping gesture. "Don't think that we are through with them yet! Evidently Uhl hasn't a shred of evidence. It was just blind luck that brought him to that house in the country. They will still try to get that evidence. Even now they may be watching the hotel, watching what move you will make next."

Donahue scoffed. "Don't you believe it. They'll lay low for a couple of days at least. They'll think that I might have squealed. They'll watch their tricks for a while. It's almost certain they were keeping an eye on your house, and it's just as certain that if you'd gone out there you wouldn't be alive now to tell about it."

"Believe me, Mr. Donahue, I am very grateful."

"You can let that slide. You paid for that service. And I'm thanking my stars I got off with only a crack on the conk. Just rest at ease. Temporarily you're out of danger. As a matter of fact, you can go out, make your official appearance, and do what you please. The time would be ripe right now to plant Shadd and his guns. You say you've got a lot of important data. In a pinch, I can swear that I heard them say they'd changed license plates. And I can swear they entered your house."

Herron's eyes danced brightly, reflectively. "By Godfrey, perhaps you're right! Indeed I think you are right, Mr. Donahue!"

"I planted the box behind the shrubbery by that rear wall. I can go out just before dawn and get it."

Herron shook his head. "That would be too dangerous, Mr. Donahue. Leave it there. I think it will be safe. In the morning, after I have had some sleep I shall decide on a course of action. And remember, I am depending on you to stand by me."

Donahue stood up. "Naturally. And I think I'll hit the hay myself."

Herron grasped his hand. "You have practically saved my life, Mr. Donahue. I am deeply grateful. Let us have breakfast at—say—ten tomorrow morning, in here. Eh?"

"Only omit the grapefruit," Donahue said.

Chapter V

AT nine-thirty Donahue awoke, yawned, swung out of bed and took a cold shower. He shaved and dressed, took a look out of the window and saw the inevitable pall of smoke and fog hanging over the city, in the streets.

Whistling, feeling bright and chipper, he went down the hall and rapped on 804. The door opened and a Negro maid looked out.

"Mr. Herron in?" Donahue said.

"Ah's just cleanin' up, suh. Party checked out o' heah."

"Checked out?"

"Yassuh."

"Thank you."

Donahue retraced his steps down the hall, not whistling, and looking very dark and somber. He swung into his room, closed the door, and stood with feet spread, arms jammed against hips. He nibbled tightly at his lower lip. His eyes became round and hard, staring fixedly at the carpet.

He chopped off a short oath, put on hat and raglan, went downstairs and out into the street. He called the hotel from a cigar store at the corner. Asked for Mr. Herron. Mr. Herron had checked out at seven that morning. Donahue hung up savagely, went out lighting a cigarette, knew that cigarettes didn't agree with him before breakfast, and snapped it away. He entered a lunch-room and ordered tomato juice, poached eggs on toast and coffee. He ate vigorously but with no great appetite. Finished, he roamed the streets, walking swiftly, seemingly with purpose but actually without it. In that manner, he was surprised to find himself at length in front of the Apollo, and entered.

He was striding across the lobby when Uhl rose placidly from a divan and laid down a rumpled copy of the *Globe-Democrat.*

"Good morning, Donahue," he said, smiling.

Donahue stopped short, his scalp contracting, a scowl starting on his forehead. But on second thought he grinned, said: "Oh, hello, Sergeant."

Uhl was alone, his hat in his hand, his white hair thick and bushy. "I would like to have a few words with you—in your room."

"Sure thing. Come on."

When they were in Donahue's room, Uhl seemed oddly embarrassed for a moment, turning his hat round and round in his neat white hands.

"Sit down," Donahue urged.

"Yes—thanks."

Uhl sat down and said: "I'm sorry you didn't tell me last night that you were an Interstate operative. I think pretty highly of your agency."

Donahue started. If Uhl's knowing he was a guest at the Apollo had startled Donahue, this second revelation was a distinct shock. But Donahue appeared to take it like an old campaigner. He even chuckled.

"Take it from me, Sergeant, the only thing I was worrying about last night—or this morning, rather—was getting away with my guts intact. I wouldn't fool you a bit."

Uhl nodded understandingly, then went on: "I hope your head is better, too."

"You know things, don't you, Sergeant?"

"Through no fault of mine, Donahue. I suppose you were surprised to find your client gone this morning."

Donahue sat down suddenly on the bed. "I like you, Uhl."

"Thank you. Can you spare the time to go out to Edgecomb's house with me to show me where the black box is?"

"A command in the form of a question, eh?"

"Well"—Uhl smiled modestly—"you know how it is."

Uhl had his own flivver downstairs, which he drove himself. Donahue sat beside him on the way out. When they drew up before the towered house on Lindell Boulevard a policeman came towards them. Uhl told him to stay by the car.

Donahue led the way into the grounds behind the house, through the arbor.

"I always wanted a garden like this," Uhl remarked dreamily. "But it costs money."

"I was born in a hotel," Donahue said.

He reached the shrubbery, no indecision in his movements. He searched for a couple of minutes, his face falling. Finally he stood up and faced Uhl, shrugged and shook his head.

"It's gone."

Uhl looked suddenly sad. "No, is it?"

"It's gone. I planted it right there, alongside that vine that comes down the wall."

"Pshaw," Uhl drawled.

Donahue began thrashing through the shrubbery, inspired by anger more than by a belief that he would find the box. Finally he stopped and came back towards Uhl wearing a brown scowl.

"What's the lowdown, Sergeant?"

"What do you mean?"

"I mean, how is it you know so much about what happened last night? Did you go out to that place in the country again and make a pinch?"

"No," Uhl said. "I didn't do anything. Your client called me up this morning. Mr. Edgecomb called me up and explained in detail. He said something had happened that made him leave the hotel abruptly. He called from a West End public booth and told me that I should communicate with him tonight or tomorrow morning at the Rex Hotel, in Kansas City."

"Why the devil did he do that?"

"He explained his hiding incognito in the Apollo and asked me to keep it a secret. He was a lot concerned over you and asked me if I would look you up and go out with you to get the box. He said you would swear that Shadd and his mob had beaten you up, taken the key and gone back to the house to look for certain important papers. I've heard a lot about Edgecomb. He's an honest lawyer. He was supposed to have left by car for Hot Springs some days ago because this mob was out to take his life. And by the way, he left an envelope with the clerk at the Apollo for you. A little gift, I suppose."

Donahue was searching Uhl's face intently. "Edgecomb's got a good reputation here, hasn't he?"

"None better. Why?"

"Well, I was just wondering if he's entirely on the up and up. Take it from me, Sergeant, this is one of the queerest cases I've ever tackled—and I've had a lot in my time."

Uhl thought for a moment. "The only answer I see, Donahue, is that Shadd's boys came back here again, maybe thinking that you might have planted the box somewhere. One of them might have tailed you to the hotel—"

"They knew where I was staying. Edgecomb—or Herron, as he was down on the books—didn't like that a bit."

"One of Shadd's men probably tailed you, planted himself in the hall, and maybe listened at the door while you were talking with your client. That's logical, isn't it?"

"I guess it is." But Donahue was not emphatic. His brown eyes wandered thoughtfully.

Uhl sighed. "Anyhow," he said, "I guess I have a perfect right to collect Shadd and his boys. You'll testify, won't you, Donahue?"

"What else can I do? Edgecomb may be a swell lawyer, but he's certainly afraid of his precious skin."

"Let's go down to Headquarters," Uhl said.

On the way Donahue stopped at the hotel. The envelope his client had left contained a hundred dollars.

He met the police car in front of Headquarters, on Twelfth Boulevard. Uhl was there, quiet, retiring. Smiddy was at the wheel. There were three other men in plain-clothes: Knoblock, Reems and Brannigan. Donahue squeezed in front beside Uhl and Smiddy. The big Packard, rated at a hundred miles an hour, headed west on Olive Street. The wind hammered the top and the side curtains. They followed Route 40 through the city and kept to it on the outskirts.

"You were out here last summer, weren't you?" Brannigan asked.

"Yes," said Donahue. "And last winter. Every time I come out here I get in trouble."

"Don't go too fast now, Burt," Uhl said. "Time enough when we have to."

The big car was doing fifty past bare fields. The curtains clapped in the grip of the cold wind, and the men in the rear kept pounding their feet on the floor to keep warm.

"Turn off here, Burt," Uhl said.

Smiddy swung into a crushed gravel road that met the state highway obliquely. The tires ground on the gravel; gravel drummed against the undersides of the mudguards; dust ballooned behind. The road was wide, smooth, and the car passed scattered farmhouses and went through small sleeping towns that looked run down and hopeless.

The road rose slightly, then dipped in a long straight run between sparse timber. It curved beyond, and Uhl pointed to the big weather-beaten farmhouse ahead, on the right, set back fifty yards from the road.

"There may be trouble," Uhl said. "Burt, drive past and then pull up alongside those woods just beyond."

The big car swished past the house and skidded to a stop in the lee of the woods. Donahue and Uhl got out. The three men sat in the back holding Thompson guns. Uhl leaned in.

"You boys stay here for the time being. Burt, I guess you'd better come with me. Donahue, you stay out of sight. Well, come on, Burt."

Uhl and Smiddy walked slowly across the grubby lawn and climbed three steps to the ramshackle veranda. Uhl knocked. He waited patiently, listening. He said something to Smiddy and Smiddy left the veranda and went around to the rear. Uhl kept knocking at intervals. Smiddy returned shaking his head.

Uhl drew his gun and knocked the panes out of a window. He and Smiddy went in. Five minutes later they came out and returned to the car.

"They're gone," Uhl said sadly. "But I want you to stay out here, Brannigan, in case they come back. Stay in the woods. If they come back, walk to the nearest town—it's only two miles—and telephone in."

On the way back to the state highway, which was distant eight miles from the house, Uhl stopped in several towns and asked questions. It was in the third town that he came back to the car smiling quietly.

"A big black Cadillac sedan, coming from the country, stopped at the filling station at ten this morning to load her tank. There were six men in it. One of them tallies with Shadd. They left headed for the state highway, speeding. The man at the filling station remembers the car had Illinois pads, because after he filled the tank he dusted off the rear plate. He doesn't remember the number, though. Ten to one they're flying west right now. Hit the highway, Burt, and go west."

At the entrance to the St. Charles Bridge across the Missouri River, the ticket agent remembered a similar Cadillac sedan. It had crossed the bridge at about ten-thirty. The Packard crossed the bridge, went through St. Charles, and struck Route 40.

"You can let her out," Uhl said.

Smiddy jammed his foot down on the throttle and the car roared at eighty miles an hour, its siren screaming at intervals. The men sat motionless while trees and fields whipped past. At the first important crossroads, Uhl called a halt.

"I want to telephone ahead," he said, "and have the news relayed. A black Cadillac sedan, with six men and Illinois plates."

He telephoned from a pretentious filling station and then came back, told Smiddy to keep to Route 40.

A mile east of Wentzville Donahue suddenly said: "Hey, pull up!"

Smiddy looked across at him.

"Pull up!" Donahue yelled above the beating of the wind.

Smiddy took his foot off the throttle and applied the brakes gradually. The Packard bumped gently on the frozen shoulder alongside the road.

"There was a car parked in a lane back there," Donahue said. "I think it had bullet holes in the rear."

"You have eyes, you have," Uhl said. "Turn around, Burt."

It was a narrow lane that met the highway at right angles. Bushes grew thickly on either side of it. The Packard swung in and stopped behind an empty Lincoln sedan.

"By ——, you're right!" Reems said.

The men piled out and stopped by the Lincoln. Donahue jabbed six bullet holes with his finger.

"There's baggage inside," Uhl said. "No glass broken. And I don't see any blood."

Donahue hauled out a yellow suitcase and tipped it on the ground. "Take a look at these initials: S. E."

"It looks," drawled Uhl, "as if they got Edgecomb."

"He was a fool to have left the hotel!" Donahue snapped.

They searched the ground around the car, finding nothing of consequence.

"I'll telephone Jeff City," Uhl said, "and check up on these plates. Knoblock, you drive the Lincoln. We'll go up to Wentzville."

Nobody had heard any shooting in Wentzville.

Uhl came out of a restaurant and said: "It's Edgecomb's car all right. I just telephoned."

Reems looked out of the Lincoln. "His bags are opened. Doesn't look as if there was any ransacking."

Donahue was looking through the bags too. Every piece of linen was spotlessly clean.

"His body'll probably turn up along the road somewhere," Reems offered.

Donahue got out of the Lincoln, lit a cigarette and stared transfixed at its red end. A puzzled shadow moved slowly across his forehead, and his lean strong fingers began to tremble, his eyes suddenly became round and hard like brown bright marbles.

Chapter VI

AT six that evening Uhl called Donahue at his hotel.

Shadd and his five men had run into trouble in Jefferson City, where they had stopped to put water in the radiator. One of the attendants at the filling station went inside while another was filling the radiator and telephoned the authorities. The county sheriff happened to be only a block or so away and he came down with three deputies and some police.

They stopped the Cadillac just as it was starting. The driver tried to speed up, but a deputy cracked him with a gun and the car ran into a tree. Shadd and his men piled out dragging two Thompson guns with them, and warning the law officers to clear out. Shadd had one of the Tommy guns.

A deputy shot him through the thigh and in a minute all the guns were in action. The gangsters were outnumbered. One of the Tommy guns jammed after having put twelve bullets in an officer and another officer emptied his gun at the assassin. The gunfight lasted three minutes, and all six gunmen were killed.

They had had fifteen hundred dollars among them. However, no black metal box was found. It was natural to assume that they had thrown that away. But there were no papers, either, though there too it was natural to assume that they had destroyed them.

Since it was likely that they had kept to Route 40 at least as far as the town of Mexico, parties were on the hunt for the discarded body of Stanley Edgecomb. Bus drivers and motorists were asked to keep an eye out also. Circumstances pointed unwaveringly to the fact that

Stanley Edgecomb had been attacked in his car, taken in the gangsters' car, relieved of important documents, then killed and thrown out somewhere between Wentzville and the town of Mexico, or between Mexico and the state capital.

Uhl concluded: "This case has many strange ramifications, Donahue, and it's going to take us a while to clear it up. Already there's a lot of people saying that maybe Edgecomb was not all that he was supposed to be. Kind of insinuating, you know, that he might have had his fingers in a dirty piece of pie. Are you staying in town a while?"

"Yes. There are a few things I'd like to clean up for my own satisfaction. I'll be seeing you, Sergeant."

He hung up and drained the highball he had started on before Uhl telephoned.

There was a knock on the door and Donahue let in the hotel's head porter, a gaunt old man in a blue flannel shirt.

The head porter said, "No, Mr. Herron didn't send down any clothes to be laundered while he was here."

"You would have handled the clothes whether they went to the hotel laundry or an outside one?"

"Yes. If they go to an outside one, the man in the receiving room pays the bill when they're delivered back and then collects from the cashier, who would put it on the guest's bill."

"Thanks," Donahue said, and dismissed the man with a quarter.

Then he returned to a collection of train and bus timetables, studied them intently, made a few notations. He telephoned the St. Louis terminal of the Central States Motor Express, spoke briefly and hung up. Then he telephoned Union Station and got a reservation on the 11:55 p.m. train for Kansas City.

At ten-forty he checked out of the Apollo, carrying his bag. A taxi ran him over to Union Station. It was raining when the Wabash train pulled out at midnight.

It was raining in Kansas City next morning. Donahue had checked his bag in the station, had eaten there in the chill early morning.

When he entered the Central States Motor Express waiting room, he said: "Will Nixon be in soon?"

"You mean Sam Nixon?"

"I mean the man who was chauffeur on your through bus from St. Louis yesterday that arrived after dark last night."

"He's out in that bus you see through that door. He's due to leave in half an hour."

Donahue went out through the door. "Mr. Nixon, I'd like to speak with you in private for a minute."

"Who, me?"

"I'm just a private cop on a tail. Come on."

They went back of the bus. Donahue said: "You made a stop at Wentzville yesterday, didn't you?"

"Sure."

"How many passengers did you pick up?"

"Three. A couple for Mexico and one for here."

"The man for here—what did he look like?"

"Hell, I can't remember exactly. Fat guy, I think. Glasses. Had a suitcase along. Or maybe he didn't have glasses."

"But," Donahue said, "he was the only man who got on at Wentzville destined for here."

"Yeah, I'm sure of that. What's the matter?"

"I don't know yet," Donahue said. "I'm trying to find out."

He went around to the taxi stand. Three cabs were there. The drivers had not been on duty last night when Nixon's bus arrived. However, Donahue got the names of those who had been. From the taxi company's garage he got their telephone numbers. He spent twenty minutes telephoning.

Then he took a taxi to the Hotel Bretton-Palace. The big lobby was noisy. It was a travelers' hotel. Donahue went directly to the desk and asked for the house officer. A page took him down a corridor and into an office. A small bald man blinked sky-blue eyes, dismissed the page.

Donahue sat down and produced identification.

"Oh, yeah, I've heard of you," the house officer said.

"I came right in here," Donahue said, "so I could put my cards on the table. I'm on a quiet little tail. It would be doing me a great favor, if you'd go out, look at the register for last night, and get me a list of names of men who arrived and registered here between six-fifteen and six-forty-five."

The house officer blinked. "No rough stuff on the premises."

"Nothing like that."

"Wait here."

Five minutes later the house officer came back into the office holding a memorandum as if reluctant to hand it over. "Remember, no rough stuff."

"Not if I can help it."

"Six men. I didn't take the women's names. Six men. I guess they were from that St. Louis bus. Here."

Donahue eyed the list closely. Room numbers were beside the names. All the names were strange.

"Look here," Donahue said, "do me another favor. Have a girl call these rooms, one by one, and let me listen in on an extension."

"I wouldn't want to get in any trouble," the house officer demurred, ill at ease.

"Be a good scout," Donahue urged. "And you won't get in any trouble. There's an unemployment drive on. Get a girl and have her ask these men over the phone if they will contribute. Anything for a stall. Just so I can hear their voices."

"Hell, I'd lose my job if the manager— Besides, there's no jane around here I'd care to trust. You know janes."

Donahue shrugged. "All right, then: never mind. I'll make the calls myself and take a chance."

He went out into the lobby, entered a booth and began calling the rooms. He said he was on the committee of the new drive to relieve the suffering of homeless men. Could he come up and collect a small donation? He tried to keep his voice in falsetto. Two of the rooms did not answer. One man refused to contribute and bawled Donahue out for calling. Donahue did not make the sixth call. The fifth was sufficient.

Stepping out of the booth, he saw the house officer leaning against one of the marble pillars at the other end of the lobby. Donahue crossed to him.

"Please, now," he said, "don't master-mind around after me."

"Only no rough stuff," the bald man said, worried.

Donahue strode to the elevators, went up to the sixth floor. He walked down a red-carpeted corridor, turned sharp right and followed another corridor. He stopped in front of a door marked 645 and knocked.

A voice said: "Who is there, eh?"

"Just Donahue."

"Donahue!"

"On the level."

Silence.

Then—"Well, well, this—this is extraordinary, Mr. Donahue!" The door whipped open and Donahue's recent client bubbled buoyantly on the threshold, saying: " 'Pon my word! Well, well, come right in—come right in, Mr. Donahue. It has been something of a travail for me." He locked the door.

Donahue moved squinted eyes around the room, said absently: "I suppose it has been. Your Lincoln was riddled all right."

"Indeed it was! By Godfrey, Mr. Donahue, I shall never be the same man again!"

"I wondered why you took the bus from Wentzville, leaving your car parked down the road, hardly a mile, and with all your baggage in it."

"My dear man, wasn't I attacked? Do you suppose I was going to linger around that spot?"

"I see you registered here as Baldwin Coombs of Indianapolis."

"A very original name, eh? Eh, Mr. Donahue?"

"You're a very original man. I'm not. I'm just a plain everyday guy trying to make a living—as honestly as possible. There's not a hell of a lot of romance attached to my business. I'm no drawing-room cop. One day I'm here—the next day, somewhere else. That's not romance. It's damned monotonous. When I take on a client, I expect a break. I expect the truth. If it is the truth, I'm just as liable to risk my neck for the guy as not. I'm a nice guy ordinarily. But when a man two-times on me, I'm a louse—the lousiest kind of a louse you ever ran across. Understand?"

"Why, yes—of course. But what is the point, eh? Eh, what is the point? After all—"

Donahue snarled: "After all, you two-timed! You're not Edgecomb. You never were Edgecomb. That baggage in the Lincoln was not your baggage. It was Edgecomb's. But you were driving that Lincoln. Edgecomb wasn't in it. You were never attacked, either. You drove the car in that lane, put the bullets in yourself. You walked the mile to Wentzville and boarded the bus and arrived here between six and six-thirty last night.

"Shadd and his mob were fogged down in Jeff City. They had nothing on them. The theory was—I didn't hold it—that Shadd and his men overtook you and mobbed you, chucked your body out somewhere farther on. I began to smell other things when we opened the baggage in the Lincoln. Every stitch was clean. I figured that a man who had made a quick getaway, like yours, would at least have a dirty shirt along, you had plenty, I imagine, because you sent out no laundry in the five days you were at the hotel."

The other clapped his hands gently. "Very, very good, Mr. Donahue. As I said once before, you are a man of parts. Indeed, that you are, Mr. Donahue. I should like to hear some more about it. But, please, if I am not Stanley Edgecomb, who am I? By Godfrey, there is a splendid side of the ridiculous to this: having assumed so many aliases, I find it hard to recapture my real name. Droll, don't you think? Eh?"

Donahue's brown face looked hawkish, predatory, keenly alert. "You may think you can song and dance yourself out of this, mister, but you can't."

"Eh?"

"I'm taking you back to St. Louis."

"Of course, Mr. Donahue. I intend going. I shall engage a drawing room for both of us. Let me see—I had a time table—in my overcoat." He picked a blue overcoat up from a divan, rummaged in the pockets. Then he dropped the coat and turned around holding a small automatic, smiling buoyantly. "You will keep your hands well up, Mr. Donahue."

Donahue twisted his lips in a sneer. "This won't get you anywhere, you —— !"

"Language, Mr. Donahue!"

Donahue shoved his hip against the telephone and deliberately knocked it to the floor.

"Pick that up," the fat man said.

"Pick it up yourself."

"Pick that up. You knocked it down."

"Horsefeathers," Donahue chided. "If you want it picked up, then pick it up. I knocked it down because I wanted it knocked down. You want it picked up. Okey. Pick it up. You better hurry up. Operator may think there's a murder going on up here."

"It's wedged between the table and the wall. You will have to bend way over to get it."

"You mean," Donahue said, "you will."

"I am no longer fooling, Mr. Donahue!"

Donahue shrugged. "Neither am I. You're not going to get anywhere with me, mister. You're not going to threaten me. Oh, no you're not. You're not going to shoot me and make a lot of noise with the telephone disconnected. You're not going to be a jackass like that."

"Mr. Donahue, pick up that telephone."

Donahue lowered his hands, chafed them together, smiling with utmost self-assurance. He turned and walked to the door, his back to the man and the gun. He unlocked the door.

"Mr. Donahue!"

Donahue palmed the knob, about faced, bowed with mock courtesy. "I'll be waiting for you. And I'd advise you, mister—spare the rod. You're in bad enough as it is. Besides, I promised the house dick there'd be no rough stuff."

The fat man stood like a man petrified, staring wide-eyed through his horn-rimmed glasses. For a brief moment he looked oafish, stripped of guile; looked like a man trying hard to believe what his eyes and ears transmitted to his brain; and believing it, in spite of himself, and still incredulous of his own intelligence.

Donahue, eying him levelly, turned the knob, opened the door behind him.

The glaze left the fat man's eyes; it was like windows thrown suddenly upward.

"Remember: spare the rod," Donahue said.

The fat man emitted a groan. His gun drooped. The actor had disintegrated; the man was present now, humble, flushing, fearful, prey to encroaching terror.

"Will you step to one side, Donahue?"

Donahue ducked, half-whirled.

Sergeant Uhl stood in the doorway, placid and sad, holding a big gun in his hand. Back of him stood the house officer.

"It was funny about that phone," Uhl said, smiling.

Donahue growled: "How the hell did you get here?"

"Oh, I've been behind you since the time you left St. Louis. I thought you might get in trouble. Is that Mr. Edgecomb?"

"That," said Donahue, "is liable to be anybody."

Uhl sighed. "Yes, Silkhat Willems always was known for inventing swell aliases."

"Is that his name?"

"It was the name he started with."

"Hell," Donahue said, "this isn't even funny any more."

"No. I never found anything humorous about murder."

Donahue looked at him. "Who's been murdered now?"

"Stanley Edgecomb was murdered," Uhl said, drawing out manacles. "Quite a few days ago."

Chapter VII

POLICE headquarters, St. Louis....
Donahue sat on a desk, dangling one leg, when Uhl opened the door and came in wearily. It was after midnight, and the sergeant, not a young man, looked pale and haggard—but still placid.

"It's all over now—practically," he said.

He let himself slowly down into a swivel-chair, drew out an old briar, began stuffing it. His gentle eyes had a faraway look.

"So he came through," Donahue muttered.

Uhl nodded. "Yes, he came through. He murdered Edgecomb."

Donahue got off the desk, paced up and down with long angry strides; stopped, flung up a fist, "And I was working for that guy!" He brought the fist swishing down. "I knew it, Uhl. By —— I sensed everything was not on the up and up! But I had to go along with him. He was smooth. Uhl—he was smooth. I was a gofor. He pulled the wool all over my eyes."

"Silkhat Willems has always been a smooth crook. It was his first murder. But the stakes were big. He must have thought it was worth the chance. But think of it: almost a hundred thousand dollars."

Donahue laughed mirthlessly. "And he had me believing they were important legal papers, notes, data."

"Whereas," Uhl smiled, "they were emeralds. Edgecomb picked them up for a song a year ago, in Siam. Willems has been an international card sharp and con man for years. He was in Siam at the time and made a note of the sale. He came here to get the emeralds. He laid pretty careful plans. He struck up an acquaintanceship with Shadd in the Lido, a gambling house in the country, and got Shadd to throw in with him. He then called on Edgecomb. He had a lot of front, you know, and it was easy for him to pose as a globe trotter. He said he was on his way to California. He remarked about the sale in

Siam, and Edgecomb was fool enough to show him the emeralds. Conditions being what they are and have been for a year, Edgecomb was holding the emeralds till better times would warrant a better price. He wasn't feeling well, and spoke of going to Hot Springs. Willems so planned their meetings that nobody ever saw them together.

"Shadd was to get the emeralds, and there was to be a fifty-fifty split. Remember, Willems had never killed a man before. But then Shadd and Willems got into an argument. Willems wanted to break. He was finding Shadd a hard man to boss. But Shadd wouldn't have anything of it.

"Willems got desperate. He worked himself into getting a ride from Edgecomb as far as Hot Springs. Edgecomb picked him up in the car. Willems wanted those emeralds. He knew they were in the house. He attacked Edgecomb in the car, choked him senseless, threw his body in the river, weighted with stones, came back in the car himself, put it in a garage, became Mr. Herron at the Apollo.

"The killing hit him hard. He had the keys to the house, he had the combination, but he was afraid it would mean another killing. Besides, Shadd was looking for him. So Willems got the idea of getting you.

"You ran into trouble. You got the box, planted it in the garden. While you were sleeping, Willems went out and got the box himself, just before dawn. He made that call on me. He also called Shadd's house in the country and said that the police were going out there on a hot tip. Shadd and his men beat it, for they'd killed Jansen, the caretaker. Willems figured that we'd spend all our time hunting Shadd. He knew someone would find the Lincoln he drove out in. Willems, of course, drove it off the road and put the shots in it. That would make us believe that Shadd had overtaken Edgecomb. As a matter of fact, it did. Up until the time I called Headquarters here when I arrived in Kansas City, I thought Edgecomb was still alive and knew nothing about Willems. And I knew nothing of Willems until I looked at him while you were standing in the door of his hotel room in Kansas City."

Donahue put his head in his hands, made a sour face. "It's sure going to take me a long while to get back my self-respect."

"Nonsense, Donahue. You really caught Willems, didn't you?"

"Where did they find Edgecomb's body?"

Uhl winked. "They didn't find it. A man in a boat picked up a toupee. It took them an hour to find the place that made it. The place identified it as belonging to Edgecomb. That was enough to make Willems confess."

Donahue reached for his hat. "Come on back to the hotel and sock a bottle of Scotch with me."

"I'd like to, but my liver can't stand it."

"Okey. Then it means looking-glass drinking for me. I'm going to get plastered and then I'm going to call my boss on long distance."

"What, a new case?"

Donahue laughed. "Hell, no. By the time I get through telling him what I think of him, young Donahue will probably be out of a job."

"I wouldn't do that."

"I wouldn't either," Donahue said, "if I stayed sober. That's why I want to get plastered!... Well, toodle-oo, Uhl."

Pearls Are Tears

A string of them, along with other things, is handed to tough dick Donahue

Chapter I

DONAHUE came in with his ulster open, the collar negligently turned up. A snap-brim tan felt leaned over one ear. He elbowed the door shut and stood for a moment leaning against it, a droll half-smile hovering on his wide, good-humored mouth.

"Your humble servant, Mike," he said.

Mueck moved forward in the carved mahogany chair and laid smooth white hands on the green desk blotter, palms down, fingers splayed. He bowed with his blonde leonine head; his gray eyes twinkled; he lifted one side of his mouth in a sly, jovial leer.

"Same old Donny."

"Same old Mike, only"—Donahue looked around—"considerably more prosperous." He dropped into a chair facing Mueck, lit a cigarette, blew smoke towards the ceiling. "Well, counselor?"

Mueck was a striking figure of a man, even while sitting. With his fingers clasped, he rubbed the heels of his hands slowly together, regarded Donahue with a bland look.

"I didn't want to speak too much with Hinkle over the phone," he said. "It's a delicate matter. For me."

"How much is in it?"

"Five hundred."

"For you and us?"

Mueck shook his head. "I get nothing, Donny."

Donahue scoffed with his brown eyes.

"Honest," Mueck insisted quietly.

The two men eyed each other steadily. Then Donahue shrugged and gushed smoke through his nostrils.

"All right, Mike."

"You've got to believe me in that, Donny. You know, or ought to know, that I've always been on the level with you. I asked Hinkle to send you over because I believe I can depend on you—implicitly."

"What's troubling you, Mike?"

"Do you remember the Jennifer jewel theft—six months ago?"

"That old eccentric dame who lost her fifty-thousand-dollar necklace?"

"Yes. But stolen. Not just lost. Well, Mrs. Jennifer happens to be a client of mine. She had me come over last night. She was, well, all of a-twitter." Mueck picked up a pencil. "She has a chance of recovering that necklace—for twenty thousand dollars. She's a paralytic, you know; never goes out of the house. A man called her up last night, offered to return the necklace for the sum I mentioned—and no questions asked."

"Why don't you throw it to the cops, Mike?"

"Damn it, I wanted to, Donny! I talked myself blue in the face trying to dissuade her. But, no. The necklace has a great sentimental value. She is willing to pay the twenty thousand. The man who telephoned her wanted to make a rendezvous with her. Of course, she can't go out. She told him to come to the house. He wouldn't hear of it. Then she said that she would appoint an agent to carry out the deal, explaining to the man why she could not meet him. He agreed to this. She told him to call back this afternoon at five."

Donahue said: "Well, why don't you act as her agent?"

"Please." Mueck held up his hands. "You know damned well, Donny, that I wouldn't dare. I have my legal reputation to think of. If something happened during the course of the procedure, if the police got wind of it, I would stand a fine chance of being accused of compounding a felony. Besides, it is out of my line. But at the same time I feel I should try to humor my client. Hence you. She wants that pearl necklace and wants it bad. The cops disgusted her just after the robbery by running around a lot, drinking her liquor, and finding out nothing. She doesn't want it to happen again."

"And I'm supposed to take the twenty thousand, meet the crook, turn over the money and receive the necklace."

"Yes—if you want to take the job."

"It sounds like a soft snap."

"I won't say whether it is or not. I've put my cards on the table, and it's up to you. You can call on Mrs. Jennifer this afternoon, get the money and receive the instructions the man will give over the telephone."

"I sure hate to turn over twenty thousand to a crook, Mike. It kind of runs against the grain."

"The same with me. But you couldn't tell Mrs. Jennifer that. She wants the necklace, she's willing to pay for it."

Donahue crushed out his butt. "It sounds so simple that I'll bet there will be a hitch somewhere. That necklace should have been fenced long ago."

"The crook might be a first-timer. Maybe he couldn't find a fence. The necklace is well known, you know."

Donahue said abruptly: "I'll take you on."

"Good. But remember, Donny, I am not your client. I have nothing to do with this. Your client is Mrs. Jennifer. When you go around there she'll settle the bill."

Donahue stood up, grinned. "Mike, I've never spoken to you about it."

"I know I can depend on that, Donny."

"You know little old me, counselor!"

Chapter II

HINKLE, the agency head, said: "How well do you know this Mueck?"

"We used to play duck on the rock together."

Donahue sat at the desk opposite Hinkle in the Interstate office and counted crisp new bills. Hinkle eyed the bills reflectively.

"That's a lot of money, Donny. I hope this chap Mueck is strictly on the up and up."

"I know, Asa. If I had any doubts—hell, do you think I'd take this job?"

He shuffled the bills together, snapped a rubber band around them and slipped the lot into a heavy manila envelope. He put the packet in his inside pocket and buttoned his coat. He looked at his strap-watch. It was twenty to six.

"The old dame made me swear to be a nice boy," he said. "I shouldn't try to flimflam this crook out of his jack. Imagine! Well"—he shrugged, scowled—"it's her dough. Though it gives me a pain to do this."

"What time do you meet the crook?"

"At ten o'clock."

Hinkle wagged his head. "I certainly hope you don't get in trouble, Donny."

"What a swell moral support you turned out to be!"

Chapter III

DONAHUE leaned against the mail-box on the corner, the belt of his ulster drawn in tightly, the gusty wind tussling with his turned-up collar, snapping at the brim of his hat. A street-light hung a wan glow over this Greenwich Village intersection, sometimes picking out Donahue's chin when he raised his head to peer searchingly.

It was a dark, dismal crossroad, blockaded by one-and two-storied houses, none of them pretentious; a meeting of the ways flanked by shadows, sapped by alleys, undermined by areaway speakeasies. Far away could be heard the sound of intermittent Elevated trains; five minutes by foot, was Sheridan Square.

Donahue drummed his heels on the pavement. He was impatient as well as cold. It was half-past ten.

Suddenly a man appeared on the opposite side, stood motionless, his hands in his pocket, his face a blur beneath a yanked-down hat brim. Almost imperceptibly Donahue tensed. Force of habit as well as the urge of precaution made his hand tighten on the gun in his pocket.

Abruptly the man started across towards Donahue, hard heels rapping the street, re-echoing.

"How the hell much longer are you going to hold up that mail-box, buddy?"

Donahue said nothing. He remained leaning against the green metal box, his chin buried in his collar, his eyes peering hard under the brim of his hat. Then suddenly he chuckled, hove his chin out of the collar, showed his teeth in a crooked grin.

"How the hell long have you been watching me, Kiff?"

The plain-clothes man reared his head, craned his neck, shoved his jaw forward, squinted as he screwed up his compact mustache. Then he put hands on hips, rocked on his heels.

"So it's you, Donahue."

"How is every little thing, Kiff?"

They let it go at that for a minute, Donahue drumming his heels, wearing an amused smile, Kiff peering at him with hard little shiny eyes.

Then: "What are you waiting for, Donahue?"

"A date."

"In this neighborhood?"

"Sure."

"What's the matter with a speak? It's warmer."

"The jane doesn't like speaks."

"Boloney!"

Donahue shrugged. "All right, Kiff. You see that dump over there? Well, a scrubwoman lives there. I'm going to rob her. Going to take her pennies away from her, Kiff. I'm sorry I lied to you about the jane, Kiff."

"Oh, that's all right." Kiff poked Donahue in the stomach, leering. "That's all right, kid. Well, hope you have luck with the pennies. I'll tell the copper on the beat to stay away."

Kiff laughed harshly, left a hard shiny look as he turned and swung off, heavy-heeled.

Donahue listened to the sound of the heels fading away. Then he exhaled a long-held breath, swore briefly. Silence and the wind again. Five minutes later the creaking of a door. A man was in the street, motionless, ten feet from Donahue.

A low mutter: "Hey, you!"

Donahue straightened, kept his hands in his pockets, started slowly towards the man.

"Yeah?" he said.

He noticed the suggestion of a crouch in the small man's attitude, the crook of his arm, the way his hand was rigid in the pocket of a blue jacket.

"Are you the guy?" the little man said.

"What kept you so long?"

"That dick's been snoopin' around. Heard you and him talkin'."

"Where's the scatter?"

The little man jerked his head. "In here."

Donahue went gingerly through a doorway one step above the sidewalk. A gas jet supplied mediocre light. The hallway was narrow, beads of damp, cold sweat stood out on yellow walls.

"Door at the end," muttered the little man. "Just open it."

Donahue turned the knob and opened the door. A tall man with a patent-leather haircomb and dull eyes stood behind a table holding a gun. His face had the dry gray look of cigarette ash. He had a long goose-like neck, wore a tight white collar, tight dark clothes, long sideburns.

The small man slipped in behind Donahue and closed the door. He was rabbit-like in his movements.

"Okey, Eddie," he said. "That shamus beat it."

Eddie said to Donahue: "If you brought that shamus with you, guy, I'll turn your belly inside out."

The little man blinked bright blue eyes in a chubby red face. "Hell, Eddie, he's okey. Ain't you heard him and the shamus?"

"Yeah," Eddie said somberly, without conviction. "Show us the color of your dough, guy."

"I've got it," Donahue said. "Show me the color of the pearls."

Eddie slipped a hand into his pocket, drew out a string of pearls, dangled them. Donahue stepped forward. Eddie drew the pearls in, lifted his lip wolf-like.

Donahue said: "I want to count them."

Eddie laid them on the table, stepped back and leveled his gun at Donahue. Donahue, ignoring both men, picked the pearls up. He moved the string slowly through his fingers. There were fifty-two pearls. He then examined the settings and the clasp. He nodded, drew the packet from his pocket, and dropped it on the table.

Eddie snatched it up while the small man stood behind Donahue with a gun. Eddie ripped the packet open, scowling, and counted the bills swiftly. Still scowling, he crammed the bills into his pockets.

He jerked his head. "All right, bozo. Beat it."

Donahue dropped the necklace into his pocket.

"Beat it!" snapped Eddie.

"Pipe down," Donahue said. "It sure amazes me how a couple of punks like you get away with twenty grand."

"Beat it!"

The small man opened the door.

Donahue bit his lip, wrinkled his forehead, looked from one to the other, exasperated, reluctant to go, to leave twenty thousand in hard cash with these punks. Not because he pitied Mrs. Jennifer. Not at all. It was just on general principles.

"Beat it, you! Beat it!"

"Ah-r-r!…" Donahue snarled, spun on his heel, his back to their guns; banged the room door savagely behind him; tramped down the hall, the pearls in his pocket, his job done practically— Practically! He laughed bluntly to himself. Reached the hall door, put his hand on the knob, paused, thinking, deliberating, still reluctant to leave. But his job was done—done! His teeth lashed his nether lip. He swore, pulled open the door and stepped into the street. The wind slapped him in the face. He yanked down his hat, looking up and down the street; buried his face in the folds of his coat-collar. He waded through the wind, long-legged, rolling his shoulders.

"Make your date, Donny?"

Donahue stopped as he saw Kiff lounge from between two vacant store windows. Kiff was smoking a cigar. Kiff looked genial, jovial, hale-fellow-well-met. He shoved his chest out expansively, wobbled the cigar in the wind from one side of his mouth to the other; snorted as sparks showered back into his face; then was genial again, oddly blocking Donahue's path, turning sidewise to keep the wind from blowing his long coat between his legs. Light and shadow danced a windy saraband around him; his big horse teeth kept showing; the red cigar end hummed and sputtered in the wind.

"You playing tag or leap frog or something?" Donahue asked.

"Just tag."

"All right, I'm it. Follow me."

Donahue started around the precinct dick, boring his head into the wind.

"Wait a minute, Donny."

Still genial, still jovial, provocative. He twisted his blunt body to sideswipe and stop Donahue. Donahue lifted his hard jaw out of the coat-collar. He glared at Kiff. He looked angry, his brown face seemed strangely malevolent. Kiff grinned with his big horse teeth, a fixed grin, while he weaved his head to keep the wind out of his eyes.

"What the hell's on your mind, Kiff?"

"What's on yours, Donny?"

"Go to hell!"

Again Donahue started forward. Kiff, instead of blocking him, fell in beside him, flanking him closely, turning his cheek to the wind.

"You wouldn't be down in this neighborhood for your health, Donny. What's in that house, Donny?"

"A still."

"Rats. They don't cook stuff in this neighborhood."

"You know better, then."

Kiff stopped, grabbing his hat as the wind uprooted it. "I'll go back in and see, just in case, Donny."

Donahue stopped. The wind had made his eyes water. He dabbed at them.

"Why be a gofor, Kiff? Hell, are you hard up for a pinch?"

"Sure. The chief's been on our necks. A pinch is a pinch—any kind of a pinch." Kiff kept backing up towards the house, holding his hand to his hat, looking awkward as the wind pushed his coat between his legs.

Donahue said: "Wait, Kiff." Went towards the precinct dick, gestured with his hand. "I went in there for a pinch myself, Kiff. That's straight. But I missed out. There's nothing in there. I was on a tail. I'll be frank with you."

"Well, I'll go in anyhow, Donny."

"——! Kiff, don't be weak-minded like that! It's nothing, I tell you. Just an idea I had."

The little guy—and the guy with the sideburns—Eddie—in there. Both heeled. And Eddie had looked hopped up. A hot rod he'd be if

Kiff went poking his nose in there. They'd smear Kiff all over the walls.

But Kiff kept backing up, then half-turned, moving side-wise towards the door. Donahue followed by fits and starts.

"It was just an idea I had, Kiff. I wanted to— Hell, Kiff, don't be like that. It's a jane all right, but don't bust in. Don't pick on her. She's a friend of a friend of mine." He crowded Kiff. "I'll go in first, Kiff, talk with her. I'll—"

It sounded silly. He knew it sounded silly. He felt his ears burning. The guy with the sideburns would cut Kiff down like nobody's business. Kiff was no great shakes as a gun artist. A snooper, Kiff was.

Kiff said: "First it's a jane—then it isn't a jane— Donahue! What do you take me for? You been hanging around that corner for something. I watched you. Then I find out it's you and I walk away. But I think—hell, he's up to something, that guy. I come back and you're gone."

"Well, can't a man stand on a street corner?"

"I'm going in there, Donahue. I don't know but what you're hand in glove with a lot of heels. Roper always figured you for a two-timer—"

"Don't you call me a two-timer, you cheap gumshoe!"

"Get outta my way!"

"Kiff!" Donahue got between him and the door, bulking.

"A jane I know is in there. That door's locked. By —— ! You can't enter this house without a warrant!"

"Warrant! Holy Mary, I never in my life bothered with a warrant! Get out—"

"Kiff, you dumb animal!"

Donahue grabbed him, desperate now. He knew that if Kiff entered that door it would be murder. They'd murder Kiff. They wouldn't be caught red-handed with all that dough on them. And for the first time he found himself reacting to a moral obligation. Not one that included Kiff. To hell with Kiff! Kiff used to work stoolies on the street girls when he was on the vice squad. It was Mike Mueck. The East Side boy who grew up to be a swell lawyer. And himself too. Oh, Donahue was thinking of himself—

Kiff cursed and whirled. A blackjack crashed down on the crown of Donahue's hat. Donahue reeled away, fell against the wall of the building, fell down to the pavement.

Kiff broke through the door. Donahue, getting to his knees, saw

Kiff disappear.

Three shots boomed out of the hallway.

A figure staggered out, slammed headlong to the pavement, lay motionless.

Donahue, half-risen, flung himself backward, fell into the recession between two store-windows. He heard two pairs of feet running— running away down the street. He got up, took his hat off, punched out the dents, replaced it on his head.

Windows grated open. Voices called. Heavy shoes came pounding from the distance.

Donahue stood on his feet, hefting his gun. He saw the two men tearing down the street, the tall one, Eddie, far in the lead. Eddie had the money on him. Donahue clamped his teeth, raised his gun, his arm out straight. Flame tore from the black muzzle. A woman screamed and a window slammed shut. Flame burst again. The little man reared, keeled over, struck a pole and spun down to the sidewalk.

Donahue broke into a run. Eddie had disappeared. Donahue reached the little man where he lay beside the pole. He rolled him over, ransacked his pockets. No money. But a small black wallet, worn and bent out of shape. Donahue thrust this in his own pocket.

He stood up, looked back. A couple of cops were over Kiff's body. Donahue walked towards them swiftly, his face drawn, his lips dry. Damn Kiff for a snooper, a busybody! Everything would have gone off nicely but for Kiff. And Kiff had cooked his own goose. And Donahue had had to shoot that little guy....

Chapter IV

THE two cops squared off, their guns drawn.

"Hello, boys," Donahue said.

"Stick your hands up! Who are you?"

Donahue didn't put his hands up. "I'm Donahue, an Interstate operative."

"What the hell are you doin' around here?"

Donahue jerked his head. "I just plugged a guy."

"Grab him, Joe!"

"Wait a minute!" Donahue said. "Not Kiff. A guy up the street."

"What guy?"

"The guy bumped off Kiff."

"Go ahead, Joe—go look at that guy he plugged."

Donahue pointed. "By that third light."

Joe started off.

The other cop put away his gun. "He's dead—Kiff's dead. How'd it happen?"

"I don't know. I came around the corner here as the shots went off. I saw Kiff falling. There were two guys running away. I yelled at them. They didn't stop. Then I fired and got one of them. The other guy got away."

The precinct station was in an uproar. Donahue was in a room with Detective-Sergeant Brannigan.

"You saw them babies, Donahue—you saw them—"

"Get me right, Sarge," broke in Donahue. "I saw them running away. Running away. I just yelled to them to stop. They didn't. So I let 'em have it."

"Why the hell didn't you get the other guy?"

"I had a job getting one. It was pretty dark. The other guy just got away. I should go running around the streets and have a cop take a shot at me!"

"He went in that house, Donahue. There's bullet marks in the walls. The damned house was supposed to be empty. No rooms was rented to anybody. The house was empty. But those two babies must ha' been in there, 'cause Kiff went in. Kiff got the works in the hall there and must ha' fell out the door. If I only had an idea why Kiff went in that house. But I ain't."

"Maybe he knew the place was empty and saw a light in there—"

"I'll get that other guy, Donahue. He'll burn for this, and before he burns he'll get the beatin' of his life. We'll beat him till his eyes pop. I got a general alarm out. We're pick-in' up any guy don't look right. We'll get that baby!"

When Mueck opened the door he was in bathrobe and dressing-gown.

"Well, Donny—"

Donahue stepped into the apartment, closed the door, said: "Well,

Mike, I got the pearls."

"Great!"

"Oh, you think so?" Donahue scaled his hat on to the divan, threw open his ulster, began pacing up and down. "Not by a long shot, Mike. There's trouble and plenty of it. Kiff, a precinct dick, got the works."

"You didn't!"

"Hell, no, I didn't. But one of the guys I called on did. And I had to plug one of the guys—to save my face. And incidentally, your face."

"——! Donny!"

"Keep cool, Mike. I knew damned well this job should have been thrown to the cops. But it's done now, and I suppose it's up to me to find a way out."

"Are—are you suspected?"

Donahue stopped. "No. Not yet, anyhow. They think I'm a great guy because I plugged one of the hoods that got Kiff. Kiff—that snooping old fool! But"—he wagged a forefinger—"the cops are throwing out the old dragnet, and if they pick up the other guy, find the jack on him— Listen, Mike, this is not going to be any bed of roses."

"But how did it all happen? Sit down, Donny. Have a drink."

Donahue sat down. Mueck poured out some Scotch. Donahue downed it straight. He told Mueck what had happened. Mueck walked up and down, eyes glued on the carpet, teeth nibbling at lips.

Donahue cracked fist into palm. "I tried to keep Kiff out of there! I knew damned well that if he went in those two hoods would let him have it. But the jackass took a swipe at me with his blackjack and I took a header. Before I could organize myself it was over."

Mueck sat down, spoke quietly: "It looks bad, Donny."

"Don't worry, Mike. I'll keep you out of it."

"Nonsense! Do you think I'd let you take the rap alone?"

"Be your age, Mike. What's the use of everybody taking the rap? And besides, shut up about a rap. So far I'm in the clear. Just act as if nothing happened. And tell that client of ours to keep her face shut."

"I shouldn't have got you into this, Donny. But I didn't dare take it myself. The legal profession is the butt of a lot of unfair criticism these days. And a lawyer found acting as intermediary for thieves is immediately suspected of cashing in on it. But, damn it, Mrs. Jennifer wanted those pearls! She would have paid more than twenty thousand for them! Oh, she's a hard client, Donny. Eccentric as blazes. They were her mother's pearls."

"Yeah?" Donahue was dangling the long string. "They're sweet—they're certainly sweet. But they're causing a lot of tears, Mike."

Mueck took them and ran them through his fingers.

"What do you intend doing, Donny?"

"The guy who got away looked like a real gun, Mike. He looked hopped up too. A tough hombre. We've got one chance of cleaning out of this."

"What's that?"

"I've got to get to that guy before the cops do."

He had lied—naturally enough—to Kiff. Kiff had tried to butt into his business. Kiff had had a hunch that Donahue had been hanging around that corner for other reasons than amorous ones. So Donahue had lied. The lie was based on many ramifications. He had had to protect himself, the crooks he later met; and he had not wanted to start something that in the long run might well have reached and drawn in Mueck.

Mueck stood up, gestured with both hands. "Hell, Donny, I don't see why you should run the chance of getting killed."

"I'd rather do that than run my chances with the cops—at this stage. I've got to, Mike. This guy is a killer and I have no qualms about going after him. You and I are fairly honest men. But that wouldn't prevent the law from having you disbarred and very likely pitching me in jail. If they get that guy—find the dough—he'll talk. And will it be rough on me? Don't ask!"

"Remember, Donny, I'm with you—I'm not trying to slide out."

Donahue laughed. "I never had any doubts about that, Mike." He pinched Mueck's arm. "And remember, let me handle it, old kid. It's the kind of work I'm cut out to handle."

"I feel sort of—"

"I know how you feel. But you couldn't help me by baring your breast to the H.Q. crowd. I'll see the old dame in the morning. She's got to bury this necklace among her other souvenirs."

Chapter V

HINKLE looked worried when Donahue breezed in at ten next morning. He looked up from the newspaper.

"I see you're a hero, Donny."

"Well, I gave the dame her necklace and she almost wept on my shoulder. I told her a few things though. I talked turkey. She swears she'll never mention the necklace. She never wore it anyhow. It's an heirloom."

"Did you stop in at H.Q.?"

"Yes. I got there in time to witness the line-up. They had dozens of guys. But not the guy I want.

Hinkle wagged his head. "What a mess!"

"I took a walk through the Rogues' Gallery. I spotted the guy. Man, he's a bad hood! So I helped myself to the dope they've got on him. He's been arrested ten times—for almost everything on the calendar: dope, felonious assault, concealed weapons, petty larceny. But he beat them all. Eddie Bishoff's his name."

"Did they identify the other guy?"

Donahue sat down, said: "No." He drew out a small black wallet, tapped it on an open palm, smiled. "I took this off that guy, Asa."

"What the devil did you want to do that for?" Donahue made no reply. He whistled to himself, emptied the wallet on the desk. "The cops," he said, "have got more than a hundred guys combing the city—not counting the stoolies these hundred guys will swing into action. I'm one guy against that mob—one guy, Asa—"

"I was leery of this job—"

"Don't crab!" Donahue smacked his palm down on the photograph of a woman. "I've got this. Picture of a dizzy broad. 'Love to Louie from his Nora.' And here—down in the corner—*'Barcelona Club.* Jan. 4th.' A cabaret girl. 'His Nora.' Okey"—Donahue waved the picture— "I'll find that dame. Louie was the little guy. He put one bullet in Kiff. Eddie Bishoff put two."

"Are they making any progress at H.Q.?"

"No. They dragged in a lot of punks and busted a lot of hose on some guys. They're mad for a pinch, what with the vice squad getting razzed these days. Here, this"—Donahue flattened a sheet of paper on the desk—"is a list of amounts of money, with dates alongside each amount. Small amounts. It's on the back of a piece of Hotel Grebb stationery. That's a one-fifty a night flop-house on Seventh Avenue. The paper looks old. But the picture doesn't."

"Who's in charge of the case?"

"That bruiser Tom Brannigan. All steamed up. I was just talking to him at H.Q. He said if I ran into the guy got away I should tip him off and he'd see I got a case of Scotch. Big-hearted Mick, that Brannigan. I told him I'd snoop around. He said it was okey by him. I said: 'Tom, suppose I smack into this bird and have to shoot it out with him?' Tom looked down-hearted. He said: 'Hell, Donahue. Save him for the boys. We want to take it out of his hide and then pitch him to the D.A.'"

"Do you want a man to work with you?"

"No. It's solo for me, Asa. And don't say anything to any of the boys. And don't mention Bishoff's name. Well"—he grabbed up his hat—"I'll be seeing you, sweetheart."

THE *Barcelona Club* was closed at noon. It huddled between two drab brick houses in West Tenth Street. Its black door was flush with the street. Donahue knocked. A man opened the door and put out a wedge-shaped face.

"Barney here yet?"

"Who is it?"

"Donahue. Barney knows me. Ask him."

The door closed. Donahue waited. A minute later the door opened and Barney De Vere looked out—grinned, opened the door wide.

"Bar's not open, Donny—"

"It's not that, Barney. Can we have a little talk? I'm hard up for a little information."

They went into the lobby, across the dim dance-floor, down a short corridor and into a stuffy office. Barney nodded to a chair and Donahue sat down.

"It's about a jane, Barney."

"Oh-oh."

"Can't remember her last name but I think she used to work in your little review. Maybe she does yet. Nora something— Nora— Nora— Well, a little brunette."

"Oh, you mean Nora."

"Yeah, Nora."

"Yeah—Nora Slaven. What did she do?"

"Nothing," Donahue said. "Not a thing. I just want to have a talk with her—a real heart-to-heart talk, Barney."

Barney sighed, shook his head. "She used to work here, Donny. Up until a month ago. She left, and she didn't say why."

"Do you know where she went?"

"No, I don't, Donny. I often thought she might have run off with a little guy used to hang around here a lot. Louie Brown—or something, I dunno. Say, I see by the paper you did the cops a good deed."

"Yeah. Ran into a gun-fight and helped old John Law. Well, thanks, Barney."

"Drop in some time."

"Sure."

"Sorry I can't help you out."

"Don't know where she lived, eh?"

"Well, she lived upstairs till she left."

Barney didn't know that Louie Brown was the man Donahue had shot last night. Neither did the cops. The corpse was still that of "an unidentified man."

Donahue walked over to Sheridan Square and caught a north-bound subway train. He got off at Penn Station and walked a few blocks north on Seventh Avenue. He took a look at the drab façade of the Grebb Hotel.

He dropped into a corner cigar store nearby and crowded into a telephone booth, got a number out of the directory. He put a nickel in the slot.

Yes, the girl at the Grebb said, Mr. Louis Brown lived there. Donahue hung up, stood for a while near the cigar stand. He didn't want anyone at the Grebb to know that he was looking for Louie Brown. He left the cigar store and went down to the Penn Station. He sent a wire to Louie Brown at the Grebb. *"Call me when you get this. Jim."* Then he left the station and retraced his steps north on Seventh Avenue, entered the Grebb.

The lobby was as drab as the façade. A dozen men sat around in wooden rockers. Donahue joined them and waited, watching the door. Half an hour later a Western Union messenger came swinging in. Donahue rose casually and sauntered to the desk, flipped tourist and excursion leaflets negligently.

"Wire for Mr. Brown."

The clerk turned from a ledger, signed the slip. He called over to the switchboard: "Brown in 408 in?" The operator buzzed.

Donahue left the desk, went back into the washroom, killed ten minutes there and then came out. He took an elevator to the fourth floor.

A master key paved the way for him. He slipped into a narrow room that had a narrow bed, a dresser, a cheap green armchair. The closet door was open. Inside were a couple of hats, a suit, a pair of shoes, a yellow suitcase on the floor. He opened the suitcase. It was empty. He searched the pockets of the suit. They were empty.

Half a dozen shirts were in one of the dresser drawers. Socks, handkerchiefs, in another, and underclothes. Odds and ends in another: a pocketknife, some pennies, a tarnished cigarette case, some poker chips, cards. Donahue closed all the drawers, disgruntled.

Then his roving glance landed on the telephone. Hanging from the mouthpiece was an oblong sheet of cardboard with an advertisement at the top and ruled horizontal lines beneath it. There was some scribbling on it. Donahue removed the cardboard and squinted. Names. Telephone numbers. *Nora.* Donahue drew his lips tightly against his teeth. He sat down and copied the names and numbers. Six names. *Johnnie S.... Pete. Nora. Kitty. Ed. Luke.* He returned the cardboard to the telephone mouth-piece, hesitated, then removed it, tore it to bits.

He left the room, locked the door, went down in the elevator, out into the street. He made a flying trip to the Agency office, in Park Row.

"Call up your friend in the telephone company, Asa," he said, "and get the street addresses of those telephone numbers."

"Oh, you've been places, eh?"

"Yeah. Louie Brown was the little guy's name. He had a room at the Grebb Hotel. I busted in."

"How you get around!"

"Well, go ahead, Asa. Those two dames on there—Kitty and Nora—have the same number. Pals, I suppose."

Asa made a telephone call, called off the telephone numbers, and hung up. Donahue gave him a resume of what he had done and the manner in which he had done it. The telephone rang. Asa answered it, pencil in hand. Beside each number on the slip of paper Donahue had given him, he wrote down an address. Finished, he said: "Thanks, Bill," and hung up. He shoved the slip of paper across the desk.

"May God watch over you, Donny."

Donahue seemed not to have heard. He stared round-eyed at the addresses, his lips moving. "Ed," he said, "may be Eddie Bishoff."

Chapter VI

DONAHUE came out in Park Row and walked over to Broadway. He turned north and was nearing Chambers Street when a bull voice haled him. Before he could locate the voice a P.D. flivver hurtled to the curb. Tom Brannigan was leaning out, waving a red, beefy hand, grinning like a fool.

"C'm here, Donny."

"Hello, Tom."

"Yah, boy—yah, boy!" Brannigan spat with gusto. "What the hell do you think? Hey?"

"Got me, Tom."

"We got that punk identified. Louie Brown's his name. That punk you give the works, Donny. Hot dog! Yah! Ain't that hot, kiddo—ain't it? Yah! Well, we got him identified all right. A pal of a pal of a pal of mine—'Sure, I seen that guy,' he sez. 'Louie Brown's his name.' All I gotta do now, kiddo, is get my stoolies workin' to find out who was trottin' around with Louie Brown. Watch the papers, Donny. You'll be seein' things."

Donahue forced a grin, not heartfelt. "Swell, Tom."

"Goin' up a ways?"

"Yeah."

"Jump in."

Donahue dropped to the seat in the rear beside Brannigan and the police flivver started off. Brannigan erupted, slapping his knees, chewing a cigarette to rags, the feel of the hunt burning in his eyes.

"Just depend on Tom Brannigan, Donny," he said. "I'll get that bum got away. Me, personal. Before sundown I'll have the name o' the guy was trottin' with Louie Brown. I'll bust everything but his windpipe. Yah."

Donahue got off at Eighth Street and walked west with Brannigan's voice still re-echoing in his ears. He did not doubt that Brannigan, who had a vast array of stoolies, would discover the name of the late Louie Brown's partner before sundown. Armed with the name of Eddie Bishoff, Brannigan would find his police record, get his underworld spies working, and eventually get Bishoff.

Donahue hardened in his purpose. It showed on his face. He knew of a private cop on the West Coast who had been engaged to turn over an amount of money to a gang of crooks in return for bonds that had been stolen from a Seattle bank. A bank official had engaged him. There was a slip-up. The bonds were returned well enough, but then the cops started in; hauled in the private cop for abetting the criminals, handed him a jail sentence, thereby setting a precedent.

Donahue knew he was headed for a jam. And he knew that if he got in the jam Mike Mueck would be fool enough to try to get him out and in so doing would entangle himself. And Brannigan was on a tear. Brannigan was ruthless, a hard cop, in his way a good one. But he would rough-house Donahue as quickly and as explosively as he had, on many an occasion, shaken his hand and clapped him on the back.

In Grove Street, near Sheridan Square, Donahue neared the address that corresponded with the telephone number Louie had written alongside the name of Ed. It was a speakeasy. Donahue grumbled his disappointment. But he entered, following a long corridor that terminated in a bar, with tables along the wall. He went to the corner where a telephone stood, looked at the number. It corresponded with the number on the slip of paper.

Donahue went to the bar, hooked his heel on the rail and ordered a highball. The barman whistled sleepily while he mixed the drink. Donahue took a few swallows, frowned—not because of the liquor but because of an indecisive train of thought. Finally he drained the glass, got change from a dollar, went out. He had decided not to bring up Ed's name to the barman, since he believed that nothing would have been gained by it. He didn't want to spring Bishoff's name until he could be certain that it would bring definite information.

He took a cab to Twenty-sixth Street. The address was that of a small apartment house. A row of mail slots was in the lobby, with names above. One was—*Miss Kitty Bradon.* Donahue pushed into a narrow, bare foyer. There was no elevator. He started up a staircase. There were two apartments on each floor, the doors facing each other across a small landing. On the third landing Donahue stopped and looked at the door marked 4B. He looked at the name under the bell-button.

He listened at the door. His right hand closed around the gun in his coat pocket. He used his left thumb to press the button. He eyed the door steadily. Heard footsteps.

A woman's voice. "Who is it?"

"Special delivery, ma'am."

The lock clicked. The door opened a matter of two inches. A blonde head appeared. A hand thrust out.

Donahue grabbed it. "Quiet, sister!"

He elbowed the door violently, shouldered in, kicked the door shut. His gun was in his hand, his voice low—

"Not a chirp, sister."

"Ow—you're hurting!"

He flung down her arm, trained the gun on her, backed her down the short, narrow corridor, into a small living-room. He nodded to a divan.

"Sit down."

She fell to the divan, drawing up her legs, rubbing her hands back and forth across her chest, her eyes wide. Donahue stepped to the door, looked into a kitchenette, saw part of a bedroom. He looked quickly back to the girl, his eyes keen.

"Where's Nora?"

"Nora—?"

"You heard me. Nora."

"She's—out."

Donahue remained standing. He pointed at the woman. "You knew Louie Brown!"

She clasped her face between her hands.

"And"—Donahue was incisive, hard—"you know Eddie Bishoff!"

She shrieked: "Who—who are you?"

"Never mind who I am. Where's Bishoff?"

She put her head back, gasping, saying nothing.

Donahue hefted his gun. "I haven't all day. Get your breath and tell me. I want to know where Bishoff is. I don't care about your girl friend—unless I have to find her to find Bishoff. But I want Bishoff. Louie Brown knew you and Nora Slaven."

"You're a cop!" she cried. "That's what you are—a cop!"

"Yeah, I'm a cop," Donahue drawled.

SHE appeared to make an effort to pull herself together. She stood up, pressed her hands to her hips, moved to a half-open window and inhaled great draughts of air, kneading her hips. Then she pivoted and faced Donahue, her face very white, very grim.

"You've got to help her," she murmured.

"Help her!"

"Nora—you've got to help her—or help me—whatever way you want to put it."

Donahue wagged his gun. "Sister, don't try to kid me."

"For —— sake!…" She clasped her hands together, moving them up and down monotonously, emotionally. "She's a good girl—but bewitched. She's a good girl—but a fool, a little fool, an awful fool. Please—believe me!"

Donahue relaxed, a shadow falling over his face, sarcasm fading from his lips, his lips softening, his eyes keening but at the same time losing their contemptuous glitter.

Yet he spoke bluntly—"Shoot." Willing to listen, yet still watchful, wary—still mindful of the fact that he had been bitten many times, the scars still on his memory. "It's got to sound damned good, my lady."

The woman had not the aspect of a hot-house lily, but at the same time she had a vague prettiness. Emotion had tensed her; she stood image-like, only her lips moving.

"I don't know what he did. He came here last night—late—around midnight. He looked murderous. But he was cool, in that cool way he has. He wanted us to hide him here. I loathed him. But Nora—well, he was a friend of Louie's. She never believed they were bad men. She met them where she worked—in a night club. She came from Utica. He said he had tried to save Louie—he was wounded—in the arm.

"But I wouldn't let him stay. I didn't know what had happened, but I wouldn't let him stay. I own this flat. I got Nora to give up that night-club life, she was such a little fool. I tried to get her away from Louie. But he had that morbid fascination for her; she pitied him—he had hard-luck stories.

"So he was wounded. And we argued. He said he got wounded

trying to save Louie. He must have known this would be a good place to hide. It's a respectable house. I was terrified. So then Nora said, like a baby: 'He's Louie's friend. I've got to stand by him.' I wouldn't let him stay here. I was furious—then furious at Nora. She went with him. He said to me, while she was in the bathroom: 'You keep your mouth shut about this or I'll kill you—and her.' So she went away with him, to nurse him."

She moved to the divan, dropped to it, rubbing her palms slowly together, elbows on knees. She stared transfixed at the carpet.

"I followed them," she said; then looked up, startled, her eyes springing wide-open. "You've got to save her—save that little fool! She's innocent!"

"Go on," Donahue muttered.

"So—I followed them. Nora took a suitcase. She looked dazed, and nun-like. The awful little fool!" She sobbed, then bit the sobs back. "First she bound up his arm—tightly. Then they went—and I followed. I followed them to the Hall Hotel, on Broadway, near Thirty-seventh Street. They registered as Mr. and Mrs. Norman. The poor little fool!"

Donahue groaned, raised his hands, looked at the ceiling.

"I swear," she said, "that Nora doesn't know what she's doing! Isn't there something—something you can do? I want to save her. I'll take her out of New York—take her back to Utica—anything. But, please, she's innocent!"

Donahue sat down. Sat down and shoved his gun into his pocket, lit a cigarette and eyed the woman for a long time through the smoke that dribbled upward. And she eyed him, eyes wide-open, frank, candid, deeply troubled. Donahue grunted. He slapped a palm to a knee, left it there, looking down at the fingers. He grunted again, making a face. Then his lips tightened. He looked up.

"You've got to get them out of that hotel," he said.

"Get them— Why?"

"If I went there and crashed in their room there wouldn't be a chance of getting your friend in the clear. It would be slaughter and she'd bounce into trouble. We've got to get them out of that hotel— that's final."

"But then what?"

He jabbed a finger towards the floor. "Telephone her. Tell her you're sorry you acted the way you did. You've thought it over—and you're sorry. Tell them to come here. Impress on them that you think it would be safer here than in that hotel."

"But"—she spread her hands—"there would be slaughter here and she'd be drawn in anyhow. And so would I. It would be an awful mess."

"Listen," Donahue said, getting up. "I can go over to that hotel and crash it. Or you can do as I say. I want Bishoff. For the information you've given me, I'm willing to try my best to keep Nora out of it. And to do that, we've got to get both of them out of that hotel first."

"But don't you see—"

"Be quiet. I see. I know. You've got to depend on me—and the breaks. Telephone the hotel. Talk them into coming over to hide out here. Leave the rest to me."

She held her breath for a long minute. Then she said quietly: "All right." She rose and walked white-faced to the telephone.

Chapter VII

THEY sat waiting, listening. Sometimes their eyes crossed, but for the most part they said nothing. The woman sat very straight on the divan, her hands folded primly in her lap, her face grave. A small clock ticked on a console. In another apartment a radio was playing.

Donahue sat with his gun hanging between his knees, his coat open.

He said in a hoarse whisper: "Now remember—convince her. Don't get out of town too suddenly. Wait a while. And never say anything about my being here. If I get him out—and I hope to—I do!—never say anything about it. This guy Bishoff has a record against him a mile long."

She whispered, "I'll do my best."

They went on sitting, listening, looking at the clock. The woman bit her lip, knotted her hands, moved her lips without audible sound. She got up and paced back and forth, feeling her throat, touching her lips with her tongue.

"Steady," Donahue murmured.

She sat down again, fanning herself with a newspaper, rolling her eyes.

Donahue muttered: "You've got to look natural when you meet them. The way you are now—"

"I know—I know," she said, trembling. "Oh…—!"

"Sh!" He looked around. "Got any liquor?"

"I never use it."

"Hell!"

She got up and went into the bathroom, washed her face with cold water. It seemed to steady her. She came back into the living-room, holding her chin up. Sat down again.

The door-bell rang.

Donahue stood up, putting a finger to his lips. The woman rose. Oddly enough, she looked calm—suddenly calm. She even smiled—grimly. She went swiftly out into the little corridor.

Donahue stepped to one side of the console, flattening against the wall. He held his gun waist-high. The radio downstairs had stopped. He could hear every sound. He heard the latch click as the woman opened the door.

"Hello, Nora, dear—Eddie."

"Oh, Kitty—you're so sweet!"

The door closed.

"Hello, Kitty," a man's voice said. "I'm glad you changed your mind. I'll lay up here for a couple of days, then breeze."

The footsteps came scuffling down the corridor. Donahue dropped to one knee behind the console. Nora came into the room first. Hardly twenty, a slip of a starry-eyed kid. Then Bishoff came in, his left hand in his pocket, resting there.

Donahue stood up, stepped out. "All right, Eddie."

Bishoff stiffened. His right hand swept towards his left armpit.

"Cut it, kid!" Donahue muttered. "Keep that hand away!"

Bishoff's lip curled; he snarled at Kitty: "You dirty little two-timer!"

Starry-eyed was Nora—still unable to grasp the situation.

"Why—why, what's the matter?" she asked.

"You see what's the matter!" snapped Bishoff. "Your friend laid a trap for me!"

"Kitty—"

"Sit down, Nora," Kitty said, breathless. "I had to get you out of this. This man's a murderer."

Nora cried: "Kitty, how could you? He's not a murderer! He tried to save Louie. He told me how the cops had been persecuting them.

He told me how cops beat poor men in station-houses with everything they can lay hands on."

"He told you a pack of lies," cut in Donahue. "This man has a fat police record. He's an old offender. And he's a killer. He came here after he killed a cop for protection, knowing what a little fool you are. This flat offered the best kind of protection. He was a louse to try to drag you into it."

"Yeah, was I a louse!" snarled Bishoff.

"I'm not wasting words on you," Donahue said. "You're going out of here with me. You're cheap, Bishoff—you're so damned cheap that you hadn't a crowd to hide out in. You had to drag in a fool jane. Why, damn you, you didn't even have a fence. I said it—you're a louse."

"Oh, Eddie, I'm sorry—I'm sorry," cried Nora.

Bishoff whirled on her, started to say something, changed his mind. She was staring at Kitty.

"Oh, Kitty, how could you do a thing like this!"

"Nora, it's for your own good. Can't you see? Do you want to go to jail? Do you?"

"We're going," Donahue broke in, moving towards Bishoff.

Nora sprang at him, blind to the gun.

"Run, Eddie!"

Donahue fell back. He saw Bishoff bolt for the door. He did not strike Nora. He tussled half-heartedly with her. Kitty sprang and gripped Nora's arms, pleaded with her. The hall-door banged.

Donahue tore free. "That's all right," he said. "I'll get him, Kitty. But keep your friend here. Knock her senseless if you have to. She's probably the dumbest animal I've ever seen. But keep her here. She's in your hands. And your hard luck. Get her out of town. She hasn't been told the facts of life."

"Thanks—thanks!"

"So long, sister."

Donahue reached the foyer as the front door was closing. He saw Bishoff heading west at a brisk walk. As he stepped from the lobby, Bishoff looked back and saw him. Donahue started after him, stretching long legs in a fast walk.

At Eighth Avenue Bishoff dived into a taxicab. Donahue broke into a run and hailed another cab at the corner.

"Follow that yellow," he said.

The yellow cab swung west into Twenty-fifth Street, and Donahue's taxi followed. The two cabs snaked among slow trucks. The yellow crossed Ninth Avenue, swung south on Tenth. Bishoff leaped from it at the corner of Twenty-second Street and headed west on foot. Donahue left his cab there and followed.

At Eleventh Avenue Bishoff ran into the middle of the street and leaped aboard a cruising taxi. Donahue broke into a run. The cab started south. There was not another nearby, but one was coming north. Donahue ran towards it, out in the street. The cab stopped.

"Swing around and tail that checker," Donahue said.

He sat on the edge of the rear seat. His cab gathered speed. The checker ahead was speeding on its way south; it struck West Street and went flying past the pier sheds. It looped around slow-moving trucks. It swayed dangerously. Then suddenly it stopped. Bishoff leaped out and ran pell-mell across the wide thoroughfare, dodging north-bound traffic.

Donahue tossed a dollar to the chauffeur and tailed Bishoff into Barrow Street. Bishoff started running and Donahue ran after him. Bishoff darted across Washington Street, across Greenwich, turned north into Hudson. He had long legs. He was fast.

He turned east on Christopher Street and then swung right into Bedford. People stopped and stared after him, only to be surprised again by the appearance of Donahue, his coat flapping about his legs. Others darted into convenient doorways, sensing trouble, the possibility of gunfire.

At the corner of Grove a policeman appeared, idly swinging a nightstick. He took one look at Bishoff, saw the light in his eyes. He shouted: "Hey, you, wait—" Bishoff's gun came out of his pocket for the first time during the chase. It blazed. The cop got it in the throat and crumpled, gurgling.

A pedestrian screamed and flung herself to the sidewalk, hugging a housefront.

Donahue leaped over the fallen policeman. He saw Bishoff crash into a store on Grove Street. Donahue crashed in after him. There was a door open in the rear. He started for it. He heard a snarl and threw himself down as a gun boomed. A bullet smashed into the wall back of him. He saw Bishoff reeling towards the front door again. He fired. The bullet shattered a window.

Bishoff plunged back into Grove Street, sideswiped a woman,

kicked over a child. The woman started to rise. She saw Donahue heaving out of the door and fell down again. The child screamed. People were on the corner—a dozen or more. But they did nothing. They stood petrified.

Blindly the chase led to Sheridan Square, across the Square while a policeman directed heavy traffic, up to Waverley Place, then east. At Sixth Avenue Bishoff turned and fired a shot. It went through Donahue's hat without budging the hat. Donahue fired and his bullet rang against an L post, and Bishoff turned up Sixth Avenue. He turned and saw Donahue taking aim again. He flung himself against a door. The door gave and he plunged into a hallway.

Donahue reached the door and saw him at the top of a staircase. He dived in headlong as Bishoff fired. He felt a jolt in his right arm and dropped his gun. He fell to the floor as another shot boomed and gouged the floor behind him. He grabbed up the gun in his left hand and started up the staircase.

Bishoff broke through a door on the second floor. A woman cried out and dropped a skillet to the stove. He struck her with the gun and she fell to the floor. His teeth were bared, his eyes blazed and sounds grated in his throat. The woman kept moaning and he cursed her. Food from the overturned skillet hissed and sputtered on the hot stove.

Donahue crept to the end of the hall, climbed out to a fire-escape, swung to the kitchen window. Bishoff saw his shadow, swivelled. Donahue fired across the woman on the floor. Bishoff's bullet struck the upraised window; glass rained down on Donahue as he fired again. Bishoff fell back against the wall, grimacing, trying to raise his gun.

Donahue jumped through the window, stepped over the woman. Bishoff cursed him, still tried to raise the gun. He groaned. The gun went off and a bullet banged into the floor. He couldn't raise the gun. He fell down, belching.

The woman was creeping towards the door. Donahue laid his gun down, tore open Bishoff's coat, plunged his hand into Bishoff's pocket. He drew out a thick sheaf of bills held together by an elastic band. He transferred them to his own pocket.

As he stood up he heard heavy shoes rapping up the stairs, hard voices exclaiming. Tom Brannigan loomed in the doorway, his gun leveled.

"Hands up!"

"Your eyesight bad, Tom?"

"Jeeze, it's Donahue! What you been— Jeeze you got him!" Brannigan tramped across the room. "I told you, Donny, to save him for us! Watcha want to go and— Say, I would ha' had that baby. I got tipped off an hour ago it was him was runnin' with Louie Brown. Louie, we find, is wanted in Denver. He cleared outta there six months ago after knifin' a woman!"

Half a dozen cops crowded in.

Brannigan bent over Bishoff. "Well, you wiper! Well— Hey, he's dead! Well, c'n you tie that!" He turned to Donahue. "How come you meet up with him?"

"Well, Tom, I was strolling up Broadway in the Twenties, when I saw him. He saw me at the same time. I said to myself: 'I'll tail him and hole him up somewhere and then call Tom Brannigan.' I tried to, Tom. But he got loose with his gun. He got me in the arm. I—I've got to get to a hospital, Tom. Look me up there." He put his gun away. "You're not sore, are you, Tom?"

"Well"—Brannigan scowled—"what's the use o' gettin' sore. I'll okey this, Donny." He jerked his head. "Beat it to the hospital before you get infection. I'll see you there later."

Donahue went downstairs, pushed through the curious mob, found a taxicab. He climbed in, fell back, called out the Agency's address. He got white on the way downtown. Getting out of the cab in Park Row, he staggered.

He walked stiff-legged into Hinkle's office. Hinkle shoved his chair back.

"My ——! Donny, what's the matter!"

Donahue flopped to a chair, drew out the sheaf of bills.

"Count them, Asa."

"But you—you—you're sick."

Donahue licked his lip. "Upset stomach, I guess. Count them, Asa."

Hinkle pulled off the rubber bands, began counting. As he counted, his eyes grew wider. Donahue sighed in the chair, dropping his chin to his chest.

Asa said: "Exactly twenty thousand!"

"Good. He must have been afraid to spend any of it so soon. See that gets back to Mrs. Jennifer, Asa. Do it now. And tell her to forget about it. I'm pretty sure I've burned all my bridges behind me. Tell Mike Mueck to come over to the hospital to see me sometime, if he's not busy."

He stood up. His right hand was red. The blood had come down his sleeve. He took a handkerchief and wrapped it around his hand.

Hinkle said, jumping up: "Why didn't you tell me you were wounded, you idiot?"

Donahue went towards the door. "It's not much, Asa. The punk just gave me a little something to remember him by."

Asa heaved towards the clothes-tree. "I'll go with you."

"You'll take that money right up to Mrs. Jennifer, that's what you'll do!"

He went out alone.

Death's Not Enough

Tough dick Donahue crashes the murder trail of a band of red-hots

Chapter I

WHEN Donahue heard the dull thump against the door he twisted around in bed and listened, pipe in one hand, magazine in the other.

The cylindrical brass reading lamp, clipped to the head of the bed, sprayed light on his neck, past his ears, picked out rumpled twists of black hair and left his face mostly in shadow.

Half a minute passed without a recurrence of sound. The tenth story room was intimately quiet.

Donahue looked at the clock on the little bed-table. It was twelve-thirty. He shrugged, pyramided the coverlet with his knees, took a drag at his briar and resumed reading.

Then another sound reached his ears: a scraping, like cat's claws on wood. Then a definite thump. Donahue sat up slowly, laid aside the magazine, reached over and placed his pipe on the bed-table. He shoved big, strong feet out of bed and stood up in gray silk pajamas. He scowled at the door, a little annoyed, a little curious.

He took a flat black automatic pistol from the bed-table drawer and released the safety. He held the gun negligently, like one accustomed to guns, and moved slowly on bare feet towards the door. Silently he threw the catch. His left hand closed over the knob, he turned it as far as it would go, then yanked the door inward and stepped back.

A man fell flat on his face across the threshold. He had been kneeling by the door. He went down so fast that Donahue did not see his face. Donahue stood motionless, covering the man.

"Well, get up," he said.

The man did not move. A muffled phlegmatic groan reached Donahue's ears. He took a step across the man and looked up and down the hall; saw no one. He stepped back in, bent down, gripped the man's shoulder and turned him over on his back. He couldn't see the face clearly, so he switched on the ceiling light.

There was a thread of blood lying from one corner of the stranger's mouth down across his jaw. The lips were pursed tightly, the face muscles taut; in the glazed eyes was a fierce white look, blind and unseeing but awesome in its fixed intensity on space.

Donahue closed the automatic's safety, knelt down, unbuttoned the blue topcoat, unbuttoned the vest. There was a wet splotch of crimson on a white shirt. Hoarse, spasmodic breathing pumped through the nostrils and the lips twitched but remained resolutely pursed.

Donahue said nothing. He somehow knew—because of the look in the eyes—that it would be futile to say anything. He stood up, ran his hand through his hair, took three long steps and picked up the telephone.

"A doctor—quick. A man's dying.... Now, now, sweetheart, never mind. Get a doctor up."

He hung up and slipped the receiver quietly into the hook. He went quickly into the bathroom, drew a glass of water and came back. He knelt down, looking at the eyes. He shrugged. He tried to get the man to drink. The man wouldn't. He wouldn't budge those lips.

Donahue set the glass down, remained kneeling on one knee, leaning with his elbow on the other. He reached down and patted the man's shoulder. But he didn't say anything. His face was somber, his brown eyes troubled.

The elevator door banged open and quick footsteps came down the hall. Donahue looked up and saw Mason, the chief night clerk— Mason, white-faced and breathless, eyes popping.

"The operator said—"

"Did she get a doctor?"

"He'll be up—he'll be right up. I called Monahan too. Good grief! What happened—what happened?"

"Ask me another," Donahue muttered, still looking at the tortured face on the floor.

"Did you do anything? Did you—is he?..."

"Keep your pants on, Mason. What can I do? He's been shot in the belly. He was lying against my door. I guess he couldn't make his own. Know him?"

"He's—why, he's Mr. Larrimore! My ——! he's Mr. Larrimore!"

"Who's Larrimore?"

"You know—you know. That—that column in the *Press-Examiner: The Awful Truth.*"

"Oh," said Donahue dully; but his brown eyes brightened. He said, "Get that doctor, Mason. He doesn't have to comb his hair. Tell him he doesn't have to comb his hair."

"Yes—yes."

Mason ran down the hall.

Donahue leaned close to the tortured face, tried to lock his glance with the man's.

"Larrimore. Larrimore, who got you? Why? I'm Donahue, Larrimore—Donahue of the Interstate Detective Agency. If you can talk, Larrimore, spill it. Listen, Larrimore—Donahue, you must have heard of Donahue. Who shot you, Larrimore?"

He gave it up. He heard the elevator door open. Mason and the house doctor appeared, followed by Monahan, the house officer.

"Get him inside," Monahan said. "We don't want to wake the hotel up.... Hello, Donahue."

They dragged Larrimore in and Mason came last, closing the door. The doctor changed spectacles and knelt down. He felt the pulse, shook his head; unbuttoned the shirt, pulled up the undershirt. He looked quickly at the man's face. He remained thus—looking at the face. Then he looked at his watch.

"Twelve-thirty-seven," he said; rose, adding: "He's dead—quite dead."

"Good grief!" choked Mason. "And we've never had a scandal—"

Donahue rasped, "That's all you're thinking about!"

The three men looked at him. He shrugged and went across and picked up his pipe, tamped it down. Monahan, a short, round-bodied man with a bald head, went to the telephone.

"Get Police Headquarters, Miss McGillicuddy. Detective-Sergeant Kelly McPard. Tell him to come right over. Mention my name.... Yes—yes, he died. And don't forget to mention my name."

He hung up and looked importantly at Donahue. "You don't happen to know anything about this, do you?"

"Not a thing."

Monahan picked up Donahue's gun, smelled the muzzle, drew out the clip. The gun was fully loaded—six in the magazine, one in the chamber. Monahan shoved back the magazine and laid the gun down.

Donahue, sitting on the bed, said: "You opened the safety, Monahan. When you monkey around with my gun leave it the way you found it."

Kelly McPard was a big fat man with a neat, sandy mustache and rosy cheeks. His eyes were bright blue, whimsical, and he smiled easily, though a man with any sense at all could see the wiliness behind his good humor. He dressed in the height of fashion, and he drifted in through the door smoking a cork-tipped cigarette and looking like a million dollars.

"Hello, Monahan. Why, hello there, Donahue. Hello, Dr. Stress.... Well, well, this is not so nice. Did you shoot him, Donahue?"

"Yeah. Twice in the belly."

McPard chuckled and laid down his hat. His hair fell back in silken, shiny waves, without a part.

"Who is he?"

"He's—Mr. Larrimore," Mason said. "He lives down the hall in 1010. You know him—I mean, that column in the *Press-Examiner.*"

"A.B. Larrimore," nodded McPard. "H'm."

"Shot twice in the stomach," Dr. Stress said. "He died a moment after I arrived here. There was nothing I could do."

Mason said: "The elevator boy said he thought Mr. Larrimore was—well, you know, a little drunk—the way he walked, I mean. He sort of staggered into the elevator, with his coat collar up. He didn't say anything. The elevator boy knew the floor."

"He never made his room," Donahue said. "He fell against my door, sank there. I heard the thump. I was reading in bed."

Mason yammered: "He wasn't shot in the hotel. I saw him come in the front, kind of staggering, his chin in his collar. He was like that a lot. But if he was shot like that, why did he come here to die?"

"He was out on his feet," Donahue said. "A man gets like that and he steers for home. Or maybe he didn't think he was hurt so bad. Some guys don't like to slobber all over in public."

"Might call that dying manners," McPard said.

"You were the guy told Scotch jokes at an Irish wake one night, weren't you?" Donahue said.

McPard had a velvet chuckle. He pulled up his trouser-legs by the knees before kneeling down. He wore sheer silk socks, starched cuffs with gold links. He pawed Larrimore's pockets casually, whistling absent-mindedly in a whisper.

"H'm—right in the guts—side by side…. See it, Donny? Tsk, tsk!… No powder burns on the coat. No hand shake kill. I think I'll have a look at the bullets anyhow. So you might call the morgue, Monahan. Thanks…. H'm, thirty-three dollars, sixty cents. And—isn't this a good-looking cigarette case?" He wrapped it carefully in a silk handkerchief. "You never know," he sighed.

There was a furious pounding on the door. Monahan swore, stuck out his jaw and yanked it open. Libbey, of the *City Press,* reeled in, turned around once and flopped down in a chair.

"My ——! He's shot too!" Mason cried.

"Plastered," Libbey said. "Bacardi cocktails again. Hello, Donny, you big tramp. Hello, Sarge…. So Larrimore got it. Where? When?

Come on, Sarge, whom do you suspect? There has got to be a suspect. Come on. I got the tip from H.Q. and I gave three other news-hawks a phony address, I think it was a lying-in hospital or a hotel for Lithuanian immigrant girls. Hello, Monahan, how's the keyhole business these nights?"

"Should I put this bum out?" Monahan said.

"You and what other two Swedes?" Libbey laughed.

"Leave him be," McPard said, still pawing Larrimore's pockets. "Only shut up, Libbey."

Donahue brought Libbey a drink and that shut him up.

McPard said: "Well, he has nothing on him worthwhile. If he walked here, he couldn't have been shot far away. Else he came in a cab. I'll find if he came in a cab. Was he drinking, Doc?"

"There was a faint smell of liquor. Not very distinct, however."

"I thought he'd get it some day," Libbey said. "That column of his was rich. He should have named it 'Private Lives—and How.' You know, my dear friends—as among gentlemen—this will create a furor. Inside of twenty-four hours the *Press-Examiner* will offer a reward. And other sheets, conscience-stricken because they have underpaid us newspapermen for so long—"

Donahue growled: "Pipe down, you fat-head."

"—other newspapers will supplement the reward and, attend—you, you and you, three enterprising master-minds: here you are, the three of you, in the presence of one foully murdered—"

"Jeeze, Sarge," Monahan grumbled, "can't I throw this stink out?"

"—Kelly McPard, Donny, and Monahan. Three of you, by a planetary coincidence, will each go his secret way with one eye on justice and one eye on the shekels."

Monahan looked guilty. McPard put a cork-tipped cigarette between his lips. His face beamed, but back of the laugh in his eyes burned a wily, speculative spark.

"But, Libbey," he said expansively, "we're all friends."

"Of course," said Donahue. He bent down, picked up a cardboard packet of matches, struck one and held it to McPard's cigarette. They smiled into each other's eyes.

"Aren't we all?" McPard said.

"Sure," Donahue said. "We're all big-hearted guys, Kelly."

The phone rang. Monahan picked it up, listened, said above it:

"The morgue wagon, Sarge."

When the body had been removed from the room, when McPard and Monahan had gone and Libbey had taken the stairway down to dodge three irate reporters, Donahue locked his door. Then he opened his hand and looked at the blue packet of paper matches. He opened the flap. Printed on the inside of the flap was:

The Venetian Cellar
West Tenth Street

Two matches were missing. One of them he had used to light McPard's cigarette. The other was missing when McPard, pawing Larrimore's coat pocket, had tossed the packet away as something inconsequential.

"Good old Kelly McPard," Donahue chortled.

He started dressing.

Chapter II

MASON was back at the desk in the lobby, his nerves jumpy. But he was at least thankful that no one had been disturbed. He sincerely believed that at night he guided the destiny of the hotel. They had taken the body out in the freight elevator, then through the service entrance, and the reporters had gone along with McPard. He looked up and saw Monahan coming seriously across the dim, deserted lobby.

Monahan had been fired from six private detective agencies, but he still believed the agencies were wrong. The hotel had hired him because he was cheap. The hotel was small and mostly residential and a house officer was a superfluity anyhow. The owners kept him mainly to quiet drunken parties and to patrol the halls at two every morning to see if all the doors were locked.

Monahan went into a huddle with Miss McGillicuddy, whom he had awed from time to time with imaginary yarns of man-hunts. Monahan, you understand, figuring as the master-mind exclusively.

"That 1005 now, Miss McGillicuddy," he said impressively under his hand. "Keep an ear open on any telephoning he does."

"You—you think he's—guilty?"

"Sh! No, not that. But he's a smart aleck and if the hotel solves the death—the brutal death, Miss McGillicuddy—of one of its guests.... You get me? So keep an ear open. You know, there may even be a reward and"— he leaned closer, winked—"I'm not a hog, young lady."

"Gee!" She coughed and blew her nose. "Got an awful cough, Mr. Monahan."

"A—uh—little pin money, you see, might fix it so you could get two weeks off and take a fling at Palm Beach."

He walked away with a pious look on his face and his palms against his round thighs. He stopped as he saw a tall man in a brown ulster and a tan, rakish hat striding across the lobby for the doors.

Donahue went out into a raw full wind that blustered down the street. He turned south into University Place, west into Tenth Street. He crossed Fifth Avenue, reached Sixth, walked beneath the Elevated, cut across Greenwich and went down Tenth Street past Waverly Place. He crossed the street diagonally towards two blue globes that burned above a blue door in an areaway sunk four stone steps below the pavement. He elbowed the door open and entered a low-ceiled restaurant that had canals and gondolas painted on the walls. The blue lighting gave the faces of people a ghostly look.

Near the door was a cigarette showcase with a cash register alongside it and a man behind the cash register. The man had a mask-like face and a receding hair line. Donahue bought a package of cigarettes. Asked for a match. The man threw him a packet. The packet was blue.

Donahue went to a table, threw his hat and ulster on one chair, sat down in another.

"Scotch and seltzer."

He leaned back, put a cigarette between his lips, opened the blue packet. On the inside of the flap it said: *The Venetian Cellar—West Tenth Street.*

Nobody was eating now, but the menu was a large one specializing in Italian dishes. The waiter brought the drink.

"Where's the head waiter?" Donahue said.

The waiter looked at him blankly for half a moment, then turned and went off. He came back with a short fat man who had black marcelled hair, who carried a cigar horizontally at right angles to his uppermost vest button.

"Yes?"

"Will you sit down?"

"I'm sorry—"

"Only for a minute."

The fat man sat down.

Donahue leaned on his elbows and looked straight into the dark pool-like eyes.

Donahue said: "Do you know Larrimore?"

"Who?"

"A. B. Larrimore."

The fat man looked down at his fat white hands, turned a diamond ring round and round; looked up and moved his shoulders in the semblance of a shrug.

"No," he said. "No, I don't."

"He was here tonight," Donahue said. "He's a little shorter than I am, slim and well-built. Clean-shaven. Derby, blue overcoat, blue serge suit. He's about forty, I'd say. Black hair, but"—he touched the side of his head—"gray along here, quite gray. Distinguished looking man."

"He was in here?"

"Yeah. In here."

"Well, sure, he might have been. There was a lot of people here tonight. I wouldn't know. I'm not out here much, only if somebody asks for me. Like you. Who's Larrimore?"

"What I want to know is, what time did he leave here, and was he with anybody?"

The fat man sat back. "How do I know?"

"Was he with a man or a woman?"

The fat man made an impatient gesture. "I tell you, how do I know?"

"I tell you, he was here. Was he alone or—"

"Listen," broke in the fat man irritably. "I don't know who you're talking about. All right, he was here. Maybe he was. If you say he was here, all right, then he was here. But I don't remember. I can't remember every guy comes in here. Or every woman—"

"Or every woman," said Donahue.

"What?"

"Or every woman. You can't remember the woman he was with."

The fat man looked surprised. "What the hell are you talking about?" He scowled suddenly, heaved up. "Go on, you're crazy." He laughed and walked off.

Donahue got up and followed him. Tables were in the way. He

had to weave among them. He followed the fat man to the other side of the restaurant and the latter was not aware of this until he was thrusting aside the rose-colored curtains leading to another room. He turned and his cigar, that had been jutting out straight from his mouth, drooped; his jaw drooped; his eyelids drooped. He looked suddenly sinister with his fat white face and his black pool-like eyes.

"This is a private room," he said. "The door to the street is over that way."

"Oh, that's all right," Donahue said cheerfully. "I just want to find out what time that man left here. Be a good egg. I'm a good egg and strictly on the up and up. I'm not trying to crash this scatter and if you knew me better you'd know what a swell guy I really am."

"Are you trying to sell anything?"

"An idea. I'm trying to sell you the idea that it would be nice for you to play ring around the rosy with me."

The fat man started a leer. "You mean—nice for you."

"No. I mean"—Donahue nicked a thumb-nail against the man's uppermost vest button—"for you."

The fat man's face drooped more; he had jowls now, sagging like wet dough in the ghostly bluish light. His lower lip sagged, revealing the lower part of his lower teeth.

He said slowly, distinctly: "I don't know who you're talking about. I don't know you. Get out."

"You feel that way about it, eh?"

The fat man said nothing. He put his cigar carefully between his lips, rolled it around with thumb and forefinger and regarded Donahue with his drooping, sinister eyes.

Donahue saw one of the waiters come up and stand beside him. He turned and saw another standing behind him. He saw a third leaning against the wall. He whistled a few bars to himself. He saw a cuspidor, squinted one eye towards it and snapped his butt into it.

"Okey," he said.

He went swiftly back to his table, gathered up his hat and coat, put the hat on but not the coat and went directly out without looking at anyone. He walked long-legged to the next corner, swung left, stopped and put on his coat. He turned and peered around the corner.

He saw a man standing on the sidewalk looking at the twin blue lights. He knew the shape, the build, the round shoulders. He saw Monahan go down the steps and through the blue door.

He put his hands on his hips and bit off a sharp, caustic oath.

He heard heavy footsteps and pivoted. A patrolman came across the street, saying: "Why the hell all the hocus pocus?"

Donahue smiled, "Hello, Officer."

"Now let it go at that. What's the idea?"

"I thought someone was following me."

The patrolman snapped gum with his teeth and stood on wide-planted feet, his arms akimbo, nightstick dangling.

"On your way. Beat it."

Donahue said: "Sure," good-naturedly and strode off. He turned left into Christopher, went around the block and was again on Tenth Street. He slipped down into an areaway across from the twin blue lights. He looked at his strap-watch. It was ten past two. The street was deserted except for an occasional late-wandering drunk or a night-hawk taxicab.

Presently a man and a woman came out of the *Venetian Cellar.* They walked towards Hudson Street, stopping at intervals to embrace. Then a man came out putting on his coat. He staggered towards Sixth Avenue, singing. A man and a woman came out, the man supporting the woman; then two men; then two men and a quarrelsome girl.

A minute later the twin blue lights went out.

Donahue looked at his watch again. It was two-thirty. An Elevated train rumbled down Sixth Avenue. A taxi barged east with someone thumping a banjo. Silence fell again. And Donahue waited on.

At two-forty-five Donahue heard footsteps clicking from the direction of Sixth Avenue: woman's high-heels by the sound of them. He saw a woman wrapped in a dark fur coat pass beneath a street light. She walked rapidly, each heelfall distinct. She turned down into the *Venetian Cellar* areaway and disappeared through the blue door.

Donahue craned his neck. He was about to climb to the pavement when he saw the woman reappear, rising quietly from the areaway, walking only on the soles of her feet. She looked up and down the street, walked a matter of ten yards and slipped behind a stone stoop that hid her from sight of anyone entering or leaving the *Venetian Cellar.*

Donahue retreated deeper into the well of shadows, his eyes keen and watchful. From time to time he saw the vague blur of the woman's face peering around the corner of the stoop. There was no street light near her. He could not get even a general idea of what she looked like.

His attention was diverted suddenly by the banging open of the blue door across the street. He heard low, angry voices. Then suddenly he saw Monahan being rough-housed up the steps by a couple of men. They shoved him and he fell down, and then the fat man appeared and stood at the brink of the sidewalk.

"Now beat it," he said. "I've stood plenty of your lousy lip. You've got this place of mine wrong."

"You'll see, you'll see," Monahan threatened, rising.

"All right, I'll see. You got no business to come in my place and act wise. So scram."

Monahan brushed his coat with his hands and reset his hat. He shook his fist.

"Don't think a dago like you can get tough with me. I got friends at Police Headquarters. You can't get tough with me."

The fat man waved a hand. "Oh, go on and beat it, for cripes sake. You're just a loud noise. You asked for a slide to the pavement and you got it." He turned to the others. "Come on, boys."

They went down the stairs and through the blue door, banging it shut.

Monahan buttoned his coat, put a cigar in his mouth and stamped off.

Donahue thumbed his nose at Monahan's back and grinned with genuine satisfaction.

Chapter III

WHEN Monahan's irate footfalls had died in the direction of Sixth Avenue, Donahue saw the woman slip from the shadows and enter the blue door. In a little while he saw four men come out and head east. They were the waiters. He waited ten minutes, then climbed to the sidewalk, darted silently across the street and descended to the *Venetian Cellar* areaway.

His right hand slipped beneath his coat to settle on the butt of his automatic. His left hand closed over the door-knob and eased it as far as it would go. He turned it in the other direction and after a firm but gentle pressure towards himself he knew that the door was locked.

His lips formed a silent oath. He turned and climbed to the pavement and returned to the areaway across the street. The fall air was cold and he turned up his collar, kept his hands thrust in his pockets.

At a little past three he heard the blue door open. After a moment the woman and the fat man climbed to the sidewalk. The man had hat and overcoat on and a red cigar-end marked his face. The woman took his arm and they started walking rapidly towards Sixth Avenue.

Donahue let them get a good lead, then followed, hugging the shadows and the house walls. He followed them through Waverly Place into Grove Street. They crossed Grove at the subway entrance, crossed Sheridan Square towards a row of three taxies parked in front of a lunch-wagon.

Donahue stopped at the north side of the Square. He looked up and down West Fourth Street. It was wide here—and deserted. He saw the fat man and the woman get into a taxi and drive off. He waited until the taxi was out of sight and then drifted across the Square and entered the all-night lunchroom.

Monahan was sitting at the far end of the counter, drinking milk, eating pie and reading a newspaper. He did not look up. Donahue gave himself a half-smile and sat down near the door.

"Cup of black coffee," he said.

Monahan looked up. His eyes popped.

Donahue grinned. "Hello, Monahan."

"Hello, Donahue."

"Out late, aren't you?"

"Came out to get the air and a bite to eat."

He thought for a moment, wrinkling his forehead in perplexed indecision. Then he picked up the glass of milk, the pie and his paper, and came down next to Donahue. He leaned over, spoke out of the side of his mouth.

"What do you think of that kill, Donahue?"

"Huh?... Oh, that. Well, Monahan, my good friend, I really haven't thought about it."

"G' on!"

"Honor bright. I couldn't sleep so I came out to the flesh-pots. What do you think about it, Monahan?"

Monahan looked uncomfortable. He stabbed a chunk of pie. "I ain't thought much about it, either."

Donahue drank his cup of coffee, stood up and said: "Well, I'll be seeing you, Monahan."

He went out, climbed in a taxi and said: "Head east." When the taxi was under way, he leaned forward and thrust a dollar bill into the driver's hand.

"Duck south at the next block and let me off," he said. "Then duck around the streets for a few minutes or go where you like. There's a dumb bunny back there tailing me."

"Okey."

The taxi swung south into Cornelia Street. Donahue leaped out, slammed shut the door and bounded to the sidewalk. He had barely reached the shadows when a second taxi turned the corner. He saw Monahan in the back seat. He laughed to himself, watched the tail-light disappear and then walked back to Sheridan Square.

Five minutes later a taxi drew up and the driver got out. Donahue approached him.

"Buddy," he said, "I'll give you five dollars if you'll take me to the address where you took that fat man and the woman."

"Says you."

"Says I. I'm a private dick and I'm hard up for an address." He peeled a five dollar bill from a cordovan leather folder.

"Get in."

Donahue gave him the bill, entered the cab and sat back lighting a cigarette. The cab cut across town to Third Avenue and then headed north beneath the Elevated structure. At the corner of Fifteenth Street it pulled up and the driver turned around, jerking his thumb.

"Up that way, opposite Stuyvesant Square. Number two hundred and ——; it's a gray brick building, kind of narrow. You want me to wait here?"

Getting out, Donahue said: "No."

"That's swell by me."

Donahue watched him drive off, took a few drags at his cigarette, tossed it away and turned into East Fifteenth Street. Across the way Rutherford Street ran its two blocks north, flanking Stuyvesant Square on the west. The south side of East Fifteenth faces the park and is walled by substantial stone houses marking a bygone period. Some of them have been remodeled with new fronts and modern façades and hold forth as small apartment houses. Such a one was that in front of which Donahue paused.

The lobby was flush with the sidewalk, faced with two glass doors.

Donahue pushed one of them in and was confronted by a large wooden door with a shiny brass knob. On the wall at the right were built-in brass letterboxes and a row of ten brass buttons with names under them. The door was locked. Donahue studied the names intently. Then he went out, crossed the street and looked up at the front of the house. There were only two windows lighted, the shades drawn. The windows were on the third floor, at the right.

Donahue re-entered the lobby, drew a ring of keys from his pocket. He used four master keys and spent four minutes. The door eased open and he stepped into a wide, brown-carpeted hall. One little amber wall-light burned at the foot of a wide staircase with a broad banister. The stairs were carpeted, Donahue's footfalls muted as he climbed.

He listened at the head of the staircase, turned, walked along the wall of the second floor corridor and started up a second staircase. On each floor burned a single amber light, sufficient to light one's way, but overlooking many shadows. Donahue climbed stealthily, leaving his hand off the banister because banisters invariably creak.

On the third floor he stopped, getting his bearings. At the front of the hall was a window. At either side, an apartment. There was a sliver of light beneath the door on the left. Donahue slid towards it and listened. He caught the undertones of a voice, and though he could not distinguish a word he recognized the undertones. The fat man....

He straightened suddenly and stepped quickly into the corner of the hall. The door opened and the fat man came out putting on his hat. The woman came with him. She had red hair and looked to be in her thirties, and she had beauty of a sort.

"All right, Tony...."

"Sh!" the fat man whispered. "Everything'll be jake. Just keep a stiff lip, Beryl."

She went with him down the hall towards the stairs, leaving her door wide open. Donahue crept along the wall, entered the apartment. He was in a comfortable living-room. Back of it was an open bedroom. He slipped into the bedroom.

In another minute the woman came in, closed the corridor door, pushed fingers through her hair. She stood in the center of the living-room, holding her hands to her head, staring haggard-eyed at the floor.

Donahue appeared and said: "Good morning, Beryl."

"Oh!"

She started, tearing her hands from her head, making fists that she pressed to her thighs, and stood suddenly rigid and white-faced, her eyes wide.

Donahue scaled his hat onto a divan, sat down with his overcoat open and flaring around his neck.

"Sit down, Beryl," he said.

"How—how—"

"Go on, be a good scout, sit down."

"Oh, my ——! My ——!"

He pulled out pouch and pipe, ran the bowl into the pouch, packed with his second finger. The woman kept staring at him while she moved, felt for a chair, gripped its back and let herself down slowly. Her face had drained so of color that her rouged lips looked like a vivid red gash. She began striking her fist on a knee slowly.

"What do you want, what do you want?" Donahue reached towards an end table for a match. He glanced at the cabinet photo of a girl. The girl was young, reminiscent of the woman in the room. Donahue lit up.

He said: "When you left Tony's last night with Larrimore, what happened?"

"I wasn't at Tony's last night," she said huskily.

"No?"

"No. I wasn't at Tony's."

Donahue smiled. "Why, when you came to Tony's alone at about three this morning—why did you come right out and hide behind that stoop?"

"I didn't."

"And why, after a man was thrown out, did you go back in?"

She said, hoarsely: "You seem to get around, don't you?"

"I'm a great little getter-around, Beryl. And I'm a great guy, too, once you get to know me. If you knew me better you wouldn't try to hand me a line. I don't even nibble, let alone swallow the hook."

Color was coming back to her face. She seemed to have got over the first shock and now a desperate, level look was in her eyes.

"I don't know what you're talking about," she said. "My actions are my own business. Who is this Larrimore you're talking about?"

"Now, Beryl...." Donahue got up and stood looking down at her with eyes in which mockery danced lightly.

"Listen, you," she said, warmly. "What business have you here? Who are you?" She stood up, trembling, her eyes burning. "You have no right here. If you don't get out I'll call the police and have you put out!"

Donahue chuckled, shook his head. "No, you wouldn't call the police."

"Wouldn't I?" Her chin rose, her nostrils quivered. "You think I wouldn't?"

"I think you wouldn't."

"You're a pretty wise guy, aren't you?"

"Pretty wise."

"Well, we'll see how good your bluff is!"

She swept past him, crossed the room to an open secretary where a telephone stood, sat down, put her left hand on the telephone. Donahue took two fast strides, caught her right hand as it was drawing a small automatic from a pigeon-hole. She cried out and heaved up, tussling with him. He twisted her wrist once.

"Not in this day and age," he said, as the gun fell to the floor.

She stood panting before him, her throat pulsing, her breast convulsing, a fierce, haunted look in her eyes.

"I knew you wouldn't call the police," he said.

"Get out!" she choked. "You have no right here. For —— sake get out and leave me alone!"

He released her, kicked the little gun under the secretary. A v-shaped crease was between his brows, his brown eyes were steady and searching, his face suddenly somber and serious.

"You're in a tough spot, sister, and don't think you aren't. And don't try to play around me. I don't like it. There's been a lot of monkeyshines between the *Venetian Cellar* and this place tonight."

"If you're a cop, show your shield. If you aren't, then get out."

"I'm without benefit of shield, sister, but that cuts no ice with me. And don't think it's going to cut any with you. You're a liar, and you know it, and I'll tell you right now that I'm a swell guy ordinarily and a mean baby if anybody, jane or guy, tries to pull a rod on me. Tuck that under your belt and grow up and be your age."

He spoke crisply, bluntly, without malice or emotion, stating facts simply and pointedly.

She defied him. "I don't know what you're talking about. You have no right here."

"All right, smarty, take that telephone and call the cops and see if you have a better right to be here or in jail. There's been murder done, little girl, and this man's town still looks on murder with disfavor, despite a lot of ballyhoo to the contrary."

"Murder! Murder!" she cried. "What—what do I know about murder?"

"Nothing. Oh, nothing. Maybe you call the death of Larrimore just an act of God."

"Death of…. I—why, my ——! I haven't murdered anybody! I haven't—Oh. For —— sake, I haven't killed anybody. No! No!"

She held out her hands and fell backward, shaking her head. Her calves struck the low divan and she dropped to it.

"And death's not enough, darling, to kill a hot clue," Donahue muttered. "Larrimore was murdered somewhere between the *Venetian Cellar* and his hotel—"

"No! No! Oh, no!"

"You were with him in the *Venetian Cellar*. You left with him. You left the *Venetian Cellar* with him and he was shot. He was shot and got to his hotel—and he died. He died and by —— he died for something—and you know! You know why he died. You know because—"

"You're a liar—a liar!" she broke in. "What do you think you can do? You can't come here and accuse me! Who do you think you are? I—"

"Never mind who I think I am. I've got that fat boy's ticket and I've got yours. And never mind what right I have to be here. I'm here and here, by cripes, I'll stay! Till you fork over, little one. It's my business—and I'm a business man."

Her voice throbbed but became at the same time one-toned and incisive—"I was with—with a man named Larrimore, was I? Can you prove it? No. Nobody can. Because I went to the *Venetian Cellar* and backed out because they were arguing with some pest…. What's that to you? I went there because a friend there is a good friend of mine. And that's none of your business, either. You handed me a jolt when I first saw you here. You handed me a jolt when you mentioned murder. It's an ugly word. But that's all there is to it. Go on. Run along. I'm getting tired of you already."

"You're like that lizard called the chameleon," Donahue said. "You change color quickly—but underneath you don't. You can't bluff me."

He toed the little gun from beneath the secretary, picked it up. It was a .25 Webley, four-and-a-half inches overall. It was fully loaded. Donahue rubbed the muzzle with his handkerchief.

"Never been used, eh?"

She said nothing.

"Oh," Donahue said, shrugging, "I don't think you killed Larrimore. But you know who did."

"I don't! I tell you I don't know what you're talking about!" She jumped up. "For the love o' —— get out—before I do something— before I scream!"

"Don't scream, Beryl," said the fat man from the door. "I'll take care of this buttinsky."

Donahue wheeled about.

The fat man stood in the open door holding a gun in his hand and looking very sinister with his drooping eyelids.

Chapter IV

DONAHUE had taken the clip from the Webley, ejected a cartridge from the chamber. He threw the lot on the desk and when he looked at the fat man again the latter had come in and closed the door.

The woman stood digging her fingernails into her palms, biting her lips to silence, looking as if she were torn between two diverging lines of thought.

"I told you to get out of one place tonight," the fat man said in a low, grinding voice.

"Tony—"

"Shut up, Beryl. This guy's pal is standing over on the corner of Rutherford. I saw him before I went out in the lobby, and stayed down there watching. I didn't know this egg was up here—until I heard him just now."

Donahue looked puzzled. He said: "What are you yapping about? I've got no pal—"

"You're just about the damnedest liar I ever ran across. What kind of a line did he hand you, Beryl?"

"Oh—oh, a lot of nonsense about a man named Larrimore."

"That's what he did me too."

"Run him out, Tony. He's been talking about Larrimore being murdered and he's trying to charge me with being mixed up in it."

"I'll show him," the fat man said. "I'll show you. I've got a mind to blow your brains out, you lousy pest!"

"Tony!"

"Nah, don't worry, baby—I won't. But I've got a friend right in this neighborhood who's on the cops. I'll show this bum if he can bust around here the way he does. He's a heel, Beryl—a dirty, rotten gunman, with his pal across the street. I'll get him pinched. Keep your hands up, bright boy."

The fat man, who looked genuinely angry and indignant, backed to the telephone, kept his gun trained on Donahue, and called a number.

"Hello—hello.... This is Tony—you know.... Well, I'm sorry to get you up, Mike, but listen, do me a favor. There's a hot shot up here at my girl friend's, you know—in Fifteenth Street.... Yeah, that's the place. He's heeled but I've got him covered, and he's got a pal hanging across the street.... Do me a favor and pick the pal up and then come here and pick up this guy.... Well, he's got an idea in his nut that me and Beryl bumped some guy off.... Yeah, imagine that!... Will you?... Thanks a lot, old pal."

He hung up. "Well, big boy, what do you think of that?"

"Swell, for the time being. But what do you think you're going to get out of it?"

"The satisfaction of seeing you get a rough deal from the cops."

Donahue looked from the fat man to the girl. Her lips were tight, she was grinding the bent knuckles of one hand into the palm of the other. The fat man looked formidable, lowering, his black fedora pulled down to his thick eyebrows.

"So you want to turn me over to the cops," Donahue said. "That's funny, because I like cops."

He went on talking, rambling aimlessly, wisecracking and chiding the fat man and the woman. He appeared cheerful and nonchalant, but deep in his hard brown eyes two tiny flames burned steadily, warily—and in the set of his neck was tension.

"Oh, shut up, shut up!" cried the woman, a note of hysteria in her voice.

"You wouldn't turn me over to the cops," Donahue said, lying his way on and on. "I know you two. I know you from cradles onward. The both of you. I know too much about you. You wouldn't be fools enough to throw me to the cops. What I know about you, Beryl, would fill a book. And you, Tony, you moon-faced spaghetti-bender. I don't care if you do know a dick named Mike so-and-so."

"Pipe down!" growled the fat man.

"Not on your natural, kid. You can't make me pipe down. You're yellow, you beef-faced jerk. You wouldn't dare use that rod. You carry it for show. The only chance I'd have of getting plugged by you would be if the gun went off accidentally. You're just a punk."

"Damn you, shut up!"

"Make me."

The fat man came forward, his eyes muggy, his lip curling.

"I tell you, shut up!" he choked.

The woman beat her temples with her fists and cried:

"Oh, ——!..." She threw herself violently on to the divan, picked up a pillow, punched it, threw it down again, clawed at her hair and rose. "For —— sake, Tony—"

"Be quiet, Beryl."

"Tony—"

"Shut up!"

She swallowed hard.

A buzzer sounded.

"Get that, Beryl," Tony said.

She went numbly across the room towards the door, beside which was an ivory push-button. She arched her back, pressed the button. Then suddenly she choked and slumped to the floor, rolled over and lay in a dead faint.

"Don't worry about her," the fat man said.

Presently there was a knock on the door.

"Come in," the fat man said.

The door swung open. A neat, tall man stood there with his hands in his pockets, chewing on a cigar, half-smiling.

"You look funny with that gun, Tony."

"Come in, Mike. And collar this bird."

"I picked up a couple of harness bulls on Lexington and we've got the other guy downstairs. What's it all about, Tony? Oh—oh, Beryl pass out?"

"Can you blame her, with this guy picking on us?"

The fat man talked at length, and the other listened and rolled his cigar back and forth and kept looking from Tony to Donahue with polite interest.

"All right, Tony," he said, "I'll take him over to the precinct."

"Yeah?" said Donahue. "Well, if you take me, brother, you'll take him too."

"Now don't give me any lip. Get your hat and come along."

The fat man said: "See if he's heeled, Mike."

"Ain't he had his rod out yet?"

Donahue said: "When I pull a rod, I mean it. Not like this guy here."

"Stick that in his back, Tony, while I take it. This guy sure acts tough. Keep your hands way up, brother."

He removed Donahue's gun from its armpit holster, hefted it and unlocked the safety in a kid-gloved hand.

"Get Beryl too, Tony," he said. "Then you better come around to the precinct and we'll thrash this thing out. On your way, you," he said to Donahue.

Donahue scowled at the fat man. "Don't forget what your boy friend just said."

"Get," said the laconic boy friend.

Donahue jabbed him with a contemptuous look, then strode out of the room and down the corridor.

"Hey, take it easy."

Donahue stopped short at the head of the staircase and spun around. "Listen; use your head. You're not getting anywhere by hauling me over the coals. I'm a right guy, copper." He began gesturing with his hat.

"Get down them stairs."

"On the up and up now, give me a break. You're just wasting your time by dragging me over. No kidding. I tell you, I'm strictly kosher. Tony's the guy you want. The fat boy and the jane. Not me." He tapped the man's chest with a forefinger. The man stiffened. "Listen, copper. Honest. Don't arrest me. Please. I ask you in a nice way. And don't press that gat in my stomach that way."

He winced and put his hand on barrel of the gun. The gun pressed harder, the men's eyes locked.

"You fool, take your hand off that gun or I'll let you have a bellyful!"

Donahue's forefinger shot forward almost imperceptibly, closing the safety. At the same time he gripped the gun hard and heaved it and the man's hand outward and upward, his finger tight on the safety.

The man snarled in his throat, tussled. Donahue hit him, with a hard short left to the point of the jaw and both went tumbling down the stairs. They landed sprawling at the bottom.

"You will, will you?" rasped Donahue. "You will try to fake you're a cop! What a laugh you hand me!"

"Let go this rod!"

They heaved up, wheeled around, crashed against the wall. Donahue cut loose with his left again. The blow caught the man on the jaw and slammed his head against the wall. He cursed and Donahue planted a hard left in his stomach, followed with another to the jaw and a third between the eyes.

By sheer force he tore his gun from the man's hand, flattened him against the wall with the gun jammed against his stomach. With lightning-like speed he took the man's own gun, a .45, from its armpit-holster, released the safety.

"Now get downstairs," he said.

The man hesitated.

Donahue clouted him with one of the guns and booted him along. People in the house were stirring. Donahue drove the man down to the main hall and kept prodding him towards the lobby. He made him open the inner door. He planted him against the wall of the lobby with his two guns.

"Now, you poor dumb heel," he rasped, "what about the other guy standing across the street?"

"Hell! Go out and find out!"

"Listen, you! So help me living—!"

"It was a stall. There wasn't any guy out there. I didn't see any. It was just a stall. I was fooling you."

"It was, eh?"

"Yeah."

"Well, pipe this, sweetheart. I don't fall for that. I want it straight."

"I told you straight."

Donahue cracked him across the jaw with a gun-barrel. "Did you?" he said, all playfulness gone from his manner. "Did you? No, you didn't, you louse! No, you didn't!"

The man crouched against the wall, his teeth drawing blood to his lips, murder and hatred and fear toiling in his eyes. He did not look so neat now, nor was he as laconic as he had been.

Sounds increased in the house. There were voices in the corridors and a bell ringing somewhere.

"Get it out," grated Donahue. "Give it to me straight."

Blood dripped from the man's cheek, from the lips he had bitten.

The inner door whipped open and a group of men in bathrobes bunched there. Before Donahue could say a word they sailed upon him.

"Here—here!" Donahue snapped. "Let go! I'm—"

From the hall yelled the fat man: "Get him! He tried to waylay me in the hall! The two of them!"

The man who had been laconic—and wasn't now—ducked out through the swing doors. The fat man barged through and tore after him.

"You damned fools, let go!" roared Donahue.

Anger in him became fury. Fury gave him wild, devastating strength and cyclonic speed. He tossed one man clear over his head, floored another with a swung gun, kicked another, drove a fourth reeling back into the hall. He still had the two guns. He gripped them hard. He kicked open a swing door and poised outside, hefting his guns.

Chapter V

THE top of his hat was crushed in. The wind caught his baggy coat and ballooned it, flapped his upturned collar. He saw the fat man and the other running side by side; saw the latter receive the fat man's gun. Beyond, near Third Avenue, was a parked car, with no tail-light. The fat man and the other ran across the street towards it.

Because the men in the lobby were picking themselves up and gathering for a new attack, Donahue ran out to the sidewalk and slid along the house-fronts. He saw the fat man and his boy friend reach the parked car. They looked back. Donahue was hiding in the shadow of a façade. His hands were hard on the guns.

He heard the roar of the motor as the fat man and the other climbed in. Donahue knelt down on one knee, raised his left arm, laid the gun in his right hand across the crook of his elbow, aimed. Three times the black muzzle spewed jets of flame, and the echoes banged violently in the street.

He saw the car start to limp off. He had ruined the rear left tire. Still kneeling, still aiming, he fired again—broke an unlighted spotlight attached to the left of the windshield. The car turned north on Third Avenue and Donahue broke into a long-legged, bounding run. He saw it bouncing up the avenue on its flat tire, swinging among the Elevated pillars. Donahue knelt between the street-car tracks, took aim again over his left arm, cut loose with the remaining three shots in his gun. He blew out the right rear tire, switched the .45 to his right hand and raced up the sidewalk.

He was half a block from the car when it swung east into Eighteenth Street. He stopped short, raised the .45 and put five shots through the long hood. He piled in a doorway as a half dozen jets of flame issued from the tonneau; slipped a fresh clip into his own gun, switched it to his right hand, gripped the .45 in his left and started off again.

Turning the corner, he saw the car half-way down Eighteenth Street. But he didn't hear its motor, and he saw men piling from its door: four men. He let fly with a shot from his left hand, and the men pounded for the sidewalk. One of them didn't reach it; he plunged headlong into the gutter. Donahue flattened against a house as one gun spoke twice and two bullets whistled past and shattered a window.

The neighborhood crackled with the dying echoes of gunshots. Somewhere far distant a police whistle shrilled. Donahue heard the pound of running feet again and saw three men racing towards First Avenue. He left the house wall and broke into a run. He had gone but a dozen steps when he saw gun flashes at the end of the street. He stopped in his tracks, saw the darting figures of three men; saw other figures—cops, uniformed cops.

He went on at a fast walk until he came to the form of the man in the gutter. He bent down. The man was on his face. Donahue turned him over. It was the man who had been laconic. He was dead, his gun frozen in his hand—the gun the fat man had passed him in Fifteenth Street.

Donahue looked up. Over on First Avenue the guns were still banging. Donahue shoved his guns in his pockets and started off on the run. He reached the intersection and looked north. He saw two cops crouched behind a truck on the west side of the street. They were firing across towards the opposite sidewalk, and jets of flame spat from a dark doorway, bullets rang in the metal of the truck.

A taxicab was parked nearby, its driver crouching in a doorway. Feet hammered up the avenue and two more cops came on the run, guns drawn. A few windows grated open but no lights appeared. Donahue leaned at the corner and watched the exchange of shots across the street. The two running cops slowed down, held their guns out, advanced cautiously. In a brief lull they broke into a run and joined the two behind the truck. The firing opened again.

The taxi driver in the doorway said: "Jeeze, those guys mean business!"

"Yeah," said Donahue.

Stray shots broke windows. Glass rained down, wood splintered, brick chipped off.

A siren moaned up the avenue and the headlights of a police car rushed through the darkness. It pulled up at the northwest corner of Fifteenth Street. Uniformed men jumped off, and two carried sub-machine guns, one carried a riot gun. The men behind the truck yelled instructions. The men from the riot car got a line on the doorway from which the flame issued and two sub-machine guns began to hammer. One kept hammering while the man with the other ran up to join the men behind the truck. Then it opened fire, its mad stutter raising unholy bedlam in the street.

Cops began to appear from all directions. Another police car arrived. People appeared warily, got bolder. Soon a crowd was formed, and the policemen had to drive them back. Nightsticks waved, commands were harsh and urgent. The machine-guns poured stream after stream of lead into the doorway. A powerful searchlight was thrown on the doorway. It revealed brick pockmarked with bullets, glass shattered, wood splintered and shining in long tears. And mixed with the bedlam of the guns were the cries and exclamations of women, the excited shouting of policemen, the arrival of more cars and the wailing of sirens.

A cop reported to a sergeant within earshot of Donahue: "A guy dead in the gutter up Eighteenth—and a car with two flats and a busted hood."

"Go up there and watch it. Anybody in the car?"

"No."

"All right, go up there."

Donahue lit a cigarette, turned and walked away. He pushed through the crowd, reached the fringe of it and headed south. The wind blew sparks from his cigarette, and there was a brown grim look about his mouth. He reached Fifteenth Street, turned east, crossed Second Avenue on the south side of the street.

He could see that many of the windows were lighted now in the small apartment house. He saw a couple of men out front. He saw a policeman twirling his stick and listening, and then he saw Monahan. He did not slow down. He kept right on walking until he reached the group and then he stopped. He stopped and he eyed Monahan with a withering hard look.

"Hello, Monahan," he said dully.

One of the men in the doorway said: "That's the man!"

The cop wheeled, gripped his stick hard. "Hey, you!"

Donahue overlooked him. He kept looking at Monahan. His face was stony, his eyes cutting, and there was a bitter twist to his mouth. He looked angry—angry and filled with loathing.

"So you did tail me after all, Monahan," he said.

"Now be reasonable, Donahue—"

"Be reasonable your sweet aunt's eye! And just like you, you went and balled up the whole shooting match. You copied every move I made, you dirty poacher. So it was you was hiding out here. Why didn't you give me a hand when there was action?"

"Jeeze, Donahue, I was in that car—"

"You were in that car too, I suppose, when you saw me look at that stiff in the street. But you didn't come out. You thought there might be more fireworks. You let me go and then you sneaked back here to try to steal a march on me. A poacher, Monahan—that's you all over your dirty face."

"Now look here, jazzbo," the cop broke in.

"And you," Donahue snapped. "I don't like that word jazzbo from any harness bull. Keep your jaw out of this."

"He was the man that struck us," repeated the man in the doorway.

Donahue looked up at him. "Oh, go inside and put your pants on."

"Did you bust these people?" snarled the cop.

"Sure I did. I had a red-hot in my hands and they jumped me. The result of that is all the banging you hear up on Eighteenth Street. Now don't take yourself serious, officer. I was on a hot tail. I had it sewed up, only this thick mick Monahan got his fingers in the pie. When the cops up on Eighteenth Street finish with the wipers they're after they won't know what all the shooting's about. I had it sewed up—get me? Sewed up! Until this"—he looked at Monahan—"until this— Oh, what the hell's the use!"

"Hell, Donahue," Monahan complained, "don't blame me. I was only trying to do my duty—"

"Duty? Why, you two-faced so-and-so, you were after the same thing I was. A pinch, to make a reputation and to get a probable reward. Don't tell any fairy stories, Monahan. It doesn't fit you at all."

The cop poked him with his nightstick. "Now cut out the arguing. What I want to know is, what was all this about? Never mind any beefing. Just spring a little information. We're trying to find out where the hell in this place the trouble started."

Donahue knocked the nightstick aside, "Don't get free with that, copper. Not on me. I'm touchy."

Monahan was nervous. "Donahue, be reasonable. We can all share—"

Donahue, his nerves raw, his temper at its peak, took one step and made a furious swing at Monahan. Monahan ducked so fast that he fell down. The cop gripped Donahue and spun him around.

"One more break like that, Donahue, and I'll crown you!"

"I never saw," Monahan said, "such a guy!"

Donahue glared at the cop. "Call Headquarters," he said. "Tell Detective-Sergeant Kelly McPard to come over."

"Why?"

Donahue said: "Grab hold of that guy Monahan and hold him!"

"Look here, Donahue!" Monahan cried.

"Grab him!" Donahue shouted.

The cop cursed and grabbed Monahan, saying: "I didn't like your story in the first place!"

They went inside to an apartment on the first floor. Monahan couldn't speak. He was flabbergasted. Far away the sounds of shooting were beginning to diminish. Baffled and angry, the cop used a telephone. He asked for Kelly McPard. Kelly McPard was over at the morgue. He called the morgue.

"Sergeant McPard?... This is Patrolman Swansen."

While he spoke Donahue looked out into the corridor. He stepped out casually, moved towards the staircase, then began climbing. When he reached the first landing he looked down. Then he went on, swiftly—climbed the next staircase two steps at a time. Listened again. Then he went down the corridor and stopped before the door at the left. He tried the knob cautiously. The door was locked. He looked around. Halfway down the hall a door stood open, the occupant of the apartment was downstairs.

Donahue stepped back, gathered his strength and rushed his shoulder against the door. He smashed the lock and burst into the living-room.

Beryl was standing in the middle of the room, holding the .25 Webley. It barked as Donahue lunged, holding out his left hand. The bullet pierced his hand, was deflected, and glanced off his cheek, leaving a silver-like streak. He crashed into the woman, grabbing her gun hand. A second and third shot thudded into the floor. He ripped the gun from her hand with his bloody left hand. He grabbed her with his right and hauled her out of the room, down the hall, into the vacated apartment. He slammed the door, locked it, turned on her and backed her across the room. He set her down in an overstuffed chair.

He took out a handkerchief and wrapped it around his wounded hand. He picked up the telephone and called the *City Press*. He asked for Libbey. He waited half a minute.

"Libbey?... This is Donny, you old soak. Hang on and get your pencil poised. I've got a red-hot here. Hang on."

He set the phone down on the oblong library table. He pulled a chair up to it. He looked at the woman.

"Sit down there," he said.

Her eyes looked green, glazed, murderous. Her red hair stood on end. She didn't move. Donahue pulled her up and shoved her into the chair, pushed it closer to the table so that she faced the telephone. Then he went around to the other side of the table, sat down on another chair and drew out both guns.

"Get it out," he said. "As I came in the door you fired and wounded me in the hand. I grabbed you and took the gun away from you."

She began to laugh hysterically, in a cracked, mad voice.

"You fool—you fool! I took poison—just before you came. I saw the knob turning. I took poison. A double overdose of veronal. Laugh that off! In a few minutes I'll be out of all this. I'll never burn, damn you!"

She seemed not to notice the telephone. She stared at Donahue with green burning hatred.

Donahue spoke in a low whisper. "You took the easy way out, but I can make it harder." He moved his guns. "I can make it messy and harder—with these."

Her eyes widened, staring at the black muzzles.

"You're a killer, Beryl. I can see it in your eyes. You killed Larrimore."

"In a few minutes—"

"I can still cut the time short with—these."

The whites of her eyes shone. Suddenly she screamed. "Yes, I killed Larrimore! I killed him—killed him—killed him!"

"You killed him."

"I said I killed him!" she screamed. "Yes, and meant to. What does it mean now? I fooled you. I'll not burn. Larrimore thought he was smart—smart. And I—showed him."

"Why? What did he do?"

"You mean what was he trying to do! The snooper. I put him on the spot."

"Why?"

Down below there were shouts and men running around, yelling up and down the stairways, trying doors.

Donahue said: "Tony and the rest just got smoked out. You heard the shooting. The cops got them."

"Tony!" she cried, with bitter scorn. "He ran out on me. I asked him to stay—pleaded with him. The lousy bum had to go down the stairs. He said he would be back. He didn't come back. And he left without paying me."

"Paying you?"

"Yes, you fool! Do you think I would have shot Larrimore for love? I was paid. You never heard of a jane yet who got a guy on the spot, did you? Well, you're hearing one now!"

She picked up a book and flung it on the floor.

"Larrimore was just a nosy newspaperman," she rattled on. "He got some dope and he tailed it down. Tony, the bum, was a pay-off man for that vice ring the cops have been trying to run down. Larrimore began to nose around the *Venetian Cellar*. He had brains, that guy. It was tough I had to smoke him—but the dough looked good."

Men were in the hall outside now.

Donahue urged: "Keep it up, keep it up."

"What will you get out of it? I can feel the heart now.... So this guy Larrimore hangs around Tony's for a few nights. But Tony didn't know who he was then. Larrimore was getting the lay of the land all the time. Every night he was there he picked up one of Tony's janes. He never picked the same one twice. After the janes began to compare notes it comes out that Larrimore would do nothing but take them to swell night-clubs and then send them away in a taxi. He always called himself Jack. He used to get them tight and then send them away so drunk they couldn't remember what they'd said.

"Tony began to get worried. So then one little dame comes back after one of those sessions with a stroke of conscience. She used to be a friend of Magistrate Paglioni—"

"Who?"

"The boss of the vice ring. Magistrate Paglioni. Or he was a magistrate till last month. He resigned because the vice ring takes most of his time and there's more money in it. He lives in class now.

"This little dame says she can't remember whether she bragged about her playmate days with Paglioni, but she thought she did. She said Larrimore got her pretty drunk. But she did remember—she did remember that some guy slapped Larrimore on the back in one of those night-clubs and called him—Larrimore.

"Tony got a line on him. Get it? Larrimore, the newspaperman. The guy that's been exposing things for the last year. Tony went to the boss. Paglioni went crazy—almost. I'll tell it. Didn't Paglioni give me the air once? I'll tell it. Paglioni tells Tony to get rid of Larrimore.

"So I'm called in. How do you like that? I'm called in and Tony says it's worth five thousand to bump off Larrimore. I angled so that Larrimore picked me up. He picked me up in Tony's."

Fists pounded on the door.

"Keep going," Donahue said.

"We hung around and drank and then he said we should go somewhere else. To a ritzy place. I said sure. See, he never figured there would be any danger from a jane. He never figured that I packed a rod. I had it, baby, in my purse. We had the cab all ready. The guy who came in and took you out before—he drove it. It was parked outside, waiting.

"Larrimore and I got in and we drove off. We went over to Third Avenue and started north. I was a little tight and nervous, because I hadn't bumped off a guy in a year and I was using a new gun. I heard an Elevated train coming up. I thought quick. I told Larrimore I would like some bourbon and pointed to a door where I said he could get some. Mike pulled up to the curb.

"Larrimore backed out, but he was suspicious. He looked it anyhow. He stood on the curb as the Elevated roared by overhead and then I let him have it. He dropped like a log. I was sure I'd finished him. I told Mike to drive off."

Donahue heard the fists pounding at the door. He heard a key grating and withdrawn. But he was transfixed by the woman. Age had crept upon her. She looked haggard and vicious and dissipated. She was no longer the superb actress she had been earlier in the morning. Donahue, who had seen crime in its many strata, looked upon a gunwoman for the first time.

"Open this door or I'll break it down!"

Green-eyed, the woman clutched at her breast. "Say, let's have a gun. Let me blow those cops apart when they break in. Give me a break—before—I go."

Donahue, who had a stomach for nasty sights, shuddered and began to wear a sickly look. Blindly, the woman flung herself across the desk, tried to grab one of his guns. He had no difficulty preventing her. She whimpered and lay on the table.

Donahue pocketed his guns, rose, picked up the telephone. "Hello, Libbey.... The name? Downstairs on the door it says Miss Beryl Mercine.... No, not mercy—M-e-r-c-i-n-e.... That's right.... She's lying on the desk now, dead, I believe.... She says veronal. I wouldn't know.... Will that make the daylight editions?... Just, eh? Good.... Oh, that noise you hear is a hot-headed cop about to break in.... Now remember, sweetheart, the Interstate Detective Agency nabbed this case, with Donahue, if you please, to be credited. Don't by any chance slip in any such name as Monahan— Just a minute, Libbey. Hang on."

The door had burst inward. The patrolman loomed there with his gun drawn. A man in plain-clothes held a gun. Behind them, looking over their heads, was rosy-cheeked Kelly McPard, and farther back,

Monahan.

The patrolman stamped in, red-faced, angry. "What the hell's the idea? I've been looking all over this dump for you!"

Monahan yapped: "It was a trick! See! He's got a woman!"

Kelly McPard came in, wearing his fixed cherubic smile. He crossed to the woman, took hold of her hair, lifted her head, looked at her face and let the head down again. Then he looked at Donahue, who was sitting on the desk, holding the phone in both hands and dangling one foot.

"Well, well, Donny, everybody is mad at you," he said. "I see your hand is all messed up. Tsk! Tsk! What's all the noise, and who's the woman?"

"Beryl Mercine, who murdered one A. B. Larrimore and then died by her own hand."

Kelly McPard almost lost his smile. But not quite. "I feel downhearted, Donny. I'm just after finding a woman's fingerprints on that cigarette case I picked up, you remember. But it was a woman who was supposed to be out in Akron now. Bernice Marks. Also Barbara Markall. Also"—he nodded towards the woman on the desk—"this woman. Good, good work, Donny."

"But, Sarge," said the patrolman, "he went and—"

"And," broke in Monahan, "he said I was mixed up in it. I want an apology!"

Wearily, Donahue spoke into the telephone. "Libbey... Say that Detective-Sergeant Kelly McPard was on the scene ten minutes after I was shot by the woman. He took full command in a very aggressive and thorough manner.... That's right. And also—also, Libbey, mention Monahan's name.... Yeah, good old Monahan. Mention the fact that I saved Monahan from being taken for a ride. He was already in the car. I shot the gunmen smack out of the car. Monahan has just asked me to apologize. I hereby apologize."

Kelly McPard laughed.

Monahan said: "I'm going. I see I can't depend on any of my friends any more." He glared at McPard.

McPard said nothing, only winked at Monahan good-naturedly, and Monahan, bristling at the wink, turned and stamped out.

Donahue said: "Monahan... on the way down the stairs, Monahan, please fall and break your neck."

Shake-Up

*"Tough Dick" Donahue
objects to having his dates
murdered and doesn't care
who pulls the strings.*

Chapter I

DONAHUE went down four steps into the shadow ridden areaway, turned left and stopped before a wrought-iron gate. He pressed a button, stood humming *Sweet and Lovely* while drawing off yellow pigskins.

An inner door opened. A girl came and pressed her face to the wrought-iron bars and Donahue, saying: "Greetings, Carmen," snapped her familiarly under the chin.

"Oh, it ees *you*, señor!"

The bolt clanged as it was thrown back. The door swung inward and Donahue followed it, a rangy tall man in a camel's hair topcoat and a brown Homburg.

"You have been away a long time, señor."

"Been slumming in the Village for weeks.... Let me." He swung the heavy gate shut, slammed home the bolt, flicked a kiss off the girl's cheek and laughed good-humoredly when she chided him. They went into the hall way, closed the inner door, and Donahue gave her his hat and topcoat.

"Listen, beautiful," he said. "A lady'll be here tonight. She'll ask for me."

"*Si*, señor."

The Spanish atmosphere ended there. Going down the corridor and through a swing-door into a small luxurious bar, the scene was made Levantine by the barman, who swung a large nose towards Donahue and grinned, waved.

"Donny, as I live and breathe!"

Donahue hooked a heel on the polished rail and plucked a potato chip from a silver bowl. "Martini—dry, Maxie."

"So where you been—where you been?"

"Oh, hither and yon.... Hello, Walter. How's the kid?"

Walter Nass, the proprietor of the place, came across past a large hors d' oeuvres table, gripped Donahue's right hand with his right and felt Donahue's biceps with his left.

He smiled. "Keeping fit, huhn, Donny?"

Donahue nodded past Nass's square shoulder. "That Klay?"

"Yeah."

Donahue turned back to the bar, planted elbows on it and lifted his Martini without taking an elbow off the bar. He drank and then suddenly turned and said: "I thought Klay was over on the West Side."

Walter Nass shrugged, lifted his well-packed face and blew out a horizontal streamer of smoke. He changed the subject, saying: "Eating tonight or just on the way through?"

"I'll want a table in one of your private rooms. There'll be a jane along later.... I thought Klay was over on the West Side?"

Walter Nass shrugged. "What am I going to do about that?"

He turned and walked towards the headwaiter, who was beckoning from the dining-room entrance. Donahue turned to look after Nass, and Klay, eating at one of the bar tables against the back wall, looked up and waved his fork. Donahue moved his chin upward in

acknowledgment, turned back to the bar and ordered another Martini.

Klay got up and came over, carrying his napkin with him and rubbing his chin free of salad oil. He wore his clothes with a theatrical elegance, carried himself erect. His cornsilk hair was brushed back in a pompadour. His face had been shaven very closely and powdered profusely, so that now it had a gray-white look. His eyes were mouse-colored, flat, and when he smiled he showed false upper teeth that made his face masklike.

"Imagine meeting you here, Donahue," he drawled in a slow crusty voice.

"That calls for no imagination, Klay."

"I've just started the meat course. Join me?"

"No, thanks."

Klay's eyelashes were almost white. "What's going on at the District Attorney's office these days?" he asked.

Donahue half-turned and looked over his cocktail at Klay. "I'm a private dick, Klay. What the hell do I know about the District Attorney's office?"

Klay laughed softly. "Yeah, I get you; I get you."

Donahue's brown eyes were frankly disapproving of the plain-clothes man. Klay nodded mockingly, drew one corner of his mouth down, turned and drifted back to his table.

Donahue finished his second cocktail and went upstairs to a telephone booth. He dialed and while waiting for the connection scowled at his wrist-watch. He crowded the transmitter with his mouth.

"Get Mr. Castleman.... Donahue." He tapped his foot for a long minute; stopped tapping it and dipped his head. "Frank?... This's Donny.... Say, I don't feel right. There's a fluke here somewhere or else old man coincidence is on the job.... Well, Klay; he's downstairs wolfing grub now.... Well, if it is coincidence I don't give a damn, but if something leaked out and this crackpot is playing me ring-around-the-rosie—... I know, I know, but I've got a date with this jane and I don't like to have Klay pulling a Dracula around here all night. If somebody in your office got loose-mouthed, it might be just too bad.... Okey, Frank. Oh, yeah, I'll tell you all right. S' long."

He pronged the receiver, shoved out of the booth and went downstairs to the bar. He had two vertical creases between his black eyebrows. Lights gleamed on his high cheekbones and light moved back and forth in his brown eyes, and his wide lips were a little tight beneath his long, straight nose.

He leaned on the bar, shook his head when Maxie reached for his empty glass. Walter Nass appeared in the dining-room entrance, looked at his back and then turned his troubled stare on Klay. Nass came over to the bar and rubbed his elbow against Donahue's.

"What's up, Donny?"

Donahue crackled a potato chip between long hard teeth. "Do me a favor, Walt. Tell Carmen when the jane comes to send her up by the front stairway."

"Jane?"

"I'm meeting a jane here. I'll go up and meet her in the room, then."

Walter Nass looked puzzled. "Cripes, Donny, I'd hate to have anything happen here. What's Klay doing here?"

"Search me."

"There's something wrong somewhere."

Donahue growled. "Don't be an old woman—" He broke off because Carmen was beckoning from the corridor door.

"A chauffeur says the lady wishes you should see her in the car," Carmen explained when Donahue reached her.

"Yeah?"

She nodded.

He said: "Get my hat and coat."

Walter Nass was at his elbow, saying: "What now, Donny?"

Donahue said nothing. He went down the hall behind Carmen. She helped him into his coat in the shadow of the stairwell, and he was slapping on his hat when Walter Nass touched him again.

Donahue said: "I don't know. I'm going upstairs and then down and out the back way."

Nass looked worried. "Cripes, I thought—"

"Keep your pants on, Walter. I may be goofy but I'm not taking a chance…. Carmen, you stay in here…. Okey, Walter; you want to let me out?"

Nass pushed past Donahue giving him a sidelong look and then climbed the carpeted staircase. Donahue followed, watching Nass's shiny heels. They went halfway down the corridor above, took a rear stairway that grounded back of the kitchen. Nass dangled keys and his face was genuinely concerned.

"Honest, Donny—I think you ought to watch your step."

Donahue prodded him. "I'll watch it, kid."

Chapter II

NASS let him out into a dark alley, stood hovering in the doorway while Donahue groped his way rearwards. Donahue reached the street that paralleled the one in which Nass's place stood. He turned left and walked a half block to a main north-and-south artery.

He turned south, the big collar of his overcoat up around his ears, the brim of his hat snapped down low over his eyes. He reached the corner and went close to the window of a cigar store. There was a man standing on the corner looking down the dark side street. He wore a blue overcoat with the collar upturned, and he was hatless. He had blonde close-cropped hair.

Donahue entered the cigar store, bought a packet of cigarettes and killed a few minutes opening it and watching the corner. The man kept looking into the side street and tapping a foot on the curb. Presently Donahue walked out, retraced his steps north and took the first right turn. He followed the side street to the next north-and-south artery and did not stop until he reached the first corner.

He entered the street, walking west; took a flat black automatic pistol from an armpit-holster and shoved it into his coat pocket. He also left his hand in the pocket. The houses here were gray stone with high stoops and areaways beneath. When he got halfway up the block he could see the hatless man standing on the corner beyond.

Nass's place was near the west end of the block. There was a sedan parked in front of it, its taillight a red eye in the darkness. Donahue walked close to the curb, and when he came abreast of the sedan he crowded his body close against it.

Nothing happened. He saw no other car nearby, heard no idling engine. But he saw the hatless man turn and cross the main drag beyond and disappear behind a fleet of moving cars. Donahue opened the tonneau door and saw the woman sitting in the corner.

"What's the idea?" he said.

She did not answer. She did not move.

His head went down between his shoulders and his gun came halfway out of his pocket. He flung a look about, up and down the street; returned it to the tonneau. He reached in with his left hand and grabbed the woman's arm. She fell sidewise—softly—and lay quietly on the seat.

He had tried to stop the fall of her body. Failing, he drew his hand back, rubbed his fingers together and then looked at them. They were smudged.

He stepped back to the curb and stood very erect. His brown eyes flashed, marble-hard, and a whispered oath slipped out of a corner of his mouth. He was suddenly warm and he pulled down the collar of his coat, drew a handkerchief and wiped the blood from his fingers.

He turned away and went down into the areaway. He rang the bell and before its echo died Carmen came out, as though she had been waiting for the sound. He saw her white, round-lipped face floating towards him in the shadows.

He said nothing. She opened the wrought-iron gate and he went past her long-legged, with a swish to his overcoat. He ran into Walter Nass in the corridor and Nass's face was a white question mark.

"Klay," Donahue said, and went down the corridor.

Klay put down a pony of brandy and laid his long, prehensile fingers on the white napery. Donahue stopped in front of the table and Klay looked at him peculiarly with half-shuttered eyes, his white eyelashes filming his stare.

Donahue said: "There's a dead woman outside."

"H'm," Klay said and stood up quietly. His glance flicked Donahue and he wiped his flat lips with a napkin, dropped it and came around the table, square-shouldered and erect. "How'd it happen?"

"Shot."

"I didn't hear a shot."

"She was shot elsewhere and some kind-hearted son-of-a-so-and-so delivered her at the door."

Klay brushed his hair back of his ears with his hands, swung on his heel and strode swiftly out of the bar, up the corridor. Donahue followed slowly and Walter Nass met him in the hallway. Nass was patting his forehead with a handkerchief and Carmen was holding her hands together just inside the door and looking round-eyed.

"——! Donny, what happened?"

Donahue grabbed his arm roughly. "Take it standing, Walt. It didn't happen here."

Donahue seemed to have grown taller, darker. His teeth bared when he spoke and there was a growling huskiness in his throat. Sparks seemed to be crackling in his eyes.

"Who was she, Donny?"

Donahue did not reply. He crossed to Carmen and muttered: "What makes you think that guy was a chauffeur?"

"He—he wore a cap like a chauffeur, señor."

"Okey. I get that too."

He heaved past her and opened the iron gate, climbed out of the areaway and saw Klay half in the tonneau, with the car's dome light on. Donahue stood on the sidewalk and waited until Klay backed out.

Klay was casual, undisturbed. "How'd you find this?"

"A guy came to the door here and said she wanted to see me."

"Where's the guy?"

"How the hell do I know?"

Klay nodded to the car. "You expecting her?"

"I was, yes. Check those plates. It's not her car."

"Who is she?"

"You know as well as I do."

Klay squinted at him. "What are you getting hot about?"

"What do you expect me to do—light a Murad?"

Klay lifted his cleft chin. "Don't get snotty, Donahue." He tried to put beef into the words but they snagged over his teeth and sounded somewhat hollow. The tonsorial pallor of his face was heightened by a glassy look that came suddenly to his eyes and as suddenly departed. He licked his dry flat lips and ducked down into the areaway.

Donahue reached into the sedan and turned out the dome light. He closed the tonneau door, looked sourly up and down the street and went down into the areaway vestibule. Klay was using a wall telephone near the checkroom and Carmen was twisting a handkerchief round and round. Walter Nass was watching Klay at the telephone but when Donahue came in Nass turned towards him and shrugged.

Through the partly open door at the end of the corridor Donahue saw three men drinking at the bar. A dozen or more people were in the dining-room. But nobody knew yet that anything was wrong—none but Nass and Donahue, Carmen and Klay and Maxie the bar man.

Klay hung up and turned from the phone. His hair shone like platinum and his gray-white face looked long and hollow in the cheeks. His nape was straight, his tailored shoulders square.

"This ain't so sweet." He looked at Donahue when he said it, then turned and walked to the iron gate, climbed to the sidewalk.

Donahue came up behind him and got in front of him. "What's the idea of a crack like that?"

"You're out of diapers, aren't you?"

"What's the idea of a crack like that?" I asked.

Klay nodded to the sedan. "Having dates with Cherry Bliss, weren't you?"

"Maybe," Donahue said, "I'm not the only guy's had dates with Cherry Bliss."

"I guess she's had dates with a lot of guys."

"Maybe you don't get me."

Klay worked his artificial smile. "I don't care if I get you or not, Donahue."

"What I've been wondering, Klay, is how the hell you happen to be over on the East Side. I thought you were working the cab-joints over on the West Side."

"This happens to be my night off. I'm just taking care of this till the precinct men get over. I'm not quizzing you, Donahue. That'll be their job. So keep your sarcasm to yourself—or chuck it at the precinct men. Maybe they won't like it."

"This is vice squad business, Klay."

Klay's lips tightened. "This is my night off, Donahue."

Chapter III

SERGEANT of Detectives, Kelly McPard was a big fat man with rosy cheeks and a neat sandy mustache. His eyes were bright blue, whimsical. He had an easy, engaging smile. His sandy hair was silken on his large head and he had a smooth, polished cleanliness that included his clothes.

He drained the glass of beer, was careful to wipe the foam from his mustache.

"Now, Donny—after all, what the hell. You're not telling me that your date with this twist was a social one."

Maxie was polishing glasses furiously behind the bar.

Donahue said: "I had a date with her, Kelly—and that's that. She was bumped off before she got here and that leaves me in the dark."

A uniformed officer came into the bar and said: "The morgue bus is here."

"Tell 'em to take the body down," McPard said. "Tell Craik to drive the car to Headquarters and have 'em look for fingerprints. The car was bent in midtown last night and after they've looked it over they can return it to the owner. I'll follow up as soon as I've finished here.... Fill that up, Maxie."

"I'm sliding," Donahue said.

"Shucks, wait," McPard said. "Your date's dead, so what's the hurry?"

Donahue eyed him levelly. "You're wasting your time and my own, Kelly. You're a swell egg, but you're up a wrong tree."

McPard was tranquil. "I'm not so sure about that, Donny. I know there's only one reason why you'd have a date with Cherry Bliss. She's seen her day, Cherry has. I know you go in for neat dames, and Cherry used to be neat but that, kid, was all long ago and faraway. There's only one reason why you'd have a date with her."

"Maybe I put her on the spot, huhn?" Donahue mocked.

"Don't be a dumb animal. You were going to meet her here because she had some dope you wanted."

"And what was the dope?"

"That's what I'm trying to find out."

Donahue said: "Bushwah, Kelly," and buttoned his topcoat.

Klay came in from the corridor, his derby in sharp contrast to the pallor of his hatchet face. His pale eyelashes quite concealed his eyes.

"Well, that's that," he said offhand. "I'll take Scotch, Maxie.... You've got all this dope, eh, Kelly?"

McPard looked into his beer. "All from you, thanks, Ken. But Donny, here, is getting his feelings hurt."

Klay chuckled flatly. "He gets that way quite often. A guy can't look crooked at him any more. He thinks that agency of his is just about the berries. I've seen a lot of private dicks lose their licenses in my time."

"Yeah," Donahue said, frankly sarcastic. "And I've seen a lot of city flatfoots lose their shields."

"Tsk, Tsk," McPard clucked dispassionately. "This is no place to bicker."

Donahue growled: "Then tell that fashion plate to keep his trap shut." He tossed a five-dollar bill on the bar. "Four cocktails out of that, Maxie."

"Listen, Donny." McPard faced him and smiled benevolently. "I'm not trying to ride you, kid. But the death of this jane is going to raise a hell of a stink and I'd like to be on the inside track. You can't just walk out on this. You had a date with the jane and the Commissioner is going to want to know how come. Cripes, I can't go down and tell him you just had a date with her."

"You tell him anything you want, Kelly. I don't know a thing. Not a thing. Can't I have a date with a jane? Is there a law against having a date with a jane?" He took the change from the five-dollar bill and crammed it into his pocket. "I like you, old socks. You're a white man, and I can't say that about some coppers I know."

His gaze passed McPard and clicked with Klay's. Klay came over close to Donahue and his flat lips took on a vicious twist.

McPard shoved them apart, complaining: "You guys make me sick with all this small-boy crap."

Donahue muttered: "Let him say what he wants to say. Go ahead, Klay, spring it."

Klay's lips shook. He said, suddenly: "Ah, hell!" and turned and strode stiffly across the room.

McPard was gripping Donahue's arm. "Now easy, Donny—for crying out loud, easy."

Donahue shrugged free of McPard's hand, said: "So long, Kelly."

He left the bar, went up the corridor.

Walter Nass was standing inside the iron gate with Carmen. He turned a harried look on Donahue.

Donahue said: "I'm sorry, Walt, this had to happen here."

"You're not in Dutch, Donny, are you?"

"Nah, not me. Somebody else might be, though." Donahue looked back down the hall and growled: "That lousy crackpot!"

"I'd go easy, Donny."

Donahue smacked Nass's back. "You know me, boy." A low laugh rumbled in his throat. He pinched Carmen's cheek. "Smile, beautiful!"

He yanked open the gate, rolled out into the areaway, up to the street.

Chapter IV

FRANK Castleman, the District Attorney, was having brandy and coffee in his library when Donahue came in. Castleman was a square-built stocky man, with crisp iron-gray hair and a rugged jaw. He didn't rise.

"Haul a chair over, Donny, and give me the dirt."

Donahue said: "There's not much dirt—yet." He carried a high-backed occasional chair to the library desk and sat down. "Kelly McPard's on it."

"Good man."

"Swell. Old pop Kelly himself—and they don't make 'em smarter. But he's a cop, Frank—and the cops is a system. The cops, may they always be right; but right or wrong, the cops: that's Kelly's credo and that's going to be hard to climb over, maybe. Klay said it was his night off."

"How'd the girl die?"

"Kerplunk in the heart—a small bore, I'd say offhand. These mugs fell on her somewhere and let her have it. Kelly shot the body to the morgue. The car she came in was swiped last night and Kelly sent it down to H.Q. for fingerprints."

"Kelly asked a lot of questions?"

"Plenty. That guy knows I didn't have a date with Cherry because I liked her. And I think Klay knows too. When I first came in the speak Klay asked me what was going on in your office."

Castleman leaned back. "Why was she coming to meet you, Donny?"

"She was going to give me the names of some guys mixed up in the vice racket. Big names. It took me two weeks, a lot of soft language and hard liquor to win her over. She called me up this afternoon and said she'd spill the works. She must have got suddenly sore about something, I don't know what. She sounded sore—mad.

"If Klay happened to be at Walter Nass's by accident, all well and good. If he was there by appointment—well, boy, that gives me something to crack, and it's not a nut. Klay might hurt me—I don't know. He was scared about something tonight. And Kelly is going to camp on my trail; he's like that."

Frank Castleman got up, went to the Georgian fireplace and shoved in a fresh log. He stood up with his back to the flames, took a hitch in his dressing-gown belt and three quick drags at his cigar.

He said: "They must have known she was going to turn over. They must have got wind of it somehow. I wonder if she had anything in writing."

"I don't know. But writing or other wise, she had the goods."

Castleman grunted. "Unh." He came back to the desk solid-heeled and sat down. He rolled his cigar back and forth between his teeth, beneath his clipped iron-gray mustache. After a minute he looked up at Donahue.

"Donny, I can't make this out. Not yet. I smell something behind this that stinks louder than we may think. But whatever you do, for —— sake man, don't let them, know—yet—that I've hired you. Fundamentally there's nothing wrong about my hiring a private detective. But I've come to the stage in this racket where I can't rely on my men when I start after something niggerish in the Commissioner's woodpile. It's a rotten shame that out of the several thousand honest cops there's got to be a few, a mere handful, that are turning vice and corruption towards their own beneficial ends. But if it's found out—now—that I've gone out of my own camp and hired you, I'll never hear the end of it."

Donahue said: "It's the system. A lot of cops know they're working with guys that are crooked, but they'd never squeal. It's like one big family. They picked up an idea a long while ago that they've got to protect the honor of the family. It's just one of those things."

"Can I depend on you to keep a tight lip?"

Donahue laughed. "What, you mean when they ask me down to Headquarters?"

Castleman nodded.

Donahue held up his hands. "Why should I worry, Frank? I'm strictly clean. I had a date with Cherry—and as for what kind of a date I had, that's my business."

"I appreciate this, Donny."

Donahue stood up. "That's business, Frank. I took this job with that understanding."

"Only business?" Castleman stood up and smiled ruefully.

Donahue shrugged. "Well, I think you're a pretty swell District Attorney, too."

"Sure, sure." Castleman came around and put friendly pressure on Donahue's arm. "I often wonder why you never went on the cops. You'd have risen high."

"I don't like the system, boy.... That brandy looks good. Do I rate?"

Chapter V

DONAHUE entered his hotel-apartment at ten-thirty whistling *Trees*. He hung up his hat and overcoat, undressed down to undershirt and trousers and was mixing rye and Perrier in the little pantry when the knocker sounded. He carried the drink into the living-room and laid his hand on the knob, his ear against the panel.

"Who is it?"

"Me, Donny."

"Libbey?"

"Li'l ol' Libbey!"

"Haven't you got a home?"

"Sure, but there's no liquor there."

Donahue opened the door and Libbey of the *City News Bureau* breezed in, said: "Greetings, Sherlock—or is it Shylock?" and took the glass from Donahue's hand. He downed half of it, smacked his lips. "Not bad," he said. He crossed the room to a console, knocked open a cedar humidor, helped himself to a cigarette and lit up. He flopped into a big club chair, planted his heels on an Ottoman, raised the glass. "I forgot: to you, old boy, old boy."

"Life's just a bowl of cherries, huhn?"

Donahue went into the pantry, mixed another drink and came back into the living-room.

"So what?" he said.

Libbey grinned boyishly, though he was not a boy. "The boss said if I came up here you'd tell me all—all, Donny."

"All what?"

"About that body in front of Walter Nass's tonight."

Donahue chuckled. "You're an optimist."

"Come on, Donny; be Santa Claus."

"You were over at Headquarters, weren't you?"

"Yup."

"You got the dope there, didn't you?"

"The bald details, but what I want—"

"That's all I know: the bald details. I had a date with a jane and somebody bumped her off. What's that make me—a know-it-all?... Nix, sweetheart. I don't know a damned thing, and if I did I'd get a ghost-writer and cash in on the tabs. Be your maturity, Libbey. Beat it. I'm turning in."

Libbey got up, considered his empty glass. "Know anything about Ken Klay, the vice squad sheik?" He did not accompany the question with an upward look.

Donahue had his trousers half-off. He pulled them up again and came over to Libbey, holding them up in front. "You're going to make cracks about me to other people maybe, and maybe I'm not going to like it."

Libbey chuckled and put his empty glass in Donahue's hand. "My error, Donny."

The phone rang and Donahue went across the room and scooped it up off the secretary. "Yes, Donahue.... Huhn?" He turned his back to Libbey and his eyebrows came together. "What makes you think so?... Maybe I could—that. Leave me your number and I'll call you in five minutes.... No; I didn't think you would. Okey, then; call me in five minutes. I'm busy now."

He hung up, got an old briar out of the desk, crammed it with bright Burley, lit up and shot fragrant smoke ceiling-ward. He swiveled and spread a palm.

"So I'll be seeing you again sometime, Libbey?"

Libbey laughed. He didn't say anything. He crossed the room cheerfully, grinned from the door, winked, went out. Donahue scowled at the door, tapped the pipe's Bakelite stem on his teeth; then started dressing. While buttoning his vest with his left hand he used his right to pick up the telephone receiver, and bent over.

"Hello, little wonderful," he said to the hotel operator. "How about doing a favor for your constant admirer?... Well, it's like this. A guy's going to call me any minute. When he does, kind of make believe things are bawled up and ask for his number, the way exchange operators do sometimes. Then remember the number.... I know it's off-color, but so is the guy that's going to call.... Thanks. I'll drop around a box of candy one day.... Oh, perfume, instead, eh?... *Chez Moi,* huhn? Little gold-digger!"

He hung up and finished dressing; was lacing his oxfords when the phone rang.

"Yeah," he said into the transmitter. "I'll listen now. Shoot.... Well, to begin with, Mr. so-and-so, I'll have to approach him. You're taking it for granted that he's my client and that's where you're all wet— soaking. But go ahead; spiel it.... I get you. Ten thousand, huhn? And I'm to act as the little old go-between?... I see. Well, call this number at nine sharp tomorrow morning."

He hung up, waited for a moment holding the telephone and then lifted the receiver. "Well, little wonderful?... Thanks." He pronged the receiver quietly and set the instrument down. He wrote a number on a slip of paper, tucked the paper into a vest pocket. He shrugged into his overcoat, grabbed his hat and went out.

It was eleven when he came out into the street. He walked north for two blocks, entered a cigar store and went into a telephone booth. He called a number and said, presently: "Did I wake you, Frank?... Good. Listen. I want you to do something for me, Frank. I can't do it myself. Get in touch with your office, have 'em check up a telephone number: Alexandria 4141. Get the address. How long do you suppose it will take?... Okey. Call me back at Waterford 9086."

He hung up, slipped out of the booth, left the door open and bought a late paper. Ten minutes later the phone in the booth rang and he got the call.

"That's not so hot, Frank, but even so it may work.... I'll tell you tomorrow morning. Can I see you at eight?... Swell."

He paused outside the booth to write an address beneath the phone number he had put down on the slip of paper. He went into the street and out of the tail of his eye saw a man move behind the corner building opposite. He turned casually east and moved down the dark side street. He did not look back until he reached the next corner; turning north, he thought he saw a figure moving in the shadows up the side street. He turned west at the next block, walked fast and when he had gone about two hundred yards ducked down, into an areaway. He stood motionless and quiet.

A few minutes later he heard approaching footfalls. He saw a man drift by. He rose out of the areaway and had taken six steps before the man spun.

"You wouldn't by any chance be tailing me, would you?" Donahue said.

Klay's gray-white face remained expressionless. "Oh, it's you, Donahue?"

"Maybe you thought it was four Hawaiians." His voice had a brittle edge.

Klay was stiff, straight. "Guilty conscience?"

"I know when I'm being tailed, Klay. I thought this was your night off?"

"It is. I'm walking off a heavy supper."

"I thought maybe you were walking off the guilty conscience you seem to think I have."

"Be funny."

"How can I, when you offer such swell competition?"

Klay said quietly: "There's something about you I don't like, Donahue."

"There's a lot of things about you I don't like and they wouldn't bear repeating in nice company. I don't know which way you're headed tonight, but whatever it is, I'm going in the opposite direction. Now get started."

"I'm going crosstown."

"Fine. You look better from the back than the front."

Klay chuckled dryly, swung easily on his heel and sauntered east. Donahue watched him for a moment, then turned around and retraced his steps.

Chapter VI

CASTLEMAN was one of those men who look ruddy and well slept in the morning; His beaver-brown suit was nicely aged and had an air about it of having been leisurely draped to his body. He was eating breakfast alone in a nook overlooking the Park when Donahue came in.

"Sit down, Donny.... Jenny, if I want you I'll ring." The elderly maid vanished. Castleman nodded to the door and Donahue closed it, then crossed the little room and leaned near one of the French windows.

"This egg," he said, "phoned last night and wants ten thousand for a list of names, a few letters and a few cancelled checks that he says ought to interest you."

Castleman set down his knife and dabbed his mustache with a napkin, looked sharply at Donahue. "What did you say?"

"I said he was mistaken in thinking that you were my client. I added, though, that I'd approach you. That was stalling for time."

"Think it's in connection with that killing last night?"

"What else?"

Castleman stuck a cigarette between his lips. He pried in his pockets for a match, but Donahue came across with a patent lighter and put flame to the cigarette. Castleman sucked in while staring intently across the table. He started, and as an after-thought said: "Thanks," nodding to the lighter.

"Klay was playing hide-and-go-seek with me, too, last night."

Castleman was absorbed by his own thoughts and he said: "I'd pay ten thousand if it's the real goods." He looked up. "I can get ten thousand by noon."

"That's why I didn't want to tell you this last night."

"Why?"

"I didn't want you to get big-hearted with dough right away."

Castleman, perplexed, seemed unable to marshal a prompt reply; and in the meantime Donahue sat down and began talking fast: "There's something screwy somewhere, but I can't lay my finger on it. If Cherry Bliss was rubbed out because some mugs were afraid she was going to spring a story, why then is some guy calling up and offering dope for ten thousand berries? Look. You'll pay the ten thousand. You'll get names and general dirt you've been looking for. You'll use it in court to clamp the lid down on some big operators and no doubt several guys on the vice squad. You'll naturally—or kick me if you don't—you'll naturally have occasion to use Cherry Bliss's name. Okey. What kind of legerdemain will you use when the defense asks where you got your dope? You got it from Cherry Bliss. Whether you admit that or not, they'll know it. Then what? Then who killed Cherry Bliss to get the information she had? Answer: our eminent District Attorney was in collusion with a gang of heels. He went to drastic measures to get information. He used criminal methods himself to bring evidence against criminals. This isn't extemporaneous, Frank. I thought it over in bed last night."

Castleman toyed with a mouthful of smoke, then shot it through his nose. "You think of things, Donny. Then what about this guy who called up?"

"I'm going after him. There's no proof yet that I'm working for you. I'm going after this guy and see what he's got. Klay's mixed up in this, but I don't know how. I've got him worrying and if I keep him worrying long enough he'll take a header."

Castleman broke out in a concerned grimace. "Hell, Donny, it sounds dangerous for you."

"My eye, dangerous! Only if this guy tries to approach you before I get to him, act dumb. Under no circumstances offer to pay for information. Okey?"

"I see what you mean. Sure." He stood up, came around the table cracking a ruddy smile. "You're doing a lot for me, Donny."

"You're paying for it, aren't you?"

Castleman chuckled. "Not for these added attractions you stage—at your own expense." His jaw tightened. "But if the worse comes to the worst, old man, I'm behind you—to the last ditch."

Donahue's rough low laugh was not unpleasantly ironic. "Get

dramatic, now, Frank; get dramatic! And I'll break down and yell, 'To the death for dear old alma mater!' Or am I thinking of something else?... Be seeing you—or phoning you anonymously. Marmalade on your chin, Frank!"

He went down in the elevator, took a side exit out and strode long-legged southward along the Park. When he had gone a matter of five blocks he motioned to a taxi, climbed in and gave an address. He got off ten minutes later on the East Side, near the railroad terminal, and walked south three blocks. An Elevated train was threshing by overhead when he entered a drug-store that specialized in books, stationery and cold drinks.

He walked on spic-and-span white tiles to the rear and found a bank of four telephone booths. He entered them and copied down the number of each. Then he called his hotel.

"Good morning, Miss Tracy. This is Donahue.... I'm fine. If anybody calls me at nine tell them to call Alexandria 4677.... Thank *you!*"

He was in the end booth on the left and he stayed there behind the closed door, his hat yanked down over his eyes. He looked at his watch. It was a quarter to nine. Men and women entered the adjacent booths; bells rang; doors opened and closed. Donahue watched the men who came to the booths. When his wrist-watch said nine o'clock the phone in his booth rang. He removed the receiver and let it hang.

He stepped out of the booth. In the next booth a girl was talking. In the next a fat old man was yelling in Yiddish. Donahue pressed close to this door, then turned about and went around back of the booths and on to the one at the extreme right. He pressed his ear to the back panel. He heard a man's voice.

"I tell you, I've been cut off.... Alexandria 4677." There was a moment of silence. "The hell you're ringing 'em!... I tell you, a party's expecting my call.... Oh, all right—all right!"

There followed the sound of a receiver being slammed into its prongs.

Donahue stepped across behind a pyramid of books. He saw the man come out of the booth; a large man in a fawn-colored fedora and a belted tweed overcoat. The man strode towards the front door, went outside and stood on the corner, lighting a cigarette with his head bent into the wind. Donahue remained in the store, watching him; and when the man swung around and headed down the side street, Donahue walked out and spotted him.

When a half dozen pedestrians, headed in the same direction, got between him and the man in the belted coat, Donahue started. They walked three blocks, until finally the man turned right and climbed a flight of stone steps between iron handrails. Donahue quickened his pace. He saw the man draw a ring of keys from his pocket, insert one in the hall door, open it. The man swung the door wide, entered; and the door began swinging shut against a pneumatic pressure. Donahue took the steps two at a time and caught the door before it quite closed.

He entered with his head down, and saw the man halfway up the staircase. He reached the foot of it and had his gun out, leveled.

"Steady, brother!"

He climbed the stairs rapidly until he was but two beneath the man, then said: "Now we'll go up to where you are going. Hands away from sides, like a nice boy."

The man stared dully at him, his lower lip beginning to protrude.

"Up—up," Donahue said.

"Who the hell are you?"

"We had a phone date, but I thought I'd call in person. Donahue's the name, you'll remember. You're blocking traffic, you tramp. Shove up!"

The man turned and went on upward, and he was careful about keeping his hands clear of his pockets. They climbed another flight and at the top Donahue stopped him.

"Anybody else in your place?"

"No."

"If there is, honeybunch, you'll get it smack in the back, no fooling."

The big man scowled and went down the hall slowly, dangling his keys. He opened a door at the rear, and Donahue was close behind him with the gun in the back of the tweed coat. They entered an apartment and Donahue kicked the door shut. The man turned with his broad heavy chin down on his chest, his mutinous eyes staring from beneath shaggy red brows.

"You're a sweet mutt, ain't you?"

"I don't want dialogue from you. I had a date with Cherry Bliss last night and it's the first time a jane's turned up dead on me. I'm not used to it."

"Gunning for the D.A., huhn?"

"No."

"Hell, fella. I didn't kill Cherry Bliss."

Donahue laughed harshly. "Maybe you think shooting people is a new kind of light entertainment.... I'm after something, mister—several things; and I intend to bail out of this thing with my hands clean."

"And mine dirty, I suppose."

Donahue lifted his chin. "Before we go into any more bright back-chat, suppose you fork over."

The man's voice was deepening. "Suppose I don't."

Donahue took three quick steps and jammed the muzzle of his automatic hard against the big man's midriff. His eyes got very dark and his lips very straight, tight.

"If you think I'm a bluff, you haven't been around much." He caught hold of a lapel of the tweed coat, ripped it open savagely. Three buttons fell to the floor. "Those hands, kid—watch 'em!" He crowded the big man against the wall. "Try clowning and I'll let you have it!"

"Jeeze, I was only—"

"You were only trying to bring that knee up," Donahue snapped. His left hand moved quickly, drew a .38 from beneath the man's left armpit, shoved it into his own pocket.

"Listen, Donahue. Listen, I got to get something out of this. I got to—"

"The only time I bargain with a hood is when I have to save my own skin."

He ripped a wrinkled brown envelope from the big man's inside pocket, stepped back and said: "Turn and face the wall, with your hands way up and palms against the wall."

The man did this and Donahue backed across the room until he came to a table. He kept his gun leveled across the room with his right hand. With his left he emptied the contents of the envelope on to the table. He did not bend over. He remained erect, groped with his left hand and raised at random a check to the level of his face, so that he could look at it and at the same time watch the man against the wall.

It was a canceled check, made out to Kenneth Klay, signed by Geraldine Bliss. He groped again and picked up a letter. It was quite wrinkled, written in the slanting hand sometimes noticed in the writing of left-handed persons. It was addressed to Cherry and signed by Ken. Its keynote was one of money. There was another check made out to a magistrate who at present was up for questioning before a board headed by District Attorney Frank Castleman. There were other checks and other letters relative to the once famous vice queen's dealings with men in the pay of the municipal government.

"This is sweet," Donahue said. Still using only his left hand, he slipped the lot back into the envelope, tucked the envelope away in an inner pocket.

The big man dared to turn around. His face looked white and peculiarly bloated and there was a glassy look in his eyes.

"For cripes' sake, Donahue, give me a break!"

"Why didn't you give Cherry a break?"

The big man stretched his neck as though finding it hard to speak. "She was going dippy, no kidding. She was going to turn all that info over free of charge. She was broke. She was out of the business and she was broke. I tried to talk her out of it. I told her she'd be flat on her back after this if she didn't promote some cash. But she was dippy. She said, 'Nix. I'm clearing out of this racket kosher.' I got mad, Donahue. Honest, it wasn't planned."

"So then you got the swell idea of dropping her in front of a place where she had a date last night."

The big man turned red. "That was Louie's idea. He figured it would chuck suspicion the other way. He figured everybody'd think she was done in by the mob she was turnin' up."

"All right. Why didn't you make a pass at the guys that were named in these letters and checks?"

"Jeeze, don't you see? Them guys are on the carpet now, most o' them. They ain't got no strings to pull. We figured the D.A.'d go far to get this junk and we'd get a clean ticket out. Listen—" He started away from the wall.

"Back, get back!"

The big man groaned. "Gawd, you don't need us! That stuff there'll incriminate enough guys to last a lifetime and put the D.A. in line for mayor for next election. At heart I'm a good guy. I didn't mean wrong. Things just happened—"

"Boy, do I hate your guts! At heart you're a dirty heel, that's what you are. And I'm not going to run myself into a jam by letting you go! Do I look dumb or something?"

The big man held his throat with one hand, stretched out the other towards Donahue. "Listen. Get in touch with the D.A. Tell him how things stand. I don't want no dough, honest. Just tell him how things stand and see if he don't give me a clean ticket out. You got there what he wants, what he's been looking for. Why pick on a poor guy—"

"You must have been dropped on your head when very young if you stand there and think I'm going to talk you up to the D.A. This is a pinch, sweetheart. Now shut up a minute."

Donahue went across to another table and lifted a Continental telephone, called a number. "Hello, Kelly there?" He waited a moment, eyes and gun trained on the big man. "Hello, Kelly. This is Donahue. I've got a nice pinch for you." He gave the street and number; added: "Snap on it, Kelly, before this mug gets ideas."

Chapter VII

DONAHUE said to the big man: "Now turn around and face the wall again."

"Gawd 'lmighty—"

"Turn around."

Handcuffs dangled, snapped shut, locking the big man's hands together behind his back.

"Now sit down in that chair there…. Smoke?"

There came the click of a lock. The door opened and a young man with blonde, close-cropped hair breezed in; stopped short and almost fell over.

"All right, goldilocks," Donahue said. "Do setting-up exercises."

"I—I—"

"You—you—*up*, baby!"

"Well, for the love o' cripes— Buck!"

"Yeah—yeah," panted the big man. "Lookit me!"

The blonde young man had a flippant smile. "Ain't this just too bad?"

Buck groaned. "Jeeze, Louie, don't crack wise like that. This guy's Donahue. He's got them papers and the cops is coming over any minute."

Louie's eyes shimmered. "Oh, so he's a police nose, huhn?"

"I'm the little boy scout," Donahue said, "who saw you up near

Walter Nass's last night, after you parked the car in front."

"The hell you saw me!"

"Standing on the corner with your hat off. I was only ten yards behind you. Cute, aren't you?"

Louie's flippant smile faded slowly and then he snapped at Buck: "What the hell did you want to let this guy put you in a jam like this for?"

"Gawd, Louie, he went and framed me! In good faith I offered him the whole dope—"

"In good faith!" mocked Donahue. "My, my, don't you see yourself through rose-colored glasses!... Hey, you, Louie, kick that door shut and keep your hands up."

Behind Louie, Klay stepped through the doorway, with his service revolver drawn and his gray-white face passionless. His gun stopped against Louie's back. In a split moment he had the manacles on. He shoved Louie, and the latter stumbling, complained: "I never seen things happen so fast!"

Klay ignored him because his interest was bent on Donahue, and also his gun. "Heel against heel," he said; added: "Huhn?" His false teeth had a flat gray-white surface not unlike his face. "So, what's your newest fable in slang, Donahue?"

"Here's something, and it's not a fable: you stink."

Louie began walking up and down with the mature irritation of the very young. "Damn it, damn it, is this an act or something? Is this an act? I'm beginning to burn up! First one thing, then—"

"Louie, for cripes' sake!" Buck groaned.

"Why should I? Who are these eggs? I ain't gonna—"

Klay turned back his lapel, revealed his police shield.

Louie stopped pacing and stared. "Then why the hell didn't you say so?" He turned and stared hard at Donahue, pointed: "And him?"

Klay smiled. "I'll take care of him. Now you get over there by your boy friend and keep that loud mouth of yours shut till I ask you something."

Donahue had lowered his gun because Klay's was pointing at him. "All right," he said. "You can take these eggs in, Klay. I'll breeze."

"Wait. Why should I take these eggs in?"

"The big one bumped off Cherry Bliss. She had a lot of dope on a lot of big poobahs in this man's city and she was going to turn it over. So he bumped her off. Then he got the dope."

"Where's the dope?"

Donahue said: "I've got to get along. Come on, we'll both take these eggs over to the precinct."

"Wait, you." Klay's gun stopped Donahue and Klay said without turning his head: "You guys, where's the dope this bird's talking about?"

Buck took heart. "He's got it! Him! He took it away from me. I was trying to get in touch with the right party but he frisked it off me. He's got it, mister; and he's gonna cash in himself on it."

Klay looked thinly at Donahue. "Shake-down, huhn?"

"Shake-up, Klay—if you get what I mean."

"Let me have it."

Donahue laughed shortly in Klay's face. "Boy, you're the berries—bowls and bowls of them."

"He's got them papers," Buck rushed on. "He's going to use 'em against a lot of guys. Your name's in there too, now I remember. He's going to cash in on 'em. Me—he double-crossed me! I thought he was representing the right guys, and then when he gets 'em he turns on me and laughs. That's the kind of a jazzbo that guy is."

Donahue made a sharp right turn, took six long steps and smacked Buck in the mouth. Klay sped after him and spun him around.

"Never mind that, Donahue. Hand over what you took from this guy and do it fast." His face was becoming livid, his eyes very pale and hard.

Donahue was steaming up. "Not on your natural. I've got those papers, right in here"—he tapped his breast pocket—"and I know who I'm going to hand them over to. And it's not you."

Klay made a left-handed pass at Donahue's pocket. Donahue caught his arm and flung it down savagely.

"Don't try it, Klay!"

Louie began snarling: "Listen, Klay, there's stuff in those papers that means you're done for if it gets out. Me and Buck's in a jam and we got to spring out of it. We know what's in them papers. Unlock these cuffs and we'll take this guy. If them papers get in the wrong hands it's bad news for you and a lot of other guys. Like Buck said, we were tryin' to do right by you but this egg double-crossed us."

Klay's gun was pressing hard against Donahue's stomach, his eyes were narrowed down whitely. "Donahue, I want those papers. I want to see them."

"You heard me the first time, copper. You've double-crossed a lot of women in your day and got away with it, but you're not getting away with this."

Buck cried: "He called up another cop! He called him Kelly. The cop's on the way over. You better step on it, Klay!"

Klay's nape stiffened. For an instant his hand shook.

"Donahue," he said, "you're going to turn over those papers or you're going to regret it."

"If you've got the nerve, Klay, reach in my pocket and get them."

Klay stepped back, tossed a key to the floor. "Buck, unlock your boy friend's cuffs."

Buck let out a joyous grunt, fell to the floor and picked up the key. He unlocked Louie's manacles and Louie smacked his hands together.

Klay said: "Get behind this guy. Take his gun.... Don't move, Donahue, or you'll get it!"

Louie whistled cheerfully as he took the gun from Donahue's hands, tapped his pockets and took also the gun which Donahue had taken from Buck, and the key to Buck's manacles. He pressed both guns against Donahue's back and went on whistling. Donahue didn't move.

Klay took the brown envelope from Donahue's pocket and backed away. Louie went over and unlocked Buck's manacles and gave him back his gun. Buck let out a vast breath and beamed.

Klay was slipping fingers into the envelope when Louie, nodding to Buck, stepped swiftly and jabbed his gun against Klay's back. Buck took the cue and trained his gun on Donahue and Louie reached over Klay's shoulder and took the brown envelope.

"You were born dumb, fella," Louie said.

Klay sucked in a breath and remained quivering where he stood, his eyes frozen on space.

Louie clipped: "Okey, Buck. We lam."

"Yeah, bo!"

They backed to the door. Louie opened it and motioned back out. Buck ducked behind him and Louie paused a moment on the threshold.

"Pleasant dreams, guys!"

He vanished, slamming the door.

Chapter VIII

KLAY whirled, his gun held level with his waist. Donahue jumped from behind, ripped the gun from his hand and sent him spinning across the room.

He snarled: "That was a swell frame you walked into, Klay. Thanks. I'm going to get those hoods and I'm going to get those papers."

He lunged across the room, yanked open the door and barged out. But Klay had the gun he had taken from Louie, and he reached the door a split-second behind Donahue, opened it and bounded down the stairs.

He caught up with Donahue at the hall door and Donahue whirled on him. "Swell, Klay! You'll be along—a cop—and that'll cover me. But remember, baby—"

Klay went through the hall door, down the steps, and saw Buck and Louie a half block away, walking east. He broke into a run and the two ahead saw him and darted across the street, their heels flying.

Donahue caught up with Klay and they ran side by side. Klay's face was white and shiny now with sweat, and little muscles worked at the corners of his mouth. Buck and Louie turned at the first corner, and when Donahue and Klay reached it they saw the other two pounding north.

Klay raised his gun and fired. The shot crashed a window and glass fell, rained noisily on the sidewalk. Buck and Louie turned east and Klay and Donahue went after them past public garages and run-down frame houses. Pedestrians scattered. Vehicles pulled up to the curb and stopped.

Donahue lifted his gun, aimed offhand while galloping and fired. Buck missed a step, swayed a bit but kept rushing head long beside Louie. Louie turned around and fired two shots past Buck's shoulder. One smacked against a fire-hydrant and the other whistled above Donahue's head. Klay fired and Buck put his hands straight out and began stumbling. He stumbled faster and faster, tried to look back, then plunged suddenly to the gutter—so hard that his legs flew upward, banged down again, as he rolled, with a ringing of heels on the pavement.

Neither Donahue nor Klay stopped to look at Buck. They knew Louie had the envelope, and Louie was beyond, fleet as the wind. Trucks were backed up against warehouses here. Louie weaved among them; plunged down an alley, and was almost through when Klay and Donahue spotted him.

Klay slowed down to fire. He missed and Donahue rushed past him and pounded his heels down the alley, reached the next street and swung east. Louie cut across in front of a horse-drawn truck, turned to fire around the back of it. The shot clanged in a refuse can and raised dust from it.

As Donahue started across the street, Klay tripped him. Donahue, who had been running fast, fell hard, rolled over and over while Klay sped on. Donahue heaved up, stretched his long legs and overtook Klay at the next corner.

"Smart, aren't you?" he called; stuck out his leg and sent Klay hurtling into the gutter.

A shot from Louie's gun tore off the lapel of Donahue's overcoat pocket, and Donahue, though off balance, fired and his shot knocked Louie against a house-wall. Louie rebounded, ran on for a dozen paces, then jumped behind a pole and fired. Klay broke into a run, firing again. Louie made the alley and Donahue reached the entrance as Klay did, and heard Klay's empty gun click. He saw Louie turning again to fire. Donahue stopped in his tracks. His gun boomed. Louie wilted and began sagging backward. Then he stopped moving, swayed for an instant, crashed down.

Donahue broke into a run, reached Louie and dropped down beside him. He tore the envelope from Louie's inside pocket, was rising when Klay fell on him, clubbing his revolver.

"I knew it was empty," Donahue said, reeling. "I heard it back at the entrance—or I'd never have come in this alley ahead of you!"

"Give me those, Donahue!"

Donahue stopped against the house-wall, rebounded and drove his fist to Klay's jaw. Klay took it and struck with his gun, crashing in Donahue's hat. Donahue grunted and jumped back, stopped the next blow with an upraised arm; cracked his own gun against Klay's jaw and drew blood. White-eyed, Klay came back at him, walloped his foot to Donahue's stomach. Donahue tried to cry out but couldn't. He had bullets left in his gun but he was not fool enough to plant his trademark in Klay. He took three blows on the head while still fighting for his breath and holding his hands to his injured stomach. Blood flew from his cheek.

Louie had started crawling. He crawled past the fighting men, and Donahue saw him and tried to push off Klay. Klay twisted, saw the gun in Louie's hand and broke with Donahue, plunged towards Louie. Louie fired, grimacing. Klay doubled up and struck the cobbles with his forehead.

Louie turned his gun on Donahue but Donahue was waiting for him. He let Louie have it. Louie rolled over quietly and lay very still.

There were running feet in the alley, and Donahue, cramming the envelope into his pocket, saw Kelly McPard and a couple of uniformed policemen. He leaned against the wall, wiped his face, looked at the blood on his fingers. He grimaced again, pressed knuckles hard against his stomach.

"Hey, Donny," McPard said, puffing to a stop.

"I think Klay's shot."

"What the hell!"

"Yeah. This mug here. He let Klay have a dose."

McPard pointed. "You and Klay working together to get these two hoods?"

"Believe it or not, Kelly. Side by side. We ran side by side all the way."

"This the pinch you called about?"

"Yeah."

McPard looked puzzled. "You didn't say Klay was there."

"He wasn't. He joined me. He's been Johnny-on-the-spot ever since last night."

McPard bent his ruddy face. "You shot too?"

"No. I got kicked in the belly. A lousy two-timer kicked me in the belly." He kept rubbing his stomach, licking his lips, making painful grimaces. "I ought to get a drink. A good shot of brandy might help. There's a speak right around the corner."

"Go ahead, then. But come back here, Donny. Now don't go sliding out on me!"

"Promise."

Donahue went on through the alley, walked a block and entered a speakeasy. "Brandy," he said. He dragged his feet into the lavatory, took the brown envelope from his pocket. He drew a stamp from his wallet, affixed it. He undipped his fountain pen from a vest pocket and wrote on the envelope: Frank Castleman—and the address.

He returned to the bar, swallowed his brandy and shouldered out into the street. He walked to the next corner, looked up and down, dropped the letter into a mail box.

When he trudged weary-footed up the alley Kelly McPard was waiting for him and one of the cops was kneeling with Klay in his arms.

McPard said: "Klay said there were papers, Donny."

"Did he?"

"Kid, I'd like to see 'em. Klay asked me to. He's a cop. I've got to give him a break."

Donahue leaned against the wall and held his coat open. "Search me, Kelly."

Kelly searched him, then dropped his hands and looked up into Donahue's eyes. "Where are they, Donny?"

"Maybe that was just an idea Klay had. Sort of rambling in his mind. I've got no papers."

"You wouldn't cheat on me, would you, Donny?"

"Not on you, Kelly. I don't cheat on white men."

He Could Take It

*Tough dick Donahue gets
caught in the inside of a jam
where he takes plenty*

Chapter I

DONAHUE came into his hotel apartment coughing. The camel's-hair coat he wore was stained, his brown Homburg was dented. He walked straight to the bed and dropped flat on it. His hat fell off and wobbled several feet across the floor. He lay for a minute swearing to himself.

After a while he got up, pushing with his arms, and stripped. He looked at himself in the elongated mirror that took the place of panels in the closet door. His flat, hard stomach was blotched with abrasions. A black and blue welt capped his right hip bone. His face was sallow beneath the brown.

He went into the little pantry that contained an icebox and a porcelain sink. He cracked a piece of ice and held it first against one abrasion and then another. His teeth chattered. It was only a little past noon but he went into the bathroom, showered—first hot, then cold.

He didn't rub down. He swung into a terry cloth robe and let it absorb the moisture. From the pantry he carried a bottle of rye and a glass with three lumps of ice in it. He poured the glass half full of rye and dropped into a club chair. The liquor rushed color to his face but two resentful lines still clung between his brows.

When a knock sounded on the door he scowled at the door but said nothing. When the knock was repeated he growled: "Who is it?"

"Me, Donny."

"Don't be so anonymous."

"Me—Libbey."

Donahue slushed red leather mules towards the door. His manner was not ingratiating when he opened it.

"What! You're not glad to see me, Donny!"

"I'm never glad to see you."

"Oh, grandma, what big eyes you have!"

"In, pest." Donahue kicked the door shut, sloshed the liquor around in his glass while eying Libbey stonily. "Hooch on the coffee table. Perrier or Canada Dry in the pantry. Wet your whistle and scram."

The *City News Bureau* man chuckled. "You'd be a nice guy to have around the house a lot. But—genius must have its moments." A thumbnail snapped a match to flame and Libbey lit up. "So Klay got it, huhn?"

"You were around, weren't you?"

"I saw Kelly McPard. Great dick, Kelly. How'd it happen you and Klay joined up against those two heels, Buck and Louie?"

"What did you come here for, Libbey?"

"To play marbles, if I played marbles, but I don't play marbles. Kelly McPard said Klay tried to help you collar these two eggs. Is that right?"

"You'd take Kelly's word for it, wouldn't you?"

"I didn't think you and Klay were on good terms."

"Maybe that was an idea someone had."

"These two eggs that were killed—I hear they were implicated in the murder of Cherry

Bliss, the vice queen with whom you had a date the night she was unkindly bumped off. There's a rumor around town that Cherry was turning some information over to an unknown party. You that party?"

Donahue smacked his empty glass down on the coffee table. "Do you want a drink?" he snapped.

"I might."

"Then take it and beat it."

Libbey took a jolt straight, without ice. "Thanks. I can't figure out how you and Klay happened to join up. I know Klay had no use for you, and you no use for him. Then suddenly you become pals against two heels. Klay goes down in a blaze of glory and you bump off the guy that did him in."

"Miracles happen."

"In Heaven maybe, but not—"

"You go," Donahue muttered. "Get out of here. I've got an awful pain in the gut and you don't do it any good." He strode past Libbey and opened the door. "Out, bozo."

Libbey shrugged, helped himself to another drink. He sauntered to the door saying: "Thanks for every little thing."

Donahue said nothing in a wooden-faced way.

Libbey cocked an eye. "Say, Donny, do you know if Cherry had a kid?"

"A what?"

"A daughter."

"I don't know."

"Of course, you wouldn't tell me if she had."

Donahue indicated the open door. "You were going out, weren't you?"

"That's right! I was! Toodle-oo!"

Donahue locked the door and poured more liquor into his glass. He sat for a while, drank half a pint of rye straight and then got up and began pacing the room, his face flushed and angry. The phone bell stopped him and he answered it.

"Where are you, Frank?... Good. Come right up."

He hung up and went over to stand by the door, cramming a pipe from a leather pouch. He was ready when the knock sounded. He opened the door and Frank Castleman, the District Attorney, said:

"You look lousy, Donny!"

"I'm feeling better, Frank. In."

Castleman was a stocky square-built man with ruddy cheeks and a good jaw. He left his hat on and kept his hands in his overcoat pockets. His face was curious but also a bit worried.

"Drink, Frank?"

"Not so early. What happened to you?"

Donahue opened his robe.

"My—!" Castleman said. "Did a horse kick you?"

"No. A horse's neck."

"Huhn?"

"Klay.… Sit down, old boy."

CASTLEMAN sat on the edge of a high-back chair and blew his nose into crisp white linen. Donahue fell back into the big club chair and planked his long legs on the Ottoman. Breeze coming in through a partly open window tossed fragrant whiffs of tobacco smoke towards Castleman.

The District Attorney lifted candid eyes. "Get the papers?"

"Yeah."

"Where are they?"

"In the mail."

"In the mail! What was the idea—"

"Take it easy, Frank. It was my only out. I figured Kelly McPard would frisk me. My gut hurt after Klay kicked me and when Kelly came up I said I wanted to slide around the corner and get a drink. I did. I sealed the envelope they were in, put your name and address on it and dropped it in a box. When I came back sure enough Kelly frisked me. Klay, dying, must have said something to Kelly."

Castleman looked at the floor. "You use your head, I guess, Donny. How did Klay get mixed up in it?"

"Well, he must have been tailing me this morning—or one of the eggs. I nailed Buck in his flat and then Louie came in. I got the papers and then I phoned for Kelly. He's a white guy. I wanted to give him the pinch. Then Klay came in and tried to take hold of things. He wanted those papers. He flashed his badge and got very sore when I wouldn't turn 'em over. We had the two heels handcuffed. Klay was afraid to take the papers out of my pocket. Afraid I'd jump him. So he released one of the heels and the heel released the other."

"Klay was going to let them go because they knew too much. But they turned on him and bailed out with the papers. He knew he had to get those papers. Well, I wanted them too. So we went after the heels and shot it out with them. Buck got killed on the way and Louie got his in that alley. I took the papers from him. Klay's gun was empty, but he tried to take 'em from me. While we were fighting, Louie came to long enough to plug Klay. Then I had to plug Louie for keeps. Then Kelly McPard turned up."

"This Louie—this Buck—did they kill Cherry Bliss?"

"Of course. She was going to hand those papers over to me free of charge. They objected. They wanted dough for them. So they bumped her off and left her in front of that speakeasy."

"Who all were mentioned in the papers?"

"Detective Klay for one. He was shaking down Cherry even after she'd bailed out of the vice racket. There were others. I was in a hurry. I didn't look at all of them. I did see Magistrate McGiff's name—and another vice squad dick named Carney. He used to be Klay's partner. But they're in the mail. You'll get 'em in the morning."

Castleman said: "You're sure no one knows you're working for me?"

"I haven't told a soul. There's enough evidence in those papers to raise hell in this city. I'm glad you'll get 'em, Frank."

Castleman stood up. "I have you to thank, Donny. What did Kelly McPard think about this scrape?"

"When he's made up his mind—he'll come and see me."

Castleman thought for a moment, blank-eyed; then shook his head and looked worried. "Kelly McPard's the whitest dick in the city. I'd hate like the very devil to see you and Kelly become enemies. Do you think he'll come back?"

"I don't know for sure. I think he will. He didn't quite get what I told him. He didn't say whether he believed me or not. He was trying to think. Because Klay, dying, must have told Kelly about the papers."

"What will you do—if he comes?"

"Tell him a fable in slang. Klay died, didn't he—two hours later? The heels are dead. Who's to prove I had any papers? Don't worry about me, old boy."

"I do, though, Donny. I don't want you to get in too deep."

Donahue scowled. "Hell, don't be an old woman, Frank!"

"I'm no old woman, but—"

"I'm sorry, Frank." Donahue made a sour face, touched his stomach. "My gut."

Chapter II

DONAHUE slept through the afternoon. Slept off all of the liquor and most of the pain. He sent the camel's-hair coat and the brown Homburg out to be cleaned and went down to the lobby at six-thirty wearing a gray fedora and a gray topcoat. The blonde at the cigar counter gave him a dazzling smile.

"You don't come around as much as you used to," she said, luscious lipped.

"I didn't know you were married, little beautiful." He added with a look of mock-fright: "And that your daddy is a box-fighter."

He bought a paper and strode to the center of the lobby, snapped the paper open and downward with a loud report. The news was there in a black streamer. *Detective Killed in Duel with Gunmen.* Donahue grunted and reached the lobby. *"Detective Klay fighting bravely to the end...."*

"Oh, hell!" Donahue scoffed out loud.

"Beg pardon?" a red-headed bellhop said.

Donahue warped a look downward. "Oh—hello, Roy."

The bellhop grinned, tossed a glance towards the cigar counter. "The blonde pooch is ga-ga about you, Mr. Donahue."

"A pooch is a dog, Roy—a little dog."

Roy chuckled. "Yeah—something you cuddle."

"Okey, boy—okey. You win."

"When do I get a job with your detective agency?"

"Stick around—and be nice to me."

Donahue went out and nodded to the chasseur. "Cab, Henry."

He continued reading in the cab by the feeble glow of the dome light. He grumbled, snorted, laughed aloud once or twice—with grating irony. His eyes thinned. They'd identified the two gunmen at the morgue. Louie Staley and John "Buck" Hubling. *"Suspected of having been implicated in the murder of Cherry Bliss, notorious vice queen."*

Donahue looked out of the window at the jostling traffic. "Poor Cherry...."

Then he returned to the paper. It mentioned him. *"Detective Klay was joined by Ben Donahue, a private operative, who at great danger to his person aided in running down the two gunmen."* It was very graphic writing, but the details were all wrong. Only two men knew for a fact that Donahue was working for District Attorney Castleman in the latter's attempt to clean up certain metropolitan bureaus. These two were Donahue and Castleman. Only Donahue and Castleman knew for a fact that Detective Klay's mad running gunfight with the two gangsters had had nothing to do with loyalty to the shield he had worn. Klay had died in his attempt to obtain evidence against himself that would be dangerous in another's hands.

Donahue got out of the cab in a quiet uptown street, went down into an areaway and rang a bell beside a huge iron gate. Carmen let him into the vestibule, saying: "Walter told me to tell you—if you came, señor, that"—she nodded towards the inner door—"that Detective Kelly McPard is inside."

He scowled, not at Carmen. Then he shrugged, grinned, and nipped her chin. "Why? McPard's an old friend of mine."

"Walter just said—"

"Yeah, I know, I know."

Donahue entered the hall, left his hat and topcoat on a table there and went on down the corridor to a door at the end. He opened it and entered the bar and saw Kelly McPard standing at the other end, drinking beer out of a stein.

"Hi, Donny."

"Prosit, Kelly!"

McPard was a big fat man, scrubbed clean, rosy-cheeked, with a neat sandy mustache following the mobile line of a genial upper lip. His sandy hair was silken on his large head, his clothes were always good, well kept.

"Dry Martini, Maxie," Donahue said, remaining at the end of the bar opposite McPard.

McPard grinned, carried his beer down to Donahue's elbow, grinned again with a genial bow, and munched potato chips. Donahue looked everywhere but at the plain-clothes sergeant, and McPard called for another beer.

"Nice place here, Donny."

"I like it."

"I never used to come around much."

"So now that I'm making it a hangout, that gives you ideas."

McPard poked him. "Good old Donny—never as bad as his bite!… Say, why don't you put me straight on what happened this morning?"

"I tried to help out a conscientious dick by the name of Kenneth Klay."

"Yes, you did."

"Doubt me. See if I care."

McPard shook with good humor. "Yes, you did."

"All right, razz me. I did this, then: I had that heel all sewed up—Buck What's-his-name. Then Louie came in. Klay'd tailed Louie. He came in. The two heels broke away from Klay and we beat it after them. Have it your way. Klay helped me."

"That's not my way either. Those guys had something—something they got from Cherry Bliss. Maybe something she was to give to you. You wanted it. Klay wanted it and because he was a cop he had a right to have it. In the smash-up in that alley you got it. Klay said: 'He's got papers, Kelly. For —— sake get them and give me a break.'"

"What do you suppose he meant by that?"

"Well, he was being rode for quite a while lately. He was on something hot. He had a chance to turn up some dope and show his boss he was working. It would have looked rotten if you'd turned up the stuff instead. He thought he was going to live. He wanted a break, the credit of rubbing out these heels and turning up the dope."

"What dope?"

"I don't know, Donny. But you do. You got it."

"You searched me, didn't you?"

McPard nodded. "Yeah. But you went away for ten minutes."

"Maybe I gave the dope to a total stranger and said: 'Here, buddy, hold this till I come back. Or maybe I hid it somewhere. Don't make me laugh—my stomach's tender!"

McPard shrugged. "There was a cop there, too, you remember. My boss is calling me names now because it's rumored around you did get away with something—right under my nose. Hell, I can't stand for that. I'm supposed to be a good cop."

"You are a good cop. A white guy."

"Thanks." McPard crunched a potato chip. "Now what did you get out of that fight?"

Donahue touched his stomach. "Welts and abrasions."

McPard turned and looked full face at him. McPard rarely got mad so that you noticed it. His mouth warped humorously and his eyes twinkled—but back of the twinkle was a wily look.

He sounded sorrowful: "Give me the run-around all the time, Donny—all the time. Why? I *like* you."

"I like you."

McPard sighed and turned away. "Fill that up, Maxie." He caught the glass of beer as Maxie snaked it towards him; drank deeply, was careful to dab the foam from his mustache. Then he hunched close to Donahue.

"The other night Cherry Bliss was murdered. These two guys you and Klay got murdered her. She had a date here with you the night she was murdered. Why?"

"We've been over that, Kelly. I just had a date with her."

McPard regarded Donahue's profile. "Suppose you did. Then how come you were mixed up in this thing this morning?"

"Simple. I tailed down the guys who murdered her. I telephoned you to make the pinch. Klay cut in on you and balled up the works."

McPard shook his head. "No, you didn't just have a date with Cherry, and you didn't just go after these guys because they murdered her."

"Why did Klay cut in on you?"

"His privilege. He was a cop."

Donahue snorted. "Oh, go places, Kelly—go places!"

"But it all narrows down to one thing." McPard had turned full face again. "What did you snatch out of the gunfight and what did you do with it?"

Donahue tossed a bill on the bar. "So then we're back where we started from.... Change, Maxie."

"What," McPard said, "was it?"

"Thanks, Maxie.... Well, be seeing you, Kelly."

"Wait."

McPard gripped Donahue's arm and eyed him with a faint twinkle.

Donahue said in a low voice: "I wouldn't try any precinct crap on me, Kelly."

"Hell, I'm just trying to do my job."

"I'm not going to have every flatfoot with an idea try to work it off on me."

McPard looked hurt. "Gosh, Donny, I'm just working for a living."

"Leggo!" Donahue ripped his arm free. "Shovel that bushwha where it hasn't been heard before. To hell with you!"

He pivoted and strode towards the door. He turned and came back and said: "I'm sorry about that last crack, Kelly."

McPard stared at the mirror behind the bar with a detached look.

Donahue shrugged and went out and down the hall. Walter Nass was waiting for him, holding a slip of paper.

"Hello, Walter."

"Hello, Donny. Here. A jane telephoned here and asked for you. I didn't give her your number. I thought maybe you wouldn't want to. So she gave me her's."

"What'd she want?"

"You."

"What's her name?"

"Search me."

Chapter III

DONAHUE made a telephone call at a corner cigar store. He came out lighting a long cigar. He stood for a moment on the curb, his face lined with thought. A taxi came up and stopped. The driver looked at Donahue with quizzical eyebrows and Donahue returned the look with a vacant stare.

The driver said: "Hell—he's screwy!" finally and meshed gears.

"Hey—wait!" Donahue climbed in, gave his hotel address.

He stopped at the lobby desk for his mail and the clerk said: "There was a man here a few minutes ago looking for you."

"Sorry. He leave a message?"

"He said he'd wait a while in case you returned. In the lounge."

"What's his name?"

"Mr. Bunn."

Donahue idled towards the lounge. He saw a small man in black clothes looking piously at the ceiling. He saw so one else. He regarded the man for a moment, then returned to the desk and said: "If he asks again, I'm not in."

He took an elevator and went to his apartment, hung up his hat and overcoat. Ten minutes elapsed when a light knock sounded on the door. Donahue looked at his wrist-watch, shook his head, but went to the door anyhow.

The small man in the black clothes was standing there, one eyebrow way up, the other way down. "I thought the clerk may have been mistaken. I am K. W. Bunn, Mr. Donahue."

Donahue was overly polite. "I'm sorry. I don't know the name. No doubt you're mistaken."

"Wait. I am an attorney."

"I'm still sorry—"

"I know. You might not be, however, after you've spoken with me a few minutes. Really"—he looked up and down the corridor—"it is very private, and for your own good benefit."

Curious, Donahue stepped aside and Mr. Bunn came in. His head was peculiarly small, with fuzzy down on the back of a stringy neck. Frail nose-glasses rode precariously and quite matched the dusty frailty of his face and body. He was ageless.

Donahue closed the door. "Go ahead, Mr. Bunn."

"Yes; yes, of course." Mr. Bunn's upper lip had a chronic twitch, giving the impression that he continually sniffed because of a cold in the head. "Certain gentlemen have delegated me to call on you, Mr. Donahue, and lay before you a plan by which you can benefit handsomely."

"Yeah?" Donahue had a hard slantwise stare on the man.

"We need mention no names. Suffice it to say that you have certain papers which you acquired today. It is the belief of my clients that you are a man of business, that you acquired these papers primarily so that you might realize a profit. It is the belief of my clients that you would not be certain whom to approach. They anticipated this, and as a result have sent me to act as their representative. What price will you name?"

Donahue growled. "I thought so!"

"Thought so?"

"I picked you for a cheap shyster the minute I laid eyes on you.... Well, you can't sell your groceries here, Mr. Bunn. You can't because I've got no papers."

Unabashed, Mr. Bunn went on: "Naturally you hesitate to take me into your confidence. I don't blame you. It may interest you that my clients, however, have offered $10,000 for those papers. This money can be placed in your hands at eleven tomorrow morning. In cash, sir, and in whatever denominations you choose to name."

Donahue held up his palms. "No can do. No can do because I've got no papers. What the hell makes you think I've got any papers?"

"A detective attached to the vice squad was shot in a battle with two gunmen this morning. He died a few hours later at the hospital. Before his death he was called upon by several friends. It is very possible, sir, that he told one of these friends that during the fight you acquired certain papers."

"If he did, he lied."

"Dying men do not frequently lie."

Donahue's face became wooden. "I'm sorry, Mr. Bunn, that you got wrong information. I'm busy. I'll thank you if you'll go."

"But my dear Mr. Donahue—"

"That's final. I've got no papers. I've got nothing to sell you and you've got nothing to sell me."

Mr. Bunn sighed. He removed his gloves, laid them on the divan, took a handkerchief and carefully cleaned his glasses. "I regret, Mr. Donahue, that I must report failure to my clients. Perhaps if you would reconsider—"

"What's the use? I've got no papers, I tell you."

Mr. Bunn shrugged. He replaced his glasses on his nose, went slowly to the door. "Good night, Mr. Donahue." He went out and Donahue closed the door, relit his cigar and started pacing up and down. His eyes dropped on the gloves that Mr. Bunn had forgot. He scooped them up and went to the door. But Mr. Bunn was not in sight. Donahue closed the door and tossed the gloves on the desk.

A few minutes later there was a knock. Donahue went to the door but did not open it. "Who's there?"

"Mr. Bunn, sir. I forgot my gloves."

Donahue turned and strode across to the desk, picked up the gloves, returned to the door and opened it. A big man in a blue ulster crowded him with a gun.

"Back, you!"

There was another behind him, quite as tall but less broad. Mr. Bunn turned and went away down the hall and the two big men moved into the apartment, closed the door.

Glitter-eyed, Donahue said: "That was a swell trick!"

The leaner of the two laughed softly. "Wasn't it!"

The broad man said: "Frisk him, Archie."

Humming light-heartedly, Archie got behind Donahue and slapped his pockets; removed, finally, the gun from beneath Donahue's left armpit.

The broad man was serious, thatch-browed. "You know what we're here for, fella."

Archie chuckled. "We came to call, you know!"

"Can that!" the broad man said.

Archie said: "You mustn't mind Homer, Donahue!"

"I said can that cheap comedy!"

Donahue, hands up, said: "What do you bums want?"

Homer growled: "You know what we want. Shell out, fella."

"Look around," Donahue said. "See if there's anything you can use."

"I wouldn't get funny, fella."

"Am I? Hell, I'm telling you to look around."

"You can find it quicker."

Donahue shook his head. "I can't find something that isn't here any quicker than you can."

"You can't?" chuckled Archie, and brought his gun-barrel down on the back of Donahue's head.

INSTINCTIVELY Donahue whirled. Instinctively his fist came up; traveled a foot, swiftly. Archie sat down on the floor, looked dazed. Then he began rubbing his chin. Slowly he began to smile. His lips smiled showing white teeth but the shimmer in his eyes was humorless. He rose and kept smiling with his lips.

"That's a nice start," he said, chuckled absently; then suddenly snapped: "You dirty —" and whipped up his gun.

Homer blocked him. "Fat-head!" Homer said.

Archie had risen quivering to his toes. Now he settled back to his heels, shrugged, smiled sheepishly.

Homer turned on Donahue. "Now how about it, fella?"

"I tell you, guys, I haven't got a thing!"

"You got papers from them two bums Louie and Buck, that's what you got and that's what we want. The Professor offered you cash dough for them but you clowned around. Clown around now and see where it gets you!"

"Search me. Search my apartment. You're haywire. I haven't got a thing. If I did, do you suppose I'd turn down ten thousand bucks? Be your age!"

Homer stepped back. "Archie, dig into this joint."

Archie dug in. He turned bedroom and living-room into a shambles. It took him half an hour, and he found nothing.

"There," Donahue said. "I told you."

"Yeah?" smiled Archie. "But you ain't told us what you did with them?"

"You hear that?" Homer asked.

Donahue scowled. "So what?"

"So we're goin' to know what you did with 'em," Homer said. "Come on. Out with it!"

"I can't. I can't because I never had them."

They grabbed him, one on either side, and their guns rubbed his ribs. They walked him to an open window.

"Look down," Homer said. "It's a long fall."

"What good would that do you?"

"What good would it do you?" Archie asked quietly.

"I tell you I never had any papers! I don't know what you're talking about!"

Homer gritted. "You're goin' to tell the truth, fella, or you're goin' to take a header."

They shoved his head and shoulders through the window. The pavement was far below in a dark side street.

"You're goin' to talk," Homer said. "Or you'll hit that street so hard it'll take days to identify you."

"God's truth, I don't know."

They shoved and now he lay on the windowsill with his waist. There was a humming sound in his ears. Blood was pounding in his head. Archie started tapping him on the back of the head with his gun. Slowly and gently at first, then faster, harder, and through the rapid knocking in his head came the thin sound of Archie's chuckle.

"Take a long look, old pal, old pal!" Archie cooed.

"So help me, I don't know!"

They shoved and his body moved farther outward, his fingers scraped against the stone of the building.

He grunted: "Haul—me—back."

"Do you talk?"

"Yes—yes."

They hauled him into the room. He fell to the floor and sat there, his face a dull red, the breath pounding hard from his open mouth. They squatted beside him.

"Tell papa," Archie said, poking him.

Donahue looked from one to the other. He knew killers when he saw them.

"I put them in the mail," he said.

"When?" Homer growled.

"Just after the fight."

"What'd you do that for?"

"I—I didn't want them to be found on me."

"Where'd you send them?"

"To—myself."

"Okey, then where are they?"

"In the mail. They ought to arrive here first thing in the morning."

Archie smiled. "Okey. We'll wait for them."

The phone rang.

Homer said: "Answer it, Donahue."

"Don't be dumb!" Archie said.

"Fat-head, the operator knows he's up here!"

Donahue stumbled to the desk, picked up the phone and held it in both hands. Homer was beside him.

"Answer it!"

Donahue picked up the receiver and put it to his ear. Homer put his head close to Donahue's, near the receiver, and Archie crowded Donahue on the other side with his gun.

Donahue stammered: "I guess—you have the wrong—"

The voice said: "But this is Frank—Frank Castleman. This is you, isn't it, Donny?"

"Oh, yes. Oh, Frank." Donahue's eyes smoldered, his throat ached.

"That stuff isn't here yet. What do you suppose—?"

"It will, Frank.… I'm sorry. I'm busy!"

He hung up abruptly and the two men eyed him strangely.

Homer snarled: "You lyin' two-faced bum!"

"What's the matter?" Archie asked.

"He was just talkin' to the D.A., the louse! He's workin' for the D.A., he is!"

"You're crazy," Donahue scoffed. "That was—"

Homer leered. "So it's the D.A. you're workin' for?"

"No. I owed him some money. I was sending it—"

"Yah!"

Homer stepped back. "Archie, you stay here with this two-timin' wiseguy. I'll go get more instructions."

"Okey, Homer. Don't be long."

"I'll phone from a drug-store and then come back. If he tries to get fancy let him have it and then lam."

"Right!"

Homer shoved his gun into his pocket, opened the door, looked up and down the corridor and went out.

Chapter IV

ARCHIE chuckled. "So you're working for the D.A., old pal, old pal?"

"Never heard of it."

"Sit down in that chair and keep your hands on the arms of it."

Donahue sat down and eyed Archie sourly. "You guys make me sick. You're dumb—plain dumb."

There was a knock.

Archie stiffened, whispered: "Who's that?"

"A lady friend," Donahue said, looking at his wrist-watch.

"A lady friend!" Archie's brows bent. "Tell her to scram!"

"Can't."

Archie came over and towered. "Tell her scram, damn you!"

"I have a date with her. If I tell her to scram she'll think there's something wrong."

"The hell she will. Tell her to beat it and you'll call her later."

"Now you are dumb."

Again the knock.

"You hear!" Archie hissed. "Tell—your—date—to—scram!"

Donahue got up, looked wearily at Archie. He went slowly to the door and Archie followed closely with his gun level. Donahue looked at the door panel.

He said: "I'm sorry I have to disappoint you. I'll call you later. I'm very busy right now."

"But—"

"I'm sorry. You'll have to go."

After a moment there was a muffled, "Oh, all right."

Archie backed up. Perspiration had come to his forehead in those few minutes. He forgot how to smile. The color had ebbed from his face.

Donahue turned and went back to the chair. He was undergoing a change in demeanor. He became self-satisfied, unconcerned. He crammed and lit a pipe and whistled a few bars.

Archie eyed him narrowly. "What are you so happy about?"

"Oh… because I didn't take that header."

Archie threw a look at the door, whipped it back to Donahue. "Who was that?"

"A girl friend." Match went to pipe and through the smoke and flame Donahue's eyes were turned upward at Archie. "I had a date with her."

"What's her name?"

"I don't give out girl friends' names."

"All at once you're getting pretty smart."

"And you're losing the sense of humor you breezed in here with. If we had a checker board we could play checkers."

Archie was white. "There's something screwy here."

"You think Homer'll be back?"

"Of course he'll be—" He stopped short, as if a new idea had walked up and hit him; then he snapped: "Say, what makes you think he won't be back?"

"Did I say he wouldn't be back?"

"You didn't exactly say but—" He stopped again, exasperated. He backed to the door and listened, keeping eyes and gun still trained on Donahue.

Donahue seemed to enjoy his pipe. Archie came towards him with a white threatening face. "I'm getting tired of this, Donahue. I'm getting damn' tired of this."

"Have it your way, then. Go ahead. Homer is coming back. Homer is coming back."

"Who was that jane?"

"All right, I'll tell you. She was the maid. She comes around at this time to turn my bed down. Why not try using your head for a change?"

"You lie, Donahue! You lie! Homer isn't coming back. You know Homer isn't coming back!"

Donahue grinned. "You're losing your grip, Archie."

"Yeah? Grip, eh?" His eyes shot around the room desperately. "I'm bailing out of this joint. Don't move, you!"

Archie back to the door, fumbled for the knob, turned it. He opened the door and threw a quick look outward. "Start after me, Donahue, and I'll let you have it!"

Donahue sat very still, holding the pipe between his teeth. He watched the door close. He did not hear Archie's footsteps because the carpet in the corridor was very thick. He let a minute pass, then stood up. He went into the bedroom, took another gun from a bureau drawer and loaded it. He thrust it into his pocket and went to the door. He laid his ear to the panel.

A quiet knock on the other side started him. His left hand froze on the knob.

He muttered: "Yeah?"

"Can I come in now?"

One eye squinted. He drew the gun from his pocket, whipped the door inward. A young girl stood there.

"Get in," he clipped.

He grabbed her by the arm, pulled her in, closed the door. It locked automatically.

"I'm Helen—"

"I know, Helen. You look like her. And you may not know it, but you just got me out of a sweet jam. Sit down. What's bothering you?"

She looked neat, clean. Eighteen or so. Quiet-eyed and a little afraid.

"My mother wrote me—just last week—that if anything happened to her, I should see you."

Cherry Bliss's girl, down from an up-state boarding school.

Donahue's voice was low—"I'm sorry about your mother, Helen."

"You *are* Mr. Donahue, aren't you?"

"Yeah." He was eying her vacantly. The daughter of one of the big town's most notorious vice queens. "What name do you go under?"

"Helen Thompson."

"Seen any reporters yet?"

"No."

"Don't. For —— sake, don't! Anybody else know you're in town?"

"No. I—mother wrote me last week that she was afraid. She told me that if anything ever did happen I shouldn't show up at the funeral. She told me—who she was. I never"—her eyes dropped—"knew. She said she'd got out of the—business—two years ago, but that a lot of men were still hounding her. Then yesterday I saw the paper. I saw her name—the name I never knew was her name. I didn't say anything. I came down."

"And you never told anybody?"

"No. Only you."

He sat down facing her and took her hands. "Now don't be frightened, Helen— What are your plans?"

She was on the brink of tears. "I don't know. That's why I came to you. Mother seemed to think a lot of you."

"Any dough?"

"I've got about twenty dollars. Mother left some, I know, but I'll have to wait till things clear up to claim it."

"No you don't!" he cut in. "What, claim her money? Come out and tell who you are? It'll ruin you!"

"I must see her—funeral."

"Nix. You came to me for advice, didn't you? All right, I'm telling you what to do. Clear out of town. Don't go near the funeral. You're the dead image of your mother and you'd be recognized."

"But I have no money."

"I owe you something, Helen—for tonight. When you knocked— well, after that a guy talked himself into a swell case of yellow fever."

"I saw him come out," she said. "I was hiding behind the stairway. I thought something was wrong when you spoke to me through the door."

His thoughts were miles ahead. "Listen. You've got to clear out of this town tomorrow. I'll get you some dough and buy you a ticket to Denver. Stay at the Brown Palace there till you hear from me. Listen. You'd better get home now. We'll talk this over tomorrow. Tonight— well, I'm busy. I'd take you home but it's best that you're not seen with me."

"When I came in the lobby—a man looked at me."

Donahue had a rough chuckle. "Don't blame him!"

"I mean, in a peculiar way. His eyes followed me all the way to the elevator."

"What'd he look like?"

"Rather fat, with a sandy mustache. Rather nice-looking man."

Donahue said: "Oh oh," and took a turn up and down the room. He stopped and looked at her. "You stay here. Stay here till I get back. Don't open that door for anybody else."

Chapter V

KELLY McPard sat on a high-back chair against one of the lobby's Ionic pillars. He held a newspaper before him. He had put on ancient steel-rimmed spectacles and looked peculiarly like a small town banker—complacent, urbane.

He saw Donahue come out of an elevator and stride with a business-like air towards the cigar counter. He let the paper droop and his lips bent in a droll half-smile. He saw Donahue buy a paper, some cigarettes. He must have known that Donahue was using the mirrors behind the counter. He raised the paper again.

Turning, Donahue's gaze landed on McPard. The newspaper didn't fool him, nor the apparent interest McPard displayed in its columns. Donahue crossed the lobby.

"Hello, Kelly," he said.

"Why, Donny!"

"Imagine your surprise!" Donahue mocked. "What are you on now, the hotel squad?"

"Oh, I move about kind of." McPard removed his spectacles, held them at arms' length, squinted. Then he put them away in a worn leather case and patted a yawn. "I'm getting weary, Donny."

"Of what?"

"Of all this dodge and double-dodge."

McPard stood up and eyed Donahue placidly.

"So am I," Donahue said. "Damned sick of it."

McPard said: "Let's go up to your apartment and have a long, friendly talk."

"Nothing doing."

"I'd like to look your apartment over."

"I'd like to know where the hell you get your sudden crust!"

McPard shrugged. "My boss over the precinct says I've got to show some results. He says if I can't get you to come across I should bring you over the precinct."

"I didn't think you'd rat on me."

"I'm a cop, Donny. You play me the run-around and you've got to expect the worst. Everything you've told me is a lie and I don't like it. I'd like to poke around your apartment."

"Or else?"

"We go over the precinct."

"And why my apartment?"

"I'm curious about apartments."

Their eyes locked and Donahue said: "If you want to look my apartment over, you go get a warrant. I'm not going to have any flatfoot rooting around my apartment."

McPard touched his arm. "Okey. We'll go over the precinct."

"Wait here. I'll get my hat."

"No. You won't get cold. I'll stand the cab fare. Come on."

Donahue shook his head. "I need a hat and coat. I'm going in no drafty cab. You wait here and I'll go up and get it."

McPard laughed, good-humoredly. "Not in these panties, Donny. I'll go up with you. Why the hell do you want to be so stubborn? Why not—"

"It's a matter of principle, Kelly; that's all. I started off by saying you can't go in my apartment and I've got to stick by it. It's the Irish in me…. But I'm going to get my hat and coat. I'll send a boy up."

"Okey. Snap on it."

Donahue called: "Roy—oh, Roy."

The young red-head came over on the double and Donahue said: "Roy, this is Detective Sergeant Kelly McPard. Kelly this is Roy McAleer…. Roy, here's my key. Go up and get my hat and overcoat— they're in the closet. Turn the lights out, close the windows and put the pooch out."

"Yes, sir, Mr. Donahue!"

The boy pivoted and headed for the elevators.

McPard said: "You're doing wrong, Donny, by going to the precinct. The boss has some rough guys there."

"You don't think they'd shellac me, do you?"

"How can I say? I wouldn't, but you know the boss—he's a go-getter."

Donahue sighed. "It's tough I'm stubborn. What the hell do you expect you'd find in my apartment?"

"Listen, kid. Walter Nass gave you a telephone number when you were there tonight. A jane called you up just before you came in."

"Walter tell you that?"

"Don't blame him. I put the screws on him. I didn't get the phone number because he didn't remember it. I bounced out after you and saw you make a phone call in the corner cigar store. Then you shot back to your hotel. Now you wouldn't have shot right back here unless you had an appointment. I've been in this lobby ever since you came home. About half an hour ago I saw a girl come in. She acted strange, like she didn't know the ropes here. Then she spotted the elevators and went up. I saw the marker stop at twelve—your floor. I haven't seen the jane come down yet."

"Well?"

"I've seen her before, a long time ago, but my memory's cloudy."

Donahue chortled. "That's a hot one! You stand there and think that every strange jane rolls into this casa goes right to my apartment. Hell, I never thought I was so hot! You're not really serious, are you?"

"Donny, I'm getting seriouser."

"You know, Kelly, I've got a mind to take you up and show you what a horse's neck you are!"

"Okey. Show me."

"This bellboy will think I'm nuts. Come on."

They went to the elevator bank. The marker was still motionless at the twelfth floor.

"Waiting for Roy," Donahue remarked.

Presently the marker began moving, and in a moment the elevator opened and Roy came out with the hat and coat.

"In, Kelly," Donahue said.

"Here's your key, Mr. Donahue."

Donahue looked down at the boy's face, pale and curious now against the freckles. "Thanks, Roy." The key was thrust into his hand—and something else. A slip of paper. Donahue's hand closed on both and disappeared in his pocket

They got off at the twelfth floor and Donahue led the way down the corridor. He whistled light-heartedly, but his eyes were glued on the door towards which they walked. He inserted the key, turned it and opened the door. His apartment was dark. He reached in and found the button, made light. His eyes flicked the living-room.

"Come in, Kelly."

McPard came in. His eyes took in the living-room with one sweep. He plodded on into the bedroom, and Donahue took his hand from his pocket, read the slip in his palm.

The "pooch" is out. I hope I did what you meant.

He crushed the paper, took a long breath, let it out and sang a bar from Chloe. He idled to the bedroom entry and saw McPard coming out of the bathroom.

He pointed: "There's a closet, Kelly. And don't forget to look under the bed."

McPard looked in the closet and under the bed. He came across the room, his brows bent, worried.

"Say, Donny, that crack about a pooch. I didn't think you went in for dogs."

Donahue was cramming a pipe. He paused, his back to McPard. His eyes dragged to the ceiling with a weary hopelessness. Then he turned and said: "I like dogs, Kelly. Always have."

"I'd like to see the pooch."

Donahue darkened. "Go to hell! I sent the pooch downstairs. The bellhop sent it down by the service elevator. He does that every night."

McPard smiled. "I want to see the pooch. I like dogs myself."

Donahue threw pipe and pouch on a table. He yanked up the phone. "Bell desk." He tapped his foot. "Hello, Roy. This is Mr. Donahue. Sergeant McPard doesn't believe I have a dog. Will you go down the basement and bring it up?… Yeah, right now."

He hung up and said: "By and by, Kelly, I'm going to get sore."

Three minutes later there was a knock on the door and Roy stood there with a wire-haired. "Here's Laddie, Mr. Donahue." He gulped and handed over a very sleepy pup. He remained in the doorway.

Donahue stroked the dog and said:

"He's just a dumb Irish dick, Laddie…. Well, Kelly, what should I do now—have the pooch stunt or something?"

McPard growled, reddened. "Do what you want with it!"

Donahue gave the dog back to the red-head. "Thanks, Roy. Take the pooch down and see they don't feed it too much."

"Yes, sir."

The door closed and Donahue spread his palms. "Now what?"

"Now that you've got your hat and coat we'll go over the precinct."

"What!"

"You're going to talk, Donny, and it's not going to hurt me more than it does you. Come on."

Chapter VI

KELLY McPard took Donahue out a side exit. He didn't bother with handcuffs; didn't even bother to remove Donahue's gun. And he wore a concerned look.

"I hate to do this, Donny."

"Isn't it the crocodile sheds false tears?"

"Oh, hell—don't ride me like that." He stopped. "Listen, Donny. Come clean. I hate like hell to tote you over the precinct. I tell you, the boss is a rough egg."

"Kelly"—Donahue's face was grave, lined—"you're a white guy. I always said you were. You can't help being a cop. Let's go to the precinct."

Two shadows behind suddenly materialized into two men with guns drawn.

"All right, you guys! Calm, now!"

Donahue and McPard turned. McPard looked at the muzzles of two guns and then at the shadowed faces.

He said: "Boys, I'm a cop. Lay off that baloney."

"We sure hate to pick on you, copper—but there's no other out. Start walking."

"Get, you!" the second man snapped.

Donahue let go of a lazy, dry chuckle.

Homer and Archie got on either side of them and began walking them down the side street towards a parked sedan. Mr. Bunn sat at the wheel, looking pious and detached.

"Cover 'em, Bunny," Homer growled.

Mr. Bunn drew a gun and trained it on Donahue and McPard as they were hustled into the rear. Archie got in and pulled down spare seats, straddled one about-faced. Homer straddled the other and Mr. Bunn got the car in motion. The car was big and possessed of serene, certain power.

McPard cleared his throat. "Strangers in town?"

Archie laughed. "Don't you know?"

"I only know that home town boys would think twice before monkeying around with Kelly McPard. I'm McPard."

"Really! How interesting!"

"Brave, huhn? I've seen your kind get shaky before."

Donahue chuckled. "Yeah, you said it, Kelly."

"Pipe down, you!" Archie snapped.

"Easy," Homer growled. "Don't get excited now."

The car cut westward across town. It struck quiet streets. A cop standing on a corner, twirled his nightstick, saw it go by but saw nothing wrong. The car turned south, sharply; hummed contentedly past dark windows and hulking warehouses. It turned east for a block, then south again; crossed a vacant square and slid down a narrow cobbled street. It passed a large square building, all lighted, from which issued the roar and clank of machinery. The sound made tremors in the street, beat upon the air like a gigantic pulse.

The car stopped a few feet beyond in front of a narrow brick building of three stories above a high basement. From the sidewalk to the front door was a flight of a dozen steps. There was a sign on the door: *For Rent or Sale.*

But Homer had a key. He got the front door open. Mr. Bunn had parked the car two blocks down the street. Homer and Archie had Donahue and McPard in the lower hall by the time Mr. Bunn returned with his quaint air of aloofness and his out-of-line eyebrows.

Archie was using a flashlight in one hand, his gun in the other. The blotched walls trembled to the beat, beat of the machinery next door. The worn wooden stairs up which they climbed throbbed and the rickety banister vibrated. Donahue and McPard were driven to the top floor and prodded into a large room containing a rusty iron cot, bare of covering or mattress. Archie lit a candle that stood on a dusty wooden mantel. Above it a heavy gas bracket jutted from the wall. It vibrated. The sound of the machinery was dull, deadening—a low mechanical roar.

Without warning Archie struck McPard on the head with his gun. McPard hit the spring on the cot, bounced and lay quiet.

Donahue moistened his lips. The yellow candlelight lapped the shadows like lazy waves, made a waving pennant of dim radiance across Homer's grim, coarse face.

"That seemed lousy," Donahue said.

"Pipe down," Homer said.

Archie came over hefting the gun he had taken from McPard. His eyes glittered. His teeth broke whitely in his half-shadowed face.

While Homer held a gun against Donahue, Archie went around behind and took away Donahue's gun. Then he took a piece of piano wire from his pocket, crossed to the cot and tied each of McPard's wrists to the spring. McPard was out—cold.

Donahue lifted his voice hoarsely: "What's the idea of taking it out on him?"

"Because, wiseguy," Archie snarled, "I'm bugs on cops. We had to take him along."

"He'll know this place."

"Who cares? This is just one of our hide-outs. We came to look at it a month ago. The agent lent us the keys to look at it. It took us an hour. In that time Bunny there made a duplicate. Then we took the others back, didn't like the place—we said."

"Smart, huhn?"

Homer crowded him. "We want the truth now, sweetheart. You pulled a fast one in your hotel, but you're in our backyard now—and let us play ball."

"What do you want to know?"

"I want to know if you're working for the District Attorney."

"No."

"Where's the papers you swiped from Buck and Louie?"

"I told you."

"Yeah, you told us a story. We want the truth."

"I've told you the truth."

Archie cursed and kicked Donahue in the stomach. Donahue fell down with a hoarse outcry and writhed on the floor. Homer knocked his knees down and straddled him with his weight full on Donahue's stomach.

"Oh—get off!"

THE floor beneath his head shuddered to the sound of the machinery. No one would hear his cries. He beat his head furiously against the floor in an effort to bring on unconsciousness. But Archie stopped that by kneeling and holding Donahue's head in his hands.

"Nice head," he cooed. "Nice Irish head." Then he hammered the heel of his hand into Donahue's face; his lips got wet and red, gleaming, and his eyes glittered.

Homer was thick-voiced: "Come on, Donahue. We're goin' to get rough if you don't come across. We want to know where we can get those letters."

Donahue spat blood from his lips on to Homer's tie. Homer cursed and bounced up and down on Donahue's stomach. Donahue yelled and struggled and McPard opened his eyes and watched. Mr. Bunn was smoking a cigarette, oddly detached. He strolled over and used a little finger to shave hot tobacco embers into McPard's face. McPard couldn't use his hands. He shook his head until the ashes fell off. Mr. Bunn twitched his eyebrows, bowed and turned to watch Archie and Homer at work on Donahue.

Donahue fainted. Archie used piano wire to tie his feet and hands. Then the three men went out into the hall, closed the door. The room throbbed, the pound of the machinery went on and on.

"Donny," said McPard.

Donahue stirred. "Huhn?"

"What's all this about?"

"Hell!" mumbled Donahue.

McPard said: "These guys are crazy, Donny. They're wipers. What are you holding out on them?"

"If you think you can soft-soap me into talking my head off, you're dumb."

McPard sighed. "Hell, you're stubborn."

"I can take it."

"Where's it going to get you?"

The men came in again. They found Donahue awake and went to work on him. It took them ten minutes to put him to sleep. Archie got up and swore and Homer said: "This thick Mick is beginnin' to get my goat!"

"I'll murder the bum before I'm through!" Archie cried.

McPard growled: "Lay off him."

Archie whirled. "Man, how I hate cops!" He fell upon McPard, hammering his face until Homer dragged him off.

"Archie, don't lose your temper that way."

McPard spat red. "He's sore, I guess, because Donahue's holding out."

"I'll kick your face in, shamus!" Archie screamed.

Homer struggled with him to the door. Mr. Bunn opened it and helped Homer get the cop-crazed Archie out into the hall. The door banged.

After a while Donahue opened his eyes, groaned between puffed and lacerated lips.

McPard said: "Donny—Donny, these eggs'll kill you. There's nothing worth dying for. I know: They're after the same thing I'm after—those papers you took from Louie—"

"You're off your nut!"

"Donny, listen. For —— sake, listen! I had you wrong. I thought you got those papers and was promoting a deal with guys they concerned."

Donahue groaned. "Shut up, Kelly! Shut up!"

"Listen, kid. You're in a tough spot. These guys are hired to get those papers. They'll kill you if they don't get 'em."

"I notice you did enough clowning around."

"Donny, I had you wrong. I thought you were angling to cash in on them with guys they concerned, like I said. Klay said Louie had them. He swore it. So you must have got 'em when you knocked Louie over after he shot Klay. If you haven't got 'em now, there's only one man'd have them."

"Go ahead—shoot."

"The District Attorney—"

"To hell with you, Kelly!"

"All right—to hell with me. But you're in a jam and you'll get yourself killed if you don't stop being so stubborn."

Donahue scowled at him. "You know why you wanted those papers! Because you're a cop and part of a system and because you knew some other cops were named in them! Because Klay was named in them! Because Klay asked you to give him a break. Because you are a cop and you're so square you think no cops can do wrong—and if they do, you want to keep it in the family!"

McPard lay back. "You're right, Donny—part of the way. Klay did ask me—"

"And you'll never get 'em, Kelly! And these guys'll never get 'em!"

"I know. But if the District Attorney has 'em—why all this strong, silent stuff?"

Donahue choked. "Because he hasn't got 'em yet. They're in the mail. He'll get 'em the first thing in the morning. And if these eggs knew that they'd have a gang up at his apartment house waiting for the mailman. Now you know! And what the hell good will it do you?"

"I'll tell these guys."

Donahue heaved. "My eye you will! That stinking political crowd sent these heels after me. They've beat hell out of me and if you did tell them they'd hold us here till they got the papers. I can take it, Kelly. I'm taking it. I'm taking it because those papers will be delivered and that cheap crowd will pay through the nose. For this beating, among other things."

"Donny, they'll murder you."

"I'll take the chance. I've taken too much to squeal now and if you squeal I'll cry it all over town what a yellow rat you turned out to be. It's not my fault that you're here. You walked into it. You keep your mouth shut. Damn you, you walked *me* into it!"

The door opened and Archie and Homer came in, rubbing their hands.

"Ready, Donahue?" Homer said.

"I can take it," Donahue said, a little crazed now. "I can take it like that pink-faced punk with you could never take it!"

McPard bit his lips to silence.

Homer grabbed Donahue by the throat with one hand, struck him with the other.

McPard cried: "Damn you, cut that out!"

Archie hissed, spun, took one leap and kicked McPard on the jaw. The bedspring creaked.

The door opened and Mr. Bunn stood there, forefinger to lips. "Listen!" he cried softly. "I think there's someone in the house!"

Homer stood up and Archie's eyes shimmered. They drew their guns. They went out and Mr. Bunn went with them and closed the door.

McPard groaned: "Who could—have—followed—them?"

Donahue's eyes were glazed, intense. "There's only one—" He stopped short.

"What, Donny?"

But Donahue was wriggling towards the iron cot. He lifted his bound wrists and began sawing the piano wire against the sharp edge of the cot. His wrists dripped blood but he kept on sawing.

"Donny, you'll tear your wrists apart!"

"Shut up!"

He sawed on and on, grunting, groaning, sucking in sharp breaths, biting his lips till they bled. The wire snapped. He looked for an instant at his red hands. Then he worked the wires free of his ankles. His socks were torn, soggy. He stood up and limped. He looked around for a weapon. He went to the gas jet, turned it on. No fumes came out. The house was ostensibly vacant and the gas had been turned off. He unscrewed the heavy brass bracket—it came off into his hands, a length of pipe a foot long. He hefted it.

"Donny, don't be a fool!"

But Donahue had reached the door, a ragged spectre of a man, his hair matted and scraping his eyebrows. He opened the door and looked out into a dark corridor. He went out and felt his way down the stairs. He reached the landing below and listened. He plunged beneath the back stairwell as he saw a beam of light sweep from a door at the front of the hall. He waited. He saw the beam feel its way down the hall, heard the creak of a shoe. Then he saw a hand holding the flashlight—and another hand abreast of it and holding a gun.

He saw the head of Mr. Bunn. He struck. Viciously. The length of brass pipe seemed like a great weight that, falling, bore Mr. Bunn to the floor. Donahue grabbed his gun, stood for a moment listening above the inert Mr. Bunn.

Then, commingled with the pounding of machinery, he heard a faint outcry—below. He found the next stairway and went down on shaky legs. His hands were almost numb. He saw the sweep of a flash's beam. "I got her! I got her!" a voice cried.

Feet pounded from another direction. Another flashlight leaped out of a door. A man followed with his gun drawn. Archie. Donahue's gun exploded and Archie looked upward with a blank stare, turned half around, like a dog getting ready to lie down; then he crumpled.

Donahue fell down the remainder of the stairs. A flashlight swept across his face. A gun boomed. A bullet broke plaster on the wall behind. Donahue fired at the flashlight, heard a groan, a thud, scraping feet and then a louder thud. He swept up Archie's flash and aimed it down the corridor.

Homer was lying flat. Helen was standing, wide-eyed, with her palms pressed to her cheeks. He toiled to his feet and sagged towards her.

"What are you doing here?"

"I—saw. I followed. I broke—in—a basement window."

He fell against the wall. "I owe you things. Now beat it, Helen."

"But you're hurt and—"

"Beat it! You can't be found here! The newshawks'll get here and your mug'll land in the papers and there'll be questions. Beat it. I'll call you tomorrow—see you get away. *Beat it!*"

She turned and fled.

The sound of the machinery was thunderous, shaking the walls.

Donahue climbed up the stairs on hands and knees, crawled into the room where McPard lay on the iron cot.

"Hear it?" he said.

"Not much."

Donahue hauled himself on to the cot.

"Who was it?" McPard said.

"Nobody. It was just an idea they had." He began working on the piano wire that bound McPard's wrists. "I'll pass out any minute, Kelly. So you ring in for the wagon. There's one guy I didn't get completely. He's sleeping down in the hall. Get this, Kelly: you fought it out with these guys. They collared me and you fought it out with them."

"Is that the way you want it?"

"You wouldn't turn down a guy who's saved your life, would you? That Archie was nuts on cops. He would have killed you before the night was out."

"You win, Donny."

Donahue said: "Thanks," and passed out.

He woke up next morning in the hospital, swathed in bandages.

Castleman sat beside the bed.

"Did you get them?" Donahue said.

"This morning."

"Jake. What did Kelly say?"

"He said you could take it." He nodded to the table. "Some flowers— from a lady."

"Who?"

"Anonymous."

Donahue muttered: "The pooch."

"Huhn?"

"Go 'way, Frank. I wanna sleep."

The Red Web

*When tough dick Donahue
makes up his mind about
anything it goes—or
something breaks*

Chapter I

DONAHUE looked at himself in the elongated door mirror. He had lost twenty pounds during the three weeks in the hospital. He showed it in his face, and it was accentuated in his body by the dark blue suit he wore. But the old lean hardness remained, and the self-assurance, the sense of steel beneath the surface.

He turned and walked across the room to a bureau, took a flat black automatic from the top drawer, jacked a cartridge into the chamber and slipped the gun into his coat pocket. He lit a cigarette and watched the door with one eye narrowed against a rising column of smoke.

Eastward, a Third Avenue Elevated train slammed its way south. The air that came in through the open window was cool, crisp. He took four steps and closed the window, looked at his cigarette, looked at the door.

He heard the elevator doors down the hall open and close. He kept his eye on the door and started forward simultaneously with the sound of a knuckle on the panel. He let his right hand lie in his pocket and reaching the door, put his left hand on the knob and turned it.

"Ragtime Bliss, huhn?"

"I'm glad you know me. I thought maybe—"

"Get in."

Donahue jerked his head and the man came in and Donahue toed the door shut and turned at the same time to keep his eyes on the gray face of the man. He had turned on the center lights so that the room would be bright. Ragtime Bliss blinked in the incandescent glare. His clothes were new, cheap, and of a youthful cut that did not harmonize with his old, warped face. He had washed-out eyes that kept flicking but did not meet directly Donahue's dark, unpleasant stare.

He muttered: "You don't seem glad to see me."

"Why should I be? I never saw you before in my life."

"I'm just out of stir. Fifteen years of it. You might at least say—"

Sit down." Donahue pointed. "Sit down there and get it off your chest. Heeled?"

Ragtime touched his pockets. Donahue said: "What's under your arm?"

Ragtime's face looked pained and Donahue clipped: "I'll take it while you're in here."

He went close to Ragtime with his own gun making a bulge in his pocket. Ragtime drew a gun from beneath his left armpit and Donahue, placing it on the desk, told him: "There's a Sullivan law in this state. Or," he mocked, "have you got a license?"

"Cripes, what are you pickin' on me for?"

Donahue said nothing for a long moment. He sat on the edge of the desk, folded his arms and studied Ragtime's face with keen disapproval.

Presently he said: "Well, what do you want?"

Ragtime moved forward to the edge of the chair, rubbed his hands on his knees, stared mournfully at the mouse-colored carpet. "I been in stir for fifteen—"

"I don't want your history. What did you come here for?"

Ragtime made a hopeless gesture. "I been readin' the papers. About Cherry—my wife—bein' bumped off by some heels and about you bein' her friend. See?—I been readin' the papers."

"So what?"

"So—so—well, hell, I been thinkin' about my kid. About Helen. I been wonderin' how she is and if I can do anything for her. I been thinkin' maybe—"

Donahue's voice was wooden, like his face: "You couldn't do a thing for her."

"Where—where is she?"

"I don't know."

Ragtime looked up. "Huhn?"

"I said I don't know. And if I did know, you're the last guy in the world I'd tell!"

Ragtime jumped up, made a supplicating gesture, his knees bent. "You wouldn't tell me—her father?"

Donahue straightened from the desk, put his hands in his pockets and took three slow, inimical paces until he stood over Ragtime. "Listen, punk. I know all about you. I took the trouble to look up Cherry's history and in doing that I naturally came across yours. You bailed out on her when she was having her kid and the next time she heard of you was when you landed in stir for a manslaughter rap two years later. She'd washed her hands of you before that. She had to make her way. You started her on the downgrade. Now get out."

The self-pity left Ragtime's face like a cinema black-out. He shrank back several steps, screwing up his hands. He croaked: "I guess I got a right to see my kid!"

"You mean," Donahue said, "that you think you've got a right to the dough Cherry left her."

Ragtime's eyes popped. "I never even thought o' that! It's my own flesh and blood I'm thinkin' of. She's got a right to a father's protection—"

"The flesh and blood you ditched before she was born." Donahue took a stride and his voice hardened, his long teeth gleamed. "I told you I don't know where she is. I wish I knew. And I'm telling you this, grifter: if you find her first I'll frame you, I don't care how—I'll frame you so that you'll go back to stir for the rest of your life. She doesn't know you exist. She doesn't know anything about you. Get that. And get this!" His hand shot up and gripped Ragtime by the throat. "It's going to stay that way. You hear, punk!"

Ragtime babbled. "I get you! I get you! You'd like that dough for yourself, huhn? You've got your own eye on her—"

"I've got plenty of women without taking 'em in their teens—and when I go in for that kind of stuff, sweetheart, my intentions are never honorable. But I like the kid. I'd like to see her get a break. Scram!"

His arm straightened violently and Ragtime, with a shocked grimace, traveled the length of the room and stopped hard against the wall. He pawed at his throat, made a few gasping sounds, then lurched toward the door.

"Wait," Donahue said.

He scooped up the gun on the desk, walked across the room and held it out, barrel first. Ragtime clutched it and stuffed it beneath his armpit.

Donahue said: "Try using it on me in a dark place some night and see where it gets you."

Chapter II

ASA Hinkle, the Agency head, was nibbling at potato chips and washing them down with an Old Fashion when Donahue, lean and a paler brown than he used to be, came into the small, discreet bar at Milio's. Hinkle was the direct antithesis of Donahue—being older, fat in a solid way, and smoothly pontifical behind delicately rimmed pince nez. Paul, behind the bar, was a dark cameo aptly set in the black marble, mahogany and chromium of the bar.

"Oh," said Hinkle, quietly, and dabbed at his lips with fresh linen. "I'm caught, eh?" He grinned, winked. Donahue said: "Getting better taste in your liquor, huhn?"

"I—er—heard the food was good here."

"I remember—I told you.... Whiskey-sour, Paul—not too sweet."

He leaned with his elbows on the bar, massaged his palms slowly together and stared at nothing, absorbed with himself.

Hinkle said, offhand: "Penny for your thoughts."

"Piker."

On the floor above, where the restaurant was, a string quartet was worrying through "Barcarolle." It was dinnertime and afterwards. Later, the strings would be put away and there would be brass and reeds and drums getting hot. The place had a surface elegance, in the best Upper East Side, New York, taste. Park Avenue was only a stone's throw away and once this house had been tenanted by an ambassador.

"That girl?" Hinkle tried, carefully—and then looked innocently at a potato chip.

Donahue said: "Ragtime Bliss showed up—sure enough."

"I knew he would." Donahue stared hard at his hands. "If I know my heels, he's way down—way down."

"What did he want?"

"What do you suppose?"

Hinkle said: "H-m-m," reflectively and then looked sidewise at Donahue. "The girl, eh?"

"His daughter."

"You treated him nicely, I suppose."

"Can you imagine," Donahue said, "that fat-head spinning me a hearts-and-flowers yarn about his flesh and blood?... Oh, yes, I treated him nice! Like an old friend! Yeah...." His voice trailed off into a harsh rasp.

Hinkle turned and got close to him. "Donny, listen. For the love of —— listen: don't be a sentimental Mick all your life. Granting the girl is good, which I don't doubt she is, why tangle yourself up in this web? Her mother was a notorious vice queen that made a last try to clean out. She was going to turn information over to you that would incriminate several vice squad men, several police magistrates and a surrogate. She got bumped off doing it. The information landed in other hands. You went through a lot of heartache and headache to get it. You got it. You turned it over to our client—the District Attorney. In the meantime this daughter of Cherry Bliss, the vice queen, turns up—broke, desolate, down from an upstate girl's school where she was known as Helen Thompson. She comes to you. Seventeen or eighteen, isn't she? She comes to you and suddenly I find you being godfather—"

"And now you're trying to be godfather to me. Pardon me, Asa, but—"

"I know, but on the other hand—"

"On the other hand," Donahue cut in, turned, raising his palm, "that little girl saved my life. Downtown that night, when those guys were ready to kill me—she'd followed me there. She got in the house. They heard her. They let up on me and that gave me a chance to fight my way out—and get her clear. But it's not mainly that. It's"—his face became warped with brown disgust—"it's that I want to see her get a break.

"Libbey, that foul-minded newshawk, has a hunch that Cherry left a daughter. Don't ask me how he found it out. But he's got his nose to the ground because his boss is on his neck and they're aching to spread it high and handsome. Kelly McPard, a good guy but a cop, wants to know who the woman was somebody or other saw coming out of the house downtown after the shots. And here's a girl who was kept ignorant of her mother's profession for years, learns about it suddenly and has her whole viewpoint knocked cockeyed.

"I liked Cherry, Asa, no matter what she was. This punk of a

husband of hers started her on the downgrade when he pleaded with
her to go to a rotten state's attorney out West to use her charms to
get him out of Dutch. And she went, the fool, and later he bailed out
on her. The kid came to me—what could I do? She wasn't on the
make. She was on the deep end—and it was partly my fault that her
mother got bumped off. I talked her into giving me that information—and, damn it, I really think she thought I was falling in love
with her. I was out after information and determined to get it at any
cost. And that's why I'm for the kid."

Hinkle sighed. "I see. I see your mind's set." He sighed again, looked
at his empty glass. "This business of ours is a pretty lousy one at times,
Donny.... Any word of her?"

"No. She sent me flowers once at the hospital. I tried to get in
touch with her at her old address. No go. I don't know where she
went—or why. But I've got some feelers out. I've got to find her before
her father does—or Libbey, or Kelly McPard. Kelly read a book once
on how to be a cop and it went to his head. And Libbey's drunk
himself to the point where he has to bring in big news all the time
or he'll lose his job. That puts me right in a nice bed of roses—with
plenty thorns."

Hinkle said: "Her old man may prove troublesome."

"You're telling me?"

Donahue tossed a bill on the bar and got a quarter change.

"Where are you going, Donny?"

"I was on my way when I stopped here.... There's a little blonde
trying to catch your eye. What would Mrs. Hinkle say?"

Hinkle reddened.

Donahue poked him in the ribs, chuckled, said nothing and strode
from the bar. He got his brown hat and tan camel's hair in the foyer
and went out into the windy autumn street. He had the rangy walk
of a long-legged man. A block farther on he caught a taxi and it took
him eastward to an opulent apartment house that rose alongside the
East River.

THE doorman looked like a character out of a comic opera. The lobby
was austere, modernistic with many angles of bronze and recessed
mirrors. The elevator was large, silent on its upward flight, and the
corridor down which Donahue later walked was bathed in silence.

A maid in a black-and-white dress opened the apartment door.

She looked like an octoroon and had very white teeth. He gave his name and in a moment the maid returned and let him in. She vanished down a small inner corridor and Donahue went on into a deftly lighted living-room and grinned at the large woman on the sofa. Three Poms crawled over her. She grinned back.

"Hello, handsome."

"Hello, Bertha."

She was Big Bertha, fifty if a day, fluffed and powdered and dressed expensively but in bad taste. She had a finger in many peculiar rackets in the city, and once had been faithful to a Milwaukee brewer until he got kittenish and ran off with a girl young enough to be his grandchild. She had known Cherry Bliss. Once she had knocked out a Filipino student who tried caveman stuff on Cherry, long ago and far away.

"You could make some woman happy, Donny," she said.

"I make a lot."

"Gee, you hate yourself—but I like you, fella!" She held out her hand, slapped it like a man into Donahue's and yanked him down to the sofa beside her.

He picked up one of the Poms and bounced it into an armchair.

"Easy!" she cried.

"If I loved you, I might love your dog. Have a cigar?"

"Don't mind if I do."

He snipped the end off a panetela with his knife. She took the cigar, clamped it between strong teeth. He struck a match, lit her cigar, then his own.

"What about it?"

He picked up another Pom that had crawled on his lap and bounced it after the first. Big Bertha bristled.

"It's the breed," he said. "Why don't you get Scotties?"

"They smell."

She heaved out of the sofa with the third Pom under her arm. She crossed to a Queen Anne secretary, got an envelope and lumbered back to the sofa. She landed heavily, and with relief. She snapped open a lorgnette, held it to her eyes and fumbled one-handed with the envelope until she had extracted a fold of paper.

"One of my girls," she said, "is indebted to me. Heavy. If I moved a finger, she'd go up. She's valuable, as it is. I use her to keep a check on the places where I run my dances. By the way, I'm opening a new place. In Harlem. Dinge. What the hell, it's business. Black hostesses and only"—she leaned towards him—"black sheiks. Here."

She passed him the slip of paper. "That girl of mine went all over town. Women's rooming houses, women's hotels. She's slick—good as a detective, only more reliable. No reflections, Donny."

Donahue looked up from the paper, his face a little weary. "Here, huhn?"

She nodded. "Ten cents a dance for sixty seconds."

He leaned back, chewed on a corner of his mouth. "That's not so good. This the name she used?"

"Mary Stone." She handed him the envelope. "The picture you lent me's in the envelope. She give you that?"

"Sent it—when I was in the hospital."

"How old you getting?"

"Thirty-four."

Big Bertha puffed on her cigar. "She's only eighteen, Donny."

He scowled at her. "I'm not out for her!"

"Just Irish, huhn?"

He stood up. "Thanks, Bertha. What kind of place is this?"

"Not the best. Lot of Filipino trade. Pretty rough—but I keep the precinct skipper smeared well."

He dragged at his cigar, dropped his voice, saying: "How well did you know Cherry's husband?"

"Who—Ragtime?"

He nodded.

"I knew him long before she did. Out in Milwaukee. He used to pound the ivories in a beer garden. I used to sing. I was a lousy singer. You see, Donny, I was always a hellion—I was in trouble for the first time at thirteen. It was through Ragtime I met Cherry—a wide-eyed kid from the sticks. She didn't know what it was all about."

Donahue nodded slowly, reflecting. Then he said: "Ragtime's out of stir."

"That's too bad."

"He's looking for Helen."

Big Bertha blinked, chewed on her cigar, spurted smoke through her nostrils. "The kid, I suppose, would be a soft-hearted slob like her mother—and fall for his song and dance."

Donahue snapped: "Like hell! He'll never get her!" He picked up his hat. "I'll be seeing you, Bertha. Thanks for every little thing, honeybunch."

She sighed. "Boy, I wish I was twenty years younger!" Then she heaved up, said: "Oh, wait; I almost forgot." She thumped into her bedroom, came out with a folded newspaper. "Pipe this, Donny."

He went over beside her and peered at a short item in *Personals.*

Helen T.—Write me or call me. What has happened?—Bob.

"Of course," said Big Bertha, "it might be Helen anybody. I know a Helen Tumulty and a Helen Torgaard. But it just caught my eye. I always read the *Personals,* hoping I've got rich relatives with diamond mines or something in Africa."

He said: "Mind if I keep this paper?"

She said: "Go ahead," and he shook her hand and went out.

Chapter III

IT said: *Dancing Academy* in red, flickering neon letters one story above an all-night cafeteria. The entrance was at the side, with a lighted façade, a wide door. Shiny, slick, too-white or too-dark youths hung around the door. Smart-alecks. Cake-eaters. Nine out of ten on the make.

Donahue was a tall man thrusting through the group. He went up the wide staircase and into the railed-off area in front of the dance-floor. Here dozens of youths and older men hung around, watched. Pale, pimpled boys from the side alleys and small, glossy Orientals from God knows where. Rotten dancers and excellent dancers. But all the girls were hoofers.

There was a large man who leaned in the little gateway, his arms folded. He watched the dancers. Donahue tapped his shoulder and the man turned, hard and blonde and remote.

"Mary Stone on the floor tonight?"

"No."

"Where is she?"

"Ask information, guy."

"Don't get funny. I just had a cigar with Big Bertha."

"Oh." The man grinned sheepishly, then said: "She quit. She called up this afternoon and said she was quittin'. I guess she can't take it. These dames have to know how to take it."

"Thanks."

Donahue turned and went out and a small, young Filipino turned and cruised dark, brilliant eyes after him. Down in the street, on the curb, Donahue took out the envelope Bertha had given him and got a second address. He stopped a cab, got in and gave the address, settled back with the last of his cigar. He tossed the stub away when he climbed out, five minutes later. It was a dark, windy tunnel of a street with narrow, three-story brick houses fronted by high stone stoops with iron rails and gloomy vestibules. Donahue climbed one of these stoops and rang a bell marked *Janitor*.

In a little while a man in a bathrobe opened the door and Donahue said: "Where does Miss Stone live?"

The man's arm went straight up. "Top. Forty-three. In the back. Way in the back."

Donahue nodded briefly, pushed past him and went up the first staircase. It had a brown, worn runner with brass strips at the edge of each step, and the banisters were huge, old. The halls were vast, cold, neat but worn to the bone with age and repeated cleanings. The top hall was the smallest and tan doors shone with cheap, glossy paint.

He knocked on a door that had 43 in tin numbers on the center panel. He waited, hands in overcoat pockets. In a minute a small voice said:

"Who is there?"

"It's Donahue, Helen."

He could hear the small, muffled "Oh!"

She wore a blue skirt and a Russian blouse of white, heavy silk and she looked clean and trim and a little white-faced, frightened. She made a halting gesture.

"Won't—won't you come in?"

He entered the bed-sitting-room that was square, high, with dark mahogany trim and old sand-colored wallpaper. He stopped by the foot of the brass bed and heard the door close quietly behind him. Then he turned and looked at her.

"What's the idea, Helen?"

Her lower lip trembled. She started a gesture with her hands that stopped halfway and then her hands dropped hopelessly to her sides and she went slowly, wearily across the room and sank into an old Morris chair. Quietly she began to cry—soundlessly.

Donahue said nothing at first. He scaled his hat on to the bed, unbuttoned his overcoat and stood regarding her bowed head with dark, troubled eyes. A little grimace passed across his lips. He may have pictured her on the dance-floor of that academy, at ten cents a dance.

"Thanks for the flowers," he said. And when she made no reply, he took hold of a chair, dragged it across the worn carpet and planked it down in front of her. He sat down, sweeping back the skirt of his overcoat.

He said: "Why'd you drop out of sight?"

She shook her head. Her handkerchief hid half of her face.

He went on: "I told you I wanted you to leave the city. A busybody of a cop is looking for you. A certain newspaperman is looking for you. They want to give you a lot of publicity." He leaned forward, elbows on knees. "Helen, you don't know what it's all about. Why did you go to work in that lousy dancehall?"

She looked up, startled. "How did you know?"

"Given time, I can find almost anybody."

She looked away. "I needed money. I went job-hunting. There was nothing I could do. At school I was taught to be a lady. A lot of help that is. But I can dance. I—I needed money."

"What was I around for?"

"I—I didn't want to ask you. You'd got yourself into enough trouble because of me. I didn't want it to go on. There was no reason why you should have done all you did. I thought it was best I go my own way."

"And why'd you ditch the dance-hall?"

She covered her eyes suddenly.

He put out a big hand but did not touch her. "I'm sorry."

But she cried out: "I couldn't stand it. The men—all the men. Especially those Filipinos. The things they said, the proposals they made. It was an awful place. Oh, most of the girls knew how to handle them. But I didn't. How should I have known? I know nothing—nothing. And I couldn't bear it any longer. I couldn't."

He leaned back and let the emotion pass. Then he said: "Well, what now?"

She held her handkerchief to her mouth, stared hard at the floor, then raised her eyes and met Donahue's quizzical stare. "I've been thinking. All day I've been thinking. There is one way out. Mother must have left about ten thousand. I'll go—claim it."

"What!"

She nodded. "Yes."

"Know what that will mean?" His eyes narrowed on her.

"Yes."

He said: "Don't be a fool! Here you're Helen Thompson. You've been Helen Thompson for years. Not the daughter of Cherry Bliss, but Helen Thompson, with a good education, a swell chance in this world. Now you'll chuck that, huhn? You'll chuck all that for ten thousand dollars. You'll go, identify yourself, claim the money and within twenty-four hours it'll be in the papers. Headlines! Pictures! Cherry Bliss's daughter!"

"I'm not ashamed of that."

He said: "You'll never live it down. I wouldn't want you to be ashamed of it, but there's no use broadcasting that to the world. Touch that money, Helen, and it's dynamite. You'll be hounded, persecuted, shamed, humiliated. You're young—you're a kid. Ten thousand won't last you a lifetime. For —— sake, don't touch that money!"

"I must. I need it."

His hand slashed the air. "You don't need it as much as that! It won't do you any good. What's ten thousand dollars?" he demanded suddenly; and his right hand knotted, all but the forefinger and this he leveled at her. "The Williamson Committee is now holding its own court. The information your mother had and I finally got and turned over to the District Attorney is now the main exhibit. Through it a lot of heads are falling. If they found out you were Cherry Bliss's daughter, they'd have you on the stand, too. It would ruin you! The sob-sisters would write columns of trash. The reporters would dog you to death. A dozen guys would be chasing you."

Her chin was up. She looked pale and beautiful. "I can stand all that. There's nothing else for me. I've lost all the friends I made, anyhow. No, they didn't leave me. But the curse of it is that I was brought up in private schools, among wealthy girls—and now I couldn't keep up appearances. So I may as well come out and say who I am. What does it matter?" Her eyes watered and her voice squeaked pitifully: "What does it matter now?"

He stood up. "Listen to me!" His voice hardened. "I can get you out of this. Our Agency has branches all over the country and I have some few close-mouthed friends here and there. I can get you a job—far away, say in Denver or Salt Lake or even 'Frisco. I'll have it all arranged. You'll go there, start over again."

"You're good," she said. "You're so awfully good…. I'm tired now. Will you go?"

He said, tight-lipped: "Will you leave this burg?"

She looked at him levelly. "I can't say—yet."

"Tomorrow will be too late, maybe."

A pulse throbbed in her throat. "Please—may I be alone now? I'm so very tired."

He regarded her suspiciously, with one eye cocked. She turned away and went to a dresser and moved things around pointlessly. It was a long minute before Donahue picked up his hat. He was still dubious, still reluctant to go; that was obviously told by the dark frown, the fretful lips.

But finally: "All right. You're tired."

He went to the door and she came over and gave him her hand. Her smile made a pale glow in her face that had no connection with happiness. Her hand trembled.

In the street, he turned up his collar against the wind and walked away with long strides. There was something savage in his gait. He walked a matter of four blocks, stopped, found he had taken the wrong direction. And then he looked at a street light reflectively and said: "Hell, I forgot."

WHEN he had gone—when, listening at the door, she heard his going-down footfalls become fainter and at last die away, she turned and went back to the dresser and looked at herself in the mirror. She began undressing, taking off one garment after another slowly, in deep thought. She was beautifully formed. She put on a blue silk nightgown and over this a dressing-gown of darker blue, heavier silk. Then she sat before the dresser and brushed her hair.

The door, which she had neglected to lock, opened slowly, then swiftly, and a slim, dark youth came in. His face was dark and smooth and when he tossed off his hat, his hair was thick and black, combed straight back. He had slant eyes and he was handsome in a small, sleek, hard way. There were rings on his fingers, a watch on his wrist held there by a slave bracelet.

"Hello, baby."

She said coolly: "Will you please leave this room?"

He laughed softly. "Yeah, I know that crap, lovely. Boy, you're a knock-out in that nightie. I do get a break, eh?"

"Get out."

He gestured. "What's the matter you don't come around the dance-hall? You're the only jane ever made me fall. You dance like the berries and that ain't all."

She stood up and faced him. "You paid for the dances and I danced with you. The price didn't include this. You're a very cheap little person. Will you please get out?"

He grinned. His teeth were white, his grin bold and brazen. He sauntered over. "You wouldn't high-hat me, would you? I've got dough, lovely. I'm no moocher. But I went nuts on you and I just had to find you.... Who's the boyfriend just left?"

There was no fear in her face. Only a lofty pallor and back of it, faintly, a look of loathing. "Please—go."

"I like them airs, lovely." His smile was crooked, in certain strata it might have been called winning. In his dark eyes a slow fire burned, and her remoteness, her cool beauty had the odd effect of whipping that fire to a greater intensity.

"Gimme a kiss, lovely. Get human."

In a flash he caught her and she was in his arms and his lips hit her tight mouth. Her fingers struck his face and he ducked but still held on and mouthed an obscene phrase and then raised a hand, grabbed her hair and held her head back while he kissed her throat. Her hand settled on a coldcream jar. She struck with it and it stunned him. He flung back savagely and ripped her dressing-gown from her shoulders. There were no words on either side—no outcry. But the whiteness had left her, and the coolness, and now red color shame, overran her face and terror burst into her eyes.

She said hoarsely: "The police will kill you for this!"

"It's worth it," he said. He went towards her, on his toes, quietly, like an animal, with his hands extended. "I want you, lovely, and I'll take the chance."

"Don't! Don't! Please, don't! Please to God in heaven…!"

The door made a sound as it opened swiftly.

She sobbed: "Oh… Donahue!"

The little dark man had wheeled and his hand flew to his hip.

"Don't," said Donahue, his own gun drawn as he walked rapidly across the room. His gun stopped within a foot of the dark man's chest.

He said: "Who is he, Helen?"

"I don't know. One of the men who came to the dancing place."

"Did you ask him here?"

"No. Of course not. He broke in."

"Get your hands up, louse."

The little man raised his hands.

"Turn around."

He turned around.

Donahue took a small automatic from his hip pocket and shoved it into his own. Then he spun the man around. Suddenly he put his big left hand across the man's mouth, held the small dark face locked in his powerful fingers. He put away his own gun. With his right hand he began hitting that part of the face that his left did not cover. He closed the man's eyes. He let the man go and the man fell to the floor.

"Get up," Donahue said.

The little dark man got up and held his head in his hand. Donahue found his hat and slapped it on the rumpled hair. He steered the man to the door.

"Try making love with that face," he said.

"Oh, oh," the little man moaned.

"Follow the banisters down."

Donahue stood in the doorway and watched him disappear down the stairway. He heard the fumbling footsteps, heard the man sobbing. But in a little while the sounds faded away. Donahue turned and faced the room, closed the door and looked at Helen where she stood, slender and transfixed, against the farther wall.

He shook his head, frowned. "That's something I shouldn't have done." He looked at his skinned knuckles, shook his head again. "No, I shouldn't have done it. I shouldn't have beaten him that way. Those guys know how to hate. They're bad actors. And once they get their mind set on a certain woman...." He shook his head violently this time and made a rasping sound in his throat.

"What would I have done, what would I have done?" she murmured.

Then: "What brought you back?"

"I thought," he said, "you might be broke."

She settled into the Morris chair. "I'm afraid. Afraid of this house. I—I'm going to a hotel—now—tonight."

"Any dough—any money?"

"A little. Ten dollars."

He looked around the room. "Get packed. Get your clothes on and I'll wait downstairs."

"Yes. I'll be down—in fifteen minutes."

He leaned against a lamp-post in front of the house. The wind showered sparks from his cigarette.

Chapter IV

DETECTIVE-SERGEANT Kelly McPard was a stout, nicely groomed man with legs that tapered thinly downward to glossy, pointed shoes. His linen was crisp against his expensive blue suit. His rosy-cheeked face beamed good-naturedly in the doorway and he jangled loose change in his pants pocket. Back of the merry twinkle in his eyes was a wily look.

Donahue said: "Now my breakfast is spoiled."

"Try a glass of hot water with a dash of lemon."

McPard closed the door, walked tranquilly to an open window and peered at the East River. Donahue pulled a long terry cloth robe over gray silk pajamas and crossing to the window, closed it.

McPard said: "Look at Tudor City. I can remember when all that coast was a dump. And look at the Chrysler Building. That spire looks nice. I hear they have a swell club up on top there."

Donahue went into the bathroom, scrubbed his teeth and used a red liquid to rinse out his mouth. He combed his hair after running a rubber sponge over face and neck. Returning to the room, he said:

"And the monkeys have no tails in Zamboanga."

McPard grinned with vast pleasure and took a cigarette from a yellow ostrich skin case trimmed with gold. "Have one?"

"Can't smoke before breakfast."

"Can't take it, huhn?"

"Oh, I can take it."

McPard lit up. "Where is Zamboanga?"

Donahue gave him a steady brown look "If this is a pleasure call, Kelly, you have bad manners. Or are breakfast calls the thing now in impolite society?"

"Same old Donny. Pleasant as a burr in a man's sock."

"Spill it."

McPard winked. "It gives me great pleasure to inform you that you're wanted down at Headquarters for a little heart-to-heart talk. We like you down there, Donny. Always like to have you drop in."

"What now?

"A funny thing happened last night. A cop picked up a guy with the blind staggers. He thought the guy was drunk, but it was something else. He couldn't see very well out of his eyes. They were smeared. One ear was up like a balloon and his cheek was open to the bone."

"Were there fights at the Garden last night?"

"You know who I mean. A guy named Manuel Christovão. A half-breed Filipino. I guess the other half is Portuguese or something. I didn't think you ever picked on little guys."

"Never heard of him."

McPard nodded. "Sure, I knew you'd say that. How's to get your pants on?"

"What's the charge?"

"A jane invited him to her room last night. You sprang out from a closet, beat him up and took a hundred and fifty bucks from his pockets. Depression in the agency business?"

Donahue said: "I'll get my pants on."

They went into the elevator ten minutes later and McPard said: "Want to grab some breakfast? I'll wait."

"I wouldn't think of making you wait."

It was a clear, bright morning. They climbed into a cab out front beneath the marquee and it sped them downtown and across. There was a square, bright office into which McPard led the way. Libbey was sitting on the desk, draining a bottle of tomato juice.

"I heard you socked a guy, Donny," he said. "Good!"

"Out a minute," McPard said.

There was no color in Libbey's face and there were dark circles beneath his eyes. He looked a wreck but his air was breezy.

"Okey." He grinned at Donahue. "What did you hit him with,

Donny, the bed?"

"Out," McPard said.

Libbey went out, blowing his nose boisterously.

McPard made a phone call downstairs and then leaned back in a swivel-chair. He removed his hat and patted his silky hair gently into place. His hands were white, the fingernails pink and neat.

"You see," he said, "there's always been something screwy about this business. Ever since Cherry Bliss was bumped off you've been doing a shadow dance. The department is looking for the woman who was seen by three citizens as she left that place where you and I were held up by those heels. They think she has some connection with them. Or with you. Anyhow, they want to make sure."

"What has this pipe dream got to do with that?"

"I don't know. I don't know a thing. I like you, Donahue. I admire you. We've always been friends. But when you come between me and my job, no matter how much I like you I've got to do my job. I hope there's no hard feelings."

"No."

"I thought so."

"I'm just crazy about the way things stand. I'm tickled pink."

"I thought you would be."

"Would you mind going to hell?"

There was a knock on the door and a uniformed cop came in leading Manuel Christovão. The little dark youth had a wad of cotton taped to his cheek and there was a bandage around his eyes. The cop eased him into a chair and McPard, tranquil, said:

"Okey, Monahan. You can go now."

The cop went out and the little dark man sat quietly on the chair with his hands resting on his knees.

"Christovão," McPard said, "what was the man's name who assaulted you last night?"

"It was Dono-something. Donnelly or Donahue."

"What did he look like?"

"He had on a yellow overcoat and a dark hat—dark brown or gray. It happened fast. He was big and dark and he had dark eyes and black hair. He held my face with one hand, so I couldn't yell or get away and he socked me half a dozen times. When I got out in the street I wanted to get a taxi but my money was gone."

"What did the girl look like?"

"She had brownish kinda hair, maybe she was a inch taller than me. She was a good-looker. Her name was Mary Stone. That was the name she gave me. But he called her Helen."

"How'd you come to go to her room?"

"She asked me. She worked at the Trianon Dance Palace and I danced with her a lot and she asked me to come to her room. She wasn't dressed much when I got there. She kissed me and the man broke in—"

"That's a damned lie!" Donahue broke in. "I never saw this guy before."

McPard said: "That sound like him?"

Christovão had stiffened. "Yes," he said.

"Come on, Donny," McPard said. "Who's the skirt? What's the racket? Be sensible."

Donahue laughed harshly. "What do you take me for, a sap? I tell you I never saw this guy before. It's just your bad mind that thought of me when he said the name was Dono-something."

"He described you, too."

Donahue pointed. "All right. But he hasn't yet identified me."

"He can't see yet. It'll be a few days—"

Donahue still pointed. "When he can see, then come after me and maybe I'll come down."

"It was a frame," the little dark man snapped. "She got me in her room and the guy slammed me and robbed me."

Donahue said nothing.

McPard said: "And this sounds like him, huhn?"

"It sure does."

McPard looked at Donahue. "And you're wearing a yellow coat."

"Come out and take a walk up Broadway with me and I'll point out a dozen like it in half an hour." He slapped his knees. "No, sir, Kelly; you can't make me get hot over this comedy. I'll be on my way."

"Hold on."

Donahue was at the door. "If you want me, get a warrant. And try getting a warrant on this half-baked charge."

"I'm going to prove, Donny, that you were in that room when this man got taken for his dough. It's going to link up a long line of shenanigans ever since Cherry Bliss was bumped off. Some day soon

I'll get you in a spot where you'll have to talk."

Donahue said: "Maybe." He opened the door and passed into the corridor. Walking away, he wore a worried frown between his dark eyes.

Chapter V

AT two that afternoon he walked into Big Bertha's apartment. The maid vanished. Bertha was on the sofa with the three Poms. She wore an old rose dressing-gown and had a wet towel around her head.

"What's the matter with you?" Donahue said.

"An old friend I knew in St. Paul blew in last night and we drank fifteen bottles of beer between us. She drank four. I've tried five kinds of pick-me-ups but they don't work. Sit down. You woke me up this morning with that phone call. I felt fine. It's when you get on your feet that the stuff knocks you. You in any more trouble?"

"I'm in enough. If that guy identifies me, it's going to be too bad. I must have been nuts to crack him the way I did. You should see his face."

One of the Poms hopped on to Donahue's knees. He picked it up and bounced it back to the divan.

Bertha said: "She ought to be here any minute."

"How far can you trust her?"

"I told you yesterday. Mabel can't afford to two-time on me."

The buzzer sounded and in a moment a thin, plain woman of forty-odd came into the room. She was dressed in black and looked spinsterish. She looked at Donahue with small, shrewd eyes.

"Well?" said Bertha. She added: "Go ahead. He's my pal."

Mabel said: "As far as I know, he has no police record. He comes from Los Angeles. Came here two years ago. He works mostly alone. He can usually tell the girls he can do business with. I made one of them come across. He never tries to make love to the kind he can do business with. This one gave me his address. She's a customer of his—or was. Heroin. He sells heroin. I had to buy her with heroin—to make her come across. I gave her an address where she could get more. She told me that that is his real name. She said he might be dangerous—that he might do anything for revenge."

"Where's his address?" The woman in black gave Bertha a slip of paper.

"All right," Bertha said. "You can breeze now."

When the woman had gone Big Bertha passed the slip of paper to Donahue. "Yes, his real name's Manuel Christovão. He's a dope peddler. There's his address."

Donahue entered his hotel room at three-thirty, carried a newspaper to the desk, sat down and marked off an item in the *Personals*. He was mixing a drink ten minutes later when the phone rang.

"Oh, you're interested?" he said into the mouthpiece. "How long will it take you to get here?... That's fine." He gave his address and hung up.

Half an hour later he answered a knock on his door. He saw a young man, tall but not quite as tall as himself—and of an age around about twenty-five. The man was slim, sandy-haired. He had a good face, a good mouth and level eyes that were now a little quizzical.

"Come in," Donahue said.

The young man entered and said: "I saw the item in the paper and called right away. It was yours, wasn't it?"

"Smoke?"

"Thanks."

They lit cigarettes, took seats and regarded each other. Donahue's stare was one that weighed, gauged, measured—frankly, candidly. The other's stare was a little puzzled.

"I can't quite make it out," he said.

"Bob what?"

"Roundsville. Robert Roundsville."

"Mine's Donahue."

The boy moved forward on his chair. "What—what do you know about her? Where is she? What's happened to her?"

Donahue's eyes were keened. "How much do you want to know?"

"More than I've ever wanted to know about anybody. I love her. I want her to marry me."

"How does she feel about it?"

"She said she would—and then she vanished."

"You're young," Donahue said. "You look neat and clean and like a swell guy. But you're young. If she got in a jam—or if the both of you got in a jam—how could you take it? Family rich?"

"Yes."

"That's tough."

"I was disowned—four years ago."

"Why?"

"I wanted to paint. They wanted me to go into business. So I went and painted. Had some luck, too—mostly in the past year. I've a swell little place in Passy, near Paris, that was just made for Helen."

"That's better."

"But what about her? You must know."

Donahue said: "I like you. I think you've got guts. Helen's all right—safe—for the time being."

Roundsville was on his feet. "What's the matter?"

"Take it easy." Donahue got up and faced him. "She vanished because she's sensitive, I guess—because she was a little ashamed. I'm telling you this so she won't have to. She's a little lady. She was brought up that way. A little while ago she learned that her mother was notorious. Her mother was Cherry Bliss, a big shot in the vice racket. I knew her. She never told her daughter and she gave her daughter the best of everything."

"Cherry Bliss," echoed the boy.

Donahue's fists were clenched. "Hurts, huhn?"

Blue eyes flashed. "Who said it hurts?" Roundsville snapped.

"There it is, then," Donahue said. "You've read the papers. You know about the Cherry Bliss case. Nobody knows about her daughter but me—and a friend of Cherry's—and a man. I'll take care of the man. I told you this to save the kid a lot of heartache. You can turn, walk out and forget about her. You're under no obligations."

Roundsville's voice got low: "You heard me say I wanted to marry her, didn't you? Where is she? I've got to see her. I've got to get her away from here!"

"Leave me your phone number," Donahue said.

"But—"

"And sit by the phone."

"Tell her," Roundsville said, "I love her."

"I'll tell her."

AT four o'clock Donahue entered the hospital and spoke with the nurse at the desk. He took an elevator to the fourth floor, asked a floor nurse questions and was given directions. On a glassed-in sunporch he found Manuel Christovão sitting in a wheel chair. Donahue carried another chair over, sat down beside Christovão and studied his bandaged face.

Presently the dark man said: "Who is it?"

"Donahue."

Christovão's hands tightened and he drew in his lower lip. "You can't touch me here!"

"That gives you a big break, louse."

"Go away!"

"Not until I've had a talk with you."

"Yeah? I don't want to talk to you. Get out!"

"Pipe down. And listen. Listen close. I just came from your room. Get that."

The little man sucked in his breath. "What right you got bustin' in my room?"

"I'll tell you what I found there. A list of addresses of girls and enough heroin to knock a couple of hundred goofy for hours."

"You didn't!"

"In your room, wise guy. Right in your room."

The little man's breath came rapidly. "You turned it over to the police—"

"No. I left it there. I locked the door. Now I'm waiting for you to identify me when they take those bandages off. And when you do identify me, I'll suggest that the cops go to your room before you do."

The small dark hands opened and closed fitfully.

Donahue leaned forward. "But I'll tell you what you will do. When I stand there, when they take the bandages off, you'll say to the cops, 'No; he's not the guy.'"

Donahue stood up and waited but the little man said nothing.

Donahue said: "Get that?"

"Yes," Christovão whispered, hoarsely.

Chapter VI

DONAHUE entered the hotel in Ninth Street by way of a discreet door and chose the emergency staircase rather than an elevator.

He came out on the seventh floor, walked around an L in the corridor and knocked on a door marked 718.

"Who is there?"

"Donahue, Helen."

She let him in and he closed the door quickly. She looked more rested than she had looked on the night before.

"You're going out of here tonight," he said.

"But—"

"That's finished, Helen. Tonight. You're going out of here. I've got it all arranged. It'll be late, near midnight. There'll be a car up the street and you'll get in it. A man will be at the wheel. The destination will be Boston, and from there you'll sail for Europe as soon as everything is settled."

"But I don't want—"

"You heard me. This town is getting hotter and hotter and if you stay around any longer there'll be trouble. I don't want any arguments. I've seen a friend of yours and he rates."

"Who?"

"Bob Roundsville."

The name was like a blow. It sent her halfway across the room, backwards, with the back of one hand against her mouth.

She cried: "But how...?"

"I'm a great little old finder-outer."

She shook her head. "I can't do it! I can't do it!"

"You can because it's all been arranged. The guy is crazy about you. He's all steamed up."

"But he doesn't know—"

"I told him. I told him everything."

She flared: "What right had you to tell him?"

"The right," he clipped, steady-eyed, "of using my own judgment and hoping to God it was good. It was good. I saw no way of fixing it so that you'd get clear and free of this mess. If I sent you on your own, far away some place, there'd always be the chance of some guy nailing you. Now it's different. This guy Roundsville you're in love with is the real goods. No pretty boy. No mama's darling. He's seen something of life and he knows what he's doing. He loves you. He told me to tell you that."

Her hands dropped. "How do you do these things? How do you

find these things out?"

He said: "You'll go with Roundsville. Tonight."

"It's unfair," she cried.

"For you?"

"No. For him. Why, Donahue—why don't you let me come out and tell everybody who I am? Why—"

He grabbed her and his voice was low, husky: "What are you doing, losing your nerve?" He gave her a gentle shove. "Sit down and be sensible. You love this fellow, don't you?"

"If I didn't, would I have dropped out of his sight?"

"I can never follow a woman's reasoning. But I'll tell you this: if you love him, you'll go with him tonight, because he's hotter than a pancake and if you disappear again he'll bust wide open and get himself in Dutch."

She stared straight ahead and after a long moment she said: "I'll be ready."

"You'll get a phone call," he said. "And if you pull a fade-away in the meantime—in fancier words, Helen, if you fail him you fail me and I'll be all washed up with you."

Her voice was hushed: "I'll be ready, Donahue."

He moved to the door and she got up and came over beside him. He opened the door, looking at her. There was a blinding flash, a sound like *pouff.*

"Okey, Mike," Libbey said.

Donahue whipped into the hall. To the girl he said: "Close it! Lock it!" And slammed the door behind him.

The man beside Libbey tucked the camera under his arm and Libbey said: "These cops are dumb. I just had to find the taxi driver who brought you and the jane here last night. He said you stayed in the cab and the jane went in. He remembered you'd said: 'Good night, Helen.'—Oh, this is Mike. Good photographer. Going our way, Donny?"

Donahue looked up and down the hall. "Yeah," he said.

They went down in the elevator and out into Ninth Street.

Donahue said: "I know a new speakeasy. I guess the drinks are on me. Come on."

Mike and Libbey fell in step and both wore bland, innocent expressions. Donahue whistled snatches of a Broadway melody but back in his eyes, way back, there was an unpleasant light. But he kept his eyes turned away from Libbey and Mike.

"So what do you get out of this?" he said.

"Well," Libbey said, after a series of hiccups. "I was sure Cherry Bliss left a grown girl. The boss had a dream one night or something and he came down to the office and said: 'Libbey, you've got to find Cherry Bliss's girl.' Why? Damned if I know. Pictures, I suppose. Big story. I went to the bank where Cherry banked, but that was a dead end. She left money, but to her 'estate.' It had not been claimed and that scared me. But then I got on your tail. And then—and *then,* Donny—I got a big break. Hot-cha!"

"If this speak is far," Mike said, "why don't we take a cab?"

"You're common people," Donahue said.

"I," went on Libbey, "got a break. I found a guy just out of stir named Ragtime Bliss. Just out of Ohio State. Cherry's husband in the long, long ago. He said Cherry was having a kid when he went up for killing a guy or something. Now here's a poor, lonesome father looking for his long-lost chee-ild. Drama! Think of it! And you're coming between father and child. Not fair, Donny!"

"You're drunk."

"Mildly crocked. So I found him. But I didn't tell Kelly. Why should I? So I got on your tail hot—me and my shadow here, Mike. Of course, I didn't know under what name that jane had registered, so I figured it would be best to follow you. I think it was real nice and clever the way we got that picture. Don't you?"

They were in a street of shabby brick houses with areaways fenced in by rusty iron.

"What good will the picture do you?"

Libbey said: "Front page stuff. Big picture, and underneath: 'Is This

Cherry Bliss's Daughter?' We won't say it is. We'll wait for you to say that."

"Me, huhn?"

"Yeah. Kelly McPard will want to know, too."

Donahue said: "She's not Cherry Bliss's daughter."

"Who is she?"

"A client of mine."

"Really!"

"And if you publish that picture, she won't like it. I'd advise you not to." He slowed down. "Here's the new speak."

They went down five steps into an areaway and pushed into a dim cubicle beneath the stoop, hidden from the street.

Donahue turned. His gun was in his hand. "Now I'll take that camera, Mike."

"Don't you do it, Mike," Libbey said.

"You heard me," Donahue said. "When you guys begin to rat on me because you're afraid of your lousy jobs, I'll get dirty. Drop that camera, Mike. Get back, Libbey!"

Libbey blinked. "Hell, this is rough stuff."

"Drop it!"

Mike did not drop the camera. He laid it down gently. Donahue shoved him back, raised a foot and drove his heel through leather, lenses, plates. He ground them under his foot.

Mike said: "Listen, that gadget cost a hundred and fifty bucks!"

"New teeth'll cost that much and more if you guys don't take your tails out of here. I'll smash this rod smack in your mouth."

Libbey, drunk, teetered on his heels. "Thanks for the drink." He threw himself at Donahue and Donahue raised an elbow, stopped him and then struck with the fist. Libbey went down in a bundle.

"Once," Donahue said, "you were halfway decent, but that cheap bathtub gin ate more than your guts out."

Mike was bending over Libbey. "Hadn't we better go?"

Donahue pivoted, climbed out of the areaway and walked away. His face and neck were red and there was sullen red color also in his eyes. He walked three blocks, entered a door flush with the sidewalk and came into a bar.

"Scotch—straight, Jerry," he said, and went on down the bar to a telephone booth. He inserted a nickel and asked for a number. In a minute he said: "Helen.... Yes, this is Donahue. Leave right away. Go to the Hotel Alacar and take a room.... Everything's all right. Remember—the Hotel Alacar, off Washington Square. I'll phone you there in an hour, so.... No, no; nothing's wrong, Helen. Register under the name of Ann Brady."

He hung up and the bartender slid the drink across the bar as Donahue came toward it. "How's tricks, Donny?"

"Tricky."

Chapter VII

HE got back to his own hotel at five-thirty and went directly to his room. He thumbed a telephone book and got the number of the Hotel Alacar. He called.

"No," said the Alacar operator. "No one by that name has registered."

He hung up and let a slow, exasperated breath steam from his nostrils. He yanked off the receiver and called another number.

"Miss Mary Stone checked out about forty minutes ago."

He pronged the receiver more slowly this time and stared quizzically at the wall. The Alacar was only four blocks from the hotel at which she had spent the night....

He called the Agency. "Hello, Asa.... Oh, you were just about to leave?... Well, listen. Who's there?... Okey. Have Jonesbury, Wills and Garfinkle stand by. If they go home, I'll clout them.... Never mind.... Oh, yeah? Well, then why did you ask?... For this reason: When I start something, I finish it—even if I'm wrong."

Bang! went the receiver on to the hook.

He got up, walked around the room three times—then barged into the little pantry. He reappeared a moment later, darkly, slushing ice, White Rock and Scotch in a short glass. He tramped up and down the room, the long skirt of his yellow overcoat slapping his calves. He finished the drink in two swallows.

He made one more call—to Roundsville. "You're there, huhn?... All right, stay there—with your hat and coat on.... Your bags in the car? Car outside your hotel?... Swell. I'll be calling you."

He went out. Like the wind.

Big Bertha was dressed up like a Christmas tree when he walked in on her. She had on ivory-colored silk far overtrimmed with sequins.

Her bare arms were white powdered boughs and she looked tremendous, comical, absurd.

"Whoah!" she said.

"Listen, you—"

"Mind your tone, Donahue!"

He made an impatient gesture. "I'm sorry, Bertha. She's dropped out of sight again. She was to move from one hotel to another. She left one. She should have been at the other an hour ago. She's not."

"Love her?"

His eyes blazed and his lips hardened. "Make that crack again and I'll bop you!"

"You will, eh?"

"Shut up, then. I'm not in love with her. I got myself into this thing. I've got an idea how it ought to be finished. I told her mother, before she died, that I'd finish it right. I hate like hell to lose. I'm the world's sorest loser. Now shut up."

She was back on her heels. "Go ahead, Donny."

"Get that woman—what's-her-name—Mabel. See if she can find Helen. It's something else this time. Helen didn't pop out of sight of her own accord."

"How do you know?"

"I know."

Big Bertha relaxed. She smiled. "It'll be all right."

The phone in her bedroom rang. The maid got it and called Bertha and the big woman went in, walking as if she were troubled with corns. She reappeared and beckoned.

"Mabel just tried to get you at your hotel. She's on the phone. You take it."

He took it "Go ahead—shoot." He had a pencil out, and an old envelope. He wrote rapidly, listened, nodded and finally said: "Thanks, Mabel. That's great."

He hung up and turned on Big Bertha. "Why didn't you tell me Mabel had her shadowed?"

"What are you crabbing about? Didn't you get what you wanted—from Mabel?"

He put his hand across his mouth, shook his head, took his hand away. "I guess I'm going ga-ga."

She lit a fat cigar. He watched her light it. Then he pulled his hat on and strode past her, out into the corridor. An elevator plummeted. He was in the street. He stood for a moment beneath the bright marquee and studied what he had written on the back of the old envelope.

"Taxi, sir?" That was the chasseur, ivory whistle lifted.

"Yes."

The whistle piped.

Donahue said to the chauffeur: "Cut through the Park. Hit the West Side and go south till I tell you to stop. Make it snappy, too."

"Yes, sir."

At Seventy-second Street the cab turned south into Eleventh Avenue. At Thirty-third it whipped around the front end of a locomotive. It took the ramp at Twenty-third Street to the overhead speedway. There were signs saying *Speed Limit: 35 miles per hour.* The cab did forty-five and left the speedway at Canal Street.

"East," Donahue said.

Three minutes later he got off at a busy corner, paid and tipped the driver and walked away. Balls clicked in a pool hall. Two radio stores, side by side, had loud speakers outside hurling different melodies into the street. There was a big sign over a haberdashery shop: *Closing Out—Bargain Prices.* There were smells, noise, the clanging of a street-car bell. Kids pitching pennies against a house wall and a boy kissing a girl in an areaway. The girl giggled.

And then all this was left behind as Donahue cut through quieter streets. He reached a dark one. He walked down it past narrow, silent houses. He stopped before a four-storied brick house whose hall door was only one stone step removed from the pavement. He looked up and down the street and then he walked around the block and found a grocery store with a telephone booth inside. He spoke for two minutes on the telephone.

He returned to the house in the dark street and walked into the vestibule. The inner door opened at a turn of the knob and he found himself in a narrow hall. A drop light hung from a high ceiling and shone dimly on battleship gray walls.

The stairway, like the hall, was narrow and crowded the right-hand side. There was no heat and the wall had little bubbles of dampness. Donahue covered the first two staircases with speed, but on the third he moved slowly and with care. He reached the summit and stood for a moment regarding the drop light that was just like the one in the lower hall and that cast quite the same feeble glow on battleship gray walls.

In the front of the corridor, where the drop light's glow failed to completely penetrate, there was a horizontal sliver of light close to the floor. It was a beacon toward which he moved on soft soles, until it glowed at his feet and before him was the shape of a door, dark-colored.

He listened for a full moment, recognized voices—one voice spoke rapidly, eagerly, breathlessly. His left hand closed slowly on the knob and he spent a long minute turning it. He pushed ever so lightly, paused, while his right hand went into his pocket and came out gripping his gun.

Whipping open, the door made one fleeting creak.

"All right, Ragtime—stay that way."

Ragtime sat on a chair, far forward. Facing him, on another chair and very close, was Helen. She had on a dark blue coat with a cape-like collar, and a small, snug hat. Her handbag stood in the middle of the floor.

Donahue closed the door behind him, with his left hand.

"What did I tell you, Ragtime?" His voice was low, stiff.

Helen started to get up.

"Sit down," Donahue clipped; and then, again: "What did I tell you, Ragtime?"

Ragtime Bliss looked at Helen, pleading. "You see now? You see how he's got it in for me? Just like I was tellin' you."

Donahue spoke to Helen: "How'd you get here?"

Ragtime jumped up, shoved his chest out. "I brought her here."

"How'd you find her?"

"I seen her on the street. I been lookin' day and night for her—to give her what she needs, a father's protection."

Donahue laughed contemptuously. Helen rose and he snapped at her: "What made you fall for his line?"

She pointed. "He stopped me on the street. He asked me who I was. I ignored him and went on and then he followed me and held his watch open and I saw my mother's picture—when she was very young. I stopped. I looked at him. He said: 'You're the dead image of her. I'm your father.' Why didn't you tell me, Donahue, that my father was alive?"

He said: "Why didn't your mother?"

She reddened. "There is no need to bring my mother into—"

"She didn't," he went on, "for the same reason that I didn't. Because your father's a bum, a louse, a dirty trickster—"

"He didn't tell you," panted Ragtime, "because he didn't want you to get any help from the place you should. I asked him on me bended knees, I did, where you were. I wanted to help you, hon. He wouldn't let me. He slammed me."

Donahue was cold, deadly. "You want, Ragtime, to drag her down to your level. You want her money. You want her to travel in the company you travel in. You're getting on in years. You want her to take care of you. And when the money's gone you'll make her support you—and maybe I've got a good idea how."

Helen was white-faced. "You should have told me, Donahue, about my father. How can I believe you now? You knew I had no one in the world to turn to. Why didn't you say my father was living?"

He said: "How do you suppose he found you?"

"I don't know."

"He was hooked up with those newspaper guys who tried to get your picture. They didn't know—they only guessed—that Cherry Bliss left a daughter. He told them—"

"I didn't!" cried Ragtime.

"You are going, Helen," Donahue said, "out of here."

She was high-chinned. "I am staying. I am going to do what I'd intended doing. I'm going to make myself known, claim my mother's estate, go with my father to California—and we both can start over again. That is what I'm going to do."

He said: "I've given myself a lot of headache, I've made a number of enemies, in order to keep you in the clear. I'm not going to let you fall for this bum's sob-story. I could walk out on this now. But I won't. I hate to lose. You keep your hand away from your armpit, Ragtime!"

"Please," she said, "leave us. Leave us—let me do what I want to do and don't ever see me again."

"No."

"Why?"

"Because this business of finding your father has knocked your common sense all haywire. You found him—and presto!—the magic word... father. Someone to turn to. But it's all the bunk. I tell you he'll ruin you, rob you, send you on the streets. I know his record. He sent your mother—"

"You are," she said, "a bad loser. All these maledictions get you nowhere. Will you please, please let me live my own life?"

His gun steadied. "I figured it out how this should end. I'm a conceited guy. I'm not going to have certain people say that I fell hard for a girl who chose the streets in the end. I hate that line, 'I told you so.' Button your coat."

Her chin was up and he watched it come coolly towards him. She laid her hand on the barrel of his gun and gently turned it aside.

"You're not going to use that gun, Donahue."

Ragtime Bliss moved swiftly. His hand brought a gun from his armpit and he darted, trained it on Donahue's back. "You get out! You leave my poor daughter alone!"

Donahue's neck got red. He turned slowly on his heel and looked at Ragtime.

Helen said: "Put your gun away, Donahue."

Watching Ragtime, he put his gun into his pocket.

Helen stepped between them, looking at her father. "Now you put yours away."

"No," he said. "If I do, he'll slam me."

"Put it away."

Fear welled in Ragtime's eyes. "No! No! I'll handle this! Get out, Donahue!" He thrust Helen aside. "You hear, Donahue!"

She flew back at him, grabbed his arms. "Please, please, put that gun away!"

"He slammed me once! I hate him, I do! I hate him like poison! Let go—me—me arms!" He heaved violently and his left elbow cracked her on the jaw. She tottered, fell, and her head grazed the corner of a table on the way down.

"Oh," she moaned.

Horrified, Ragtime's glance whipped towards her.

Donahue's fist traveled like a piston. Ragtime went over the bed backwards and landed on the other side. With one hand Donahue grabbed up Helen's handbag. He was able to use both hands in raising her from the floor. Her eyes looked fogged. He sped to the door with her, into the hall, while Ragtime was scrambling on the floor.

Donahue went down the three stairways swiftly, with Helen moving in his arms. He reached the street door and outside the street looked dark, deserted. But when he reached the step, he saw the red light of a car a few doors up the street. Then a shadow moved towards him.

"Donahue!"

He stood the girl on her feet. She put a hand to her forehead and then what had been a shadow was now Roundsville, very close.

"Helen!" he cried in a hoarse whisper.

She was a little dizzy, but she must have seen his eager face. "Bob—Bob—"

"Scram!" Donahue muttered.

Roundsville's hand gripped Donahue's arm hard. "Old boy… !"

"Beat it!"

Roundsville half-walked, half-carried Helen up the dark street. Donahue watched—saw them disappear into the car—saw the car move off and vanish. He backed across the street and dropped down into an areaway. His gun was trained on the opposite doorway.

He murmured: "He asked for this. It's waiting for him."

A minute passed and no shadow moved in the doorway. Donahue rose a bit. The sound of three shots, muffled, drove him back into the areaway. The echoes died away. The street was silent. Donahue walked out of the areaway, walked west. A man came out of the doorway and yelled:

"Help! Police!"

Donahue ducked into an alley, followed it to another street that was dark and as yet unaware of the cries. He took his overcoat off and carried it under his arm. He zigzagged through the streets and after a while, blocks away from the narrow house, he climbed into a taxi.

Chapter VIII

A T eleven next morning he walked into Big Bertha's apartment. She was playing Russian Bank with Mabel. Mabel did not look up but Bertha waved a hand, shouted:

"Hello, handsome!"

"Hello, kid," he said. "I was just down to Headquarters. It was funny—that Filipino failed to identify me. Was Kelly McPard mad? Boy!"

Big Bertha said: "I see Ragtime got his belly full of lead last night."

"I see," Donahue added, "that his assailant left by the back window and the fire-escape. And no fingerprints. But on the platform outside the window—a flower pot was overturned and they found a woman's footprint in the dirt. A long, narrow shoe with a worn spot on the ball of the foot."

Mabel—thin, dark, dark-clothed—laid down her cards and got up. "I guess," she said, "I better burn those shoes."

She walked out of the room.

Big Bertha reached for a cigar, cocked an eye at Donahue. "You see, Donny, I never told you that Mabel was the first girl Ragtime started on the downgrade.... Got a light?"

Red Pavement

Tough dick Donahue crashes into a load of grief

Chapter I

DONAHUE had stopped in the dark, windy street to cup his hands over a match. He heard the door bang, and looking up from the match's glow, he saw the drunk reel towards him across the sidewalk. He stepped aside, still maneuvering his hands in the wind to get a light, and had the flame leaning steadily towards his cigarette when he heard the grunt and the sound of the man piling headfirst into the gutter, near a fire-hydrant.

The door opened again. Tossing the match away, Donahue saw a head thrust out, the shadow of a face beneath a fedora; then the head withdrew and the door banged shut. He stood for half a moment quite complacently enjoying the first drags of smoke and watching the drunk's awkward efforts. The wind came from the west, up West Tenth Street and smack against his back, flapping the long skirt of his belted camel's hair and humming past his rigid Homburg.

"Here," he said, at length.

He swung to the curb, grabbed a wandering arm and hauled the man to his feet. He grinned good-humoredly.

"Steady, brother. Another dive like that and— Stead-y!"

" 'S all right—'s all right, brother. Must have been somethin' I ate. 'S trouble with restaurants these days: you can't depend on nothin' any more."

"Come on; I'll steer you to a subway."

The man grunted. "Idea." He reeled around and poked Donahue's arm. "An' not only restaurants, brother." His lower lip pouted; he teetered back on his heels. " 'S damn' shame, 's what!"

"Come on; snap out of it."

"Sure. Where was we goin'?"

"Subway. I'll pilot you to Sheridan Square."

"Swell idea. Le's go…. You goin' uptown, too?"

"Yeah."

They went along the dark street, past the pale glow of a speakeasy areaway; went on—the man bouncing along on his heels like a marionette and Donahue keeping a firm grip on his arm. He was no great bundle to handle; short, bony-faced, with a gray, hard pallor. New clothes, cheap but substantial. And he was very drunk. The whites of his eyes rolled into view frequently. They reached West Fourth Street and the drunk stopped resolutely.

"T' hell with subway. Le's get taxi. *Taxi!*" he yelled.

Brakes squealed and a cab stopped on the opposite side of the street. Donahue hadn't bargained for this, but traffic was flowing past and he did not care to see the drunk run down. He steered him through the traffic and put him into the cab.

"Where d' you want to go, friend?"

"Hell. You're comin' uptown, ain't you? Come on!"

Donahue shrugged and climbed in and the man said: "Penn Station, Jymes."

The cab started off and the drunk leaned against Donahue's shoulder. "Gonna meet her, brother. Gonna make her my wife. Penn Station,

train at 9:02. She come a long ways. To meet me." He poked himself, hiccoughed. "Be my wife."

He swung away, heaved over on one side and dragged awkwardly at a hip pocket. He drew out a small wallet and a big .38 revolver. His lip drooped and he said:

"Here, hold this rod a minute, brother."

Donahue took it, hefted it; guns were in his trade and he liked the feel of this one.

The drunk had taken a small snapshot from his wallet. "Her picture, mister." He looked, oddly enough, like a yokel just then.

Donahue glanced sketchily at it, then said, hefting the gun: "You want to look out for this rod. What the hell are you packing a cannon like this around for?"

"Ah," the drunk said, and winked with tremendous spirit. He closed his hand over his gun and thrust it into his overcoat pocket. His teeth bared in a drunken grimace and he stared grimly before him. "I gotta pack it," he said.

Donahue was good-humored, twisting a smile off his lips. "I know, but look at it this way: here you show me, a perfect stranger, a rod the State of New York says you're not allowed to pack. Of course, personally I don't care who packs a rod, but if I'd turned out now to be a city cop instead of a private dick—well, where'd you be?"

"Uh," said the drunk. "Yeah, I get you. I gonna be careful. I gotta—" He stopped short, fell against Donahue, gripped his arm. "You—you're a private detective?"

"Yeah."

"Good! Listen, brother—now listen." He tugged at his wallet, counted out some bills. "Here. Here's a hundred bucks. Listen, now. I gotta meet this gal. But I'm drunk, see? I'm stewed. Some swell lousy pals o' mine got me stewed. Tell you what. You meet my gal, tell her I been detained on business. You take her to a hotel—make it the Grandi, and see she gets a room there. Me, I'll get me a Turkish bath, get straightened out. Hey, wait now! How the hell do I know you're a private dick?"

Donahue chuckled, showed him plenty of identification. He was frank. "This is easy money," he said.

"A hundred bucks. Count 'em. I—jeeze—I got to get straightened out. You see, I just come back from South America—struck it rich— and these fine, nice, lousy pals o' mine...."

Grinning, Donahue pocketed the hundred dollars. "Now wait, brother. You'd better lend me that picture of the girl. Tell me her name. Also, I'll have to have your own name."

"Sure! Sure I'll"—he sought his wallet again—"lend you the picture. Name's Laura and she's—"

Donahue had his little book out. "And your name."

He turned, by instinct more than anything else, and saw the long black shape of the touring car draw up and crowd in close. But he hadn't time to get a word out of his mouth. He hadn't time to snap his hand to his gun.

A gun crashed four times.

Donahue flung back against the side of the cab, ducking. The driver ducked and slewed in his seat and the cab careened, brakes screamed, but at the same time there was a tremendous bounce as the wheels went over the curb. The right front mudguard crashed against a building wall. The car recoiled and glass shattered.

Donahue was pitched forward out of the seat. He struck the glass partition between tonneau and driver's seat and collapsed on the floor, facing backwards. The drunk piled down on top of him violently and Donahue felt something warm and liquid slap his cheek. He straight-armed the drunk off, hauled himself up and dropped to the seat, hot and shaking all over. His client was gurgling on the floor, in the darkness there.

The driver was pressing his forehead down on the upper rim of the wheel. The man on the cab's floor was groaning and gurgling, and up and down the street autos, trucks, were stopping; the shots, the sound of the crashing taxi had frozen a few pedestrians into immobility and they remained thus.

"Brother...."

Donahue got a flashlight on and sprayed light down on the man's face. He shut the flash off immediately, grimacing.

"Brother...." The tone was curiously sober.

"That's all right—that's all right."

"Listen. Go meet her. It'll be tough, her comin' alone. Go meet her. Here... take this wallet. Key inside—for bag—"

Donahue snapped: "Cut out talking."

"Here, take it"

"Will you shut up!"

He felt a hand pawing at his own.

"Take it. You'll recognize her by the picture. There's some dough in it. Give it to her. Here. There's a baggage check in it. I got a bag at the station. Get it. Give it to her. Tell her to get out of town—go home again—I'm sorry—"

Donhaue found himself taking the wallet shoving it into his pocket.

And he heard the broken voice go on: "Don't tell—the—cops. It ain't her fault. She—don't—know—and—"

"For —— sake, shut up!"

It was hard to listen to the gurgle of a dying man. There was no reason why he had to listen to it. The man was a stranger.

"Hey, there!"

That was a voice outside the cab—loud and challenging.

Donahue pushed open the door and climbed out and a cop came up to him, stopped and eyed him with a hard stare.

"What the hell happened?"

Donahue's thoughts were on the sprint. In his pocket lay the hundred dollars representing his fee for promising to meet and conduct to the Hotel Grandi one named Laura something. He did not know the man's name—nor the girl's. He had a rather thorough opinion of a harness-bull's imagination. To tell this cop the truth as it had happened would, in the clear sound of words, seem fantastic. He would not expect the cop to believe him. Part of the truth might get by. The fact of the matter was he had seen an easy way to make a hundred dollars, had taken the case as a joke; and the joke had turned into tragedy.

"Take a look in the cab," he said.

The cop snapped on a flashlight and poked into the tonneau. Donahue watched him, his eyes narrowed.

"Hey!" the cop yelled; then he backed out, spun around. "That guy's dead."

Donahue said: "A curtained touring car yanked up alongside us and let go. The guy inside got it."

"Who's the stiff?"

"I'm damned if I know."

The cop towered with rage. "What the hell are you trying to hand me?"

"I picked him up in a gutter downtown. He was soused. Like a drunk, I couldn't get rid of him. So we took a cab."

The driver looked out, choked: "F-four shots!"

"You," the cop said to Donahue, "are lying!"

"So what should I do now? Break down?"

There was no turning back now. He had the man's wallet. To turn the wallet over now would be to put himself in a very serious jam.

The cop twirled his nightstick and laughed unpleasantly.

"Okey, guy, okey. Be wise, be wise…. Hello, Coake," he said to another cop who had come up on the run.

"Hello, Donlin. What the hell?"

"A stiff inside."

"Who's this?"

"A wise bimbo."

Donahue said: "You cops!" with hopeless irony, and chuckled.

A car drew up at the curb and a stoutish man alighted without haste and came across the sidewalk slapping gloves he held in one hand across the palm of the other.

"I heard shots."

"Yeah," Donlin said. "Pike what's inside."

The stoutish man looked into the cab, backed out and said: "Well, well," in a merry voice. "And who's—"

Donahue was leaning against the building wall, eyes cold but watchful.

The stoutish man said: "Well, well, Donny!"

Donahue's "Hello, Kelly," was not enthusiastic.

"He's a wise bimbo," Donlin growled.

Kelly McPard grinned broadly. "Hell, he's all right. Just has a habit of being Johnny-on-the-spot. So what happened, Donny?"

"Ask precious," Donahue said, indicating Donlin.

Donlin told him, and then said: "And this guy right away starts to act dumb like a Dago."

McPard made a face, as though all this was unpleasant business. "Tsk! tsk! Well—well, suppose we get the morgue bus. Did you frisk the stiff?"

"No," Donlin said.

"Better." He backed away from the cab, turned casually and looking up the street, said to Donahue: "What about it?"

"It's blind to me." Donahue shrugged. "I told the cop everything I know."

Kelly McPard kept looking up the street and said thoughtfully: "Ye-es, I suppose so.... Well?" This was directed at Donlin, who had come out of the cab.

"Only this." Donlin held the .38 auto in his hand.

"Full?"

"Yup."

McPard sighed and said to Donahue: "Mind running over the station house?"

"I gave the cop all the dope. I was headed uptown. You know where I live."

McPard shrugged. "Okey."

"What!" yelped Donlin. "You gonna let this ape—"

"Ah," drawled McPard, "he's all right. We don't need him." There was curious laughter back of his voice, a wily dip to his head. "Run along, Donny. I wouldn't think of pestering you." And there was still that curious sense of laughter.

Donahue walked away.

Chapter II

HE had decided a dozen times in the space of as many minutes to turn the wallet over to McPard. And in the end he hadn't. He was Irish, and that may have accounted in some measure for the sentimental streak beneath the tough hide. That—or the fact that he and Kelly had a habit of playing hide and seek with each other. Within limits he trusted McPard. Kelly was square. But he had long wanted something on Donahue, and this would have been too good a chance.

It was two minutes to nine when he heaved out of a taxi at Penn Station. He slapped swing doors open, went down into the main rotunda. The only 9:02 train would arrive downstairs. He went down and saw a man in a cap marking on a blackboard that the 9:02 was expected to arrive at 9:15. He worried a cigarette between his lips and cast a quick glance over the waiting people. The small wallet felt hot and oily in his palm; he kept that hand religiously in his overcoat pocket. Shop windows were bright and cheerful in this subterranean cavern, but the air was always stuffy, second-hand, winter or summer. He prowled around, looking. He pushed into a soda counter, entered a telephone booth, took out the wallet. It contained two hundred and twenty dollars. There was the girl's picture. She looked young, brown-haired, nice. On the back was inscribed: "Love to Charlie from Laura." The snap wasn't very old. And there was a baggage check. He replaced the articles in the wallet, the wallet in his pocket.

"Tough," he said, thinking of the picture.

He went out and looked at the blackboard again. His watch checked with the electric one above: 9:12. Then the man with the cap was megaphoning: "Blah... from... blah... Columbus... Wheeling... blah... was due at 9:02...blah... Track... blah!"

People got up and moved down the corridor. Donahue tailed along, looking around. His eye lit on a small young man leaning against a stone pillar. There was a sensation of something clicking as the little man's eyes met his own. Then they dropped, a foot ground out a cigarette and the little man sauntered off, whistling. Donahue tried to catch sight of him a moment later, but was unable.

People were coming up the stairway from the train level below. Donahue watched and saw her but did not immediately go to her. She was very small, with a startled, pretty face. A porter was beside her, holding a bag and asking something. She kept shrugging and peering eagerly at the faces. It was minutes before the crowd went away, and then she stood there alone with the porter drooping beside her. Donahue cast another look around, then went over to her.

"Laura?"

There was a frightened smile. "Yes!"

"He couldn't meet you. He sent me.... I'll take that, porter." He took the bag and gave the porter a quarter. "This way, Laura—"

"But—"

He was pointing: "We have to go to the checkroom first." He flung a look over either shoulder.

"How is Charlie? Why couldn't he come?"

"Yes," he said, making believe he misunderstood. "The checkroom's upstairs. Have a nice trip?"

"Oh, long. Lonesome."

"There it is over there."

He gave the check to the man at the counter and received a small yellow handbag that looked new. Gripping it in his left hand, the girl's suitcase in his right, he started off.

"Come on. We'll get a taxi."

They got one in the tunnel and rode out into Seventh Avenue. Donahue had given the address of his apartment-hotel. He was glad the girl didn't talk. She sat quietly in a corner. He sat in the other, his arms folded and his face in a hard, brown study. Presently the cab stopped and the hotel doorman let them out. Donahue lugged the bags and they went up to his apartment. He could tell by the way she looked when they entered his rooms that she expected to see Charlie there. She turned on him as he was closing the door.

She said, weakly: "Something—something's—"

"Ssh!" He skated the bags into one corner and scaled his hat on to a divan. He went on into the bathroom, looked at himself in the mirror and thought: "Of all the saps, Donahue, you're the berries—with all the trimmings." He turned, strode out of the bathroom with his coat's long skirt slapping his calves. He walked straight to the center of the room and stood there grinding the heels of his hands slowly together and regarding the girl with a glazed introspective look.

There was a little cry—"Oh!" And small white fingers suddenly against cheeks from which the color was ebbing.

He took a step and laid a big hand on either of her small rounded shoulders. "He's dead, Laura." That was the easiest way—right out with it. He felt the rounded shoulders twitch and he saw her looking up at him with a peculiarly abstracted expression. Then she stepped back and began walking up and down the room, swiftly, quietly, with her eyes fixed on the carpet. Suddenly she dived on to the divan and lay there—still, motionless, without a move, without a quiver.

He grabbed the back of a chair and dragged it across the carpet, planked it down in front of the divan. He sat down and scrutinized the palms of his hands, turning them this way and that.

He said, as if talking aloud to himself: "He asked me to meet you. That bag there: he asked me to give it to you. He said you should go home again. He said he was sorry he couldn't meet you. He gave me some money to give to you—to get back on, I guess."

She broke into sobbing and he got up and entered the bathroom and washed his hands. The running water dimmed the sound of her sobbing. He washed his hands over and over again, throwing secret glances at his image in the mirror. After a while he turned to the room and saw her sitting up. Her hat was askew, her face smeared with tears. She sniffled, stared straight ahead of her with blank, wet eyes.

"Where can I see his body?"

"I wouldn't," he said.

"I want to."

"You can't."

She looked up at him. "Why?"

"It was his dying wish that you shouldn't."

Her tone was dull: "How did it happen?"

"He was shot. I guess it was an accident." He tossed the wallet to the divan. "His money's in that and the key to his bag. I'll get you a room in the hotel. I brought you to this apartment because I thought it'd be easier."

"Who—who are you?"

"My name's Donahue. I'm a private detective."

"You knew Charlie well?"

"I never saw him before. I just saw him when he was dying."

"And—and you did this—for him—for me? You did this for strangers?"

He frowned and turned away. He was glad she didn't rave and carry on hysterically. She wasn't that kind. All her emotion remained inside, locked up, torturing her. You could see that much in the stunned white face, tell it by the dull, listless monotony of her words. Then she was feeling at her throat.

"Do you—you mind if I stay here till I can get a train?"

He shivered. He wanted to get her into another room, out of sight; he wanted to get her out of the city as soon as possible. He had done enough. He didn't want to have a strange girl on his hands.

She was saying: "I hate to ask it. I—I'm not that kind of a girl, you understand. But—but I'm afraid to stay alone. I'm just—afraid. Coming like this—from a small town—I've never, been in a big city. And I'm afraid to be alone. I'm ashamed to ask you, but..." She moved her shoulders wearily and then covered her face with her hands.

"Okey," he said after a while. "Sure. Stay here. I never thought of that." He nodded. "Bedroom's in there."

He picked up her suitcase and Charlie's bag and carried them into the bedroom. He frowned and muttered, to himself, but when he reappeared in the living-room these manifestations of his ill-humor were absent. She was standing, a small, lone, pitiful spectacle.

"In there," he said.

She smiled wistfully. "You're so good, Mr. Donahue—so good." She dragged her feet past him and entered the bedroom, closing the door quietly.

He crammed a pipe and lit up, took to pacing with slow, long strides, his face wrapped in thought. A few moments later he heard a sharp outcry. His nape bristled, his eyes narrowed and he whipped to the connecting door, flung it open.

She was on her knees, shaking, her eyes wide. She looked up at him and grimaced and pointed downward. He crossed the room and looked down into Charlie's open bag.

It was crammed with money—hundreds, thousands of dollars.

Chapter III

THE connecting door was closed—locked. He had heard the girl turn the key quietly on the bedroom side. It amused him more than anything else. There was a single in-a-door bed in the living-room, if he wanted to use it later. But the divan would do. He was interested in neither, though, at the moment. Coming out of the little pantry that contained nothing more than an icebox and a sink, he tried the Scotch highball while heading for a mohair easy chair. Dropping into the chair, the dim glow of the floor lamp behind made his smooth black hair shine but kept his face mostly in shadow.

Fourteen thousand five hundred dollars. He looked at the connecting door: the money was behind that door. He drew on his pipe and heard, far away, the thresh of a southbound Elevated train.

Charlie Stromson was his name. It was like this: He'd known her in Revelation, Ohio, six or seven years ago. She was the cashier in the

Center Square General Store. Charlie worked in the Sportsman's Exchange, the game and fish store; he was a wizard at repairing guns and fly rods and mounting fish or birds. Then he got it into his head that there was gold in South America. They became engaged, and he went off to find a fortune.

He wrote her three months later from New York, that he was leaving for South America to get their fortune. That was the last she heard of him for three years. Then there was a letter from Montevideo. He'd made his fortune and he named a date when she was to meet him in New York. She sent a letter care of the General Post Office, New York, saying she would meet him on the appointed date. She'd shown Donahue the letter post-marked at Montevideo. It told of hardships in the jungle, of privation, months and years away from any civilized town.

Donahue muttered: "Um," and took a long drink. The sound of a knock on the corridor door made him lower the glass slowly and stare. He had removed his shirt—his suspenders looped around his hips—and was in worn leather slippers. He got up, went to the secretary, put the drink down and picked up his gun. He crossed to the door.

"Who's there?"

"It's Kelly, Donny."

Donahue thrust his gun into his hip pocket. He threw a look at the closed bedroom door, then turned the key in the one before which he stood and opened it

McPard looked neat in his blue overcoat and soft gray hat. His shoes shone. His cheeks were pinked up by the wind outside and his smile bloomed whimsically in his cherubic face. He wandered in, cast his smiling, twinkling eyes around the room. Donahue closed the door and stood for half a moment eying McPard's back.

"Park, Kelly…. Drink?"

"No, thanks." McPard sat down on a straight-backed chair, drew a white linen handkerchief from his pocket, unfolded it and blew his nose quietly. "That guy who was bumped off, Donny…." He patted his nose gently, put away the handkerchief.

Donahue drew his eyes away from the bedroom door. "Yeah?" He walked across to the secretary and scooped up his drink and carried it on to the divan. "Yeah, Kelly?"

"Hell, now, Donny"—he made a palliating gesture with his hands—"why not give me the straight of it?"

"I did, Kelly."

"I know, I know. Straight as a crooked list I don't say you had anything to do with his death, Donny; you know I wouldn't say a nasty thing like that."

"I know; you wouldn't like to hurt my feelings."

McPard grinned. "Exactly!" He leaned back, crossed his legs. "It didn't take us long to place him. I didn't expect much, but anyhow I wandered through Rogues' Gallery and—sure—there was his mug—there it was."

Donahue snapped a look at the bedroom door. "I don't believe it, Kelly."

"So his mug led to his record. He did a three-year stretch."

Donahue stood up, growled: "That's something you thought up!"

McPard chuckled absently. "Yeah, I thought you'd say that. But it's no go, Donny. I guess you weren't so hot as a bodyguard."

"Bodyguard?"

McPard stood up and regarded Donahue affectionately. "Come, now, Donny—don't try to kid me. I just want the truth. When did this mug hire you, where did he live, and who bumped him off—and where," he added, smiling whimsically, "was the dough bunked?"

"You know so much about this, Kelly: tell me."

"There was around twenty thousand involved. This mug blew into New York from the wide open spaces about three and a half years ago. He got tangled up in the wrong end of town. One night this egg and two pals walked into a gambling joint uptown and collected twenty thousand bucks in a handbag they swiped from the joint's office. In the mix-up one of the customers got shot and spent a month in the hospital. One of this egg's pals did the shooting. They scrammed out with the dough, this egg hauling the bag. Cops were bearing down. The two pals got big-hearted and told the egg to take the bag and beat it—they'd meet later.

"Well, he beat it. He waited in their hide-out for a week, but they didn't show up; they were waiting for the tail to cool and besides a couple of dicks were working that street and the pals were afraid. The egg finally leaves the hideout. We pick him up two weeks later on a loitering charge, not knowing who he is—and then he's identified by the guy who was shot. But he won't squeal on his pals—no names, nothing. And he swears he doesn't know where the money is. He gets three years. He comes out six weeks ago and tonight he's bumped off.

He was afraid of that, I guess, so he hired a private dick."

Donahue shot back: "The only reason a guy like that would hire a private dick would be so he wouldn't have to pack a rod himself. Well, this guy packed a rod. You saw it. And besides, since when have I been so hard up that I'd rent out to a heel?"

"You mightn't have known."

"I didn't know what he was. I picked him out of the gutter down near Sheridan Square. He was plastered. He couldn't stand up so I thought the best way to get rid of him would be to shove him in a subway train. Well, I walked him a couple of blocks and then he got the taxi idea. I didn't want to go with him, but you know how drunks are—and, anyhow, I was headed uptown and it meant a free ride. I never saw him before in my life. I didn't know his name."

McPard seemed politely bored. "Anyhow, Donny—anyhow, what I came here for in the first place was to tell you that Inspector Overhill wouldn't take my word for it that you were on the up and up. So you better put a shirt on."

"Listen, Kelly—"

McPard shrugged. "What's the use? Overhill wants to see you. I'll wait." He added: "Meantime, if I were you, kid, I'd think it over. This Charlie Stromson left some dough. Overhill's very eager about knowing where. Besides, when a guy hires another for a bodyguard he usually tells the bodyguard the names of the guys that are after him and what they look like."

Donahue swung around, glowering: "I told you—"

"That's right, that's right. You told me you weren't hired. Tsk, tsk! I keep forgetting." His eyes danced with a wily blue twinkle. "I'm waiting."

Donahue cursed him, put on a shirt and tie. His eyes darted to the bedroom door. No sound there. McPard had not even noticed the door.

"Okey," Donahue said, swinging the overcoat over his arm.

They went down in the elevator. Going across the lobby, McPard pulled out a packet of cigarettes, took one, said: "Have one, Donny?"

Donahue took one and McPard struck a match and they lit up from it. Outride, they climbed into a taxi. It turned left into a side-street, then down Park Avenue, which lower became Fourth.

OVERHILL, a blonde man with big ears, a Roman nose and a wicked pair of eyes, said: "There you are, Donahue," and kicked shut a desk drawer upon which his foot had been propped. He scanned some sheets, leaned back and made a pyramid of his fingers.

"Well, Kelly, what's the dope?"

"Donny's in the dark."

Overhill planted his elbows on the desk. "You knew this man, Donahue. You were riding with him and the cock-and-bull story you handed Kelly doesn't go over—not at all. Now I'm not here to waste my time or patience on a private dick. I don't want a song and dance. I want to get the guys that killed him and I want to recover a certain amount of money. This Stromson cached about twenty thousand before he was imprisoned. He got it when he came out and these two heels went after him to get it. He hired you—"

Donahue broke in: "As for wasting time, Inspector, mine's as important to me as yours is to you. Kelly went over all that and I told him what I'm telling you: I never saw this guy before until I picked him out of the gutter tonight."

"You're lying, Donahue."

"Did you get me down here to pinch me?"

Overhill frowned. "Of course not. I got you down—"

"I know—to hand me a lot of crap. Well, keep it. Any time something happens within a hundred blocks of where I happen to be, you damned blockheads get me down here and put on an act. I'm getting fed up on it!" He glared. "And if I'm lying, you prove it. You go ahead and prove that I knew this bird, that I was acting as his bodyguard when he was bumped off. Prove it! And when you prove it, get out a warrant for my arrest or a subpoena as a material witness—"

"Here, here!" Overhill said. "Don't get all steamed up—"

"Oh, don't get all steamed up! Maybe I should take it as an honor!"

McPard shook his head. "Tsk, tsk! All over nothing. We're just your friends, Donny—"

"Oh, yeah!" Donahue said, nodding his head. "Yeah. Like"—he drew a forefinger across his throat—"this."

He pivoted and strode to the door.

"Hey," Overhill said, "where you going?"

But Donahue did not reply. The door banged after him.

Overhill shrugged. "No use, Kelly. We haven't anything on him. He knows it."

Kelly McPard smiled whimsically and rosebuds bloomed on his cherubic cheeks. "Some day, Ed… some day I'm going to make Donny say Uncle."

Chapter IV

WHEN Donahue sailed into his apartment the first thing he noticed was that the bedroom door was open. The next thing he noticed was that the bed had not been slept in.

The girl was not there.

Both bags were gone—the suitcase and Charlie's handbag.

His eyes brown and hard, he cruised around the apartment. There was no sign of a struggle. Nothing was overturned, no rugs had been scuffled. He stopped in the center of the living-room and his thoughts went round and round. She had listened, heard Kelly and himself talking. Afterwards she had slipped out. No note of thanks, no note of explanation.

The phone rang and he answered it. "No, don't send it up. I'll be right down."

The clerk at the desk was mysterious when Donahue confronted him downstairs. "A lady left this letter for you with instructions that I should give it to no one but you." He smiled. "She emphasized—'no one but Mr. Donahue.'"

"What time was that?"

"About forty minutes ago."

"Thanks, Herbert. You're a great guy."

He walked to a corner of the lounge and opened the letter beneath a shaded wall light. It read:

> *Dear Mr. Donahue:*
> *I heard the conversation between you and that man. He was a detective, I guess. I am sorry. I wanted to open the door and tell him you were in- nocent but I was afraid. I am taking the bags to the Penn Station. I thought that I better get Charlie's bag out of your apartment in case some policemen came back. I will wait at the information booth in the station until midnight, in case you come back. Then you can come over and tell me what to do. If you don't come, I will check the bag and throw away the check. I don't want it. Then I will take the first train home I can get. The way you talked to that man, I know you would not want me to show up. But I am very*

grateful to you for everything.
   Laura.

He crumpled the letter and stuffed it into his pocket. She had used her head, taking the bag out. But—he cursed—it would be like her to throw away the money! He stalked out of the hotel, hailed a taxi and climbed in. Ten minutes later he climbed out at Penn Station and made his way to the information booth. She was not there. He looked all around, ventured into the waiting-room, came back to the information booth. He sought out every nook in the station, re-covered the waiting-room and returning to the information booth stood with his hands in his pockets and regarded the floor darkly.

It began to occur to him that his position was not as secure as he had felt it to be when he walked out of Overhill's office. Certain people had seen him take the girl into the hotel earlier that evening. The clerk was a good fellow, but the cops could make him talk. If she turned up a corpse, they would be able to get a fair likeness of her for the tabs. Certain people in the hotel would recognize her....

He shook his head, made a sound in his throat and strode long-legged out of the station. He stood for a moment on the curb, the wind hooting and clapping about him. A cab drew up.

"Taxi?"

Donahue said: "Maybe that's a good idea." He climbed in and said: "Sheridan Square."

He leaned back, his hands way down in his pockets and his shoulders hunched. The more he thought of it, the less he liked it. He took the letter out of his pocket, tore it up into little bits and let them fly out the window. He did not go quite as far as Sheridan Square.

"Stop here," he said, and got out at Hudson Street and West Tenth.

He made his way slowly down West Tenth Street, bending his head into the wind that blew from the river. He was frank with himself. No mock heroics. The guy with the death gurgle in his throat asked you to do something, and like a sap you did it. The girl turned out to be a pop-eyed little thing from the sticks. You broke the news to her as gently as you could. You didn't have to be gentle about it, but you were, anyhow. Then you felt relieved: it was simple, and you'd put her on the train back, tomorrow, brush your hands together and—finish. Hell! —— you would. The yellow handbag turns out to be a plant, the girl is more shocked than you are. You still are able to get over that. "Take this dough, little one, go home and bury it for another five years. Then use it." But then Kelly had to turn up....

No. No mock heroics. Not tonight. Not now, especially. There was one thing essential, paramount, vital: this girl must not turn up a corpse. Not under any circumstances must the cops find her; not alive, if possible, certainly not dead. So Donahue was frank with himself. He was not being gallant—not now. He was intent on saving his skin, his license to operate, his sense of superiority born of his always having been on the right side of the fence when the cops got gay. When you got right down to it, the girl as a personality meant nothing to him; she was significant only for the fact that her death would bring the cops down on him. And, he reflected, a girl wandering around with almost fifteen thousand dollars was certainly a potential corpse.

He recognized the glow of the areaway speakeasy across the street. He moved on, and in a minute he saw the fire-hydrant. He continued to the end of the block, crossed to the southeast corner and came back up West Tenth on the south side of the street. By this time he had his gun in his overcoat pocket, his fingers gripping it loosely.

He remembered the door, not because it was unlike the other doorways in that block but because it lay diagonally across the sidewalk from the fire-hydrant. He remembered considering how neatly the drunk would have opened his head had he struck the hydrant.

Going up to the door, he put his left hand on the knob and turned it. The door gave but he did not immediately throw it open. He stood deliberating for half a minute. He threw a glance up and down the street. Then he opened the door swiftly the length of his arm, stepped in while his right hand came out with his gun; shifted deftly and quietly on his feet and in a second had the door shut behind him, without a sound.

For the space of a minute he did not move. He stood rock-still, his gun held level with the lapel of his coat pocket, his breath bated and his ears straining. The hall was black as pitch but there was, beyond in the darkness, an oblong of slightly lighter darkness that seemed familiarly like the night outside. He went towards it. The oblong was a door. The door was open. It led into a small yard. Standing not too close to the doorway, he could smell the damp earth. After a moment he slipped into the yard and hugged the outside wall.

It was a sort of hollow square. A high board fence separated it from the yard back of the house on the next street. The house he had entered had a wing extending on either side as far as the fence. These wings made the east and west side of the hollow square, the fence made the south, the part through which he had come made the north.

There was an outside wooden stairway up the front of the west wing, with a platform at the top, and a door. On this door was a spider-web of light, as if a green shade, cracked with age, had been drawn down over the glass panel. Otherwise there was no light, no sound of life or even hint of it, within the hollow square.

He crossed to the foot of the wooden stairway, looked on the building for a button. There was none. A railing went up the outside of the stairway, supported at intervals by a post. He started up, keeping close to the face of the house. He paused on the next to last step and listened. The night had an emptiness about it; street sounds, not nearby, had a bell-like clarity.

He took the last step rapidly, rapped soundly on the glass panel. His right hand shoved the gun back into his pocket and remained there. The door opened, a blowzy fat man in an undershirt stood there outlined against light made hazy by skeins of tobacco smoke. He was sleepy and halfway through a yawn, and Donahue shoved him backward, stepped in and said:

"Now sit tight, everybody."

It was a large room, dusty, smelling of liquor, tobacco, old perspiration. There was a round table in the center with a drop light, green-shaded, above it. Poker chips were on the table, stacks of silver and bills; and around the table three men in shirt sleeves. The skeins of tobacco smoke wound sluggishly around their heads. They did not move. The three of them leaned with their elbows on the table. One had a deck of cards, ready to deal. They had about them the beady-eyed immobility of rats at bay.

"Sit down, you," Donahue muttered.

The fat man pawed his way around to the fourth chair and sat down. His fat eyes popped and he wore an injured expression.

Donahue said in a dead-level voice: "I may be up the wrong alley. Who runs this scatter?"

The fat blowzy man looked very pained.

"You?" Donahue said.

"Well, that is, now—as you would say—if some boys want to play a little cards and drink a bit—" He stopped and sat back and looked injured again. "I don't see—that is, as I would say—"

"Hell," chopped off the man at his left. He had a face the color of cement and looked quite as hard. His pale hard eyes were steady on

Donahue. The man next to him made whistling lips but no sound came forth. He wore a gray hat and an innocent, youthful expression. The man on his right had a bald head and a red neck.

This man fidgeted and then said: "You a dick?"

"Suppose I am?" Donahue said.

"Well, I'd say, then, we only spoke to the skipper last week and he said he'd lay off. He's gettin' his cut. He and Henry—"

"Of course," the fat man nodded. "Me and Bill there—" He looked around indignantly. "Me and Bill are okey with the skipper."

The man with the pale hard eyes growled: "This guy ain't no dick! Damn it, this guy ain't no dick!" He shoved back his chair.

"I wouldn't do that," Donahue said.

The man subsided, but his pale eyes glowered. The youthful man in the gray hat went on making whistling lips but still no sound was heard. He kept looking at the cards in his hands.

Donahue said: "It's about Charlie Stromson."

The man in the gray hat choked. This startled everybody at the table. The man broke into a violent fit of coughing and the pale-eyed man towered in his chair. The other sneezed, choked, and finally sat with his eyes running water.

Donahue said: "You get up, put your coat on."

The man rose, put his coat on and stood sniffling and wiping his eyes.

"Pull your hat down a little more." The man did so.

"Okey," Donahue said. "Now sit down again and—and this goes for all of you—keep your hands on the table." His voice lowered, his eyes were fixed hard on the man in the gray hat. "When Stromson pitched out of the street door tonight, why did you open the door and then duck back?"

The man sneezed. "I didn't open no door."

The fat man and the bald man both looked very innocent and the pale-eyed man stared hard and bitterly at the man in the gray hat. He seemed about to explode but didn't. Instead, he tore a card in two and slapped the pieces angrily down on the table.

Donahue was grim. "No song and dance. I'm in the right scatter and I'm going to get what I came after. I'm looking for the woman. I'm looking for fourteen thousand five hundred bucks. I'm looking for the guys that bumped off Charlie Stromson."

The pale-eyed man forgot himself. He jumped to his feet and his chest swelled, his eyes got doubly large and hard and they had a white whiplash look in them.

"Who the hell bumped off Charlie Stromson?" he bellowed.

"Sit down, you."

The man sat down—but sitting, he towered, his jaw thrust out like a slab of cement.

The blowzy fat man insisted: "This man's a dick! I tell you he's a dick! Listen, now listen—" He stopped and threw a peevish look around the table. "May as well tell him. I'm going to tell him." He looked up at Donahue. "This Stromson was here. He got tight here. He was here, see, and about eight-thirty he goes. He goes out about eight-thirty. He gets halfway down the steps and falls. Louie"—he nodded towards the man in the gray hat—"Louie goes out and sees. I guess he picks him up. Anyhow, in a few minutes Louie comes back. This is on the up and up. Louie comes back and says, 'Hell, Charlie's in bad shape.' I say, 'Well, Louie, maybe you and Beef ought to look after him.' And Louie says, 'I told Charlie. I said we ought to look after him, but he says he can take care of himself.' So we think, well, Charlie'll be all right and we sit down to play. That's God's honest."

Donahue said: "Why did Charlie come here?"

The fat man shut up like a clam. The pale-eyed man had undergone a considerable change of expression. He stared at the table with a bright, concentrated look. He was thinking—hard. He looked up suddenly to find Donahue eying him with keen scrutiny.

"You," Donahue said, "and this mug in the gray hat were the two pals that stuck up that gambling joint with Charlie. He banked his dough before he went up to stir and you two smart sweethearts chiseled in when he came out."

The man in the gray hat choked on this and went into another fit of coughing.

"Will you stop that!" the pale-eyed man cried.

Donahue's voice picked up an edge, swiftly. "I'm not going to monkey around here. I'm no precinct dick. I'm just a sap that walked into a jam out of which I'm getting nothing but a headache and a swell chance of taking a rap for a stunt you eggs pulled off tonight. Well, I don't take raps. Where's the jane?"

The pale-eyed man leaned back. "Guy, we been here in this joint since eight o'clock. You ain't worryin' us. We didn't know this umpchay was bumped off till you told us." He grinned, seemed confident and suddenly sure of himself. "We're strictly kosher, and there's a phone over there if you want to call the cops. See if we care."

The fat man began fussing like an old woman: "Now, now, Beef, don't go makin' the gentleman mad. Of course, that is to say, well, I'm okey with the skipper and all that—but if I cause him any trouble, it'll mean a bigger cut. Me and Bill here"—he indicated the bald, red-necked man—"like to play square with everybody."

Louie, the man in the gray hat, moved nearer to the pale-eyed Beef, and the pair assumed an attitude of mixed hostility towards the operators of the joint. And Beef said:

"I don't care. This palooka ain't goin' to faze me none. I'm clean. You guys know me and Louie been in this dump since eight or before."

Donahue remained silent for a long moment. Then he shrugged, grinned and put his gun in his pocket. The fat man sighed and smacked his hands together.

"Now, now, sir, that is what I would call—well, so to speak, that is—"

Donahue was at the door. He said: "Fourteen thousand five hundred bucks are floating around somewhere." He was noisy going down the stairway. He did not go far. There were many nooks in the dark hollow square. He pressed back into shadows and waited.

Chapter V

TWENTY minutes elapsed. Then Beef and Louie appeared on the landing. Both wore hats and coats. The door closed behind them and their feet came down the stairway. They did not go towards the door leading to West Tenth. They went around the bottom of the stairway and passed through a hole in the board fence. Donahue went after them. In the street, they walked into a cigar store. Donahue went on, walking rapidly. At the corner he climbed into a cab and said:

"Just wait here a minute."

He watched through the rear window, and when he saw Beef and Louie come out of the cigar store accompanied by two others, he said:

"Drive around the corner and park."

In a minute the four men, walking briskly, crossed Hudson Street and got into a cab on the east side.

"When that Checker starts," Donahue told the driver, "swing around and tail it. Don't get too close—but don't lose it."

The tail led up the West Side, went across town at Fortieth as far as Madison, and then north. It made a right turn into the Fifties, swinging in with a few eastbound cars. The Checker stopped at the next block and Donahue, passing in his cab, saw the four men get out. He let his cab cross to the east side of Park, then got out, paid up, tipped generously and walked back to the west side of the avenue. The four men, he saw, had started walking west. They walked in pairs, Louie and Beef in front. A little farther on, they turned and climbed a brownstone stoop, opened a door and disappeared. Donahue waited a couple of minutes, then went up the steps, opened the door there and entered a high, narrow corridor.

There was the sound of a piano being played lazily. Muffled drone of voices. A girl reached for Donahue's hat and coat. He gave her a quarter but kept both. At the end of the corridor was a wooden door with a glass port high up. He went down and looked through the glass. There was a chummy bar inside, half a dozen men. Beef and Louie and the others were not present

Donahue pushed open the door. There was a wide door at the right, a dim-lit room beyond. A man was drowsing over piano keys, playing lazy rhythm. A girl was leaning on the piano singing in a whisper.

Donahue said: "Rye high," to the bartender. Turning, he caught a glimpse of a small young man leaving the other end of the bar, heading for a curtained doorway at the rear. Donahue moved slowly, then a little faster as the curtains opened and closed. He pulled them aside. There was a small lighted sign halfway down the hallway: *Men's Room.*

Donahue took two long running steps. The small man turned around. Donahue had his gun out. He did not stop. With his left hand he grabbed the small man by the collar and hustled him into the men's room. The door swung shut.

"Quick, you!" Donahue clipped in a hoarse whisper.

"Look out now—"

"You're the nice-faced punk I saw at Penn Station tonight! Where is she?"

"I don't know what—"

There were voices coming down the hall. Donahue rushed the man into one of three closets. The cabinets had half-doors, with two feet of open space at the bottom. Inside, he snapped the catch and kept his gun jammed in the small man's back. Several men entered. He heard them talking, laughing. In a few minutes they went out.

"Now," Donahue said, "spill it!"

"You're hurting me!"

"Oh, am I? Listen, you! There's an open window leading to an alley. If you don't yap, I'll let you have a bellyful and take that window out. Quick, now!"

"Honest, I don't know anything."

Donahue took a big gun from the man's pocket "You're just an angel, I suppose. You're going to be an angel for me, sweetheart. Where's the jane? By —— where is she?"

He had the man by the throat now. He pressed hard, while his knee kept the man pinned to a sidewall of the cabinet. The man twisted and writhed, his tongue stuck out and his eyes bulged.

"Where is she?"

"Leggo."

Donahue eased up. "Now."

"Upstairs."

"How'd she get here?"

"I—brought her."

"Who wanted her?"

The man shook his head and Donahue went to work on his throat again.

It came out—choked: "Hagin...."

"He upstairs?"

"Ugh—yeah."

Donahue said: "Okey, sweetheart. Now don't think you're going to waltz right after me and...."

He struck with the man's gun—on the head, a short, hard chopping blow. The man sank without a sound. Donahue pushed him against the back wall of the cabinet. He did not unlock the door. He got down on hands and knees and crawled out. Looking at the outside of the door, he saw that the indicator said: *Occupied.*

He put a gun in either pocket and left his hands on them. He went out into the corridor and began climbing the stairway. In the hallway above, he stood for a moment, then went to the rear and peered through a windowpane there. He unlocked and opened the window. There was a fire-escape outside, leading to a court below. He left the window open. The lazy sound of the piano seemed far away.

Moving up the hall, he listened at doors. At the third from the rear, on the left, he listened longest. Then he retraced his steps to the door nearest the rear window. He tried it. It was open and he entered a large bedroom. A small bed lamp glowed. The room was empty, and an open door gave into another room that was dark. He moved into it on soft rugs and saw a long, thin sliver of light where sliding doors had not quite closed. He returned to the bedroom, took stock of his bearings, then turned out the bed lamp. All was in darkness now. Looking through the open door, he could see the thin sliver of light. He moved towards it.

The slit was not large enough for him to see through. He counted four or five different voices. There was a heated argument, everyone was talking at once. He pried the doors apart, a bare half-inch, noiselessly. Now he saw Beef and Louie and the two men they had picked up downtown. The four were in a dangerous huddle around a blonde burly man, at the far side of the room.

Donahue pulled out his guns. He worked the doors apart another inch. No one noticed him. Bit by bit he got them far enough apart to enter. He entered and stood quite silent. He saw the girl on a couch. She looked unconscious. Her hair was down and her clothes were twisted. He stood waiting, the guns in his hands, level with his hips.

It was the burly blonde man who saw him first. The others stopped talking.

"Hold that pose, all of you," Donahue said.

"It's him!" muttered Beef.

Donahue said: "So you and Louie were just a couple of home-loving card players. Fighting over the split, huhn?"

The burly man began: "These mutts—"

"You're Hagin," Donahue said.

"I'm Hagin. These mutts walked in on me. Let me walk out of this huddle and it's worth a thousand bucks to you."

"Put the thousand on the table."

Hagin took out a wallet, emptied it. "I got only nine hundred here. I'll get the rest up. Now lend me one of those rods and I'll teach these grifters a lesson."

"You sit right down in that chair," Donahue said. "You other guys hold that pose."

Hagin dropped down into the chair, his eyes wide. "Why, you

dirty—"

"Pipe down. There's a lot of dough flying loose around this burg tonight. Most of it I can't touch. So I'll touch what I can." He moved slowly to the table, caught up the sheaf of bills with the two end fingers of his left hand. "Somebody's got to pay my taxi fare. You, Hagin—you were the guy ran that joint Stromson and these two heels crashed that night. Right?"

"Right! And now these two bums tango in here with a couple of punks—"

"Pardon me. I want to get this straight. It figures, then, that the little punk downstairs was the guy you sent after Stromson. He got Stromson and then he went to Penn Station to head off the jane. You didn't know just where the dough was bunked. You figured the jane might know. I got to her ahead of the punk. The punk tailed us, camped on my doorstep. I went out. The jane went out later and he clamped on to her and brought her here. What I can't figure out is"—he looked at Beef—"where you guys horn in."

Beef growled: "Stromson took the rap for us and kept his trap shut. When he come out, we crowded him. He bunked the dough in the country before he went up. We knew he took the rap and he kept his jaw shut. We dickered and he offered us two grand apiece and that was okey by us. Then for some goofy reason he takes a boat to South America, soon as he's out of stir, and comes back on the same boat. We try to roll him for some dough by gettin' him into a card game. We get him drunk three nights runnin', but he won't play. And we don't know where he's bunked the dough.

"There was a little guy hangin' around Bill and Henry's for a week. Bill says he's hidin' out. This little guy leaves about half an hour before Stromson does tonight. Stromson was belly-achin' about a jane he had to meet at Penn Station. When you bust in there tonight we know there's only one guy'd be after Stromson. Hagin. So up we come, after Stromson's dough. The little guy's Hagin's punk. We saw him downstairs but didn't let on. You drop them guns, fella, and you get a third of the dough. Hagin's got it."

"You're a damn' liar!" Hagin said. "I haven't got it."

Beef snarled: "You bum, you got it! When we crashed in here the jane was out cold!"

"If I got it," Hagin growled, "why the hell would the jane be out cold?"

She was lying now with her eyes open.

Donahue said to her: "Get up, put your hat and coat on and go out. Got the wallet?"

She shook her head.

Donahue said: "Hagin, give her the wallet."

"It's in the desk drawer," he said.

Donahue said: "Get it, Laura. See he hasn't taken anything out."

She got up and made her way to the desk, took out the wallet, examined it. "It's all here."

"Where're your bags?"

"I checked them at the station. I thought it would be best to check them. After I checked them a little man followed me to the information booth. Then he said he'd shoot me if I didn't go with him. He brought me here."

Hagin said: "I only tried to get the checks out of her."

"He's got them!" Beef snarled.

"No," the girl said, "I've got them." She turned down the left cuff of her coat sleeve. She said to Donahue: "I couldn't make up my mind whether to give them up or not."

Donahue said: "Which one is for the little bag?"

"This one," she said, holding up a cardboard square.

"Put it on the table. These rats would run you down for it, no matter where you went"

She sighed. "I guess you're right. I don't want it anyhow."

Hagin stared at it. Beef and the others stared at it—hungrily.

The girl had her hat on.

Donahue said to the men: "This hurts, but it's my only out." He motioned to the girl. "Come on. Go through those rooms and into the hall. There's a back window open. Go down the fire-escape, through the alley. Get a cab, get your suitcase, go to a hotel and leave on the first train you can get. I won't be seeing you again."

She came very close to him. "Thanks," she said. "Thanks for everything."

He waited fully two minutes, then began backing out. The men remained like images. They couldn't understand his letting almost fifteen thousand dollars slide by. He reached the next room, turned and sped swiftly to the bedroom. The hall was empty. He went out the window, down the fire-escape, through the alley. He breathed thankfully. The girl had gone.

He grabbed a taxi and rode to Penn Station. The driver passed a stop-light and was held up for five minutes by a long-winded cop. Presently he moved on. It was dark and deserted in front of the station. No trains were moving, and inside the station it was quite deserted also. He didn't see the girl. She would have been here already, he reasoned.

He saw four men heading for an exit. He started, then stopped. The four men walked swiftly in close formation and passed out through the doors. Donahue broke into a fast walk. He reached the doors and pushed one open when a vicious snarl of gunfire broke loose in the street. The mad sound of a sub-machinegun was touched up with the bark of heavy pistols.

He saw four men lying on the sidewalk. A car roared on the getaway. One of the four figures moved and the gun in his hand blazed four times. The car turned suddenly, heeled over on its rubber, hurtled diagonally across the street with full power on. It struck a building and seemed to bounce back into the street. He couldn't tell definitely. Because the car exploded in a sheet of flame. The fourth man on the sidewalk was motionless again, on his back now, his arms outflung. It looked like Beef.

Donahue was on his way, blocks north, by the time police arrived, to find the pavement red.

Next day the papers had it. Hagin and the punk had shot it out with the other four, using a Thompson gun. But their getaway had been tragically incomplete. Six dead men in the street....

One of the papers got waggish. "Apparently," it said, "there was something sentimental about it. It would appear that the gun fight started over a suitcase containing a lot of woman's clothes, no piece of which bears any identification."

Donahue, reading it, said: "These women... these women!"

Save Your Tears

*Tough dick Donahue explodes
in a large way a double set-up
on a killing*

Chapter I

THE Champ, Harrigan, took one on the chin and piled into the ropes above the press-box. Three blows made sopping sounds against his ribs. He laughed. It was an intimate laugh, close against Tripp's face, as they clinched. The referee bounced in, slapping them. The champ tossed Tripp off. The referee waltzed backward, bent over, fingers splayed, his monkey face screwed up tensely, his lower lip jutting upward over the upper.

It was only the third round. It had been noised around that the fight would go the limit—fifteen. The odds were seven to five in the champ's favor. He was a big fellow, a kid—twenty-one or two, fighting out of Giles Consadine's stable. He was not particularly sweet to look at, but he had a nice smile, a nice laugh, and he was the champ.

Rushing Tripp to the ropes, slamming him with both hands, he looked over the challenger's shoulder, smiled at Token Moore. She waved, showed her fine set of teeth between luscious lips. The champ was crazy about her. But there was something peculiar in his smile. Giles Consadine, lean, slightly gray, sat next to Token Moore. He sat wooden-faced, his hands folded on the silver knob of an evening stick. The bell broke up the clinch.

They came out for the fourth, reached the center of the ring. Harrigan ducked. Then he piled two hard ones into Tripp's face.

Tripp clinched, muttered: "Yuh mug!"

Harrigan laughed, danced away. He began dancing backward around the ring. He looked down over the ropes at Token, at Giles Consadine. Tripp jumped him but the champ was nimble for a big man. He tied Tripp up, broke, tossed him away, went after him. He stopped smiling and his jaw set, bulged. He carried Tripp to the ropes above the press-box. The wet gloves smacked, sopped; they were the champ's gloves. Blood flew, spread like a comet across a newshawk's

cheek below. And suddenly the gloves stopped.

The referee was bending over Tripp.

The champ was not looking at him. Nor at the man on the floor. He was looking through the ropes, down at Token Moore, at Giles Consadine. He wore a dizzy grin. And he was laughing. The short, idiotic laughs thumped his chest, pumped his cheeks out and in. Nobody heard the laughs. He just looked as if he had the hiccups.

Giles Consadine was standing, expressionless, lifting a match to a long thin panetela. Token Moore was round-eyed. About them, Consadine's yes-men jabbered, gesticulated. But you couldn't hear what they said. Shouts, roars, screams, laughs, rose to the distant dome of the Arena, cascaded down again.

The newsreel cameras were in the ring, turning. Tripp was on a stretcher; two men carried him from the ring. The champ was glassy-eyed and trying to poke his way clear of the mob in the ring. A man was holding up a microphone, shouting for him. The champ did a breast-stroke for the ropes, swung through.

Consadine, inhaling deeply, let smoke languish from his nostrils. He was laconic, a little abstracted. "That's that, then," he said, half to himself.

Token Moore gave the impression of a bird fluttering, looking for a place to alight. She fell on Consadine's arm. He hardly noticed her. But a tap on the shoulder made him turn, look around.

Donahue, lean and brown-faced above a single-studded stiff shirt-front, said: "Greetings, Consadine. The kid's a natural."

Consadine was short with him, clipped: "Thanks." Turning front, the fight solon bent his wiry gray brows, frowned thoughtfully. He turned around again.

But Donahue was gone.

Token said: "Who—who was the handsome well-wisher?"

"A private dick."

Chapter II

DONAHUE made his way to the back of the Arena, opened a door marked private. A short hallway lay beyond. It contained but one door. The door was broad, of metal, and had no knob. Donahue pressed a buzzer.

In a moment the door slid open and Donahue walked into a large elevator.

"Deep down," he said.

His overcoat was over his arm. He wore a black velour hat slanted over one ear. Humming to himself, he drew from time to time on a cigarette as the car descended. When the car stopped, opened, he drifted into a severely modernistic foyer. A girl in trim black and white took his hat and overcoat and he drifted to one end of the foyer, pushed open a door and entered an elaborate bar. It was crowded, noisy; and beyond, in the vast dining and dancing-room, a Negro band was playing. The allegorical murals on the walls were in keeping with the name of the *Suwanee Club*. Giles Consadine did most things lavishly.

Donahue pushed into a telephone booth, dialed a number. A woman answered the phone and he asked for Karssen; waited, tapping his foot, whistling to himself. When Karssen answered, Donahue said:

"The champ put the works to Tripp in the fourth.... A knockout is right.... Well, there's something screwy about it. I'd have bet my shirt Tripp was to win.... Not a chance. When the champ got busy Tripp didn't have a chance.... That's all so far, Alex."

He hung up, squeezed out of the booth and came face to face with Detective-Sergeant Kelly McPard.

"Donny, as I live and breathe!"

"Me and my shadow. How're you, Kel?"

"Just swell, just swell." He used a neat, manicured fingernail to snick Donahue's single shirt stud. "You look like a million. I never knew you went in for following the fights in a big way. Seems I've seen you at all of them for the past three months. Cleaning up, old kid?"

Donahue said: "I got this suit for a Christmas present. I don't like the theatre. I had to wear it somewhere."

McPard squeezed Donahue's arm affectionately. McPard was a large man—large in the torso, thin in the legs. His feet tapered off in pointed shoes forever aglow with a high polish. He wore a tailored suit, a tailored overcoat. His starched collar was snug about his plump neck. He was a clean-looking, pink-cheeked man, wily behind the merry twinkle in his eyes and the amused smile that never quite left his lips.

He poked Donahue's ribs, said: "I picked up a hundred bucks on that little brawl, Donny. Not bad for a copper, huh? Hey... once I was a roundsman when Danny Harrigan was a kid. He was nuts about my uniform. Wanted to be a cop. Now look at him! Champ!... Come on, Donny; I'll buy you a drink."

The head bartender was signaling. "Oh, Mr. Donahue there!"

"Yeah?"

"Mr. Consadine wants to see you."

"It's free. Tell him to come down."

"He says upstairs—his office."

Donahue, leaning elbows on the bar, said: "I can't. My pal's buying me a drink. It might never happen again. Make it a double Scotch, Rudolph, with a bottle of Perrier on the side."

The head bartender looked pained. "But I'm hangin' on the phone here and the boss—"

Kelly McPard chimed in: "Why act like that, Donny? Go up and see him."

"I just came down. You think I'm going to spend the rest of the night chasing up and down in the elevator? Tell him," Donahue said to the bartender, "I'm engaged. No—wait a minute. I'll go up. Tell him I'll be up."

McPard said: "Tsk, tsk! What a man!"

Donahue stretched his long legs to the foyer, entered the waiting elevator and said "Top" to the attendant. The car rose to the top floor. Sliding doors opened and Donahue entered a carpeted anteroom on either side of which stood a Grecian urn. Three doors faced him. He headed towards the one marked Private, opened it. He did not hurry.

Consadine was seated in a tremendous red leather chair. He was fully dressed, hat on, white silk muffler bunching between the lapels of his black overcoat. He sat well back, legs crossed, and he tapped the patent leather toe of one foot with the end of his walking stick. Kempler, a small, chubby man with a squashed nose and close-fitting ears, sat on the mahogany desk spinning a small penknife at the end of a platinum watch chain. He looked as if he had been shoehorned into his evening clothes.

Donahue elbowed the door shut. "Mohamet comes to the mountain, Consadine."

Consadine's face was wooden. "Win any dough on the scrap?"

"Didn't bet."

"Since when did you begin to follow the fights?"

"I take it in spells."

"This spell began about three months ago, didn't it?"

"You figure close."

"I noticed you behind me in every scrap I attended in the past three months. Kempler noticed it, too."

"Yeah," said Kempler.

Consadine said: "You've been dropping in at the gym, too."

"Sure," nodded Donahue.

"Going to write a book or something about the game?

"No."

"Why the sudden lively interest?"

"Hobby," said Donahue, good-humored.

Consadine said: "Take a tip. I don't like strangers hanging around my stables."

"I get tossed out if I show up again, huh?"

"That's the idea. And that goes for the *Suwanee Club*, too. You've been practically living there. Stay out of it."

"In other words—"

"In other words," said Consadine, wooden-faced, unemotional, "keep your nose clean."

"Yeah," said Kempler.

"Finished?" Donahue said.

Consadine said: "Yes, you can go now."

Donahue turned, opened the door. He stood for a moment on the threshold, smiling at Consadine.

"Keep yours clean," he said.

Kempler thumped off the desk, lumbered over and said: "What?"

"I wasn't talking to you."

"What?"

"Nerts."

"What?"

Consadine said: "Lay off, Kempler."

Kempler lumbered back to the desk, turned, scowled at Donahue.

Donahue said to Consadine: "B-r-r-r! He scares hell out of me, Consadine." His voice dropped: "You do, too."

He chuckled, went out, closed the door.

Chapter III

A**LEX** Karssen was head of the Boxing Commission. He was a small bag of bones, five feet four, and he had a lopsided, leathery face, a tyrant's bright eye tempered by an amazing sparkle, crooked teeth that nonetheless could produce a winning, dynamic smile. He spoke quickly, sharply, out of his warped mouth.

"In here, Donny, my boy."

He shoved and punched Donahue into a small study whose door, now closed, muffled the music in the salon. Karssen was socially prominent. His Fifth Avenue house was the scene of many bright affairs and it was said of him that he entertained every night.

He was eager. "What happened, Donny?"

"Nothing much. Only Consadine's wise. He may not know for sure, but he's got a bug in his brain—he suspects me. I was told"—he grinned slowly—"to keep out of his gym, out of his *Suwanee* scatter."

Karssen's bright eyes darted about in space, he rubbed thumb frantically against forefinger. "What do you think, boy?"

"Only this: something went wrong. I don't say Tripp was to've knocked Harrigan out. Nothing like it. But I do say Tripp was to've stayed the fifteen, to a close decision. The fight started out like big-time. The two guys smacked hell out of each other. Tripp's been the only logical contender for the past two years. He was built up nicely. I say he was to've lost this scrap, but by such a slight margin that a return bout would have been down on the books before their gloves were dry. As it is, Tripp's a has-been. There's no contender on the horizon. Consadine is going to lose dough on the champ. Why? Because there's nobody for the champ to fight."

Karssen bobbed his shriveled head. "Right! Right! That sounds reasonable. The fight was to have been in the bag. Both sides in agreement. A close, fast fight. A close decision. A return bout inside of six months and the public milked of another several hundred thousand dollars! Capital!"

Donahue dug in "Referee fixed, judges spoken to. Not only in this fight but in the other fights Tripp had preparatory to the championship match. He's a good man—but the champ is a wow. He's the best—Tripp is—of the white hopes."

Karssen rattled on: "Somebody double-crossed the inner ring. Forgetting the actual money transaction of the bout itself, there must have been thousands bet on the outside. Get this, boy: Giles Consadine either lost a fortune on this bout—or made a fortune. It could have worked either way."

Donahue frowned. "What I'm worried about is, Consadine's got an idea I've been soft-shoeing up his alley."

"Scared?"

"I'm not bragging I'm not. His keeping me out of his stable and out of his *Suwanee* is going to cramp my style. I'm not afraid of Consadine personally. I mean him—the guy. He's a pushover. But there's a lot of mugs—"

"I see." The eager, darting eyes sparkled; the crooked grin spread. "Chuck it, boy. Send me a bill tomorrow."

Donahue walked around the room scowling. He shrugged. "Hell, I might as well stick."

"Why? What's the use of inviting a bullet?"

"I'd hate my guts if I gave it the go-by now."

Karssen slapped him. "Boy, you've got what it takes!"

"Cut out the bouquets, Alex. Give me a drink."

"But remember"—Karssen pinched his arm, tightened down his voice—"you've got to keep my name out of this. Unless you get the real low-down.... What'll you have?"

"Anything that burns on the way down."

AT 11:40 Donahue breezed into the Hotel Whitestone, where he kept a small bachelor apartment. Hinkley, an assistant editor of the *Sporting Sphere,* rose from a straight-backed chair in the lobby. A scrawny, young-old little man, dressed in flashy clothes, a low-crowned derby, he always affected an unpleasant leer that was, obviously, intended for a smile.

"Brother, can you spare a dime's worth o' your time?"

Donahue said: "Oh, I mistook you for one of the potted plants," and kept heading for the desk.

"Frequently potted but never a plant. Say, kiddo...." He lolled languidly after Donahue.

Donahue received several letters from the clerk, turned, moved towards the elevator. Hinkley fell in beside him, rose in the car with him and paced him down the fifth floor corridor. All the time Donahue was reading a letter. Reaching his door, he unlocked it, entered his small apartment and turned on the lights. Hinkley, lolling in, kicked the door shut with his heel.

Donahue took off hat and overcoat, carried them into a closet, said from the closet: "Well, what's on your mind?"

Hinkley helped himself to a cigar. He nipped off the end, said nothing.

Donahue reappeared, saying: "Well, what's on your mind?"

"I was up the *Suwanee* tonight. Kelly McPard said you had an interview with Consadine."

"Did he say interview?"

"Call the italics mine."

Donahue went into the bathroom, washed his hands and reappeared carrying his tuxedo jacket over him arm.

"What about Consadine?" Hinkley drawled from the depths of a wing chair.

Donahue, sitting on the divan, removed his shoes, clamped in shoe-trees. He carried them into the bedroom, called out: "He likes me. He just wanted to shake my hand." He appeared in the doorway clad only in shorts. "You better toddle, Hinkley." He disappeared again.

"*The Sporting Sphere,*" Hinkley said, "is aching to pay you a little cash for a little good turn."

There was a moment of silence, then Donahue came into the living-room buttoning his pajama coat, holding a pipe in his teeth. He crammed the pipe, lighted it while peering down keenly at the man in the wing chair.

"About what?" he asked.

Hinkley sent up a toy balloon of cigar smoke. "You've been tagging Consadine's fights for the past three months, Donny. That's common gossip. When one of the best private dicks in the city—and one of the best known—does that sort of thing, it's news in the bud. Catch on?"

"No." He puffed up. "Tell me some more."

"My sheet's interested. What have you got on Consadine?"

"What's it worth?"

"Anything within reason. We know you're not tagging his fights for the fun of it. Who's behind you? Who hired you?"

"That goes in the deal, huh?"

"Sure. We've got to know where we stand."

"What's your top price?"

"How about ten thousand?"

Donahue sat down and began chuckling, wagging his head. "This is rich," he said. "Rich!" He stopped chuckling and his face began to darken. "That rag you work for, if it paid out ten thousand it'd go broke."

"Says you."

"Says I!"

"Why get tough?"

Donahue puffed, took the pipe from his mouth and sighted down the stem. "Hinkley, I'm so far ahead of you that it's a crime to take advantage of you. Listen, boy scout: I don't know a thing. I just follow the fights. I don't like bridge and I don't like jig-saw puzzles. So I follow the fights. Consadine's pugs put on some swell dances." He made a brusque gesture. "Okey, Hinky-dink; take the air."

Hinkley stood up. "Listen, Donny—"

"Peddle it where you've got an audience." Rising, Donahue flapped a hand. "I need some shut-eye. Skid out."

"Donny, look now...." He moistened his lips. "This is hot. Be a pal. *The Sporting Sphere*— Listen, kid; how about twelve thousand?"

Donahue suddenly appeared thoughtful. "How about fifteen?"

"Maybe I could arrange it."

"Fifteen?"

"Okey, fifteen. But that's the limit."

Donahue laughed shortly. "Now scram. I just wanted to know how much you were holding out."

"But—"

Donahue's voice snapped. "You deaf? Slide out!"

Hinkley colored. "That's a lousy trick, fella!"

Donahue took his arm, escorted him to the door. "Thanks for dropping around, Hinkley. You must come in again some time. Come in for a drink some time. Bring your own liquor."

"I hate wiseguys!"

"So do I—when they go flat." He opened the door. "And do you know why the *Sporting Sphere* can't bribe me?"

Hinkley made no reply.

"I'll tell you," Donahue said. "Because I happen to know—and I'm one of the few guys who know it—I happen to know that Consadine dough is behind it. And I can guess—don't break down, Hinkley—I can guess that it wasn't your editor who sent you here. Should I tell you now who sent you here?"

Hinkley rasped: "Things happen to guys like you!" He swung out, strode swiftly down the corridor.

Donahue called after him: "Consadine sent you, dope!"

Chapter IV

THE Hotel Chancellor lifted its pale, severe beauty into the cold winter starlight. Traffic moved sparsely on Park Avenue, slipping out of the ramp that hurtled Forty-second Street and wound its way among the cluster of skyscrapers. The outward serenity of the Hotel Chancellor was massive, overwhelming.

In the lobby, shaped like a tremendous bell, deftly lighted by radiance that seemed to float beneath the high-domed ceiling, a page boy moved swiftly, vanished down one of many corridors. The chief hotel clerk spoke quickly into a telephone; he was hunched over the instrument, his eyes intent. The liveried doorman, who should have gone off duty at twelve—it was ten past twelve—lingered beneath the heart-shaped marquee, blowing white breath into the cold, tapping cold heels on the sidewalk.

A man came out of a door in a corridor on the main-floor. He was buttoning his vest. He had combed his hair quickly, and a slab of it, at the crown, sprouted upward like a recalcitrant weed. His face was puffed from sleep. He poked irritably at his sleep-drugged eyes, wheezed. He headed for the lobby, and gradually, as he walked, he straightened, squared his shoulders. He was Adolph Elms, the resident managing director.

Before he attained the lobby he ran into a short, rotund, bald man. Both men stopped, regarded each other. The bald man sighed, spread his palms. The managing director grunted irritably. Both men fell in step, reached the lobby, where they were joined by a third man who looked as if he had seen a ghost. The three men marched towards the elevator bank, vanished in a car.

The lobby door opened and two men headed across the lobby,

paused at the desk. As they went towards the elevators, they were joined by several uniformed policemen. All entered an elevator and were whisked upward.

The lobby was vacant, then. Two drunks staggered in, singing. They wore top hats. They fell into an elevator car. A man came in with a lot of baggage, signed the register. The operator was telling room so-and-so that the hotel did not supply liquor.

Donahue entered swathed in a belted camel's-hair coat, his lean face riding beneath a brown felt. He was slapping pigskin gloves against his thigh as he reached the desk.

"Where's the trouble?"

"I'm sorry. Press not allowed—"

"I'm not the press. Sergeant McPard phoned me."

"Oh. It's 1406."

Donahue found a waiting car. It carried him silently to the fourteenth floor, and stepping out he swung his legs down a wide corridor that smelled remarkably of fresh air. He turned several corners, came to a door that had 1406 inscribed in bronze on its dark panel.

A cop opened the door, said: "What do you want?"

"Kelly called me."

He stepped into a spacious foyer. To his left was a Lancet arch. Beyond was a large, luxurious room, almost baronial in size; at the farther side was a narrow mezzanine. Many lights were sprinkled about. There was no glare, yet there was sufficient light. Bluecoats were standing about. Several hotel officials, jabbering. Kelly McPard, spic and span, working his provocative smile, his eyes wandering but his mind—Donahue knew—certainly at work.

"Thanks, Donny," McPard called.

Spengler, his assistant, came in through a French window. He had been wandering about on the broad terrace that overlooked Park Avenue and the East River. He was a roughneck, badly dressed, good-humored, loud, who regarded his job as a joyous hobby.

He yelled: "Hello, Irish!"

The hotel officials looked up in unison, a little shocked. But Spengler was never self-conscious. He banged the windows shut with great gusto, smacked his big hands together.

"What do you think, Donny?" he bawled on good-naturedly. "Somebody give Giles Consadine the works. Ain't it just like life, though? There's a mug with everything to live for—swell joint here—

nice flower garden out front—"

McPard broke in quietly: "Okey, Dutch."

Spengler was expansive: "Okey, Kel. Excuse it."

Kelly McPard beckoned to Donahue. They climbed to the mezzanine, and McPard pushed in a door that had been standing slightly ajar. He leaned in the doorway, jerked his chin.

"A honey, eh, Donny?"

Donahue stood beside him, looked down at the body of Giles Consadine. It lay on the floor, in front of a huge canopied bed. Clad in gray silk pajamas, it lay on one side, head pillowed on arm.

McPard's voice was low, almost confidential: "Two slugs smack in the chest."

"Anybody hear the shots?"

"No. Radio was going loud."

"How'd they find out?"

"They knew he was in. He'd told the operator he was expecting a long-distance call from Chicago. When it came, she got no answer. She sent a hop up. He knocked hard. No answer. And he heard the radio playing. So he got a clerk with a pass key. Found him at exactly midnight. It was eleven when he came home."

"Between eleven and twelve, huh? Any ideas?"

McPard looked vacantly at the body on the floor, spoke in a detached manner: "Yeah. My first idea, I suppose, was to ask you over."

"What am I going to turn out to be now—a strange interlude?"

McPard rarely became angry, rarely raised his voice. "I guess you were one of the last men to see him alive. He never came down to the *Suwanee*. Took the Arena service entrance out and went straight to his hotel."

"How do you know?"

"That elevator boy at the Arena saw him leave at 10:45. It'd take about fifteen minutes, traveling fast."

"He come in alone?"

McPard nodded. "The clerk said.... Look here, Donny. Consadine wanted to see you earlier tonight. Pretty bad. Or he'd not have paged you in the bar. What did he want?"

"Wanted to know if I'd won any dough on the fight."

McPard chuckled faintly. "Quit kidding."

"All right; you tell me what he wanted."

McPard fooled with a button on Donahue's overcoat. "He hired you for something, didn't he?"

Donahue walked six paces away, turned, laughed and wagged his head. "That sure panics me!"

McPard grinned, showing small pearly teeth. His eyes twinkled, radiated. You could never tell what was going on behind that smiling, cherubic face. Kelly McPard should have been an actor; he had all the qualifications.

"Honest, Donny, I've got to know."

Donahue came back to face McPard and said, seriously: "Consadine couldn't have hired me for a million."

"That sounds nice and big and strong, kid, but I'd hate to've had him wave the million in front of your face."

Donahue smiled, shrugged. "All right, Kel; I exaggerated. But get this: he didn't hire me."

"Was he scared?"

"I didn't ask him."

McPard sighed. "What a pal!" Then he was suddenly grave, his voice low and quiet: "I've got to know, Donny."

"I told you."

"Listen, kid." He touched Donahue's arm. "You know the champ—you know Danny Harrigan…. I used to, well—you know, I kind of brought him up. In a way, I mean. I mean when he was a kid I used to steer him clear of the hoodlums. When I was a roundsman. Once I let him have his picture taken wearing my hat and shield…. Listen, kid; this is no song and dance, no soft soap. Listen, Donny"—his voice dropped lower—"the champ was here tonight."

"Go on."

"He was here. The kid runs the hotel elevator—he couldn't help recognizing him. Danny was here. Came here between eleven and half-past—nearer half-past. Came out again in about ten minutes." He withdrew his hand from his overcoat pocket. A .32-calibre revolver lay in his palm. "Danny's gun."

"How do you know?"

"I helped him get a license to carry it—six months ago, when he had an idea some mugs were trying to kidnap him. See the chip on the butt?… Danny's gun."

Donahue was silent for a moment, eying McPard steadily. Then he said: "What am I supposed to do? If it's Harrigan's gun, what's the matter with getting Harrigan?"

"I phoned his hotel. He checked out at 11:15. He must have taken his bags and checked them at the station. Then he came here."

"Where is he now?"

"I don't know whether I'd like to know or not—but I don't know. I want to know if Consadine hired you. I want to know if he was afraid of Harrigan—or anybody else."

Donahue said: "Consadine didn't hire me."

"Did he try to?"

"No."

McPard sighed. "I'm not going to like it—pinching that kid."

"Hey, Kel," Spengler shouted. "The camera guy from H.Q. is here. He wants to mug the stiff. Ask the stiff if it's okey."

Donahue said to McPard: "I imagine Spengler's comedy goes over big with the hotel help."

"Spengler's all right at heart…. Listen, Donny—"

Donahue held up his palms. "Nix, Kel. We've been all over that. Consadine didn't hire me."

Chapter V

DONAHUE walked north. Park Avenue was wide, empty, in the winter starlight. Even in the dark its smartness was obvious, insistent. The purr of a passing automobile's tires made a loud sound in the wide, windowed canyon.

Donahue cut east to Lexington Avenue, entered a drug-store and pushed into a telephone booth. He thumbed a directory, dialed a number, made a whistling mouth but no sound. The operator at the Hotel Eden answered and Donahue said:

"I want to speak to Miss Moore in apartment 44."

"We have no Miss Moore in apartment 44."

"You must have. Look it up."

There was a pause and then the operator said: "I'm sorry, sir; we have no Miss Moore in apartment 44. The only Moore we have is in apartment 606."

"I must have made a mistake," Donahue said. "Pardon me."

He hung up, whistled his way out of the booth and bought a malted milk at the counter. He drank only half of it, left the drug-store and walked north on Lexington, then west to Fifth. In a nearby side-street he entered the small, chic Hotel Eden, crossed to the open elevator car and mentioned the sixth floor. The operator yawned on the way up.

Donahue hummed on his way down the sixth floor corridor, bowed before 606, listening, and then rippled his knuckles down the panel. He seemed quite satisfied with himself, teetering back and forth from heel to toe.

A breathless voice broke on the other side of the door: "Who's there?"

"Is Harrigan in there?"

"No!"

"I don't believe it."

"He's not here!"

"I heard him in there."

"You didn't! Who are you?"

"A detective. Harrigan's in there."

"He isn't!"

"You've got to prove it."

A lock grated. The door was flung open. Token Moore was not so sleek as she had been at the fight; but she was no less beautiful. She looked stunning in a black sheer peignoir, black pajamas beneath. She was flushed, her auburn hair rumpled, and her eyes bloodshot. And she was drunk.

Donahue shouldered in, shouldered the door shut and snapped the lock. He passed her where she stood swaying, went into the living-room, the bedroom, the bathroom, the closets. He reappeared to find Token flip-flopping her way across to a divan. She made a peculiarly pathetic spectacle. Changing her mind about the divan, she brought up in the center of the floor, rubber-kneed, dabbing at loose ends of hair.

"What you want?"

She hadn't a bad voice; there was nothing particularly coarse about it; but liquor made her tongue thick, her lips clumsy. She bounced from one foot to the other, her arms darting out at eccentric angles in an effort to strike a balance.

Donahue said: "Where's Harrigan?"

"Don't know."

She made a headlong dive for the coffee table, grabbed at a bottle of gin, raised the bottle to her lips. She had had more than enough. Donahue knew it. But he didn't move, he didn't offer advice. She gagged and slammed the bottle down and went dizzily around the room holding her throat. He seemed keenly, clinically interested in her haywire maneuvers. Suddenly she wound up in a heap, on the divan, and lay there shaking violently, panting hoarsely.

Donahue sauntered over, sat down beside her, ran his big hand familiarly through her hair.

"Little girl shouldn't drink gin that way—!"

She slapped at his arm and went spinning to the floor.

He sighed. "The things I walk into." He picked her up and stood holding her in his arms. She was small, pliable, and he liked the feel of her in his arms. He sighed again. "Business, though, is business," he remarked as he dropped her to the divan.

She crouched there, staring up at him out of wide-open eyes. He rubbed the back of his neck. He sat down beside her and she shrank back farther, tugging her peignoir across her small breasts.

"Listen," he said. "What kind of a deal was made on that fight? You're in the know. You'd know. Was Harrigan supposed to lose that fight or what? What went wrong?"

She gave an agonized groan, sprang from the divan and went hurtling across the room. She carried down a tea-table, sprawled with it, her legs flying.

Donahue said: "Tsk, tsk!"

She scrambled up and ran crazily into the bedroom. He followed her. He found her hiding beneath the bed. Pulling her out by one leg, he lifted her to her feet, held her erect. She looked horror-stricken.

He shook her. "Pull yourself together."

Her teeth began chattering and her face became so white that Donahue was uneasy. He was annoyed, irritated. He laid her on the bed and she buried her face in a pillow and began sobbing and moaning.

He thought she might be out of her mind.

He went into the living-room and walked round and round, angry one moment, puzzled the next. Her moaning was unpleasant to hear. He was standing in the middle of the room, cogitating, when she came stealthily out of the bedroom and crept across the living-room.

Fascinated, he watched her. She appeared to be unaware of his presence and kept creeping towards the hall door. Finally he jumped, caught her as she was about to open the door.

Her voice was hoarse: "Lemme out!"

"Listen—"

"Lemme—" She tussled, kicked, clawed in sudden fury.

"Now, Token, take it easy!"

She tore away from him, fell on the doorknob, managed to unlock the catch. But he grabbed her by the arms, lifted her, swung her about and whisked her across the living-room, into the bedroom. Her feet did not once touch the floor. He dropped her to the bed, his shirt cuffs protruding, his hair rumpled and several bloody scratches on his face.

He rasped: "Cut out this damned nonsense!"

She tried to heave off the bed, but he caught her, flattened her on the bed, held her down.

"Listen," he said earnestly, "I'm not going to hurt you. See? You understand? I want to know what happened to Consadine. I want to know where Harrigan is. I want to know if that fight was framed. I want— Wait a minute. Stay here. Stay on this bed. I want to lock that door."

He rose, swung into the living-room. He stopped short. Two men were coming across it towards him and both had guns leveled. They were young men, impeccably dressed. One was tall, handsome and hard in a pale-faced, red-lipped way. The other was small, anaemic, and the .45 automatic he held looked huge in his skinny little hand. They were bent on business.

"Back up, you," the tall man said.

"Wait a second—"

"Back up!"

The two men crowded Donahue, and he backed into the bedroom. The smaller of the two had a nervous affliction; his upper lip kept twitching while the rest of his face remained cold, stony. His eyes were as cold as a lizard's.

The tall man snapped: "There she is!" He leaped after Token Moore as she staggered towards the bathroom.

The small man kept Donahue covered.

The tall man, rough-housing Token across the room, said: "Where's

Harrigan, brat?"

"Oh, my—!" she moaned.

"Where's Harrigan?"

"I—I don't know."

He held her up with his left hand. With his right he slapped her face. She choked and groaned and he backed her up, slapping her hard, first on one cheek, then on the other. Meanwhile he wore a hard, tight smile. He stopped slapping her, took hold of her left arm and bent it behind her back. She grimaced. Her eyeballs bulged, rolled, showed the whites as she bent backward. Her knees gave way and she slumped. He let her fall to the floor.

Donahue offered: "She's just drunk."

The tall man spun on him. "You're Donahue," he rasped.

"Okey."

The tall man took one step, one swing. Donahue crashed against the wall. His eyes blazed.

"What the hell's the idea of that?" he exploded.

"For being funny," the tall man said.

The little man grinned with his twitching lip, but the gun he held did not waver.

The tall man went into the bathroom, came out with a glass of water which he threw in Token's face. She stirred and he hauled her to her feet, shook her.

"Where's Harrigan?"

"Please—" Tears began to stream from her eyes.

He said: "Stop yammering, brat! Where is he?"

"Please—honest—so help me—"

He scoffed: "Crap!" The hard flat of his hand whanged against her face. Furious, but coldly so, he pitched her to the bed. As she tried to crawl off, he walked around the foot of the bed, waited a second, then struck her full in the face. She toppled back to the other side of the bed, fell to the floor, groaning weakly.

The little man giggled. "Jeeze, she's frail, the dame!"

Donahue said: "In about a minute I'm going to get sore."

"In about a minute," the tall man said, "you'll be sore—all over."

"What's the sense of slamming her around that way? Any punk can do that."

The tall man pointed. "You got yours coming, bozo! So keep your trap shut!"

"What have I done? Hell, I'm looking for Harrigan, too."

The tall man narrowed his eyes. "What for?"

"Murder of a guy named Consadine?"

The tall man and the small man flicked a glance at each other. Then the tall man said: "What's she told you?"

"Not a damned thing. She's pie-eyed. I couldn't raise a peep out of her. Harrigan's vanished."

"Who says so? Who says Harrigan murdered Consadine?"

"The cops. Kelly McPard found Harrigan's gun in Consadine's apartment—the gun that killed Consadine. It's open and shut. The cops'll have him inside of twenty-four hours, and it's a murder rap."

The tall man quieted down. He said: "Is this straight?"

"Phone Kelly McPard and check up."

The tall man looked sharply at Donahue, at the little man. He turned and walked to the other side of the bed, stood there looking downward. Token was on the floor and Donahue, from where he stood, could not see her. Several times the tall man raised quizzical eyes, flicked them at Donahue. Then he leaned down, picked up the girl and flopped her on the bed. She lay sacklike, unconscious. The tall man slapped her cheeks briskly, not roughly, in an attempt to bring her around. But she remained unconscious. He cursed, shrugged. He blew his nose sharply. There were diamonds on his hands. His clothes looked expensive. He blew his nose again, looked from the girl to Donahue, frowned, went through the apartment like a dog on a scent.

Presently he stopped in front of Donahue and frowned seriously. "We're breezing," he said. "You're walking down and out with us. Get your hat.... Watch him, Midge," he added to the small man.

Donahue went into the living-room, scooped up his hat. The small man played shadow to every move. The tall man joined them and they went out into the corridor.

The tall man said: "We'll walk down a couple of floors, then take the elevator. Act nice, Donahue."

Donahue looked at their bulging pockets, said: "Wouldn't you, in my place?"

The tall man was not in a jocular mood. "Pass up the cracks."

Three floors below, they buzzed for an elevator. The car dropped them smoothly to the lobby. The lobby was deserted except for the clerk at the desk. He looked up, saw them, looked down again and kept on writing in a ledger. They went out, walked as far as Madison Avenue. On the corner the tall man stopped.

He said: "Okey, Donahue; keep going. Fade."

It was cold and deserted on the corner, and he looked at their white, humorless faces, their bulging pockets. A lump caught in his throat. He looked up and down the avenue. No one was in sight. He returned his gaze to the motionless white faces.

The tall man said: "Well, get going—west."

He nodded. He turned on his heel and started across the avenue. His jaw was clamped, his shoulders hunched a bit. He went through all the imagined sensations of a man being shot in the back. He didn't dare look around but walked on—not too rapidly; though he had to grit his teeth, almost, to stop from breaking into a run.

But nothing happened. He reached the next corner, stopped, looked around. He was in a cold sweat.

He became suddenly angry. He could feel heat rushing through his body and in an instant he was striding back through the street. He broke into a run, up on his toes, the long skirt of his overcoat flapping about his knees. Reaching Madison, he peered south. Several blocks distant, two men passed beneath a street light. But Donahue wasn't sure. He was angry enough, however, to take a chance.

He flagged a loafing southbound taxi and climbing in told the driver to take it easy. He drove four blocks south, called for a right turn, passed the driver a coin and jumped off.

From the shadow of a stone stoop he saw the tall man and the small man stride past the corner, heading south on Madison.

Chapter VI

KELLY McPard sat on a desk in his office. The office was warm, and the sound of steam whistling from a radiator was not unpleasant. Spengler, his assistant, leaned against the wall; he looked wide awake and kept jabbing industriously at his teeth with a shaved-down match. Kelly looked preoccupied.

Harrigan, the champ, sat in an armchair and scowled at the floor. Out of fighting togs, he was less prepossessing. He had a good face, far from handsome, and coarse-featured; but he gave the general impression of being clean-cut, honest, straightforward; a fine animal at the peak of his power, aware of his standing, a little obstinate.

When Donahue came in, McPard looked up, twiddled his thumbs, said absently: "Hello, Donny."

"Jeeze, you still up!" bawled out Spengler. "Hey, look, we got Harrigan here!"

Donahue closed the door, leaned against it. The brown of his lean and chiseled face was ruddied by the cold. His coat belt was yanked tight, the loose end dangling. He looked at Harrigan, who scowled; at Kelly, whose face was steeped in thought.

"Quick work," he said.

"Ah, say," Spengler said, flapping a big hand, "it was a snap, it was. He just went to another hotel."

Kelly McPard said: "The champ says he didn't do it!"

Harrigan's jaw jutted. "Of course I didn't do it!"

"An old refrain," Donahue remarked.

"What?" the champ barked.

"I was just thinking," Donahue said; and to McPard: "Who did it, Kel?"

McPard said: "The circumstances say Danny did it."

Harrigan heaved up, his thick brows bending. "That there's a lie, Kelly!" He spun on Donahue. "What the hell are you butting in for? You keep your mug out of it!"

Donahue, leaning against the door, said: "Don't shoot your mouth off at me, Harrigan. You're a nice guy and a real champ, but don't get tough."

"Now, now," McPard chimed in. "None o' that…. Donny, he said he went there, all right. He went to Consadine's apartment. He had an idea Consadine had his girl there. He had an idea the jane and Consadine were cutting corners on him. He was all steamed up and he went there with a gun. But he didn't find the girl. Consadine was scared about Danny holding the gun and he kept talking to him and after a while Danny threw the gun on a sofa. Danny was all shaken up. Consadine wanted him to have a drink, but Danny was too balled up to enjoy a drink, so he just turned around and went out, leaving his gun there." McPard paused, then added: "That's Danny's story."

Harrigan blurted: "It's the truth!"

McPard shrugged, strolled around the office. There were no melodramatics about Kelly McPard, but you could see he was deeply disturbed, indecisive, caught in a web of duty and sentiment.

Harrigan's face worked. "That's what I did! That's why I polished Tripp off in the fourth tonight. I could have done it in the second—but I was making up my mind!"

Donahue's eyes steadied. "Why?"

"Why?" Harrigan roared, swinging around. "Because I was sure Consadine was taking my girl away from me. No guy can take a jane away from me!" Some of his self assurance fled and his shoulders hunched, his big face looked pained, his eyes wandered. "I didn't kill him. I guess I went there to do it. If she'd been there, I guess I would have done it."

Donahue felt his way cautiously. "You did a nice job on Tripp."

"Sure. Tripp's okey, but I can lick him. Maybe I did surprise him a bit. I guess I surprised him a hell of a lot!"

"I see. You were to let him stay the fifteen, huh?"

"Stay!" Harrigan laughed. "The tramp was supposed to win!"

Donahue, tingling all over, merely said: "H'm."

"I was supposed to lay down in the twelfth! But I seen my girl down there with Consadine and I went nuts. I couldn't stand it. I was afraid it was a trick. I was afraid that if I lost the fight I'd never get another come-back chance. Consadine promised me a fight in six months when I was supposed to flatten Tripp. But I was scared. I was scared he was framing me and trying to get Token. I went nuts. I was afraid if I wasn't champ she wouldn't like me any more."

Donahue suddenly felt sorry for Harrigan. The champ was just a kid with the mind of a kid. There was something touching in the way his voice broke hoarsely, in the way his face muscles strained and his eyes darted about, harried and uncertain. A splendid machine in the ring; outside, a babe in arms, a sap. "If I wasn't champ she wouldn't like me any more."

Donahue said: "What are you going to do, Kel?"

"Hell, I guess I've got to chuck him in the hold-over."

"I didn't do it!" Harrigan cried hoarsely. "I tell you I didn't do it, Kel! I meant to do it, but I didn't. Token wasn't there and I didn't do it. And then I felt like a louse and I didn't have the guts to go back and see her! I felt like a louse!"

Donahue became engrossed in his own thoughts. His train of thought went into reverse, traveled backward over the ground he had covered.

Presently he said: "You going home, Kel?"

"I was thinking of it."

"Hang around, will you?"

"Why?"

"I may need you."

McPard squinted. "What's on your mind?"

"Something goofy as hell." He opened the door. "Hang around, will you?"

"Sure, I'll hang around."

Chapter VII

DONAHUE was surprised, anxious, when he found the door of Token Moore's apartment unlocked. Entering, he closed it quietly, locked it. He made his way towards the bedroom, reached the doorway.

She lay on the bed, sprawled. It seemed to him that she lay exactly as she had lain when he and the two men had walked out. Drawing nearer, he could see that she was breathing. This reassured him. She was sleeping, soundly. There were marks on her face put there by the tall man. Her sheer garments were torn in places and there was a bruise on her shoulder, another on one wrist. Obviously she had not left the bed.

He sat on the bed and began shaking her shoulder. She roused slowly, turned over, away from him, sighed deeply. He kept shaking her and presently she turned back again, opened her eyes quite candidly. In an instant a rush of memory must have come over her, for her eyes widened, her brows shot upward.

Donahue said: "Take it easy. You're okey. Those guys went away. Now take it easy. Do you want a drink of water?" He saw that she was moistening her dry lips. He rose. "I'll get you a drink of water."

He brought a tumbler full from the bathroom. She was sitting up, white-faced, quivering now but giving no hint of being hysterical. He sat down on the edge of the bed, held the glass to her lips. As she drank, her eyes regarded him steadily. Finished, she looked away. Donahue set the glass on the bed-table. He did not say anything for a while, choosing to allow a few minutes for her to compose herself. He didn't say anything when she rose, went to a mirror and looked at herself. He heard a gasp. Then for a moment she seemed stricken, as if remembering. He went over and offered a cigarette. She made a face, shook her head.

"Too much hangover, huh?" he muttered casually.

She let herself down on to the chair in front of the dresser. Donahue dragged over another chair, sat down beside her. Instead of looking directly at her, he studied her image in the mirror.

He said in a conversational undertone: "They've got Harrigan for the murder of Giles Consadine."

She looked up quickly, at her own image, at Donahue's. Her eyes remained round, wide. Then she turned her head and looked at Donahue. He regarded her image, noticing that she had a nice profile.

"What?" she said.

"Harrigan."

"No!"

"Would I kid you, Token?"

His voice remained low, conversational, almost intimate.

She looked back at the mirrored images. The fact that she was able to see the change in her own features, startled her.

He said to her image: "I dropped around again, Token, to tell you. Harrigan hasn't got a chance in the world. The cops found his gun— fired twice—in Consadine's apartment. He admits having been there but he says he didn't kill Consadine. He says he left the gun there."

She shook her head. "No—no! He didn't kill Giles!"

"I thought you might know."

"Know?"

"Know he didn't."

Her eyes shimmered as she stared at his image. "I mean—I mean I believe him! He couldn't have—"

"He could have," Donahue said pleasantly. "He meant to, in fact. He went there with a gun, expecting to find you with Consadine. He didn't find you there."

"No—of course not," she panted.

"Were you there?"

"No!"

He sighed, was silent for a moment. Then he said: "You and Consadine were crossing corners with the kid, weren't you?"

In an instant she was on her feet, quivering. "That's a damned lie!"

He rose and leaned back on his heels, dropped his chin, regarded her sorrowfully. "You were true-blue to the kid, huh?"

"Yes!"

"Didn't Consadine try to make you forget him?"

She stuttered: "It—it w-wasn't my fault."

"He did, didn't he?"

After a moment she said: "Yes."

"You hated him?"

"I—well, I couldn't show it—account of Danny. He was Danny's boss more or less."

"Did you know Harrigan was to throw the fight—and didn't?"

She looked startled, confused; but she managed to say: "I thought something went wrong. I didn't know just what it was."

"Harrigan was supposed to lay down in the twelfth. He didn't. He didn't because he thought you and Consadine were cheating him. He was afraid that if he lost the championship he'd lose you. Token, you were cheating on the kid."

She shook all over. "I was not! I didn't! Danny meant everything in the world to me! I love him!"

Donahue was mournful. "He's sure in a tough spot right now, Token. It's murder. Say the word over to yourself a lot of times and get the real sting of it."

She gripped his arm. "N-no! He didn't! They can't prove he did! He says he didn't! How can they prove he did? Oh, he didn't kill Consadine!"

"He's got to prove he didn't. Or somebody else has to prove it for him…. How about yourself, Token?"

She choked out: "Me?"

He was eying her keenly. "When I first came in here you were practically out of your mind. You were raving drunk. You were going around this apartment like a mad woman. You were mad. Off your nut. You hardly heard me and you hardly saw me. You were crazy, deranged—horrified about something. I couldn't talk you out of it."

She shrank back from him.

He went on: "You knew Consadine was dead. You knew he was dead and if you'd been in this apartment since you left the Arena you wouldn't have known that he was dead. Because nobody knew. Not even the press. You couldn't have found it out from Harrigan because he didn't see you or phone. Besides, he didn't know Consadine was dead. He didn't know till the cops nabbed him. Yet you knew. When I got here, Token, *you knew that Consadine was dead!*"

"No!" she screamed, fleeing to the other side of the room.

He did not move to follow, but he lifted his arm, wagged his forefinger. "You knew! You were trying to drug yourself with liquor. *You were in Consadine's apartment when he was killed!*"

She choked and shook her head violently. She backed up against the wall, spreading her arms, spreading her hands against the wall. Words deserted her and she could only choke, gasp, grimace.

Donahue was asking gently: "Did you kill Consadine, Token?"

She groaned "O-o-oh!" miserably and slid down the wall, her eyes rolling upward, showing the whites.

Donahue crossed the room, knelt down in front of her. She sat in a crushed, broken huddle, tears streaming down her cheeks. He took hold of her chin, raised her face.

"Come on, Token," he said. "Who killed Consadine?"

Chapter VIII

IN a street off Lexington Avenue, in the Thirties, Donahue went along counting brownstone houses. It was too dark to read the numbers. At three in the morning the city was deserted. The swift passage of a taxicab could be heard blocks away. A cough echoed, and you were aware of your footsteps. Earlier, Donahue had come down this street, trailing the tall man and the small man from Madison Avenue. He had counted houses then, oriented himself pretty thoroughly.

He entered a vestibule, found the inner door locked and tried several skeleton keys. None worked. The lock was old but good. He tried again and again, working as quietly as possible, but with no success. He knew the house contained furnished rooms, apartments, and he had an idea as to what apartment he wanted. After the two men had entered earlier, he had seen a light appear in a front window, second story, where no light had been before. There was, now, a hint of light in the same window—behind drawn dark blinds. He was almost certain he heard a radio playing.

After a few minutes he gave up the hall door and soft-shoed down the stoop to the sidewalk. There was a shallow areaway belonging to the house, three steps below the sidewalk. Unlike the main floor door—which was equipped with a snap lock—the door in the areaway had only a keyhole beneath the knob. Donahue got in, locked the door from the inside.

He was in a hallway. Groping through the dark, he came to a boxed-in narrow stairway and climbed to the main floor, where a dim light glowed in the hallway. He listened for a moment, heard no sound; and then he began climbing the carpeted stairway towards the second floor. A radio was playing, softly. He tracked down the sound to the front of the hallway, heard the low mutter of voices behind a door on the left.

Standing motionless for a long moment, listening, cogitating, he finally drew his gun from its shoulder-holster. It was a .38 revolver, and he cocked it. Then he cat-footed halfway up the next stairway, turned, and made considerable noise coming down. He went directly to the door and knocked insistently.

A voice asked: "What's the matter? Who's it?"

Donahue assumed a high, petulant, rasping voice: "You going to play that damned radio all night? How do you expect a person to sleep?"

"Okey, okey."

"If you don't cut it out I'll find a way to make you! Who do you think you are, anyhow? You think maybe you own this house? Other tenants want to sleep! I want to sleep!"

"I said okey, didn't I?"

"I'm just getting tired of it! You play it again and I'll bust your door down and bust the radio, too!"

"Oh, yeah!"

"You heard me!"

There was an oath, a furious rattling of the key in the lock. The door whipped open.

Donahue went in like a gale wind. Briefly he saw the little man before him. The little man went down like a struck weed. The tall man was sitting in a big armchair with a girl on his lap. That handicapped him. He dropped a glass of whiskey and the girl, frightened, threw her arms around his neck. The little man began scuttling across the floor like a whipped cur, but at the same time he clawed frantically at a shoulder-holster. Another girl stopped squirting seltzer into a glass, opened her mouth wide but didn't say anything; her mouth remained open.

"You on the floor!" Donahue snapped.

The little man flattened, his right arm buried beneath his body. He remained that way, motionless, his breath whistling. The girl who had been squirting the seltzer began backing up, wooden-legged.

Donahue said: "You on the floor, slide that rod out from beneath you and be careful when you do it."

The tall man rose, lifting the girl with him. He set her down in the chair. He was in shirt-sleeves. His coat hung on the back of a chair several feet away; on the chair, also, hung his gun and holster. He put his hands on his hips. The diamonds on his fingers sparkled. The room was large, luxurious; a door, open, led to other rooms beyond.

"Is my face red?" he drawled.

Donahue said: "It looks pretty white to me." He barked at the man on the floor: "What did I tell you about that gun!"

The little man's hand shot out, still holding the gun.

"Take your hand off it," Donahue said, "and crawl."

The little man was reluctant. Donahue took a step, put his foot down on the man's hand. There was a yelp. The little man crawled away. Donahue picked up the gun, hefted it, shoved it into his overcoat pocket.

"Get up now."

The little man rose, crouching. His upper lip twitched madly, his lower hung motionless, and the rest of his face was cold, stony, gray.

Donahue said to both men: "This is a pinch, sweethearts.... Half-pint, get over alongside your pal. Get over, I said!"

When the little man had joined his companion, Donahue moved to a small table, reached for a French telephone.

The girl who had been sitting on the tall man's lap cried: "What are you doing?"

"Cops."

"No! No! Listen, I can't be caught here! Listen, I got a husband! He'll beat hell out of me!" She jumped up, wild-eyed. "Listen, for —— sake! Irene and I are supposed to be in New Jersey!"

Donahue said: "So I hope he beats hell out of you."

"Oh, please Oh, listen! N-no!" She stumbled across the room towards him, shaking her head. "You don't know Bill! He'll murder me! Irene and I are supposed to be in Bill's cabin near Woodport! Bill couldn't come account of work! He'll—"

"Get back!"

"Oh, won't you listen! My —— ! The cops! I can't—"

"Get back! Don't get in my way!"

Panicky, breathless, she swayed before him, wringing her hands.

He saw the little man move—lightning-fast—towards the chair on which the other's holster hung. He saw the woman reeling in front of him—her contorted face, her frizzy hair. He struck with his left hand and she reeled, took a floor lamp down with her, screamed. He saw the slight twitch of the holster as the little man freed the gun. Saw the gun swing.

Donahue fired twice. The two explosions interlocked, welded; there was only a split-instant's interval between them. There was no third report. The little man shook, sank—and Donahue saw that his eyes were closed tightly, that his upper lip convulsed, baring his teeth in a macabre grimace that almost looked like a grin.

The tall man's face was white as death.

Donahue said to the tall man, grimly: "Ambitious, wasn't he?"

Then he raised the telephone.

Chapter IX

TOKEN Moore sat in Kelly McPard's chair. She looked very lovely and grave and injured, with her downcast eyes, her fingers worrying a crumpled little handkerchief.

Donahue, taking drafts from a bucket of hot coffee, regarded her critically. Kelly McPard, though he hadn't slept for many hours, looked spic and span, alert, wide-awake. There was a sound in the hall, and then the door opened and Spengler, grinning, shoved the tall man into the office.

Spengler said: "He's Joe Ackerman. The little guy's Midge Reider. Close friends of King Padden, the St. Louis number one man."

Kelly McPard looked at Token Moore. "This the guy?"

She raised her eyes, then lowered them. "Yes."

McPard sighed. "Okey, Dutch; take him out."

Spengler shoved Ackerman into the hall, closed the door.

Token had remained stoical too long. She burst out: "I'll go crazy, I'll go crazy!"

"You should have reported this," McPard said. "It would have saved a lot of grief."

She cried: "I couldn't! I was there when Danny came and I hid. I hid behind the sofa. And then Danny went out and about five minutes later there was a knock and I thought it was Danny again, so I hid behind the sofa again. I heard them come in. I heard one of them say: 'Consadine, you and Harrigan double-crossed the chief. King sent us here with three hundred grand to bet on Tripp because you told him you and Harrigan were chucking the fight. You double-crossed us, you rat. We're getting you and we're getting Harrigan.' And then—it happened. And I got a look at them. And then they went out and I saw Giles—dead—bloody—and I ran out and went home to my hotel."

"When you knew we had Harrigan here for the murder, why didn't you tell us the truth?"

She gasped: "I—I—" And then she broke into sobbing, covering her face.

Donahue set down the bucket of coffee. "I'll tell you, Kel," he said, his eyes still fixed on Token. "She and Consadine had been two-timing on the kid. When Consadine was knocked off, she skimmed out because she couldn't take it. When she learned from me, later, that you guys had Harrigan, she knew then that he was out of danger of the two men that had killed Consadine. So she told me she loved Danny. She must have had an idea that somehow or other Danny would be freed. With Consadine dead, she thought of Danny again—and his dough. If she'd come out in the open to explain who'd killed Consadine, Harrigan would have known she was in Consadine's place. So she kept silent. She probably had a vision of herself standing heroically by Danny during the trial—getting her mug in the papers, getting nice sobby write-ups, and getting—if he was freed—her hooks into his dough. She—"

Token screamed: "Stop! Oh, how I hate you—hate you! I—I—" She choked, then broke out in a flood of new tears, stamping her feet.

Donahue picked up the bucket of coffee again. He said, with a dry smile: "Dumb as the kid is, he fooled you and he fooled Consadine. Mainly, though, he fooled you. He'll have a hard time of it for a while, but he'll grow older, forget; and after a while you'll be just another day wasted away."

She buried her face in her hands. She was overwhelmed by chagrin, humiliation, self-pity.

"Save 'em," Donahue said. "Save your tears, Token."

Song and Dance

Tough dick Donahue plays nurse to a champ who has more dollars than sense

Chapter I

THE wind was raw, cold. It beat the skirt of Donahue's long camel's hair like a pennant, rapped the brim of his fedora against the crown. He walked into it, against it, bent over. Ahead, farther up the dark street, he saw the winking sign of the *Suwanee Club*. He stretched his legs, ducked down beneath the white marble façade, opened the heavy wooden door; and instantly the sound of the wind was gone, the warmth of the foyer enveloped him and he stood for a moment blowing his nose, wiping his eyes. Beyond the heavily draped doors, a band was playing.

A theatrical blonde in a trim little uniform took his hat and coat. He stood in the center of the sumptuous foyer, a lean brown man, neatly dressed in dark clothes. He lit a cigarette, puffed, and the first balloon of smoke hung languorously above his head. There was a frown on his forehead, a lowering look in his eyes, and a tautness of lip that indicated he had not come here for pleasure.

As he started forward, one of the black drapes parted magically and Arnholt, the manager, stopped and squinted towards Donahue. A light flashed in Arnholt's eyes, and was instantly extinguished, but it left on his face a sudden pallor. A silly, jerky grin jumped to his pulpy lips, and in an instant he was flounderingly ingratiating.

"Well, well, Donny—" He clapped pulpy white hands together, came forward.

Donahue said dryly: "The old *Suwanee* still going strong—in memory of Giles Consadine." He laughed softly, went past Arnholt, drew aside one of the black drapes. He walked down a short, broad corridor. He looked over his shoulder and saw Arnholt standing with the drape drawn, with his lower lip hanging open. Donahue went on, bending his brows in a frown. He pushed open a wooden swing door, and the sound of a band rushed at him. He stepped into the crowded

bar-room, crossed to the bar and slid a foot onto the brass rail.

"Old-fashioned, Rudolph."

"Ain't seen you in a couple weeks, Mr. Donahue."

"I wouldn't be surprised."

Waiting for the drink, Donahue turned, leaned his back against the bar, hooked a heel on the rail. Through the archway he could see the broad expanse of the dining and dancing-room, the swaying couples, the flashing brasses of the band. The bar itself was noisy—noisy with drunks and with men trying to make themselves heard above the bedlam of the band.

Out of the corner of his eye he saw Arnholt come in. He did not turn, but he could see Arnholt coming hesitatingly towards him. He turned in the opposite direction at the sound of his drink landing on the bar; he raised it, sipped, and found Rudolph eying him sharply. But Rudolph dropped his gaze, whistled, moved away. And then Arnholt was at Donahue's elbow.

"Just—ah—killing a little time, Donny?"

"Just," said Donahue.

"I—I'm trying to keep the place going since Consadine was killed. I guess I'll make a go of it." His voice sounded strained, and there was a nervous, unnatural little laugh in it.

Donahue looked at himself in the mirror, shifted his gaze and saw, farther down the bar, Rudolph tapping fingers and eying him intently. Donahue turned around and saw that Arnholt had gone, but he caught sight of the manager heading for the dining-room, saw him stop and talk with a head-waiter. Donahue finished his drink, moved away from the bar, reached the archway and stood there, back on his heels, his eyes narrowed down, searching the crowd.

A minute passed before he saw, through the shifting, shuffling dancers, the girl moving alone. He saw Token Moore moving swiftly, with a wrap over her arm, and the headwaiter at her heels, pointing towards one of several doors. A tight, malicious grin spread over Donahue's face, and he nodded to himself. He pivoted back into the bar, went down the bar to the swing door, pushed it open and entered the corridor. He strode swiftly down the corridor, flung aside the drape and saw the last of Token Moore going out the front door. The headwaiter had opened the door, and now he was swinging it shut.

"Open that," Donahue said.

The headwaiter turned and raised his hands, said: "Listen, now—"

"Get out of my way."

"Listen—" He fumbled around in front of the door, killing time.

Arnholt was standing with one of the drapes held back, his mouth open, his eyes wide.

Donahue grabbed the headwaiter, lifted him, threw him. The man let out a frightened squeal, and then Donahue had the door open. He ran to the sidewalk, across it, and caught a cab door as it was swinging shut. He opened it wide and looked in at Token Moore.

HIS voice was low, sarcastic: "You're why I came here, sweetheart." He climbed in, closed the door. "Okey, driver—shoot."

"Where?"

Donahue looked down at Token Moore. "The Hotel Eden, I guess."

She had not moved, had not spoken. She sat pressed in one corner of the seat, her face drained of color, her eyes wide and rolling with a kind of subdued horror. She was small, beautiful; and as the cab drove off, she rocked with the motion of it and kept staring wide-eyed at Donahue.

"Scared, huh?" he muttered, boring her with a dark stare.

"What—what do you want?"

He laughed ironically, remained silent for a moment, worrying her with his dark stare. "You know what I want, baby. Not so long ago you were Harrigan's mama—the champion's love life. And at the same time you were playing around with Giles Consadine, the champion's manager. And Giles Consadine was killed, and the champ found out you'd been playing around with him—and you lost your meal ticket."

She moved uncomfortably, looked away from him.

He leaned closer to her, his voice low and caustic: "It's just come to me that you're going to sue him for breach of promise. Four hundred grand, which means you hope to get three hundred. Listen, sister, use your head. Lay off. I'll crucify you if you try to go through with it."

She turned and stared hotly at him. Her lips moved, then tightened. She said nothing.

He went on, tapping her knee: "Donahue sees all, hears all. Consadine was killed by a couple of wild St. Louis hoods because a big shot out there figured that Consadine double-crossed him. Consadine had told this St. Louis big shot that Harrigan, the champ, was to chuck the fight to Tripp. Harrigan was—but at the last minute he changed his mind. He changed his mind because he was afraid Consadine was taking you away from him—and he was afraid that if he wasn't champion any more you'd chuck him. So he knocked Tripp out. And that knockout cost the St. Louis big shot exactly three hundred grand and—"

"Stop this cab!" she breathed, like one stifled.

"You little tramp, listen to me!" he dug in. "I'm still hired by the Boxing Commission to see Harrigan gets in the clear. Listen, you— sit down! And get this, sister," he went on in a low, bitter tone. "I saw you riding down Fifth Avenue yesterday in a big limousine. I know you haven't the dough to ride in one like that. You were alone, but I checked up on the license plates. I found—"

"Driver!" she yelled. "Driver, stop this cab!"

Donahue barked: "Keep going!"

"Driver, stop—stop!"

The driver braked, pulled over to the curb, stopped.

Donahue snapped: "By ——! I told you to keep going!"

Token Moore was trying to open the door, and she cried: "Don't! This man is trying to attack me!"

The driver was a large, beefy man. He swung down from his seat, opened the right-hand door, and Token Moore fell out. Donahue leaped after her, and the driver grabbed the lapel of his coat, swung him around.

"Listen, buddy, maybe this ain't no business o' mine, but I got a daughter o' my own—"

"You lug, stay out of this!"

Donahue heaved him off, bent and caught hold of Token Moore as she staggered to her feet. It was a dark street far on the upper East Side, tenantless at this hour. Token kicked and scratched. The taxi driver set his jaw and got under way with both fists cocked.

Donahue rasped: "You big sap, lay off! This dame—" He heaved back, dragging Token with him.

"Leggo her!" the driver roared.

With one hand Donahue swung Token behind him; with the other, knotted, he slammed the driver between the eyes. The man sat down on the sidewalk, cursed, and got up and came at Donahue with a low bellow. Donahue let go of Token and she fell to the street. He weaved beneath the driver's blows, came up under them and gripped the man.

"Listen, guy—you're wasting time! I tell you this dame—"

Donahue stopped talking and looked up the street. A car was speeding towards them, only low cowl lights glowing. Token was getting to her feet.

Donahue's voice rushed down at the man: "Let go!" He wrenched and tussled violently, but the man hung on grimly.

Suddenly a spotlight sprang to life, flooded them. Token Moore raised her hands to shield her eyes. Donahue dragged the man with him towards the taxi. The car swooped nearer. Donahue caught a glimpse of a hand thrust through one of the sedan's windows. He yelled into the driver's ear and tried to pitch with him behind the taxi. A gun exploded three times from the window of the speeding sedan.

Going down, Donahue felt the weight of the driver slam against him, heard a strangled moan. Donahue landed on his back and the driver was on top of him, still gripping, but fiercely now. Blood slapped Donahue in the face, and he turned his face, gripped with a heel on the sidewalk and turned himself and the driver over. But the man held on grimly, and Donahue, grunting, panting, struggled to free himself. He could hear the vanishing sounds of the sedan, and he could hear, too, vanishing heels—the clicking sound of Token Moore's running heels. Suddenly the driver let go, sighed, fell back—and as his head hit the sidewalk his eyes rolled open like a doll's, and remained open.

On his feet, Donahue saw no sign of the sedan. Far westward, he saw the dim shape of Token Moore; but in an instant she disappeared around a corner. The driver, Donahue saw, was dead. He heard somewhere distant the sound of a police whistle—eastward, he thought. And then his gaze swung west again, and he broke into a run. He reached the corner where Token had turned; he turned also, beat his heels up a narrow street. He stopped short as he saw, down another street, two blocks distant, a woman climbing into a taxi. He heard the sound of the taxi getting off.

He looked in all directions for another cab, but saw none. A block away, he saw a uniformed policeman pass, running, beneath a street light, disappear. Far away, a police whistle shrilled again.

Donahue stood for several minutes in the windy street. His breath pumped from his lungs, and presently the cold wind began to chill the sweat that had come out on his face. He started walking. He walked away from the scene of the shooting.

Chapter II

ARNHOLT strode up and down his office in the *Suwanee Club.* His office was on the ground floor, in the rear of the bar. The club itself was part of the great Arena. It had been Giles Consadine's idea; he had built first the fight arena, then built into it the nightclub which Arnholt, following Consadine's death, had taken on his own shoulders.

The headwaiter was having a drink. Donahue had thrown him hard, and the headwaiter had sustained a cut cheek which he now patted delicately with a handkerchief.

Arnholt had in his shiny eyes small nervous ghosts. He was essentially a nervous, flabby man; and as he paced back and forth he also patted his cheeks with a handkerchief, but it was sweat he patted, not blood.

"That fellow—that fellow'll be the ruination of me!"

The headwaiter sneered. "He's a bum—just a big Irish bum."

Arnholt stopped, spun. "Whether he's a bum or not, he's dangerous! He gets to know things, and if he finds out that—" Arnholt blew through his teeth, held his palms to his temples and began pacing again. He stopped short, drew a watch from his vest, stared at its face. His voice jittered: "I wish— I wish—" He broke off, sighed, bent harried eyes on the floor and went up and down the room like a man going through a drill.

When the door opened, he stopped so short that he almost lost his balance. The headwaiter gulped and pressed his bloody handkerchief harder against his cheek.

Donahue came in, kicked the door shut and stood breathing heavily. Every muscle in his lean brown face was taut, his brows were bent till they met above his nose, and beneath them his dark eyes were dead-level, hard with a hard brilliance. He gave the effect of steel drawn. And as he stood getting his breath, saying nothing, the room became very quiet. The first sound was made by the knocking together of Arnholt's knees. The second sound was also made by Arnholt.

"Don—Donahue—"

Donahue's "Yes?" had a sandpaper rasp, but it was evident that he was not interested in Arnholt's preliminaries, for he said: "You're a swell example of a Greenwich Village bartender that got big ideas and moved north."

The headwaiter rose and said idiotically: "I—I think I'd better g-go and wuh-wash my face." But he did not move, though he ached to. Donahue standing in the line of the door intimidated him.

But Donahue said: "Get out. I don't talk to the help."

The headwaiter scooted out like a whipped cur.

Arnholt made a few silly gestures with his hands and began: "You see, Donny. You—ah—uh—see—well—"

"Oh, shut up!"

Arnholt shut up and landed in a chair. He landed so hard that the chair moved a few inches, and then he gripped its sides till his knuckles grew white. He writhed under the look of dark disgust that Donahue had fixed upon him.

Then Donahue said: "You broke your neck to get Token Moore out of my way, Arnholt." He came closer, slowly, his dark eyes growing wider, shining with a harder brilliance. "I want to know who followed us."

Arnholt's voice leaped high: "Followed you!"

"I want to know what dumb bunnies followed us and cut loose with their rods."

Arnholt's eyes popped. "Cut loose with—"

"Damn it, are you going to repeat everything I say? I asked you a question, you fat slob!"

The courage of stark fear came to Arnholt and he stood up, his face doughy but suddenly grim, his voice hushed in the quiet room. "I don't know what you're talking about. You know damn' well I don't keep a staff of gunmen here."

"This I know, though, Arnholt." Donahue leveled a finger towards the floor. "We were followed." He was silent for a moment, and then he said: "Was there anybody with Token Moore?"

Glassy-eyed, Arnholt shook his head several times before saying: "No—no one."

"Why did you break your neck to get her out of here?"

"I—I didn't want any trouble in my place."

"What made you think there'd be trouble?"

"I knew you were riding her, and when you came in here first, I saw you were after something."

He was quiet now, deathly quiet—dry-lipped and glassy-eyed, staring straight at Donahue but seeing him through a dazzling haze. Suddenly he saw Donahue come at him, felt his wind choked. He heard the hard beat of Donahue's voice.

"You lying rat, there was somebody here with her! We were followed. Followed! And if you'd like trying to sleep on something—the guy that drove the cab was bumped off!"

Arnholt's face purpled, his knees gave way and he slumped to the floor. He did not really faint, but he pretended. He lay on the floor, holding his breath, not moving. Donahue stood over him; he stood well back on his heels, his body relaxed now. He heard the rhythm of the jazz band, muted by the heavy walls. He gazed down at Arnholt with a weary, twisted, half-vacant expression.

He drawled: "You're good at playing 'possum, Arnholt."

Arnholt tensed on the floor, pressed his body against it. He would not budge, would not get up. He was afraid—physically afraid—of Donahue, and he was tense, waiting. The sweat fell from his face to the carpet.

Chapter III

DONAHUE chuckled briefly to himself, turned and made his way slowly to the door. It opened as he reached his hand towards the knob, and he looked up to find Kelly McPard, eyes twinkling, slow smile drawing his mouth engagingly awry.

Kelly said: "Hi, Donny, old kid, old kid. I just dropped in."

"Swell."

"What's Arnholt doing, posing for animal crackers?"

Donahue turned to look at Arnholt, then brought his dark, disturbed stare back to McPard. "I wouldn't know."

McPard was genial, conversational. "Yeah, I was on my way up from Engelhoffer's *Brauhaus.* I seen Danny Harrigan down there with Margaret—you know Margaret, the little school-time chum from Chillicothe." He sighed pleasurably. "Yup, Donny—I guess the champ's going to marry that little girl."

"I wish somebody'd marry him and talk him into buying a sheep ranch in Australia or something."

"Tut, tut; you're too hard on Danny."

"He's been nothing but grief to me ever since I took the job of dry-nursing him for the Boxing Commish."

McPard made a good-natured deprecatory gesture. "You old fault-finder, you!" He chuckled, poked Donahue playfully in the belly; then he sighed, blinked and said: "Oh, yes—I want to see Arnholt. There was a killing a little while ago over on the East Side. Cab driver. Owners say it was a cab did a regular stand in front of this club."

Arnholt scrambled to his feet, yammered: "I didn't have nothing to do with it! I didn't!"

"Ah, dramatics!" McPard said softly, brightening.

Arnholt was panting out: "I didn't! She left here. She was here alone. I told her to go because—" He choked, felt his throat with twitching hands.

Donahue was eying him sorrowfully.

McPard said gently: "Who? Who left?"

"I'll give it to you in a nutshell, Kelly," Donahue rapped out, his dark eyes still riveted exasperatingly on Arnholt. He told it in two minutes, never once taking his eyes off Arnholt.

McPard wagged his head, clucked: "Tsk, tsk!"

Donahue said: "I saw the guy was dead and I tailed out after Token. I lost her. Maybe I should have gone back to the scene, but you know what I think of the general run of cops. So I sailed over here, and this fathead's been handing me a song and dance ever since."

"What did you want Token for?"

"Wanted to straighten her out. A lawyer—Barron Yerkes—dropped in on me today and out of a lot of baloney I discovered that this awful little tomato, Token Moore, was going to start breach of promise against Harrigan. Yerkes wanted to know how I stood—and I told him."

McPard murmured "M-m-m" and stepped into the office and then said to Arnholt: "Well, what do you know about this? It's as plain as the nose on your face that some guys tried to bump off Donahue because he snaked off the woman—and got that taxi driver instead. The chase must have started here. Break clean, Arnholt."

Arnholt was almost in tears. "I tell you, Kelly—I tell you I don't know. She was sitting here alone. I can prove that. There's a hundred people out there can prove that for me. Honest to God, Kelly! Ask anybody—ask the whole crowd out there. I—I just liked Token kinda.

And I knew Donny was riding her. And I just went over and told her he was here—and she beat it." At this point Arnholt did break into tears. He slumped into a chair, abject, woebegone, tears streaming down his doughy face.

McPard motioned Donahue out to the corridor. He said: "There is something screwy here, Donny, but I've got a hunch Arnholt's okey."

"We may as well start disagreeing now as later."

"What should I do, drag him over to Headquarters?"

"Should I tell you your business?"

"Okey, be funny."

"Funny, hell! I almost get my guts blown out and I come back here and this yellow tramp song-and-dances me and then you come around spreading peace and good-will!... Listen, Kel. This guy knows something. And I'll tip you off to something else you don't know. The other day I saw Token Moore riding alone down Fifth Avenue. I knew she was broke so I checked up on the plates. It was King Padden's chariot."

"What! Is he in this burg? Why the hell didn't you tell me he was here?"

"He's here, Kelly, and so is his number one man, Albino Will Olsen—and two other boy scouts."

"But why didn't you tell me?"

"My ——!" Donahue exploded. "Am I supposed to tell the police department what they ought to know?" He stopped short, laid a palm against McPard's chest. "Wait. If you're thinking Padden and his boys had a hand in this—and I'm thinking the same—you may as well consider yourself licked. Because nobody saw that gun car. I didn't. Nobody did. There's only one chance. No, maybe there're two. Token Moore or"—he nodded towards the door—"Arnholt."

"How did you figure Arnholt in it?"

"Three years ago King Padden tried to get his hand in the fight game in St Louis. He flunked. There's no disposition been made yet of Consadine's Arena and stables. I'm not off my nut when I say that it's likely King Padden might be making a bid—and using some other guy as a front."

Kelly McPard rocked back and forth on his heels. "Donny," he said, "I think I'll taxi Arnholt down to Headquarters."

Donahue said: "I'll go collect Token Moore."

"But listen, kid; no rough stuff on the *femme.*"

"Me rough?" He chuckled and then went past McPard and said under his voice: "I'll be sweet as the roses in May."

He went on up the corridor, entered the bar. The music was loud. There were fewer intermissions now. The members of the floor show were doing turns more frequently. The entire staff of the night-club strove to let no note of tension reach the guests. Donahue passed through the bar, reached the foyer as Harrigan, the heavyweight champ, came in with Margaret on his arm. The big boy was sober; he liked the bright lights but not the booze. And Margaret was swallowing in great gulps her first tour of the city's night life.

"Oh, Mr. Donahue!" she said, smiling brightly.

Donahue did not smile, but he said good-naturedly: "Hello, Margaret." And to Harrigan, in an aside: "See you in the washroom."

"Huh? What's up?"

"Dope! Do you have to go telling—the world? In—"he jerked his thumb—"the washroom." He pivoted and crossed the foyer, went down three steps, opened a solid swing door.

Harrigan came in a moment later. He was big, young. His shoulders rolled. His face was never free of a not unpleasant scowl, as though at all times there was something going on which he did not quite understand.

"Huh? What's up, Donny?"

"Listen, boy," Donahue said in a low, quick voice. "Suppose you take Margaret out of here and beat it home."

"Why? Ain't we having a swell time?"

"Listen…." Donahue got very close to Harrigan and told him the recent happenings, something of his talk with McPard. He spoke in a low, rapid-fire tone. He concluded: "King Padden and his boys are in town. So watch yourself. Remember, when you neglected to chuck that last fight, you lost Padden three hundred grand."

The champ spat, curled his lip. "Look here, Donny. I'll bust that guy in the kisser if he tries—"

"You'll bust hell in the kisser!" He was silent for an instant, narrowing his eyes shrewdly. "Listen. Have you seen Token lately?"

"Me? Nah."

Donahue gripped him. "That's on the up and up?"

Harrigan flushed. "Sure it's on the up and up."

"Okey," Donahue clipped. "Kelly's here and he's going to run

Arnholt to Headquarters. I'm going out after Token. Take Margaret and get out of here. Take her home. And you go home."

"Ah, listen, Donny—"

"You listen!" Donahue barked. "There's something rotten brewing and I want you off the streets till we can get it straight. D'you hear?" He shoved Harrigan towards the door, clipped: "Go on, now. For once in my life do as I ask you."

Big Harrigan pouted, "Jeeze, it's like I was a kid in diapers or something."

"You're not so far wrong at that."

Donahue cut ahead of him and went over to Margaret. "I just talked to your big he-mans," he said. "See that he gets home, will you?"

"What's the matter?"

"Enough." He paused, dropped his voice earnestly: "I wish, Margaret—I do wish you'd marry this kid and take him away somewhere—anywhere, faraway. Only take him off my hands. When I took this case for the Boxing Commish I started a song and dance and my legs are getting tired and I—"

He stopped, turned, saw Kelly McPard and Arnholt on the way to the door. He said in undertone: "Get him out of here, Margaret," and strode to the check room, got his hat and overcoat. He saw Kelly McPard and Arnholt go out.

The jazzband was playing a rumba.

Chapter IV

AT half-past eleven Donahue got out of a taxi in front of the Hotel Eden, off Fifth Avenue. He crossed the sidewalk, opened the heavy glass door and entered the quiet, luxurious lobby. The lights were dim, hidden in glass-enclosed crevices, and the man on duty at the desk was amusing himself with a small radio which he had tuned very low.

Donahue did not stop at the desk. He made his way to the elevator bank, found one car open. Entering, he said, "Six," and leaned back against the rear wall. The car rose quietly, stopped gently. Donahue got out and walked down the sixth floor corridor. He stopped before a door marked 606 and knocked. Waiting, he drummed with the toe of his shoe on the carpet. He knocked again, listened; and when no response came he knocked a third time.

Three minutes later he turned and retraced his steps up the corridor. He rang for the elevator, was taken to the lobby. He went across to the desk and said:

"Is Miss Token Moore in?"

The clerk turned from the dial of the radio. "Why, she isn't staying here any more."

Donahue frowned. "What do you mean?"

"She left." The clerk returned to the radio.

"When?"

"About an hour ago?"

"Where'd she go?"

"I'm sorry, I don't know."

"How about her baggage?"

"I don't understand."

"I mean," Donahue said, "didn't she leave an address for her baggage?"

"She took it with her, I believe, in a taxi."

"And left no forwarding address?"

The clerk snapped: "I told you she left no forwarding address, didn't I?"

Donahue looked at him. "Keep your shirt on. Do they pay you to take care of this desk or fiddle around with that radio?"

The clerk reddened.

"As a class," Donahue said, "you desk wallopers burn me up."

He swiveled and strode out of the hotel, stood for a moment in the windy street, letting the wind hammer him, balloon the skirt of his long camel's hair. He cursed under his breath and headed for Fifth Avenue. Reaching the Avenue, he stood there for several minutes, wasted six matches lighting a cigarette, and then burned the cigarette up the side, cursed and tossed it away.

"Taxi!" he barked.

Brakes squealed and a cab pulled up alongside the curb. Donahue climbed in, banged the door shut and slid down to the small of his back.

"Hotel Elsinore."

The Elsinore was only ten blocks distant. Donahue climbed out of the cab, pushed through the revolving doors and went swinging his legs across the large lobby to the desk.

"Mr. Harrigan come in yet?"

"About five minutes ago. Who shall I say—"

"Never mind."

He took an elevator to the seventh floor and a minute later he was knocking at the door of Harrigan's apartment. He had to knock several times before the door opened and Harrigan shoved his head out.

"Huh? What's up now?"

Donahue shoved in and walked to the center of the living-room before saying: "Token's disappeared." He turned and put his dark, fretful eyes on Harrigan. "She get in touch with you?"

Harrigan looked concerned. "Me? No. Where'd she go?"

"If I knew where she went—" He broke off with a disgusted groan, then said: "Please don't start asking profound questions. Got a drink?"

"Yeah. Over there."

Donahue walked to a table, picked up a glass, a bottle. He said as he poured: "I thought you don't drink."

"I don't."

"So I imagine."

Harrigan colored. "Oh, that—that—" He laughed, nodding to a half-drained highball. "I—I just took a snifter."

Donahue was eying him crookedly. "Token didn't get in touch with you, huh?"

"I said she didn't!" Harrigan growled. Donahue drank, still eying Harrigan.

"What the hell you looking at?" Harrigan demanded.

Donahue shrugged, sauntered into the bedroom, came out again, his eyes roving around the living-room as he took sip after slow sip.

Harrigan blurted: "I'm getting sick and tired o' having my personal life busted into!"

"Maybe you think I'm not sick and tired of busting into it. Calm yourself, champion.... Mind if I look around?"

"Yes I do!"

Donahue squinted.

Harrigan came over to face him. "I ain't gonna have you or anybody else telling me what to do! I ain't going to have you crashing in here anytime you feel like it! I don't care if the Boxing Commish did hire you! I ain't no kid. I can take care of myself and, by ——! I want to be left alone!"

Donahue said wryly: "There's no liquor on your breath."

Donahue was a big man, but he suddenly felt himself lifted and rushed to the door.

"Get out," Harrigan rasped.

Donahue's face had darkened. He showed his teeth. "Why, you dirty big tramp—"

"Get out!"

Donahue turned, whipped the door open. He looked Harrigan up and down contemptuously. He said with quiet deadliness: "Okey, boy. I'm going out now. And I hope you get what's coming to you—right smack in your thick neck!"

He stepped back into the hall, gripped the door knob, banged the door shut He strode swiftly up the corridor, his cheeks burning, his eyes humid. He was through, he told himself. Job or no job, he was through dry-nursing Harrigan.

NEXT morning the ringing of the telephone bell roused him at eight. He turned over on his side and regarded it sleepily, and when it kept on ringing, rasping on his nerves, he made a violent pass at it and swept it over to the bed.

He barked: "Hello!" And then, dropping his voice: "Oh, hello, Margaret…. You did, eh? And then what?" Listening, he scowled, his lips tightened and he said: "Listen, Margaret I'm through with that potato. He may be the moon and the stars to you, but to me he's an accident that should have happened at birth. I'm through with him, washed up. He's one of my sour memories. He—" He swung his feet off the bed, shook his head, worked his lips, stamped his foot, rolled his eyes. "No. Listen, Margaret. I feel sorry for you. But it ends there. Call Kelly McPard. Kelly knew him when he was a kid and is still soft on him. Call Kelly. Me, I'm through."

He hung up, rose and set the instrument down on the table. He went to the windows, snapped up the shades and went yawning and growling into the bathroom. He showered hot, then cold; rubbed himself dry with a big Turkish towel. The sun was bright, the air cool and crisp, fresh-smelling, blowing in through two open windows, kiting the curtains.

He dressed and was on his way to the door when the telephone rang. He sighed, pick it up.

"Hello, Kelly.... What about?" He looked down at the mouthpiece, dropped his voice: "Okey. Maybe in an hour."

He went down to the hotel dining-room, drank half a pint of tomato juice, ate two lamb chops, four pieces of toast, and drank three cups of coffee. Outside, he climbed into a taxi and said:

"Police Headquarters."

He found Kelly McPard in his office. McPard was freshly shaved, his linen was clean, crisp, and his clothes were, as always, well pressed. He had just begun a long, dappled panetela.

"Margaret called me up," he said.

Donahue flopped into a chair. "Me, too."

McPard said: "She's worried. She phoned Danny at 7:30 this morning and found he wasn't in. Nobody at the hotel knew where he was. So I phoned and asked them to send someone up. His apartment looked all right, but he wasn't there. But he'd slept there."

Donahue stood up, bowed. "I see you got me down here to talk about that dumb-bell Harrigan. Well, I'm through with him. Good-day, Kel."

"Wait."

Donahue turned at the door. "Go on."

"Look here, Donny. For —— sake, don't get your Irish up. The champ's a good lad—"

"Listen." Donahue came back to the desk, laid his fist on it. "I went up there last night after I found Token had disappeared. Harrigan put on a swell act. Listen." He thumped the desk. "Token was there, too."

"How do you know?"

"There was a half-drunk highball on the table. Harrigan doesn't drink. When I wanted to search the apartment he wouldn't let me. He got nasty. Gave me the bum's rush. I don't take a bum's rush from anybody and like it!"

"Donny, hold on." McPard stood up, trying to spread calm with his hands. "You can't chuck this now, Donny. We held Arnholt over night and couldn't get anything out of him. I got King Padden down here, and his boys, but"—he shook his head—"it's a dead end there. There's a murder on our hands, but there's Danny, too. He's good. He's just hot-headed. And there's Token. And take 'em all together, there's a hook-up somewhere."

Donahue went to the door. "Okey. You find it."

McPard grinned, crossed the office and took hold of Donahue's arm. "Donny, you're getting temperamental as a chorus girl. How do you know Token was there last night? Maybe Danny was just sore. He had a right to be—"

Donahue lashed in: "And I've got a right to be told things that this mug insists on hiding!"

McPard looked down at his fingernails. "Suppose Token was there? You don't mean to stand there and hint around that he went off with her—leaving Margaret?"

Donahue was finding it hard to breathe. "Listen, Kel. Nothing that guy would do would ever surprise me. He ought to hire a small boy to tell him the time and tell him when it's day and when it's night."

McPard's smile was persuasive. "Anyhow, Donny, agreeing with all you say, you can't slide out of this. It's not right."

Donahue opened the door. "I'm sliding, Kel. I know Padden and Albino Will Olsen from my St. Louis days, and I'd like to go up against them—but Harrigan sticks in my throat. Happy days, Kelly."

Kelly grabbed his arm. "Donny, if I asked you to hang on, what about it? Me, I'm asking you. Forget about Harrigan. I'm asking you personally, Donny."

Donahue sighed and stared at the floor. He stared a long time, chewing on his lip. Then he looked up at McPard, and he didn't smile.

But he said: "So I guess you win, you heel."

Chapter V

BY noon there was still no word of Harrigan. Donahue learned this by phoning McPard from a booth near Sheridan Square. He also got in touch with Margaret, frankly apologized for the way he had talked to her over the phone that morning, and wound up by telling her to stay in her hotel room.

He took a West Side subway to Times Square, where he got off and boarded a crosstown shuttle for Grand Central. He walked down Lexington, entered his hotel lobby and asked at the desk if any message had been left for him. None had been left. He went up to his apartment and found an oldish maid cleaning up. He intended eating downstairs in the dining-room, but first he mixed himself a Dry

Martini in his small pantry. The maid went out, saying she would return with fresh towels, and Donahue stood in the center of his living-room sipping the Dry Martini. He drank down two and was pouring a third when there was a knock on his door.

He said: "Come in," and emptied the cocktail shaker.

It was not, as he had supposed, the maid. The Albino came in first, with both hands in the pockets of his coat and his cap slanted over one eyebrow. With him came two other men. They were well-dressed, neat, and cleanshaven; the one short and muscular, dressed in a fashionable raglan coat and a brown Fedora, the other taller, though not quite as tall as the Albino, but dressed with equal care. This man, coming in last, closed the door and locked it

Donahue put his cocktail glass to his lips, sipped, ran his tongue back and forth between his lips and said, not pleasantly: "I thought it was somebody else. The gate for you."

The Albino was smiling politely, his emaciated face a little on one side. The other two men separated, taking up strategic positions and showing a keen but silent interest. The Albino looked from one to the other, nodded, and removed his hands from his overcoat pockets.

He said: "We were waiting for you to come in, Donahue."

"Why didn't you bring Padden along, too?"

"He's got a kinda bilious attack this morning." The Albino smiled softly, almost sweetly; then he arched his eyebrows, put his lips sweetly together, said: "You know, we're looking for Token Moore."

"Swell. So am I. Let's get together on it."

The Albino again smiled sweetly, folded his long, fragile hands primly against his chest. "We are together, ain't we now?" From his manner, his lips, you expected him to speak precise English; he did speak precisely, but there it ended. "We think you know where she disappeared to."

Donahue shook his head. "Not me, Olsen."

The Albino sauntered across the room, turned on the radio. He let it warm up, and when the first sounds came, he increased the volume. Smiling daintily, he went very close to Donahue and said with a precise movement of his lips:

"We ain't, you know, kidding."

"Neither am I. I don't know where she is."

The two other men caught Donahue from behind; each grabbed one of Donahue's arms and he dropped glass and cocktail shaker to the floor. Back of him, the radio thundered. The Albino drew a blackjack from his pocket, smiled, and struck Donahue on the head. Donahue jerked at the two men who held him.

Donahue's eyes flashed. "I told you I don't know. I've been looking for her myself."

The Albino struck again. Donahue sagged, grimaced, while the Albino craned his swanlike neck and looked on with a brightly clinical interest.

"T'll hurt next time," he said.

Donahue began tussling violently, swinging the two men about the room with him. They all went down in a heap, arms and legs flying. The Albino stepped nimbly, raised his blackjack, struck. Donahue straightened out on the floor, put his hands to his head. The two men jumped up, dusted themselves briskly. Donahue took his hands from his head but did not move his body. Fury and anger were in his eyes, and his face was gray, his lips curved wolflike over his clenched teeth.

The three men stood looking down at him, down into his face. They did not see the door open, did not see the oldish maid standing on the threshold with a pass key in her hand. Her eyes popped and her jaw fell. Only Donahue, looking between the archway of the Albino's legs, saw her.

He yelled: "Run! Call the police! Run!"

The Albino whirled in time to see the maid pitching away from the doorway.

She screamed: "Help! Police!"

The Albino snapped: "Beat it!"

The two men turned and darted into the hall. The Albino, his pink eyes suddenly furious, waited a moment to kick Donahue's head, ribs, and then his head again. And then he, too, turned and sped into the corridor.

Donahue lay with his hands pressed against his face, groaning. After a minute, he turned over, got to his knees, then to his feet. He took off his coat and vest, ripped off his shirt. He went heavy-footed into the bathroom, turned on the cold shower and held his head beneath it. Bits of red color mixed with the water in the tub.

He pulled his head out of the shower, ripped off his blood-stained undershirt, looked at himself in the mirror. Water still poured down his face from his soaked hair. He spat it from his lips, cursing.

Chapter VI

BARRON Yerkes looked at the card which his secretary placed on the glass top of his flat-topped desk. He ran a forefinger slowly across his lower lip, leaned back, put his fingertips together and shook his head.

"I'm not in," he said.

The girl picked up the card, returned to her outer office. Barron Yerkes took a cigarette from a red lacquer humidor, placed it between his lips. There was a rattle at the door. The door whipped open and Donahue strode in. Yerkes looked up, smiled, lighted his cigarette.

"I thought you wouldn't be in," Donahue said. He banged shut the door. There were several black and blue marks on his face and a neat strip of adhesive tape on his right cheekbone. He came slowly across the office and stopped by the desk, his hands in his overcoat pockets, his eyes boring down at the attorney.

Yerkes cleared his throat, smiled. "You look rather worked up, Donahue."

"Lay off the jokes. I'm sore. These lousy hoodlums you represent came around to my place and played house, with me on the receiving end."

"I'm genuinely sorry, Donahue."

"You look all broken up. Listen, Yerkes." He knuckled the desk sharply. "If you don't want to get hurt, you'd better break with that crowd."

"H-m-m. It was unfortunate."

"And another thing." Donahue dropped his voice way down. "Where the hell is Token Moore?"

Yerkes raised his palms. "I certainly wish I knew. Don't you know?"

"So now you're going to start in. No, I don't know. And I don't know where Harrigan is. But this I do know—I do know that if you play along with this case you're going to get hurt and I'm going to hurt you. No dirty St. Louis bum can sail into this town and play kick-the-wicket with me."

"Donahue—"Yerkes stood up. "I'm genuinely sorry this happened. Something went wrong somewhere, but I assure you I had nothing to do with that beating and I don't know where Token Moore is.

Times are hard, and it looked like easy money. I regret I took the case, and I hereby tell you that I'm dropping it—now—this minute."

Donahue laughed. "Yeah—I'd like to believe that."

"Believe it or not."

"All right. Then why do you think she disappeared?"

"It's possible that Token and Harrigan made up and went away together. That's the only answer I can find."

Donahue said: "The answer's so simple that I don't believe it. Not that I think Harrigan wouldn't be dope enough. But the lay of the whole thing doesn't seem right." He looked steadily at Yerkes. "And remember, stay out of it. Or you'll get hurt."

He went uptown to the Hotel Elsinore, and found the clerk beaming.

"Mr. Harrigan is in."

Donahue stood back on his heels, then settled. "Don't bother ringing."

By the time he reached the elevator he was worked up. By the time he reached the seventh floor he was cursing to himself. His jaw was set, and dark lights moved in his eyes. He strode long-legged down the corridor and worked the knocker on 707 violently, stood simmering, impatient, licking his lips. He knocked again and then beat upon the door with his fist. Several minutes passed before he heard the click of the lock. The door opened and Harrigan stood swaying back and forth in the foyer.

Donahue stepped in quickly, closed the door, narrowed down one eye and said vindictively. "What the hell happened to you?"

Harrigan turned and went leaden-footed into the living-room. He dropped to the divan, stretched out and planked a wet towel down on his face. He groaned. His collar and tie were in rags. Several buttons had been ripped off his vest and one pocket of his coat was torn.

"Oh! Oh!" he groaned.

"Listen, Harrigan—"

"Oh! Oh!"

"Listen, will you?"

"Yeah. What?"

Donahue bent over. "What happened to you?"

"What's it look like? I was hit with the Chrysler Building."

"Where?"

"All over."

"I mean, where did it happen?"

"In here. Oh! Oh!"

"In here!"

Harrigan removed the towel. "Listen, Donahue. Go wet this again, will you?"

Donahue took the towel into the bathroom, soaked it, wrung it out and carried it back to the divan. Harrigan placed it on his face again and sighed, "Ah, ah!"

"Listen, Harrigan. Who did it? Cut out acting like a baby. Who did it?"

"Three guys. They used blackjacks. I come in here, and then I heard a knock and I opened the door and there they were. First they held me up, and then they landed on me with blackjacks."

"Why'd they use blackjacks?"

"They wanted to know where Token was."

"Where is she?"

"I don't know."

"Listen, Harrigan. Where the hell were you all day?"

"I got up early. I couldn't sleep, so I got up early and went for a walk. I walked up to Central Park and sat down and fell asleep there."

"Harrigan," Donahue said hotly, "I think you're a damned liar. You know where Token is."

"Gawd, now you're picking on me! I tell you I don't. I don't give a damn where she is. Lemme alone, will you!… Oh, my head!"

"Damn your head!"

Donahue walked violently around the room. From a far corner of it he said testily: "I'm getting sick and tired of you, Champ. You're not on the level. You've made up with Token and you're going to skin out with her. You're a sap and a blockhead. Here Kelly and I worry our nuts off about you, and what do you do? Sleep in Central Park? Bah!"

Harrigan sat up, flung the wet towel to the floor. "To hell with you! You think I care what you think about me? Well, I don't! Get out o' here and leave me alone!"

Donahue shook a finger at him. "You can yell all you want, Harrigan. But there's one thing you won't do—you won't run away with Token Moore. I promise you that."

Harrigan's face reddened. He stood up. He held out his hands, palms up. "Listen, Donahue. I ain't. I swear I ain't."

"Then where is she?" Donahue crossed the room swiftly and stopped in front of Harrigan. "Where is she?"

Harrigan's jaw set. "I don't know," he ground out.

The two men measured each other for a long moment. Then Harrigan ducked his head, turned and barged into the bathroom. He banged shut the door, locked it.

Donahue's lips moved in silent oaths. He pivoted, went to the foyer door, opened it and passed into the corridor. He rang for the elevator and stood waiting, wrapped in thought. Presently the doors opened, and he stepped in, was dropped to the lobby. As he stepped out he ran into Margaret.

"Oh, Mr. Donahue."

He took hold of her arm, walked her to a quiet corner of the lobby and motioned to a chair. She sat down, wide eyed, and he pulled up another chair and sat down facing her.

She gasped: "Danny—"

"He's all right."

She slumped. "Thank God!"

"Listen," he said in a low husky voice. "You love that guy, don't you?"

"But of course! Why, what makes you—"

"Never mind. Listen to me. When are you going to get married?"

"We haven't set a date."

"You've talked about marriage, though, huh?"

"Ye-es."

He tapped her knee. "Look here, Margaret. I wish you'd go upstairs, take that big overgrown kid and marry him right now."

"Oh, but—"

"I know, I know. But never mind what's proper and what isn't. Marry him and get out of this city with him tonight."

"But why?"

"Because there's a few mugs running around this town that don't like him. Because if you love him, you'll do as I say. Take care of him. He needs someone to look after him. I'm getting tired of it…. Do that, will you? For his sake, for your own sake—and, yes, for my sake. Drag him down to City Hall, put him over the jumps and haul him out of town tonight. I'm serious, Margaret. He needs a girl like you. By himself, he just can't stay out of trouble. Go up now, will you? I'll wait down here and see how you make it."

She was a little white-faced now. "All right," she said quietly, and stood up.

He walked with her to the elevator, saw her in, then strode to the newsstand, bought a newspaper and sat down in a lobby chair. He liked Harrigan, as everyone liked Harrigan, but he was becoming fed up; Harrigan's inability to handle his own personal affairs was beginning to exasperate Donahue beyond endurance. Donahue knew that Harrigan had a fatal weakness for women, and he knew that Token Moore had a way with men of Harrigan's type.

Fifteen minutes later he saw Margaret come out of the elevator. He rose and headed her off. She had her chin in the air.

"Hey," he said in a low voice.

She did not stop walking, but she looked at him and said: "I guess I'm not wanted." She went on swiftly, her high heels clicking rapidly on the tiles.

Donahue stopped, watched her disappear through the door. He took a coin from his pocket, tossed it in the air, caught it. He sighed, wagged his head, thrust the coin back into his pocket and strode out to the street.

"The stuff," he muttered ironically, "of which champions are made!"

Chapter VII

KELLY McPard was eating an early dinner in Englehoffer's *Brauhaus* when Donahue walked in. Kelly looked benign, cheerful, and on good terms with the world at large. He was radiating good nature. "Well," he said, "I see Danny's back again. I got him on the phone and he said he went for a walk this morning and fell asleep in the Park."

Donahue sat down, said to the waiter: "A mug of beer, August, a couple of sausages, cabbage and two boiled potatoes." And then to Kelly McPard: "Harrigan makes me sick, and you don't act as an antidote yourself."

"Tush, tush, Donny," Kelly McPard said. "Little food will make you feel better."

Donahue began talking with restrained viciousness: "Listen, Kelly. He may be a swell guy, a fine guy, good to his mother and with a kind face. He may have a heart of gold and you may have known him since he was kid. But to me, Kelly, he's a wash-out, a honk-out, a boob and a moron. I don't think he knows his elbow from a hole in the ground, and he knows less about women than the thousands of infants that will be born in this country between tonight and tomorrow. I can like a boob for a while, if I don't have to be around him too much; but when I'm around him too much I start to feel homicidal. Right now, I wouldn't care if Harrigan was bumped off."

"Tush, tush! Of course you would."

"I wouldn't!"

"Tush, tush!" Kelly took a long swallow of beer, sighed pleasurably. "What's eating you now, Donny?"

"I put Margaret up to ask him to marry her this afternoon, and the flat-footed bum turned her down."

"H'm!" Kelly put down his knife and fork. "This is getting serious, Donny."

"And if you ask me," Donahue went on, "he didn't go for a walk this morning and he didn't sleep in the Park. This wench Token Moore has got her finger into him again and he's falling like a ton of brick!"

Kelly McPard began to frown. "Donny, I'm beginning to think maybe you're right."

Donahue bowed deeply. "Thank you so much."

"No kidding. You finish your dinner and then we'll go up and I'll talk to Danny like a Dutch uncle."

"You can go, Kelly. But me"—he held up hands, shook his head—"not me. I'm through with that guy. Washed up. I hope she takes him for his whole roll so I can walk up to him some day and say, 'Well, I told you so.'"

"Nonsense, Donny! Danny's a swell kid, but young. He's no match for Token Moore. Listen, I saw that kid grow up. Okey. Never mind. I'll go alone."

"Swell! And you'll probably get your face caved in for your trouble. He's worse to handle than a dog with the rabies."

Kelly McPard finished his meal rapidly, got up and took down his overcoat from a hook, slipped into it. Donahue was plowing savagely through his meal, his head bent way down.

McPard said: "Okey, Donny. I'll go it alone. I didn't think, though, that you were the kind of a guy would give up. Well, so long, kid."

"Wait!" Donahue shoved back his plate, heaved up and grabbed his coat. "You make me sick," he growled. "Come on. And if I break a chair over his head, it's your fault—remember that."

"One thing I like about you, Donny—you're so calm and collected all the time. You never get mad."

They boarded a taxicab and headed uptown. Kelly McPard lighted a Turkish cigarette, inhaled in the manner of a man who really enjoys his nicotine. The cab turned off Fifth Avenue, wedged into slow-moving eastbound traffic; and as it neared the Hotel Elsinore Kelly leaned forward and said:

"There's Danny coming out now—"

"Wait a minute," Donahue cut in. "Suppose we follow him. I mean, if we light on him now, it'll be all off. He'll shut up like a clam."

"Ah, he'll listen to his Uncle Kelly—"

"I tell you no!" Donahue shoved Kelly McPard back in the seat. He said to the driver: "Follow that cab pulling away from the Elsinore."

They followed the cab to Fifty-fourth Street, where Harrigan swung out and disappeared through a doorway. Donahue and McPard got out and stood on the corner and Donahue said:

"It's a speakeasy and— Hey, look!"

"What?"

Donahue, craning his neck, did not reply for a long moment. Then he said: "A guy just dropped off a cab beyond that door, piped the address and—I can't see him now."

"You're imagining things."

"Have it your way."

Kelly McPard lighted another cigarette. "Listen. I think we ought to go in and talk to Danny. I can handle him."

"Kelly, I tell you—"

But McPard started off. Donahue cursed and followed him, and they found Harrigan leaning against the bar and frowning at himself in the mirror.

"Danny," said McPard, "I'd like to have a talk with you alone."

"Kel," said Harrigan, "I'm sick and tired of being talked at. Beat it."

"Danny, it's your old pal Kelly McPard asking you."

"I'm sorry, Kel."

Harrigan finished his drink, paid up and strode out of the speakeasy. Kelly McPard went as far as the front door, peered through the peep-hole. He saw Harrigan enter a cab, and when the cab moved on Kelly McPard opened the door and Donahue followed him out. They jumped into a cruising cab and McPard said:

"Tail that black and white ahead there."

Donahue laughed. "Oh, you can handle him all right!"

They followed Harrigan to another speakeasy in West Fortieth Street but did not enter. They waited on the corner, in a cigar store, and an hour passed before Harrigan reappeared. He took another cab and headed east.

On Lexington Avenue he got out and entered a drug-store. The cab waited. He came out in a few minutes, reentered the cab and drove north, turned east at Thirty-eighth and entered a brownstone speakeasy east of Third Avenue. Donahue and McPard waited in a garage across the street. Harrigan reappeared half an hour later and walked west to Lexington, where he boarded another taxicab.

The taxi headed west on Thirty-ninth Street; crossed Madison Avenue, Fifth, Sixth, and Broadway—went on to Tenth Avenue and then swung south. At Fourteenth Street Harrigan alighted and went ahead on foot. It was a noisy, traffic-ridden intersection, and Donahue and McPard, on foot now, had a hard time keeping track of Harrigan. Finally they saw him enter a transatlantic steamship pier.

Donahue stopped. "I told you. He's skipping. The *Montania* sails tonight for Cherbourg. Stay back!"

He could see Harrigan standing behind the glass doors and peering into the street.

Donahue cursed. "Oh, he's a nice guy all right. He gets Margaret all worked up and then leaves her flat for this Token Moore! Boy, do I like his insides! Do I!"

"I'm going right up to him—"

Donahue grabbed Kelly. "Like hell you are! You stay here and wait!"

Taxis were arriving and departing in great numbers, and a crowd was gathering out front and inside the terminal. Porters were hauling baggage. The crowd was animated, laughing; an air of impending departure electrified the air. The space in front of the terminal was not well-lighted. The broad street was dark. Trucks rumbled past, taxis sped. Newsboys hawked papers. Telegraph messengers darted in and out of the terminal, and all the time the crowd kept growing. Trunks thumped and iron-wheeled hand trucks banged.

"Pipe that!" Donahue muttered suddenly.

"What?"

"Token!"

A taxi had drawn up and from it Token Moore alighted while two porters dived for her baggage. Token stood in the clear, in the glare of a floodlight, taking change from her purse. Harrigan started out of the terminal, elbowing his way through the crowd.

"I'm going to get her," Kelly McPard muttered.

"Let's," Donahue said.

The motor of some automobile roared. Instinct made Donahue and Kelly tense, look around. Three shots rang out. Women screamed and pitched this way and that. Donahue caught a glimpse of Token going down, another glimpse of Harrigan knotted up in a crowd of men and women. Donahue drew his gun.

Kelly McPard squinted his eyes and his gun leaped magically into his hand as he heard the door of a car slam. He heard rubber tires rasp, looked between two taxis and saw a black sedan lurch forward for the open street. McPard raised his gun and its muzzle blazed in the shadows. A small hole appeared in the right side of the windshield, and instantly the car yawed, its rear end whipped violently.

There was a crash of metal as the sedan sideswiped a taxi. The taxi seemed actually to jump in the air and the sedan slewed, turned completely around. Brakes of another car screamed as it plowed into the sedan's radiator, blew one of the sedan's front tires. Its doors whipped open and three men leaped out, raced towards the east side of the street.

Donahue started off and Kelly McPard raced beside him. McPard fired and one of the three men turned without stopping and fired back. Donahue ran with his arm outstretched before him, his right eye sighting. His gun bellowed and one of the three men teetered but kept on running, and all three ran north on the east side of the street and dived into Fifteenth Street.

McPard stopped on the corner, took aim and fired twice. The man who had teetered turned around, fell backward; he fell so violently that his legs leaped into the air, slammed down again. His two companions did not stop. McPard fired again and one of these started toppling but regained his balance, turned half around and fired three times. McPard took a step backward, shook himself. He tried to take a step forward and stumbled, rolled to the gutter.

But Donahue was on his way, running across the street. The man who had shot McPard was now backing up and reloading. Donahue fired once and this man stopped reloading and sat down in the middle of the street. Brakes squealed as a taxi swerved to avoid hitting him.

The third man ran faster, and Donahue went after him with strides equally long. The man turned left, and Donahue, nearing the corner, pressed close against the building and bent over as he looked around. A shot rang out and chipped the corner of the building a foot above his head.

He saw the man wheeling beneath a lone street light, leaping for a doorway. Donahue went around the corner and fired at the same time, heard a short outcry, the scraping of feet on the pavement. He went swiftly along in the shadows of the buildings, heard the blast of a police whistle somewhere distant. He saw the man trying to break through a door, but the man heard him coming and swiveled.

Donahue saw the glint of metal and without stopping he emptied his gun. The man staggered away from the door, tried to run but only hobbled. He reached the center of the street before he pitched to his face. His gun bounced, rang on the pavement, and he turned over on his back and let out a long sigh.

He was not entirely outside the radius of the street light. His hat was off, and his pale hair was splotched, and now he was grunting and tearing at his collar. Going towards him, Donahue could see that it was the Albino.

Chapter VIII

HARRIGAN walked up and down the back room of the precinct house. His hat was crushed down over his forehead. The room was full of detectives, and there were other detectives and policemen in the central room, and some newspaper men. The house was noisy. Telephone bells jangled and men yelled into the telephones; men arrived and departed and twice a reporter was thrown bodily out of the back room.

Suddenly there was loud and violent talking in the doorway, and Donahue talked his way in. Harrigan bumped into him, stopped, blurted out:

"Holy ——! Donahue!"

"Holy your grandmother!"

"Listen, Donny—listen now! How is Kelly? How is poor old Kel, Donny?"

"He'll pull through, but it's not your fault. Shut up! Listen to me, you awful dumb-bell! What was the idea of running away with Token Moore?"

"So help me, Donny, I wasn't running away with nobody. Honest to gawd, I wasn't. Listen, Donny. I wasn't, see? I was only making sure she got off. That's all. I was only making sure."

"You're a liar, Harrigan. Besides being God's foremost dope, you're a liar and a double-crosser!"

"No—no!" He grabbed hold of Donahue's lapels, shook him. "You got to listen to me. I wasn't going away with her. It was like this. Look now, Token came to me and said how she got tied up with King Padden, not knowing what she was in for. It was King Padden put the idea in her head."

"What idea?"

"Look now. It was King Padden put her up to sue me for breach of promise or something. She asked—she was gonna ask for three hundred thousand, but she was only to get twenty-five grand out of that. The lawyer was to get twenty-five too and King Padden was to get two hundred and fifty grand. See? So she got scared. She got scared of him and his guys and she come to me and told me the whole thing, and told me the danger she was in. She didn't want to go through with it, and she cried and she said she'd have to get out of the country and would I give her about twenty-five grand."

"So she was a double-crosser again."

"No! Look now. She was all busted up and I was sorry for her. Besides, I didn't want no case in court. So I said I'd give her the twenty-five grand, and this morning I did—I got it out of the bank and give it to her and she had her passport and all she had to do was get a ticket. I was sorry for her, and maybe I should ha' went back with her again, but I'm gone on Margaret. And I was scared about Token getting away. So I come down to the pier to make sure she got on the boat all right. I wasn't going anywhere. And then them guys came along and killed her."

Donahue wagged his head, sighed. "Boy, you sure need someone like Margaret to look after you. Token lived a double-crosser and died a double-crosser. Kelly shot King Padden in the belly tonight—in the sedan. And Padden talked a bit before he died. It was Padden and his mugs killed that taxi driver last night. They drove up in front of the *Suwanee* as Token and me drove off in the taxi. And they followed. They thought she was in a tough spot and they tried to shoot me up. Arnholt knew who followed us, but Padden and his boys hadn't been in the club that evening and he knew he was safe if only he kept his mouth shut. Besides, Padden was buying into the club, into the Arena.

"Your sweet Token Moore was yellow," he rasped on. "A couple of days ago Padden gave her ten thousand bucks. She was broke and he advanced that amount against the twenty-five grand she hoped to get out of the breach of promise suit against you. He also advanced the lawyers several thousand. But she got cold feet. She was afraid of me. She was afraid of what I'd say in court. So she double-crossed Padden and came to you with a long sob story and got twenty-five grand out of you. Imagine the grifter!"

Harrigan stared. "She done that!"

"She did that."

Harrigan looked sick. He felt his throat and sent his harried eyes about the floor. He looked abject, stunned.

"Gosh, Donny—I—I— Listen. Uh—d' you think I can see Kel yet?"

"Not yet. My advice—and don't take it if you don't want to—is to go and see Margaret. Your body's all right, Harrigan, but it lacks a head. Try using Margaret's."

"Uh—listen—uh—will you call her up and—uh—ask her if I can come up and see her?"

"Anything," Donahue said, "to get rid of you."

They went into another room and while Harrigan fidgeted and shifted from foot to foot, Donahue telephoned Margaret's hotel.

"Margaret?… This is Donahue, Margaret. The penitent champion wants to call on you. For my sake, for his sake, and for the sake of all his friends, please take care of him. See that he doesn't get his feet wet and keep him out of drafts. Keep him clear of grifters. Never let him sign a check. If he ever tries to use his head, remind him that he hasn't any. The big lug—"

He stopped short, frowned, listened. His face grew red, he held the receiver slightly away from his ear, looked at it. His eyes flashed. He placed the receiver tentatively to his ear again. His lips worked, trying to interrupt. Suddenly there was a click, then silence. He hung up.

Harrigan gulped: "Huh?"

Donahue patted his ear, wagged his head. "I guess she told me a few things. I'm this and I'm that and I'm those and them."

"But—but how about me?" Harrigan cried hoarsely.

"You," Donahue said, going past him, "seem to be the apple of her eye. She loves you, you big palooka. Go up and get it."

Champions Also Die

*A box-fight setup that looks
sour to tough dick Donahue*

Chapter I

DONAHUE came into the lobby of the *Suwanee Club* with his black Chesterfield over his arm, his black velours hat aslant his forehead. The hat-check girl moved to take his things, but he shook his head, said: "I won't be staying," and went on down a corridor. He looked lean in his dinner suit, but the broad expanse of the white shirt, single-studded, made his face look very brown.

He slapped open the swing door, pushed into the noisy bar. The radio was on, and a dozen-odd men, standing at the bar, were listening intently. Donahue leaned on the end, said offhand: "Scotch and Perrier," to the bartender.

Ken Teebolt, the new owner-manager of the club, came over, clicking a half dozen quarters together. He was a big man, blonde and clean-looking, with flat but thick pink cheeks and large, good-humored eyes.

"How's she look, Donny?"

Donahue sent a glance roving casually about. "Nice."

Both men paused to turn an ear towards the radio loudspeaker. Half a dozen shouts rose in the bar and were followed by lusty laughter, hard back-slapping.

Ken Teebolt grinned: "Kid Lenox out in the fourth. Well, Harlem's getting it on the chin tonight! And me up fifty bucks. You betting?"

Donahue, drinking, looked at Ken above the rim of his glass, shook his head, said into the glass: "Uh-huh."

Ken sighed. "Well, I got a grand on the Emperor Brown."

"Sentiment?"

Ken frowned. "What do I look like?"

Donahue set his glass down, patted his lips with a handkerchief. He lit a cigarette and said out of the cup formed by his hands: "Got a hunch you'll lose it."

Ken smiled. "I've seen King Brown and I've seen Young Boston. It's a push-over for the Emperor."

"Okey," Donahue said lightly, and tossed a fifty-cent piece on the bar.

"Say—" Ken put a hand on Donahue's arm, searched Donahue's face candidly with his round blue eyes. "What's in the wind? You wouldn't lay dough on Young Boston, would you?"

"Uh-huh." Donahue took the cigarette from his mouth, added: "Or the Emperor." He replaced the cigarette in his mouth, took a deep inhale, looked with a direct but provocative gaze into Ken's eyes.

"Say, Donny—"

"I don't know a thing," Donahue said. "But if you can get that bet called off, put the dough in some bourbon."

He turned from the bar, spurted a breath at the end of his cigarette, knocking the ash off. He made his way back to the lobby, walked down a wide corridor and entered an open elevator. Two men besides the operator were standing in it. One was Sam Beckert, King Brown's manager, and the other Pete Korn, a small, slight man with a dry-skinned hatchet face and wet, red-lidded eyes. Sam Beckert was rotund, jovial, with a voice like a fog-horn, cheeks like red cherries and with a bulblike chin to match. In the center of his massive face was a small, pointed nose that seemed to have got there by mistake.

"Gonna see my Emperor clean up tonight, Donny?"

"Yeah."

"I hope you laid all you got on him, Donny. He'll take that Boston wildcat by the ears."

"By the ears," supplemented Pete Korn in a dry, cracked voice.

The car started upward.

Donahue looking at the ceiling, said: "He's the fastest lightweight we've seen in this town since Benny, and a real champion."

"You're telling me?" boomed Beckert.

Pete Korn cackled: "Telling me?"

The car was slowing. Beckert slapped Donahue on the back and rumbled: "Yessir, boy, I hope you laid all you got."

"I don't bet on fights, Sam."

The door opened and as they walked out Beckert laughed: "You oughtta, boy, when I'm telling you! Be seeing you, kid!"

"Seeing you, kid," Pete Korn said.

Donahue, making his way up the corridor, could hear the din of the Arena crowd. When he opened a heavy door, the din bellowed at him. Moving on, he came to the upper tiers, saw the massed crowd below, howling and roaring, waving arms, hats, handkerchiefs. Far down, he saw the white pool of the ring; saw King Brown, the ebon lightweight champ, taking his bows. Donahue went down through the roars and cheers, took a seat ten rows from the ringside and pinched out his cigarette beneath his heel.

A little group was in the ring, talking. Brown and Young Boston were looking at each other, smiling tight, insincere smiles; the black boy showing a mouthful of dazzling teeth, the white boy curling his upper lip. They went back to their corners, and the ring emptied, the fighters stretched arms, gripped the ropes, braced toes on the floor. Quiet descended upon the Arena.

THE bell shot them out. The black boy was not smiling now; he looked serious, with a scowl on his forehead, a catlike, stealthy look in his eyes. He struck. Young Boston landed on his back. Scattered shouts rose, uncertain. Boston got up, touched his nose with his left glove. He slid a blow up the Emperor's left arm; the blow was tossed off snakelike. They clinched, but the black boy broke, pranced on his toes, swung his head beneath a hard overhand shot and went up under Boston's guard. Boston tied him up. The referee broke them. Boston struck on the break and the black champ teetered, laughed aloud; the laugh was smothered by a crack on the mouth and Boston followed with hard body blows.

The champ took them, absorbed them, came into them with his shiny black arms driving. He began to beat Boston back across the ring. His neck was taut, the nape like a gleaming column of gun metal. Sweat flew from the wet gloves. The boys were exchanging blows furiously at the bell. The challenger could take it. Most people knew King Brown could.

They came out fast for the second. The crowd was settling down with an attitude of satisfaction. It was a fast, good fight. The fighters hammered each other through the second round, and the counts looked even. The Emperor had a split lip and Young Boston had a bad eye. Half of black Harlem was in the Arena rooting for the local boy who was lightweight champion of the world.

The Emperor came out for the third with an elastic bound. He grinned broadly, feinted, ducked, cut viciously into Boston's guard. He cut through Boston's guard, carried him to the ropes, hammered his blows in with terrific speed—a cross-fire of body blows and snapping shots to the face. His teeth were bared, his lips flattened back, his breath whistling and hissing out. The crowd murmured. Cries rose here and there. It was as if the black boy had played tag during the first two rounds and was now getting down to business.

Pain contorted Boston's face. He writhed and squirmed against the ropes while the black boy grunted, crowded him with an endless fusillade of smashing blows. The scattered cries rose to shouts and the shouts welled in volume; the voice of the radio announcer was crackling into the microphone. The judges looked at one another. The black boy's seconds grinned.

Boston managed to clinch, to hold at last. The referee jumped in to break them, and the Emperor fell back, his mouth bursting open to suck in a great lungful of air. One leg sagged. His neck muscles bulged and his eyes rolled as he started in again, Boston, looking through eyes that were almost closed, swung mightily. The blow hit the black boy on the chest; it stopped him for an instant but then he was driving in again. But now Boston seemed to be taking the blows with ease, and he began fighting back. He began driving the Emperor back across the ring. The shouting wavered, became a low, distant hum.

The Emperor was covering up as he hit the ropes, and Boston, his lip curled, was hammering him. The black boy did not clinch. He struck back, but his arms lagged, his knees wabbled. Boston covered the black face with blows and with blood. He was still swinging blindly when King Brown fell to his knees. The referee jumped in. The Emperor fell on his face.

He was counted out.

"Ladi-e-e-e-s-s-s... Gen-tul-men-n-n-n... the new cham-p-e-e-e-e-n...."

Young Boston fell down trying to help, in the established custom, his vanquished foe. The Emperor's seconds brushed him aside, picked up the black boy. Boston's seconds rushed him to the microphone.

"Hello, folks. I'm d' new champeen. Hello, Ma...!"

The Emperor was standing, looking very dazed and solemn. "Whut happened?" he muttered. Then he scowled, when they told him to shake hands with the new champion. "Wha' fo'? Dat boy's no champeen. He can't fight wo'th a damn."

"This way, King."

He shoved them off, climbed through the ropes, a glaze in his eyes. He trotted up the aisle, shaking his clasped hands above his head, grinning with his great white teeth.

Donahue made his way out of the madhouse, took the private elevator to the *Suwanee Club,* strolled into the bar and ordered a Scotch and Perrier. The bar was boiling with the fight news.

Ken Teebolt touched Donahue's arm. "What happened, Donny?"

"Happened?" Donahue picked up his drink, looked over it at Ken, said: "The Emperor was decrowned."

He put the glass to his lips as a man rushed in shouting: "Hey! King Brown just died!"

Twenty-odd voices exclaimed: "What!"

The informer threw up his arms. "Died!"

Donahue kept the glass to his lips, but did not drink. After a moment, he drank.

Chapter II

KELLY McPard, the plain-clothes sergeant, finished with his pearl-handled penknife, held up his left hand, with the fingers splayed, and eyed the pared fingernails critically. Then he looked through his splayed fingers at Donahue.

"Fifty," he said.

"Some day you're going to learn not to bet."

"The Emperor looked good to me."

Donahue turned and scowled at the floor. "Boston cut him down like hay."

"Listening on the radio, the beginning of that third round, I was counting my winnings already." He took his hand down, closed the fingers into his palm and laid the fist on his office desk. "What'd he die of, Donny?"

Donahue jerked a thumb to his chest.

"H'm," mused Kelly regretfully "Heart." He sighed. "Too bad. The Emperor was a real champion."

Donahue stood up, stared down at Kelly and said firmly: "Get an autopsy, Kel."

"Huh?"

Kelly looked up quizzically, half-humorously. Donahue said nothing, but kept staring at the sergeant.

Kelly drummed with his fingers on the desk and stared vacantly at the desk's surface, chewing his lower lip reflectively. "What's the idea?"

"I may be bad-minded, but that fight ended, not too suddenly, but up the wrong alley. Get an autopsy. If you don't, I'll go over your head and make a squawk."

Kelly grinned, showing his neat white teeth beneath his neat, clipped mustache. "My old pal Donny again!"

"I'm serious," Donahue muttered. He began knocking with a knuckle on the desk, and spoke to fit the rhythm: "That—dinge—went—down—too—fast."

Kelly lit a cork-tipped cigarette. "I'll look into it, kid. But I wish to hell you'd break with the Boxing Commission. You're always imagining things."

"You just imagine I imagine."

Kelly polished the nails of one hand on the heel of the other. "Where d' you think things are crooked?"

Donahue put on his hat, went to the door. "Get that autopsy and maybe we'll see."

HE took a cab uptown, got off in one of the East Sixties and entered a tall, narrow apartment house. A cream-colored elevator lifted him to the fourteenth floor, and getting out he swung his long legs leisurely down the corridor, drawing off gray capeskin gloves. He rapped on the door of 1412, and as it opened a babble of voices rushed out at him.

"Yeah?" said Pete Korn.

Donahue looked over his head, walked past him and, passing through the foyer, entered the large and ornate living-room of Sam Beckert's apartment. Six men besides Sam were in a noisy, talkative huddle: men in the fight game, well-dressed hangers-on. To one side, a medium-sized Negro wearing decent evening clothes and horn-rimmed spectacles, stood wiping his hands on a handkerchief.

"Hello, Donny!" Sam Beckert boomed.

"Sam," Donahue said offhand; and then: "Tough about the Emperor."

Beckert's big face got very mournful, his thick voice shook: "Donny, that boy—that boy—" He wagged his head dolefully. "I brought him up in the fight game, Donny. Need I tell you how I feel about all this here?" He spread his bough-like arms, his broad palms. "I'm kinda busted up, kid."

"Kinda busted up," Pete Korn said, his dry lips twitching.

Donahue said: "I just dropped in on my way home. I hear they're going to ask for an autopsy."

"Yeah?" Sam Beckert said; he looked around goggle-eyed at the men, then looked back at Donahue, nodded. "I guess that's their privilege. Sure. Why not? Unless"—he waved to the Negro—"George there objects. That's King's brother."

The Negro dipped his head. "Of course, if the police want to perform an autopsy"—he shrugged—"I shan't object. My brother's"—his lip shook—"death was sudden and unexpected, but in that sport—well, those things happen—"

"That was an awful sock to the heart Boston handed him in the third," Beckert boomed in. "You seen that, Donny—huh?"

Donahue nodded. "Yeah."

Beckert stood back on his heels, threw out his stomach. "O' course, I ain't got nothin' to say about if they c'n or can't pull an autopsy. King's brother it's up to—him being the head of the heirs or something. Smart guy. Teaches school, huh, George?" He added: "O' course, take it was blood o' my blood, I'd kinda hate to see them autopsy him. But"—he shrugged hugely—"it ain't up to me here."

The Negro poked his handkerchief back into his breast pocket. "I have no objection. After all, King—King's dead and—well, what's the use?" He turned, picked up his hat.

A tall, slim man with white hair and black eyebrows came strolling in from an adjoining room. He was idly polishing a pair of rimless nose-glasses.

Beckert said loudly: "Oh, Les, meet a pal. Meet Donahue here."

"Hello," said the thin man absently, without looking up. Then he held his glasses up to the light, seemed satisfied and placed them on his nose.

"My lawyer, Lester Paisley," Beckert explained.

Paisley yawned: "Yes—Donahue; I know the name. How do you do." He went to a table, turning his back, and poured a drink.

Donahue said negligently: "Any truth, Sam, in the rumor the Emperor was going to change managers?" A match flamed off his thumbnail, rose to a cigarette in his mouth.

Beckert guffawed. "If there was, I sure ain't been around. Who gave you that hooey?"

Donahue deprecated his own statement with a frown, a shrug. "Speakeasy gossip.... Well, I'll roll along, Sam."

Beckert tossed up a big hand, yelled: "Glad to seen you!"

"I'll go along too," George Brown said. "Good night, Sam."

" 'Night, George. Give the old woman my deepest symp'thy."

"Thanks, Sam."

Donahue and the late Emperor's brother rode down in the elevator in silence, crossed the lobby and reached the street.

"I go uptown," George Brown said.

"Me down.... Say—" Donahue dropped his voice. "Don't squawk about the autopsy. Let 'em pull it."

George Brown looked quizzical. "You talk as if you think something's wrong."

"Listen. Did your kid brother ever say anything about changing managers?"

"No. You see, we never saw him much in Harlem. He stayed in midtown when he was here. He trained down South and on the West Coast. Who told you?"

Donahue said: "Well, I'll grab a cab and go home."

"You're connected with the Boxing Commission, aren't you?"

"They hired the agency."

"What makes you think—"

"Taxi!... S' long, Mr. Brown."

ALEX Karssen was a small man, five feet four; he had a leathery, lopsided face, a bright, tyrannical eye, and crooked teeth in a crooked but engaging mouth. He had a habit of spurting words sharply out of a corner of his warped mouth. He weighed about a hundred pounds. He was head of the Boxing Commission.

"Sit down, Donny. Want a drink?"

"Not now, thanks." Donahue remained standing in the library of Karssen's Fifth Avenue mansion. He was drawing on a cigarette, holding it with his fingers, and gazing down with a rueful smile at the diminutive Boxing Commissioner.

Karssen bit him with a keen, windy look. "Champions come and champions go, eh?" He took a quick, snapping puff at his cigar. "And some champions die."

"In his dressing-room," Donahue said in a low voice pregnant with implication. "Five minutes after he left the ring."

"Five minutes."

"Black Harlem went nuts. I heard it was a blow to the heart."

Karssen leaned back, put his cigar in his mouth, took three quick puffs while his keen, bright look hunted back and forth across Donahue's face.

"So what, Donny?"

"Kelly McPard's going to crab for an autopsy. I told Beckert. He seemed agreeable. Paisley was there—in Beckert's apartment, I mean."

Karssen leaned forward, took the cigar out of his mouth, kept his eyes fastened on Donahue's face. "What are the chances?"

"I bribed that bank clerk once. I guess I can again."

"What about the autopsy?"

"I hope to find something there. Beckert wasn't knocked over when I hinted—but you know that lug." He paused, reached down to grind out his cigarette in a tray. "Mike Dolan's in San Francisco. I'm going to get him on long distance tomorrow morning. If it's true that King Brown spent an hour on the phone with Mike in a Los Angeles hotel a month ago, there's only one reason why he should have."

A crooked, wily grin captured Karssen's face, and he nodded, puffed jerkily but made no comment.

Donahue brushed the dead ash from his fingertips. "If a stink is up Beckert's alley, it's going to mean murder. Which means that if we get hot, somebody's going to get hurt." He paused, dropped his voice, held Karssen's eye. "If it gets to that, I'll have to shoot first and go around asking bright questions afterwards."

Karssen nodded.

Donahue said: "Is that okey with you?"

Karssen stood up, came around the desk, dug his bony fingers into Donahue's biceps. "I'm behind you, boy. I won't be Boxing Commissioner much longer, but while I am"—his crooked jaw shot forward—"I'm going to see if I can't weed out a lot of this lousy double dealing."

Donahue picked up his hat. "Les Paisley first," he said.

Alex Karssen linked his arm in Donahue's and walked to the door with him. He clipped: "Okey, then, Donny. Get Mike Dolan on long distance tomorrow. If Mike comes through—and I'll bet my shirt he will—we'll have a motive to start on." He pressed Donahue's arm, said with sudden earnestness: "Watch yourself, boy. I'd feel lousy if you turned up some morning in the obituary column."

Chapter III

THE alarm clock woke Donahue at eight next morning. He phoned the lobby newsstand to send up the morning papers, went into the bathroom and showered hot, then cold. He walked in his underwear to the door, received three papers from the bellhop. He poured himself a glass of Canadian ale, sat on the edge of the bed and spread the papers.

The death of the Emperor Brown was news. The sports writers had liked him, had always gone for him in a big way. The Emperor had been an unusual Negro, with many of his kind's virtues and very few of its vices. He'd had the heart of a lion in his black body. He had been engaged, at the time of his death, to one Mary Hartley, a high-yellow Bronx school teacher. His death outshadowed the crowning of the new champion.

Donahue paused to reach for the phone. He said to the hotel operator: "I want to get Michael J. Dolan, at the Hotel St. Luke, in San Francisco. Person-to-person." He hung up, resumed reading, turned a page and then darted his head downward. His eyes snapped, his jaw hardened. He reached for the phone, said: "Listen, never mind that call…. Yes, cancel it." The receiver smacked into the prong and Donahue stood up, still holding the newspaper.

He re-read the stick that had roused him:

> San Francisco, February 8: Michael J. Dolan, well-known boxing figure, manager of Jack Turck, was found dead late tonight in an overturned sedan, which he had been driving. The fact that none of the tires was blown, and that a cursory investigation showed nothing wrong with the brakes or steering gear, caused police to begin an investigation into the cause of the accident. The car left the road and crashed into a tree. Dolan's skull was fractured, according to police, when he was thrown against the windshield. The accident occurred on a lonely suburban highway, and there were no witnesses, according to the police. He was dead when found, apparently shortly after the accident, by a passing motorist, at 8:30.

Donahue tossed the paper across the bed. He dressed quickly, automatically, with his gaze fixed intently on space. He went downstairs, ate breakfast in the hotel restaurant, swung his long legs out to the street and hopped into a taxi.

Kelly McPard had all the morning papers spread before him on his desk when Donahue walked in.

Kelly McPard said: "The Emperor sure had a swell press, didn't he?… Tough. I see he was only twenty-three."

"Did you see anything else?"

"Huh?"

"Page two, right-hand column."

Kelly McPard turned the page. "Oh. Oh, you mean Dolan. Yeah. Apparently he wasn't drunk, either."

Donahue rasped: "He never touched a drop in his life, believe it or not."

"Pretty early to get steamed up, isn't it?"

Donahue sat on the desk. "Listen, Kel." He paused, waited until Kelly McPard looked up at him. "I was going to long distance Dolan this morning. A month ago a West Coast columnist ran a squib that ran something like this: 'What gentleman of color, sojourning in Hollywood these past two weeks, talked on the phone with what sporting tycoon at what hotel the other night for one solid hour?' Catch on?"

"Tell me."

Donahue shrugged. "The Emperor was in Hollywood at the time. So was Mike Dolan."

"Tell me more."

"I'll guess. Dolan and Brown talked over a contract. A week later the columnist ran an apology to the anonymous gentleman of color, saying he had been misinformed. I'll guess again. Dolan paid him to." He stood up, pointed. "If this death of Dolan was an accident, I'll be a moron. Dolan and Brown had to be cagey. So cagey that nobody but Dolan and Brown was to know that they'd talked. Brown's dead. So is Dolan. Who's to prove, now, that they talked for an hour?"

McPard fooled with his neat mustache. "But who would care—enough to murder? Don't forget, Donny, murder is a pretty big thing. Besides, they wouldn't have bumped off Dolan before the Emperor died. That wouldn't make sense even on your crazy idea."

"They didn't. That 8:30 in the paper is Pacific Coast time. It was 11:30 New York time, an hour after the Emperor died. There was a San Francisco radio hook-up." He pivoted off the desk, smacked fist into palm, ground the fist in. "This burns me up. If I'd phoned last night—" He shrugged, made a sour face. "But I knew if I phoned early I'd get him in. He wouldn't've been up yet."

McPard grinned. His mouth was small, his teeth small and very white and even. "I'm beginning to wake up, Donny!" He grabbed a phone, called the morgue. "Jake there?... Hello, Jake. Kelly. That autopsy coming along?... Okey, kid; call me when huh?... Swell." He hung up, looked at his fingernails.

He said: "What about that columnist?"

"I doubt it. If his dope was straight he must have got it from a hotel telephone operator stooling for him. If he turns her up, it'll mean a penal offense against her and he'd lose his face and his job and go around hearing 'rat, rat' on all sides." He stared with hard intensity at the floor, chewed on a corner of his lower lip. Then he snapped out of it and said: "I'll run along, Kel. Be seeing you."

Kelly pointed to the newspaper. "Did you see that picture of Sam Beckert taken near the dead Emperor's body?"

Donahue said from the door: "The one where he's crying?"

"Yeah," McPard said, with a wry grin.

"The lousy crocodile," Donahue said.

LOMARD'S was a quiet chop house in East Fifty-Fourth Street. It contained a few dark, secluded booths, and in one of these Donahue sat down at a few minutes to twelve and ordered Blue Points on the shell. He was impaling the sixth oyster when a young, pale, weak-chinned man approached the booth. Donahue nodded and the man slid on to the bench opposite.

"Chicken broth and an omelette," he said to the waiter.

The waiter went away and Donahue leaned his elbows on the table. "How goes it, Trent?"

Trent kept his eyes lowered while he thrust a hand into an inside pocket of his coat. He withdrew a folded piece of paper, opened it, spread it on the table and put on a pair of glasses. He leaned forward, lowered his voice nervously.

He said: "This morning he deposited eight checks made out to himself. They totaled eighty-seven thousand dollars and were signed by eight different persons. All the checks were drawn against New York banks and bear dates as far back as two weeks ago."

Donahue grinned. His grin faded and he dropped his voice, bent a sharp eye on Trent. "If I could only find out who made out that check for a hundred grand he deposited three weeks ago."

"I'm sorry. We can't check that up."

"But you're sure before that his account was only ten thousand?"

"Yes. Of course, he may have had accounts in other banks, and it may have been a transfer."

"It might have been," Donahue mused, but his tone bore a negative implication. He sighed. He drew from his pocket a fifty-dollar bill, passed it across the table.

Trent colored. His fingers fumbled with the bill, thrust it away into his pocket.

Donahue was saying: "Watch that account. See what happens to it."

"I—I—" Trent moistened his lips. "I'm getting nervous—"

"What the hell for?" Donahue muttered, darkening. "You started it. Finish it."

"Y-yes, of course."

Donahue said quietly, but threateningly, "Bail out on me now and...."

The waiter brought chicken broth.

IT was almost two when Donahue walked in on Kelly McPard. The sergeant turned from a window. A slow grin made bright spots on his rosebud cheeks, put a tantalizing twinkle in his blue eyes. He shrugged, held his arms out, palms out, then shook his head.

"Poor old Donny," he sighed.

"Poor old Donny, why?"

McPard suddenly looked sad. "The autopsy is all washed up, pal. What do you think the Emperor died of?"

Donahue kept a sharp eye on McPard. "Go ahead."

"Heart failure."

"Quit kidding."

"I'm not kidding, Donny. They didn't find anything. He wasn't poisoned and he wasn't needled. The old heart just folded up."

Donahue snarled: "That's a lie!"

McPard was tranquil. "There were three doctors working on him. No two of them were close friends. But they all said the same things. It's open and shut, Donny. The Emperor was like a lot of high-priced thoroughbred horses. They suddenly blow up."

"I don't believe it."

"Hell, man, you can't go against the findings of three good doctors. An autopsy's the last court of appeal." He came over, took hold of Donahue's arm, shook it good-humoredly. "Trouble with you, Donny, you been working for the Box Commish so long that you see dirt in every corner. Drop it, kid. You can't go farther than an autopsy. That's a good kid—drop it."

Donahue shrugged off McPard's hand, walked to a window. He stuck a cigarette in his mouth, snapped a match on the nail of his thumb. He lit up, scowled down at the street. McPard crossed to stand beside him—a genial, scrubbed-looking fat man in well-made clothes, crisp, clean linen.

He said: "It was just a tough break for the Emperor, Donny. Don't be a sap. You can take it, I know you can. We got to admit we're wrong now and then; you know, take it on the chin—like the Emperor did—"

"Ah, lay off the stuff," Donahue rasped. He pivoted, strode across the office and went out. He slammed the door.

McPard looked pop-eyed at the door for a moment, then broke into a chuckle. Still chuckling, he sat down, poured liquor from a flask into his mouth. He chuckled again, capped the flask.

"Same old Donny," he mused. "Same old palsy-walsy."

Chapter IV

THE Negress was tall, dusky tan rather than black. She had an unusually high forehead, a good chin, and there was nothing Negroid about her nose. Her eyes were intelligent. She wore a short brown jacket, a longish brown skirt that tapered from the hips smartly to well-shaped ankles. She wore smooth black hair over her ears; it was rolled in a loose doughnut on her nape.

"I'm Donahue," Donahue said, leaning in the doorway; he added: "I work for the Cosmos Detective Agency. The Boxing Commission's been using us for several months."

"Won't you come in?"

He nodded, walked past her to the center of a small, well-furnished living-room; stood twirling his hat slowly on his index finger and turned when he heard the door close. The customary nonchalance with which he went through life was gone now; there was a hard, shrewd depth in his eyes, and an innate stubbornness had found its way to his lips, tightening them at the right-hand corner.

"Won't you sit down?" she said.

He liked her voice. There was a drained look in her face, as though she had cried for many hours; but now her eyes were dry, gentle with a brown, deep warmth—and curious, expectant. He took a seat, hung his hat on one of his bony knees. She sat down near him, watchful, leaning forward, with her small brown hands in her lap.

He frowned at his hat. "I don't like to bring up an unpleasant subject, Miss Hartley... but it's about the Emperor."

She pursed her lips, nodded; after a moment she said: "Yes."

He suddenly looked at her with his round, candid eyes. "You were as close to him as anyone. Did he ever mention shifting to another manager?"

She shook her head. "He never said anything to me." She spoke like an educated white girl. She looked away vacantly across the room. "I'd have remembered," her voice said, trailing off.

"Did he seem dissatisfied with Sam Beckert?"

She nodded. "Yes, he did. But I suppose that was natural. The more money King made, the more he had to give to Beckert. King was a frugal man. He didn't want to fight Boston in the first place. He said it was a setup. But Beckert wanted to make the money. It's ironic. Now—now Beckert's lost a lot."

He looked at her. He saw that she believed Beckert had lost a lot.

She sighed. "I like Sam Beckert. He's rough and all that, but he was always lots of fun. He used to make fun of King being so serious. Sam Beckert always took life as a big joke. And then when King

died—Sam looked like—well, he looked like a man seeing ghosts."
She clasped her hands together. "I don't know why—why I feel—feel—
Oh, I'm silly," she broke off.

Donahue leaned forward. "Feel what?"

Her eyes turned on him. "I—I feel King didn't die naturally!"

"Why?"

"I don't know. I just *feel!*" She jumped up. "But I'm silly. George
called and said they'd performed an autopsy and that nothing was
wrong." She quieted down. "Maybe we were all wrong. Maybe King
was done. A month ago Les Paisley, the lawyer, said so. He said: 'I
may be your lawyer, Sam, but I'd lay my dough on anybody but King.
He's cracking. Black boys are good so long, but they can't take it.' He
said that in King's presence, made King worry for days. But Sam
knows fighters. He said King was better than he ever was. So did Dr.
Helvig. But I remember—that blow to the heart—it was terrific."

Donahue said: "I remember that blow to the heart, too. You were
all for King, emotionally. You wouldn't have noticed the funny look
that came into his eyes *before*—a few seconds *before*—that blow hit
him."

She started. "You don't believe that blow did it?"

"I wouldn't want to be quoted—but I don't."

"But the autopsy proved—"

He was nodding. He sighed, stood up, said: "I know."

"Then why do you say—"

"I'm damned if I know. But once get an idea in a Mick's head and
even an autopsy won't knock it out." He tossed up his hat, caught it
deftly and walked to the door. With his hand on the knob he turned
to say: "Forget it. Every now and then I get illusions of grandeur and
think I'm St. Patrick driving the snakes out of Ireland."

She remained standing in the middle of the room, looking dumbly
at him. He saw that her eyes were beginning to shine with tears. He
said: "Well, good-day—and thanks," and left the apartment.

ON the way downtown he dropped off at his hotel and the clerk at
the desk said: "A Mr. Trent phoned and left a number for you to call."

"When?"

"He phoned at about three-thirty—half an hour ago."

Donahue took the memorandum and went to a lobby booth. He
dialed the number and in a moment heard the bank clerk's nervous,

squeaky voice.

"Yes, this is Donahue…. I get you…. The Keystone Realty Company…. What's the address?… Never mind; I'll look it up myself. And I'll be seeing you. Keep your lip tight, Trent. I wouldn't let you down."

He hung up. He let his hand remain on the instrument, stared intently at it, while faint little lines appeared and disappeared at the corners of his eyes. He went out of the booth, bought a newspaper, sat down and read the latest news on the death of the Emperor. He turned to the Keyhole Kid's daily column and the first item that struck his eyes was:

> It's being noised around that a certain private detective told a certain uptown speak owner that the Emperor Brown was due for a fall. The dick told the speak boss this enlightenment twenty minutes before the Emperor's death, little children!

Donahue crumpled the paper savagely. His lower lip shot out and an angry, sullen look welled in his eyes. He tossed the sheet down, strode darkly across the lobby, rode in the elevator upward. He reached the door of his apartment, dangled keys, got the door open. He stumbled at sight of a small square of paper that had evidently been slipped beneath the door.

He bent down, picked it up. It was a newspaper clipping. It was the same item he had read a minute before in the lobby.

But across it was drawn, in black crayon, an X.

DONAHUE sloped into the foyer of the *Suwanee*. Ken Teebolt was standing talking with the hat-check girl and clicking a half dozen quarters in his hand. He grinned, said: "Hello there, Donny!"

Donahue went past him with a swift gait and a dead-ahead dark look in his eyes. He followed the corridor to the swing door, punched it open, went up to the bar and jammed his heel down on the rail. He leaned on his elbows, clasped his hands together and stared down at them.

"Whatcha have?" the bartender said.

"Scotch—straight," Donahue clipped, staring at his hands.

It was five. The dining-room was not yet open, and the bar was almost empty. A radio, tuned low, brought in tea-dancing music from a midtown hotel. The bartender rolled back down the bar, planked down a bottle and a glass in front of Donahue, eyed him curiously through thick eyebrows. Then he hummed to himself and wandered back up the bar.

Ken Teebolt opened the swing door, let it swing back, and sauntered to the bar. He leaned sidewise against it, on one elbow, crossing his legs and keeping them straight up and down. He looked grave, puzzled.

"What's eating you, Donny?"

Donahue downed his drink, poured another, held it up and eyed it with narrowed-down lids.

Ken Teebolt said: "Okey; sulk." He sauntered off into the darkened dining-room.

Donahue swallowed his drink, rasped his throat. He kept his gaze on the bottle as though it were a crystal ball. The bartender polished a glass and kept a sidelong gaze on him. Donahue poured another drink.

Ken Teebolt came back to the bar, stood alongside Donahue and said: "What's the idea of the looking-glass drinking?"

Donahue drank, slapped down the empty glass. He tossed a dollar and a half on the bar, buttoned his coat, pivoted and strode past Ken Teebolt. He kicked open the swing door and vanished. Ken Teebolt leaned back, said half-aloud: "The guy's nuts." The swing door slammed open again and Donahue came towards Ken Teebolt with a narrow, vicious look and a hard, fast walk.

He said coldly but viciously: "So you're stooling for that tabloid columnist."

"I'm what?"

"Go ahead; act the Boy Scout!"

"Look here, Donny—for crying out loud—"

"For crying out loud your sweet grandmother's neck!"

He turned violently on his heel, went through the swing door like a blast of wind and was striding hard-heeled down the corridor when Ken Teebolt called. "Hey, you Irish tramp!" Donahue stopped and Ken Teebolt caught up with him.

"Well?" said Donahue.

Ken Teebolt was warming up too.

"Make it clear, Donny. For —— sake, don't act like a ten-year-old. What the hell have I done?"

Donahue pulled the newspaper clinping from his pocket. "Pike this."

Ken read it. His jaw hardened; he reddened. "Who—what's this X mean?"

"What d' you think it means?" Donahue cut in. "I found it under my door."

Ken Teebolt looked up, and his face was very red. "I—I didn't spring that, Donny."

"A birdie did, I suppose."

"Listen, kid—" His voice became husky, his eyes stared into space, then suddenly clouded. "Jeeze!" he muttered hoarsely. "I must have— that jane I picked up— *Jeeze!*" he snarled, and lunged towards the checkroom.

Donahue grabbed him. "What are you going to do?"

"Break a jane's neck. Lemme go!"

Donahue wrestled him against the wall. "Use your head," he said.

"I'll cave in her face—"

"What good will it do?" He shook Ken, cracked a grin. His voice softened a bit. "I just thought you'd two-timed on me. A dame, huh? Talked in your sleep—"

"No. I was a little likkered—"

"Same thing." Ken Teebolt was sincerely moved. "My —— Donny, I'd bite off my hand rather than pull a squeal on you!"

"Listen. Paisley drops in here every day on his way from the office, doesn't he?"

"Yeah."

Donahue nodded to the bar. "Come on. I want to talk to you." He added: "And I want to ring Kelly."

Chapter V

THE bar was crowding up. The dining-room was still dimmed, but more lights had been turned on in the bar, a second bartender had joined the first. The radio had been turned up a notch, bringing on the daily news flashes of a local newspaper. Men arrived in business suits with newspapers under their arms. They kept on their hats and coats. Cocktail shakers made a cool, icy sound. The cash register rang more frequently.

Lester Paisley came in at five past six. His white hair seemed whiter beneath the brim of his black hat. He wore a belted dark blue coat with raglan sleeves, carried a dark stick. He gave the impression of looking above the heads of all persons, but he rarely missed anything. He saw Donahue at the far end of the bar, but you would not have guessed it.

"Whiskey-sour—plenty sour."

He unfolded a newspaper, took off his nose-glasses, polished them, held them to the light and then replaced them on his nose. He turned the newspaper over, folded it twice one way, once the other, took out a pencil and fixed his eyes on a cross-word puzzle. In three squares he wrote three letters that spelled *Yak*.

"Hello, Paisley."

Donahue had walked over, but Paisley did not even look up. He said abstractedly: "Hello, Donahue."

Somebody turned on the lights in the dining-room and Ken Teebolt stood in the broad entry-way, his hands behind his back. He was watching Donahue and Paisley.

Donahue said: "You picked a winner, didn't you?"

"Guess I did," Paisley said, filling in five vertical squares and getting the word *Yodel*.

Donahue said: "I'd like to have a little talk with you. We can take it easy in a room upstairs."

"Sorry, Donahue. I've got to run along."

The radio boomed: "And a news flash from San Francisco. Central office detectives working on the death of Mike Dolan, nationally known boxfight solon who was killed in a motor accident last night, discovered a spent .38-calibre bullet imbedded in a tree near the spot where Dolan crashed. The theory is that someone may have fired at Dolan, missed, but that Dolan, ducking, might have lost control of his car and smashed up.

"Since all the windows in his sedan were shattered by the crash, a theory that one of these windows was broken by a bullet cannot be verified. No bullets were found in the body of the car. The police are seeking a motive, urged by the facts that the car was proved to have been in excellent mechanical condition, that Dolan had not been drinking, that the road was wide and, at the time, free of rain. Dolan also is reputed to have been an excellent driver...."

"*Idiom*," said Paisley.

"Pardon?"

"I'm working this out."

Donahue lit a cigarette. "Knew Mike Dolan, didn't you?"

"Met him."

"I wonder who could have tried to bump him off—and why?"

Paisley finished his drink, paid up. "Well, see you some time, Donahue."

Donahue held on to his arm. "How about now?"

Paisley looked down at Donahue's hand reflectively. Then he took it off. "Some other time. Friends due at my hotel."

Donahue held his arm again, said in a low voice: "You'll regret it if you don't see me now, Paisley. I'm not kidding."

Paisley looked through his thin shell-like glasses. His face was hatchet-thin, wooden. He said liplessly: "Come on, then."

They went up two flights of stairs, walked down a corridor. Donahue opened a door, stepped aside and let Paisley walk in past him. Then he closed the door. Paisley walked to the middle of the large, mannish living-room, sat down on the edge of a straight-backed chair, took off his glasses and, polishing them, looked up politely and wooden-faced at Donahue. With his white hair, his thick black eyebrows, he seemed a strange and provocative man.

Donahue said: "When did you work up an interest in real estate?"

"It's always a good investment if you get in on the ground."

Donahue nodded. "It sure is. It's like everything else, though. A guy wants to sink his money in a gilt-edge investment. For instance, you wouldn't think of buying bonds in a tank bank. If you had a lot of dough, you'd sink it in something with a solid foundation, some organization that has a reputation."

"I suppose. Now we're talking banking, eh?"

"No. Real estate. For instance, suppose you had between one and two hundred grand. You had the choice of several banks or corporations in which to sink this dough. You'd sink it in the best you could find, wouldn't you? I mean, in these times—when it's dangerous to speculate on a dark horse. You'd do that, wouldn't you?"

"I suppose I would."

"Just as an example. I'll take something offhand. Take the Keystone Realty Company. A small outfit with a dump of an office on Sixth Avenue—one man in the office and a ten-bucks-a-week typist. This outfit opened shop exactly twenty-eight days ago. It's not a member of the City Realty Board. It started with a cash deposit in a West Side bank of three thousand dollars. Its owner-manager used to run a road-house and tourist cabins on the Boston Post Road until two years ago, when he was knocked off by the cops on a liquor charge. There's an example. Now you wouldn't sink your dough in an outfit like that, would you?"

Paisley's wooden face did not change its expression. "What is this, a new kind of game?"

"Yeah."

Paisley stood up. "Hell, I thought you wanted to talk to me about something sensible. I never thought you had a screw loose, Donahue. I've got to get along."

Donahue went and stood in front of the door, folded his arms, leaned against it. "You're not really in a hurry, Paisley." He wore a dark, mocking smile.

"I really am," said Paisley.

"I'm not. I'm not going to touch you. But before you get through this door you've got to get through me. I want to know why you sunk one hundred and eighty-seven thousand in the Keystone Realty Company."

"I believe that's my business, Donahue."

"Is it? When you never before had at one time more than ten grand to your name?"

Paisley made an impatient gesture. "You bore hell out of me. I tell you I've got to get along. Don't be a mug."

"You'll talk first."

Paisley drew a small automatic pistol from his pocket. "I hate to do this, Donahue, but you're a bigger man than I am and I couldn't knock you down. Keep your hands up and move away from that door."

A closet door opened and Kelly McPard said: "Got a permit to carry that rod, Mr. Paisley?"

Paisley stiffened, looked over shoulder. McPard was holding a gun in one hand, his badge in the other. The badge caught the light, gleamed.

Paisley lowered his gun. He said: "This man wouldn't let me out."

"He didn't try to stop you. He just said he'd stand in your way. You pulled your gat on him."

Paisley's nose-glasses shimmered. His dry, cold voice said: "A frame, huh?"

"I wouldn't think of framing you, Mr. Paisley. The laws of this State—"

"I know the laws of this State!" Paisley snapped.

"Then I suppose you'll come along down to Headquarters with me." Kelly McPard came towards Paisley and with his left hand took the gun from Paisley. "I won't put cuffs on you, counselor. We'll walk out just like we were old friends."

Paisley said dryly: "Just a couple of rats," eying both men.

"That ought to make you feel at home," Donahue said.

"Tsk, tsk!" McPard said. "Is that nice, Donny?... Let's go, Mr. Paisley."

They went on out of the room.

Donahue lit a cigarette, inhaled deeply, let the smoke idle from his nostrils. After a moment Ken Teebolt opened the door.

He breathed out: "Everything okey, Donny?"

Donahue grinned, nodded.

Chapter VI

THE bolt clanged. Ken Teebolt let Donahue out into the alley, said: "You think it's wise?"

The tilt of Donahue's hat brim made a diagonal dark shadow across his face and only half of his tight grin was visible.

"No," he said. "But I figure they'll come after me eventually. I hate suspense."

He turned and went rearward through the alley, cut around the wall of the Arena, hit a side street and followed it to a main drag. A taxi came along and he stepped into the street, held up a finger. Brakes squealed and Donahue was inside before the cab stopped. He clipped out the address as he dropped into the puffy leather seat.

He did not smoke. He hummed absent-mindedly, but kept a dark, intent eye on space. The cab finally stopped and a few seconds passed before Donahue realized it had stopped. Thrusting a bill through the window, he climbed out and received the change through the front door. He tossed back a dime.

The lobby of the hotel was rectangular. There were many people in the lobby, sitting or moving about, but all talking; yet there was no din. Severe, unostentatious doorways led to arcades.

Donahue rose in a black enameled elevator studded with narrow beveled mirrors. When he got out, thick carpet absorbed his footfalls. He took his gun out of his pocket, took his hat off. He placed the gun in the crown of his hat, crumpled the hat and held it carelessly in his left hand. He stopped and knocked at a door, leaned indolently with his right shoulder against the right side of the doorframe.

Pete Korn opened the door. He was in evening clothes. Voices bubbled in the living-room beyond. Pete Korn was getting ready to say something when Donahue walked past him. The scene in the living-room was a gay one. Sam Beckert and a tall, gaunt man wore evening clothes. At a glance the tall, gaunt man looked distinguished; he had a shock of iron-gray hair, wore rimmed nose-glasses with a black ribbon attached. There were three girls present—none of them was over twenty-five. All were drinking cocktails.

Sam Beckert threw up a boughlike arm, boomed: "Hi there, Donny, old kid! Come on in, old pal! Have a cocktail! We're all waitin' for Les Paisley. All gonna see a show.… Meet the girls. Girls, meet Ben Donahue, a great guy!… And Donny, you ever met Doc Helvig? This is Doc Helvig, the Box Commish's doctor."

Fifty if a day, Helvig looked as if he had taken a lot of liquor on board. "It's a pleasure, Mr. Donahue," he said with profound gravity. "Mr. Paisley will be home soon."

Beckert poured a cocktail. Donahue wandered across the room, laid his hat on top of the radio. The radio was making a lot of noise. Then he walked across and took the cocktail Beckert held out.

Beckert looked suddenly gloomy. "Thinkin' about King, Donny, I gotta drink myself outta the dumps. Y'know, even though your heart is bustin', laugh, clown, laugh. It was a play I seen or somethin', once.… Sit down, Donny. Les'll be along any minute."

"Any minute," Pete Korn muttered.

Donahue finished the drink, set the glass down. Beckert started to pour another, but Donahue made a gesture, shook his head.

"No, Sam. I've had enough today." He stood wiping his lips and gazing idly about the room. Thrusting his handkerchief into his breast pocket, he said: "Send the janes out of the room a minute, will you, Sam?"

"Huh?"

Helvig swayed over. "I remember now, Mr. Donahue. I think I met you at the Arena once, a couple of years ago. When Bat Brady and Jo-Jo Link were weighing in."

Donahue nodded but looked at Beckert, and said: "Want to talk to you."

Beckert shrugged expansively. "Sure thing, Donny." He pivoted hugely, jerked a thumb. "Girls, scram into the other room a minute, will you? Me and Donny's gotta talk."

The girls rose, went into an adjoining room and closed the door. Pete Korn sat on the arm of a chair, put a match between his lips and began chewing it with his little peglike teeth. Helvig stood spread-legged, swaying like a tree in a gentle wind; his mouth and eyes hung open oafishly, and he did not look distinguished.

Beckert's eyes got round, very watchful and curious, and he took several gulps at his cocktail but did not take his eyes off Donahue for a second.

Donahue's eyes had a dark up-from under look. "Heard the latest from San Francisco, Sam?"

"Huh?"

"The cops out there think Mike Dolan was put on the spot. They found a bullet near where Mike crashed."

Helvig looked at Pete Korn. Pete Korn was nibbling the match to shreds and his eyelids were so narrowed that it was impossible to tell at whom he looked.

"It came over the radio," Donahue added.

"Yeah?" Sam Beckert droned, his eyes dull.

Donahue nodded. "I understand the Emperor had a long talk with Mike on the phone—out on the Coast, some time ago. The Emperor and Mike were going to hook up, weren't they?"

Pete Korn spat shreds of the match to the floor.

Beckert rolled out a laugh. "I ain't ever heard."

"I did," Donahue said. "Mike Dolan was killed an hour after the Emperor died."

Sam Beckert walked heavily across the room, set down his glass and came back heavily. His forehead was wrinkled, his heavy features began to sag dully.

"Look here, Donny. You makin' cracks or ain't you? Seems to me you're gettin' damned steamed up over nothin'."

Donahue said coldly: "I'm not half as steamed up as I ought to be. I don't like having X notes shoved under my door. They scare me and make me sore as hell."

Pete Korn put another match in his mouth. Helvig's eyes got rounder.

Sam Beckert's loose lips flopped as he said: "For —— sake, what you talkin' about?"

"You know what I'm talking about, Sam. We're all thinking about the same thing—the Emperor Brown. Did he fall or was he pushed?"

Sam Beckert roared with laughter. "Oh, that! Ho-ho! You can't kid me, Donny. Poor old King just smashed. You oughtta know that from the autopsy report."

"It's the first autopsy report I never believed."

Sam Beckert's face got heavy again and his brows shot together. "Boy, you're makin' them dirty cracks fast!"

Pete Korn got up, chewed faster on the match, flexed his little legs. Helvig's mouth hung agape, and he mopped sweat from his forehead, drew the handkerchief up under his chin. He crossed the room and took a long slug of whiskey straight.

Donahue said: "Sam, it's a long story—"

"Shut up!" Beckert growled. "I don't have to clown around with you and I ain't. Les Paisley'll be here any minute and you can talk to him. I'm a plain man and I ain't up to sparrin' words with a wise Mick like you."

Donahue grinned. He grinned first at Sam Beckert, then at Pete Korn, then at Helvig. He said: "You'll be wasting time, Sam."

"Huh?"

"Paisley won't show up."

Sam Beckert took a loggy backward step. Helvig gulped down another strong shot of whiskey. Pete Korn stopped chewing and closed his dry lips. The stub of the match jutted like a fang. Bracing himself on his huge legs, Sam Beckert's eyes stared and a cloudy look overtook them.

Donahue said: "Paisley's down at Headquarters. Kelly McPard picked him up. I turned him over to Kelly. It's about money, Sam. About a lot of money that was juggled over the fight. And about the Keystone Realty Company—"

Helvig choked, took a drink of water. Sam Beckert turned to look at him, then looked back at Donahue with his wide, foggy eyes.

He roared: "I don't believe it!"

"Call Headquarters and see. I told Paisley I'd come up here and tell you to come down. He's in a tough spot and he'll need you." He nodded. "We're going to find out that the Emperor was pushed—he didn't fall. Better make it snappy, Sam. Paisley's up against it and he's expecting you."

"Yeah?" roared Sam Beckert. "Okey. We'll all go down. Come on, boys, get your duds on. The janes can stay here." He stamped across the room, took a big overcoat out of a closet, heaved into it.

Pete Korn lifted an overcoat from the back of a chair, draped it over his left arm. He was chewing on a match again.

Helvig said: "I'll stay here." He was very drunk, his face loose and his mouth twisted, his eyes glazed. "I—I'll wait."

Sam Beckert was bluff: "Come on; you get your coat on. We'll go down and show them mugs. All of us."

Helvig sagged to a chair. "I'll stay here, Sam. I got to."

"You'd better come," Donahue said.

"You hear me!" Sam Beckert boomed.

Helvig's eyes flashed. He gripped the arms of the chair. "I'm not going down. You don't need me. I—I'll stay here and keep the girls company."

Sam Beckert thumped across the room, reached down and hauled Helvig to his feet. "We're all goin' down—you hear!"

Helvig broke away and ran across the room, crouched in a corner, his eyes blazing. "I'm not!" He made a bee-line back across the room, slopped whiskey into a glass.

Sam Beckert punched the glass off the table. Helvig sucked in a breath, rasped: "It's a trick! It's a trick this fellow's playing! I don't believe Paisley's down there! I won't go!"

"You're drunk," Sam Beckert said. "The air'll do you good. I tell you we're all goin' down!"

A glassy, cunning look came into Helvig's eyes. He cackled. "You can go. But"—he shook his head—"not me. I tell you it's a trick! You don't know if Paisley's there, do you? It's just this fellow's say-so. I tell you it's a trick! It's a frame!"

"Shut up!" Sam Beckert roared; he growled to Pete Korn: "Come on, Pete. We got to take Doc down. It's for his own good."

"Take Doc down," Pete Korn muttered.

They started for him. But Helvig reeled backward across the room, hit the wall hard. A slab of iron-gray hair jumped down over his forehead. A gun jumped into his hand.

"I'm not going," he said.

Beckert snarled: "You dope, put down that rod!"

"You heard me, Sam. You and Pete go. But not me. Go on!" he grated. "Get out of here!" And to Donahue: "And you, too!" His breath pumped hoarsely from his wide-open mouth. Sweat shone on his contorted face.

Donahue said: "You're going, too, Helvig."

"Am I? No, I'm not! For —— sake, get out! Get out!"

Sam Beckert's face was white, grave. "Doc, pull yourself together. You *got* to go with us. You *got* to. Don't you understand you *got* to go?"

Helvig's eyes shimmered. "Sam, for the love o' gawd get out. Get out before I let you have it!"

There was a moment of silence, and then Sam Beckert said: "I guess we got to go. Come on, Pete."

But Pete was chewing viciously on the match, and his eyes looked almost shut. His dry voice crackled: "I know what that baby's up to! I know! And if you think I'm gonna stand for it—"

"Pete!" roared Sam. "You're all goin' nuts! *Pete!*"

Pete Korn drew fast. Helvig fired first, but missed. Pete's shot drilled him, crashed him to the floor. There were screams in the other room.

Pete Korn whirled on Donahue, snapped: "And you hold everything!… Sam, frisk him."

"I'm not heeled," Donahue said, holding up his hands.

"Frisk him, Sam."

Sam Beckert crossed to Donahue went through his pockets. He said: "He ain't heeled, Pete."

The match bobbed in Pete Korn's mouth. He rasped: "Doc's croakin'. Donahue did it, Sam."

Sam Beckert gaped.

"Donahue did it," Pete Korn repeated, making the match bob. He snapped to Donahue: "Turn that radio louder, you!"

Donahue took three steps, looked at the dials. He turned one. The radio blared, screeched. Pete walked over to Helvig, toed him. Helvig was rolling to and fro on the floor, moaning; a wild, steady stare in his eyes. Donahue picked up his hat from the top of the radio, turned. With his left hand he switched off the radio. His hat dropped from his right, and he held his gun.

"Don't drop it, Pete," he said. "Hold it—and hold that pose, darling. There'll be no prints on the gun but yours. Stay where you are, Sam. Move, Pete, and you'll get jarred."

Donahue moved sidewise, three steps. With his left hand he picked up the Continental telephone. The hotel operator answered. Donahue said: "Send up a flock of cops to Lester Paisley's apartment. A lot of people went nuts up here."

KELLY McPard stood behind his desk, with eight fingertips resting on it. The nails were pink, clipped, clean. Rosebuds bloomed on Kelly McPard's cheeks; his eyebrows were arched high, his blue eyes twinkling. A chuckle began deep in his throat, rose and flowed out liquidly.

"Good old Donny," he said.

Donahue was eating a banana, the skin peeled in four strips and draped down over his hand.

"Helvig started it," he said. "It was funny. You can't always tell about liquor. Helvig kept taking slug after slug—to brace him up, I guess. Instead, it let him down. He became a raving maniac, raving with fear. He was afraid to come down here. He lost all his reason. Then Pete Korn figured Helvig was making to pull a fade-out and a double-cross—and so Pete lost his head. Sam Beckert never had any head to lose, so it remained where it was. Nice people." He took a bite of banana, chewed.

The door opened and Alex Karssen came in, swinging a stick. "I heard briefly over the phone," he said, "that fireworks broke out in an uptown hotel."

Kelly McPard sat down, shook with chuckles. "Pinwheels, rockets, Roman candles...."

"You see, Alex," Donahue said. He paused to swallow a lump of banana, went on: "As far back as a month ago they planned to frame the Emperor into losing not only this fight but his life as well. I think I got an inkling then that something wrong was in the wind, because Paisley started going around town making cracks against the Emperor. Up until then, Paisley had always said good things about King Brown.

"The facts now are these: The Emperor was to chuck Sam Beckert and throw in with Mike Dolan. Sam and Paisley and your Commission's doctor, Helvig, talked it over. They were going to needle the champ. Helvig was to get a cut of ten grand.

"When that Hollywood gossip column ran that item, Sam Beckert went to Mike Dolan and called him, but Mike admitted nothing. However, Sam was sure, and not without reason, that Mike Dolan was to get the champion. In a heated argument Sam said to Dolan: 'You're muscling in, Mike. If ever you get the champ away from me, you'll get him dead. I won't give him up.' So when Sam confronted the Emperor, the Emperor beat about the bush, but Sam knew. The Emperor was a bum actor.

"And finally Sam managed to bribe the hotel telephone operator who had overheard Mike's and the Emperor's conversation, and then he knew. Sam started out for revenge, and meanwhile he planned to rake in a lot of dough while getting his revenge. The trouble was, in order to do away with the Emperor he had to do away with Dolan— because he had promised Dolan the only way he'd get the Emperor would be dead.

"Of course, Sam Beckert couldn't be caught openly betting against his man. So what? So he turned over a pile of dough to Paisley. Paisley would bet against the champ, clean up. But then it would be risky to turn the winnings back to Beckert through open banking channels. They got the idea of a front and so formed the Keystone Realty Company.

"When Paisley cleaned up on the fight, he wrote out a check to the Keystone Realty Company for the amount he had received from Beckert to bet with plus the amount he had won. Later, the money was to dribble back to Beckert. All this we got from Paisley's lips. Down at the hospital, we got the rest from Helvig, your Commission's honorable doctor who okeyed the Emperor just before he went into the ring."

"But the autopsy," broke in Karssen, "proved that nothing had been done to the Emperor."

Donahue said: "Nothing had. All these plans I mentioned had been laid a month before the fight. Gunmen were hired to go West and camp on Dolan's trail, to be ready for the go-signal. The Keystone Company was formed. Beckert was all primed to bring vengeance against Dolan and at the same time make a big winning. Then a week before the fight Helvig discovered something wrong with the Emperor's heart. He didn't tell the Emperor but he told Beckert. The

Emperor was through training and had been ordered to rest. Helvig told Beckert that any exertion would kill the champ. He told Paisley. None of them told the Emperor.

"It was Beckert who said that there was no need then to do away with Dolan. But Helvig was scared. He knew he would examine the Emperor before the champ entered the ring. He wanted not the slightest suspicion to fall on him. He figured that if Dolan lived he would come out with the news that Beckert had threatened to turn the Emperor over to him dead. This would bring down a lot of investigation and cross-examination, and the only examination Helvig wanted was an autopsy, which he knew would be safe. So Helvig refused to send the Emperor into the ring unless Dolan was taken care of. He was afraid of Black Harlem as well as the law. Beckert knew of only one way to take care of Dolan and he gave the word. If Brown keeled over, that was to be the signal!"

"My ——!" said Alex Karssen.

"The Emperor was okeyed by your Commission's doctor and went into the ring to die. He fought like a madman. It got him."

Karssen rasped: "I'll see that those fellows get life!"

"They will," Kelly McPard said cheerfully.

"They'd better," Donahue said. He tossed the banana peel into a basket, added: "Black Harlem's honing its razors, Alex, and it's life or"—he was wiping his mouth—"else, Southern style."

Ghost of a Chance

*Tough dick Donahue struck
him behind the ear with a
hard left fist*

Chapter I

DONAHUE pulled open a side door of the Hotel Coronet and came into the arcade with a gust of raw wind that kited the long skirt of his blue ulster round his rangy legs. He went swinging on past smart shops towards the lobby, one hand pocketed, the other rapping a newspaper against his thigh at each step. From the breast pocket of his ulster a handkerchief protruded in two overlapping triangles. He wore a gray hat well off his face.

As he neared the lobby entrance, he heard the sound of Cuban music at the *thé dansant* in the Flamingo Room and picked up the tune with a whispered whistling. He reached the lobby and was cutting diagonally across towards the elevator bank when Phalen, the *Post Express* legman, turned from trying to date the brunette at the cigar counter and called out:

"Hey, look at Handsome."

"Poison in your soup, Red," Donahue said cheerfully, on his way.

Phalen tossed a wise-eyed wink at the brunette, popped a cigarette butt into a sand-filled urn and set off after Donahue.

"What's the rush, Donny?"

"Date."

"Who is she?"

"What's the matter; did little beautiful at the counter give you the air?"

Phalen was pacing him. "Me, I'm her everything, bo." His thin face was the color of sand and it was dry like sand. His smile was slow, twisted, and his eyes were sharp, brazen, and he had a dandified way of wearing his clothes. He spoke glibly: "No kidding, Donny. I've been trying for hours to stir up news."

"So what?"

"So news is where you are, usually. You wouldn't kid me, would you, pally?"

They stopped in front of the elevator bank and Donahue said in a mock-confidential voice, "Keep it under your hat, Red, but"—he put a hand significantly alongside his mouth—"there's a blonde upstairs who doesn't want to be alone."

One of the elevator doors opened and Donahue swiveled away from Phalen and strode into the car.

"I mean," Phalen said, following, "on the level."

Donahue chuckled with rough good humor, said, "Don't be a horse's neck, Red," and straight-armed him out of the car. And to the elevator boy, "Shoot me up, will you?" And when the car had started—"Five."

Number 545 was at an L in the corridor and Donahue used a small bronze knocker shaped like a crouching cat. In a moment the door

was opened by a short, heavy-set man dressed in a dark, speckled-gray lounge suit. He was holding a pair of rimmed nose glasses chest high, and with a slight inquisitive dip of the head he said:

"Mr. Donahue?"

"Yes, sir."

"Good. Come right in."

Donahue entered a small foyer and laid his hat on a small table there. He saw, beyond, through the Lancet arch, a girl standing sidewise to him; her chin was tilted upward and she was peering into a small vanity mirror and adjusting a brimless dark hat. She wore a three-quarter length black lapin coat, and as Donahue followed the middle-aged man into the large living-room, she made a quarter turn, gave him a brief, hesitant smile of greeting and turned again to her mirror.

The middle-aged man led him to a far corner of the room and said: "Pardon me just a moment, Mr. Donahue." And Donahue nodded, unbuttoned his overcoat and stood gazing down on to the boulevard below. There were several apartment houses and a tall, lean hotel across the street. He heard the man and the girl talking in the foyer but did not catch what they said; he did not try. The sound of the door being opened and closed was followed shortly by the man's return.

"Sorry to keep you waiting, Mr. Donahue."

"Not at all, not at all, Mr. Loftman."

"There; take a seat, please; that one, any one."

He looked fifty-odd and wore his snow-and-iron hair like a plume, unparted. His clothes were loose, sack-like, but obviously expensive, and when he replaced his glasses upon his nose he looked scholarly and a little older.

He said: "I've had occasion to use other branches of your agency and found them all dependable. That's why I telephoned you to come over. What I really want this time, however, is a messenger. I wanted to get you here and make tentative arrangements with you. The messenger is not to be sent yet, but when the time comes I want to be certain of having him ready—instantly—to board a plane for the East. He will fly, meet my wife at a bank I shall name. She will turn over to him a certain amount of money and he will fly back with it and deliver it to me at this hotel."

Donahue leaned forward. "It might be simpler and less expensive for you to have it wired here."

Loftman gazed down absently at his unlit cigarette. "Possibly you don't care to undertake it?"

"It was just a suggestion. I can have a man on call, any time you say. There's always at least one man on reserve. No retainer's necessary."

Loftman rose. "Within the next twenty-four hours I shall know definitely. You say there is always someone at the agency?"

"Night and day. And if you want to speak to me personally, they can always locate me, any hour."

"Good, I'll telephone you."

Chapter II

LOFTMAN stepped back, tossed his unlit cigarette into a tray, put his heels together and dipped his big head.

Donahue went towards the foyer saying, "Thank you for the opportunity, Mr. Loftman." He picked up his hat from the table and made his way out into the corridor. As he was walking away from the closed door he heard hurrying footsteps and turned to see Phalen coming towards him rapidly. Behind Phalen, slower-gaited, was Bickford, the house officer.

Phalen jerked a thumb back over his shoulder. "Blondie want to be alone again?"

"Funny, you are," Donahue muttered, taking long strides.

"Blondes are the curse of the working classes, Donny."

"One of the curses of my life is a red-headed legman with a nasty mind."

"No fooling, pally. Is there anything in the wind? I'll do right by you in the paper."

Bickford caught up with them and said in a hoarse, grave voice, "Hello, Mr. Donahue."

"Hello, Mr. Bickford," Donahue said, and they all got in the elevator and rode down to the main floor.

Phalen poked Bickford in the arm and said, "Donny's a pain in the neck. Ever know that, Bick?" as they left the elevator.

The house officer wore a neutral stare. Phalen sauntered off towards the cigar counter and then Bickford turned to Donahue and said, "Mr. Donahue, could I have a few words with you?"

"Sure thing."

Bickford jerked his shiny bald head. "My office."

When they were seated in his small cubbyhole, Bickford planted his hands on his broad knees and stared gravely down between them. "I don't want to pry in your business, Mr. Donahue, but could I just ask you if you think the 545 business is okey?"

"What do you mean—okey?"

"Well, sir, I mean, whatever the business is, it won't make a stink in the hotel, will it?"

Donahue chuckled. "I think not. It's just a matter of messenger service. No tailing, no shadowing."

Bickford let go a large sigh. "Well, I'm glad to hear that," he said, but still looked a little troubled. "Because that 545 caused us a headache a couple of days ago. It was on the fourth, the day before Loftman checked in." He shrugged. "It's a job, keeping monkeys out of this hotel, Mr. Donahue.

"You see—and this is under the hat, Mr. Donahue. I seen a couple of guys in the lobby from time to time and I got to wondering about their faces. They were down in the register as Herbert Gearman and P. T. Lancaster, but that didn't mean a thing. So finally I shot over to Headquarters and went over the mugs there. And sure enough—they were Marty O'Fallon and Jess Fauls, a couple of con men and gamblers and a lot of other things, with a record longer than a coast-to-coast railroad ticket.

"So I got McCartney from Headquarters—he's a good friend of the house here—and we walked in on O'Fallon and Fauls and Mac said, 'I'll give you birds just fifteen minutes to pack up.' They tried to stall but Mac planted himself right in the living-room and they had to pack. Well, we didn't want any notoriety here in the hotel and Mac said the best thing to do would be put 'em on a train. Which we did. We made 'em pack and then Mac walked 'em over the station and made 'em buy tickets all the way to California. And he stayed there till the train pulled out. It was a close shave but with the help of Mac we did well."

"But what makes you sorry about the new tenant?"

Bickford sighed. "Just an idea, I guess. Just the kind of goofy idea a guy gets sometimes. I guess it was seeing a private dick coming out of there so soon after this other mess." He slapped his knees. "Well, thanks, Mr. Donahue; thanks."

"If I thought there was anything wrong, I wouldn't touch it—and I'd tell you."

"That's the way I figure. Has this—um—Red Phalen anything against you?"

Donahue shrugged. "I just tossed him out of my office once for trying to pull a fast one on my files. He probably once read a book about how reporters have the free run of the town and it went to his head."

Bickford nodded. "I have trouble with him myself sometimes."

"Oh, Red's all right," Donahue said, going towards the door, "except when he gets in your hair."

Bickford raised a forefinger. "Don't give him any dope on what I told you, Mr. Donahue."

Donahue chuckled. "I wouldn't even give Red the right time," he replied, backing out of the office.

"Wouldn't you, pally?" said Phalen, leaning against the corridor wall. His expression was not pleasant.

Donahue pivoted. He went on his way saying, "Go roll your hoop, nuisance."

DONAHUE went to a Greek place in Sixth that night for dinner. The walls were covered with large photographs of wrestlers and boxers; a famous Italian tenor; a radio crooner. There was one of those pianos that work when you feed it nickels.

Sam came over to the table and said jovially, "Hey-lo, Meester Donahue. Whatcha you have, hahn?"

"A double Martini, steak, French fries, tomatoes and salad."

"Huk-key, Meester Donahue."

Donahue spent half an hour over the food, another half hour over Turkish coffee and brandy and a long heavy cigar. He looked lean, smooth, in a blue serge suit, his face well-shaved, a bit hawkish, beneath the hard black sheen of his hair. As he was leaving Sam gave him a brandy on the house and plucked a piece of lint off the back of his overcoat.

Outside, there were two cabs at the curb. The nearest had its engine purring and Donahue got in, slammed the door behind him, said: "The hockey games," and sank back into the seat. It was a ride of ten minutes. He was early and went around to the lavatory, and he was standing in a corner lighting a cigarette when he felt a hard object thrust against the small of his back. His eyes flicked upward at the bare wall, he finished lighting the cigarette and let the match fall.

"Spill it," he said, raising his hands half-way.

"That's very clever. You're Donahue, ain't you?"

"I'm Donahue."

"Donahue the private cop?"

"Sure."

"I thought so."

"Who are you, the big man from the South?"

"Keep your puss to the wall, Donahue! And skip the funnies!"

Donahue, his cigarette between his lips, inhaled, let the smoke lag from his nostrils. He stood straight, well-planted on his feet, looking even a little debonair. "I'm keeping my puss to the wall."

"The door's latched," the low, stern voice went on. "I latched it. So don't try to stall thinking someone'll waltz in."

"Who's stalling? If you've got something on your mind, get it off. I don't want to miss the games."

"You'll miss the games, handsome, if you don't talk. What were you doing in 545 at the Coronet?"

Donahue inhaled languidly, though he did not feel languid. He said offhand, "Who sent you—that pup Phalen?"

"Never mind who sent me! I asked you—"

"I heard what you asked me. What did Phalen pay you, fifty bucks? Or could he raise fifty bucks?"

A crack on the back of his head made his teeth shake and he pressed his eyelids close together, wincing. He swayed a trifle and the cigarette fell from his lips.

"That's just the barrel of it, Donahue. The muzzle's used for something else."

Donahue made himself sway a little more. He made his legs break at the knees and let himself fall against the wall

"Snap out of it!" the voice behind him rasped.

"Ugh," said Donahue.

When he was half-way down the wall, his body looking limp and useless, he felt the man's hand tussle with his shoulder. Donahue suddenly shot one foot backward and threw himself down to his knees. He connected. But instantly the lights went out and he figured that he had driven the man against the light switch. He heard the man groaning, heard feet scraping on the floor. He drew his gun, swiveling on his knees and trying to get a bearing by the sounds the man made. His gun was cocked and he felt wide awake, tight-drawn. Then there was a moment's silence during which the man apparently made no move. Donahue continued to remain motionless, on his knees, sitting back on his heels.

Then he heard a loud click and instantly the door was flung open, dim yellow light poured in. Donahue caught a glimpse of an overcoated shape diving out through the doorway. Donahue raised his gun but in that moment the fleeing man collided with two others.

There was a short, violent tangle of bodies. Donahue let down the hammer of his gun, shot to his feet and lunged towards the door. The overcoated man had broken away and vanished, and Donahue, piling through the door, got tangled up with the two men who had tried to enter the lavatory before. They made no attempt to fight with him, but they simply were unable to get out of the way. Donahue finally broke between them, leaped for the lobby and found himself wading through the crowd there like a man trying to run in water.

When he reached the street, hundreds of men and women were arriving. He stopped, his eyes dagger-sharp and whipping about in all directions. But he had not seen the man's face, he had only a vague idea of what the man looked like from the rear. After a moment he relaxed.

He took his hat off, reset the crown, placed it back upon his head. He dusted off his overcoat, his knees, popped a cigarette from his leather case and lit up. It had all the earmarks of the kind of thing Phalen would do: send a gunman after him to get information. Yet Donahue knew that he could not successfully point the finger at Phalen. You have to have evidence.

Chapter III

ON his way from the hockey games, Donahue dropped in at the *Casa Caliente*. He tossed hat and overcoat on to the checkroom desk, pushed aside black drapes and made his way around the edge of the dining and dancing room to the bar. The bar was situated in a long, open alcove, two steps up from the main room.

"Hello, Mr. Donahue," the barman said. "Been around to the games?"

"Yeah. Scotch, Julius, with soda on the side."

"Was the games good?"

"Swell."

Julius turned to get the Scotch and a syphon and Donahue turned to hang his elbows on the bar, prop his back against it. Walter Hazen, the owner, came up and said: "Haven't seen you since Repeal, Donny."

They shook hands and Donahue asked, "How's it feel to be legal, Walt?"

"I sleep better, anyhow."

"That's something. Who's that girl over there?"

Hazen turned. "Which?"

"Walking across the dance-floor."

"Search me. Maybe I can fix—"

"Uh-huh. I just asked."

His drink was ready and he turned around, poured the Scotch into the glass of iced soda and jigged the glass swizzle stick. He ate some potato chips and finished half the drink at a swallow. Julius was showing him a new match trick when the girl climbed on to a high stool beside him. Both looked at each other at the same time and the girl smiled.

"Hello," she said frankly, warmly.

"Greetings."

Julius picked up his matches and went down to the other end of the bar.

"See what you did," Donahue said. "He'll pout now."

"Oh, I'm sorry."

"Buy you a drink?"

"Oh, no; no, thanks."

She turned to regard him with a shy little smile twitching at her lips. He wasn't looking at her; he was hunched over the bar making wet circles with the bottom of his glass. But presently she said towards the side of his face:

"About—this afternoon…."

He looked at her. "Huh?"

"I—I hope you didn't think anything wrong."

"About what?"

"I mean—well, the way it happened. The way you walked in and found me primping and then the way I went out. He's forgetful about those things, though—about introducing people. But he's a dear old man."

"Oh, that. I hadn't thought of it." He finished his drink and beckoned to the barman. "Do it again, Julius."

Julius reached for his matches.

"The drink, I mean," Donahue said. Julius looked disappointed.

The girl blushed a little and said: "I guess I was foolish to speak to you this way. But what did you think when you saw me there?"

He raised his palms, looked at her. "I tell you I didn't think anything."

He had to laugh at her earnestness.

She regarded him curiously. "Don't you care what people think of you?"

"Of course not."

"But don't you think it might help sometimes if a person thought good of you rather than bad?"

"Listen," he said, pretending to slump, "maybe we'd better dance."

A man, a tall, very young man in dinner clothes, came up and said: "Pardon me," to both of them; and to the girl, "We didn't know where you'd gone, Fern. Isn't this my dance?"

She slid off the stool, leaned over and said close to Donahue's face: "It matters sometimes," in a grave, anxious whisper. He put his glass to his lips and over the rim of it watched her walk off with the tall young man. The young man had pink cheeks, wavy golden hair.

Donahue turned to Julius. "Know that girl was sitting here?"

"Nah. The guy with her is Judge Emmett's son. I thought you knew her."

Donahue raised his drink. "I do," he lied. "I was just asking you."

He left the bar and headed for the lounge and was putting his scarf round his neck when Phalen came in with a couple of other legmen and three girls. The crowd was pretty high and Phalen, gesturing flamboyantly, shouted:

"M'gawd, gals, look! It's Handsome himself!" And then sententiously: "Look, out, gals. Get within ten feet of that maiden's prayer and you're lost. Lost!"

A little straw-blonde cried plaintively, "I wanna get lost!"

"Did you say ten feet?" another asked, plucking at Phalen's sleeve. "I want to make sure."

Walter Hazen came through the black drapes and said, "Please, not so loud, not so loud."

"Go hang your neck, Walt," Phalen called to him.

Donahue had his hat and coat on by this time and, drawing on his gloves, he was detouring towards the door.

The little straw-blonde cried, "O-o-o-o, you big handsome mans!"

Phalen lurched between Donahue and the door, screwing up his face. "Too good for us, hey?"

"Look out, Red."

"Too almighty good for us, hey?"

"Beat it, Red; you're plastered."

"Hah! Big, young, successful private dick too good to 'sociate with working boys and girls, huh?"

Donahue, still drawing on his gloves, raised his chin towards the other two legmen and said: "Take it before I do something with it, boys."

They swayed over and grabbed hold of Phalen. "Come on, Red; cut it out," one urged. "Walt'll think we're drunk and—"

"Lemme at him," Phalen croaked, his eyes blazing.

The two legmen held on to him.

Donahue said over their heads: "See you sometime, Walt," and went out, closing the heavy door quietly.

"Ran away!" Phalen exulted. "He couldn't take it!"

"Ah, my big brave star reporter!" one of the girls cried.

Chapter IV

DONAHUE went to court next day, to testify in an insurance fraud case, and when he got back to the office, at three-thirty, Miss Laidlaw looked up from her typewriter.

"Lieutenant Kelly McPard telephoned about ten minutes ago and asked if you would kindly come over to apartment 545, the Coronet."

Donahue stopped getting out of his overcoat and asked, "What'd he say?"

She moved prim precise lips. "Just that you should come over."

He shrugged his shoulder back into his overcoat and stood looking quizzically, a little darkly, at the surface of his secretary's desk. Louie, the office boy, was methodically stamping envelopes.

Then Donahue said: "I'll be there if anyone calls," and left the office.

He went downstairs and looked up the line for a street car. There was none in sight, so he flagged a taxi and rode out towards the West End. Donahue got out of the taxi near the Park and took the front entrance into the Coronet. He went past the desk, caught an upbound elevator and got off at the fifth floor. The long skirt of his ulster slapped his calves as he swung long legs down the corridor. He knocked on 545 and a uniformed policeman opened the door, saying:

"Oh, hello, Mr. Donahue."

Donahue did not remember his name, so he just said, "Hello," and passed from the foyer into the living-room. A couple of policemen were standing about, and across the room, at the entrance to the bedroom, there was a group of men gathered behind a police photographer, who was taking a picture of the bedroom. The man from the coroner's office was shoving things into a black satchel.

Phalen was standing on his toes, peering over the photographer's shoulder. Plain-clothed Kelly McPard was taking neat little drags at a cork-tipped cigarette, and when he turned to knock some ash into a tray, he saw Donahue and raised his eyebrows, smiled. Donahue moved his chin upward, in greeting, and then McPard left the others and came across the room.

He was a tall man, and pretty stout, but the dark tailormade clothes he wore lessened the effect of his stoutness. His pale hair was neatly slicked down and he had a round, pink face; but nose, eyes and mouth seemed concentrated over a very small portion of it. His eyes were shrewd and at the same time genial. White, starched cuffs crowded his plump, pink hands.

"I break into your routine, Donny?"

"Not at all, Kel," Donahue replied, his eyes fastened on the group at the bedroom door.

Kelly McPard smiled and nodded towards the partly open pantry door and Donahue followed him into a small, rectangular room, tiled, and fitted with an electric refrigerator, a porcelain sink and a high white porcelain stool. McPard drew the door shut. He pressed his cigarette into the sink and it sizzled briefly against the wet.

"I hear you were up here yesterday, Donny."

Donahue sat on the stool, propped his heels on the metal foot-rest and leaned comfortably back against the wall. He nodded.

"What did Loftman want?" McPard asked, his voice quiet, unhurried.

"He wanted us to send a messenger East. It wasn't definite at the time I saw him. He just wanted to make sure we'd have a man on call."

"Messenger, what for?"

"To fly there, get some cash from his wife and fly back here with it."

"How much?"

"He didn't mention the amount."

"What was he doing here?"

"Search me, Kel."

McPard leaned over to look at the polished tips of his pointed black shoes. "Just what were the conditions?"

"There weren't any. Everything was tentative. Details were to be given when he decided definitely our man'd fly."

"Did he phone again after you saw him?"

"Nuh-huh."

McPard wagged his head. "This looks like a funny one, all right."

There was a knock on the door and McPard opened it and a policeman said: "Doc wants to see you a sec, Lieutenant."

McPard walked out, leaving the door open, and Donahue, sitting on the stool, frowned down his nose. In a minute Gus Lankford, McPard's partner, thrust his dark, rawboned face through doorway and said:

"When'd you get in?"

"Minute ago."

"What you been doing, Donny, getting mixed up in murder?"

"Me mixed up?"

Lankford had a loud foghorn laugh. "You're a one for getting mixed up in things, Donny! Boy, if you ain't a one I never seen the like…. What, was this here now Loftman hiring a body guard?"

"The whole agency, Gus."

"Red says you was kidding him about a blonde."

"Yeah."

"It's like my wife always says— Hey what'd you think! My new kid began walking last night! Did I tell you?"

"Great, Gus."

"Took four steps and then flat on his kisser!"

Phalen came up and said over Lankford's shoulder in a voice that was not apologetic: "They said I was trying to smack you last night, Donny. Sorry. I guess I was stinko."

"That's okey, Red," Donahue said; and then to Lankford, "What did the coroner's man say?"

"Instantaneous!" Lankford boomed, his eyes popping. "A blunt instrument…." He tapped his left temple. "He musta been laying there for two hours. It was the hotel maid found him. She come in with some clean towels and there he was laying in the bedroom." He added a slab of gum to some already in his mouth and his big, knobby jaw moved from side to side. "Kel says—"

Kelly McPard called him and Lankford turned and walked across the living-room, a bony scarecrow of a man with deep hollows behind his ears. Kelly McPard addressed him, using small, nimble-fingered gestures.

Donahue wandered into the living-room as the coroner's man and the police photographer left. A minute later two precinct detectives came out of the bedroom and headed for the corridor door after the manner of men who knew definitely where they were going. A uniformed sergeant and a couple of patrolmen were still in the bedroom, and Phalen was bent over the radio, dialing it, while the loudspeaker rasped, squawked.

"Sh, sh," Kelly McPard said.

"I was trying to get the Rhythm Twins," Phalen explained. "They're friends of mine."

Donahue thought he heard a knock on the corridor door. He was nearest, so he stepped into the foyer, opened the door and looked down into the face of the girl. Before she could open her mouth he said:

"You'd better beat it."

"But I just wanted to—"

"Beat it." She didn't know yet. "Later—later."

He closed the door in her face and strolled back into the living-room.

"Was that somebody?" Kelly McPard asked.

"No."

Lankford had gone into the bedroom again.

"Listen, Donny," McPard said, smiling persuasively, "you sure that's all took place between you and Loftman?"

"That's all, Kel."

McPard nibbled on his lower lip. "The man's had at least a two and a half hours start. The clerk gave a pretty good description of him and I've notified all air lines, train terminals and bus lines. Far as I can figure out, he left his baggage behind—one suitcase."

"Who?"

"Loftman, Loftman."

Donahue brought his lips together and swung his gaze towards the bedroom door.

Phalen went past saying, "Well, I've got to buzz off." The door slammed behind him.

Lankford came back into the livingroom planting his feet slowly and heavily, his hands behind his back, his head lowered and a mournful scowl on his face. Then he threw his arms outward, let them flop back to his sides.

"Well," he said heavily, impressively, "that's life: here today, gone tomorrow, and the devil takes the hindermost. They tell me Bickford was a good egg, a hard-working house dick. Tough. I hear he has a wife or a mother or something over in Terre Haute, Indiana. He comes from Terre Haute, Indiana. I was there once, the time I was contradicting Goo-Goo Dorshinsky, for murder. Goo-Goo won four bucks offa me on the ride back, playing poker. I had a awful time with Goo-Goo's wife the day the State gives him the works. I sits up with her all night account of she wanted to commit suicide. It takes me just eleven hours to talk her out of it. Six years ago. She always sends me a Christmas card."

Chapter V

MISS Laidlaw's horn-rimmed spectacles were large and her thin, triangular face was small. Her eyes were calm. Her neat, flat haircomb carried out the motif of her prim lips, her chaste dress, her large low-heeled shoes. She was shadowlike and competent.

"It all sounds very involved, Mr. Donahue," she said. "I don't see any reason why the agency should meddle with it. After all, Mr. Loftman didn't really engage you, and he is not on our files. Therefore, since you asked me, I think you ought to leave well enough alone."

He sat in a deep brown study. "It's clearly a police job," he said.

She nodded primly. "Of course. If you don't think the girl is actually involved, it would be unfair to mention the fact that she was there. I hate the way newspapers like to involve pretty women in these things."

"You and me both." He sat up, leaned on his elbows, frowned down at his big strong hands. "It was just an impulse that made me send her away. Part of the impulse, I guess, was because I didn't want her to see Loftman all smashed up. At the time, of course, I thought it was Loftman who was dead. I think that was the main part of the impulse." He picked up a pen, began signing correspondence.

Miss Laidlaw returned to her office, closing the connecting door. But a minute later she opened it, to say:

"Mr. Phalen."

Donahue was eying a small bronze effigy of Jack Dempsey. "I'm busy."

"Yes, sir."

She closed the door but after a moment opened it again and shrugged. "He says it's of vital importance."

Donahue sat back. "Okey," he sighed wearily.

Phalen strolled in wearing a sly, insinuative smile. He shut the door with a backward kick and said, "Was she really a blonde, Donny?"

"D'you know only one joke, Red?"

"I mean, was she really?"

Donahue clasped his hands behind his head. "Go ahead, Red; get it off your chest."

Phalen threw a small, neatly folded handkerchief onto the desk and sat down. "Exhibit number what?" he said, with exaggerated complacency.

Donahue did not remove his hands from behind his head. He glanced casually at the handkerchief, then up at Phalen. He didn't say anything and his face showed a large lack of interest.

Phalen gestured languidly. "Pick it up. Look at it. Go ahead. It won't bite."

Donahue picked it up, looked at it, saw the initials FC on it and then tossed it negligently back to the desk. "Now go on from there, Red."

"I think maybe it's your move now."

"Are you going to horse around or are you going to tell me why you came in here?"

Phalen chuckled dryly. "You know, the funny thing about it was that I thought you really were kidding about some woman. That's you all over; a guy never knows whether he's coming, or going with you. Where does the blonde fit in, Donny?"

"You're still horsing, Red."

Phalen leaned forward and said intimately, "Listen, Donny; you've always had me wrong. You could never take a joke. Just because one time I thought it would be a great laugh to purloin some information from your files, why"—he looked astonished—"you're down on me for life. We could do a lot for each other. I could help you and you could help me."

"I'll worry along solo, Red."

"That's where you're wrong. You never know. Look, I could have taken this handkerchief right around to Kelly McPard. But did I? No. I wanted to be a right guy. I brought it to you."

"Why me?"

"Now *you're* horsing. Over the apartment, while I was fiddling around with the radio trying to get the Rhythm Twins—friends of mine—you went to the door. When you came back in the living-room Kel asked you if anyone had knocked and you said no."

Donahue nodded.

Phalen went on: "I picked up this handkerchief as I left the apartment. It was lying just outside the door. It wouldn't have been there five minutes before some cops went out and one of them would have seen it and picked it up. It was during that time you went to the door, when Kel thought he heard a knock." Phalen pointed. "There was a dame out there, Donny. I'll eat my hat on it!"

"Eat it."

"I haven't told Kelly anything about it. I haven't said a word about it." He laid his hand on the desk, palm upward. "I came here to put my cards on the table. Why be an Airdale?"

"You came here figuring to get in on the ground floor."

"All right; say I did, say I did. I'm still giving you a break. If I was a wrong guy, I'd have run to Kel in the first place."

Donahue shook his head. "No you wouldn't've." He leaned forward. "Kel's in the dark. You think I'm in the know. Kel couldn't have given you anything. You think I can. That's why you came here, Red, like a Greek bearing gifts."

"Horsefeathers!"

"When you're sober, Red, you make a good show at liking me. When you're tight, the truth comes out."

"Ah, hell, a guy tight's liable to say anything."

"Anything he means, yes."

Phalen jumped up and snarled, "Okey, have it your way! But you'll trade, sweetheart, or"—he scooped up the handkerchief—"I'll bounce this in Kelly's lap!"

Donahue put his hands behind his head again. "I've nothing to trade, Red. Just because you pick up a woman's handkerchief in a hotel corridor, you get ideas."

"What a sweet liar you are!" He thrust the handkerchief out at arm's length. "Do you or don't you?"

"I wish I could, Red, but I can't. I've got nothing."

Phalen jammed the handkerchief into his pocket and went out like a blast of ill wind.

After a minute, Miss Laidlaw came to stand primly in the connecting doorway. "You're too generous, Mr. Donahue, to even let that man inside your door."

Donahue's forehead was wrinkled darkly with thought. "Maybe I should have told him—but it stuck in my throat. I hate that guy, I guess."

Chapter VI

HE lived in a two-room apartment on the South Side. There was a small kitchenette and sometimes he made his own breakfast, but not often, and sometimes, when some boys came in to play poker, he made steak sandwiches, late at night. He was lying on the divan at eleven that night, with newspapers strewn about him, when the telephone rang. He got up and went into the bedroom and unhooked the instrument.

"This is—is me," she said.

"What's the matter now?"

"I—I'm in a drug-store around the corner. Could I see you a few minutes here?"

"What's the matter with my apartment?"

"Well… all right."

"Four-one-four. You run the elevator yourself."

He hung up and wandered into the bathroom, where he splashed cold water in his face and ran a comb through his hair. Going to the bedroom again, he put on an old robe. Then he went into the kitchenette, put ice and a jigger of bourbon into a tumbler and sloshed in ginger ale.

The buzzer sounded and, carrying the drink to the door, he let her in. She had on the black lapin coat again but a different hat. Before he had quite closed the door behind her, she said in a breathless voice:

"I—I heard the late news bulletins on the radio."

He extended his hand towards an armchair. "Sit down."

She sat down and then he crossed to the divan and made the newspapers crackle beneath his weight. He let the hand holding the drink hang between his knees and he regarded her curiously but not anxiously. He was patient, and took a few sips at his glass.

Sitting on the edge of the chair, with her ankles crossed, she was not at ease and her face was flushed from what apparently was a combination of an inner excitement and the cold out-of-doors. It made her look very attractive in a fresh, wholesome way, like frost in the early fall.

"I understand now," she said, nodding, looking gravely at him, "what you meant when you chased me away from the apartment door."

He was candid: "I thought it was Loftman."

She did not understand quite what he meant and her eyebrows lifted.

"I mean," he said, "I thought it was Loftman was dead."

"Did you send me away because you thought I had something to do with it?"

"I just did it on an impulse. Besides"—he shrugged—"I didn't think it would be pleasant, seeing him."

She clasped her hands together and a shudder, hardly perceptible, passed over her body. "I'm a little afraid," she said.

He looked down into his glass and did not ask why.

She looked frankly at him. "I mean, I'm afraid of being involved in this. Not that I'm guilty of anything. I just—well—you know..." She inhaled, then let out a little sigh, and then she was thoughtful for a moment, her eyes downcast; but presently she said: "I came to ask if anything had been found out since—" She made a little gesture which indicated "the crime."

"I don't know," he replied, still looking down into his glass. "The police may have found something, but I'm not in on it."

Her eyes lay gravely on him. "Did you tell them about me?"

He shook his head.

"I had to see you," she told him earnestly. "I wanted to know where

I stood. I thought you might have told the police. What puzzles me, though, is your apparent total lack of curiosity about all this."

He bent his brows and walked up and down the room. "I don't see why I should get steamed up about it. I don't want to get mixed up in the case because there's no reason why I should. I don't think you're in any way involved in the criminal angle of it, because if you were, you wouldn't have popped up outside the apartment door yesterday."

"But they insinuate Mr. Loftman is a murderer! I can't, I can't believe it!"

He said: "You can't blame the police. They find the house dick dead in Loftman's apartment. They don't find Loftman. So naturally they draw conclusions. It's human nature."

She stood up. She stood very straight, like an athlete, though you felt she was not athletically inclined. "Tomorrow," she said, "if nothing turns up, will you work for me?"

He looked at her.

"I mean," she explained, "as a detective. I haven't much money but I imagine I can pay you. Will you try to find out where Mr. Loftman is?" And then she asked immediately, "Does a private detective have to reveal everything to the police, if he works for a client?"

"It's about like a lawyer and his client. Only we've got to use a little more discretion and we like to have faith in the client."

"Have you sufficient faith in me?"

He stood spread-legged, gazing down at the floor. He felt a sharp personal angle creeping into things. He could not help liking the girl, she was so deadly in earnest. And yet more than anything he wished to keep his hands off this case, he wanted to know as little as possible about it, for he felt that somehow, sometime, he might have to tell the police that she was acquainted with Loftman. And he had already burned a couple of bridges.

"Well, I'm sorry," she said, in a slightly injured voice, and started towards the door.

"No. Wait a minute. I was just thinking." He paused and looked at the back of her head. "Suppose we wait until tomorrow. I guess we can do something about it."

She turned and said gravely, "But you've got to have faith in me first."

"I have," he said.

There were male voices in the hall and an instant later a knock on the door. Donahue raised a finger to his lips. He took hold of the girl's hand and walked her swiftly, silently into the kitchenette, and pointed to a door about two feet square in the lower part of a white cupboard.

"That's for service delivery," he explained. He opened the door, revealing a square compartment whose back was another door. "That one leads to the hall. Wait about a minute, then move that snaplock back and crawl out. Close the door again."

She was anxious. "What's the matter?"

"Police, I think."

HE turned, stepped back into the living-room and closed the kitchenette door. They were knocking again. He rumpled his hair and then walked noisily to the corridor door. It was Kelly McPard. Lankford was with him.

"Wake you up, Donny?" McPard asked with polite concern.

Donahue was rubbing his eyes. "I guess I fell asleep. Come in."

As they walked in, Lankford craned his long neck and said in his loud, foghorn voice, "Nice place you got here, Donny."

"Sit down," Donahue said. "Drinking? I've got nothing but bourbon."

McPard held up thumb and forefinger, close together, and sighted between them. "Just a wee drappy."

"Same here," Lankford said.

"Straight?"

They nodded and sat down and Donahue brought in the bottle, glasses and some ginger ale for a chaser. Both detectives took full measure and Donahue took a short one. Kelly McPard said: "Well, happy days," and they all downed the drinks neat and then McPard dabbed at his lips with a large, snowy handkerchief.

Lankford turned to him and said with hoarse approval, "Donny always did have swell liquor."

McPard nodded towards Lankford in polite agreement, while the expression on his face suggested that his thoughts were up another alley.

"Well, we haven't got anywhere, Donny," he said, leaning sidewise and thrusting his handkerchief back into his hip pocket. "Looks as if it's going to be a nut to crack and we haven't a ghost of a chance of cracking it. We had all trains, buses and planes covered and we even checked up in these drive-a-car-yourself places. Not a peep. This

Loftman was down on the Coronet register as from Greenwich, Connecticut, but we checked through and there's no Henry W. Loftman in the Greenwich directory. That in itself is a swell beginning, I don't think so."

McPard sighed. "A few days ago Bickford got McCartney to toss out a couple of con men by the name of O'Fallon and Fauls. It was under the hat, of course, though when this murder happened Mac told me all about it and said it was the same apartment."

"Bickford told me about it," Donahue said. "He saw me coming out of 545 and asked me if I thought Loftman was a square guy. I said I thought he was."

McPard said: "I don't for a minute think there's any connection between those two con men and Loftman, because Mac ran them smack out of town. I think it's just coincidence that this 545 figures twice in a row. To my way of thinking, Bickford was still up in the air about the O'Fallon and Fauls scare, and when he saw you come out of Loftman's suite, why, he began to wonder.

"Maybe he sneaked in there while Loftman was out and was rooting around in Loftman's baggage when Loftman came back in. He wouldn't know right offhand Bickford was the house dick and maybe he pasted him right off the bat. Then maybe he found out who Bickford really was, got panicky and ran out. If he had something to conceal, this would be natural. And the fact that we can't locate his name in Greenwich seems to show it was an alias, and if it was an alias then you've got to conclude that he had something to conceal. Don't you think so, Donny?"

"It sounds reasonable."

McPard leaned forward, elbows on knees, and regarded the polished tips of his pointed black shoes. "Red thinks maybe there was a blonde mixed up in it after all. He thought at first you were kidding."

Donahue went around the room looking for a cigarette. He found one and stood in the center of the floor, lighting it.

McPard stood up, kicking the creases free of his knees. "Red says he thinks there was a blonde at the apartment door the time I asked you if someone knocked and you said no." He took his hand out of his pocket. "Red found this woman's handkerchief outside the door a couple of minutes afterwards."

Donahue nodded. "He tried to sell it to me first, for a beat. When I told him he was screwy, he ran it over to you."

Lankford looked indignantly at McPard. "Red didn't tell us that, Kel."

McPard slipped the handkerchief back into his pocket, smiled ruefully to himself. "But Red's pretty certain—"

Donahue whipped his cigarette into an empty metal waste basket. Sparks showered upward and he blurted out, "Red seems to be your prize stool!"

Lankford raised a hand. "Now don't get sore, Donny. Kel was just remarking—"

"Kel's remarks are beginning to annoy me like hell!"

Lankford looked with long-faced regret from one to the other.

Dull red color had seeped into Donahue's cheeks and a dark, sultry look was in his eyes.

"Well, now we done it, Kel," Lankford sighed hoarsely. "When he gets sore, he gets stubborn as a mule."

Kelly McPard nodded regretfully.

Donahue pointed in the general direction of downtown. "That legman thinks every crime has to have a chemise in it and you guys play along with him like a couple of half-baked potatoes!"

McPard made gentle, placatory gestures. "Sh, now, Donny; sh!"

Donahue swiveled, said: "I'm going to bed," and strode into his bedroom, slamming the door.

"Now he'll blow up any time you just look at him," Lankford said morosely.

McPard sighed. "Well, I guess we may as well go, Gus."

Lankford nodded and they went out together and rode down in the elevator in silence.

Chapter VII

FIVE minutes later Donahue opened the bedroom door. At the same time the kitchenette door opened and the girl stood there, not on her toes yet seeming to be poised. Her eyes were warm, disturbing.

"I—I heard it," she said.

He was biting his lip and he didn't say anything. She ran across the room, took hold of his hand impulsively, said in a warm, rushing whisper, "You're grand—grand!" There was no smile on her face, but a rich, a wide-open expression, pathetically ingenuous.

He muttered, "I just got sore."

Her eyes hurried anxiously back and forth across his face and she gripped his hand harder. "You ought to know my name. Do you realize you don't? It's Fern Chester and I live with a maiden aunt—Bethia Samson—at twenty-six Westminster Road."

He was darkly preoccupied, but he said, "I knew it was Fern something."

She suddenly wilted away from him, grimacing. "But I know, I know you're getting into something you don't want to. And I got you to do it. Why don't you just throw me out and tell them—tell the police?" She ran to a chair and sat down on the edge of it, her toes turned in, her hands clasped between her knees and a wet look in her harried eyes.

He regarded her stoically for the space of a minute—he still looked preoccupied—and then suddenly he took a few long strides, picked up a chair and slapped it down in front of her. He sat down and said point blank:

"We may as well get down to business. I've stayed out of it as long as I can. Personally I'm not curious, but the agency's not mine, I only work for it, and the home office is pretty tough. They've got a reputation they're proud of. I can go just so far with the cops, but there's a limit. I can't clown around with them any longer unless I get some details from you. Kelly McPard is beginning to bear down on me and there's a certain newspaperman in town would like to see me take water."

"I'm sorry," she said in a small, plaintive voice.

"Loftman's suspected of having committed a crime. You believe he didn't do it, but that doesn't really count."

"I know, I know," she grimaced. "I feel I want to tell you certain things. I feel you ought to know certain things and I feel I can trust you. How far can I trust you?"

"You've got to leave that to my judgment. I don't know yet what you know, so I can't make any promises. I'm not one of these rich amateur detectives you read about. I work for a living and I work for an agency that allows its district men a lot of leeway but lands on 'em like a ton of brick if there's an unhappy ending. Do I understand that you're not personally involved in this—I mean criminally?"

She started. "Of course not."

"All right. Then I'll promise that I'll keep you out of the limelight if it's humanly possible. Is that what you want?"

"That was one of the things—the least, really, I suppose, when you get right down to it."

"What else?"

"Well"—she dropped her eyes—"I made a promise to Mr. Loftman."

He lit a cigarette and said offhand: "What's his real name?"

She stared miserably at the floor. "That's what I promised: that I wouldn't tell his real name."

"If you're sure he's not guilty, what does it really matter?"

"Oh, it's not that. He was in the city under an assumed name for business reasons, but I don't know what they were."

"How do you know then that his so-called business reasons were not really criminal reasons?"

"Because I've known him a long time. He knew my father and mother and when they died he took care of their affairs and what little money was left. The money lasted until I was about eighteen and I had to go to work. He gave me a job in his office and I soon became his secretary and worked for him a little over three years.

"Then my Aunt Bethia came into a little money and asked me if I would like to come out and live with her and take charge of the house. That was two years ago, and I came out. He and I corresponded from time to time and then he wrote me that he was coming out and that he would like me to call on him. So then you saw me at his hotel apartment. He'd told me he was expecting a Mr. Donahue, but we kept talking and talking and I didn't get away before you arrived."

"Did he ask you point blank not to divulge his real identity?"

"He said, 'Fern, under no circumstances whatever tell anyone I'm here. Or that I was here, after I go. I'm on a secret business mission and I expect to be here only a day or two longer, when I'll return to New York.'"

"Did he mention any local names?"

"He didn't mention any names at all. I—" She paused, then began again, "I saw—" and then stopped, troubled.

"Come on, come on."

"Well, I happened to see a memorandum on his desk. He'd written the name Flannigan on it, and an address. But I don't remember the address. After a while, after I was there a while, he tore the memo into bits. He didn't act guilty or troubled or anything like that."

Donahue squinted at her. "What's his real name?"

The hunted look in her eyes deepened and she looked up at him imploringly. "Marcus Rathbun. He used to be a congressman."

Donahue stared intently at her for a long moment, then rose and murmured, "Um," and walked thoughtfully about the room.

She cried: "A lot of important men use assumed names sometimes."

"Of course, of course," Donahue nodded. "There's no harm in that—except when a thing like this crops up."

She slumped where she sat, bit her lips and looked very miserable again.

"Red would break his neck over this," Donahue said, but only half aloud and more to himself than to the girl; but then instantly he said to her. "You'd better beat it home now." And, as she rose, "What business is he in?"

"He's a director of the Centaur International Engineering Company. You can see," she cried desperately, "that he wouldn't be a man to go about killing people, hotel detectives!"

"Flannigan was the other name, huh? Any initials?"

She shook her head, then said: "Will you have to tell the police now?"

He was candid: "I may have to. But I think I can keep you out of it." He smiled down into her troubled eyes. "I'll try."

"I believe you."

He said cheerfully: "Well, just take it easy," and walked with her to the door.

"I guess I do imagine things are worse than they are."

"Sure, sure you do," he said, feeling that actually things looked pretty bad. "I'll give you a ring tomorrow."

When she said good night there was a mixture of embarrassment and warm thankfulness in her manner; the clasp of her hand was warm and close and a little disturbing.

"I—I feel I've known you a long time," she said, and then instantly blushed.

He grinned. "I hope I won't have to let you down."

She turned and hurried away and he stood in the doorway, watching, until she disappeared in the elevator.

Chapter VIII

GRAY dawn was outside the window when the ringing of the telephone bell roused Donahue. His bedroom was in semi-darkness and, sleepy eyed, he groped around for a while, yawning, before he found the instrument and drew it into bed with him.

He said: "Hello," on the tail end of a noisy yawn; and then: "Don't you ever sleep?… Sure you woke me up…. Well, I don't care about worms…. I'll bite: what?" He listened and presently he sat upright. "Says who?… All right, go ahead; I'm listening." He listened for two minutes, motionless. Then he said in a dropped voice, "I'll be right over," and hung up.

He washed and dressed in ten minutes, and went out. There was no taxi in sight, so he walked across to a car line and then walked eastward until he heard a car coming. He boarded it and it was cold too and the only other passengers were three laborers with metal lunch boxes. They sat staring dolefully into space. The car made loud, clanging sounds in the empty street.

It was a ride of twenty minutes. Donahue got off in the heart of the business district and walked south. Pretty soon he was out of the business district. He passed some warehouses, an empty parking lot, a row of drab rooming houses, a Greek restaurant. The smell and the feel of the river were near. The light in the east was lifting slowly over the rooftops. In an alley a man was making a lot of noise with ashcans.

Donahue turned a corner and saw, a few yards beyond, a couple of police cars and an ambulance drawn up to the curb. A narrow, three-storied red brick house was sandwiched in between a garage and a pool hall, and in front of the house a uniformed policeman was standing. A weatherbeaten sign hung alongside the door; it said: Furnished Rooms.

"Looking for somebody?" the policeman asked.

"The lieutenant phoned me."

"Upstairs—all the way."

Donahue climbed. Some people were standing in the second-floor hallway, gossiping in low voices. Some wore bathrobes in which they huddled. One man wore drooping trousers and a long-sleeved undershirt. The gossiping died down as Donahue drew nearer. They looked aside—or towards him, but covertly. A few electric bulbs lit the way and there was the smell of plaster that had been damp a long time. The banister was black and did not slide smoothly beneath the hand.

When Donahue reached the top-floor hallway, he saw several policemen standing outside an open doorway. One called into the room beyond, "I guess here comes Mr. Donahue."

Donahue stopped in the doorway of a small, dilapidated room. He saw a uniformed sergeant, a couple of policemen, the ambulance doctor, Kelly McPard and Lankford, and a man named Stratford, from the District Attorney's office. They made a crowd in the small room.

"Thanks for coming," McPard said. He beckoned with his finger. "Can you identify him?"

Donahue shouldered his way to the side of a large, lumpy bed. On it lay the man he had known alive as Loftman. Loftman lay quite peacefully, quite naturally, as though he slept. His skin had a peculiar pinkish tinge.

"Loftman?" McPard asked.

Donahue turned and nodded.

McPard tossed a tagged key into the air, caught it deftly. "We thought so, account of the hotel key, but we wanted to make sure."

"How long's he been dead?"

"Offhand"—McPard nodded towards the ambulance doctor— "about since the night of the day Bickford was killed. Monoxide." He moved across the room, wedging his way through the group, and pointed to a small coal stove. "This did it, Donny." He pointed upward, where the stove pipe careened far to one side, disconnected from that chimney hole. "The coal gas couldn't get up the chimney."

"Accident?"

"Ha!" laughed Lankford hoarsely.

McPard toed some crumpled, sooty newspapers that lay on the floor. "These were stuffed in that hole," he said. He withdrew a torn piece of newspaper from his pocket and extended it towards Donahue. "Take a look at this, Donny."

Donahue stood beneath the single electric bulb and peered down at an item which was encircled by a pencil marking. The caption said:

Coal Gas Kills Sleeping Youth

The account went on to say that one John Leffler, aged twenty, a houseboy in the employ of Ferdinand Ashmun, of Blue Ridge Road, was found dead in bed of carbon monoxide poisoning. The supposition was that in shaking down the stove before going to bed he had jarred loose the stove pipe. No one else was in the house at the time. The Ashmuns had gone to Phoenix. There was furnace heat throughout the house, except in the room occupied by Leffler. In this room there was a small coal stove. The body was discovered when paperhangers, who arrived next morning to redecorate several rooms, received no response to the doorbell and notified the police.

Donahue turned the piece of paper over, gazed down abstractedly at an advertisement, then handed it back to McPard.

"We found it in his pocket," McPard said.

Donahue said: "Power of suggestion, huh?"

"That's all we found," McPard continued. "No identification. Except the hotel key."

Lankford boomed good-naturedly, "You sure pick swell clients, Donny! Boy, you sure pick 'em!"

"From what I hear," the District Attorney's man said caustically, "you've been doing plenty of shadow boxing around town."

Donahue turned. "Oh, hello, Mr. Stratford."

"Didn't you hear what I said?"

Donahue looked around the room. "What am I, on the carpet or something?"

"I just thought," McPard said, in his friendly way, "you'd want to have a look. He came here the other night with a woman. The old man who runs this place said he met them at the front door and the woman hung in the background. Loftman asked for a room for a week and the old man took them up to this one. He's very nearsighted and he didn't pay much attention to the woman. The room was all right and they didn't have any baggage, so Loftman paid a week in advance.

"The old man brought up some kindling and some coal for the stove, and that's the last he saw of them. He came up next day about ten, to bring some towels and make the bed, but there was no answer. He thought they were out and tried to use his own pass key, but there was a key in the other side of the door. He tried once again, later, in the afternoon, but still no luck. So he gave it up, I guess.

"Then this morning, at five, a drunk wandered in and wanted a room and the old man brought him up to this floor and gave him one, up front. He stopped to listen at this door and then he tried his key again, he was beginning to get curious, but the key was still in the other side. He began to get worried, so he went downstairs, got a screwdriver and went in the next room. He'd screwed shut that connecting door sometime ago. So he took the screws out, opened the door—and there you are."

Stratford snapped, "Kel says he thinks Loftman was using an alias."

"That's what Kel told me," Donahue nodded.

"Maybe Loftman told you his real name."

Donahue shook his head.

"The thing is," Stratford rasped, "find the woman." He looked sharply at Donahue. "It's highly possible you'd know her."

"Maybe—but I don't."

"I'd like to be sure of that."

"Try hard."

"You talk like a guy with a pretty swell opinion of himself."

Donahue turned to Kelly McPard and said: "Did you get me down here to take a lot of guff from him?"

"You'll take it and like it!" Stratford ripped out.

Kelly McPard patted down the troubled air with his plump hands. "Now, Mr. Stratford, please don't let us get worked up so early in the morning. Donny probably hasn't had his breakfast yet and it is kind of an imposition to drag a man out of bed at dawn—"

"Have I had my breakfast?" demanded Stratford.

McPard rolled his eyes ceilingward.

"Besides," Stratford hammered on, "you were the one gave me this long spiel about what Red Phalen thought and what you thought."

"Sure, sure," said McPard placatingly. "I like to keep all my cards face up with the D.A.'s office. But it's just that if you rub Donny the wrong way he goes off the handle."

Stratford snapped peevishly, "You're not so considerate of most guys you drag in that favorite back room of yours."

"Now listen here, now," Lankford barged in, goggle-eyed. "That ain't fair. Besides, Mr. Donahue ain't no mug. And have I had my breakfast yet? No! And did I pound the floor half the night with my new kid? Yes! And am I getting on my high horse? No!" he roared.

"Sh, sh, Gus," Kelley McPard implored.

Stratford muttered under his breath, turned his face into a corner and folded his arms.

McPard said: "Well, Donny, you can run along now, if you want. I'm having a fingerprint man down, just in case. There's a chance the woman left some prints around. Meantime, if you happen to recall anything you forgot about, well, wise me, wise me."

Donahue said he would, and left.

He went to a restaurant in Locust Street and ordered a baked apple, two three-minute eggs, wheatcakes, toast and coffee. He killed an hour eating and reading the morning papers, and when he walked into the street again business was picking up. He went around to the post office and bought a stamped envelope which he addressed, in large block letters, to Police Headquarters. Across a money order blank he printed: *Loftman Is Ex-Representative Rathbun.* He slipped this into the envelope and dropped the envelope into the mail slot. He left the post office and walked up Olive.

Chapter IX

WHEN he entered the agency office, his night man was putting on a tie and Donahue asked:

"Anything new?"

"Nothing."

"You can go home when you want, Joe."

Donahue passed on into the inner office and, still in his overcoat, carried a telephone directory to his desk, sat down and turned to the F's. He wrote down the telephone numbers of the various Flannigans, excluding the female members of the clan. Then he unhooked the receiver and asked for a number; and when the connection was made:

"Is Mr. Flannigan in?... Mr. Flannigan, are you acquainted with a Marcus Rathbun, one-time congressman?... You aren't. Thank you very much."

He hung up, waited a minute and then called the second number on his list, putting forth the same question. He repeated this procedure several times, until finally, in response to his question, a man's voice said:

"Who—who is this?"

Donahue leaned forward and said: "Mr. Flannigan, I'd like to have you drop by my office as soon as possible."

"But who is this?"

"I can't talk too much over the telephone." He gave his office address and room number, and added: "It's vitally important and I suggest you come down immediately." He hung up, rose, removed his overcoat and draped it on a wooden hanger.

When Miss Laidlaw arrived, a few minutes later, he said: "Good morning, Miss Laidlaw. I'm expecting a man named Flannigan. When he comes, show him right in."

A messenger arrived with a telegram and Miss Laidlaw placed it on Donahue's desk. It was from the home office:

> *What Are You Into Now Stop Clear It Up or Else.*
> *Hackett.*

He muttered, "Nerts," and tore it into strips, tossed them into the waste-paper basket. But his forehead was wrinkled with concern and his teeth worried his lips.

At a quarter past nine Miss Laidlaw opened the inner-office door and said: "Mr. Donahue, Mr. Flannigan. Go right in, Mr. Flannigan."

Flannigan was a short man with a torso shaped like a football. He had a chubby chin, chubby cheeks, and thin brass-colored hair, strategically combed, to camouflage a bald spot. His legs and arms were blunt and he looked fiftyish. He was a bit disconcerted, a little winded; his China-blue eyes tried to be friendly but appeared too worried to succeed. A neat, scrubbed-looking little Irishman dressed in dark, inconspicuous clothes.

Donahue sat on his desk, leaning on one braced arm. "You've probably been reading the papers, Mr. Flannigan. What's your idea about it?"

"About—what?"

"We're talking about Marcus Rathbun: Henry W. Loftman to the police."

Flannigan swallowed. "How did you get on the track of me?"

"I phoned the Flannigans in the directory. You were the first to show any interest in the name of Marcus Rathbun. He came to this city to see someone and I ran across your name on a memo slip."

Flannigan's chubby face looked miserable. "I haven't got a single idea what happened to him."

"Could you afford to get mixed up with the police?"

Flannigan started. "Why should I get mixed up with them?"

"The point is, could you afford to?"

Flannigan looked around for a place to sit down. He sat down and ran a harried glance back and forth across the floor.

Donahue said: "Did you know Rathbun arranged to engage the services of this agency?"

"No!" Flannigan shook his head vigorously. "Positively no!"

"Well, he did." Donahue stood up and jabbed a forefinger towards the floor. "He did. I saw him the day before that house dick was killed and he disappeared. He wanted us to fly a messenger East and bring back some money and obviously that money was intended for someone in this city. Before he could say definitely whether or not the messenger was to leave, the crime happened." He leaned on the desk, both arms braced straight from the shoulders. "Apparently you're the only man who knows why he came here."

Flannigan looked at him with scared, jigging eyes, with his jaw shot tremulously over to one side.

Donahue stood up straight and held his arms out from his sides. "And now I'm beginning to get in a spot. With the home office on my neck, with the police and the D. A.'s office and the press waltzing around me, I, Mr. Flannigan, am beginning to be in a spot. I've got to know why he came here, and you"—he dropped his voice to a note of finality—"can tell me."

Flannigan's chubby jaw shivered. He jumped up and cried in a stricken voice, "I had nothing to do with this! I don't see why you should—you should—" He broke off, tried to harden his jaw, make his stare bold. "I—must get—to—work!" He lunged towards the door.

Donahue said: "Okey. I'll have to turn your name over to the cops."

Flannigan's hand fell on the doorknob, but he did not turn it. His round body wilted heavily. He turned and came dragging his blunt feet back to the desk, and there was twisted anguish in his chubby face, a childlike fear in his eyes.

"You're being very cruel, Mr. Donahue."

"I don't mean to be. But I've got to know."

"If I tell you, you'll tell the police anyhow."

"Not if you're innocent of any complicity in connection with the death of Bickford."

"Bickford! I never saw the man!"

"Or the death of Rathbun."

"Rathbun!…"

"He was found dead a few hours ago in a cheap rooming house near the river. Apparently a suicide."

Flannigan's eyes shimmered. "What a blow, what a blow this is!" He placed a hand against the side of his head.

"Under the circumstances"—Donahue moved several articles about on his desk—"the cops might get very tough."

"My Lord, man, I—I had nothing to to do with it!"

Donahue sat down in his swivel-chair, put his elbows on its arms and built a pyramidal fretwork of his fingers, "If that's the truth, then there doesn't seem to be any reason why you should hold out on me."

"No—no—no. It's not the crime I'm afraid of. I can prove I had nothing to do with either of those crimes. It's not that. Not that at all. It's"—he swallowed—"something else."

"What else, Mr. Flannigan."

Flannigan stared at him with quaking eyes. "If you tell—if it becomes known that he came here to see me—the talk about the money and all—I'll be ruined. I'm in debt as it is. Sickness. Stocks. My wife and four kids." He put his head far back, as if he found it difficult to breathe.

Donahue said in a deep, sincere voice: "If that has nothing to do with these crimes, Mr. Flannigan, you can trust me to say nothing about it to anyone."

"But it hasn't! I swear it hasn't!"

Donahue leaned back. "What business did Rathbun come here on?"

Flannigan slumped in his chair and when he spoke his voice was dull, miserable: "Rathbun was a director of the Centaur International Engineering Company. Well, I'm with Midwest Structural, in the president's office. Years ago I worked with Rathbun and we always wrote letters afterwards, from time to time. He was a fine man, a great businessman, and he usually got what he wanted.

"Well, maybe you've heard about this new Blue River Dam that's going to be built. A tremendous job, and a lot of money in it. Sealed bids were asked for it, and the general opinion is that either Centaur or Midwest will do the job. There are a few others bidding, but they couldn't hope to compete successfully.

"I think I've been treated pretty badly by the company I work for. Maybe I haven't. But I think I have. I've taken cuts, demotions, and so on, and what with my expenses and all, I guess I took these things more bitterly than I would have otherwise. I needed money badly. I knew Centaur wanted this job and I knew it was worried about Midwest's bid, the same as Midwest was worried about their bid. I knew what our bid would be. I offered to sell out to Centaur. When a man's desperate, I guess he'll do anything.

"I wrote Rathbun about it and he said I should not write again but that he would come here and talk it over with me. So he came out, informing me beforehand that he would travel as Henry W. Loftman and that as soon as he arrived here he would send me a special delivery letter telling me where he was staying.

"I went to see him at the Coronet and we talked it over and I guess I began to feel a bit shaky, and guilty too. Rathbun was the same as ever. He offered me twenty thousand dollars and took out his checkbook. I said I couldn't accept a check, not because I didn't think it was good but because checks can sometimes be traced. Then he said that he would get me cash. He didn't want to wire for it because as Loftman he had no identification and he didn't want to use his real name. But he said he would get it to me somehow. Then I asked him to wait a little while. I was shaky. He said that was all right and I went home and thought and thought and thought. Then the news of his disappearance—and I haven't slept a wink since. That's all—that's all. For God's sake, don't betray me, Mr. Donahue. I had nothing to do with those deaths."

"Did he express any fear of being watched?"

"None. None at all. While he was congressman he was rarely if ever photographed. He won a reputation for that."

"The police say he was seen in that rooming house with a woman."

Flannigan shook his head wearily. "I can't understand that. He was never the kind. I can't understand anything. It all seems unreal. There doesn't seem to be any connection anywhere." He looked forlornly at Donahue. "Is there anything else you want?"

Donahue stood up. "No. That's all, Mr. Flannigan. Thank you very much."

Flannigan walked to the door in a half daze, groped for the knob.

"I'll never get over this, I'll never get over this," he mumbled. "And now I'll have more sleepless nights, wondering if you'll tell the police."

"It's under the hat, Mr. Flannigan—unless your story breaks up."

"God knows I've told the truth."

When Flannigan had gone, Donahue stood at his desk tapping the ends of his fingers on it. His eyes were bright, intense with thought, and one corner of his mouth was sucked in against his teeth. He let it go with a slight popping sound, sat down and looked up Bethia Samson's telephone number. Fern Chester answered.

"This is Donahue," he said. "You'd better run down and see me…. At the office, yes…. Say in an hour…. Plenty!"

He pronged the receiver, rose and put on his hat and overcoat. On his way out, he said to Miss Laidlaw, "I'm going around the corner for a shave. Be back in half an hour."

Chapter X

TWENTY minutes later he was returning up the corridor towards his office, humming to himself, when he saw vague silhouettes wafting back and forth on the soapy glass panel of the agency door. Sunlight would be streaming slantwise through the general office window and on to the glass panel of the door. Drawing nearer, he squinted, put his hand on the knob but waited. He heard scuffling sounds beyond the door. He turned the knob very slowly and discovered the snaplock was fast. He drew his keys from his pocket, and with the same hand took out his gun, while his other hand still held the knob turned full to the left. With the gun gripped in the crotch between thumb and forefinger, he was able to handle the keys with the remaining fingers of his right hand. He turned the lock and went in fast.

One man was struggling with Miss Laidlaw, another with Louie, the office boy. The man struggling with Louie was nearer and Donahue struck him behind the ear with a hard left fist. The man went down like a felled tree as Donahue swung his gun on the man breaking clear of Miss Laidlaw. Miss Laidlaw sat suddenly down in her chair white with terror. Louie fell violently on the felled man.

The other was darting a hand towards his coat pocket. "No you don't, punk," Donahue said. "Up."

Miss Laidlaw's assailant raised his hands.

Miss Laidlaw panted, "Ugh, ugh."

The young man facing Donahue smirked.

Donahue smacked him on the side of the face and said: "What's so funny?" And to the office boy, "Got it Louie?"

"Yeah, yes, Mr. Donahue. Gee whiz!" Louie stood up with the gun he had taken from the man on the floor.

Both were young, hardly twenty, and the one on the floor wore a cheap camel's hair coat and spats. The other wore dark, close-fitting clothes and a derby. His skin was swart and his hair was long, black.

"Spill it, Louie," Donahue said.

"Wuh-well, about five minutes after you went out, about five minutes, they walked in. The gink in the yellow coat held a gun on us while this other gink began going through our card indexes. Then he went through our file boxes and letter files, and when he couldn't find what he wanted, he turned on Miss Laidlaw and wanted to know where the dope was on somebody named Loftman. Miss Laidlaw said there wasn't any and then he began twisting her wrists. So I took a swing at him and then the other gink jumped on me and Miss Laidlaw began struggling with that one there and then you came in."

Donahue stared balefully at the two youths. He said to the one on the floor, "Get up," in a low, chopped voice.

The youth got to his feet and stood rubbing the back of his neck.

"Who sent you birds?" Donahue demanded.

"A man," said the youth in the dark clothes.

"That's a help, isn't it? Who sent you, I said?"

The two looked warily at each other.

Donahue pointed a long forefinger at them. "His name and you bums walk out of here. No name and you get a couple of cops on your neck. Well, snap on it!"

The dark-clothed youth said haltingly, "A man with—with red hair. We don't know his name. Honest, we don't. He just come up and talked to us."

"Where?"

"Poolroom over in Fifth."

"Snappy dresser? About your size?"

"I guess, yeah."

"Have you two ever been up before?"

"Uh, no. That is, just for little things. Petty, once. And once I got potted and by mistake drove a guy's car off."

Donahue nodded to the desk. "Okey. See that stamp-pad over there? Well, both you bums place the fingers of your right hand on that pad and then place them on a sheet of paper there."

"That ain't fair, mister."

"Do what I tell you!"

They shuffled reluctantly over to the desk, and when each had placed his fingerprints on a sheet of paper, Donahue nodded to the door. "Now beat it. Take a tip and steer clear of that red head. If he runs across you, say you couldn't get in here. And if I run across you again— Go on. Out!"

They slouched out.

Miss Laidlaw said: "You—you let them go, Mr. Donahue?"

He picked up the two sheets of paper. "I got these, didn't I?... Louie, run over to Police Headquarters and go down the Bureau of Criminal Identification. Ask Sergeant Bauer to check up on these and mark down the records beneath each set of prints. Be careful you don't smudge them. Miss Laidlaw, take a note. When Collins comes on duty, have him make photographs of those prints.... Did that egg hurt you very much?"

"No, sir; I guess not."

"You hurt, Louie?"

"No, sir; I'm not hurt none."

"Swell."

Chapter XI

FERN Chester remained sitting motionless in the chair for a long interval after Donahue told her of Marcus Rathbun's death. Her face was very white, and this made her eyes seem darker, deeper, and brought out the color of her lips, a warm rose-pink. Donahue lounged with a lanky leg thrown over an arm of his chair, his chin mashing the knot of his tie, his face long, brown, hollowed out beneath the high, strong cheekbones.

She murmured in a remote voice, "What will be the end of it?"

"It's a sticker," he muttered.

"Now his wife will have to be notified."

"I faked a message to the police—anonymous. They should know by now his name isn't Loftman. No use concealing that any longer. The thing is"—he gave her an up-from-under look—"they say he went there with a woman."

She looked at him.

"I know it was the night you were at the *Casa Caliente,*" he said. "You might have to prove you were there. You like this Judge Emmett's son?"

"Well—sort of. Nothing serious. Ralph's professed—oh, well, he's an ardent boy, very intense. But"—her eyes widened—"surely we won't have to drag Ralph in. The family's so—strait-laced." Her face clouded. "Or maybe you've told about me?"

"No, no; nothing like that. But there's no telling where this thing may lead to, who'll get dragged into it. Kelly McPard and his partner Lankford are a couple of swell cops, but they're cops, and you can't blame them for that. Then there's this Red Phalen, the legman—a glutton for news, especially where decent names are involved. And Stratford, of the District Attorney's office."

"Such a mess, such a miserable mess," she cried, grimacing. "But this woman angle—I can't believe it. He was so straight about things like that and there seems to be no reason for the woman. It's all beginning to look a little mad. Where's the reason for everything?... Oh, I can see the lurid headlines already." She stared straight ahead, her breast beginning to rise and fall rapidly. "And I know, I'm sure they'll be untrue, utter falsehoods."

She leaned forward and placed her hand on the desk and said in a sunken voice: "Should I go to the police after all? Should I tell them everything? Everything I've told you? About the memo I saw, about how I knew all along his name wasn't Loftman? I'll do it, I'll do it. And I'll tell them that all this lurid stuff about Mr. Rathbun can't be true, can't possibly be true."

He sat up straight, his fingers raised. "No." He leaned on his elbows, his eyes dark, fastened on the effigy of Jack Dempsey. "You'll get in for a lot of unpleasant notoriety, you may even be charged with withholding vital evidence from the police. The kick-back will hit me—the agency. And that's not all." He made a fist, remembering Flannigan: he'd struck a bargain with Flannigan.

She opened her handbag. It was oblong, of black patent leather, and had a leather flap with the large initials FC attached in chromium plate. Taking out a small handkerchief, she said: "You would never have become involved so deeply if it hadn't been for me."

He made a brusque gesture. "Probably would have. I seem to have a talent for it."

Miss Laidlaw brought in a telegram. It said:

Well What About It Wiseguy.

The home office again.

Donahue balled it up and whipped it violently across the room. Miss Laidlaw raised her prim eyebrows.

"Wait," Donahue muttered. He wrote on a piece of foolscap in a bold broad scrawl. "Wire this back," he said.

His reply advised:

Do Not Believe All You Read Stop Give Me Time

It took him a minute or two to calm down, and during that interval Fern Chester sat with her eyes dutifully turned the other way.

He shoved things around on his desk and said: "Excuse the blowoff." And then he went on in a deep, quick voice: "The thing now is, we're involved and we can't expect the cops to treat us with any great amount of consideration. It's a case of our knowing too much and yet not enough. If we knew less, we'd be much better off. But the 'if's' don't count. Loftman's true identity will clear up one angle but on the other hand it will magnify the whole thing over and over again.

"I might be able to keep the cops off our neck for a while by coming out with the statement that I think Marcus Rathbun was murdered. There've been some balmy ideas floating around in my head for the past several hours and I think I could put up a good front. I've no concrete ideas, only theoretical ones, which as a rule I don't like, but in this instance I've got to break a rule. I want to start the investigation up another alley, mainly to draw their attention away from this theoretical blonde."

"But wouldn't you have to name someone you thought might be guilty of the murder?"

"I've got that in mind too."

She made a wry face. "All because of me. All my fault. It's so unfair to you!" She hung her head and twisted her handkerchief round and round.

He stood up and leaned on his braced arms. "Say, do you ever eat dinner out?"

She nodded. "Sometimes."

"I know a place where they make a filet of sole that'd melt in your mouth."

"I love filet of sole."

He laughed with rough good humor. "Well, I can see this thing hasn't got you down completely. And frankly," he continued, slightly out of the side of his mouth. "I think the Judge's son looks a little on the rah-rah side."

"Do you always mix business with pleasure?"

"I did once in my life and look where I am."

"You'll likely regret it," she said ruefully.

He tossed a coin into the air, slapped it, palmed it. "I was only kidding."

She sighed. "You're a funny man. I can never quite make you out." But she didn't seem displeased about it.

Chapter XII

DONAHUE strode into Police Headquarters with his long legs swinging purposefully. He went past the elevator, took the stairway up to the second floor, walked to the front of the corridor and entered Kelly McPard's office.

"Hey, Donny, what'd you think?" Lankford boomed.

"The new kid can say 'Pop.' Right?"

"Loftman's a ex-congressman named Rathbun!"

"What's this, a joke?"

McPard was sitting comfortably in his chair and drawing thought-fully on a long panetela. "No joke, Donny. We received an anonymous message a little while ago. I chased over to one of the newspaper offices and found out when he was a congressman. Then I rooted around some more there and finally found a picture of him. They said it was only one of three the news photographers had ever got. And it was him, alright—it was Loftman."

"Boy, ain't that a break!" exclaimed Lankford, slapping his thigh. "Boy, that's a break!"

McPard said: "You mean to tell us, Donny, you never knew who Loftman really was when you interviewed him?"

"Cross my heart, Kel."

McPard frowned. "The D. A., I think, is going to have you over on the carpet. You got Stratford sore. He's not satisfied with your position in this case and I think they're going to put you over the hurdles."

"Swell."

"I wouldn't be too cocky, Don," Lankford advised sagely.

Donahue laughed. "Maybe I killed Bickford, huh? Maybe I killed Rathbun too?"

"No," said McPard. "But maybe you've got an idea who the woman in the case is. Red swears you meant it when you said you were going up to see a blonde, and now that we find a woman was with Rathbun when he took that room down near the river, why, it looks as if Red might be right. It occurred to me that maybe when the date was made for you and Rathbun, a woman made it."

"Rathbun himself made it, Kel."

McPard smoked in troubled silence for a while, then asked absently, "You come here for something, Donny?"

Donahue sat down, bending his brows darkly. "There's an idea been getting the best of me."

"I'm glad to see someone's getting ideas around here."

"I don't think Rathbun committed suicide."

"Oh, phooey," Lankford said, sour-faced.

"Why, Donny?" McPard asked.

Donahue looked from one to the other intently before continuing. Then he said, "Well, I've never heard of a suicide yet who deliberately destroyed all evidence of his identity. Usually they leave notes. Even though Rathbun was traveling under an assumed name, ten to one he carried a wallet; ten to one that wallet contained money and plenty of identification. And the fact that you've just told me who he really was makes me more certain that the identification was destroyed by someone else."

"Why?" McPard asked.

"Because when an unidentified man is found dead, the wheels move slowly and sometimes it takes a long while to identify him. That gives the killer more time to put distance between himself and the scene of the crime. If the deceased's name was found out right away, you might be able to check up immediately on his acquaintances."

McPard looked at his cigar. "I was kind of fooling around with a similar idea, but in this police work, you know as well as I do, the unexpected always happens."

"Tell me this, Kel. Tell me why Bickford crashed the apartment of an ex-congressman and give me some good, logical reason why an ex-congressman should haul off and brain a house detective."

"I've been thinking of that too, all along. But facts are facts. Bickford was killed and then we find Rathbun a suicide."

Donahue shook his head. "Let's say that he wasn't a suicide. I'm going to stick to my contention that a suicide wouldn't destroy every ounce of identification."

Lankford asked: "He left his hotel key, didn't he?"

"That only identified him as Loftman."

"But then who knocked off Bickford?" Lankford demanded.

Donahue laid a hard fist on the desk. "Let's go back a bit. Let's go back to those two guys who occupied 545 before Rathbun did: O'Fallon and Fauls."

"Whoops! Listen to the man!" Lankford guffawed.

"Razz me," Donahue said, "but keep your ears open. They were tossed out on the fourth. Rathbun checked in on the morning of the fifth, as Loftman. You know as well as I do that McCartney remained in the apartment while he made O'Fallon and Fauls pack, in fifteen minutes, and then ran them over to the railroad station. Has it ever occurred to you that O'Fallon and Fauls may have buried a lot of dough in that apartment?"

McPard laid his cigar aside, folded his arms. "Go ahead, Donny."

"All right. Now say a woman came up to Rathbun's apartment and knocked. Say she pretended she was some kind of welfare worker—I've had it happen to me in the best hotels. Or even say that she came into the hotel with a hat and coat on, but over a uniform such as hotel housekeepers wear. Say a man was with her and they went up to the fifth floor by the stairway. She took off her street things when they got there. The man held them and then she knocked and when Rathbun opened the door she said she was the housekeeper and wanted to check up on the linen.

"As he let her in, the man also went in with her. Then the woman held a gun on Rathbun while the man got the money, wherever it was hidden. As they were leaving, Bickford came down the hall, saw them, and they backed into the apartment again but Bickford crashed in too. He chased them to the bedroom, where they struggled, while the woman continued to keep Rathbun covered. In the struggle, the man smacked Bickford on the temple with the butt of his gun and Bickford went down. Then they waited a while, to make sure no attention was drawn in the corridor. Before leaving, they took a look at Bickford and found he was dead. Murder. Rathbun would remember them. So they took Rathbun along with them."

Lankford was jovial: "Boy, what stories you make up!"

McPard was attentive: "But McCartney swears he saw O'Fallon and Fauls off on a California-bound train."

"Which means, I suppose, that they'd have to go all the way to California."

"But it sounds farfetched, Donny. It's not the kind of angle a man can set his teeth in."

"If I could think of any other angle, I'd discard this. But the thing sticks in my nut. And the suicide angle sticks in my throat. Especially since you've told me who Loftman really was. Listen, let me see that newspaper clipping again—the one you found on Rathbun."

McPard opened his desk drawer, passed the clipping to Donahue. Once more Donahue scanned the account of how one John Leffler had died of carbon monoxide poisoning.

"There's no date line with the item," McPard offered.

"That usually means it happened in the city where the paper was published. There's no Blue Ridge Road in this city. Now look at the back of this clip: there's part of an ad for furniture, and the names of the store is Kinderman Brothers. It advertises a club chair and ottoman: 'For Sale—Saturday only.' All right, call a wholesale furniture dealer in this city and ask if they know of a store named Kinderman Brothers, and if they do, where it's located. Go ahead."

McPard looked in the classified telephone directory and put through a call. When he hung up, he said: "Kansas City, Missouri."

"Now call Kinderman Brothers in Kansas City, describe this ad and ask 'em on what date it was published in the newspaper."

Lankford's face was dark brown with interest now.

McPard put through the long distance call and in a few minutes was in communication with Kinderman Brothers. He made notes as he listened, and said, presently: "Thank you a great deal, sir," and hung up. "On the fifth of the month," he told Donahue. "In all Kansas City papers."

Donahue got up from the chair and leaned on the desk. "All right, now. It was on the evening of the fourth O'Fallon and Fauls were put on that westbound train. Rathbun arrived in this city on the fifth, from the East. From the East, mind you, not from the West. I will bet this: I will bet that O'Fallon and Fauls got off that westbound train late the night of the fourth, spent the night at a hotel there and came back to this city next day, possibly with the woman. I'll bet that clip came with them from Kansas City and I'd like to bet it was planted on Rathbun. It was a good idea for the suicide angle."

The telephone rang and McPard answered it. "For you, Gus," he said.

Lankford took it. "Yeah?... Yeah, Sophie.... Hah?... No!... Yes?... No, Sophie! You don't tell me!... Be home for dinner, hon!" He smacked the receiver into the hook and beamed on McPard and Donahue. "My new kid just walked the whole length of the bedroom! Imagine!"

Kelly McPard chuckled.

Donahue grinned. "Chip off the old block, huh, Gus?"

"A man's man, that kid, Donny!" Lankford puffed.

McPard rose and said: "Suppose, Donny, you and I take another look at 545."

"I was just about to suggest that myself."

"You, Gus," McPard said, "hold down the desk till I get back."

Chapter XIII

DONAHUE and McPard rode out to the Coronet in a police sedan. They got one of the assistant managers, a man named Floom, to take them up to 545. The apartment was unoccupied. Rathbun's baggage, of course, had been taken to Headquarters. MacPard stood in the center of the living-room, his hands on his hips, his eyes swinging nimbly and curiously about the room.

"Well, Donny, what would be your idea?"

Donahue said: "If they had a lot of money hidden here, and if it had been easily accessible, they could have got it into their bags while Mac and Bickford were waiting. We ought to assume that the money was not easily accessible, that they didn't have time to get it. It's highly probable, Kel, that they ran some stiff games here and won a lot of dough. If they did, there was always the chance of being knocked over by some of their guests, especially the sore losers. So they would have bunked it deep."

"The bed?"

"Never. That's a cinch. Same with the carpet, or behind the pictures, or in the divans or the chairs. Just think of all the average places the average mug would hide it and then forget those places. Then think of some place where it would be difficult to bunk it and just as difficult to get it out."

"The wall," suggested Floom.

"That's good, Mr. Floom—only the wall's made of plaster. Let's look at the doorway frames."

They spread out and it was Floom who called, "Look at this a minute," from the pantry doorway.

In the crevice between the outer strip and the base of the doorway frame the paint was slightly chipped.

"Get the house carpenter," Donahue said.

A Swede appeared in five minutes with a kit of tools, and to him Donahue said: "See this? Have you done any fixing on this very recently?"

"Me? No, sir."

"How long have you worked here?"

"Three years, sir."

"This chipping looks fresh, doesn't it?"

"It does, kind of."

"When was this apartment last decorated?"

Floom put in, "About eight months ago, completely."

Donahue turned to the carpenter. "Pry that panel out, will you?"

The carpenter took a chisel from his kit and pried the panel out. The space it disclosed was empty. Kelly McPard sighed.

"Did that seem to come off easily?" Donahue asked.

"Yes, sir, it did."

Donahue looked at McPard. "A great deal of money *could* have been planted in behind that panel, Kel."

"But in getting the panel back," Floom said, "they would have had to hammer it. I don't see any marks on the paint."

Donahue went into the bedroom and came back with a pillow. "Let's borrow that hammer," he said to the carpenter. He then placed one corner of the pillow against the panel and hammered the pillow until the panel was again secure. The hammering had left no mark.

"Think it over, Kel," he said.

"It listens," McPard nodded, his voice very soft.

Donahue turned to Floom. "Who has the apartment beneath this?"

"It's vacant at present."

"How long?"

"Well, it may seem to be a curious circumstance, but it was vacated at about noon of the day Mr. Bickford was killed. But wait a minute." He smiled, shook his head. "No connection with this. The occupant just moved to another suite, on the other side of the hotel. She said the main street was becoming too public, too noisy. So we moved her. She's quite old."

Donahue eyed McPard quizzically. "Should we, Kel?"

"No harm, I guess."

Floom took them to the eighth floor, on the north side of the building, and knocked on the door of 816. It was opened by a small, frilly old woman with a high, knotty haircomb.

Floom bowed and said: "Excuse me, Mrs. Telfair, but the police would like to ask you a few questions."

Her head went back. "Ask me a few questions?"

Kelly McPard's smooth, smiling voice crept in: "Just a few, madam. It's in connection with what happened in the apartment above the one you used to occupy. Did you ever hear any hammering there, or a sound like wood being pried apart?"

"I don't think I did," she replied indignantly.

"We just thought that perhaps you had your apartment changed because of the noise upstairs."

"Well; there was noise sometimes, but it wasn't because of that I moved. No, it certainly wasn't because of that."

McPard was gentle of voice and gesture. "Something else, madam?"

Her mouth screwed up, her eyes flashed. "Well, if you must know, yes. My only pleasure in life nowadays is reading. I used to sit by that large window in 445 practically all day long, reading. I'm a very nervous person and I suppose very irritable at times. Well, sir, I became tired of being gaped at."

"Gaped at?"

"Yes, gaped at. In that cheap hotel across the street. A busybody kept continually using binoculars and I know he trained them on my favorite window."

"For how long?"

"It must have been for a couple of days. I finally became exasperated and had my apartment changed."

"Was it a man, madam?"

"I think it was."

McPard and Donahue looked at each other and then Donahue said: "Do you mind coming down to 445, madam, and pointing out just what window the binoculars were used from?"

"It seems silly, but I don't mind, I suppose."

They all went down to 445, and standing at the window, the old woman pointed. "That one."

"How many windows up and how many from the left?" Donahue asked.

She counted, then said: "Six up and the fourth from the left."

"It's practically on a level," McPard observed, "with the fifth floor of this hotel."

Donahue nodded. "It's very much so."

Chapter XIV

A S they walked across the street to the Hotel Malvern, McPard said: "If it's so, maybe they left around some fingerprints. And if they're O'Fallon's and Fauls' prints, it's a hundred to one they had something to do with it. And then I can shoot an alarm for them, nation-wide, if I have to. They could be anywhere by this time."

McPard had with him the card on which O'Fallon and Fauls had registered at the Coronet as Herbert Gearman and P.T. Lancaster, of Dodge City, Iowa. McPard addressed the clerk at the Malvern's desk:

"I'm from Police Headquarters. Looking at your hotel from the front, what room number on the sixth floor would be the fourth window from the left?"

The clerk turned to a framed plan of the hotel. "That's a double, number 627."

"Who is in it?"

The clerk referred to the register. "Two gentlemen—Philip Cranston and R. B. Escott, of Milwaukee."

"When did they register?"

"On the afternoon of the fifth."

McPard leaned forward and said very quietly: "They're still here, are they?"

"Of course."

The lieutenant looked at Donahue. "Now it doesn't get warm anymore, Donny."

"Look at the handwriting."

McPard looked. Donahue looked also. They checked it with the handwriting on the Coronet's card, and McPard shook his head. "I'm no expert, but I'll swear it was never made by the same man."

"Maybe O'Fallon registers sometimes, Fauls others."

"Now that makes it a little warmer again." And to the clerk: "Have you any idea what these men look like?"

"No, sir. I see by this record that I checked them in, but I don't remember what they look like. I work the cashier's desk too and I've noticed that all their meals have been served in the room, and they used a lot of ice and mineral water."

"Tell room service that when this room rings again, they should say, yes, the stuff will be brought right up. But don't send it up. Tell me. We'll sit over there and wait. Come on, Donny."

An hour and fifteen minutes later the clerk came over to say, "There was a call for cracked ice and a syphon."

McPard stood up. "Okey, mister; thanks to you."

Donahue and McPard rode in the elevator to the sixth floor, got off and walked slowly down a narrow corridor.

"Better take out John Rosco," McPard murmured, "just in case."

Donahue withdrew a revolver from beneath his left arm and Kelly McPard knocked on the door. They stood side by side, their guns held low, down against their thighs. The door was opened by a tall, yellow-haired man and McPard jammed his gun hard against this man's stomach and said:

"Raise them, Fauls."

The yellow-haired man almost fell over backwards, with a sharp inarticulate cry high in the roof of his mouth. A man lying on the bed, with a bandaged foot, whipped a gun from the pocket of a blue silk robe and fired. The bullet whanged into the transom above the door.

Donahue, standing sidewise in the doorway, fired and hit the man in the chest and plastered him back against the pillow. The man set his mouth and tried to swing his gun down but Donahue strode towards him, his own gun leveled, his low voice saying:

"Don't do it, O'Fallon."

"Did you get him, Donny?" McPard asked.

"Plenty."

O'Fallon let his arm and the gun drop to the bed. He groaned, closed his eyes, gritted his teeth.

"I'm sorry, O'Fallon," Donahue said, "but you should have known better."

Fauls was breathing noisily, red color high on his cheeks.

Kelly McPard smiled up into his blonde face. "It's just one of those things, Jess," he said in his friendly way.

Chapter XV

MISS Laidlaw held up a slip of paper as Donahue came into the office. She said: "Miss Chester phoned about twenty minutes ago and left this number and said she would wait half an hour."

And Louie said: "Them fingerprints and all are on your desk, Mr. Donahue."

"Thanks, Louie. Miss Laidlaw, ring this number. I'll take it in my office."

He was sitting at his desk studying the records of two petty criminals named Michael O'Hara and Dominick Cairoli, alias the Kick-In Kid, when Miss Laidlaw said: "Miss Chester is on the wire."

He unhooked the receiver. "Your favorite detective," he said.

"Listen," her low, anxious voice came over the wire. "I'm calling from the dressing-room in the Fisk Theater. I don't know what to do. When I stepped into the street from your office building, a man was standing on the curb. I thought he looked curiously at me. Then I noticed he was following me."

"What's he look like?"

"Well, red hair—"

"Then what did you do?"

"I went into a department store and fooled around in there for a about half an hour, but when I came out, after I'd walked a while, I saw he was still following me. I didn't want to go home, because that would have meant perhaps getting Aunt Bethia involved, and she's a bundle of nerves as it is. So I stopped in a restaurant and frittered away about an hour. But when I went out, well, he was still around. Then I went into the Fisk and spent about two hours and a half watching two very stupid pictures, but when I came out into the lobby, I saw him standing outside. So I went into the dressing-room and phoned you and I've been here ever since. What *should* I do?"

"Come right over here."

"But—"

"Right over here. Let him follow you."

"Are you sure?"

"Yes."

Her "All right, then," was breathless and confused.

She came in about fifteen minutes later and almost instantly she cried, "He did! He followed me to the outside of the building and I think I saw him come in as I started up in the elevator."

"You look rattled. Sit down and try to be calm."

"Calm! After I've been followed—"

He smiled, made soothing gestures. "Down… and easy; take things a little easy."

She sat on the very edge of the chair. "But why do you suppose he followed me?"

Donahue pointed to her handbag. "Your initials on that bag are big enough to attract attention."

"But it's supposed to be rather smart."

"I don't doubt it. But Red saw them as you left this building. He remembered the initials on the handkerchief you dropped in the corridor of the Coronet."

"Oh, dear. Oh, dear, what'll I do? What will I do?"

"For one thing," he said, leaning forward on his elbows, "you can listen to me. I want to tell you that we got the fellows who killed Marcus Rathbun and Bickford."

"You—*what?*"

"In the Malvern Hotel. While they lived at the Coronet they ran some pretty high card games and made a lot of money, but they were wise donkeys and buried most of it behind a doorway panel. They were kicked precipitately out of the apartment by Bickford and a metropolitan detective and bounced on to a westbound train. They hadn't the time to pry open the panel and get their money. It was about thirty thousand dollars.

"They got off at Kansas City and came back here and took a room in the Malvern, across the street from the Coronet. From their window they could watch the apartment from which they'd been thrown out. With binoculars, of course. They used powerful ones. They wanted to become familiar with what the occupant looked like. Then they saw me in there and Fauls recognized me from newspaper photos. He stuck me up in the lavatory at the hockey games and tried to find out why I was in the apartment. Rathbun kept close to the hotel, but finally they saw him get dressed for the street. Fauls with his hat way down, his collar way up, hurried over and parked just inside the Coronet door. Rathbun left, taking his key along.

"Fauls followed Rathbun, who walked rapidly—obviously he was out for the air; for he took to the park. O'Fallon by this time was up ahead of Rathbun. They worked it nicely. On one of the quiet lanes, O'Fallon stopped and bent down to adjust a shoelace. Rathbun came up. O'Fallon stopped him and then Fauls came up. Fauls took Rathbun's hotel key and O'Fallon said to Rathbun, 'Now you and I will just continue to walk in the park until my friend rejoins us.'

"Fauls went back to the Coronet, ducked in a side entrance and took the stairway up. He had a chisel and a hammer with him. He pried out the panel in 545, jammed the money into all his pockets and into the lining of his overcoat. He was stepping back into the corridor when Bickford happened along and jumped at him. Fauls ran into the bedroom, with Bickford after him. He turned on Bickford and cracked him with the butt of his gun. Bickford went down. Fauls waited a while, listening. Then, before leaving, he took a look at Bickford. Bickford was dead. Murder.

"Fauls slipped out, walked up the street and stole a car. He drove out to the park and picked up O'Fallon and Rathbun. O'Fallon was as surprised as anyone at the sight of Fauls in a car. Fauls drew him aside and explained what had happened. They were in a jam. They'd intended all along returning the key to Rathbun and letting him go. But now there was murder. Rathbun could describe them to the police.

"It was O'Fallon who got the bright idea, after several hours of riding around, of doing away with Rathbun and making it look like suicide. He was the one who'd clipped an item from a Kansas City newspaper about carbon monoxide poisoning. He had a complete woman's outfit at the Malvern, and while Fauls waited in the car with Rathbun, several blocks away, O'Fallon went back to the Malvern and dolled up. He rejoined the others and they began driving around, finally working down near the river. Then O'Fallon told Rathbun that they were going to rent a room. Rathbun would do the talking—or else. O'Fallon showed him the gun. So they left Fauls.

"What O'Fallon wanted was a room with a coal stove in it. They looked in three places and finally found one in the fourth. Then O'Fallon told Rathbun that he would not be harmed. He was to be detained for a couple of days and would then be released. He must have been pretty reassuring, which he meant to be. Because after a while Rathbun, who probably was fagged out from the nervous excitement, fell asleep on the bed.

"Fauls swiped his wallet and burned it in the stove. Then he put some coal on the fire, pulled the stove pipe from the chimney and stuffed up the hole with newspapers. He left the room, after unlatching the rear window, and for three hours waited in a stairwell on the floor below. Then he went out, around back, climbed the fire-escape and opened the rear window. He waited there for ten minutes. Rathbun did not move. Finally O'Fallon climbed in and saw he was dead.

"He replaced the key in the inside of the door, went back out the window, closed it and climbed down the fire-escape. He had on high-heeled shoes and he was almost to the bottom when he fell, turned his ankle. He walked several blocks, limping, and got into a taxi and returned to the Malvern. By the time he reached the room he could hardly walk. Fauls had discarded the stolen car half a mile from the hotel. Well, the ankle got worse and worse. O'Fallon could not stand on it. They couldn't get away. But they didn't worry much, because they figured they had done a smooth job. They had. They'd never have been caught if I hadn't started to make up a fairy tale that turned, before long, into a true story that even I began to believe. It just goes to show what the forces of necessity will sometimes lead to."

Miss Laidlaw stood in the connecting doorway. "He's in again," she said hopelessly.

Fern Chester, her eyes transfixed on Donahue, said: "It's awful, it's terrible," in a low, cluttered voice.

AND then she looked up and saw Red Phalen standing in the doorway, a small, sly smile on his lips. "In again, out again, in again," he said laughing softly.

Fern Chester sat breathless, staring straight ahead.

"Sing your song, Red," Donahue said, leaning back comfortably. "Though I know the words and music by heart."

Phalen sauntered up to the desk, smiling insinuatively down at the girl. "If the young lady wears 'FC' on her handbag, she likely wears it on her handkerchiefs. Catch on, Donny?"

Donahue put his hands behind his head. "Red, would you like to lose your job?"

"I'd love to, Handsome."

"Would like to get tossed in the jug?"

"Just cur-razy to!"

"The thing is, Red, I'm not kidding. Take a look at those two sheets of paper."

"These?"

"Those."

Phalen picked up the two sheets of paper and lounged back on his heels with an exaggerated air of nonchalance. He considered the fingerprints and the petty criminal records of two youths named Michael O'Hara and Dominick Cairoli. Presently he did not appear so nonchalant. His eyes lifted towards Donahue as he let the two sheets of paper slide from his fingers. His lips twitched a little while the rest of his face grew dull.

Donahue said cheerfully: "I can pick those punks up in a minute, Red. It's up to you."

Phalen's mouth went over to one side. "Fast, aren't you?" he croaked.

Donahue laughed. "Or maybe you're slow. Why, you cheap little sensation-hunting fathead, you've been scooped by every legman in town. While you were shadowing a will-o'-the-wisp practically all afternoon, history's been made. Roll your hoop over to Headquarters and they'll tell you who killed Bickford and Rathbun—and why."

Despite himself, Phalen began to look a little ill.

Donahue roared with laughter.

Phalen turned on his heel, his face and neck crimson. He rushed out of the office, a blind, dizzy look in his eyes.

Fern Chester had not yet relaxed. "What does it mean?" she asked in a tense whisper.

"It means a little deal that's not on the records. He sent two bums around to crash my files and I nailed them. Instead of arresting them, I turned them loose. It just means that he'll never ring in that handkerchief gag again, because if he does, I'll ring in the two bums and Red will lose his job and land in jail. It's just the way we play house sometimes."

She relaxed at last, and a tired but warm smile came to her face. "How good, how so very good you've been to me. I don't see why."

"Maybe I liked your face right off the bat."

"It's quite an ordinary face."

"Maybe it's the way you wear your clothes."

"They're quite ordinary clothes."

"I was talking about the way you wear them."

She looked up at him. "Honestly, did you believe in me implicitly from the first?"

"I don't think I did."

"When did you begin to?"

"I can't remember exactly."

She said with sudden warmth, "That's what I like about you—you're so downright honest."

"Listen," he said, clasping his hands together. "Let's cut out all this and make a date. I've got a cheap car and I never drive while drunk but sometimes I go around ringing strange doorbells."

She broke into a gay little laugh. "I think we'd have fun. And if you got tight—well, I could drive."

"That's a pal for you. That's a real pal!"

Miss Laidlaw came in with a telegram. Donahue read:

> *Details Instanter or You Are Canned Dummy.*
> *Hackett.*

Donahue chuckled to himself and wrote out a reply. "Send this right off, Miss Laidlaw," he said.

Miss Laidlaw, in her front office, read the reply. Her small prim mouth grew round with astonishment.

> *Horse on You Funny Face Stop Read Press Tomorrow Morn.*

Publication History

Bibliography of the Works of
Frederick Louis Nebel

GROUPED by magazine title chronologically. Compiled by Rob Preston.

Ace High Magazine: "Pound for Pound," 2-27-31, rpt. *The Danger Trail* 11-28.

Ace High Novels: "Wolves of the Wild," 4-32.

Action Stories: "Raw Courage" (by Lewis Nebel), 12-25; "Sunken Sovereigns" (by Lewis Nebel), 1-26; "The Bluff That Worked" (by Lewis Nebel), 2-26; "Doom Lagoon," 3-26; "Some Grudge" (as by Eric Lewis), 3-26; "Somewhere East of Singapore," 7-26; "Claws of the Jungle," 1-27; "Captain Fortune," 4-27; "Isle of Lost Men," 11-27; "The Crimson Diamond," 4-28; "No Law Beyond Khyber," 12-28; "Typhoon McQuade," 1-29; "Flame Island," 11-29; "The Coast of Hate," 1-30; "The Darjeeling Diamond," 4-30, "The Skin Game," 9-32; "The Ice Giant," 10-32; "The Tumbleweed Kid," 6-38.

Air Adventures: "Boomerang Barnes," 1-29.

Air Stories: "Flyers of Fortune," 8-27; "Birdmen of Borneo," 9-27; "Flying Jade," 12-27; "The Shanghai Jest," 1-28; "Sky High Nerve," 2-28; "Yangtze Yellow," 3-28; "Wings of Doom," 4-28; "The Hard Fly Hard," 5-28; "Birdmen of Passage," 6-28; "Outcast Ships," 7-28; "Sky Trap," 8-28; "Proud Eagles," 9-28; "Bolt from the Blue," 10-28; "Wings of Mercy," 11-28; "Winged Chivalry," 12-28; "High Prey," 1-29; "Plane Nerve," 2-29; "Sky Wise," 3-29; "Eagles of Ind," 4-29; "High Flying Chance," 5-29; "Crate Crashers," 2-30; "High

"Flying Highbinders," 3-30; "Siren of the Wind," 4-30; "Winged Salvage," 5-30; "South of Saigon," 6-30; "Fighting Wings pt. 1," 10-30; "Fighting Wings pt. 2," 11-30; "Fighting Wings pt. 3," 12-30; "Fighting Wings pt. 4," 1-31; "Sky Blazers," 3-31; "Sky Spoilers," 4-31; "Sky Scrappers," 5-31; "Skyline Two," 8-31; "Flyers of Fortune," Spr-37.

American Magazine: "All the Good Times," 9-41; "No Time for Tears," 1-42; "Remember the Good Times," 6-42; "You Owe It to Yourself," 2-46; "Unfinished Marriage," 6-47.

Argosy: "The Creed of Sergeant Bone," 2-14-31.

Black Bat Detective Mysteries: "The Missing Car," 10-33.

Black Mask: "The Breaks of the Game" (as by Lewis Nebel), 3-26; "Grain to Grain," 11-26; "Dumb Luck," 1-27; "China Silk," 3-27; "Hounds of Darkness," 4-27; "A Man With Sand," 7-27; "Emeralds of Shade," 8-27; "A Grudge is a Grudge," 9-27; "With Benefit of Law," 11-27; "The Penalty of the Code," 1-28; "A Gun in the Dark," 6-28; "Hell to Pay," 8-28; "Raw Law: Crimes of Richmond City pt. 1," 9-28; "Dog Eat Dog: Crimes of Richmond City pt. 2," 10-28; "The Law Laughs Last: Crimes of Richmond City pt. 3," 11-28; "Law Without Law: Crimes of Richmond City pt. 4," 4-29; "Graft: Crimes of Richmond City pt. 5," 5-29; "New Guns for Old," 9-29; "Hell Smoke," 11-29; "Tough Treatment," 1-30; "Alley Rat," 2-30; "Wise Guy," 4-30; "Street Wolf," 5-30; "Ten Men from Chicago," 8-30; "Shake Down," 9-30; "Rough Justice," 11-30; "The Red-Hots," 12-30; "Gun Thunder," 1-31; "Get a Load of This," 2-31; "Junk," 3-31; "The Kill" (as by "Grimes Hill"), 3-31; "Beat the Rap," 5-31; "The Spot and the Lady" (as by "Grimes Hill"), 5-31; "Death for a Dago," 7-31; "Spare the Rod," 8-31; "Pearls Are Tears," 9-31; "Death's Not Enough," 10-31; "It's the Live Ones That Talk," 11-31; "Some Die Young," 12-31; "The Quick or the Dead," 3-32; "Backwash," 5-32; "Shake Up," 8-32; "He Could Take It," 9-32; "The Red Web," 10-32; "Red Pavement," 12-32; "Doors in the Dark," 2-33; "Rough Reform," 3-33; "Farewell to Crime," 4-33; "Save Your Tears," 6-33; "Song and Dance," 7-33; "Champions Also Die," 8-33; "Guns Down," 9-33; "Lay Down the Law," 11-33; "Too Young to Die," 2-34; "Bad News," 3-34; "Take It and Like It," 6-34; "Be Your Age," 8-34; "He Was a Swell Guy," 1-35; "It's a Gag," 2-35; "Ghost of a Chance," 3-35; "That's Kennedy,"

5-35; "Die Hard," 8-35; "Winter Kill," 11-35; "Fan Dance," 1-36; "No Hard Feelings," 2-36; "Crack Down," 4-36; "Hard to Take," 6-36; "Deep Red," 8-36; "The Green Widow," 1-51 rpt. *Detective Fiction Weekly* 2-11-33.

Black Mask (UK): "The Breaks of the Game" (as by "Lewis Nebel"), 3-26; "Grain to Grain," 11-26; "Dumb Luck," 1-27; "China Silk," 3-27; "Hounds of Darkness," 4-27; "A Man With Sand," 7-27; "Emeralds of Shade," 8-27; "A Grudge is a Grudge," 9-27; "With Benefit of Law," 11-27; "The Penalty of the Code," 1-28; "A Gun in the Dark," 6-28; "Hell to Pay," 8-28; "Raw Law: Crimes of Richmond City pt. 1," 9-28; "Dog Eat Dog: Crimes of Richmond City pt. 2," 10-28; "The Law Laughs Last: Crimes of Richmond City pt. 3," 11-28; "Law Without Law: Crimes of Richmond City pt. 4," 4-29; "Graft: Crimes of Richmond City pt. 5," 5-29; "New Guns for Old," 9-29; "Hell Smoke," 11-29; "Tough Treatment," 1-30; "Alley Rat," 2-30; "Wise Guy," 4-30; "Street Wolf," 5-30; "Ten Men from Chicago," 8-30; "Shake Down," 9-30; "Rough Justice," 11-30; "The Red-Hots," 12-30; "Gun Thunder," 1-31; "Get a Load of This," 2-31; "Junk," 3-31; "The Kill" (as by "Grimes Hill"), 3-31; "Beat the Rap," 5-31; "The Spot and the Lady" (as by "Grimes Hill"), 5-31; "Death for a Dago," 7-31; "Spare the Rod," 8-31; "Pearls Are Tears," 9-31; "Death's Not Enough," 10-31; "It's the Live Ones That Talk," 11-31; "Some Die Young," 12-31; "The Quick or the Dead," 3-32; "Backwash," 5-32; "Shake Up," 8-32; "He Could Take It," 9-32; "The Red Web," 10-32; "Red Pavement," 12-32; "Doors in the Dark," 2-33; "Rough Reform," 3-33; "Farewell to Crime," 4-33; "Save Your Tears," 6-33; "Song and Dance," 7-33; "Champions Also Die," 8-33; "Guns Down," 9-33; "Lay Down the Law," 11-33; "Too Young to Die," 2-34; "Bad News," 3-34; "Take It and Like It," 6-34; "Be Your Age," 8-34; "He Was a Swell Guy," 1-35; "It's a Gag," 2-35; "Ghost of a Chance," 3-35; "That's Kennedy," 5-35; "Die Hard," 8-35; "Winter Kill," 11-35; "Fan Dance," 1-36; "No Hard Feelings," 2-36; "Crack Down," 4-36; "Hard to Take," 6-36; "Deep Red," 8-36.

Black Mask (Canada), incomplete listing: "Song and Dance," 7-33; "Fan Dance," 1-36.

Blood 'n' Thunder: "Death Alley," Spr. 2011 rpt. *Dime Detective Magazine*, 11-31.

Boston Post Sunday Magazine, The: "Remember the Music," 8-27-39 rpt. *Collier's* 5-13-39.

Collier's: "Dance No More," 9-23-33; "Scoundrel's Choice," 12-23-33; "The Man Who Couldn't Spell," 6-30-34; "Unfriendly Call," 4-7-34; "Protecting Monica," 10-5-35; "The Grand Manner," 3-6-37; "Woman at Bay," 3-13-37; "The Real Thing," 5-8-37; "Never Sing Again," 6-5-37; "Reprieve at Eleven," 6-26-37; "Case Against Women," 7-17-37; "The Human Side," 8-7-37; "Dreams Are Real," 9-4-37; "The Bars Between," 10-2-37; "The Hard Way," 4-2-38; "Accidental Night," 10-22-38; "Chance is an Enemy," 3-11-39; "Remember the Music," 5-13-39; "The Simple Life," 1-6-40; "One Cold Night," 2-17-40; "A Girl Must Be Sure," 8-17-40; "The Man Who Lost Everything," 10-12-40; "The Girl With the Blonde," 11-16-40; "Something to Remember," 11-30-40; "Best of Luck," 4-5-41; "When the Time Comes," 6-7-41; "Case for Innocence," 11-1-41; "The Great Big Hearted People," 1-31-42; "No Shadow of Doubt," 8-22-42; "Wait Till I'm on My Feet," 12-26-42; "Give Me This," 4-17-43; "Scandal in St. Louis," 2-18-55.

Columbia: "The Secret Vanity," 4-29; "Behind the Shield," 8-29.

Complete Adventure Novelettes: "Passage to Macassar," 5-32; "Malayan Peril," 11-32 rpt. *Five Novels Monthly,* 12-28.

Complete Mystery Novelettes: "Forbidden River," 4-33 rpt. *Five Novels Monthly* 6-30.

Complete Stories: "Hands," 3-15-33; "The Command to Kill," 5-36.

Coronet: "Rendezvous With Treason," 2-42.

Cosmopolitan: "Nothing to Lose," 1-37; "Moment in the Dark," 1-44; "You Haven't Changed a Bit," 5-45; "You Can't Have Everything," 7-45; "Roses in the Rain," 11-45; "The Woman Who Changed Her Mind," 1-47; "The Web," 6-47; "The Bribe," 9-47; "Nightfall," 12-47; "White Villa in Rio," 4-55.

Cowboy Story Magazine: "Soda-Pop Mary," 9-26 rpt. *Lariat Story Magazine* 1-26; "High Jinks at Sky High," 6-27 rpt. *Lariat Story Magazine* 11-26; "The Drifting Kid," 7-27 rpt. *Lariat Story Magazine* 12-26.

Daily Mail Sunday Magazine, The (West Virginia): "The Human Side," 1-23-38, rpt. *Collier's* 8-7-37.

The Danger Trail: "Doom Drums," 10-27; "Pound for Pound," 11-28.

Detective Action Stories: "The Mystery at Pier 7," 9-31; "The Crooked Spot," 10-31; "Whispers of Death," 12-31; "The X Circle," 1-32; "The Crimson Fist," 3-32; "Murder by Ballot," 4-32.

Detective Fiction Weekly: "Call It Justice," 2-15-30; "Muscle Man," 6-10-31; "Nobody's Fall Guy," 8-8-31; "The Pinch," 9-17-32; "The Devil's Slouch," 12-10-32; "The Green Widow," 2-11-33; "The Lemon," 5-6-33; "Strangle Hold," 7-29-33.

Detective Tales (UK): "Hell's Pay-Check," 1-62, rpt. *Dime Detective* 12-31; "Death Alley," 2-62 rpt. *Dime Detective* 11-31; "Tailormade Clue" 3-62, rpt. *Dime Detective* 6-32; "Rogues' Ransom," 4-62 rpt. *Dime Detective* 8-32.

Dime Detective Magazine: "Death Alley," 11-31; "Hell's Pay Check," 12-31; "Author Profile," 12-31; "Six Diamonds and a Dick," 1-32; "And There Was Murder," 2-32; "Phantom Fingers," 3-32; "Murder on the Loose," 4-32; "Tailormade Clue," 6-32; "Rogues' Ransom," 8-32; "Lead Pearls," 9-32; "The Dead Don't Die," 10-32; "The Candy Killer," 11-32; "A Truck Load of Diamonds," 12-32; "The Murder Cure," 1-33; "Me—Cardigan," 2-33; "Doorway to Danger," 3-1-33; "Heir to Murder," 4-1-33; "Dead Man's Folly," 5-1-33; "Murder Won't Wait," 5-15-33; "Chains of Darkness," 7-1-33; "Scrambled Murder," 7-15-33; "Death After Murder," 8-15-33; "Murder and Co.," 9-15-33; "Murder à la Carte," 11-15-33; "Spades Are Spades," 1-1-34; "Hot Spot," 3-1-34; "Kick Back," 4-1-34; "Read 'Em and Weep," 5-1-34; "Red Hot," 7-1-34; "Not So Tough," 8-15-34; "Too Hot to Handle," 9-15-34; "Pardon My Murder," 11-15-34; "Leave It to Cardigan," 12-15-34; "Hell on Wheels," 2-1-35; "Hell Couldn't Stop Him," 4-15-35; "A Couple of Quick Ones," 6-1-35; "The Dead Die Twice," 8-35; "Death in the Raw," 10-35; "The Curse of Cardigan," 12-35; "Blood in the Dark," 1-36; "The Sign of Murder," 3-36; "Lead Poison," 4-36; "Murder By Mail," 6-36; "Make Mine Murder," 11-36; "Behind the 8 Ball," 3-37; "No Time to Kill," 5-37.

Elks Magazine, The: "The Brave Tradition," 11-27; "Proud Youth," 12-28; "The Makings of Command," 10-29; "Ask Me No Questions," 9-38; "Welcome Home, Soldier," 1-44.

Ellery Queen's Mystery Magazine: "Too Young to Die," 11-42 rpt. *Black Mask* 2-34; "Dead Date," 4-46 rpt. *Black Mask* 8-32; "Chance is Sometimes an Enemy," 4-56 rpt. *Collier's* 3-11-39; "Try It My Way," 6-56; "You Can Take So Much," 10-56 rpt. *Women's Home Companion* 12-40; "The Man Who Knew," 12-56 rpt. *Liberty* 3-9-40; "That's Just Too Bad," 5-57 rpt. *Collier's* 11-30-40; "No Kid Stuff," 4-58; "Wanted: An Accomplice," 7-58; "Pity the Poor Underdog," 8-58; "The Fifth Question," 1-59; "Killer at Large," 9-61; "Needle in a Haystack," 8-62.

Ellery Queen Mystery Magazine: "Overseas Edition for the Armed Forces: Dead Date," 4-46 rpt. *Black Mask,* 8-32.

Ellery Queen's Mystery Magazine (UK): "Chance is Sometimes an Enemy," 4-56 rpt. *Collier's* 3-11-39; "Try It My Way," 6-56; "You Can Take So Much," 10-56 rpt. *Women's Home Companion* 12-40; "The Man Who Knew," 12-56 rpt. *Liberty* 3-9-40; "That's Just Too Bad," 5-57 rpt. *Collier's* 11-30-40; "The Fifth Question," 3-59; "Needle in a Haystack," 12-62.

Ellery Queen Mystery Magazine (Australia): "Too Young to Die," 5-49 rpt. *Black Mask* 2-34; "Dead Date," 7-49; "Chance is Sometimes an Enemy," 6-56 rpt. *Collier's* 3-11-39; "Try It My Way," 8-56; "You Can Take So Much," 12-56 rpt. *Women's Home Companion* 12-40; "The Man Who Knew," 2-57 rpt. *Liberty* 3-9-40; "That's Just Too Bad," 7-57 rpt. *Collier's* 11-30-40; "No Kid Stuff," 6-58; "Wanted: An Accomplice," 9-58; "Pity the Poor Underdog," 10-58; "The Fifth Question," 3-59; "Killer at Large," 11-61; "Needle in a Haystack," 2-63.

Esquire: "Night Shift on the Lunchwagon," 11-37.

Family Circle: "The Man You Love," 4-58.

Far East Adventure Stories: "The Devil's Souvenir," 11-30; "Hell's Back Door," 2-31.

Five Novels Monthly: "Malayan Peril," 12-28; "In a Blue Moon," 3-29; "A Gambler Passes," 1-30; "Forbidden River," 6-30; "The Roaring Horde," 4-32.

Flying Stories: "Scourge of the South Sea Skies pt. 1," 9-29; "Scourge of the South Sea Skies pt. 2," 10-29; "Scourge of the South Sea Skies pt. 3," 11-29.

Ford Times: "Old Put's Camp Ground," 12-53; "The Island Nobody Knows," 2-58; "Israel Putnam Camp Grounds, Ford Times Special Edition" #2, n.d.

Frontier Stories: "Empire of the Devil," 3-30.

Good Housekeeping: "The Man Who Promised Not to Tell," 11-40; "Something Like a Dream," 2-43; "You Know How Women Are," 1-44; "Just Leave Everything to Me," 5-44; "Round Trip," 12-45; "You Owe It to Yourself," 2-46; "Wayward Journey," 5-46; "Rebound," 10-48.

Ladies' Home Journal: "Not a Care in the World," 9-50.

Lariat Story Magazine: "White Evidence," 11-25; "Soda Pop Mary," 1-26; "High Jinks at Sky High," 11-26; "The Drifting Kid," 12-26; "The Come Back," 2-27; "Leave it to Loppy," 3-27; "The Hell Bender," 4-27; "The Drifting Kid Strikes," 5-27.

Liberty Magazine: "Shanghai Stopover," 1-18-36; "All the Answers," 10-29-38; "You Go Your Way," 9-23-39; "Man-Crazy," 12-30-39; "Bet Your Life," 3-9-40; "Any Boy Can Be President," 8-23-41; "Grampa and the Spirit of '76," 9-6-41; "You Got to Think of the Kids," 8-22-42; "The Woman in Shadow," 3-31-45; "Your Face Looks Familiar," 6-16-45; "Back in Town," 10-48.

Life's Romances: "If You Can Take It," 6-41, rpt. *Woman's Home Companion* 12-40.

Maclean's Magazine (Canada): "The Thing to Do," 3-15-36.

McCall's: "Week End to Kill," 6-38; "Guess Again, Lady," 2-51.

Mike Shayne's Mystery Magazine: "Sudden Life," 8-58.

Mystery: "Murder Off Stage," 2-34; "Killer After 10P.M.," 8-34; "At the End of the Alley Was a Door," 11-34.

Mystery Stories: "Law Alone," 11-28.

North West Romances: "Chechako Plunder," Fall-37; "Black Fury," Win-37; "Builders of Empire," Spr-38; "Voyageur of the Wasteland," Sum-38; "Tundra Gold," Fall-38; "Code of the Iron Fist," Spr-39;

"Lair of the Gun Wolf," Sum-39; "The Hell Drivers," Fall-39; "The Tenderfoot Girl of the Yukon Trail," Win-39/40; "The Valley of Wanted Men," Spr-40; "Whelp of the Timber Wolf," Fall-40; "Girl of the Golden Snows," Win-40; "The Girl From Golden River," Sum-41; "White Woman," Spr-41; "The Outcast Breed," Sum-42; "Boomerang Bonanza," 2-43; "The Tundra Tamer," 4-43; "The Tundra Tamer," Win-49 rpt. *North West Romances* 4-43.

North-West Stories: "Trade Law," 7-25; "The Firelight Patrol," 9-25; "Stuart of the City Patrol," 12-25; "The White Peril," 1-8-26; "Eskimo Sorcery on Baffin Island," (misc.) 2-22-26; "Defiance Valley pt. 1," 3-8-26; "Defiance Valley pt. 2," 3-22-26; "The Freight of Honor," (true story) 3-22-26; "Defiance Valley pt. 3," 4-8-26; "The Black Fox Skin," 4-22-26; "Trail Tales of the North: Law of the Trapline," (true story) 4-22-26; "Trail Tales of the North: Patrol of Courage," (true story) 5-8-26; "The Big Moon Lake Patrol," 6-22-26; "Trail Tales of the North: Alone," (true story) 8-22-26; "Trail Tales of the North: Cache Law," (true story) 9-22-26; "East of Big Moon," 11-8-26; "The Frontier of Vengeance pt. 1," 12-8-26; "The Frontier of Vengeance pt. 2," 12-22-26; "Tell It to the Mounted" (as by Eric Lewis), 12-22-26; "The Lovable Tramp" (true story) 12-22-26; "The Frontier of Vengeance pt. 3," 1-8-27; "The Frontier of Vengeance pt. 4," 1-22-27; "Courage of the Strong," 3-22-27; "A Man Must Fight," 4-22-27; "Return of the Exile," 7-8-27; "Red Night," 8-8-27; "The Raw White Edge," 10-8-27; "It Takes a Man," 10-22-27; "Sun Dog Gold," 1-22-28; "Red Coat of Tradition," 6-22-28; "Far North of Chilkoot," 9-22-28; "Die Hard Donovan," 8-29; "The Yukon Trail, pt. ? of ?," 8-29; "The Trail to Caribou," 12-29; "Chechako Trail," 4-30; "King of the Yukon," 8-30; "The Law Dies Hard," 2-31; "Yukon Wings," Spr-36; Valley of Greed," Wtr-36.

North-West Stories (UK), incomplete listing, all reprints are for the matching exact US edition: "Trail Tales of the North: Alone," 2-late-27 (true story); "Trail Tales of the North: Cache Law," 3-late-27 (true story); "Trail Tales of the North: Law of the Trapline," 10-late-26 (true story); "The Black Fox Skin," 10-late-26; "Defiance Valley pt. 3," 10-early-26; "Trail Tales of the North: Patrol of Courage," 11-early-26 (true story); "Eskimo Sorcery on Baffin Island," 8-early-26 (misc.); "The Big Moon Lake Patrol," 12-late-26; "The Frontier of Vengeance pt. 1," 6-early-27; "The

Frontier of Vengeance Part 2, 6-late-27; Tell It to the Mounted (as by Eric Lewis,) 6-late-27, ; The Lovable Tramp , 6-late-27(true story); The Frontier of Vengeance Part 3, 7-early-27; The Frontier of Vengeance Part 4, 7-late-27; Courage of the Strong, 9-late-27.

Quick Trigger Stories of the West: The Driftin' Kid Draws Fire, 6/7-30.

Real Detective Tales and Mystery Stories: Cops Are Dumb, 10-29.

Redbook Magazine: The Best with the Worst, 6-35; Magnificent Gesture, 12-36; Change of Heart 4-37; All the Way Back, 10-51.

The Saint Detective Magazine: Reprieve At Eleven, 6-55 rpt *Collier's* 6-26-37; Ghost of a Chance, 4-56 rpt *Black Mask* 3-35.

The Saint Detective Magazine (UK): Reprieve at Eleven, 10-55 rpt *Collier's* 6-26-37; Ghost of a Chance, 7-59 rpt *Black Mask* 3-35.

The Saturday Evening Post: The Wheel, 4-9-32; The Things You Say, 2-3-45; Forbidden Affair, 1-10-53; Mask of Murder, 10-8-55.

Sea Stories: The Seed of Caution, 6-29.

Short Stories: Stand Up and Fight, 9-10-28; Fly By Night, 8-10-31; The Easy Mark, 12-57.

Short Stories (UK): Stand Up and Fight, 1-mid-29 rpt *Short Stories* 9-10-28; Fly By Night, 12-mid-31 rpt *Short Stories* 8-10-31.

This Week: Last Question, 4-22-45; The Girl on the Big Drum, 1-10-54; Money, Money, 2-14-54.

Today's Woman: Appointment in Rio, 1-49.

Toronto Star Weekly: Proud Youth, 6-22-29, rpt *The Elks Magazine* 12-28.

Triple X Magazine: The Devil's Double Cross, 3-28.

War Stories: A Knight of the Bath, 12-8-27.

Wide World Adventures: Wolves of Dismay, 2-30.

Wings: Skyrocket Scott, 3-28; Wolves of the Wind, 8-28; Wind Patrol, 11-29; Isle of Lost Wings pt 1, 3-30; Isle of Lost Wings pt 2, 4-30; Isle of Lost Wings pt 3, 5-30; Isle of Lost Wings pt 4, 6-30; Flying Freebooters, 9-30; Brood of the Wind, 11-30; Bloodhounds of the

Sky pt. 1," 12-30; "Bloodhounds of the Sky pt. 2," 1-31; "Blood-hounds of the Sky pt. 3," 2-31; "Bloodhounds of the Sky pt. 4, 3-31."

Women's Home Companion: "The Legend," 12-39; "If You Can Take It," 12-40; "The Big World," 10-44.

Young's Magazine: "Out of Stir," 11-29.

Books:

The Adventures of Cardigan: A Dime Detective Book, The Mysterious Press, NY, 1988, tp. "Murder à la Carte," *Dime Detective* 11-15-33; "Spades Are Spades," *Dime Detective* 1-1-34; "Hot Spot," *Dime Detective* 3-1-34; "Kick Back," *Dime Detective* 4-1-34; "Hell Couldn't Stop Him," *Dime Detective* 4-15-35; "The Dead Die Twice," *Dime Detective* 8-35.

But Not the End, Little, Brown, Boston, 1934.

The Complete Casebook of Cardigan, Volume 1: 1931-32, Altus Press, 2012. "Death Alley," *Dime Detective* 11-31; "Hell's Pay Check," *Dime Detective* 12-31; "Six Diamonds and a Dick," *Dime Detective* 1-32; "And There Was Murder," *Dime Detective* 2-32; "Phantom Fingers," *Dime Detective* 3-32; "Murder on the Loose," *Dime Detective* 4-32; "Rogues' Ransom," *Dime Detective* 8-32; "Lead Pearls," *Dime Detective* 9-32; "The Dead Don't Die," *Dime Detective* 10-32; "The Candy Killer," *Dime Detective* 11-32; "A Truck Load of Diamonds," *Dime Detective* 12-32.

The Complete Casebook of Cardigan, Volume 2: 1933, Altus Press, 2012. "The Murder Cure," *Dime Detective* 1-33; "Me—Cardigan," *Dime Detective* 2-33; "Doorway to Danger," *Dime Detective* 3-1-33; "Heir to Murder," *Dime Detective* 4-1-33; "Dead Man's Folly," *Dime Detective* 5-1-33; "Murder Won't Wait," *Dime Detective* 5-15-33; "Chains of Darkness," *Dime Detective* 7-1-33; "Scrambled Murder," *Dime Detective* 7-15-33; "Death After Murder," *Dime Detective* 8-15-33; "Murder and Co.," *Dime Detective* 9-15-33; "Murder à la Carte," *Dime Detective* 11-15-33.

The Complete Casebook of Cardigan, Volume 3: 1934-35, Altus Press, 2012. "Spades Are Spades," *Dime Detective* 1-1-34; "Hot Spot," *Dime Detective* 3-1-34; "Kick Back," *Dime Detective* 4-1-34; "Read

'Em and Weep," *Dime Detective* 5-1-34; "Red Hot," *Dime Detective* 7-1-34; "Not So Tough," *Dime Detective* 8-15-34; "Too Hot to Handle," *Dime Detective* 9-15-34; "Pardon My Murder," *Dime Detective* 11-15-34; "Leave It to Cardigan," *Dime Detective* 12-15-34; "Hell on Wheels," *Dime Detective* 2-1-35; "Hell Couldn't Stop Him," *Dime Detective* 4-15-35.

The Complete Casebook of Cardigan, Volume 4: 1935-7, Altus Press, 2012. "A Couple of Quick Ones," *Dime Detective* 6-1-35; "The Dead Die Twice," *Dime Detective* 8-35; "Death in the Raw," *Dime Detective* 10-35; "The Curse of Cardigan," *Dime Detective* 12-35; "Blood in the Dark," *Dime Detective* 1-36; "The Sign of Murder," *Dime Detective* 3-36; "Lead Poison," *Dime Detective* 4-36; "Murder By Mail," *Dime Detective* 6-36; "Make Mine Murder," *Dime Detective* 11-36; "Behind the 8 Ball," *Dime Detective* 3-37; "No Time to Kill," *Dime Detective* 5-37.

East of Singapore, Black Dog Books, Il, 2004, chapbook. "East of Singapore," *Action Stories* 7-26.

Fifty Roads to Town, Little, Brown, Boston, 1936. American Mercury Book #33, 1940.

Pulp Tales Presents #29, Flyers of Fortune, Pulpville Press, 2011. "Yangtze Yellow," *Air Stories* 3-28; "Wolves of the Wind," *Wings* 8-28; "Sky Scrappers," *Air Stories* 5-31; "Sky Blazers," *Air Stories* 3-31; "Flyers of Fortune," *Air Stories* 8-27.

Six Deadly Dames, Avon #264, New York, 1950. Gregg Press, Boston, 1980. "The Red-Hots," *Black Mask* 12-30; "Get a Load of This," *Black Mask* 2-31; "Spare the Rod," *Black Mask* 8-31; "Pearls Are Tears," *Black Mask* 9-31; "Death's Not Enough," *Black Mask* 10-31; "Save Your Tears," *Black Mask* 6-33.

Sleepers East, Little, Brown, Boston, 1933.

Tough as Nails: The Complete Cases of Donahue, Altus Press, 2012. "Rough Justice," *Black Mask* 11-30; "The Red-Hots," *Black Mask* 12-30; "Gun Thunder," *Black Mask* 1-31; "Get a Load of This," *Black Mask* 2-31; "Spare the Rod," *Black Mask* 8-31; "Pearls Are Tears," *Black Mask* 9-31; "Death's Not Enough," *Black Mask* 10-31; "Shake Up," *Black Mask* 8-32; "He Could Take It," *Black Mask* 9-32; "The Red Web," *Black Mask* 10-32; "Red Pavement," *Black*

Mask 12-32; "Save Your Tears," *Black Mask* 6-33; "Song and Dance," *Black Mask* 7-33; "Champions Also Die," *Black Mask* 8-33; "Ghost of a Chance," *Black Mask* 3-35.

Week End to Kill, Century Publications, 1945, Century Mysteries #30 with Hugh Pentecost *Secret Corridors.* "Week End to Kill," *McCall's* 6-38.

Anthology:

Action Stories, Desmond/Wiener/Howard/Howard/Murray, Odyssey Publications, Inc., 1980, O.P. #11. "Coast of Hate," *Action Stories* 1-30.

The Arbor House Treasury of Detective & Mystery Stories From the Great Pulps, Bill Pronzini, Arbor House, NY, 1983, hc, tp. "Red Pavement," *Black Mask* 12-32.

The Black Lizard Big Book of Black Mask Stories, Penzler, Vintage Crime/Black Lizard, 2010. "Doors in the Dark," *Black Mask* 2-33.

The Black Lizard Big Book of Pulps, Penzler, Vintage Crime/Black Lizard, 2007. "Raw Law: Crimes of Richmond City pt. 1," *Black Mask* 9-28; "Dog Eat Dog: Crimes of Richmond City pt. 2," *Black Mask* 10-28; "The Law Laughs Last: Crimes of Richmond City pt. 3," *Black Mask* 11-28; "Law Without Law: Crimes of Richmond City pt. 4," *Black Mask* 4-29; "Graft: Crimes of Richmond City pt. 5," *Black Mask* 5-29; "Wise Guy," *Black Mask* 4-30.

The Black Mask Boys, William F. Nolan, William Morrow & Co., NY, 1985, hc. Mysterious Press, 1985, hc., tp. "Rough Justice," *Black Mask* 11-30.

Detectives A to Z, McSherry/Greenberg/Waugh, Bonanza, 1985. "Take It and Like It," *Black Mask* 6-34.

Ellery Queen's Awards: 11th Series, Queen, Simon & Schuster, 1956. Try It My Way, *Ellery Queen Mystery Magazine* 6-56.

Hard-Boiled: An Anthology of Crime Stories, Adrian/Pronzini, Oxford University Press, 1995. "Backwash," *Black Mask* 5-32.

Hard-Boiled Dames, Drew, St. Martin's, 1986. "Murder by Mail," *Dime Detective* 6-36.

The Hard-Boiled Detecitve, Herbert Ruhm, Vintage Books, NY pb, 1977. "Take It and Like It," *Black Mask* 6-34.

Hard-Boiled Detectives, Robert Weinberg, Stefan Dziemianowicz and Martin H. Greenberg, Gramercy Books, NY., hc., 1992. "Hell's Pay Check," *Dime Detective* 12-31.

The Hardboiled Dicks, Ron Goulart, Sherbourne Press, CA, 1965. "Winter Kill," *Black Mask* 11-35.

It's Raining More Corpses in Chinatown, Don Hutchison, Adventure House, MD, 2001, tp. "Lead Poison," *Dime Detective* 4-36.

Pulp Fiction: The Crimefighters, Penzler, Quercus, 2006. "Wise Guy," *Black Mask* 4-30.

Pulp Fiction: The Villains, Penzler, Quercus, 2007. "Raw Law: Crimes of Richmond City pt. 1," *Black Mask* 9-28; "Dog Eat Dog: Crimes of Richmond City pt. 2," *Black Mask* 10-28; "The Law Laughs Last: Crimes of Richmond City pt. 3," *Black Mask* 11-28; "Law Without Law: Crimes of Richmond City pt. 4," *Black Mask* 4-29; "Graft: Crimes of Richmond City pt. 5," *Black Mask* 5-29.

Scarlet Riders, Don Hutchison, Mosaic Press, Ont. Canada, 1998, tp. "The Valley of Wanted Men," *North West Romances* Spr-40.

Tales of Mystery, Pronzini, Bonanza, 1986. "Red Pavement," *Black Mask* 12-32.

Tough Guys & Dangerous Dames, Robert Weinberg, Stefan Dziemianowicz and Martin H. Greenberg, Barnes & Noble, 1993. "Chains of Darkness," *Dime Detective* 6-15/7-1-33.

Screenplays:

The Isle of Lost Men 1928, film; *Ships of the Night* 1928; *Sleepers East* 1934; *Meet McBride* 6-13-36 CBS radio drama, written by Charles Tazewell, based on the Kennedy and MacBride stories by Nebel; *Smart Blonde* 1936, film; *The Adventurous Blonde* 1937, film; *Fifty Roads to Town* 1937, from novel AKA *Fifty Races to Town; Fly Away Baby* 1937, film; *Blondes at Work* 1938, film; *Torchy Blane in Panama* 1938, film; *Torchy Gets Her Man* 1938, film; *Torchy Blane in Chinatown* 1939, film; *Torchy Plays With Dynamite* 1939, film; *Torchy Runs for Mayor* 1939, film; *A Shot in the Dark* 1941, film; *Sleepers West* 1941 film from *Sleepers East; The Bribe* 1949 from *Cosmopolitan*, 9-47.

Note: The "Torchy Blane" movies were based upon a concept/characters created by Nebel, but he did not write the movie scripts.

This bibliography is in a nonstandard format to limit pagecount to a reasonable length.

The lone newspaper appearance from *Daily Mail Sunday Magazine* suggests there may be more Nebel to be found in this form. *North West Stories* is not completely indexed so expect more stores to surface from this source. Any corrections and additions would be appreciated. This is the first substantial collection of Frederick Nebel in 20+ years, hopefully this and the bibliography will start a resurgence of interest.

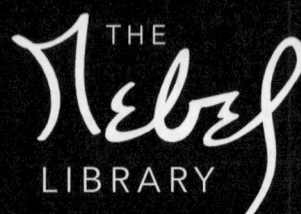

THE
Nebel
LIBRARY

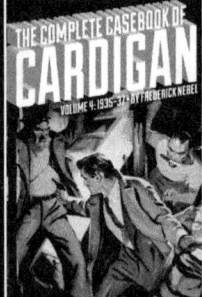